A Journey Toward The West

Legends of
The Dragon's Blood
book 7

T.L. CARLYLE

✦ΛNTELLUS.

A Journey Toward The West
Legends of The Dragon's Blood book 7
Copyright © 2020 by T.L. Carlyle, *all rights reserved.*

Cover design by T.L. Carlyle ©2020
Published by **Antellus**, Los Angeles, California USA
Catalog no. 07 ISBN 978-1-7352389-2-0

Other books in this series by T. L. Carlyle:
The Path of The Red Dragon - The Legacy of Mars -
Destiny's Forge - The Queen's Marksman - The Pirate's Pledge
The Children of The Night - A Bad Night In Soledad

Foreword

This book is loosely based on a collection of short stories I wrote during the 1980s and 90s. The original series, *Blood Songs*, was a string of epic adventures of espionage, fellowship, betrayal, murder, conspiracy, political intrigue and a host of other snippets about the human condition within the confines of a rigidly defined universe established by precedent; one which did not leave much room for innovation.

As a result of this outpouring of creativity, I went on writing more speculative science fantasy stories featuring my own characters in a universe which is as real for the reader as I can make it. These are fresh and original stories and as such I have designed them to stand alone.

There are many facets to this fantasy universe that are as yet unexplored. The whole has become greater than the sum of its parts as each new idea for a story springs into being to add to the saga. I hope that you will be fascinated and entertained by the legend of its people, who are the descendents of the first one of their kind and the inheritors of the dragon's blood.

A Journey Toward The West covers the saga of two alien vampires, one a fullblood and one a hybrid who is his son. The book is rife with conflict and adventure, because the 17th century is a time when war will soon make way for the enlightened time of the Renaissance and the Reformation periods in Europe. – *T. L. Carlyle*

"History can serve the present as a mirror of the past."
Hsu-ma Kuang (1018-1086),
a Chinese statesman and historian of the Sung dynasty.

Nihon (Japan)
September, 1645

1

The rain fell steadily, throwing up a mist among the volcanic rock, the scrub thickets, the trees. Thunder rumbled faintly to counterpoint the loud hiss of the downpour.

A man climbed carefully up the steep, muddy path toward the top of the mountain, clad in a large oilskin and a wide brimmed bamboo hat to repel the cold water. His face was pale against the dim light fighting its way through the dark clouds. His almond shaped eyes were silver grey, glowing slightly. The long fingers of his left hand curled around the woven grip of a katana, while his right grasped at the branches of the brush lining the path to help him keep his footing on the mud cascading down the incline before him. His backpack and tabi were already soaked but he did not care; all would dry quickly when he could get to dry ground.

When he reached a natural landing on the steep stairs he paused and looked out over the island. The green landscape around him seemed to glow with life beyond the veil of rain, just as it always did to one of his kind. He glanced back up the path and saw that there was only a little way to go before he arrived at the cave. There was little chance of meeting anyone in this inclement weather, and the path was not well known.

The stranger resumed climbing until he reached another landing. Here he found the entrance to the cave he sought. It was large, almost warm compared to the outside, but there was no hearthfire nor even a candle lit inside.

The master's sleeping futon was rolled up and stowed in a corner, and the large pot he used for cooking rice, his teapot, and a wooden spoon rested on the cold hearth. His clothing and other personal effects were gone.

The stranger had come too late, and stood silently wondering what he should do next. He could smell sickness lingering on the damp cold air, a hint of blood. The master had shown only a single moment of weakness in the months he taught his pupils the craft of the sword.

There was a sound of footsteps outside. The stranger flattened himself against the inner wall next to the dripping mouth of the cave and waited. A moment later a man wearing a poncho made of grass entered and walked toward the hearth, where he began to pick up the rest of the cooking utensils. As he turned around he looked up and beheld the tall dark shadow standing before him, and his breath caught in his throat. He peered closely as he said, "who is there? Who are you?"

The stranger moved closer and replied, "it is only me, Teruo," in perfect though accented Nihonese. He made a short polite bow.

Teruo's shoulders grew slack. "You startled me, Karasu" he said, as he put the pots down and gave a return bow.

"I returned to see the master and say goodbye," Karasu said. "What has happened?"

The smaller man's voice was sad as he said, "Musashi collapsed soon after you left. He is gravely ill. We took him to the hospice in Ungen so that he could die in comfort. I have returned to collect the rest of his things and take them to his home in Miyamoto."

"I had no inkling that he was that ill," Karasu said. "Is he in any pain?"

Teruo shrugged. "He hid it well."

Karasu nodded soberly. "I cannot stay, or the Daimyos will have my head. They still mistake me for a Christian no matter that I am not. Please do me the honor of conveying my goodbyes to him."

"I will," Teruo replied.

"I have learned much that is good from your people," Karasu said. "Perhaps one day I will return to visit."

"If the gods will it," Teruo said with another courteous bow, which Karasu returned. "I must go now," he said. The others are waiting for me on the footpath above. Good fortune go with you."

With that, Teruo Nabonojo picked up the pots and exited the cave, leaving Karasu Hane, Alexander Corvina, standing alone in the dark.

Alexander looked around, taking in the smallest detail of the cave to remember. He spotted something lying on the reed mats covering the dirt floor, bent down and picked it up. It was a small horsehair brush for writing, blackened with old dried ink. It looked lonely; the single sign of the master's art left. The ink cake and the tray for grinding and preparing it were already gone, and Alexander's thoughts traveled back to the day he received instruction in the making of the ink.

Musashi placed a pile of burned vegetable oil mixed with pine resin, powdered charcoal, and a small amount of camphor onto the grinding tray, which was a large piece of lava worn smooth by rubbing. He took another piece of stone and, stirring the mixture carefully, ground the drying gum until it reached a rich smooth consistency. Then he put the mixture into a small mold made of bamboo and set it aside to dry completely. He took another cake, scraped a small amount into a cup and mixed it with water, then dipped the brush into it, bringing up a small amount of black.

"You must apply the ink with smooth but gentle strokes, like this," the master said, as he pointed the brush down and dribbled a tiny amount into a small group of characters. "Never hesitate. Never rush the strokes you use, and never load your brush too heavily with ink or it will form a blot on the paper." Then he pointed the handle toward his pupil and said, "now you try."

Alexander took the brush in his hand with a doubtful glance, but did as he was shown and managed a few clumsy strokes. Mushashi nodded and clapped his hands. "If you would only learn to write as we do, you will indeed become Nihonese. But you must study for many years, for our kanja is not easy to learn. Even I have trouble with it from time to time."

No matter. It was a treasure to Alexander, a souvenir of a time which would never come again. He tucked the brush into a fold in his dark grey kimono, hitched his pack higher on his back, and stepped out into the rain once again.

2

After making the long perilous climb down the mountain, Alexander walked into the village at its base. The rain had stopped an hour before, and the parting clouds warned of sunshine too soon. He had to find shelter from the unforgiving light before he could go on to the harbor, as his pale skin was sensitive and burned easily. But luck was with him when he found a small sake parlor at the end of the road and entered it.

The manager was a small thin man who was cheerful in greeting until he saw the tall stranger come in through the sliding door and place his pack on the floor. His smile fell as he looked up, and his eyes grew wide with wonder and fear. "Wohhh. You are shimigami. What do you want?" he asked. He backed away from the crude wooden counter between them, his worn features twisting and producing a pronounced squint in one eye.

Alexander took note of this with little surprise, having seen this reaction before on his long journey through the lives of the humans. "Hot sake. Please," he said. "I will pay you well." As he spoke his long fingers withdrew a newly minted copper coin from a pouch in his sash and placed it slowly and carefully on the counter. "I wish to drink a toast to my sensei before I leave this place."

The older man grunted, approached again and gingerly picked up the piece. He turned it over, then put it in his mouth and bit down, noting the taste. "Ah," he said as he removed it. "Sake. Coming right up." He seemed to recover his cheer quickly, leaving Alexander feeling more content with staying, if only for that hour.

When the sake came to hand Alexander took a tentative sip. His thoughts returned to a time a year before, when he had come to Musashi and begged on hands and knees to receive instruction in the way of the sword.

He had admired the balance and heft of the katana, an elegant weapon made for a more civilized age. The techniques used were passed down over the generations, and were as artful as the sweeps of ink on the rice paper he saw throughout the land. He had seen other men of Nihon wield their katanas with grace and speed, and he knew that his own crude swipes with a cutlass were clumsy and lacked finesse.

Musashi was already an old man and did not want to take on anymore pupils for fear of leaving the world with one not prepared to fight honorably. But Alexander said that he did not wish to dishonor the name of his family by staying a barbarian. He wished to know the way, and swore on his mother's spirit that he would pass on the tradition to his forebears.

It was that last statement that caught Musashi's interest. "You do me an honor by swearing thus, for I am about instructing the future generations of my people in the true way. I dislike the modern ways of warfare. By what name are you called?"

"Alexander Corvina, master," the young man replied.

"You have the aspect of shimigami. Indeed, you are paler than any European I have ever seen," Musashi replied as he looked him over. "You move like a ghost, for I did not hear your feet on the ground outside. Your hair is black and fine like ours, but your eyes glow with their own light. What other things must I know before I take you on as my pupil?" He said it without an ounce of fear in his voice, and Alexander thought it an encouraging sign.

"I am but a man like other men, master, but I have certain… um… peculiarities that I must explain," he replied carefully.

"I assure you that I will not share this with anyone else. But I must know your spirit," Musashi insisted.

Quietly, Alexander spoke of his birth, his family, his need to avoid prolonged exposure to the sun, his need for blood. Musashi listened in silence, and betrayed only a mild look of dismay when he heard the story of Alexander's ascension, the traumatic shock he experienced at learning that he was different from other men; his need to come to terms with his true nature in a world already frightened of other men like him.

When he had finished, Musashi sat quietly contemplating all that he heard. When he spoke, his voice was even and calm. "Tell me. Have you ever killed in the taking of blood?"

"With respect, yes," Alexander had replied with his head bowed in shame. "But I had no wish to. I was forced to by the spirit of my own blood. In time I learned to control it, and killed no more."

"And yet, now you wish to learn to kill with a blade in your hand, not with your teeth," Musashi said.

"I am not a killer in my heart," Alexander said. "I wish to learn how so that I can know a man's mind in battle. So that I can defend those I love with skill and honor."

The older man nodded quietly. "Those are worthy reasons. You appear to be an honest man, and I can always tell when a man lies. I must think on all you have told me. Come again to me tomorrow, when the sun is down, and I will tell you what I decide."

After making a humble bow Alexander obeyed.

3

That evening his blood hunger came again, so he fed his fill on the blood of a deer in the forest, stripped its flesh from the bones, packed it into the last of his rice paper for writing and buried the packets in the snow. Then he retired into the branches of a tree and slept the day there.

When the sun went down and dyed the snows of Fujiyama pink, Alexander rose from his sleep, retrieved the packets and took them down to the cave, where he found Musashi resting and cooking rice after a long day of training his two pupils.

Alexander laid the packets down on the floor before the master as he went to his knees and bowed forward, touching his head and hands to the reed mat covering the floor. "Please accept this meat, master," he said.

Musashi regarded the packets as if they were gold, but did not make a move toward them. "You honor me with a gift. But a gift will not change my mind," he said.

Thinking that the master was about to turn him down, Alexander replied, "I apologize. I thought only to reward you for listening without prejudice or fear, for I too can tell when a man lies."

Mushashi chuckled. "Share your company with me then, and I will cook this excellent gift. It is not often that I can have a conversation with a man without drawing a sword. You must tell me more about the world beyond the sea, for I have never seen it, and probably never will."

Through the long evening Alexander talked while the old man cooked and consumed the venison and rice he prepared, then shared a small bottle of sake he kept for the rare occasions when he had guests.

"The only vice I am permitted, for it is not good to dull the senses," he said. "Do you drink?"

Alexander said, "I allow myself to indulge from time to time. But my blood tells me when it is too much."

Musashi laughed, revealing teeth dull with age. "Other men your age are not as blessed," he said, as he poured a small amount into a cup and passed it to him.

"Some would say it is a curse," Alexander replied soberly as he took a sip.

"Then they would be wrong, for a man's nature is that he is what he is. There is no shame in it. The shame would be for you to abuse the gifts the gods have bestowed upon you by doing things without meaning. By killing without a good reason for doing so. True, when you enter battle you must kill, but you must think differently from what you have been taught about killing. You do not kill a man out of hatred, or disgust, or prejudice, but to stop him from killing you and to win the battle."

Alexander realized then that his instruction had already started, and his heart grew warm with the idea. "Other men kill for those reasons alone," he said.

"Yes," Musashi agreed as he took a sip of sake.

"But, are you saying that a man must kill another without feeling those things?"

"Yes. Just as one kills animals for nourishment. If you wish to live well you must recognize the difference between the motivations for war and the war itself. The soldier on the battlefield must accomplish the goal of stopping an enemy, or to vanquish him. There is no other motivation for him but that."

"What about pity? Compassion?"

"Perhaps after you have won the battle you may have those feelings, if your opponent is worthy and has fought honorably, even unto his death." Musashi followed that with another sip. "Feelings are natural, but a man who has feelings during battle will lose. He becomes too distracted by them, and that is a weakness another can exploit to advantage."

"Ah. I think I understand now," Alexander replied.

"Good." Musashi put down his cup. "And now, it is getting late."

That was Alexander's cue to leave, and he rose to his feet, adjusting the scabbard at his belt. "When may I return, master?"

"Tomorrow evening, after my other pupils retire. I will show you the proper way to hold a sword, and the difference between the blades."

"Thank you, master," Alexander replied as he paid him a courteous bow, then left the shelter of the cave.

4

That night the moon was full, and as he looked up at the dappled orb Alexander reflected on what the old man said. Then he turned his gaze on the four stars that formed the points of the cross he knew from his studies in astronomy, and a tiny star placed roughly near the center. A pang of longing pierced his soul as his blood remembered where his kind came from, never seen but never forgotten. Yet Alexander's home was also on Earth, and his body was born of a human woman.

His thoughts shifted to his father. Lucien had left him with a woman who raised him as her own until she died, her younger sister taking up his care with stoic acceptance. Both had been secretive about their association with his father. They thrived on the gold he sent them to provide for Alexander's care, and he grew up in relative prosperity and comfort, but he always felt as if he was responsible for his father's absence.

Each of them assured him that this was not so.

There had also been letters from Lucien during that time, and in each he professed his paternal love. They were a treasure to a young man who was a virtual orphan. He was subject to the normal manly desires of women, but these quiet declarations of remorse and care were a treasure more precious to him than any woman's love.

Now the boy was a man, and had endured almost two centuries living alone among other men; making friends and enemies in the way of other men. But when Alexander had to move on before his true age was discovered, the time between letters grew longer.

Lucien's last letter was long overdue and difficult in coming, transported with a priest traveling on a trading ship from Manchuria. It spoke of contrition for not having kept up, an invitation to come and visit, and a map of the temple's location, dated three months before its belated arrival. It was full of regrets at not having the courage to emerge from isolation, and sorrow for the death of his wife.

Alexander had read the words over and wondered how such loving grief could last so long. He had never known her kind heart, but only brief spasms of pain and misery he would never forget, so far back in his memory that he could not imagine how he could remember them. He had known them all of his life. Lucien had never discussed it, and would never answer his questions why, but he had the sense that there would come a time when he would. And that alone kept him hopeful.

5

The next evening, Musashi gave a pair of wooden practice swords to Alexander, who had changed from his European clothes into a simple grey kimono shirt and black pleated trousers called *hakama* in the Nihonese manner. His long hair was tucked up into a topknot, though he refrained from putting pomade into it. That was something samurai did, after shaving off a significant portion of hair from the tops of their heads. It was fashion but Alexander did not keep to it or regard himself as samurai. He could not really do so unless he earned the right, as the classes of Nihon were subdivided by the rigid wall of social convention; and he was still considered a barbarian from a foreign land.

Musashi looked him up and down with an air of satisfaction. "You have adopted our way of dress well. Your Nihonese is rough but you will learn more as I instruct you. You will yet become a man of Nihon if you take your instruction well, but you do not have a proper name."

"A proper name, master?" Alexander said, thinking his own ought to be good enough.

"Your name is too hard to pronounce," Musashi explained.

Just then, a raven appeared on the fly and came to rest on the branch of a tree nearby, calling raucously for its mate. Musashi started at the sound and stood studying the bird. Musashi liked birds, as was apparent from the artwork he left carefully tacked to the cave walls with small dobs of rice pudding.

"Ah. That is what we will call you," he said. "You shall be called Hane Karasu, for the feathers of that bird are like your hair."

"Raven Wing. It has a poetic ring, master," Alexander replied.

"Later I will teach you to compose haiku, if you are of such a mind," Musashi said. "And if you are very good, perhaps we will move on to tanka, which is more difficult."

"Thank you, master," he said with a small bow.

Over the course of the next hour, the master swordsman taught Alexander how to hold his swords, what positions were right to use, how to use his feet. Alexander learned faster than expected, and retained everything he learned, so that Musashi rarely needed to repeat himself.

Then there was a brief bit of sparring, during which Musashi learned something of his pupil. Alexander was a little faster than his other students at adapting what he learned into new moves. At one point, Musashi had to fall back to raise his hand and say "stop!"

Alexander froze where he was, uncertain. "Did I do something wrong, master?" he asked.

The old man leaned forward, breathing hard, and placed his hand on Alexander's chest. "No," he chuckled. "You are doing far better than I had expected. I am not used to teaching someone like you, and it surprised me." Then he looked up into the darkening sky and said, "I think that will be all for today. Come to me again tomorrow and we will begin your next lesson."

It was then that Alexander realized that Musashi was ill, but he could not divine the nature of the illness because cancer was not discovered yet, and only a few could recognize the signs. He looked into the master's dark eyes and saw a fatigue which was not natural, and smelled blood sweet as apricots. He determined to go more gently on Musashi out of respect. "Thank you, master," he said.

He began to hand back the wooden blades but Musashi said, "they are yours now. When I carved them there was more hair on my head than there is now. Keep them as a gift for being a good and attentive pupil."

Alexander bowed. "I am honored, master."

6

Gradually, days became weeks, during which Alexander learned all he could about the way of the sword until his and the master's sword strokes matched to the instant. He came away every evening feeling more content with his own heart and more sure of himself. He could not help but like Musashi because he was a patient teacher and his spirit was humble, and dreaded the day he would have to part company with the old man.

But when he heard in the village one day that the Shogun had commanded all foreigners to leave the islands of Nihon on pain of death, Alexander knew that his happy days of swordplay, calligraphy and poetry were coming swiftly to a close. Reluctantly, he packed his things together and told Musashi he had to leave.

The old man gave out a small grunt of acceptance when he heard this, then went to a long wooden box sitting on the floor nearby, opened it, and took out a pair of steel swords in their scabbards, wrapped in a length of rough homespun silk.

"These belonged to my father," Musashi said. "Please do me the honor of wearing them, as I will soon have no need of them myself."

Alexander's hesitated, and his fingers trembled with quiet excitement as he took the bundle. "You honor me again, master, but I do not deserve this. Why do you give them to me? Surely Teruo has earned the right."

"Because of all my pupils you are the only one who taught me that a man from another land can be civilized," Musashi replied. "I must confess that when I first met you I feared what you were, but you have never given me reason to. I can now look upon the spirit of a man, not his appearance or the things he has been taught. A valuable lesson indeed, which I will take with me to the underworld which is waiting for me."

Alexander felt a kernel of fondness as he looked into the old man's eyes. "If I could change anything about that you know that I would," he said. "But it is ever your choice."

Musashi shrugged and smiled. "It would not profit me to be immortal now. Look at me. I am too old to change, and what woman would have me anyway? No. I prefer to die when I am destined to."

Alexander said he would be back to say goodbye, and left the cave with hopes that Musashi would be there when he returned.

Alexander went down to the harbor and arranged for a ship to take him to Pusan, which was the only port of call closest to Nihon. From there he would have to hire another ship or travel by land, but those details were far from his thoughts just then. Since the ship would not leave for two days yet, Alexander spent time hiking in the woods and absorbing the beauty of the island before he went back to the village to wait.

He had become so comfortable with his own skin that he forgot what he looked like, until he ran into a group of young men carousing down the narrow street running through the center of the village. One of them stopped and stared as he passed by, then called out, "Shimigami! What mischief do you bring here!?"

The words stopped Alexander in his tracks. He turned slightly and saw the drunken eyes confronting him with an accusing stare. Ordinarily he would ignore such jibes but the mistake he made was in looking back without fear. "You mistake me for someone else," he said, then turned away and began to walk on.

"Oh! Then you must be one of those white devils. *Gaijin.* What are you doing dressing like us?" the youth asked loudly.

Alexander froze again, sensing that a confrontation was inevitable. As he turned around to face the boy his right hand went for the grip of the katana tucked against his abdomen, while his left thumb eased the blade out of the scabbard a millimeter, freeing it from its lock. "That is not your concern" he said. "By what authority do you ask?"

"I am the boss here. I asked you a question. You will answer," the boy demanded, "or I will cut your ears off."

As Musashi had taught him, Alexander said not a word in reply but sized up his challenger. His opponent was thin and rangy, and tottered slightly where he stood fighting to keep his balance. His eyes were glazed over and his mouth was slack. Even at that distance, the scent of fermented rice alcohol on his breath was hard to ignore.

The drunken youth did not keep him waiting long. He staggered back to get his distance while his companions formed into a rough semicircle to watch, but none dared to try and stop him. His sword came out of his scabbard without much grace at all. He raised it with both hands and a high screech of rage, and ran forward to bring the force of his misguided hatred down on the stranger's head with the blade.

Alexander merely waited, and when the boy was in range, leaned into the attack as his sword came out from the scabbard in a flash and swept in an arc, dashing the other blade aside. The steel resonated strangely and almost sang when it made contact. Then he angled the point of the blade forward and pierced the boy's sword arm with a single short stab before he could recover.

The youth's eyes went wide with surprise as he dropped his sword, staggered back and nearly fell, clutching at the wound staining his kimono sleeve dark with blood; then fell and landed hard on his buttocks uttering a keening sound of agony.

His companions began to draw their swords and move toward Alexander, but he stepped back and waited for them while the red stain began to ooze down the bright curved steel in his hand. His voice rang clear but echoed slightly in the darkness, lending an even more ghostly effect to his appearance as he said, "*take your drunken friend home. I have no quarrel with you.*"

The other young men paused, exchanging fearful glances, then thought better of attacking and went to help their friend. Emboldened by drunken anger and wounded pride, the boy struggled with them, shouting that he wanted to kill the stranger for his insolence, but they quietly dragged him away before he could follow through.

Alexander calmly flicked the blood from his blade with a quick dash, then resheathed it with reverence and walked on.

His thoughts returned to the present, just as the panel behind him slid open and three men entered the shack. The leader rested his eyes on the gaijin in front of him and said, "are you the one who fought with a young man but an hour ago?"

The hand that held the cup froze in midair. Alexander turned his head slightly as he replied, "yes. He provoked the fight. He was drunk. I was forced to defend myself."

The leader said, "I understand. He is the son of the prefect here, and has been known to challenge other men to fight before. He thinks he is Musashi reborn."

"I think that would be difficult, since Musashi is still alive," he replied.

At that the man started to laugh, then recovered his grim demeanor quickly as he said, "his father views any resistance to his son's volatile nature as an insult. I came to warn you that you invite death with your presence here. Finish your drink, but you must be gone from the village by dawn."

"Then I will be happy to accommodate you, because my ship sails in yet another hour," Alexander said. "Thank you for the warning."

"Good," the man said. "I will leave you in peace, then." With that, he threw a glance around the shop and then led his friends out.

The old shopkeeper looked out the open door after them and said, "how rude. They did not even stop to buy anything."

Alexander smiled. "Would you rather they had attacked me, and destroyed your shop in the process? I was prepared to fight."

"No. You are right," the old man said with certainty. Then his face grew hopeful. "More sake?"

Alexander shook his head, then finished the cup, gave the keeper a generous tip and then disappeared out the door in a flash.

He made his way quickly toward the harbor. There he found a tackle hut and entered it to change back into his European clothes. He took down his hair and put on his broad brimmed cloth hat, doffed the kimono and drew on his long overcoat, tied the silk swathed swords to his back with a length of sinew, then tucked the kimono into his pack for safekeeping.

Then, after tying his cutlass to his belt and straightening his clothes one last time, he left the tackle hut and walked toward the dock, where he boarded the junk that would take him away from Nihon.

As the ship glided toward the west, Alexander Corvina gave a last lingering look at the snow capped shadow of Fujiyama, said a silent goodbye to Musashi, then retreated from the red light of the rising sun before it caught him.

Manchuria

7

Alexander was barely noticed when he stepped off the gangplank onto the dock at Pusan, as it was dark when the ship arrived. He kept to the shadows as he walked along the wharf and the road running through the center of town, aimlessly wandering until he found an inn catering to European travelers tucked among the ramshackle buildings.

He entered the double doors and a tavern tucked to one side off the lobby. There, he took a table in a dark corner and ordered ale, and for the next hour learned the situation in the country by listening to the Spanish and Dutch traders as they conversed over their dinners and tankards of beer.

The news was not good. Manchuria was embroiled in a civil war, its progress and its eventual outcome shaped by the latest Chinese emperor, named Dorghun, who had the same mind as the Shogun Tokugawa when it came to foreigners. He valued their coin and their goods but not their religion or their cultural arrogance, and he was about putting down any resistance to his rule by the natives, who had their own distinct cultural values and customs. His arrogance extended to making imperial edicts about abandoning Manchurian culture and adopting Mandarin as the official language, which the Manchurians resolutely ignored.

As a result, Dorghun marched a battalion of Chin soldiers into the country to enforce them.

The Dutch East Asia Company was shipping out, and so were all the rest of the Europeans except for the English, who thought that they could maintain the upper hand. There appeared to be no profit in trying to conduct trade under such risky conditions, but the English were known for their bulldog determination to exploit whatever opportunity came to them wherever they found it. Their optimism was backed by several regiments of disposable troops and a good sized navy, as well as generous bribes to make the local officials look the other way.

Then Alexander's attention riveted on a group of gentlemen taking seats at the table nearby, and their manner was both hushed and furtive. Their speech was difficult to follow for any ordinary man, but he could hear them clearly as if they were right in front of him. They appeared to be either merchants or soldiers of fortune; he could not readily distinguish which.

They were planning to leave the country as quickly as possible. Their goal was to reach the lands to the west, and they spoke of Mongolia and Russia but argued briefly about the risks involved with traveling through lands where raiders were known to beset travelers for their goods and possessions. There was also concern shared among them about the presence of soldiers everywhere they went.

Their leader, who was a gentleman clad in dark leathers and a deep blue cape, said that there was little choice to be had, as shipping in the Indian Ocean was dangerous due to the presence of pirates patroling its waters. He stressed that no matter what they did the way was dangerous and bore great personal risk. Then he took a poll, and in the end the group voted quietly to go by land.

Alexander decided to introduce himself and try to join their group. But before he could move to approach them they got up from the table en masse and left the tavern. He abandoned the drink quickly, tossed a silver coin onto his table and went after them, hoping that he would not lose them among the milling crowd outside; but by the time he stepped out onto the busy street they had already parted and gone their separate ways. He marveled at their stealth and speed, and told himself to gain more practice at tracking prey.

He looked around, then sniffed the air and found the blood scent of their leader mingled with the pungeant scent of his pipe smoke drifting on the cold air. He turned his head and spotted the dark hat sporting a pheasant feather, and the blue cape moving down the road through the crowd. He adjusted his own cape and began to follow him, hoping to catch up with the man before he disappeared completely.

Alexander was able to keep up easily and caught up in a few minutes, then waited until the stranger turned right at the corner and went down a narrow course between buildings before he decided to close the gap.

Something in his blood told him it was a trap just before the stranger turned abruptly and drew his sword halfway out of its scabbard. The man growled, with anger in his voice. "You. You will stop where you are and tell me why you were following me."

"I mean no harm to you, good sir," Alexander replied as he moved his gloved hands slowly away from his body and sword. "Grant me but a brief moment to speak with you."

The stranger looked him up and down, and his face blanched with both fear and surprise as he edged away slowly. "What are you? Are you a demon? Your skin is paler than any I have ever seen. And your eyes!"

Alexander could have easily taken over the man's mind, but it would be difficult to rekindle any trust later. He raised a hand in supplication and pleaded, "I am no demon, I assure you. Would a demon ask of you a conference from which you would emerge unharmed?"

The man hesitated, considering, then resheathed his sword but kept his gloved hand on the hilt. "What would you say to me?"

"I overheard you and the other men talking in the tavern. You are organizing a caravan to go into the west," Alexander replied. "I am but a humble traveler seeking the very same company, as I am bound for Tibet. I can pay my way, and have such coin as would cover any expense." He stretched his gloved hand forward and showed a small group of gold coins laid out on his open palm.

The stranger stared at the gold, then slowly relaxed a little more. "May I ask why you are going into Tibet?"

"My father is a guest of the lamasery at Shangri-la. Perhaps you may have heard of it," Alexander said. "I have had an urgent letter from him, and I would perforce visit him there and give him comfort."

"That area is sought after by the emperor, and there are raiders and many obstacles we must avoid. The mountains are high and the passes treacherous. But we may pass through it on our way."

"That is why I sought to approach you," Alexander said.

"Can you handle an arquebus as well as you handle a sword?" the stranger asked, pointing toward the cutlass Alexander wore.

"Aye. I have many skills which you may find of use," he replied. "I can bind wounds and prepare poultices and medicaments against infections and disease. I can handle a bow and crossbow beside, and I can track any animal easily to obtain meat for the cooking fire."

"Useful skills indeed," the stranger mused, his hand stroking at his short goatee. "But, you may frighten my companions. What gives your skin such a ghostly appearance? Were you imprisoned?"

Alexander improvised quickly. "Nay. I was ill, and have had to amend my life to suit the effects. My skin is sensitive to the light of the sun. Worry not. My condition is not one that would afflict another man."

"Aye, I know well the way of such things," the stranger agreed readily. "Very well. I know not your history, but you comport yourself like a gentleman. Might I know your name, so that when we meet the others I can introduce you properly?"

He stripped off his right glove and stretched a long fingered hand forward. "Alexander Corvina, at your service, sir."

The stranger stared down at the strange sheen on the fingernails, which were tapered slightly, then moved closer and took it gingerly. "Sir John Henry Duggens, trading representative for His Majesty King Charles."

"You are a long way from England, sir. I have not been there since..." he cut himself off, unwilling to reveal his true age. His eagerness at meeting an upper class Englishman so long after the death of Queen Elizabeth would have given away his longevity, and he could not afford that. "Well, as the days go, a long time indeed. Not since I was a boy."

"But you are not English, as your foreign manner of speech does attest," Duggens said.

"Aye. My family is from Transylvania. I had the privilege to know a man of your country who taught me your language and customs, and tutored me in letters and sums. Later I studied in Oxford."

"An educated man. Even better," the man in blue said. "I feel now that we would profit a great deal from your participation. I will vouch for you to the others and prepare them. But, for a time, will you adopt some disguise that does not reveal your ghostly appearance?"

Inwardly Alexander rolled his eyes, but replied, "I will dress like a Berber, if you will allow me."

"Good. Meet me at dawn at the Inn of The Golden Dragon, and we will depart from there. Are we agreed?"

"The Inn of The Golden Dragon," Alexander echoed him, nodding.

"Then I give you a good night, sir," Duggens said.

As the Englishman strode away into the darkness, Alexander caught the faint scent of urine on the cold air, the scent of fear. Many men he had encountered before reacted that way, but it was familiar enough by now that he dismissed it with a small shrug and walked back to his inn.

That evening, he thought to reinforce his strength against the long trek to come and was offered a shy young thing who had just been sold to the brothel keeper by her father. Women were devalued as a family burden and treated like property, no matter that the men who engaged in trading human flesh had mothers themselves. Alexander thought the practice barbaric but had little choice in the matter because his blood was clamoring for nourishment to the point of distraction, and he could ill afford to make any mistakes in judgment now.

He and his selection were escorted to a small room in the back of the house. Once he was sure the brothel keeper was gone, he had to work hard to assure the quaking, terrified virgin that he was not a demon, and that he needed very little blood. He assured her that he would be gentle, and that it would only hurt for an instant. He used his eyes, his breath and his voice to calm her. He stroked gently at her cheeks, her shoulders, her arms, until she grew used to the cold touch of his skin.

It was slow going but worth it. The girl began to respond and allowed him to take her into his arms. When he bit her, the girl did not cry out, then lost all fear of him and clung to him for comfort, then pleasure from the passion that overtook her. After he had drunk his fill, Alexander stayed with her and sheltered her in his arms while she cried herself to sleep.

An hour later, Alexander tucked the sleeping waif among the linens of the flat bed and covered her with the crude blanket. He placed a gold coin on the low table next to her and tucked another into her pocket, collected his hat and pack and slipped out quietly.

8

The next day, a group of men assembled in front of the inn surrounded by a small army of porters and armed men, boxes, horses and a pair of supply wagons. Alexander met Duggens at the head of the driveway.

"I have told the other men who you are and where you are going," the Englishman said. "They are amenable to your company. Do you have a horse?"

"I landed at the port but the same day that I met you, and had not yet arranged for a suitable mount," Alexander replied.

"Then we will obtain one for you at once," Duggens said. As he spoke he looked around with suspicion and an air that spoke of desperate haste. Alexander took note of this but said nothing. That look was also familiar, for it seemed that during these times a man could not live his life without being pursued for something. His blood had taught him that early on.

Once he was introduced to the others and furnished with a horse he took his place among them.

The caravan started down the road out of the port and northward into the wilds of Manchuria, following an ancient road which paralleled the Yellow Sea through mountainous jungles toward the Mongolian Steppe. They met with few people on the way, and it seemed that the jungle had never been tamed. The road was overgrown at times with ferns and other plants, making the way difficult, so that the men were forced to hack their way through the foliage to make room for the animals and wagons.

For the next few days, Alexander kept to himself and communicated only to Duggens, who seemed quite willing to accommodate the stranger's eccentricity. The other men avoided him but also respected him. Often he disappeared into the darkness, only to return with a brace of rabbits or the occasional small boar or deer. They took the bounty with thanks, and did not question why the bodies were so empty of blood. At night, he kept watch while the others slept near the campfire, and could see and hear strange animals in the dark watching him back.

But once the caravan reached the border and the vast plain at the edge of the forest, there was some resistance from the porters. Their leader said they could not go further because they were at war with the Mongols. Duggens offered him more gold, then cursed him when the man refused. The argument soon escalated until he started to draw his sword.

The porters promptly dropped the boxes without ceremony and retreated into the jungle as fast as their short legs would take them, disappearing into the green dark like ghosts.

The Englishman was beside himself with fury at this betrayal but there was little he could do about it. It appeared to be a common practice among the natives, whose lives and labor could be bought for less than an English pound. But once the coin was in their hands they did not hold to any contract the foreigners swore them to. Tales of the ferocity of the Mongolian Horde, however, only gave legitimacy to their haste to be gone.

The travelers were forced to pick up the boxes themselves and load them onto the supply wagons before moving on. For Alexander this would have been a very simple task, but he could not demonstrate his greater strength to the others for fear of alarming them. So he huffed and puffed like the rest and handled one box at a time.

Mongolia was a vast open grassy plain with small groves of forest crowding the low hills. Here one could see from horizon to horizon, and Alexander proved his worth even more. His enhanced night vision spotted Mongol raiding parties camped on the grasses. He would tell Duggens where to find shelter, and the caravan managed to avoid the marauders as they passed by more than once. No one questioned how he could do this; or perhaps they did not dare.

After a few more days of this the others in the caravan thought nothing of his sleeping in the shelter of a supply wagon during the day. In time Alexander began to reveal more of himself at the campfire, first by telling stories of his sojourn in Nihon, and then by gradually removing some of the dark clothes that concealed him. When the Europeans in the party saw that his white skin and features marked him as one of them, they accepted him even more, and his story of the disease that forced him to take these measures became more plausible to those in doubt.

When the second week had passed, the caravan was forced to alter its course southward by the harsh conditions and the cold of approaching winter. By now it was late October, and the mountains were already sporting heavy caps of snow, while the steppes were scoured by a fierce north wind that seemed to blow constantly.

The travelers went south and followed the passes through the foothills into the lower ranges of Tibet, where Alexander parted company with them, taking only his horse and his pack with him.

Duggens appeared both sorry and relieved to see him go.

Tibet

9

The open country was marked by mountains so high and cold that no one lived there. Alexander spent his days sheltered among the pine trees crowding the timberline, and his nights riding toward what his blood assured him was his destination. Here, there was little food to find and his blood was wise enough not to press him. Even the wolves did not bother him, preferring to chase down the goats and horned sheep living in the lower canyons.

The sky became dark with clouds most of the time, so he was able to travel in comfort during the day and gained a little time.

Two days later, he came to a mountain pass and looked down toward the valley below. The snow had already started falling, and an east wind picked up into a howling squall. His tired horse shifted under him, uttering a whicker of protest as she was buffeted by the gusts of icy cold blowing among her legs.

"Yes, I know you are tired and cold," Alexander replied softly, patting at her neck. "Come. It is just a little farther to those rocks, where we will find shelter."

The horse tossed her head with a small snort and plodded on, stumbling her way carefully through the drifts of snow. When they reached the grotto, Alexander dismounted and led the horse deep into the shelter of a cave, where he removed the saddle and his pack but left the blanket on. He rubbed at her legs, trying to restore warmth, and noted how she trembled as if she would collapse at any moment.

He walked back out into the cold, looked around at the rocks and found only a few bare scrubs and twigs among them. He yanked them out of the dirt and took them, roots and all, back to the horse.

The animal sniffed cautiously before opening her mouth, then bit cautiously at the frozen vegetation. She stood chewing gingerly, favoring one side of her mouth.

The sharp scent of warm but sick blood came to Alexander's sensitive nose, and he realized that the animal had developed an infection somewhere in her mouth, or a tooth had gone bad. There was no way to heal that.

He ruffled at her coarse mane while she continued chewing, then moved away to build a fire using whatever he could find on the cavern floor so he could melt snow for her to drink. After that he settled down near the fire and listened to the wind howling outside until sleep overtook him.

When darkness came Alexander woke suddenly and found himself alone. Puzzled by her absence, he felt around for the animal's spirit but could find nothing. She was dead, having wandered off into the storm, gone off the cliff or fallen into a numbing frozen sleep wherever she went. Alexander could do nothing now but wait for the storm to pass on.

In this weather, even his own kind would find the cold unbearable, so he dressed in a second layer of clothing, then sat back against the cold stone of the cave wall and wrote about his travels by the light of his own eyes and the weak flame of the campfire. For his instrument he used a stick of graphite around which a strip of paper had been wound, a clever invention developed by the Manchurians. When the sky outside lightened he put his journal away and leaned back to sleep.

10

By the evening of the third day the snow stopped falling, and the wind calmed to a slight breeze. When Alexander finally emerged from the cave he could barely make out the surrounding topography, and could not tell the difference between rock and open space. Everything around the cave was covered with a blanket of pure white. The sky was still clouded over, so there were no moon and stars for finding direction.

It was dangerous to travel at night in these conditions. But Alexander knew that if he did not find fresh blood soon he would weaken and die.

He looked around and found a dead tree sticking out of the rocks over the mouth of the cavern, took one of the branches and pulled it off, stripping it of dead leaves and smaller shoots. He used it to poke at the snow ahead of him like a blind man with his cane, searching for solid ground to place his feet on. Slowly and carefully, he made his way down the steep path toward the valley below.

Alexander felt the heavy weight of sleep drag at his bones as he trudged through the piles of white up to his knees, then climbed slowly toward the head of the pass. He felt sure that the lamasery was just over the next hill, and pushed himself to stay awake long enough to reach it.

The snow began to fall again. Alexander felt his strength begin to go. He could no longer feel his feet, and his gloved fingertips were numb, as was the tip of his nose. Even the heavy clothes he wore were not adequate insulation against the deep cold beginning to suffuse his bones, and the pack strapped to his back felt heavier. He felt drained of stength, but did not dare stop to rest for fear that he would freeze where he was. When he felt that all was hopeless he admonished himself grimly to find his strength and forced himself to go on.

When he reached a break in the snow at the top of the trail, his cane gave way at the tip. He lost his footing and fell, tumbled a short way toward the edge of the canyon and landed on his stomach just inches from the precipice.

After a few minutes struggling to catch his breath in the thin mountainous air, he climbed up on his hands and knees and reached out blindly to find his balance. He found wood instead, and looked up through eyes glazed over with cold to see the blurry shadow of a carved post sticking up from the icy ground. It looked like a dragon, curled into an upright fighting pose, glaring at friend and foe alike. It was the last thing he saw before his eyes closed and the world went dark.

Alexander woke slowly, and found himself lying on a mattress of straw placed on the floor of a simply furnished room, covered by layers of fur and loomed wool blankets. He could feel his fingers and toes again, and they tingled slightly as they continued healing. He was clad in dark and silken pajamas not his own, though they fit him perfectly.

The steady droning sound of chanting, drumming, and the tolling of small bells beyond the closed door penetrated the silence. The scent of temple incense permeated the air with its sweet floral fragrance. He turned his head and saw a small oil lamp sitting on the low table beside him, its flickering flame the only source of light in the room. The single window had bamboo shutters which were closed tightly against the howling wind outside.

He heard footsteps in the hall through the closed door and laid back quickly, not sure what to expect.

A man clad in yellow and orange robes entered the room. His head and face were cleanshaven, and a towel was draped over his left arm. He carried a bowl in one hand while his other hand closed the door behind him. The lama turned and started briefly, then smiled and said, "ah. Yu awake."

He walked calmly toward the bed, sat down on the mat next to it, set the bowl down and dipped the towel into it. He began dabbing at Alexander's cheeks and forehead. The water felt pleasantly warm and smelled of olives.

"Where am I?" Alexander asked quietly.

"Shangri-la," the lama replied. "Wi find you, bring yu here. Yu like dead man, but you live."

"How long ago?"

"Five days. Yu sleep long time."

"I am ever in your debt," Alexander began. "Tell me, do you know Lucien Arkanon?"

"Ah. Bodhisattva Lu-shen. One hu live forever. Yes."

"Would you please let him know I am here? I have come a long way to see him."

"Hi know yu here," the lama said with a gentle smile.

Alexander puzzled briefly. "Why has he not come to see me?"

The priest said, "hi not tell me. Yu rest now. I bring yu food."

"If you know Lucien, then you should know that I am like him," Alexander ventured carefully, not sure what to expect.

The lama nodded calmly, then put the wet towel down in the bowl and stretched out his right arm toward Alexander, rolling his cassock sleeve up. "I give before," he said, smiling again. "Yu take now."

Alexander looked down and saw old spots, signs of feeding. The lama did not seem to mind, or had already been properly conditioned not to resist. Alexander grasped the arm carefully, then dipped his head, clamped his lips over the warm golden flesh and the pulse beneath and bit down.

The rush of hot liquid was comforting, and told him how things were in this place.

Shangri-la was the last bastion of an old order, rapidly becoming more endangered by the onslought of barbarians from every quarter; from the Turks and Tartars to the west, the Nepalese from the south, and the Chinese from the east. The only insurance against invasion was the lamasery's placement in a mountainous area so impassable and dangerous that few even knew it was even there. In the fall and winter, the snow camouflaged the temple complex and made the road treacherous, subject to avalanches. No army could hope to prevail against the barrier of the deep freezing cold, a wall almost as sure and impenetrable as stone.

This lama had come to the temple ten years ago, and had fed Lucien several times. He had been told that the Bodhisattva needed blood from a living being, and that the act of giving blood was a necessary sacrifice to maintain the harmony of the lamasery. He viewed it as both an honor and a duty, with the understanding that it was for the good of another.

That may have been why Lucien chose to come here; or perhaps he, too had been caught in a snowstorm and was rescued by the lamas. But that did not explain why Lucien would not see his own son.

Alexander withdrew and kisslicked the monk's arm to heal it. The monk placed his hand over the wounds, nodded and smiled. "I tell

26

him yu awake. Rest now." Then he rose, took the bowl with him and left, closing the door softly.

Alexander could do nothing now but lay back and let the energy of the feed do its work. The place felt peaceful and serene, and he could not fight it even if he tried. Gradually, his eyes closed again in sleep.

12

The next evening Alexander woke alone. He rose carefully, feeling shaky and weak at first, but when he stood up straight the dizzy feeling vanished.

After he relieved himself in the urinal vase, Alexander found his reflection in a polished plate of metal hanging over the small commode. There, he saw patches of pink on his skin where the frost had gotten to his face, along with the shadow of a beard.

He looked around for his pack and found it resting on the floor at the foot of the bed. The cinched straps were fastened just he had left them. He opened it and withdrew the knife he used for skinning, moistened his cheeks with the water he found in a pitcher nearby and began scraping the stubble from his face. When he was done he combed out his long dark hair with his fingers, ruminating on the calm silence in his mind.

He turned and found his clothes neatly folded and placed on the floor next to his boots. They had been laundered and smelled faintly of lemons. His boots had been brushed clean and the toes repaired where the cold had eaten its way through the leather. And lying next to them, still wrapped in the length of silk, were Musashi's katana and companion sword. He thanked the stars for the Buddhists' honest spirits as he stripped off the pajamas and took up his old clothes.

When he finished dressing he ventured out into the hall and found a wonder in stone and wood.

The temple was large and expansive. Its walls were adorned with carved friezes and brightly painted with scenes of the Buddha performing various miracles. He could not understand their representations, but they were beautiful to him, having found the wisdom of appreciating a foreign culture for the mere fact that it was foreign. He had long outgrown austere English country fashion which demanded banal simplicity and craved anything different which would replace it.

Alexander had gone about fifty feet down the corridor when he found a large library off the main hall. The cabinets lining the walls were alternating honeycombs filled with scrolls of goatskin, and shelves with books hand written on folded strips of parchment and bound between wooden boards.

Always the curious sort, he entered and wandered aimlessly, then approached the tables where the lamas worked with the parchments. Some were painted, others were covered with symbols of a language he did not know. A few looked yellowed and brittle with age, and were laid open next to new parchment. The novices were kept busy copying them to learn and to preserve the knowledge and traditions passed down from the beginning of recorded time.

Alexander saw the ink pots and hawk feathers which were the instruments for writing; the trays where pots of dried tempera sat waiting for water to free the bright colors they contained; and the ceramic vases that contained brushes, their horsehair heads wrapped tightly to their handles with bits of brightly colored silk. Some were so fine that they held no more than a few hairs, others were broad and flat, round and pointed.

He stood wondering at the sight until he heard someone coming into the room behind him. Alexander turned around as a small old man approached. He was also clad in yellow and orange robes and had the aura of authority about him, but a calm smile. His voice was smooth and even, and his English diction was nearly perfect as he said, "welcome to Shangri-la. I am glad to see you have recovered."

"I am feeling much better now. Thank you, master," Alexander replied, affecting a courteous bow.

The lama chuckled. "No one is master here. We are all the same, no matter the outward signs of difference between us."

Alexander replied, "then I stand corrected. My name is Alexander Corvina. I came to see my father, Lucien Arkanon."

The old man's dark eyes flashed in the lamplight. "I am Naglara Rinpoche, abbot of this lamasery. Your arrival was foretold to me by your father, so you were fortunate that we found you in time. The mountain passes are closed now, and will not open again until the spring."

"I am very grateful for your welcome. I am new to your lands, and misjudged the weather," Alexander replied. "Can you tell me why my father has not come to welcome me? Did I do something to displease him?"

"It is not our fashion to know another man's thoughts until he is ready to reveal them," the old man said. "Lu-shen has not said more than a few words since he came to us a century ago. He stays in his own house and does not share himself with us unless he has a need for the blood which sustains him, and he works alone in his own garden in the spring and summer."

Alexander bowed his head sadly. "I see. It has been a very long time since my mother died. It is not healthy for him to maintain his guilt over her death. I had hoped to convince him to rejoin the world of men and take up his life again."

"From my experience of him, that may be a mistake," Rinpoche replied gently. "Lu-shen may not be ready to face the world outside, and we cannot make him go against his will. He alone will decide when that shall be."

"What am I to do, then? I am trapped here until the spring," Alexander said. "Is there something I can do for you, to compensate you for your hospitality?"

The old man placed a calm hand on his shoulder and replied, "you are welcome to bide your time with us under no obligation. We could use another hand at our labors, but only if it is what you wish to do. You will be free to pursue whatever study interests you. Or you may meditate or pray alone as you will. I will go to Lu-shen and talk to him. Perhaps he will be willing to see you. It may not be now, or tomorrow, or in a week, or yet in a month's passing, but when he feels the time is right."

"Then I will wait for his answer," Alexander said. "Thank you for your generosity."

"Good," Rinpoche said calmly. "I will leave you now, as I have another matter I must attend to."

The old man turned away and disappeared down the hall. Left with little more than hope, Alexander strolled the halls alone, then retired to his room and slept a little while more.

At suppertime the next evening, Rinpoche came to him and said, "he is not yet ready to see you. I am sorry, Aleksand'r. You will have to wait a little while longer."

Alexander stared at him as if he had been struck in the face. "What has happened?"

"I know not the reason for the delay. He does not always confide his innermost thoughts to me," the abbot replied. "There have been times when he is silent as a stone, and others when he speaks only when spoken to. We have chosen to indulge these whims with patience, for his moods and humors change like the wind. And though he has never been violent, his appearance reflects some inner battle which often leaves him bruised and beaten as if he has been at war. It puzzles me, but I have learned to accept these spells with the hope that they, too, will pass."

His hopes dashed, the young man said, "It would appear that I have little choice but to wait. Please allow me some little time to be alone."

"As you wish," the abbot replied with a calm smile and a short bow, then left the room, closing the door behind him.

Alexander collapsed onto the thin futon and brooded quietly until the knot of concern in his stomach dissolved away, and comfort came when the soft voices of his blood assured him that his father still loved him, no matter the circumstances of his birth.

13

The next evening, Alexander went back to the library to explore it, and perused the books he had found there. He could not read them yet but there were pictures in them and he found a vague understanding of the words from those. They spoke of cycles and creation, destiny and karma, life and death, and how to treat everyone with dignity and reverence. "The life of another is as sacred as the life you own," one of them said. He tried to take that axiom to heart.

Rather than isolate himself from the lamas, Alexander joined them at their meditation, their prayers and rituals of offering. The sonorous chant they uttered in the late afternoon was an interlaced harmony of musical sound like the resonance of the universe. He could hear it even in sleep.

It was the heartbeat of the world, very like the heartbeat he heard in his mother's womb before he was violently wrenched from it and ushered into the unknown plane of existence that was life.

He spent most of the next few weeks learning something of the Buddhism the lamas practiced from their oral instruction as they prepared their acolytes for the priesthood. They spoke in Tibetan but it was no longer hard to follow since he had fed from the lama that first day. He asked no questions, but slowly picked up the threads of tradition the sect practiced.

It was a nonviolent religion, professing a neutral accepting attitude toward all things great and small, and rejecting any reason for war, hate or intolerance. It professed that all of mankind was perfect as part of the universe, but was not aware of it and could not divest the need to clutter their lives with possessions or wealth; and that living was a bardo that one passed through on the way to realizing that perfection.

He watched the lamas create mandalas; ritual paintings with colored sand which illustrated the universe in all its complexity. Each mandala was completely different from another in its design, but the overall meaning of each was that the universe was the whole of creation itself; and the gods and goddesses depicted therein were but aspects of the whole, which mankind was allowed to experience in order to understand his place in it. And as each mandala was finished and the last prayer said, the painting was destroyed and the sands scattered to the four winds.

He was skeptical about reincarnation, but what he knew from his own blood was that the only thing truly eternal was the universe itself, having no beginning and no end; and he also knew that of all things, change was the only true constant in the universe.

Every evening Alexander worked to express his joy and sorrow in his feeble attempts at poetry. He wrote and experimented, discarded what he did not like, kept what he did, sometimes threw it all away and started over. One evening he showed his rhymes to Rinpoche, and after having read them the lama said, "these are very good. The rhythm is smooth and unencumbered by unnecessary words."

"But, they will never be perfect, will they?" Alexander asked.

The younger man chuckled quietly. "Perfection is not your goal, is it? Satisfaction comes not in the destination, but in the journey," he replied. "You must write because you enjoy doing it, no matter the reward or lack thereof."

"But if no one ever reads my work, then it matters not that I write," Alexander replied, puzzling.

"It matters to you, for what would it profit you if your words are for your eyes alone? You write to show others the depth of your feelings, to educate them in the artistry of your heart. To color the world with shades and textures they do not yet know or appreciate. Yes?"

After a moment of reflection, Alexander said, "yes."

"Then write until there is no more to write. You will know when to stop," the abbot said with a calm smile, then handed the thin sheets of parchment back and walked away.

Alexander took his words to heart, and resolved to write only when the muse struck him. He began to practice yoga and kept his body fit by chopping wood for the cooking fires; hunted for meat in the snow-covered meadow at dusk and brought back rabbits and deer to add to the stewing pots.

He learned how to cook and what herbs and spices were used to bring out the most savory flavors and in the right proportions. He occupied himself with learning how to read sanskrit until the snow began to disappear from the rocky ground and the river at the bottom of the gorge ran free of ice again.

But when the trees began to sprout fresh green shoots and the songs of the mountain birds filled the skies, Alexander decided that it was enough time for waiting, and approached Rinpoche to ask the inevitable question. "I have waited long enough. Will he see me now?" he asked.

The abbot faced him with an appraising eye and nodded. "I will ask him yet again, after supper."

Alexander then said, "this is the last time I will ask. If he will not see me tonight, I will pack my things and go. He will never see me again if that is his wish. It was he who invited me here, and it vexes me that he makes me wait thus. I cannot wait forever."

The head lama nodded again. "I will tell him."

Supper was torturous. Alexander picked listlessly at his rice, barely paying attention while the lamas laughed and told stories, shared bits of philosophy, and practiced drumming with their fingers on the wooden tables to maintain their rhythm. He gritted his teeth against the months of frustration built up in his blood even as he used the joyful noise around him as a distraction to dampen it.

Rinpoche appeared to notice this, then gathered his robes and stood up, walked toward the door and disappeared down the hall. Alexander watched him go and hoped that this time his patience would not be denied.

A few minutes later, the abbot returned. "He will see you now. Come with me," he said.

Rinpoche led Alexander down a long corridor, then out of the temple. The two crossed the gardens in silence and approached another house on the compound. It was smaller than the others, made of stone blocks like a crypt, with a roof covered in rattan and ivy. It was set well back among a bower of trees, almost invisible among the vegetation surrounding it.

"This is Lu-shen's house," he explained.

Alexander wondered. "I have lived here for months, yet I have not seen this place before," he said.

"That is because he did not wish you to see it," Rinpoche replied patiently. He pushed open the ancient door and led Alexander into darkness so profound that the moonlight outside could not penetrate it.

Rinpoche pitched his voice louder as he called out, "Lu-shen, your son is here to see you."

The voice that greeted him was deep and accented, fluid with melodic echoes. *"Thank you, Rinpoche. You may go now."*

The lama bowed to the darkness, then went back out, leaving Alexander standing alone. The young man forgot his anger as he stood waiting for some sign from his father.

The voice came again, without the echo. "You have grown into a fine looking young man. I am glad to see you are well, and that the years have not diminished your spirit."

"Father, why would you not see me before?" Alexander asked. He searched the darkness with his eyes but could not see anything.

"I…could not face you yet. My heart was so heavy with sadness that I could not even think you still loved me, after all that you endured in my long absence. I left you alone to grow without a father to guide you, to help you through your transition. I dared not stay by your side, for I feared that I would infect you with my sorrow."

"Then come out of the darkness and face me, man to man, for I would see you as you are," Alexander demanded. "I am a child no longer and would know my father's image, so long has it been that I do not know it in my heart."

The dark grew silent. Then a tall figure in black walked toward him from seeming nowhere. His skin was pale, almost blue white. Long hair as white as the snow on the mountains cascaded down over the black toga like a waterfall. The almond shaped eyes were silver grey, and the bright red lights at their centers told of his alien nature. No man Alexander knew had eyes like those but himself, and he stepped back briefly at the shock of seeing them.

"Come. Be not afraid," Lucien said softly. "I can never harm you." He opened his arms and the drape of his robe became dark wings.

Alexander approached and threw his arms around Lucien's body, hugging him fiercely as if he would never let go. "Father, I missed you so much. Please forgive me for doubting your love for me," he said.

The wings closed around Alexander, and the smooth skin of Lucien's fine boned cheek touched his as his voice rumbled pleasantly in his ear. "I missed you, too, Alexander. It warms my heart to see you again. Not since you were a babe did I look upon your face. And from what Rinpoche said of you I know that you were raised to manhood well."

They stood hugging each other tightly for another silence until Lucien released Alexander and studied him from head to toe. "Look at you," he said. "You have grown tall and strong. But you are dressed strangely. Has fashion left me behind? It has been over a century since I wore leggings."

"There have been some changes," Alexander replied. "Men wear such things which mimic the accoutrements of war, while the women's skirts have grown wider and fuller, like blossoms, until one can scarcely know they have legs."

34

"But we know they have legs, do we not?" Lucien replied with a soft wink.

"As you say," he laughed. "But, your hair... I have a vague memory that it was black at one time."

Lucien twisted a lock of his fine white hair between his fingers. "I have been fasting and testing my need for blood. I have succeeded in controlling my hunger but there is a price to pay for my resistance. I did not want to prey too often upon my benefactors, for they would have turned me out into the snow if I did. The monks are kind as their sect demands, but as humans they fear my alien nature. Thus, the dragon's blood has seen fit to drain my hair of its color to appease its appetite."

"When I was first found and brought here, the lama who tended to me did not appear to mind giving me his blood," Alexander said.

"Tell me, how many times have you availed yourself of the lama's generosity?" Lucien asked.

"Only once," he replied, feeling a little confused.

"That is good. How have you managed to avoid feeding?"

"I feed on animal blood, father," Alexander replied. "I have been tempted at times to feed on the others, but I feel uncomfortable with taking what is not offered to me."

The older Xosan studied his son's face, and a sudden dismay crossed his features. "You have killed to feed before," he said. "What happened?"

"She was my best friend of all. I loved her, but her love tempted me beyond my capacity for control. I took too much by accident. To this day I feel great shame and sorrow for what I had done."

"Yes. . . Good. . . There is hope," Lucien murmured absently.

"Father, I do not understand," Alexander replied.

Lucien's smile was smooth, so unlike the decaying malodorous dentition of humans, and his canines were longer than the rest of his teeth. "I had thought... I do not know how to express this. You are so unlike your uncle. I feared that his madness had passed on to you."

"I wish to have nothing to do with my uncle,," Alexander declared hotly. "He killed my mother, and I felt it in her blood as she died slowly."

At this, Lucien's mouth dropped open. "You... felt it? But you were not born yet. How could you feel it with such clarity of understanding?"

"I do not know, nor do I understand how. I only know the pain she felt when he took her, and the death of her mind afterward. It is etched onto my soul like a sword thrust through my bowels." As he spoke, his hands clenched tightly into fists.

Lucien placed his long fingered hands on his son's shoulders and replied, "then you must find the strength to push that memory to the back of your mind, for it will do you damage to dwell too long upon it."

"How came you to this place? I had thought..." He paused when Lucien made a short wave with his hand, then walked a few steps away.

After composing himself, Lucien said, "after you were born, my mind was unbalanced by her death, and my remorse too painful to bear. So I left you with Hortensia and her sister. I wandered aimlessly and could not find a place to settle. For a time I even contemplated ending my life but my blood prevented me, and told me that my lonely exile was punishment enough for my sins. In my peregrinations I became hopelessly lost in the mountains. Then I was found by the lamas of Shangri-la, just as you were, and have remained here ever since."

"Father, your letters never told me this," he replied.

"Alas, I wanted to avoid adding more to your boyhood than you could endure. In time my heart was mended by life among these good people. Naglara's father reminded me that I was a man of their future, and that I had a singular purpose for living."

Alexander gave him a sharp look. "I do not understand," he said.

"He said that I had transcended the cycle of reincarnation through my immortality, and that I must live to save the world one day."

"But if that is true, then why stay here? Why not visit the world and change the course of the future?"

"I... I feel that my efforts would not bear fruit now," Lucien replied softly. "The time is not yet right. I have heard things among the travelers who pass through the valley, and I fear that the world is not yet ready for someone like me."

Alexander reflected on that for a moment, then said, "I am a man of that world. I cannot bide here and meditate, chant and study forever. Come with me. You need not do more than look at the changes men have wrought in the last two centuries to see that things are better now than they were before."

"Then counsel me, and tell me all that you have seen and heard," Lucien said. "I must not go into the world without preparation. Live with me here for a short time, and enlighten me. I have kept my mind closed from the thoughts of men for such a long time that I have almost lost the practice."

15

Alexander moved his things into the cottage and began his father's instruction. He talked of the wars and the factions, of the advances in science and art, and about the wondrous places he had visited on his way. Lucien was a patient listener, and only stopped him when the sun came up. Then they slept the day long like corpses and resumed their discourse the next evening.

But of all the things Alexander showed him, it was the curved blade of the katana that truly fascinated Lucien. He took it into his hand and swung it as if it was an extension of his arm, making a few practiced swipes as if he knew every lesson Musashi had imparted. He said, "this weapon is very like our own. When did these people learn to forge them?"

"Musashi said the practice was handed down for centuries, and where it came from is shielded in antiquity and oral tradition," Alexander replied. "But he taught himself everything about using a sword to fight."

Lucien ran his long fingers along the flat of the blade and examined the wavy pattern that marked the metal with its uniqueness. He turned the blade up into the lamp's dim light and scrutinized the markings carved into its surface.

"I wonder how much that is Xosan has been retained over the years," he remarked softly. "The technique of forging swords is preserved among us even though we no longer make them, and that tradition has endured for thousands of years in human reckoning."

That comment surprised Alexander. He had never heard of beings from another world making a contribution to the history of mankind. No one at Oxford had ever even mentioned it, nor even knew what happened before the time men started to set down their journey through history in writing. All was illuminated through the Bible, which was only then beginning to circulate among the upper classes in Europe through the Gütenberg press.

"Father, I do not understand my own blood when it speaks to me," he remarked candidly. "I know a man's entire life through his blood, and yet I know nothing of what it is to be Xosan."

Lucien smiled calmly as he resheathed the katana and handed it back. "In that, you are more Xosan than I am."

Alexander rocked back on his heels. "What?"

His father chuckled. "We are Xosan, but we were men once. Surely your blood has told you this?"

"No. It has only told me what I must do to survive. It warns me when I am in danger, and it forces me to go on living when I have nearly lost all hope. It has told me nothing of the past."

"That is as it should be," Lucien replied. "Such knowledge is preserved against the day when it is needed. Come. Sit down." He sat down into a half lotus on the reed mat nearby and gestured toward another.

As Alexander put the sword aside and obeyed he puzzled even more. "Mean you that it would have caused me harm to know it?"

"The shock to your young mind would have been great indeed, so your blood bided its time until the moment you were prepared to understand. Now you are a man, and ready to face the changes that were thrust upon you by your ancestral heritage."

Lucien hesitated, and turned his attention to the closed door of the room as if he heard something outside. Then he continued, "there are worlds that you have never seen. There are people who live on other worlds like this one, and machines, great and small, that serve them as if they were living also. These humans with whom we live are just taking their first steps toward the cosmos, and like infants they falter, and stumble, and sometimes fall down. They are not ready to see all there is to see, and you are just like them in that you were not given to know your true potential in your youth. But in time you will know and understand all."

"And yet, I knew my mother's pain as if it were my own," Alexander said. "That much I was given to remember."

Lucien sighed. "That was unavoidable."

"Please tell me why it was ever thus."

Lucien took a deep breath and then continued. "Your mother was an intelligent woman who lived in a world that was not ready for new ideas. When she dreamed, she dreamed of a time where people were no longer at war and everyone was happy. For my part I nurtured her visions as best I could, but she could not tell anyone else because they would not have understood."

"They would have seen her as a witch," Alexander said. "I have seen what superstition has done to many in my travels. The Christians say that we cannot suffer a witch to live."

"That is because they do not understand the wonders the universe has to offer, or the capacity of the human mind to trandscend its physical limits. Hardship and want rules the earth now, Alexander. Starve a man, and all he can see is food. Starve a man of ideas, and he cannot hope to see the future."

"Rinpoche and the others have taught me something of the religion they practice here," Alexander said. "They believe that the universe is but one of many, and that we live through many lifetimes, learning and growing with each death and rebirth. But you are immortal, and not bound by such a ring. How does that make you feel?"

"If that were true I should feel blessed," Lucien replied with a small shrug. "But no one is ever truly immortal. I may outlive all the lamas at this lamasery, and all the people living in the world now, but I will die, and even I cannot foretell when that will happen. Everyone dies sooner or later, but as I am sure Rinpoche has told you, the soul lives on forever. It is so similar to what my ancestors believe."

Lucien paused to let that sink in, then added, "and we are not alone in this."

"But you have lived for more years than anyone I know. That is akin to immortality, is it not?"

"I was speaking rhetorically."

"Why must we hide what we are? How many of us are there?" Alexander asked.

"That matters not. What matters is that we are here, and as far as history is concerned, we have always been here."

"I still do not understand."

Lucien replied. "A few years before you were born, we came to this world in a great machine which transported us across time and space. There were but a hundred of us who survived the voyage. Our craft, intelligent as it was, could not avoid collision with an asteroid. It crashed to earth in the mountains, close to our home in Transylvania. We few who survived were forced to scatter over the world by privation and war. But it has happened once before. When I was a child, my grandfather told me the story of a group who were sent to rescue another, but they were never seen or heard from again. That happened long before I was born, and I am now almost six thousand years old."

"Six thousand?!" Alexander exclaimed, then tried to calm down. "I am sorry I shouted, father."

As he spoke Lucien's flapped his right hand languidly, a casual dismissing gesture. "No need to apologize. I had the same reaction myself when I took count of my birthdays."

"I can scarcely imagine living such a long time," Alexander said. "How do you spend your days without growing tired of life?"

"I live my life one day at a time. I take all things in equal measure, as the lamas have taught me. I do not dwell overlong on regrets, save for those I have for your mother. The past is a reminder, just as the future is a plan. But those like us must weather the changes of season just as other men do."

"And what of history?"

"There is no need to think of the past or the future as long as you pay attention to the present. But do not forget the past. Your memory will play tricks upon you if you are not careful."

"As you say, father. I will think on all you have told me," Alexander said. He did not ask what Lucien had decided about leaving Shangri-la and reasoned that his father would let him know when the time was right. "The hour is late, and the sun will be up ere long. I will leave you now to your meditation, and see you tomorrow evening."

The next evening, Alexander said, "I learn a great deal about a man from his blood. But I am curious. What does the blood of Xosan taste like?"

Lucien replied, "I will let you feed from my veins, and from the sharing you shall know all you need to know." He stretched his arm out to Alexander. "My blood is pure Xosan, and he who was the first one of our kind is a part of me, just as he was part of my fathers. Come. Drink."

His son went to his knees and took his arm. Carefully, he bit into the cold wrist. Lucien gasped sharply and tilted his head back, closing his eyes. Alexander tasted cold fire, metal and honey, ambrosia. Then he went blind and deaf. Visions filled his mind with images of space, stars, planets, all merged together into explosions of light, color and sound, which faded into a black silence so profound that it was frightening.

The black gave way to an image of a man and a winged dragon facing each other in the darkness of a cavern. The creature glowed blue along its scaly skin, and its eyes were red as the fires of hell. In the next moment, it leapt forward with an unearthly shriek and knocked the man onto his back. It pinned him there with its scaly claws and opened its mouth, revealing two long sharp teeth. The man screamed once with terror, and struggled, but the dragon held him down easily until he calmed into limp compliance, dipped its head and bit his throat.

After only a few seconds the dragon released the man, then scored one of its arms with a long sharp talon and allowed the blood to flow. The blood was blue, dark as the sea. Its voice came out thunder and bells as it said, "*drink now, and receive the remedy you seek.*"

The man struggled to his feet and staggered weakly toward the monster before him. He clasped the bleeding limb and took a tentative lick at the blue liquid, then clamped his lips over the wound. When he had drunk enough, he stopped and drew back.

The dragon licked the wound like a cat to heal it, then said, "*thy body will change and thy blood will tell thee how to live. Go now and bear my blood to thy progeny, so that thy kind may know the march of days without end. Strong shalt thou be henceforward, and thy sons and daughters shall become my children.*"

The dark enveloped the scene in its embrace, and seemed to be liquid, like water; yet Alexander could still breathe. He swam upwards and fought his way to the surface. Then as awareness returned he opened his eyes. He looked up and saw that Lucien's eyes were still closed and his face was calm, and as he withdrew from the dark flood he said, "that was… so real. I could hear the dragon's voice in my mind," he said. "I could taste the dragon's blood. Fire and ice. And the power.... it is all far beyond my ability to comprehend."

Lucien's eyes opened, and the red fire in them damped down to a dull flame as he took a deep breath. "It is the memory we all share as Xosan, from the moment our race changed and ascended. Xosan was the first and the bravest of us all, who sacrificed his humanity to save our race from extinction. The dragon's blood is our blood, and it has been so since that day."

"But, I was born of a human woman, and my blood is red as other men's. What am I, father?"

"You are the best of both worlds, of Antellus and of this soil which we call Terra. You have a responsibility to protect this flock of prey from harm. We must bear witness to history, and pass the traditions of our ancestors to our children, just as Xosan passed it to us."

"Tell me how it came to this," Alexander said eagerly.

"Ah," Lucien said. "It is a wonderful story." He shifted to get comfortable. "Eons ago, by earthly reckoning, the red sun which gave us life and death lashed out and struck Antellus, just as a frog snatches a fly from the air. Our astronomers saw the danger coming and warned of the catastrophe, so our people went to live in the deep caverns beneath the surface to escape its terrible wrath.

"Xosan was just a boy then, a prince of the royal blood. He grew to manhood in darkness, and feared not the underworld which protected him. But as time passed, the people grew restless and wished to return to the outer world. But scouts sent to the surface never returned, and when others followed they found a world so destroyed that there was nothing left to call home. Food and water began to run out, and disease infected the people. When his father died, Xosan inherited little more than a few thousand starving and half-mad creatures to rule. He knew that something had to be done to save them, or they would all die out to the last child."

"How did he meet the dragon?" Alexander asked.

"Xosan was driven to search for a way out for his people. In the quest for an isolated place to meditate on the problem he took a wrong turn and became lost. He wandered for a time before he found himself in the cavern where the dragon lived, and awakened it by accident. The dragon knew him almost from the first moment they met, and it showed him what he had to do to save his people. Now, all the dragon's powers are in your blood, and will be to the end of your days."

Alexander said, "but, the dragon cannot have lived in the dark all that time. It does not seem possible."

"We believe that it slept there through the ages, and that it was waiting for the blood of a human to fulfill the purpose for its existence," Lucien replied. "The sacred dragon was immune from the effects of age or disease. The blood Xosan was given was filled with the living seeds that gave us the power to survive. It was the catalyst for change in the lives of all Xosan who came after him, and they were human no longer. We were transformed into blood drinkers ourselves, like the dragon who lived in the dark."

When he had finished Alexander stared at him, astonished. "So, in order for our race to survive we had to give up our souls," he breathed, not sure whether he should be outraged or not.

"Nay. It was not that simple a fate for us, for ours was a legacy written in blood. We multiplied and prospered just as the dragon said we would, and learned to use the darkness to our advantage. In time we were able to live on the surface as long as the night lasted, and made our world prosperous again. We took our powers for granted, grew arrogant and full of pride. We forged a mighty empire that spanned the sky you see at night. We were invincible, and one day our lust for power grew so great that we dared to look upon ourselves as gods." Lucien paused to lick his lips. "But more reasoned minds decided that we had gone too far, that we had lost our way, and tried to restore us to the simple life Xosan had ordained for us. And so we made war upon each other just as other men do, and I followed my brother blindly into the folly that brought us here."

"So you were not perfect."

"Aye. You do not know what horrors I visited upon our enemies in my brother's name. But it was your mother who gentled my soul and showed the way out of my miserable and pointless existence. She conquered me with love and compassion, not with a sword. She taught me how to live in the open and use the daylight rather than cower in perpetual darkness, how to feed without killing, how to conquer my fear of my brother and so gain my freedom from his ambitions."

Alexander sat and considered, then said, "then I have much to be thankful for, if she had such power, for she forged in you a good heart."

Lucien reached over and grabbed his hand to squeeze it. "You are so kind to say so, but I am so filled with guilt for her death that I can scarcely feel any but the most abject self loathing."

"And my uncle?"

"Aye. I wished that it were so with your uncle, but he is my mirror image in that respect. He had no compassion when he took your mother, no matter that he claimed to love her. It was not love but an unnatural obsession for what he could never have. He preferred to destroy her rather than give her up, and for that I cannot forgive him."

"Nor can I," Alexander agreed. "But I would remind you that it has been almost two hundred years since her death, and your guilt has lasted beyond all comprehension."

Lucien sighed, and look away with an expression of futility. "I cannot forgive myself for leaving her alone for so long and allowing him the opportunity to find her. I could have stopped him if I had returned in time."

"Surely there was no choice in the matter," Alexander insisted. "You could not have been with her every moment of every day."

"That may be true, but…"

"If I can absolve you of a human mistake, then you should absolve yourself. I am certain she would have done."

Lucien smiled faintly. "How well you put it. But the loss of her love and companionship is like the loss of my own right arm, or an eye. She and I were the same soul, the same breath, the same life. I do not know when I will ever be whole again."

"Father, you must purge your sorrow or you will fall into madness," Alexander insisted. "If you will not come out of this place with me, then I must know that you will consider the alternative."

Lucien studied him quietly, then said, "your words have merit. Let me think on your proposal a little longer."

So Alexander did not press the matter, and passed the evening telling his father more about the outside world until the cock's crow began to herald the coming dawn.

17

Alexander woke suddenly with the sensation of profound silence banging at the door to his consciousness, sending all his senses into battle readiness.

He rose quickly and padded on bare feet into the small common room, then ventured down the short hall toward the back and the darkest part of the house. There he found the door to Lucien's bedroom wide open. The room had no windows, and the futon on which his father slept was disturbed as if he had just left it.

He sniffed, and found a trail of honey and rust drifting on the still night air. Alexander followed it outside and spotted the tall lean figure in black sitting on a boulder. His face was turned up toward the light of the rising moon, wearing an expression of serene contentment like the Buddha. Then, as if he sensed his son approaching, he turned his head. His eyes were glowing, two small pinpoints of red fire in the dark.

Alexander halted, feeling as if he had just intruded on a private conference with the infinite. "Forgive me, father. I did not mean to disturb your meditation," he said.

"Come closer, Alexander," Lucien said with a flourish of his long fingers. "I have just been gazing on the Moon. She is my guide in all things."

Alexander perched himself on the rock next to Lucien, looking up at the full orb just cresting the mountains. It was bright pale blue against the scattered clouds, turning the dark night into a dim silvered day.

"Tell me. What do you see when you look upon her?" Lucien asked.

"I see shadows and light. The lamas call the shadows the great hare."

"She reminds me of your mother. She looks upon the earth with sadness and reproach."

Alexander cocked his head to try and see it his way, and finally agreed. "She does look sad."

Lucien turned himself around on the rock and pointed toward the northwest. Alexander followed his pointing finger as he said, "do you know what the people here call that formation of stars? The four that form a diamond with a point at its center?"

"They call it the Great Swan," Alexander said.

"That may be so in other parts of the world, but here they call it 'The Child of The Dragon'. And see, the stars of Draco just above it."

Alexander saw that the two constellations seemed to follow one another toward the southern sky. "Ah. I see."

"These people believe that the dragon is the god of creation, and that the moon is his mistress. He chases after her every night, but he can never catch her."

"My blood has no knowledge of these things."

"It is myth, therefore your blood does not acknowledge it. Among these people, myth resides side by side with reality. They accept it as if it was truth. But these ideas were passed down from a time in antiquity, so far back that no one remembers where they originated."

Alexander recalled his lessons at university. "In Greek myth the Titan Gaea created the earth, and the stars were created by the gods. But I gaze upon the stars often and wonder what agency is truly responsible."

Lucien smiled gently. "The universe created itself. It has been here long before this planet was formed from the drifting matter among the stars, and will be here long after it has gone dark or been destroyed by the forces that created it. No one can ever discover all the complexities of its nature, nor understand its purpose, but it has endured all this time to light our way. The universe is part of us, just as we are part of it. We, you and I, are made of star stuff, ever mutable, ever changing. We need not fear death, for it is the supreme agent of change, and nothing is ever lost."

46

Alexander paused before speaking, not sure what he meant. But Lucien continued. "You are right, Alexander. I must learn to forgive myself, and resume the work I deserted years ago."

As the mantle of dread lifted from his shoulders, Alexander gave his father a tight hug of affection.

Later that evening, Alexander went to Rinpoche and told him of Lucien's decision. The abbot smiled and replied, "that is good. I am glad to see that Lu-shen has decided to move on with life. You have succeeded where we could not."

"He is my father," Alexander said simply. "No one could convince him but one of his own kind."

"Then on the morrow we will guide you both to Tsangpo, at the pass into Nepal," Rinpoche said. "The journey will take us three days."

18

April, 1646

When Alexander and Lucien were packed and ready to go, Rinpoche dispatched several lamas to guide them. As they had no horses everyone walked. The small procession left the ancient stronghold to go into the valley, stopping twice in the small villages they found erected along the way. The road was clearly marked as a rough but well trodden footroad through the wild mountainous terrain.

The lamas' only possessions were their begging bowls, their walking sticks and the clothes on their backs, so there was little chance of being set upon by the bandits that lived in the hills. Even if they did, the walking sticks could be quickly turned into quarterstaffs with a moment's notice, and the lamas were fit and well trained in the art of self defense.

The Tibetans were mostly nomadic people who followed their flocks from pasture to pasture, and they shared whatever they had when the lamas stopped for food and sleep. The mountain air and the hardship these people endured were actually good for them. With rare exceptions they were fit and strong, and their peace was preserved by the fact that they trained in the martial arts as vigorously as any Spartan. All the men wore swords at their belts next to their prayer beads. The women, besides bearing swords themselves, could turn their scarves into lariats or garrottes.

Both genders rode their mountain ponies with the expert skill of circus performers, and their spring celebrations included war games, played sometimes with a ball. They were all equal partners in war and in other aspects of Tibetan daily life. There was no room for sloth or indolence, and their imaginative folk tales educated and entertained the children at their campfires.

Alexander and Lucien kept to themselves or hunted for blood among the flocks, while the lamas ate their fill of the meat, yoghurt and khipu offered them, all staples of the Tibetan diet. They watched for danger while the lamas gave blessings to newborns among the flocks and the families or ministered to the sick or dying. Then the group would reassemble and walk on until the sun set below the jagged line of the mountains.

The lamas stopped to preside over the funeral ceremony for an old woman who had just died, escorting the long procession of mourners to a place set well apart in the hills. Alexander was told that her flesh would feed the vultures who lived there. The natives disposed of their dead this way because the ground was too hard to dig a grave and there was no wood to waste on a fire for cremation. Resources were scarce and valuable, and the body was considered to be nothing more than a vessel for the spirit.

A man from the village brought a large sword forward and set to work dismembering the corpse in front of the villagers and a growing crowd of vultures, who watched with stoic patience. As he threw the pieces to the birds they descended on them, turning into flapping, churning masses of avian hunger to feast until only the bones were left.

Then the bones were gathered together and wrapped in a piece of cloth to be set inside one of the tall brick towers that dotted the land. No one here knew who made them or when, but they suggested good strategic planning on someone's part. They were probably watchtowers put there to warn the whole valley if invaders were seen. But many had already fallen into disrepair from great age, and others were now used as storage bins for food and other dry goods.

Once the final prayer was said, the people dispersed to return to their homes and the lamas walked on, leading Lucien and Alexander on toward Tsangpo.

A day later, when the group arrived at their destination, the lamas wished Lucien and Alexander good fortune, bowed deeply, then walked away down the narrow trail and back toward Shangri-la.

Alexander lost no time looking around at the houses, the animals and chickens grazing in the yards. Here there were three towers overlooking the village, speaking of prosperity and importance fallen on harder times. But the air felt strange, and a sensation of chill ran up his spine.

The place seemed almost deserted. Those on the road had retreated inside and watched the two strangers from the shelter of their lintels with guarded curiosity, their faces speaking of tension and suspicion. "There is something wrong here," he said, sotto voce.

Lucien sniffed. "Aye. The scent of blood and fear is unmistakable. This village has seen trouble before. Come. Let us find a place to stay and learn the story. Someone here must know what happened."

They walked at a deliberately casual pace through the village until they found a ramshackle inn and entered it.

The owner was a short rotund man with piercing dark eyes, and when he saw them he started as if he was caught by surprise. Then he quickly came to them and said, "welcome to Tsangpo," in halting Tibetan. "My name is Shenporu. This is my place. You hungry? Thirsty? I get you food. Please, sit."

He indicated the long wooden table in the center of the room, where two other men sat rapidly spooning at the porridge in the bowls between them. They glanced up, startled, then resumed eating in silence. When they were finished, they left the empty bowls where they were and left the inn as if they were in a great hurry.

Lucien sniffed with distaste, then shrugged. He had seen it all too often before.

"We are not hungry," Alexander replied. "We wish to know when you expect the next caravan to arrive."

Shenporu hesitated, a gesture not lost on them, then scratched at the thatch on his head. "We do not get many travelers here, my lord. The last traders went through our village over a month ago, and we do not know when more will come. We have little to offer you but warmth and the hospitality of our inn."

"We would find a place for ourselves," Lucien said. "Is there a cave or grove nearby where we may camp in safety?"

The innkeeper blanched, and his wide eyes went wider. "You must not go into the hills alone, my lord. It is too dangerous," he protested.

"We can take care of ourselves," Alexander assured him. "What concern is it that sows such fear among you?"

The innkeeper swallowed, then said, "no one is safe, my lord. The yeti is there. Please. Stay here, where it is safe."

"Yeti? What is a yeti?" he asked, frowning.

"A demon, my lord. A great white ape that craves manflesh. It comes in the night and raids our village when all are asleep, steals our food and kills our people. At nightfall we hear a howling that can freeze a man's blood, but when we try to track it or set a trap for it we are always too late. In the morning, someone is found dead, torn to pieces. Eaten." He gestured with trembling fingers toward his own mouth.

"Are you also plagued by wolves?"

"Nay. We know wolf song well, and this is no wolf."

Alexander and Lucien exchanged helpless glances. Then Lucien said, "we will rid your village of this... yeti. Will that earn us shelter for the day?"

The man's eyes welled up with grateful tears. "If you can do that, all that I have is yours!"

"Your thanks are more than we require," Alexander assured him.

The innkeeper directed them to a large room on the second floor. Once the door closed, Alexander and Lucien threw their packs into a corner, undressed, climbed into a large single platform bed placed in the center of the room and fell promptly to sleep.

19

When the sun went down behind the mountains, Alexander and Lucien went down into the village. There they were met with friendlier eyes, and Alexander guessed that the innkeeper must have told everyone what was afoot. Some of the villagers moved quickly away to avoid them, but an old man approached timidly and said, "I am Devarta Nibleg. I am to show you what the yeti has already done. Please to come with me."

He led them to an isolated group of yurts and huts set at the edge of the compound, and stood by watching while Alexander and Lucien roamed among the dwellings and saw some of the damage. After a thorough examination there was enough evidence to conclude that the innkeeper was only partly right. The random distribution of things and furniture in the structures indicated the attack of a native animal, not a demon, and the strong scent of animal spoor drifted on the cold air around them.

"Father, the creature appears to know the habits of these people," Alexander remarked as he kicked at a loose timber.

"Aye. It is clever, but to a point," Lucien replied. "If it were truly wise it would confine its hunting to the hills, but it has aquired the taste for manflesh. Perhaps it has young ones to feed." He examined the remnants of the bedding before him, kicking delicately at the blood soaked linens. "I smell the youth in these stains. What a pity. I understand its need to find food wherever it can, but it invites death here." Then he asked Nibleg, "how long has this been going on?"

The old man shrugged. "A long, long time. Eh... twelve seasons." In terms of the times, three years was indeed a long time.

Just then, a strange sound echoed among the rocks in the ridge above the village; a low growling roar that ascended into a loud whining keen. For a moment Alexander's blood actually seemed to freeze, and the hackles on the back of his neck stood up before reason reasserted itself and brought his human instincts to heel. He turned to study the high peaks surrounding the valley and marked how the sound echoed and rebounded, lending it a ghostly effect.

Alexander remarked, "that must be the creature, and never have I heard such a sound before. Now I know why the villagers have such a fear of it." He glanced out the broken window and spied the old man scurrying away like a wharf rat in the gathering gloom. "Our new friend Nibleg has deserted us."

Lucien replied, "let us try to stop the animal before it takes another villager."

Together, they scrambled up the slope to a place high above the village, but close enough to the narrow trail to intercept anything that came through. There they waited in silence, frozen like shadows in the growing dark as the campfires and the lights in the village went out and the town settled down for an uneasy sleep.

An hour later, the faint moonlight fought to be seen through gathering stormclouds, and Alexander was almost ready to give up when something came ambling down the trail from the slope above. His night vision revealed no demon or great white ape, as the innkeeper claimed; but a large bear with mottled grey fur which only looked white compared to the snowclad stones around it. Its muzzle looked like it had been burned at one time, and scar tissue had grown over the wound to make its muzzle look apelike. It kept to the shadows and the underbrush, and the color of its fur helped it to blend in well with the snow, rendering it nearly invisible.

The creature must have learned in its lifetime that the best time to forage for food was when it was darkest in the night and the villagers were fast asleep. It paused twice to sniff cautiously, its breath coming out puffs of white vapor in the cold mountain air, then continued on toward the isolated cluster of huts in the general vicinity of the ruined yurt and walked around toward the rear of one of the others.

Lucien gestured quickly to Alexander. Their boots made no sound on the snowy ground as they moved forward after it, split apart and flanked the bear's path on both sides, drawing their swords at the same time.

The creature reared up on its hind legs and begin to scrape and batter at the yurt's wall with its massive paws until it produced a small tear.

The sound of screaming came from inside, and two women emerged from the yurt calling for help. One of them cradled an infant in her arms. The bear ignored them and continued to rip away the goatskin wall in search of its imagined prize, unaware of the pair of dark ghosts pursuing it.

Lucien ran forward and struck the bear in the leg with his blade, then danced back to gain clearance and circled the animal warily. The bear tumbled to the ground uttering a loud yowling roar of pain, scrambled to find its feet again, and almost succeeded.

Alexander came forward and struck it in the other leg, then fell back quickly to dodge a swipe of its claws. It's maw opened to display its huge broken teeth as it tried to rear up again, but the pain of the effort brought its bulk back down, transforming it into a scrambling roaring heap of angry bleeding animal.

Some of the villagers had come running at the sound of screaming, and soon the conflict with the bear became a spectacle of sport as they cheered the two strangers on. The bear scrambled back up, then started to charge the crowd, but Alexander quickly interposed himself and sliced the bear's throat open. The creature fell back and tumbled into a graceless heap on the cold ground, bleeding, refusing to die, groveling in pain. Alexander hesitated, then stayed clear while Lucien stepped forward and staked it to the ground with the point of his blade, ending its misery.

The crowd threw up a thunderous roar of approval. Alexander and Lucien stood together in the circle of humanity in silence, their blood flooded only with pity and remorse for the animal.

There was no such pity on the part of the villagers. Several of the men came forward and set to work skinning the carcass, carving the raw meat into portions which they distributed to the crowd until the animal was literally dismantled to the bones.

Then the villagers dispersed and drifted away toward their homes, leaving the stripped skeleton lying in place as a warning to any other demon who dared to invade their village.

The innkeeper approached Alexander and Lucien with something in his hands wrapped in a small piece of cloth. "Such courage I have never seen before! The peace of our valley is restored," he gushed, handing it to Alexander. "I present you with a token of our gratitude and respect."

Alexander took the parcel and opened it. It was the bear's penis, swollen and still engorged with blood. He stared at it in shock as the innkeeper said, "if you eat it, the bear's spirit will pass into you and give you its strength and stamina. You will be able to give a woman all that she desires and more. You could pleasure many woman at once, and all through the night. Come. Let us celebrate your victory." He gave them a beckoning gesture and walked away toward the inn.

Lucien began to follow him, but Alexander hung back and said, "father, I think I have lost my appetite."

His father returned to him and murmured, "let us take what is offered to us and think on the tragedy of the animal's life later. We must feed, and we do not know when the next opportunity will come. Or do you wish to be lectured to by your blood again?"

Alexander conceded that point and silently followed them to the inn. There the innkeeper ordered that food and khipu be brought them and then led them up the stairs to their room, talking of glories and rewards to come.

When he opened the door, two women were already there waiting for them, trying their best to look alluring and eager for sex as they lounged among the linens of the bed. But their eyes spoke of shyness and reluctance.

"They are young and healthy, and will do for you whatever you wish," the inkeeper said. "They are yours until the morning, or for however long you wish to stay with us. I will leave you now, and bid you good night."

When the door closed, Alexander and Lucien faced each other. Lucien said in English, "do not feel shamed because you hesitated."

Alexander replied, "I feel shame because I did hesitate." He looked down at the bundle oozing blood in his hand and asked, "what am I to do with this?"

Lucien stared at it and said nothing at first. For a moment he suppressed a smile along with several comments. Then he ventured, "come, Alexander. Surely I have no use for it."

His son promptly took aim and tossed the grisly package out the open window far into the night. "Let the crows have it, then."

A moment later, there was a knock on the door. An old woman stood at the threshhold with a large tray loaded with food and drink in her hands, tottering from the weight. "I bring you food," she said with a pedantic tone.

"It must be heavy. I will take it, grandmother," Alexander said cheerfully as he grabbed the tray. "Thank your master for this fine feast." He closed the door before she could say or do anything more, shutting her out, and as he laid the tray down the smell of the grilled meat only added to his queasiness. "I cannot find my appetite with this," he said.

Lucien calmly began to unlace his clothing and reached for a plate of food. "I think we should leave this village tonight, rather than stay to the morning and face any more needless adulation," he said. He went to the women and handed the plate to the older one, speaking to her in Tibetan. "You must be hungry. Eat your fill."

As the women looked up at the tall stranger sudden fear caught them. They started to scramble out of the bed, but Lucien raised two

54

of his long fingers. They stopped suddenly, their eyes becoming blank. *"There is nothing to fear,"* he insisted. *"No harm will come to you."*

The older woman of the pair blinked, then smiled shyly as she reached up and took the plate. "You are most kind, my lord," she said. Then she and her sister fell to feasting, tearing ravenously into the cooked meat like savages. It was clear that they did not get this kind of food often. They shared the khipu between them, and before long they were drunk and laughing like delighted children.

In their alchoholic haze, the women gave a feast of blood to their saviors. Lucien and Alexander drank as much as they could without draining their donors, then told the women to sleep.

Afterward, they gathered their things together, crept down the back stairs and walked out into the darkness.

When they had gone several miles down the road, Alexander and Lucien stopped and made camp in a tumble of boulders for the day. When the sun went down behind the mountains, Lucien roused Alexander, and together they resumed walking.

Along the way they passed by small camps of humans tending their flocks, but did not do more than ask for directions, and did not stay longer than absolutely necessary.

Kashmir

May, 1646

20

It was a journey of several days when Alexander and Lucien rounded the foothills of the western Himalayas and found a pass through their jagged peaks at a lower elevation.

At the dawn of the 8th day they walked into the outskirts of a fairly populous town, and the first that had more than one or two permanent dwellings among the shanties erected along the rough dirt road.

There, they came upon on an old man tilling the soil in front of his hut. He was so thin that his ribs were prominent through his dark skin, and he was clad only in a light colored loincloth with a mantle draped over his shoulders. He looked like he had seen poverty all his life, and his hut was made of little more than a few tree branches gathered together into a dome; tied off with a strip of leather and with a flap of sheepskin for a roof. The whole affair threatened to cave in on top of the small earthen oven that was his fireplace.

Upon their approach the old man started with fear when he looked up at them. One of his dark eyes was clouded over by a cataract. He dropped his hoe and backed up toward his hut.

Alexander raised his hands in a calming gesture and said, "we will not harm you, my friend. What place is this?"

He blinked, then pressed the palms of his hands together and touched his forehead, then his chest. "Namaste. You are in Srinagar, in the province of Kashmir. Who are you?"

"Namaste," Alexander replied as he mimicked his greeting. "We are strangers to your land. We are in search of a caravan to go into the west. Do you know where we may find one?"

"Aye," the old man said. "They come and go through here. But the Persians will not allow strangers into the Khyber without a special permit. For that, you must first visit the Raja of Kashmir."

"We have traveled far, and cannot be deterred by such matters," Lucien said. "Where may we find him?"

The old man turned and pointed toward the houses crowding the mouth of the pass. "Go down this road until you come to the end of it. There you will find the house of Shivali Todar. He will welcome you if you are a Hindu, but he will not welcome you if you are a Moslem."

"We are strangers to both faiths," Alexander said.

"Then he will welcome you anyway, because you are not a Moslem," the old man declared.

"Thank you," Lucien replied. "Namaste." Then he and Alexander walked on.

Even in the light of early evening the streets were bustling with activity, and there were even Europeans wandering among the natives, traders who bought the goods made in the shops for sale elsewhere.

The charcoal and incense manufactured here were precious commodities, and the woods used to make them each had their own distinct fragrance, blending into a perfume that masked out any other smells. But the atmosphere of mistrust and suspicion was even stronger than the perfumed scent permeating the air.

As Alexander and Lucien strolled through the center of town, Alexander looked at the signs posted in front of the shops. There appeared to be a clear dividing line between Hindu and Moslem. The more prosperous shops had signs in farsi, or arabic, while pockets of hovels with signs in sanskrit occupied the other side of the road. The people who mingled on the streets, though they shared the same color of skins, eyes and hair, appeared to segregate themselves according to their faith.

Alexander saw an argument break out between two shopkeepers over a customer's trade. One wanted the man to buy from his shop, while the other came across the narrow road and grabbed him by the arm, trying to pull him toward his. In the end the man broke free and ran away, frustrating both, and they stood with the passing crowd acting as a buffer between them as they shouted insults to each other.

"The situation here appears tenuous," was his cautious remark. "In my studies at university, I learned that the Moslems would like the whole world to embrace Islam. Here we are the infidel."

Lucien grunted assent. "Thus it is with the Turks. I smell fear and enmity through the floral effluvium. These humans are but a candle's length away from erupting into open warfare, and need little provocation for it. I will be grateful to be away from here before that happens."

Lucien and Alexander walked on through the district until they arrived at a large palace. It had a high stone wall to keep out invaders and separate the estate from the poverty of the village crowding the road. The portcullis at the gate was carved with elaborate friezes in the Hindu style, and the door set in it was a massive double portal made of solid weathered teak.

The house within rose on heavily carved columns to three stories of cantilevered roofs covered in dark painted wood and clay tile. The stepped terraces and verandas were made of the same yellow limestone which dominated the land, and there were dark streaks on the walls where the rain had deposited more fertile soil as it dripped. Awnings made of green Madras linen shaded the large windows, each with its own balcony.

Peacocks strolled aimlessly on the expanse of flowering lawn and pierced the quiet with their strange calls, and Alexander marveled at the sight of a male displaying his tail fan for a group of hens. There were no men at arms posted anywhere in sight. Either Todar was not as rich as the mansion suggested, or they were so used to the danger encroaching on their walls that they could afford such laxity.

"It is quite impressive," was Lucien's quiet remark as he peeked at it through a small gap in the wooden gate.

Alexander found a bell set in the wall next to the gate, took the woven rope attached to the clapper and rang it. The bell was ancient, made of bronze with a patina of green. Its tone was a dull clank, hardly audible in the distance between gate and door. "I doubt if anyone inside will hear this," he commented quietly. "We may have to climb the wall."

The distant sound of an elephant trumpeting caught their attention. "Perhaps he is not at home," Lucien remarked. "I sense a great assemblage of men and animals in the forest. He may be there. Let us go in."

They climbed the high wall easily and ventured out onto the open lawn toward the dark copse of thick trees climbing the hill. At first the way was difficult, made so by the thick brush, until they found a trail overgrown with weeds passing through a narrow gorge.

Just beyond that the trees thinned a little into a charming grove of myrtle. Here the air was filled with sounds of men shouting, punctuated by a steady drumming sound. The racket was almost deafening to more sensitive ears, made more so by the screeching alarm calls of monkeys scrambling about in the treetops above their heads.

Together, they walked cautiously forward until a break in the trees admitted them to a clearing, where Alexander could see groups of men beating with rhythmic strokes at the brush, driving something toward the small herd of elephants standing at the end of the gorge. The pachyderms had large platforms strapped to their backs, where other men sat on them and waited patiently. Their mahouts were perched on the elephant's necks and held them still with the application of small hooked rods and soft commands.

One of the hunters was a dark-skinned man. A black beard obscured half of his face, and his hair was tucked up into a turban.

Unlike the majority of the villagers in Srinagar, his clothes were elegantly cut, but he wore no jewelry anywhere on his body. He had a curved bow aimed carefully at something with an arrow nocked in the string.

Alexander could see flashes of sleek orange and white fur with black stripes parting the sea of vegetation. Three tigers were trapped in the circle of men, trying to escape the noise and heading straight for the hunting party. The elephants ahead of them started shifting and becoming restless, and one discharged a bellow of distress.

Suddenly, the third tiger in the trio broke away and charged the lead elephant, while the others scattered into the brush and broke through the human line.

The lead elephant reared up and trumpeted, discharging her human cargo instantly before he had a chance to shoot, then ran off into the forest before her mahout could stop her. Her rider fell to the ground and laid still, stunned and unaware of the cat coming toward him at breakneck speed.

The other hunters struggled to control their own elephants for fear they would trample their master, but the panicking animals turned tail and fled en masse, taking their passengers with them.

"Come on. There is no time to waste!" Lucien exclaimed suddenly as he ran forward, his speed increasing rapidly until he became little more than a dark blur tearing through the green.

Alexander followed as best he could but was not as fast as a fullblood. He watched the blur halt and change into his father, standing between the charging tiger and the man on the ground with his sword gripped in his hand.

Alexander's heart skipped a beat. What foolhardiness spurs him to do this? he asked himself.

The tiger almost collided with the tall alien and fell back quickly. It snarled, revealing sharp white fangs in the growing dark, then gathered its haunches and leaped. Lucien's hand was swift as he halved the creature in mid air. The two portions fell to the ground bleeding profusely, rolled about and twitched until they were still.

When Alexander finally caught up with him, Lucien was already kneeling next to the hunter, who struggled to rise with his help. The man winced with pain and a sharp breath halted him as his hand went to his ribs. Clearly he had broken something. He looked to be about forty, with long black wavy hair escaping the turban now hanging askew on his head. A small henna diamond adorned a spot just between his eyes, which were almond shaped and grey, not black. That caught Alexander by surprise.

The man looked up at his saviors and blanched, looked down at the hands holding him up, then at the tiger's remains lying a few feet away. "Who... who are you?" he asked in Hindi, his voice tremulous. "Where did you come from?"

Alexander felt a quiet flush of warmth surge through his blood as understanding of the man's language surfaced through all the tonal inflections. The other men in the hunting party gathered around them and raised their bows with arrows nocked. But their master quickly raised a hand and said, "no. Do not shoot."

The leader of the servants shouldered his bow and returned his arrow to the quiver. "We feared that the tiger had got you, my lord," he said as he offered his hand to the fallen hunter and hauled him to his feet..

"This man saved my life," the man replied, balancing gingerly on his left foot. He turned to Lucien. "I thank Shiva for his divine intervention, to send such a one to save me from my folly. I think I will hunt on the ground from now on."

"Such wisdom will grant you a long life, my lord," Lucien said quietly with a humble tone in his voice, as he gave a small bow of respect.

The man blinked with surprise. "You speak my language like a native. Who are you?"

"I am Lucien Arkanon, and this is my son, Alexander Corvina."

He replied, "I am Shivali Shankara Todar, Raja of Srinagar. I thank you most humbly for your speed and courage, for I would have had no chance against the tiger alone."

Alexander resisted the impulse to tell him that had he left the tigers alone he would not have been put in such peril. But he had learned long ago that trying to change a man's mind was often like shouting into the wind.

"But come," Todar continued, breaking into his thoughts. "We will return to my home, and after my healer tends to me I will give you a feast of welcome."

With that he gestured to his companions, who picked him up carefully and guided him limping toward the horses sheltered nearby. Todar appeared to be a man used to pain. One had to be in order to survive in a world beset by war and privation. His face barely registered another wince as he was aided into the saddle of a dark roan.

"Ranhu, Kelshan, give these men your horses," Todar said to his aides. "You two can stand to walk back and reflect on your mistake in judgment, since your idea of hunting tigers on elephants has met with such disaster."

"My lord, we..." Ranhu began, but Todar held up two fingers to silence him, a gesture familiar to Alexander. It was as if his father had dark skin, piquing his curiosity even more. Todar said, "yes, we all know you are sorry. That is understood. But do as I say."

Reluctantly, the young men handed their reins over. The shorter one turned his head and regarded Lucien with mild curiousity as the stranger mounted his saddle, but remained silent. The others mounted up and began to ride back toward the compound, the two servants taking their place at the rear. Alexander could feel them glaring at the back of his neck. Clearly these two young men did not approve of Todar's sudden show of favor.

He leaned over to Lucien and whispered, "father, those two are not as loyal to him as Todar would believe."

Lucien nodded subtly but kept his eyes on the path ahead. "I sensed that also. The hunt was organized by them," he husked sotto voce. "Todar must suspect them also. But I can scarcely imagine..."

Todar's voice caught their attention. "Come, I would know you better," he insisted. "I have never seen men before with skin as pale as yours. What country are you from?"

"We are from Transylvania," Lucien answered, somewhat truthfully.

"Transylvania? I have never heard of it," Todar said.

"It is a country so small and so far away that it is hardly worth mentioning, my lord," Lucien replied. "I have it from one of your villagers that you were the man to approach to arrange our passage out of India."

"Alas, my power extends as far as the walls surrounding my estate. The grand Shah Jahan has seen to that," Todar said. "Have you not seen the intrusion the Mughals have made into my motherland?"

"We are hard pressed to understand how this can be so," Alexander said. "Was this a sudden event? Was there a war?"

"The Persians said they wished to trade, so they moved in under the cover of treaties and agreements, bringing with them their religion, their stubborn demands that all worship as they do, to obey the will of their Allah, or we would suffer a war more terrible than we ever fought before."

Todar paused to take a deep weary breath. "We capitulated, so now we suffer their arrogance and their harsh law. Jahan allows me the freedom to administrate in the village but does not allow me the freedom to move among my own people or to act according to our traditions. Shiva protect us," he added, and pressed his fingers against his forehead as he suppressed another gasp of pain. Then he straightened himself and said brightly, "but that does not matter now. My palace is yours. We will feast, and my women will entertain you with their song and their dance. Everything I have is yours for saving my life."

"Excellence, that is hardly necessary," Alexander protested mildly. Then regreted his remark when he saw Todar's dark face grow even darker with indignation. "What I mean is, we are not worthy..."

Lucien leaned over and clasped Alexander's shoulder to give him a small shake of warning. "Forgive my son's humility, Excellence," he said. "He meant no offense. We would welcome your hospitality."

Todar appeared to stand down from his anger, and said, "good. Then it is settled, and I will see what I can do to help you on your way. It would not do to have the Persians delay your journey, for they are arrogant fools with naught but their own concerns in mind, and I would be an inattentive host if I allowed you to be harmed by them. But for the next few days you will be my honored guests."

21

When the hunters arrived at the palace, Alexander and Lucien were escorted to a sumptuous apartment on the second floor. It was generously large, with three rooms and a small lavatory. Alexander wondered at the running water that came from small narrow spigots set in the stone wall, and the seat which carried waste into a chamber deep below the palace; as well as a large porcelain bathtub fitted with a pipe which stood above it. The end was a cup pierced with holes, and as he fiddled with the valve set at the base of it was nearly drenched in water. He had never seen such inventions in engineering anywhere else before.

"Father, these people are more advanced than the English," he said. "How is it that they have these things and cannot retain their culture against the storm brewing in their land?"

"Their machines are wondrous for the fact that they exist at all," Lucien replied calmly while unpacking his bag. "Wars are devastating to all who live through them, and much of history is lost. But it is the resilience of their culture that enables them to rebuild when the war is over, and when history is remembered, for it is the doom of men that they forget."

Alexander was about to ask something else when there came a knock on the door, and a small elderly woman clad in a dark sari came in bearing a pile of clothing and slippers. She kept her eyes cast to the floor and bowed according to custom as she said, "namaste, my lords. My master hopes that you will find these clothes to your liking. If you wish to bathe, there is time before supper."

She placed the pile on the table nearby and then looked up. Her eyes went wide, and she started to back up toward the door. Her mouth worked soundlessly. Lucien's voice came out reverberant against the stone walls as he threw out his hand and said, "*wait. We will not hurt you. Do not fear us.*"

The woman froze where she stood, blinked once, then took a deep cleansing breath and said, "yes, my lord. Is there anything you require before I go?"

"Nothing, thank you," Lucien replied with a pleasant smile. "Tell your master that we will join him soon."

"Yes, my lord," she said with a meek bow, her hands clasped together. Then she turned and escaped into the hall.

Alexander watched her go with trepidation. "Father, her fear is most disconcerting. I have lived for a hundred fourscore years and I am still not used to it. I feel no different from any other man, and I often forget what I look like, until reminded so unpleasantly."

"It is difficult to bear at times." Lucien sighed gently as he turned to his son. "I know you yearn for companionship. I understand that more than you will ever know, and my sorrow for your mother is an example."

"Then what can take her place, now that she is dead?"

Lucien considered. "Perhaps the love of another woman, as wise and accepting as she was," he replied. "Now, let us bathe and dress, and go down to meet our host. And you must be less humble from now on. You are not inferior to any man on this planet."

"Thank you, father," Alexander replied with a rueful smile. "I'll try to remember that."

An hour later, the two vampires walked down the long corridor to a staircase leading down into the inner court of the hall, looking resplendent in their damascene waistcoats and trousers, and their feet shod in slippers with curled toes. Lucien had braided his white hair into a long Chinese queue, and Alexander tied his dark hair back into a ponytail with a shirt length of silk.

When they entered the hall they found other men and women already seated at a long marble table set with a sumptuous feast of food and wine. The table stood on short legs, with pillows arranged around it so that the guests could sit on the floor.

The platters on the table were filled with a variety of meats, including roast chickens and peahens, steamed elephant trunk, tigers' testicles marinated in wine, lambs' eyeballs stuffed with garlic, mutton, monkey, prawns in butter sauce, and finally steamed rhinoceros beetles.

Of beef and pork, however, there was none. Cattle were considered sacred to the Hindu sect, and pork considered unclean. Other platters were heaped high with fruits and vegetables, and still others with breads and sweet pastries.

Todar waited for them at the head of the table, seated with his injured leg tightly wrapped in bandages and propped up on a mound of pillows. He smiled as he raised his goblet and said, "ah, there you are. Come. Sit. Feast and be welcomed. Everyone, this is..." his voice trailed off. "Oh, this is terrible. You rescued me from death but in all the excitement I forgot your names. Please tell me at once."

"Lucien Arkanon, Excellence," Lucien replied with a short bow. "This is my son, Alexander Corvina."

"Excellence," Alexander said, mimicking his father.

"Everyone, please welcome my guests," Todar said, his face and voice holding a glow of satisfaction. "They are strangers to our land but they are good men. I owe them much for saving me from the tigers during the hunt today. Come. Sit at my right hand."

The assembled courtiers applauded and made noises of welcome while Alexander and Lucien seated themselves as he directed. They were handed large napkins to catch the dribbles. A long three tined fork, a knife and a spoon were placed at their right hands, and a golden goblet placed to their left. Despite the poverty apparent in the village the nobility here still ate and drank their fill with the gusto reserved for the rich.

Alexander watched quietly and learned what there was from this experience.

At length Todar appeared to notice that his guests were not eating, and said, "come, come. Is there nothing here that interests you?" he asked as he forked a large chunk of food into his mouth. He appeared to have a healthy appetite but was not rotund as most healthy eaters were, as his body was hardened by years of battle.

Lucien smiled sheepishly and said, "Excellence, it is all so wonderful that I do not know where to start. My appetite runs to more modest fare."

Alexander said, "I too am at a loss to choose."

"And the drink? What may whet your thirst?" Had Todar known what his guests drank he would have reacted quite differently.

"Excellence, I never drink wine," Lucien replied. "Perhaps… a little tea will suffice."

Todar wiped his greasy hands on a towel, clapped his hands and said, "tea for my guests. At once!" As the servants scrambled to obey he leaned closer to Lucien and asked, "now, you must tell me something of this journey you are on. How came you here? You appear to be nobles yourselves. But where is your retinue? Your servants?"

"Excellence, we have no such burdens," Lucien replied drily. "We travel alone." He paused when a servant placed a pot of hot water in front of him, next to a small ceramic cup. "I confess that the world is as wondrous as the one I have left behind. There is much to discover, and I find myself illuminated by what I have seen."

As he spoke he dipped a spoon into a ceramic box of tea leaves and put them into the strainer, then poured the hot water over the mesh so that their juice could drain into the cup.

Todar asked, "where have you been?"

Lucien replied, "Tibet."

"And, where do you plan to go? Will you return home to this .. em.. Transylvania?"

Alexander said, "we would go to France, Excellence."

"Not to England? We have heard them express an interest in trading with us."

"The English are at war with the Spanish and the French, so I have been told," Alexander explained. "The Turks are seeking an inroad to conquer all three. We would perforce avoid such entanglements if we could, for our hearts are free of warlike sentiments."

Todar grunted as he took a swig of the wine in his cup. "It seems that there is war to be had everywhere. It is as much a part of a man's life as his birth and his death."

"It does seem unavoidable," Lucien remarked

"I sense that you were once a leader of your people. What tragedy befell you, that you traveled all the way to Tibet to find peace?"

"I spent some little time at Shangri-la to recover from a great sorrow. I recently lost my wife."

Todar paused. His eyebrows rose as he said, "most unfortunate. I lost my twelfth wife last year. So, you will marry again, yes?"

That question seemed almost too eager. Was Todar looking for an alliance? Alexander admonished himself for even thinking it, and dismissed the question as a product of his overactive imagination or an impertinent suggestion from his blood.

"When I have found someone as strong and beautiful as she was," Lucien said, nodding. "But I would not destroy the festive mood of this moment with my personal concerns, Excellence."

Alexander stared at his father with veiled astonishment. It was as if the lion he knew in the forest had shrunk down to a small mouse. Then his fascination was interrupted by Todar's voice.

"Yet, you carry yourself like a soldier," Todar said. "You have great skill with a sword, yes?"

"That part of my life is over," Lucien replied honestly with a small shrug. "It has been a long time since I took up a sword against my fellow man. Above all, I am a man of peace."

Todar appeared to be satisfied with his answer, and raised his voice. "And now, the players will come and give us the gift of music and dance, and in so doing honor the divine Shiva, who is the lord of the universe."

A group of musicians entered the dining hall and seated themselves on pillows nearby. Alexander grew entranced by the assortment of instruments they carried: a mandolin, a flute, a tabla, a sitar, small taiko drum and a set of bells. The players were all young and dark skinned. As they set up and began to play, the sounds coming from the instruments was unlike any he had heard before, yet reminiscent of the sonorous mantra of the lamas.

A faint jingling of bells sounded, and a troupe of four women clad in wispy clothes entered dancing from another door. There were small bells at their ankles and wrists, and another set somewhere amid their veils. The tantalising scent coming from their smooth brown skins was tinged with jasmine and gardenia, pungent with the heat of their blood cutting straight through the fragrance of the incense burning in the stands nearby, and almost as hypnotic as the music.

Then one of them separated herself from the other three and began to dance alone, her body moving sinuously. She had finer features than the others, and black hair bound up into a pile held by a tiara of gold. Her large and expressive almond shaped eyes were grey like Todar's. Her body was rounded like the statuary and the carved friezes on the walls. Her fingers, arms and legs wove an intricate tinkling pattern as she danced. It was like sign language. Her lips were generous and held a gentle smile while her hips moved in time to the music, then settled into a gentle rhythm that enhanced her sensual grace.

Alexander watched her with rapt fascination, then glanced toward Lucien. His father sat with his gaze rooted to this dancer's movements as if her dance was for him alone; while she in turn gazed at his father as if he was the only man in the room. The dancer made her way toward the banquet table until she was standing before Lucien. She took one of her veils off and placed it around his neck, then danced away again.

But Shivali Todar's reaction was electric. He frowned and clapped his hands abruptly. The musicians stood down from playing and the dancers froze in mid step. The room quieted down to silence. Todar's face was almost red with anger and disapproval. "Go. Away with you!" he exclaimed. "No more dancing! No more music!"

The musicians collected their instruments quickly and retreated, while the rest of the troupe dispersed and ran into the back of the house. The half-clad beauty in the middle stood her ground, her face blanched, trembling, as he said, "daughter, are you trying to make me angry? We will have words about this later. Go to your room and await me there. At once, do you hear? or I will have you whipped!"

Alexander resisted the urge to protest. As a guest he had no right to say anything about another man's customs, and he knew that as soon as he opened his mouth he and his father would be ejected, or worse. He stayed quiet, and looked to his father. Lucien's eyes were dangerously close to flashing their characteristic red, and he looked annoyed with the exchange. For her part, the young woman's eyes were now brimming with tears. She turned and ran into the darkness of the palace interior without saying a word, tinkling as she went.

Todar turned to his guests and said, "I apologize for her shameless behavior. She should not have done such a thing. It is not her place to choose her intended husband."

"I was not aware that such a thing had taken place," Lucien replied calmly. "I was not offended."

"Nor I," Alexander added quickly, eager to defend her.

Todar appeared to deflate, and his voice was softer as he explained, "it is seen as an act of defiance, as it is a father's task to appoint her husband. She has no say in the matter. You do not know our customs well, so I do not lay blame upon you."

"I understand. Then by all means, whip her, but not for my sake," Lucien said. "Among my people, such a practice is considered… barbaric."

The last word lingered on the air like a faint wisp of acrid smoke. Todar's fists bunched, but said nothing in reply. Alexander quickly understood that Todar needed to maintain civility in front of his guests. It would be bad form to punish his rescuer for speaking his mind. But a wedge of mistrust had already been placed where it did not belong, and now he fervently wanted to be gone from there before something else happened to destroy the delicate thread of safety slowly tattering away.

"Then I will wait, and talk to her as father to daughter. You have my assurance that she will not be punished," Todar said. "But now, let us drink and eat, and in the morning I will make the arrangements to help you resume your journey."

"I am most grateful, Excellence," Lucien replied, then raised his cup to his host, with a sidelong glance of caution to Alexander.

In another moment the guests resumed eating and talking as if nothing had happened.

22

After the banquet had ended, Lucien and Alexander returned to their apartment and made sure to bar the door when they closed it. Alexander could hold back no more and vented his feelings. "Father, what was all that about? I feared the worst."

Lucien turned and looked at his son. A delighted smile turned his rose lips upward. "She did choose me. I could scarcely believe it. She is a most remarkable woman. She dared to approach me in a room full of guests and mark me as hers in front of her father."

"To what end?"

"Just as he said," Lucien replied. "He has already selected a husband for her, and she has defied him most boldly. Such a move could not be played better. It is beyond anything I have ever seen before!" He chortled with delight, a sound that raised Alexander's neck hairs with unnamed dread.

"You think this is a game, father? If Todar knew what you were thinking he would have our heads."

"You think I have lost my mind, do you?" Lucien said, ruffling the hair on top of Alexander's head. "Fear not. I am in complete control of my faculties. It took the clever mind of that beautiful young woman to jog me loose from my sorrow, and I am relishing the adventure. Confess it, my son, that you too are feeling the excitement, the thrill of the hunt?"

"There is excitement, and then there is foolhardiness," Alexander replied. "I scarcely know what to think."

"Let go of your concerns. You know that Todar cannot touch you, or hurt you in any way. You are the most brilliant and skilled swordsman of the day, and you could carve him into small nodules of flesh before he even came close. But you do not have to do anything. He will not risk losing our protection."

"Our protection?" Alexander echoed. "What are you talking about?"

"Did you not sense it before?" Lucien asked. "You did observe the behavior of his two malcontented servants?"

"Yes," Alexander said with growing puzzlement.

"They are plotting something sinister against him. Todar must have seen this and is courting our aid. He must know that he is surrounded by enemies in his own court."

"Can you read his mind so clearly?" Alexander asked, agape with astonishment.

"In a manner of speaking," Lucien replied with a small shrug. "It is more easily done by observing their faces. Their expressions, the way their bodies tense or go lax, the way they smell, even to the movement of their eyes and the way they blink. I could readily read Todar's mind but there was no need. His response to his daughter's rebellion was statement enough of his thoughts. Some day, when you have more practice and have lived a little longer, you will know how and when to use the talents you possess. But now, I must visit Todar's daughter and determine the truth of her intent."

"Determine the... you want her. Oh, do not look at me with those innocent sheep's eyes and tell me nay. I am beside myself with worry, and you want to feed on her. Say you will not, for my heart pounds, sir!"

"Alexander, you are becoming distraught," Lucien replied. "Take a deep breath and count to ten."

"One..."

"In Greek."

"Uno. Due. Trio. Tetra..."

As Alexander counted, Lucien went to one of the windows and climbed out onto the narrow ledge, quickly scaled the wall up to the roof and disappeared. Alex resigned himself to the inevitable, sat down on the divan and waited with bated breath.

An hour later, Alexander had begun pacing back and forth, arguing with himself as he went, muttering and running his fingers frantically through his hair. He stopped when he spotted Lucien leaning against the framework of the open window with his arms crossed, watching him with a soft confident smile on his lips.

Alex discharged the breath he had been holding and said, "do not frighten me like that again. You were gone for almost an hour."

Then he peered closer and said, "you look like the cat who swallowed the canary. What said she to put you in such a mood?"

"We shared more than words," Lucien replied as he jumped down onto the floor. "She is a most remarkable young woman. When we leave, we must take her with us. It would not suit me to have her stay here and remain subject to her father's whims. He would have her marry a man older than he is, a cousin, who does not love her and has twenty wives already to call his own. Such alliances can lead to much sorrow and tragedy, and I found her most uncommon."

Alexander noted the disturbance of his father's clothes and hair, sniffed, then frowned. "You did the deed with her, did you? A fine example you are to a young man. You speak of age, when you are old enough to be her... and what happened to your love for my mother?" Then he corrected himself in the same instant. "Aye, I've sown the seeds myself, I'll warrant. Perhaps it was too soon that I pulled you out of the lamasery. Had I known you would fall in love by the drop of a hat..."

"It will happen to you one day, have no fear," Lucien replied calmly. "And when it does, I shall cheer for you. You have no inkling how it feels, Alexander, how important this is to me." He paused and raised a hand to still the coming remark. "Pray, do not preach to me of restraint. That argument is old and stale already. You wanted me to stretch out my wings and taste the wind, so I have, and it was a moment of pure exhiliaration. I am still young and have not lived a tenth of the life I have yet. My father, your own grandfather, was still potent when I left his side centuries ago. Nay, Alexander, leave aside your judgment of me and accept that what happened was fate."

"Fate was it?" Alexander said. "Now she will become an impediment to our escape from this place. Must we be burdened with family when the road is dangerous enough?"

"You caution me against that which I know already," Lucien replied. "Yet in time you will love her as much as I do. She is not a simpering courtesan, she is a queen in the making."

"A queen?" Alexander gasped, his mind reeling with shock. "Father, she is not one of us. How can you..."

Lucien said, cutting him off, "when I tasted her blood, it was like unto our own. You have seen her eyes, Alexander. What did you think when you saw them?"

"I did, for an instant, think that. But surely it is an accident of birth. Todar himself has eyes that color."

"And what is Todar? He must have a sprinkling of the blood of Xosan himself to have the ancestral traits."

"You are saying that he. . . that she. . . ?" Alexander sputtered. Then as the thought sank in he sat down on the divan and blurted, "dear God."

Lucien smiled. "So now you see why she must go with us. She is one of us, though she knows it not." As he spoke, he went to the window and looked out as if he had seen movement in the darkness outside. He turned his head from side to side, then waited a moment before pulling his head back in.

Alexander started to say something but Lucien placed the tip of his finger against his lips to gesture for quiet. He said quietly, "I have said too much. I sense the presence of too many eyes and ears in this household. We must be circumspect from now on."

Alexander knew better than to doubt his judgment, and nodded. "What do you think Todar will do if he finds out?"

"What any father would do, I expect," Lucien replied. "Come. Let us prepare for bed, but keep watch through the night."

23

The next morning, there came a sound of pounding like a sledgehammer at the locked doors to the apartment. Lucien emerged from his room, his white hair looking touseled from sleep, and stared at the closed panels like a man ready to defend the breach. Alexander climbed out of his bed and joined him. "Father, what is amiss?" he asked with a yawn, still half asleep.

"We are betrayed, as I feared," Lucien breathed. "Someone must have overheard us talking last night. Oh, dragon's breath! We must bustle."

He went back into his room to dress while Alexander began to draw on his trousers, tripping twice as he reached for his short caftan. Then he remembered that their traveling clothes were still hanging on the line in the courtyard. Recovering some of his sleepy wit he faced the door and called out, "who is there?"

The voice coming through the panel was unmistakable. "Unbar these doors and admit me at once!"

It was Todar, angry and inconsolable, no doubt wanting blood for the violation of his daughter's virginity. If she was a virgin to begin with. Given her affect on his father's willpower, Alexander doubted it.

He finished dressing, drew his cutlass quickly and went to the door. He could smell the fermenting rage in Todar's blood through the closed teakwood panels. "For what reason do you disturb our sleep?" he asked.

"Open these doors at once, I say!" Todar thundered again.

Lucien came in again and nodded to Alexander. The iron bar was withdrawn, and Todar pushed his way in, trailed by four of his household guards.

"You will answer for this insult," Todar fumed. "You dare to violate my daughter in my own house?"

"Who told you that such a thing has occurred?" Lucien asked him calmly. "Ask your daughter to tell you the truth."

"Sarasvati is not your concern," Todar flashed. "She will be dealt with at the proper time. But now you will answer my questions, or I will have you put to the screws."

"You will not lay a hand on my father, or your head will fly like a bird," Alexander growled as he drew his sword and assumed a middle position between them, returning the glares of the guards around them with a daring gaze.

"Alexander, put that weapon away," Lucien commanded. "There is no need for violence. I can defend myself."

Reluctantly, Alexander stood down and resheathed his sword but stood ready to draw it again.

"Come," his father continued. "What scurulous tales have Ranhu woven for you, that you would turn against us so?"

Todar wavered uncertainly. "How did you know that Ranhu had told me anything?" he asked.

"He has sued for your daughter's hand before, has he not?" Lucien replied evenly. "Ranhu's designs are not for her happiness but for his own. He would take her hand so that he can usurp your position as Raja of this province. He has no desire for her beyond

73

what he can use as a tool against you, Excellence. Think on this. You must know in your heart that this is so. If you love her at all, you would allow her to choose her husband herself, or her spirit will be dead to you as if you had killed her."

Alexander watched as Todar's mouth worked soundlessly, agape. Then the Indian said, "I love my daughter, but I cannot take the word of two strangers against the word of one of my own. Ranhu has been a faithful member of my household since he was a mere babe. We grew up together."

"Then I cannot vouch for your safety, Excellence," Lucien said. "I have only warned you of what I see. Any man with two eyes would have come to the same conclusion. Think on the many accidents that have befallen you in the time that Ranhu has served as your retainer, and you have your answer there. Did I not hear this from your own lips but yesterday, when you spoke to him?"

Alexander could almost see the clock gears turning in Todar's mind as he considered. Then the Raja said, "come down to the great hall with us, and we will see what the truth is." He turned to one of the guards and said, "bring Sarasvati down to the hall. Then locate Ranhu and Kelshan, if you can find them, and summon them to me."

"Aye, Excellence," the elder guard said, and ran quickly from the room.

In short order, the main hall of the palace was filled with servants, retainers, guards, and other household functionaries. Lucien and Alexander sat in the center, while Ranhu and Kelshan sat to one side. Todar and Sarasvati sat on the side opposite.

The old man sitting on the chair next to the throne was Todar's steward, and next to him sat another old man who looked like he was fast alseep, no doubt the intended husband of whom Lucien spoke. Alexander could see why Sarasvati did not want to marry him. One slight tip toward any kind of sex and he would keel over dead.

Sarasvati's eyes remained fixed on Lucien, as if there was a lifeline stretched between them. Her life was now entirely dependent on Lucien's testimony, his powers of persuasion, and his love.

Alexander realized that Lucien was right about her. A fullblood had a better sense of what churned in a woman's breast than a half human fledgling. But nothing had prepared him for Lucien's sudden

74

transformation from a reclusive widower into a lothario. This was a side of Lucien he never knew before, and the knowledge was at once disturbing and exciting.

As it was, he always felt like he was traveling with a brother. Lucien looked no older than about thirty five, his lean face showing the merest hint of wrinkle against the snowy whiteness of his long fine hair. And his features were of a kind that no other man could hope to compete with for a woman's attention. A flash of jealousy ran through Alexander before he brought his emotions to heel.

His reverie was interrupted by the steward, who said, "Ranhu Chandraputi, do you stand by the statements you have made to his Excellency concerning the strangers? Did you say that you had seen the stranger Arkanon enter Sarasvati's chamber last evening? Did you say that you heard the strangers plotting to take her away against her will?"

"I did," Ranju declared confidently.

Alexander kept silent though he wanted to shout his indignance. He looked to his father for a reaction. Lucien's eyes were calm, as was his face. Surely if there was a time to protest it was now.

"May I be allowed to speak," Lucien asked suddenly.

The old man peered at him. "You may speak," he said.

"Ask Ranhu how he was able see all these things taking place," Lucien said. "For what reason would he undertake to spy on the guests of his Excellency, while he was supposed to be alseep in his bed?"

Alexander felt a sudden surge of cheer as Ranhu's face took on a distinctly pale and sickly expression. The small court erupted into whispers of shock until the steward clapped his hands for silence. "Answer the question, Ranhu," he commanded.

Ranhu stood slowly, and said, "I was walking in the garden when I did see this. I followed the stranger to his window so that I could know what reason he had to go into Sarasvati's chamber. I heard him and his son say many things."

Todar spoke up. "You were walking in the garden which I bade you not to visit," he said. "What were you doing there?"

Ranhu's face blanched again, as a small trail of sweat traveled down his cheek. "I... I wished to summon Sarasvati to her window so that I could talk to her, with a proper distance between a man and a woman, but he!" and he pointed with venom toward Lucien. "He climbed into her window. Such sounds did I hear that shocked me. She was taken, forced against her will by that monster!"

"I was not!" came from Sarasvati, and she stood up against her father's restraining hand. "You lie, Ranhu Chandraputi! He loves me as you never will, for your heart is hard as stone, and your mind filled with hate. You think only of yourself, while I must wait on my father's word for the life given me by my mother!"

"Sarasvati, be silent!" Todar commanded her.

She started at the sound of his voice, sat down quickly and began to weep, covering her face with her hands. Alexander stared in shock. Had Ranhu violated her, and she had kept silent all this time? No, it could not be so simple as that. But it was clear that she did not like Ranhu.

"Ranhu, you had no permission to court her," Todar declared. "You were not my choice. You had no reason to be in her garden at such an hour when all were asleep. But I begin to see what everyone has been talking about. What other plans do you have for my family?"

"Excellence, I..." Ranhu began, but hesitated, clearly frightened by his master's anger. "I only sought to learn the truth of these strangers, so that you would be safe from their malice."

"And yet these men saved my life in the forest," Todar responded impatiently. "You wish me to believe that they placed their own lives in peril to protect me from the tiger out of malice, while you two ran away and made no effort? No. Ever since I laid eyes on you, Ranhu Chandraputi, I have been met with one catastrophe or another. You furnish me with one excuse or another. I will not listen to your lies and whispers anymore now that I know the truth!"

Ranhu tried again. "Excellence, I only meant..."

"Be silent!" Todar thundered. "Enough, I say. Now I will hear the truth from my daughter, who has the right to be heard."

Sarasvati raised her head slowly, her large grey eyes now red with weeping, and wiped the tears from her cheeks as she said, "father, do not ask me to speak against these men. I will not."

"I do not ask that," he insisted gently. "I ask only for the truth. Why did you pick this man Arkanon to wed? Was it to prevent your marriage to Dharshiva?"

76

At the sound of his name old Dharshiva woke from his nap, glanced around the crowded room with only cursory interest, then settled back in his chair and went back to sleep.

"Father, Dharshiva is old and already has many wives," Sarasvati replied. "He can no longer give any woman his protection. I would have a man who has many years ahead of him, to love and to bear him children. Is that not why we are given by our fathers to wed? I saw in Lucien Arkanon a sire of a long line of Rajas, born of my loins with love and happiness. How can you deny me this? What have I done to earn your hatred?"

At this, Todar seemed to melt. He spoke softly, without the harshness of a ruler. "Daughter, you are dearer to me than my own heart. Perhaps my desire to keep you close to me caused me to err on the side of caution. Dharshiva is old, it is true, and I may have cast his continued presence into my thoughts of seeing you wed. But you know that I cannot bend the rules to suit me. If I did, I would betray the ancient traditions of our people, who were put in place for a reason. I must choose your husband for you."

"Then choose, father, and I will abide by the ancient law. But I pray thee, do not choose Dharshiva," she pleaded.

"No, of course I will not," Todar replied. "Very well, then. I choose..."

Everyone in the room leaned forward, including Ranhu and Kelshan. The tension was palpable as they waited on his word.

"Lucien Arkanon," Todar said.

Lucien closed his eyes, while Alexander let out another pent up breath. But Ranhu surged forward and declared, "no, Excellence! Have you not seen his eyes? He is not a man! He is a demon! Kali must have sent him to torment us, to drive us apart!"

"I will not believe your lies anymore. You are no longer a part of my court," Todar declared. "Plot against me, will you? Kali will send you to the darkness as you deserve. You and your monkey Kelshan will be taken to the elephant camp, where we will train you to serve as mahouts. And if the elephants do not kill you, I pray the tigers will. This is your punishment for presuming upon my position as Raja. Away with them. Take them from my sight, for they sicken me!"

The steward clapped his hands together and the guards came forward, seized the two men and dragged them struggling and protesting the whole way toward the back of the palace.

"As for you," he said to Lucien and Alexander. "I will give you horses and equip you with such goods and weapons you require to continue your journey to the west. My men will escort you to the border of the province. Take Sarasvati with you, for she has made her choice. Only promise me that you will keep her safe. I have always wanted her to be happy. Give me but one or two grandchildren, and the bargain is sealed."

"We are most grateful, Excellence," Lucien said calmly with a small bow. "And I promise that I will do all I can to grant your wish."

"Good. That is settled then. Come, everyone, and we shall make a feast of this day, that it is another good day to live."

Then Todar turned away and walked toward the steward, leaving Lucien, Sarasvati and Alexander standing alone together. But Sarasvati looked troubled, and wrung her hands nervously as she watched him go.

Lucien asked her, "come, my new wife. What is wrong?"

She replied, "I fear he will never see the family we can bestow upon him. Some evil will befall him, and I will never see him again."

Her words suggested a rare insight. "It is true that your father's house is encroached upon by the Persians and their people, lady," Alexander said. "He lives in imagined comfort and security while surrounded by enemies."

"His prowess in battle is legendary, but a legend will not protect him from the future," Sarasvati said. "Jahan is merciless. He had my uncle Shri executed, and I fear it is only a matter of time before the Persians invade and rob my father of all he has left."

"If we let it be known that your father is in need of succor, his countrymen may rally to his side," Alexander suggested.

"Aye, but discretion is now paramount," Lucien said. "I sense that our young troublemakers Ranhu and Kelshan are not easily dissuaded from their campaign against their master."

"What is Ranhu to you, that he disturbs you so," Alexander asked Sarasvati. "Did he touch you against your will?"

Her eyes filled with tears again, and she collapsed at Lucien's feet to kiss them. "Pray, do not beat me, husband!" she exclaimed.

"I lost my maidenhood to his charming words, and it was my fault it was so, for I should have seen his nagalingam sooner."

Lucien rolled his eyes and drew his new wife to her feet. "Why should I beat you for the beguilement you suffered?" he asked. "That does no harm to what we have now." He drew her into his arms and kissed her forehead like a doting father. "I am wise enough to know the truth of this, even if you did seduce me like a skilled courtesan."

Sarasvati melted into his arms and giggled quietly through the tears.

"Do you think that Ranhu will try something else against us?" Alexander said.

"I should not be surprised," Lucien replied. "Come. Let us prepare to leave while Todar is in such a mood to celebrate, and I must give him fair warning of his destiny if he does not act to reinforce himself against the wolf at his door."

So another banquet commenced in a little while, and it turned into a wedding party. Sarasvati sat in the center of the crowd of courtiers and guests, clad in a resplendent beaded sari and jewelry of gold. As was custom, a veil was drawn over her face, held in place by a crown of flowers. Lucien sat next to her wearing a crown of gold and a garland of flowers draped around his shoulders and neck.

The music coming from the corner was joyous. The feast was raucous and everyone laughed and drank a great deal of honey mead and wine. Lucien spoke and laughed with them, while Alexander watched and recorded the event in his mind, never knowing when he would see his father this happy again. Sarasvati had touched his soul with joy, and had accepted him as he was. Alexander regreted his jealousy and accepted that this was fated to be.

24

A day later, Alexander woke suddenly to the sounds of men shouting outside, mingled with the sounds of horses' hooves clattering on the paving stones in the courtyard. It sounded like a clarion call to do battle. He rose quickly, went to the window and threw the casement open.

There was a large group of men assembled at the outer gate to the compound, while the men inside the walls were scrambling to defend the palace. He turned away, grabbed his clothes and dressed quickly, snatched up his sword and went out almost at a dead run to rouse Lucien, who had been moved to more sumptious quarters.

His father was already up and dressed; fitting himself for battle, even as Sarasvati was just rubbing the sleep from her eyes. Alexander barely took note as he said, "Persians are at the gate."

"I know. There is no time to waste," Lucien said. He turned to his new wife and said, "hurry, my love. Make haste to dress and prepare for travel, for we must leave before we are caught up in an altercation we cannot easily escape."

He and Alexander went down the hallway toward the stairs, where Shivali Todar met them. "The Persians are at the gate," he said. "What could have brought them here? I have been careful to avoid a confrontation with them in order to preserve the peace."

"Your young miscreant Ranhu Chandraputi may have woven another web of lies to them in an attempt to preserve his own ambitions," Lucien replied. "Why else would they have come here?"

"I will have that wolf's head killed for his mischief!" Todar snarled. Then he turned away and called out, "master at arms! My armor! At once!"

When he was prepared for battle, the Raja threw open the door to the palace and marched down the long causeway toward the wall. Alexander tried to ignore the oppressive light of the sun beating down on his head as he and Lucien followed him, ready to draw their swords at a moment's notice; while twenty of Todar's personal guard trailed them and took up positions along the battlement, drew their bows and crossbows and prepared to shoot.

Todar stood well back from the gate as the lead sentry called out, "open the inner door!"

One of his guards threw the bar off and opened the narrow panel slowly. Todar called, "for what reason do you wake my household this early in the morning?"

The leader of the Persians detached himself from his men and rode forward, then stopped about twenty feet away. "We have news that you are planning a rebellion against the grand Shah Jahan," he called back. "I would have the truth from your own lips."

"Who is responsible for this lie?" Todar demanded. "I have no such plans. I just celebrated my daughter's wedding this evening last. Come, I would know who has spread this malice against me."

"That is none of your concern," the man said. "Open wide the gate and admit us at once, or we will take action."

Todar frowned as he replied harshly. "This is my home, and I will not allow you in. My family has been here since before your people ever invaded our land. You are trespassers here! If you try to come in, my archers will not spare you."

The Persian glanced up at the line of soldiers aiming their bows and nodded, then turned in his saddle and gave a signal. The soldiers behind him advanced ten steps and prepared to shoot their own arrows. "I say again, open your gates," he called back.

Lucien turned to Todar and said, "they mean to do it, Excellence."

"Take Sarasvati out of here," Todar murmured softly. "I can no longer keep her safe."

"We are prepared to stand with you," Lucien replied. "You will need all your might to repel them."

"No. I promised you safe passage and that is what you shall have," he insisted. "This is not your war, and I would not have you sacrifice your lives for a cause you do not own. Save my daughter and I will be honored to call you brother for it."

"But, you do not have enough men to hold the line," Alexander said.

"That does not matter. Go, both of you, as quickly as you can, and you have my wish that you return one day. Thank you for saving me for the most glorious of battles. It looks like a good day to die."

Then Todar turned to the lieutenant of his guards and said, "Arpanandra, go with these men. Gather together the servants and prepare a caravan. Take your leave by the northern gate."

The young lietuenant nodded and replied, "aye, Excellence," then stood by, waiting.

"May the stars grant you victory," Lucien said with a small bow, then turned and followed the young soldier toward the rear of the compound. Reluctantly, Alexander turned his back on the sight and tried to ignore the shouts and saber rattling exchanged among the combatants as he followed them.

In less than a half hour, a party of armed men and horses, women and asses carrying parcels, emerged from the compound by the north gate and paraded at a gallop up the dusty road toward the Khyber

Pass. When they had put some distance between them and the estate they slowed down to conserve energy. After that the group was silent, so that the only sounds heard were the creaking of the wood staves on the wagons and the tinkle of the bridle traces amid the clopping of the horses' hooves. The road threw up fine lake dust among the animals' feet, showing that drought came frequently to this region.

Arpanandra Suresh was a handsome man, a little thin but wiry and strong, with an intelligent face, large expressive dark eyes and a shock of thick black hair. His livery made him look like a Raja in his own right, and he sat his horse like a hero at the head of the file. Lucien and Alexander rode on horses among the escorts while Sarasvati, as custom demanded, rode in a large horse drawn box wagon with a pair of her maids.

The air was dry and warm, the sky was cloudless and the sun bright and hot. It was only May but it seemed more like July. Alexander's eyes were not used to this torture, and he was forced to tip his broad brimmed hat lower on his head to shade his face. But he could not imagine what his father was going through at that moment. He glanced at Lucien's face and was startled.

Lucien had narrowed his eyes until they were mere slits as nictating membranes cast a filmy cloud across the silver grey irises, making him look like a blind man. A drift of fine white hair escaped his braid and flagged in the warm breeze, while he kept his cloak close about him like a shroud. His hands were shod in leather gloves, and a scarf was drawn across the rest of his face so that nothing was exposed to the light.

When the travelers reached the top of the hill, Alexander looked back and could see the palace grounds just beyond the trees, and spotted men fighting among the dead and wounded littering the ground. A pall of black smoke billowed from some parts of the building. Despite his enhanced vision he could not see Todar's commanding figure among them. Then a stand of trees obscured the view, forcing him to give up looking and concentrate on the road ahead.

Afghanistan

25

The caravan traveled on for two days through the mountains following a trail through windswept canyons and narrow valleys. All were alert to attacks from brigands among the rocks above the road, or from Persian soldiers camped among the ruins of settlements long abandoned during the wars between the tribes.

On the afternoon of the third day they passed a goatherd tending his flock among the rocks above the path. That night they took shelter in a cave, where they lit no lamp or campfire for fear that they would be detected.

Arpanandra, Lucien and Alexander took turns watching the road and the mountains above while the others slept. They barely exchanged more than a word or two, and shared the same mind about the need for stealth. Alexander sensed that he could trust the young soldier with his life, and that made the long vigil ever more bearable.

When the group reached the head of the pass they were met by a party of Persian guards, stationed there to bar any attempt by Hindus to cross into the Khyber. But they were few in number, and the caravan was large and fortified enough that they would have no chance to stop it by force.

Yet Arpanandra brought the caravan to a halt.

Their leader approached Arpanandra, and they spoke in quiet tones to each other for few minutes. It appeared that the two men knew each other. Alexander watched silently, as did the others, hoping that some accord could be brought with peace. Then the Persian soldier signaled the others to move out of the way, and the caravan traveled on.

The road remained clear until they reached the top of the pass and the remote village of Peshawar, where several men met them with water and greetings. As the sun started to go down below the line of the mountains, Arpanandra insisted that they stop there and rest for the night.

"I have it from one of the men that the way foreward is more treacherous than the way we have come," he said soberly. "The animals need to rest, and we will need to take on more provisions."

"I understand," Lucien replied. "I trust you to make all the arrangements. Tell me, Arpanandra. Do you have family here?"

"My cousins live here," the young man replied. "We are the last of an ancient family that has held this land for centuries. The Mughals have all but destroyed our tribe, but some of the Moslems living here are part of it, and we would not divide ourselves."

"Then you are a prince of your people, to hold such a high regard for the spirit of peace."

"You honor me, sir," Arpanandra said, with one hand across his chest. "I have pledged to honor my duty to the Raja, but while we are on this journey I will do whatever you wish. You have awakened the adventurer in me, who has never been beyond the Khyber. Command me, lord Arkanon."

Lucien smiled and placed his hand on the young lieutenant's shoulder. "I do not require your fealty. But I will call you friend if you will allow me."

Arpanandra smiled with white even teeth. "I would like that, my lord," he replied. "Now, I am off to find a good place to make camp." He turned away and walked toward the others. There was a distinct spring in his step that suggested a surge in confidence.

Alexander asked, "what do you think he would do if he found out what we truly are?"

"I know not," Lucien murmured softly. "Such a strong and intelligent spirit as his should not be quashed by a disagreeable fate. What if we retained him as a companion on our journey?"

"You would turn him?"

"Only if it is absolutely necessary. But I will offer him the choice if it becomes so."

"I would like that very much," Alexander said. "He did say he has never been beyond the pass, so let us broach the subject with him when he is ready."

At the tinkling sound of small bells they turned and saw Sarasvati approaching. She was swathed head to toe in a black Muslim burqa, a necessary inconvenience for an Indian woman used to going half naked in the heat of the day. Alexander could not see more than a glimpse of her beautiful grey eyes through the dark veil covering her face.

"My husband, how long must we remain here?" she asked quietly, an edge of urgency in her voice.

"Only until we take on more provisions, and we must allow the animals to rest," Lucien replied.

"I fear that if we stay longer we may be set upon. I overheard the men talking. They said that there is a den of thieves but a day's journey hence who are known to attack travelers in the pass. They said that some of them are here in the village now. They may send word ahead of our approach."

Alexander looked toward the caravan escorts helping the servants to unload the asses so that they could lie down. They all looked just as nervous as she sounded. "Arpanandra assures us that all is well here, but we will stay on guard through the night. Have no fear, lady. No man living will invade our peace."

Sarasvati fell silent as she considered. Then she said, "perhaps I am painting shadows where they do not belong. But I cannot shed this foreboding which weighs on my spirit."

"What foreboding is this?" Lucien asked her. "Nay, do not let these matters distress you. Return to your women and rest. There is a long journey awaiting us on the morrow."

"As you wish, my husband," she said. Then she walked back toward the group, leaving Lucien and Alexander staring after her.

"I think you should tell her what we are," Alexander said.

"I suppose I must impart the truth, but I fear what she will say or do. She has captured my heart as keenly as a huntress in the forest, and I do not want her to turn away from me."

"She will turn away far faster if you hide it," Alexander said.

Lucien looked toward the dark outline of the hills in the deepening gloom and said, "aye. In matters of love you may be wiser than me."

26

The next morning, the travelers set out for the harsh moonlike nakedness of the open country. Arpanandra was dressed in clothes like those the mountain tribes wore, and everyone in the caravan wore a similar disguise, while the women remained inside their wagon out of sight.

Alexander and Lucien rode among the soldiers and wore their cloaks with their hoods pulled down over their eyes. They resembled monks more than fighting men, though they kept their hands close to their swords at all times.

The trail became steep at one point, and as the party topped the crest of the hill Alexander could see the other end of the pass looming before him.

The way through was a meandering dry river bed, narrow and craggy in places; in others wide as a small valley, with a well traveled trail made by wagonwheels among the thick brush. Just beyond it lay the open desert and the mountains to the north.

Then a sensation washed over him, and danger prickled at his neck hairs. Instinct told him not to look up. Subtly, he leaned over to Lucien and whispered. "Father, we are being watched."

"Mmhmmm," Lucien replied softly. "Since the last mile. Go forward and tell Arpanandra, but do it gently, or they will set upon us at once."

Alexander nudged his horse forward and worked his way to the front, where he joined Arpanandra. "The rocks have eyes," he said.

The young soldier nodded subtly. "I too had that feeling. I will send a scout forward to throw them off the scent." He twisted in his saddle and gestured to one of the men. "Ride on ahead and test the trail for rockslides."

The man said, "yes, my lord," spurred his horse and galloped into the canyon to disappear out of sight.

"That ought to break their focus on us for a time. Meanwhile, let us increase our pace a little, and prepare for battle," Arpanandra said. Then he raised his voice. "Let us go in. Here we must travel at single file. If we go at a faster pace the way through will be safer to the other side."

He spurred his horse into a gentle trot until he disappeared among the rocks, the rest of the party following him. Alexander fell back and waited for Lucien, then followed him into the file, keeping a weather eye on the way they had come.

The caravan traveled on through the steep walls of the canyon until they came to the scout, who was waiting for them at a sharp turn. "The way is difficult after this," the man said quietly. "There is an open bowl of land just ahead, and it is lined with many great rocks. A likely place for an enemy to lie in wait for us. We will be trapped if they attack us there."

"But you saw nothing of them," Arpanandra remarked. The man nodded subtly. "Then we have a chance to get through if we go now." He raised his voice again and called out, "quickly now! We must run this through."

The other riders kicked at their mounts to make them run, and the asses were beaten. Sarasvati's wagon was pushed ahead while Alexander and Lucien stayed to the rear, ready to strike back at their invisible enemy.

For a few frantic minutes panic seemed to rule as the party rode swiftly to pass through the hazard, as there was a risk that the bandits might rain rocks upon their heads at any moment. As he let his horse have her head, Alexander watched the canyon walls on either side of the trail and finally caught sight of men among the rocks, scrambling frantically to keep up, but they could not negotiate the rough terrain fast enough and were left far behind.

The canyon finally opened onto a wide valley, the last segment of the Khyber before it emerged onto the desert sand to the west. There, Arpanandra called a halt and looked around and above for movement while his horse snorted softly for breath and shifted about. "Hah! We left them breathing our dust. There was no chance they could catch us up."

Lucien shaded his eyes with his hand as he gazed upward and around. "Of that I have little doubt. Excellently played, Arpanandra. What is your next move?"

"We must stop and rest. The horses must be watered and fed, or they will drop dead under us."

Their scout added, "there is a small abandoned fortress which lies but another league ahead of us. We could shelter there for the night."

"Think you the bandits would find us there?" Arpanandra asked him.

The scout shook his head. "It is far better than camping out in the open and inviting an invasion with our fires. The added strength of walls would enforce our defense."

Arpanandra turned to Lucien. "Your opinion, my lord?"

He replied, "it appears we have little choice. Very well, let us use what is available, and maintain our usual guard through the night."

Arpanandra signaled to the file, and the caravan moved on.

Alexander ventured to ask Lucien, "but what lies ahead for us?"

"I will talk of the future with you in a little while, but now the heat has sapped my strength. I must find rest and nourishment soon, or I fear I will melt like wax." He turned his horse quickly and joined the wagon, unhorsed with a bound and almost dived into it.

A moment later, the two maids were flushed out like quail, squealing with mild panic and amusement, to join the others on the road. They dusted themselves off and burst into laughter, then walked along next to the vehicle talking about love and patience with men.

Alexander knew them only as Ruthinda and Charanditha, two orphaned slaves who served Sarasvati but who protected her like sisters. The younger one, called Charanditha, was pretty in a provincial way, and her eyes were large and dark as a fawn's. She glanced at Alexander, and as she did so a shy friendly smile crossed her lips. Then her attention was drawn away by the older maid, who leaned in and whispered something into her ear.

Alexander smiled back, chuckled briefly at the thought of Sarasvati finding herself with a handful to mind, then turned away and rejoined Arpanandra to talk of friendship and travel.

The fortress the scout spoke of was as he described. It was situated on a hillock overlooking the road, large enough to have ample room for everyone. No one had lived there for years, and the scout said everyone in the area thought it was haunted by ghosts and evil spirits. But he himself had stayed there a night the year before, and he never saw anything.

"Noises, yes," he said. "But of things moving freely in the wind, and doors left open. I slept quite well once I made sure all was secured."

So the travelers moved into the courtyard and sheltered there, and were not disturbed all night.

27

When they passed through the last leg of the canyon onto the first patch of sand the travelers stopped to rest. The other men set up small slats of canvas to rest under and wait until the heat of the day passed into the late aternoon. Alexander chose to sleep in the shade of a group of boulders, while Lucien remained sequestered in the covered wagon with Sarasvati and her maids.

The sun was a ball of molten lava as it dipped below the hills. The stars appeared one by one in the gathering dark, while the moon rose as a pale crescent above the eastern line of the mountains.

That evening would be the caravan's last under guard. Lucien and Alexander would continue on with Sarasvati, her women, the wagon and three asses loaded with supplies; while Arpanandra and the other men in the escort would return to Peshawar. Lucien and Alexander discussed the route, and Lucien asked the scout, "we are strangers to these lands. Might you give us a map to follow?"

His smile was friendly. "Yes, my lord," he said, then knelt down and drew a rough map in the sand at their feet as he explained the lay of the land. "We are here," he said as he drew a ragged line in the sand with a point at the northern end. "That way lies Kandahar," he said, pointing to a spot to the southwest, then up toward the horizon. "It is the stronghold of the Ghazi chief ibn Mohammad Sadr. He is not kind to strangers, least of all to their women. The Ghazis are at war with the Persians. They regard anything they see as theirs, and do not honor the boundaries agreed upon among the other tribes. They claim to be sons of Alexander."

Then he glanced upward and smiled. "It is no reflection on you, my young friend," he said to Alexander, who smiled back.

"What is to the north?" Lucien asked as he pointed to the vast expanse of sand above the line.

"Kabul, the capitol city," the man said, putting a dot a few inches away to the northwest. "Caravans pass through there on the Silk Road to Mecca, and the trading there is very good. I have been there only once, and never before have I seen such magnificence. Even the poorest of the people there live in palaces. But they are peaceful, and tolerant to all who pass through their territory."

"Then we will travel on to Kabul," Lucien agreed. "I thank you."

The man stood, gave them a short bow and said, "good fortune to you." Then he walked away to prepare his horse for the trip back through the pass.

Alexander asked Lucien, "have you talked to Arpanandra about continuing on with us?"

Lucien occupied himself with tightening the cinch on his horse's saddle as he said, "apparently his fealty extended only as far as the end of the pass. He said he had a dream in the middle of the night, which told him he must return to Peshawar and help his people. Truly, he will meet his fate with all courage."

Alexander turned to watch the young lieutenant talking to the other men, and laughing at some joke shared between them. "Then he will die in battle, will he not?"

Lucien sighed patiently. "Alexander, I realize that you have few friends in this world but it will not do to have you mourn him before he is in the grave. It is a fact of life that all men die, sooner or later. Cherish what you take with you, because that is all you may have of him."

Alexander considered this, then approached Arpanandra as he stood watching the other men. "May I have a word?" he asked politely.

"Certainly," Arpanandra replied with a smile.

"My father says that you are going back to Peshawar. Is this the truth? I had hoped you would travel with us as a friend."

"You will always have my friendship," Arpanandra said. "But you and I know that destiny has made different paths for us to travel. I am a man, and I know my place in the world. In the last few days I have traveled farther and learned more than I ever imagined, and I will remember you and your father long after you have gone from my sight. Your father has inspired in me the strength of will to defend my people. Would you have me go with you on your journey knowing that I had abandoned them?"

"No," Alexander said. He remembered what Musashi had said about crossing the ford, and knew that this was what he meant. It was time to let go. He offered his hand and said, "thank you. You are a man of the future. Go now and be a hero to your people, and I will remember you long after you have gone from this world."

Arpanandra took it, and when he released it the young man turned away quickly and walked to his horse. Alexander caught sight of a tear trailing down his cheek as he mounted up and began to lead the men away into the pass. When they had gone thirty yards the young soldier turned in his saddle and waved goodbye. Alexander followed suit, and that was the last he saw of the man as he disappeared around the bend.

He stood watching the empty trail in mourning until Lucien clapped a hand on his shoulder. "There goes another good man," Lucien declared mildly. "Come. Let us go on."

28

The small caravan moved along the line of the mountains to the north and west for two days, until they reached a wadi nestled among a stand of date palms and olive trees at sunset. There were signs that men had been there recently, and a fresh trail of footprints in the sand leading to the west showed that they had gone earlier in the day.

By now the animals were tired and thirsty, and the asses promptly walked down to the water's edge and began to drink with the packs still on their backs.

Lucien and Alexander dismounted and allowed the horses to join them as they helped the women out of their wagon, then unhitched the horses and led them down to the water's edge. As ever there was a need to stay alert, so Alexander settled down to watch the horizon for signs of riders or a caravan approaching, while Lucien helped to set up a small camp with the women.

When he rejoined Alexander, Lucien stood studying the night sky to get their bearings, and said, "Kandahar lies that way," as he pointed to the west. "If we are careful, we may yet avoid the Ghazis."

Alexander turned to look. "Do you think the man was lying? I saw no subterfuge or guile in him."

"I have learned over the years to trust but verify the word of a stranger," Lucien replied. Then he changed the subject. "Do you know why I named you Alexander?"

Alexander replied modestly with a faint shrug. "I have thought it is as good a name as any other."

Lucien chuckled. "I named you after the greatest explorer of them all, who had his eye on the future. I see in you the great untapped potential that you, too, can make your mark on this world."

"It is difficult to govern myself at times, let alone an empire," Alexander remarked.

Lucien turned to him and studied his face. "What is this doubt that troubles you so?" he asked.

He fidgeted briefly before replying. "It is hard to dream of conquest... in love... when my own father can sweep a woman off her feet in a single moment of meeting. I confess that I feel a little jealous of what you and Sarasvati share. I fear I will never find someone like her."

Lucien replied, "you will one day. I have faith in you." Then he said, "now I am off to tend to my new wife, or she will be cross with me."

He hugged his son and then walked away, leaving Alexander to watch him go with his thoughts in disarray. And after he had a long talk with himself, Alexander turned his mind to focus on obtaining fresh food for the women.

An hour later he came back with a wild goat, which he stripped and gutted, then placed the carcass on a grill fashioned of stones arranged over the firepit. Ruthinda insisted on helping, and carefully rubbed a small amount of herbs onto the goat's flesh, while Charanditha searched among the rocks for wild onions, greens and radishes to make a salad.

Sarasvati watched Alexander work with interest, and peppered him with questions about cooking. Apparently she had been groomed all her life for the position of a Raja's wife, and knew virtually nothing of the culinary arts. "Such things are for menials," she commented quietly. "But I must learn to please your father."

Lucien overheard this, and said, "you do not have to learn to cook to please me. But if you find pleasure in learning please yourself."

She smiled shyly back and nodded.

Alexander showed her how to mix spices with flour into a loaf of unleavened dough and put it into a small oven he found nearby, and before long the aroma of baking bread filled the air. When he had pulled the loaf out and set it aside to cool, Sarasvati helped

Charanditha toss the salad with oil and a small amount of balsamic vinegar.

When the women settled down to eat, Alexander retired to his saddle blanket a short distance away from the fire and watched the dark horizon, while Lucien entertained the women with the story of their trek out of Tibet. The tale about the bear was like a ghost story, and at some point they began to laugh as he danced and gesticulated wildly, imitating its movements.

For his part Alexander did not find it at all amusing, having been there. But Lucien's warm melodic voice was hard to ignore, and he was soon so distracted by the storytelling he dropped his guard, until the sensation of a presence behind him snapped him back to attention. Startled, Alexander turned quickly and had a dagger drawn halfway out of its sheath before he caught himself.

It was Charanditha. She started back a step, then froze with her hands over her mouth, her eyes wide with fright.

"I am sorry I frightened you," he said, resheathing the blade quickly.

Charanditha watched him carefully for a long moment as she lowered her hands, then said, "I am not frightened." She hesitated, then asked, "why do you not sit with us? Are you not hungry?"

"I have already eaten, and someone needs to keep watch," he replied.

The girl toed at the sand, looking down. "I have been watching you, and… I do not know how to say this. You seem… lonely."

"Lonely?" Alexander replied with mild surprise. "I do not think of myself often, but I am not lonely." Then he patted the blanket next to him and said, "please. Sit."

The girl was engaging, if a bit forward. He knew nothing of her yet he began to feel comfort from her voice and presence alone. Charanditha hesitated, then gathered herself and sat down. She kept her eyes averted from his, and her hands kept fiddling nervously with a lock of her long black braided hair. Her skin was a little darker than Sarasvati's, and the caste mark at the center of her forehead was a trio of small white dots.

"My mother and father are both dead," she said. "My mistress is all the family I have now. I have never been this far away from my people before. Ruthinda wants to go home, and I am afraid of what lies ahead. I have heard stories about great monsters, with teeth which would make an easy meal of me."

"There is nothing to fear except what you take with you," Alexander assured her. "But leave the monsters to me. I will protect you."

"Then, I am no longer afraid," she replied uncertainly. Then she took a soft breath and plunged on. "Do you have a wife?" she asked.

"No," he replied. "Do you have a husband?"

"Among my people, it is common to be married to someone at our age. Our fathers choose our mates for us. But my father and mother died when I was very young, so I have no one."

Alexander smiled. "And I am betrothed to no one, for I have not found her as yet."

"Your father has not chosen anyone for you?" the girl asked.

"Among my people we choose for ourselves," he explained patiently. "Sometimes with disastrous results."

Charanditha smiled, then giggled sweetly, and Alexander liked the sound. Then her smile vanished almost the moment it appeared as her uncertainty returned. "Then you must be very lonely," Charanditha ventured. "I cannot imagine how you can endure it."

"I must confess that I have given such matters little thought in the last few days," he said. "I would like to be wed one day, but I live the rough life of a traveler and I have never sought the interest of a woman before."

That was not quite true. Elsa Blanchett, whom he had taken in a fit of starving desperation and drained her before he could stop himself. He loved her as much as she loved him, but he did not learn how she felt about him until it was too late. That memory alone made him cringe at the thought of repeating the event.

Charanditha's eyes grew wide with surprise. "But, what woman would refuse you? You are so... pretty." She reached out and touched his cheek with a finger. Then she drew back again quickly. "Oh, my mistress is right. Your skin is very cold, like your father's."

"It is our nature to have such skin," he replied. "My people are from different climes."

"I am sorry," she said. "I was only curious."

"Be not so apologetic. It is no sin to be curious," Alexander said. "Curiosity is what leads to learning, and sometimes wisdom."

"Then, may I kiss you?" she said.

Alexander turned his head and looked into her eyes. Yes, there was curiosity, and romantic interest beside. The blush coloring her cheeks did nothing to hide the sensuous thoughts in her mind. Alarm surged into his blood like a cold winter's tide even as his thirst kicked up into sudden ravenous hunger. His blood spoke to him then, a chorus of voices in his mind. *Take her*, it said. *You need to feed. There may not be another opportunity for a long time to come.*

He warned her gently, "Charanditha, I am not a man like other men. If I kiss you, I may be tempted to take something else beside, and I do not want to hurt or frighten you."

"My mistress has already told me you must take blood for your food, like your father," she said.

Her statement rocked him back with surprise, but his blood pushed him into compliance. Alexander leaned over and planted his lips on Charanditha's, giving her a chaste little peck. He drew back and studied her face for some sign of fear, but it was calm as a mountain stream. Slowly, carefully, he pulled Charanditha into his arms and kissed her mouth gently, then with growing desperation.

She melted against him even as his hands pulled the drape of her sari from her shoulder, lifted her slightly and dipped his head until his mouth found the rapid pulse in her throat, where his lips clamped to her skin and his teeth drew into the red flood beneath. Then he went blind to all but the life force flowing into him, her strength and youth. This was willing blood, full of fire and ice, and he clung to her fiercely as she flung her head back and gasped with arousal. He drew her down with him onto the sand and pinned her there as he drank greedily.

Then awareness flooded back like a breaker on the shore. He withdrew, fearful that he had taken too much, kisslicked Charanditha's throat to heal her and watched her face for signs of trouble.

She had fallen into a languorous swoon, a satisfied smile playing on her lips. Then she opened her eyes and looked up at him. Her smile was reward enough. "I have never felt like that before," she said after a few moments of reverie. "It is as if I made love to Vishnu. What my mistress said is true. I will never meet another man as well endowed with such power to please a woman."

Alexander asked her, "you do not fear what I am?"

"A slave like me has seen worse," she replied. "But I believe in accepting the world around me for what it is."

The sound of Ruthinda's voice calling for her in the darkness alerted them. "You should go to her," Alexander insisted. "It is late, and you must rest, for we have a long journey ahead of us."

Charanditha gathered herself and stood, then looked down at him with a quiet nod. "I will treasure the memory of this night, even if we never touch again. It will be our secret, and ours alone, for I would not share it with anyone."

Then she was gone, and Alexander was left to nurse the warm glow in his heart as he resumed watching the dark beneath the river of bright stars shimmering in the sky.

29

When the sun rose the next morning, the sound of camels lowing roughly and the twittering of birds in the thickets woke Alexander. He scrambled to his feet quickly and looked for his father. He found him standing in the shade of a tree nearby fully dressed and already wrapping his head in a length of Indian cotton. He finished his disguise by pulling a length of the cloth across his face to cover his pale skin.

Alexander hastened to follow his example, while Sarasvati and the other women grouped into a huddle near the covered wagon, clad in their concealing burqas. Sarasvati held a scimitar close to her body, ready to fight by her husband's side.

A long file of people on camels and horses, and a few wagons, approached the wadi from the east. A man on horseback broke from the head of the line and appoached at a canter. He was dressed elegantly, with an embroidered cloak covering his head and body, and his face was obscured by a scarf to keep out the sand. He dismounted and led his horse to the water's edge, then spoke quietly to an attendant who joined him there. Then the attendant approached.

"Salaam alleichem," he said to Lucien, touching his heart, then his head. "My master's name is Suliman, Prince of Arkkady, from the mountains of Kashmir. And who are you?"

"Alleichem salaam," Lucien replied, mimicking the gesture of greeting, and emphasized his humility with a short bow. "I am named Lucien Arkanon, of Transylvania. This is my son, Alexander Corvina. My wife and her maids are with us also."

"My master bids you welcome to join us for tea," the servant said. "We have journeyed far, and he would enjoy your company."

"We will be most honored," Lucien replied.

The servant bowed and returned to the prince, who dismissed him with a short gesture. Then the prince approached them and looked them over with the air of a man used to danger. "Come. Remove your veils that I may see your faces, and I shall remove my own." He enforced his suggestion.

His face was already obscured by a black well trimmed beard covering the lower half of his face. Reluctantly, Lucien drew his cloth aside, as did Alexander. The prince betrayed a mild look of surprise, but did not react with fear. "Never before have I seen skins of such a color. Where is this Transylvania?"

"It is far to the northwest, highness," Lucien replied with a small bow.

"Where may I ask are you going?"

"We are on our way west to the European lands and our home."

"While we are but humble pilgrims on our way to Mecca. We would rest here for a while, then journey on to Kabul," the prince replied readily. "It is our obligation to ask permission to enter the lands to the west, and we must render tribute to the grand Shah Jahan."

Alexander and Lucien exchanged careful glances. Lucien said, "then our meeting is fortunate. Would you consider allowing us to join your caravan, and travel with you as far as the city gates?"

"You and yours are most welcome to come with us if you are men of peace," the prince said. "Even more if you can help defend the caravan on our way. This is my first expedition to Mecca, and I desire to reach my destination with a minimum of delay."

"We will pledge our lives to defend your people in return for the pleasure of your company, your highness," Lucien replied with a small bow. "This would be a mutual benefit, would it not?"

Suliman appeared to relax. "Excellent. We will camp here for the night, then continue on our way in the morning."

He turned away and spoke to one of his retainers, who began shouting orders. His servants moved to obey quickly and began to group the wagons together, while the other members of the caravan dismounted and gathered to set up their tents.

The prince's companions were an eclectic mixture of men and women with a few children among them, and despite their peaceful inclinations were armed to the teeth. Once they saw that it was safe to settle, they turned to unpack their animals, while the women seated themselves on the rocks nearby and fanned themselves against the fierce heat of the morning sun. The camels and horses were corraled under the shade of the trees, where they could find rest and good grazing among the undergrowth and branches.

As he watched the prince directing his servants, Alexander turned to Lucien and said, "he seems the friendly sort, father."

"Aye, and I hope that he remains that way," Lucien replied quietly. "Yet even now we must remain circumspect in our dealings with him. There is some unnamed mischief at work here. I can sense it."

"You mean, he is not a free man even in his own household, like Raja Todar. Spies are an ubiquitous evil we must all deal with in these perilous times," his son remarked.

"In that, no man is an island," Lucien replied, then walked away to rejoin Sarasvati and her women. When he told them of Suliman they slowly relaxed their guard and moved away to find conversation among the other women, while Lucien and Alexander prepared the campground area for breakfast.

The servants took up buckets of water from the nearby well to douse themselves and wash away the dust of travel, then set to work erecting a rough kitchen, while others poked sticks into various holes in the ground to flush out whatever lived there. Food was food, no matter what form it took.

There was a brief upset when one of the men found a large cobra and the others started to make a game of goading the creature. Someone produced a mongoose, and soon the game turned into a betting match; quickly ended when the captain of the guard dispersed the boisterous crowd with a flourish of his sword and shouts to get back to work.

The cobra was beheaded for its trouble and given to the skinner, who set to work stripping off its skin, then its flesh. The meat was thrown into the stewing pot while the skin was straightened and pounded with a rock until it was supple and clean, to be turned into a belt or other accessory. Nothing went to waste.

At midday, Alexander watched the men set up their mats and perform their ritual abeisance to Allah. There was no question about his faith, or lack thereof, from anyone. At length he asked one of the prince's retainers why this was so, and the steward replied that among his people, many different faiths were practiced with tolerance, and that prejudice was considered ill mannered. Yet, cleaving to no god seemed more socially acceptable than to a pagan god. Alexander found that refreshing compared to the Persians' treatment of the Hindus.

After an hour's repose, Sarasvati complained of a stretch of nausea, and Ruthinda and Charanditha took her away out of sight. When they returned, she climbed into the covered wagon and begged to be alone for a while. She looked sickly and pale, but said nothing about it. Even Lucien was ejected from the wagon, and retired under the shade of a tree to rest using his cloak as a tent and a rock as his pillow.

At the end of a relatively uneventful day of leisure and prayer, the caravan members settled down to sleep under the stars, and the moon rose a thin crescent in a dark sky.

As usual, Alexander took up the watch with several of the other men, but after a time found himself spending more time trying to sense which of them was most likely to betray Suliman then watching for bandits. It was more than simple unease with strangers, and so unlike his experience with Arpanandra.

He could not call himself paranoid because the word had not been invented yet, and would not be for centuries. But his senses warned him that the price for complacence or laxity could be a knife in the back.

Lucien stayed close to the wagon and stood guard over the women, a solitary yet commanding figure concealed among the shadows. Alexander alone could see him, and he watched two of the guards go by within a foot's breadth without noticing him once. Then it seemed as if Lucien disappeared altogether, blending into the background like a chameleon. Alexander felt a stroke of envy.

How useful it would be to travel through the whole world like that, he thought.

When he turned his head again he spotted movement near Suliman's tent among the tall grasses, and saw two dark shadows creeping flat on their bellies toward it. He looked beyond them and noticed that the guards posted in front of the tent were missing. He nudged the man next to him and said, "what has become of the men guarding the prince's tent?"

The man peered into the darkness and replied, "I can see nothing from here."

"I can. Stay here and maintain the watch."

Alexander went to his feet and walked toward the men, then hunched lower to the ground as he crept swiftly and silently, closing the distance with a single bound as he pounced. He seized them both by the necks, hauled them quickly to their feet and held them fast before they could react, brought their heads together and knocked them out. The two spies hit the ground as he went toward the front of the tent to examine the guards.

They were out cold. Their breath was rank with something alcoholic; perhaps wine; and bitter with the scent of cloves. Alarmed, Alexander went for the tent flap and raised it carefully. He could hear Suliman's calm breathing in the dark, and saw his bearded face composed in sleep, lit by a single oil lamp set nearby. Relieved, he closed the flap again and went back to the two spies lying in the grass. He knelt next to them and rifled through their clothing for some clue to their origin and purpose.

When they finally approached, one of the guards asked, "what happened, my lord?"

Alexander quickly gestured for silence. "These men were trying to go into your master's tent," he whispered. "The guards were put to sleep by something they drank. The prince is safely asleep, and will remain so if we move quietly. Tie these men up and hold them for questioning."

As they complied, the lead man said, "we are most grateful for your eagle's eye and quick intervention. You will be greatly rewarded."

Alexander brushed it aside modestly. "I did only what any of you would have done. Now let us resume the watch, and we will have the answers we seek in the light of day."

30

When Alexander finally woke again, it was at the sensation of his father's hand on his shoulder. "My, you slept most soundly," Lucien said with a smile. "The prince would like to see you."

"Aye?" he mumbled, still half asleep. He rose and rubbed his eyes to clear them, then said, "how late is it?"

"It is but midmorning, and the prince has already said his prayers. He would like to thank you for your actions of last evening. The two spies you caught were most cooperative once their tongues were loosened."

"Persians?" he ventured.

"Nay. Turks. Agents of the Sultan. They knew nothing of importance. They were ordered to assassinate Suliman in a place far from his kingdom, and where word of his death would travel slowly back to his people or not at all. He may have acquired a fatua against him."

"Who ordered it?"

"They did not know. Orders were passed to them through another. But that is not important now. Rouse yourself now, and dress. The prince must not be kept waiting."

A few minutes later, Alexander made his way across the wadi toward Suliman's tent. There he found the young prince seated and reading from his Qur'an while a servant worked to shave away the dark beard from his face.

"My prince, you sent for me?" he asked, affecting a polite bow.

Suliman looked up and marked his place as he closed the book. "Yes. I wanted to thank you for saving my life. I was not made aware what happened until this morning. Such stealth on your part was quite... extraordinary, for I sleep lightly if at all."

"No thanks are necessary, highness," Alexander replied. "I only did what any other man of peace would do."

"You are too modest," the prince said candidly. "You are a hero, and it would be a sin to deny the talents Allah has given you."

"You honor me, your highness," he said with another bow.

"I would like to give you a position in my retinue. I would have you by my side as a part of my personal guard." He turned his head to allow the servant to get at a spot on his throat. "What say you? Will you accept?"

Alexander felt a flush of surprise, but hesitated. He did not know what to say that would not offend his host. But if luck was with him, Suliman would not take offense.

"I am afraid that I must refuse your generous offer," he repied. "I am constrained by my commitment to my family, for they would be in danger without my protection."

The prince considered silently while the servant scraped away the last vestige of the beard and then wrapped his face with a hot moist towel. "I am finished, my prince," the servant said.

"Leave us," Suliman replied.

When the man had gone, Suliman removed the towel and finished wiping the last of the shaving oil from his face. His beard had concealed the faint scars of smallpox, but beyond that he was rather handsome. His large almond shaped black eyes were a result of the blending of tribes in the far east of the Hindu Kush. His olive skin was also slightly yellowed, either from Mongolian traits or from jaundice at birth.

"My friend Alexander," he continued, "I understand. Family is important to every man, and your destination is very far away. I know not what Allah had in mind when he created you, but you are a very interesing man indeed. Why, with ten men such as you, I would feel safer than a pot of gold. But I will accept the knowledge of you rather than compel you."

"My thanks for your wisdom," Alexander said, "but, why have you shaved off your beard?"

"The attempt on my life last evening justifies the need for a disguise," Suliman replied. "While beards are customary among my people they can also be a hazard, and I had already developed an itch from the sand fleas I picked up on the road. I will travel among my people and become a fish among the other fish, at least until we reach Mecca."

"A wise precaution, highness," Alexander said. "Who else knows what you plan to do?"

"Only my closet minister and the household guard, your father and yourself. I am counting upon you to watch for any other incursions by our enemies while we are traveling to Kabul, if you are of such a mind."

"I am happy to do so," Alexander replied with a small bow.

"Good. We are ready to continue our journey. Take your place with me, then, and your women will travel with ours."

So Alexander told Lucien what the prince told him, and his father appeared pleased with the arrangement. When the time came to leave the Arkanons integrated themselves and their animals into the caravan and left the wadi behind.

The only signs the travelers had been there were trampled sand, animal dung, a buried latrine and the bodies of the two hapless spies, left there with their hands bound behind their backs and exposed to the vultures circling overhead as a warning to those with assassination on their minds.

31

The caravan traveled northward for three days until they reached the city in the desert.

Kabul was the highest city in the world, situated near the Euphrates river, and boasted a cluster of palaces surrounded by a vast warren of mudbrick houses and apartment buildings surrounded by a high wall festooned with narrow palisades and watchtowers. Alexander could see the tall spires of minarets rising above the top of the wall, and as the human train stopped just outside the city's southern gate, he could hear a melodic wailing fill the air with the call to prayer.

The men and women dismounted their horses and camels, took their prayer mats and spread them onto the sand, knelt and faced to the west, then performed their ritual. It seemed that the city came to a standstill for a few minutes of prostration to the god of the prophet Mohammed; a precious few minutes of peace in a land where tribal conflicts set brother against brother almost daily, and where honor and revenge danced together in a waltz of death.

When they were done, the men set to work erecting the prince's tent as well as their own while his servants supervised them. When the tent city was built, Suliman declared that he would visit the Shah in the morning. But as the last tones in his smooth voice died away, the city gate opened, and a file of guardsmen rode out to greet the travelers. The leader rode straight toward Suliman, dismounted and addressed him directly with a formal bow.

From where he stood, Alexander could not hear what the leader said to him, but by the expression on the prince's face he could tell it was grave news, mixed with a bit of consternation. He could not help but sympathize, as he was beginning to like the young prince and his civilized manners.

When the guard remounted and stood by, Alexander approached Suliman. "Has something happened?" he asked quietly.

The younger man turned to him. "I must go to the grand Pasha Aurengzeb now instead of in the morning. He is most insistent, and I have not had time to make myself presentable. I must go into the city with these men without my personal guard. I am told that Aurengzeb is acting in his father's name while he is in Delhi. Jahan is building a tomb there for his wife Mumtaj and will not return for some time."

"Could those two spies have had friends in the Shah's court? Perhaps you made a mistake in killing them. We could have secured their cooperation differently had you not," Alexander suggested.

Suliman replied, "if that is the sole reason for Aurengzeb's displeasure, I will not suffer much." He did not elaborate on that, and placed a gloved hand on Alexander's shoulder. "If I do not return to you in three days, you and your family must go on with the rest of the caravan without me, for I shall be soon be dead."

"Surely not!" Alexander blurted. "You are a prince, of royal blood. Aurengzeb would not dare harm you. What will your people do once they hear of your death?"

"They will do what any man would do, rise up and try to rescue me. But they are but a few, and his army is three times our number. Fear not, my friend, for my fate is written in the stars, and the prophet Mohammed, blessings be upon him, is watching over me. If I am to die today I will take my place with him in Heaven, and he will rain down his wrath on Aurengzeb in my name." His face was calm as he said it, as if he had already made peace with himself and his god.

Alexander simply stared with lack of comprehension at this fatalistic acceptance of death. "Among my people we make our own fates," he said.

"I am but one man. What can I do against an army? I may not reach Mecca now, but I will reach Paradise, and that is all any man may hope for. Fear not for me, friend Alexander." With that,

Suliman turned away and remounted his horse, then rode away into the city flanked by the Pasha's soldiers.

Alexander watched him go determined to do something to help the prince, but he did not know what.

"There goes another good man," Lucien's voice said from close by. He had approached on silent feet, so quiet that Alexander could not hear his footsteps on the loose gravel.

"Father, I do not know the Pasha or his designs, but I fear that the prince will not return from this visit."

"What can we do about it?" Lucien asked, and his voice was soft but encouraging. The hint in that question was unmistakable. Alexander's heart leapt at the chance, and he replied, "we could wait until nightfall, then find a way in and extract him from his prison."

Lucien leaned closer and winked. "We are both of the same mind in this. Let us try, and we may yet be able to free him from Aurengzeb's grasp before some grievous harm befalls him."

Alexander and Lucien spent the day napping, then waited until the stars came out before they left the camp, and together they strolled casually along the city wall until they were well out of sight. Lucien found a tall arrow gap in the thick stone about ten feet above the ground, leapt upwards with a bound and climbed in.

 By a stroke of good luck the shaft was open to the other side. He turned and sent a soft whistle to Alexander, who followed after him. When they climbed out, they stood on a wooden platform mounted next to the inner wall with a view of the narrow course below. The area was deserted, and the guard manning the wall stood several yards away with his back to them. Lucien crept toward the guard, then reached forward and pinched his shoulder at the nerve until he fell unconscious, caught him before he fell and placed him sitting up against the wall.

He and Alexander then leapt down to the courtyard below and concealed themselves in the shadow of the platform, watching for movement from the other guards. But by now it was too dark to be seen and no alarm was raised.

When they were certain that the coast was clear, Alexander and Lucien made their way swiftly toward the center of the city. With their dark cloaks drawn over their heads it was easy to blend in with the last of the crowd moving along the road toward their homes, and no one even noticed them when they left the main road and cut through the narrow files between buildings.

They learned from the conversations around them that a curfew had been called for the time from sunset to sunrise, by order of the grand Pasha himself. But few of the people were happy with this arrangement.

When they arrived at the palace, Alexander and Lucien lingered a few moments across the way to reconnoiter and plan their assault. It was just a matter of slipping past the guard. They found a large tree whose branches extended over the palace wall. It was easy to climb, and afforded an easy drop onto a well tended lawn. The garden was lush and verdant but there was no cover to be found among the flowering thickets of oleanders and bougainvilleas; well armed with deadly poison and sharp thorns.

Lucien led the way to a small arbor overgrown with bougainvilleas, where they took cover in its concealing shadow.

"I sense fear," Lucien said, closing his eyes. "It is so strong I can smell it."

"Suliman?" his son asked anxiously.

"No... Yes... Perhaps not. There is so much pain here. I think the dungeon is just below us." He pointed down, then suddenly flattened himself against the trellis and pulled Alexander there with him.

A man dressed in courtly garments rounded the corner and walked straight toward them, bearing what looked like a pile of cloth. Losing no time, Lucien intoned, "*do not see us*." The courtier walked by without turning his head, and Alexander's mouth fell open with amazement. When the man was out of sight he whispered, "father, you have to teach me how to do that."

"Come, Alexander. You know how to do it already," Lucien hissed. "Has your blood not told you what to do?"

"No," Alexander replied in a soft whisper. "My blood and I have an understanding. It did not warn me what the hunger would be like the first time I fed, and I have no forgiveness for it. We have not spoken since."

"Then trust yourself, and it will come to you naturally when you have need of it," Lucien said, then abandoned the arbor and turned into a dark blur again as he ran swiftly down the path toward a door set in the wall. When Alexander caught up, he reached out and pulled gently on the handle, and found that it was not barred. He and Alexander slipped inside quickly and closed the door.

The place was a vast network of rooms and hallways arranged in a floral pattern. Somewhere inside that warren was the door to the lower floors and the dungeon, where the prince was held prisoner. Alexander could smell the strong stink of fear wafting on the still air, mingled with the putrescence of human tragedy, decay and death.

They moved with silent stealth down the hall until they found a door which was shut tight, perhaps locked or barred from the other side. After testing its strength, Alexander murmured, "there is no way in unless we push it down."

"Then we will combine our strength," Lucien replied. Alexander nodded, and made himself ready. "On the count of three. One. Two. Three!"

Together, they kicked the door in. The wood exploded inward with a startling **crack**. Shards and splinters flew ahead of them as they passed through and landed on the platform to a flight of stairs leading down into darkness. The rest of the panel fell on the steps ahead of them, and Lucien kicked it aside and down the narrow spiral shaft as they ran down into the darkness.

They were intercepted near the bottom by a group of guards who had heard the sound and come running. Alexander and Lucien slammed their way through, scattering the humans like bowling pins. Then the cries of ailing and desperate men filled the air, the clattering of chains, shouting and anger.

Lucien looked around, then closed his eyes. When he opened them again he pointed down the right passage. "He is there," he said, and led the way in.

Alexander only glanced at the array of prisoners reaching out to him through the small opening of each door as he passed by. He could not understand more than half of what they said as their voices mingled together and rang loudly against the walls. There was no time to stop, and sympathy for their plight grew in his heart as the flood of their emotions bombarded him from every quarter.

When he caught up with Lucien, his father was already busy pulling the pins from the hinges of the wood panel separating them from their goal. Then he wrenched it from the frame with his bare hands and threw it aside. Together, they entered a small cell stinking of mildew and human waste, and there was no light or window to let in fresh air.

There, they found the young prince huddling on a rough wooden cot covered with straw. His face was bloodied, and he held one shoulder at a strange angle. His princely clothes had been stripped from his body, and his undergarments were grimy with a mixture of blood and mud. He had been tortured, and pain contorted his face into a mask of misery. He shivered and shook like a top out of control as he looked up at their entrance. "Allah be praised," he moaned quietly.

Alexander went to him quickly and felt the prince's forehead for fever. Suliman's skin was warm, and sweat covered his face, but he was not ill. "Highness, what have they done to you?" he asked.

Suliman flinched at the touch of his cold dry skin. "How... how did you get in here?" he husked.

"That is not important now," Lucien said. "We must get you out before the guards recover. Are you able to walk?"

The prince hesitated, then said, "I think so." He tried to rise, then caught himself, wincing as the pain in his shoulder worsened.

Alexander said, "hold still," then took his arm and straightened it with a sudden jerk. Suliman's clenched his teeth and grimaced briefly, then relaxed with a grateful sigh. "Thank you," he said.

Ignoring the stains smeared on his clothes, Alexander lifted him to his feet and said, "lean on me. If you cannot walk I will carry you."

Suliman went slowly to his feet, tottering with exhaustion, then leaned against his rescuer and walked unsteadily at first. "I think I can," he said. Some confidence returned with every step, and he nodded quietly.

Lucien led the way out and they went back down the hall toward the entryway, bombarded again with pleas for help from the other prisoners.

Suliman stopped and said, "when I came to the palace, I was not allowed to meet with the Pasha. Instead I was seized and brought here directly, and asked all manner of questions for which I had no answers. Nothing I said granted me mercy. These poor wretches have all tasted of his generosity. They are not criminals, but good men who trusted him all too well. Can we not free them, too?"

Lucien turned to Alexander. "Do you concur, my son?"

"Aye. I would not abandon these men if they are innocent," Alexander replied readily.

"Very well, then. I will go in search of the keys." With that, Lucien marched off into the darkness ahead.

"Who prevented your audience with Aurengzeb?" Alexander asked.

"I think it was Aurengzeb himself, or one of his ministers," Suliman replied. "He is an ambitious man with dreams of empire. I heard the others talk of his treatment of others of high rank in his court, who spoke up when he did things against the teachings of the Qur'an. Who knows what else he has done in his father's absence?"

"That, I think, is a topic to reserve for another time," Alexander said. "Now we must focus on returning you to safety."

Lucien returned quickly. He said to Alexander, "the alarm has spread through the palace," and tossed a ring of keys to one of the prisoners, who said, "may Allah bless you," then set to work freeing himself and the other men.

The three blended in among the crowd of prisoners escaping through the narrow file and up the stairs, where they spilled out onto the garden and engaged the palace guards. Alexander, Lucien and Suliman were able to slip past in the ensuing melée, returned to the arrow gap without incident and returned to the camp, where some of the men had heard the noise and were already stirring the pilgrims up. Suliman was placed in his doctor's care, and despite his injuries would not rest until his orders were obeyed.

"Bid them prepare to leave with all haste. We must be gone from here before the soldiers find us," he said. "Quickly! Or we are all lost!" Then he collapsed into a dead faint.

Sarasvati waited for Lucien by the opening to their tent, and when he approached she was not smiling as she pulled him into her arms. "Lucien, what have you done?" she asked. "You invite danger with this reckless action. Why did you not tell me you were going into the lion's den?" Then she sniffed and made a face. "Oh. You must bathe. Never have I smelled such an odor before."

"I have just been in a dungeon," Lucien chuckled. "I was there to honor the prince's generosity by extracting him from a cage. Besides, I did not want you burdened with needless worry for me."

"Needless!?" Sarasvati drew back with her eyes wide. "You and Alexander were courting death! Will this be the way of things with you? You endanger your family with daring and adventure, and all when we need you most?"

"We? You mean, you and your sisters? Or...?" Lucien's voice trailed off. He stripped his right hand of his glove and placed his long cool fingers on her belly. He closed his eyes, and smiled as he opened them again. "Sarasvati, my love. You are with child. When did you learn of this?"

"Some days ago, when we were camped on the wadi," she replied. "Ruthinda has some knowledge of childbearing, and told me it was so." Then she put her hand to her nose and mouth and turned away. "Go, please, and put on some clean clothes! I am like to lose all composure. You men and your games. And you can wash your own clothes from now on."

Smiling, Lucien made an expansive bow with a flourish of his hand, and said, "yes, your Highness."

Alexander felt like a third wheel at that moment, the useless cog in the machine. "Congratulations, father," he said. "I will go and make myself useful, if you will allow me."

Lucien turned to him, and his mouth opened to speak, but he hesitated. Then he said, "by all means, do."

As Alexander turned away he had a feeling that things would never be the same between them. It was not logical to feel that way, but he did.

As the caravan stole silently off into the sheltering darkness of night, the army Suliman feared was fully occupied with a brief revolt amidst the citizens of Kabul, and no one saw which way it went.

32

The sun was high above the desert sand when Suliman of Arkkady decided that he could safely emerge from hiding and mount his horse. He had been bathed, and the cut of his traveling clothes concealed the dark bruises on his ribs, arms and legs. His eyes were dark with pain, and he looked drained of strength, but he kept up a brave façade for the benefit of the other pilgrims.

And Alexander was waiting for him, though sleep kept dragging at his bones as he joined the prince's side. He scanned the desert for signs of pursuit from the Pasha's soldiers, and saw that the trail they left behind was being erased by the strong desert wind. That alone give him some measure of comfort.

As they rode together, Alexander kept silent while thinking how to extricate himself from the sensations assailing his mind; from twinges of muscular pain to the self-recrimination and doubt radiating from every pore of the prince's body and mind. He wished there was something he could do to alleviate his friend's suffering, but did not know what.

But Suliman was nothing if not observant. "Is there something wrong, friend Alexander?"

"My thoughts are nought to concern you, my prince," he replied. "I was just reflecting on the events of the last day."

But Suliman would not be put off. "Come. I see the worry written upon your face. Share your thoughts with me if it will give you comfort."

"I should think that you would prefer to tell me about what happened in the dungeon, or better still, what you did or said to make the tyrant your enemy."

There was a long moment of silence. The prince winced, then shook his head. "I would rather not," he said. "It is a matter between him and me which is private and best forgotten."

After another moment of hesitation, Alexander asked, "what would you do if you were separated from your father by his fatherhood?"

Suliman said, "if he were my father, I would rejoice for the gift of the child Allah has bestowed upon him. But you do not?"

"It is difficult to explain," Alexander replied. "I spent most of my childhood without knowing my father. And now that I have a chance to be with him, I am jealous of the attention Sarasvati enjoys. She has taken him entirely to herself while I am left outside. In fact, I have felt outside even when I had his attention. Now, I am thoroughly confused. There are times..."

"Do you think he is not your father?" Suliman ventured.

Alexander drew back at his cogent remark. "It is a thought I have often had, though I know not why."

"But, friend Alexander, you resemble him in every way," Suliman replied. "He says he loves you as a son. Is that not enough to assuage your questing heart? My mother died when I had seen eight seasons of Ramadan, and no memory did I have of her, no keepsake but a lock of her hair kept in a gold locket, on a chain around my neck. My ministers told me she was very beautiful. Now, I have lost that, too."

"My condolences go with you, highness," Alexander said, as he thought of his own mother.

"It is so often true that a man cannot go through life without death crossing through with him. But as the Buddhists say, change is the only constant in the universe."

"My father said that too, once. And so did my…" he caught himself about to say "blood", then thought better of it. "I mean no disrespect, but it seems that religion is a crutch to lean on when times are bad, and many men claim to have faith when they sin the most."

"Religion was made to make men remember. I prefer to believe that ritual is necessary to honor the divine entity which is Allah, to whom other men offer their faith and sacrifice, whether it is with libations, flowers and incense, or blood."

Alexander turned and studied his face carefully. Did Suliman know what he and Lucien were, or was it an incidental comment on religion? And the man's mind now seemed opaque to his light probing. "What do you mean, Highness?" he aked.

"Men give their lives in service to Allah, whether with the sword or by dying for their faith, if the prophet Jesus of Nazareth is an example. He was a martyr. He took on a great jihad against his oppressors, and was sent to Paradise for his beliefs."

Alexander relaxed his guard at that remark. "Aye, my prince."

"Still, I am curious. You have never mentioned worship, and you do not partake in our prayers. You mentioned Tibet but I observe that you are not a Buddhist. I wish only to understand you better."

"It is difficult to explain," he replied carefully. "I worship no god of man, highness, but look to my heart and the stars for guidance."

"The stars!?" Suliman exclaimed. "I, too, rely on my astrologer."

Alexander hesitated. He never spoke of his birthright or childhood to others out of the need to survive in a world not his own, but something about Suliman spoke of trustworthiness and discretion. He said, "nay. I do not speak of astrology, but of science. I believe in a universe full of worlds like our own, with beings which inhabit them also. That for each star in the sky there is a place for them to live, just as we do here."

"I have often wondered about the stars," Suliman said. "But my position leaves me little time for such study. All I have learned of life on the path to enlightenment is through the lives of my people."

"A man's life is often measured through his deeds, my prince," he replied. "Then is his mettle and quality tested."

"I agree. And I have striven to be all that my people expect of me. But there are many things I must know which are not contained between the pages of a book. My experience in the dungeon tested my faith, and brought me memories from a time long past of a question for which my wisest ministers have no answer."

Alexander regarded him closely. Where was this coming from? But the next question caught him by surprise.

"I have seen many works of art in which strange objects float in the sky, great stars and comets, men, angels, and strange machines placed there by the artists. No one knows what they are, or why they are there. They show us things which are not of this world but of another. You are a traveler and have seen much of this world. Might you know what they mean? Is it possible for such things to exist?"

Alexander hesitated, uncertain how to reply. Then he ventured, "I have seen them, my prince. But only the artist knows why he has added them to his canvas. I believe that... if beings from other worlds had visited us, they would never have allowed their discovery so easily, or left clues of their existence for us to find. Each star is so far away I can scarcely imagine how or why they would come here. To what purpose, my prince?"

"I would hope that they would learn as much from us as we would of them. But I have often wondered what such beings look like. Could they look like us, or like the strange beasts who live in the sea? Do they fly, or do they walk on two legs?"

"The possibilities are endless, my prince," Alexander said.

The prince's eyes grew suddenly round, and he went agape with wonder and shock. "Friend Alexander, what are you telling me? Your skin, your incomparable strength and speed... Aha!" he exclaimed, causing his horse to shift nervously until he brought her under control.

Alexander regarded him with sudden dread, fearing that the prince would react with prejudice.

But Suliman returned to his calm demeanor and said, "nay, do not fear that I would speak of this to the others. But please tell me more, as I am on fire with curiosity. I only wish to know. It is not enough to live a life without being open to the wonders Allah shows us every day."

Alexander thought quickly and fashioned a response which would put him off the track. "Highness, you mistake me. I was born of a woman just as you were, and my appearance is natural. Surely you cannot believe that I am one of them."

"But you alone have given me the answer which all my ministers could not in their combined genius divine. I would have you help me understand the other worlds better," Suliman said. "Think of the knowledge I can bring to my people, the advances in science, the machines which would make their lives better..."

"Weapons? Machines of war?" Alexander asked, suppressing a sudden shudder of dread. He had heard enough about a man called da Vinci, who kept his drawings locked up in a wooden box. Few men ever saw them, but those who did said they were of weapons and other inventions of war, inspired by the devil. Then when the old artist died the box disappeared. The question arose about who took it, but it was commonly believed that the church had a hand in its disappearance for ecumenical reasons.

"To protect my people better," Suliman insisted, bringing him back to the present. "Never to cause war with my fellow man."

Given that the prince had just been through a harrowing experience, Alexander began to wonder what he had in mind. He shook his head. "I cannot speak of them, highness, for I do not know such things and would not lead you astray. Even if I did, such knowledge, used badly, would result in disaster for your people. I know you want to ensure their protection, but what you speak of would bring their destruction instead. These matters are best left to the philosophers."

The prince considered for a few moments, then said, "you think I would endanger them by using the knowledge without wisdom."

"Aye. The temptation would be too great. And as you have seen already, there are too many men who would use it for their own ends, and make war on their fellow men to obtain it."

Suliman sighed with resignation. "You are right. Our lives are threatened by evil every day, and sometimes it is hard to continue on without hope of the outcome." He paused as his hand went to his side and his face expressed a brief wince. "But please tell me that there is a future for which we fight, or our efforts are worth nothing."

"In that we agree, my prince," Alexander replied. "Though I cannot predict the future. I can only speak of my own hope, that we see a day free of hardship and pain, of bloodshed and war. That men turn away from greed and ambition and embrace peace."

"Then I have chosen well in confiding in you, friend Alexander," Suliman said. "Your words reflect what is in my heart. But later, when we stop to camp, you will instruct me further on the worlds of the stars."

It was not quite an order, but more than a request. Alexander took his words at face value, and replied, "as you command, my prince." Then the subject shifted, and the two men conversed at length about the history of the region and the factions at war with each other.

That evening, when the camp was bedded down for sleep, Alexander skipped his guard duties and flopped down on his blanket near the wagon. He laid back and looked up at the stars, warring with himself how to broach the subject of Suliman's questions to Lucien.

Then his father's voice rumbled pleasantly near his ear. "Come. Not as bad as that." He had appeared at Alexander's side like a ghost. "I saw you coming, and you have not spoken a word since mid day. You look terrible."

"I feel terrible." Then it all came out in a rush, a gush of words as if a dam had burst. "Father, Suliman knows what we are."

Lucien drew back and examined his face, his almond shaped eyes narrowing to slits. "Are you so certain?"

Alexander shrank back trying to escape those probing grey eyes and said, "By happenstance I let it slip that we were not of this world. The prince seized upon it, and told me he wished to know more. I tried to deflect his curiosity, but I did not know how to put him off without attracting further suspicion."

"What did he say, exactly, that caused you to slip?"

"He spoke of the marks some artists place in the backgrounds of their canvases, of comets, stars and other things. In all innocence I spoke of the fantasies and imaginings some men enjoy. Yet somehow he made the connection on his own."

"Then you have done nothing wrong," Lucien replied with a short smile. "He is an intelligent man, and intelligent men are often more inquisitive and imaginative than others."

"He wants me to instruct him about the worlds of the stars. I could not forestall his insistence."

"Fear not. I will take care of it." He patted Alexander on the shoulder and continued, "rest now, and catch up with your sleep. You are but half human. Your body requires rest, and you cannot burn the candle at both ends."

"Thank you, father," Alex replied, yawning. Then he could not keep his eyes open, and in another moment he fell into warm comforting darkness.

33

Alexander woke rested and refreshed the next morning, and participated in tearing down the campsite, then helping Lucien to prepare Sarasvati's wagon for travel. After that he took his customary place next to Suliman, and together they led the pilgrimage into the desert, where they found the Silk Road and began to follow it toward the western file of the mountains.

All the day long the prince did not bring up the subject of stars and alien beings, nor did he even speak for a long time through the morning. Alexander reasoned that his father must have used his mindvoice to tease the notion from his thoughts before they brought him to a sticky end. For his part, Alexander never mentioned it again.

Three days later the caravan arrived at Herat, a small village sheltered on the banks of a narrow river. To the north was a low range of mountains leading toward the Caspian Sea, called the Caucasus, and to the west lay the lands in the heart of the Parthian and Persian empires.

"It is the last water we will find before we enter the desert, my prince," one of the men remarked as he dismounted his horse. "Do you think it a fit place to set up camp for the night?"

Suliman glanced around him, squinting into the sunlight, and after a moment of reflection he nodded. "I think we have put enough distance between us and the Pasha's army."

When the camp was built and all settled down for the heat of the day, Alexander thought it a good moment to leave his side. "It has been a long ride, and I am greatly fatigued. I beg leave to take my rest now."

Suliman turned to him with a faint smile and said, "you have always had the freedom to do as you please. By all means, take your rest."

Alexander took his things a short distance away, erected a small tripod of staves and draped a goatskin over it, where he retired under its shade and fell promptly into a deep and dreamless sleep. He was senseless to all but the sun setting below the horizon, and when he woke finally to an indigo sky he was not alone. Charanditha sat a few feet away, watching him anxiously.

"Charanditha, what are you doing here?" he asked.

"Your father sent me to you," she replied. "He said you would be hungry." She punctuated her reply with a quick tug at her sari, baring her shoulders, and she moved her long hair back to expose her throat.

"I will not take it unless it is by your own will," Alexander replied. "I hunger, but you must make the choice."

"I know," she said, her lips tremulous. "I have missed you. It was agony to stay away."

He reached up and tugged her down into his arms. "I did not know," he replied. "I have been so preoccupied at times that I have quite forgotten myself. I am sorry to have neglected you."

"That is not important now," Charanditha said. "Take me, and let me feel the love you gave me before. I ache for your touch, your need. My blood is on fire for you." She removed her thin top and freed her breasts, then took his head in her hands and kissed him desperately.

He pulled her close and kissed her lips, her throat, then bit her gently. Her blood was full of fire and ice, hot and delicious, and Alexander found himself wanting more than before.

Then awareness returned suddenly, and Alexander pulled out gently, kisslicked her throat and held onto her for a few long, languorous moments to absorb the full force of the energy filling him with strength. It seemed that Charanditha had become the perfect feeder for him. Their chemical attraction was mutual, even if there was no deep emotional bond between them.

Charanditha laid still against him, her eyes closed. Then she snuggled closer. "My lord, you are more man than any woman could want," she breathed.

"I am pleased you think so," Alexander replied with a faint smile. "How does Ruthinda feel about this arrangement?"

"She is jealous," the woman said. "I have taken pains to avoid a discussion which would give her suspicion wings. But she grows more and more disagreeable. What should I tell her?"

"I shall leave that entirely up to you. But I do not want you two to fight over me. It is more important that you keep to the harmony of your sisterhood."

"Hmmmm. You are a strange man."

"How so?"

"You understand women. Most other men are... are brutes, with only their own needs and wants in mind."

Alexander felt a faint flush of puzzlement, thinking it strange that she should confide this with him. "My own mother instilled in me an appreciation of women that other men seem to have forgotten. A woman is and always will be the center of a man's soul," he said.

"Your mother must have been a wonderful woman."

"Aye," he replied. "She was. I miss her very much."

"Where is she? Is she dead?"

"She died a long, long time ago."

Charanditha looked away for a moment, then said, "I do not want to leave your side. It is farthest from my own wish, but Ruthinda wants to return home to Lahore. Ruthinda's cousin lives there. Our lady Sarasvati, she has said that we are now free to choose our own lives, but Ruthinda does not understand how far away we are from there, how far we have traveled."

Alexander's practical mind took over, and he said, "she would brave the desert alone? she would face the mountain bandits alone? she would face the Persians alone? Charanditha, I do not think she appreciates the gravity of her situation. She has come too far already to ever return."

"I know. I have been telling her that myself, but she will not listen," Charanditha replied with a charming pout on her lips. "It is for her sake that I would go with her, to protect her as a sister should."

"Then Ruthinda will learn a lesson she will perforce regret," Alexander said. "She cannot go back. We must all go forward because it is the only thing we can do. My father and I have no more choice in this than you do."

"She is at her wits' end, and she has even said she would kill herself rather than go another step. Even your father has tried to dissuade her with little success."

It was true that the power of an Antellan extended only so far, and Alexander knew that if Lucien could not convince her with words he would not waste his power to force her. "Then, let me try," he said. "Wait here and rest, then return to your mistress." He stood and straightened his clothing, then strode away into the darkness.

When Alexander inquired of the others, a few said that Ruthinda spent a great deal of time sitting with her back to the campsite, watching the way they had come. And so he found her, after a few moments of searching. He made sure that she could hear him with heavy steps in the gravel to avoid frightening her as he approached at a leisurely pace.

"Here you are," he said. "Your mistress has been looking for you."

The woman looked up at him and said simply, "I want to go home. I am not happy here."

"You should have revealed your desires sooner," Alexander replied. "Why did you not?"

"I... I was not told we would be going this far," Ruthinda said. "I came because my mistress convinced me that it would be a grand adventure. Instead, all around me I see only sand, and feel heat and misery, and loneliness. I miss my home in Lahore. I want to go home."

Alexander could empathize, but his home was wherever he was, with a past that required no ties to hang on to. Clearly reason and patience were needed. He sat down next to her on the sand and asked, "and if you went home now, what would you find there?"

Ruthinda looked down and stirred at the sand beneath her feet with a stick. "My cousin and I were close until my parents died," she said. "Then my uncle sold me to the Raja, and I have been with my mistress ever since. I thought that if I went home now my uncle might take me back."

"He might? Hope is not certain, lady. Think on the possibility that he might not. You would turn your back on your mistress, who is heavy with child, and pin all your fortunes on a hope? You have chosen a path which will bring you misfortune and more of the slavery you have endured, Ruthinda. Your life is here, if you will but take the time to remember it."

Ruthinda said, "I know... but at night I think on the future and see nothing for me. I am a slave, and will die a slave. It is my karma."

"It would be the height of disrespect to yourself to think so," Alexander declared. "You are a slave only as long as you think you are. There is no power on earth which could make you so if you do not want to be. You have always been free to make your own way."

The woman turned to him, and looked into his eyes for a long moment. It was a bold move, made even more wondrous for the fact that she dared to. "You are strange, but kind to say that," she said. "What would you have me do?"

"Return to your mistress and stay by her side," he said. "There is nothing to leave behind but the life of a slave. Face the future with your head held high and you will never endure loneliness again."

Ruthinda's eyes welled up suddenly with tears, and she threw her arms around Alexander's neck. He held her gently while she sobbed her anguish away, then helped her to her feet and escorted her back to the campfire.

34

An hour later, Lucien came to him and sat down on his blanket. "You did what I could not. Sarasvati bade me to thank you for your help. I do not know what you said to Ruthinda, but she is much happier now than she has been for quite a long time."

"Charanditha merely acquainted me with her feelings. I did only what was necessary to restore harmony to your family."

"My family? It is your family as well, Alexander. Sarasvati is asking for you. I thought you might enjoy spending a few minutes with us, instead of constantly watching the horizon for the enemy."

Alexander did not dare admit that he relied on it to make himself feel more useful to his father. "I... I feel it necessary to keep the watch. I have been doing it for so long that it is almost a habit."

Lucien leaned closer and winked. "Habits were made to be broken, and you could bear a small pause in your vigilance," he said. Then he climbed to his feet and extended his long fingered hand. "Come on."

Alexander went with him to the wagon and climbed in. The space was a little cramped, filled as it was with all manner of feminine things, but the women made room for him on the thick mattress lining the bottom among a cluster of large embroidered pillows.

"We are so glad you chose to join us," Sarasvati said as she handed a cup of tea to him. "It has been a long time since we have spoken to each other, but there has been no time of late, has there?"

"In truth I have scarcely found time to change my mind, my lady," Alexander replied. He took the cup, found the tantalizing scent of lemon grass in the steam and took a tentative sip. It was warm and comforting, much like her voice, and it was delicious. A tinge of honey clung to the tip of his tongue.

"I have been reflecting on the journey," she said, "and Lucien has been educating me on the ways of the outside world. I do hope that you will call me mother, as I have grown quite fond of you."

"As you wish... mother," he said with a short smile. He took another sip of the tea. "I am told that you are with child."

"Your father has exceeded all expectation in that regard," she gushed, with a faint blush coloring her cheeks as she looked shyly down and smiled.

Alexander tried to chase the vision of their romantic meeting from his mind and the attendant memory of the events that caused their hasty exodus from Kashmir. "Have you chosen a name for it yet? Do you think it will be a boy or a girl?"

She looked to Lucien, who said, "I think it is too soon to decide on that. I think it will be a girl, but Sarasvati hopes it will be a boy. It is important for us to establish a more familiar bond now that we must leave the caravan."

Alexander put the cup down quickly and swallowed before he would choke. "Are we not going with Suliman to Mecca?"

"I thought we would turn toward the Caspian Sea, which lies yet a few leagues from here. I am somewhat familiar with it, having passed through the lands to the north on my way to Tibet."

"There is the question of whether we will be so fortunate to find another caravan as accommodating as this one. Can we not travel with the prince to Mecca, and depart from him then?"

"There is no prospect for finding another once we are there," Lucien replied. "No. We must find our own way. We may yet encounter other travelers who would allow us to journey with them."

"You like Suliman, do you not?" Sarasvati asked.

Alexander nodded. "As I am at heart a traveler it is hard to keep friends. I found a friend in Arpanandra Suresh but he had other plans for his life, and I could not in good conscience forestall him."

"But you agree that the prince is a good man, and he has been a friend to you," she said.

"Aye. What of it?"

"Could we not impose on your friendship and ask him to lend us an escort as far as the sea?"

Lucien interjected, "my sweet, you must agree that it would be disadvantageous for the prince to divide his forces now. He will need all the protection he has, and more, to survive the desert between here and Mecca."

"What other recourse do we have, then?" she asked. Then her face brightened suddenly. "Oh. What if Alexander were to train us in weapons and fighting? I would escape my confinement from this rolling prison and be able to see more of the lands we travel."

Her women laughed and clapped their hands with glee. "Oh yes, mistress," Ruthinda said. "An excellent idea!"

Lucien seemed to accept the idea readily, and asked Alexander, "what say you? Will you take these young ones under your wing and teach them the way of the sword?"

"Father, it would take months to bring them to battle readiness," Alexander said. "I warn you now, ladies, that it will be hard work, and you must toughen your bodies. What disciplines do you follow?"

"We dance, and practice yoga," Sarasvati said. "We use such methods to strengthen ourselves and to find the centers of our spirits. It is how I have been able to survive riding in this cursed wagon without going mad with boredom."

Alexander considered. The question of their gender did not enter into the equation. The question of the child to come did. "Very well, I will draw up a plan and we can begin as soon as you are ready."

Morning found Alexander thinking how he would tell Suliman about the decision to move on. As he walked across the compound toward the prince's tent, he could see that preparations were already underway to continue the journey into the Persian desert, and the prince himself was supervising them from his horse.

Upon seeing him approach, the prince smiled and turned to him. "Ah, friend Alexander," Suliman said. "I hope you are feeling well."

"I am quite well, thank you, my prince," Alexander replied with his customary bow. "And how do you fare?"

"I am mending well, thanks to your father, who has provided me with a most excellent salve to reduce my aches and pains. Are you prepared to join us?"

Alexander brushed a strand of windswept hair from his eyes as he said, "I regret I come to you with sad tidings."

Suliman's eyebrows crimped slightly. The bruise below his hairline was still purple, and only emphasized his tan skin even more. "Aye? What are they?"

"My family and I have decided to part with you here, and journey on toward the sea to the north."

Suliman considered, then dismounted. "Aye. Allah has willed it so," he said. "Let us say farewell now, for we are leaving. You will always have my friendship." He opened his arms and took Alexander into a tight embrace, squeezing briefly, then kissed him on both cheeks according to custom. "May you have the protection of the angels on your journey, wherever your path takes you."

"Thank you, my prince," Alexander replied as he returned the hug. "I pray that the stars guide you through the rest of your days."

"In that I shall be doubly blessed," Suliman said, then kissed both his cheeks again and released him. "Allah be with you."

Suliman remounted his horse and rode toward the head of the assembled travelers, where he took his customary place. At his command, the file of travelers and wagons began to make their way across the desert toward the western horizon and the range of mountains beyond.

Alexander watched him recede into the heat waves rising from the sand for a long while to record his image in memory before returning to the covered wagon, where Lucien was waiting for him.

"There goes another good man," Lucien said.

"Would that there were more of them on our way," Alexander replied softly. "Let us go now before the sun heats the day."

Lucien climbed aboard the covered wagon and took up the reins, while Alexander mounted his horse, and as the sun climbed high into the sky they continued on their way toward the file of jagged mountains to the northwest and into the unknown.

35

For the next few days, when they were not traveling the women spent their time learning the art of the sword. Each of them had a mind of her own, and the thought of shedding blood for the sake of their men was tempered with a desire for a peaceful and gentle life.

Sarasvati set the example, and led the other two in their exercises, meditation and whatever brief pauses they could share in praying to their gods. The women divided the household chores among them so that there was no idleness, but no acrimony. Their melding as sisters was reinforced by a growing affection which dissolved the cultural barriers marking the difference between castes in a very short time.

Ruthinda discovered a natural gift for languages, which had long been buried beneath her self-identity as a slave; while Charanditha had an artistic eye and set herself to learning the crafts she saw along the way, using everything she could to make things to sell.

Sarasvati began to spend more time in less energetic activity as the humors of her pregnancy started to burden her. She confined herself to the wagon again; helping Charanditha sort through beads and pieces for this or that project, or mending clothes which had become worn and threadbare from travel.

Lucien was pleased with this development, and remarked to Alexander that it was much like the way things were done on Antellus. But he was also concerned that the women's rapid evolution into beings of extraordinary intelligence and practical accomplishment would also be their undoing.

"How could it be so?" Alexander asked with an innocent frown.

"There are men in this world who do not feel comfortable with women or their gentle manner," Lucien replied. "Instead they feel their manhoods threatened with their competition in matters of importance. And there are still others who, for whatever reason, share an antipathy, and see women as their worst enemies."

"I do not feel that way," his son said, his tone emphatic.

"Aye, but you are not like other men," Lucien said. His smile was gentle and encouraging. "You are half of one world and half of another. Your mind came into its own on a different plane. And I sense that Charanditha is attracted to you because of that difference. I have seen you together in my mind, and I am pleased with your bonding. You seem well suited for each other."

Alexander almost blushed as he looked down at the dirt before him, and toed absently at the ground as he said, "I am not so certain. I am drawn to her by my need for blood alone. It is akin to feeding on my sister, and I feel shame for it. I have thought of telling her how I feel so that there was no question of my intent. But... I know not how to tell her without hurting her, or the trust we have formed between us."

Lucien looked into his eyes, then nodded quietly. "I misjudged my own perception and mistook your closeness for affection. But now that you confess this doubt to me, I think you should tell it to her. The truth can often be a level which clears the path to acceptance of things as they are. Did you not give me the same advice but a few fortnights ago?"

Alexander cleared another windblown strand of dark hair from his eyes as he replied, "Aye, father. But I fear I will be responsible for whatever rift forms between us once the truth is revealed."

"That is for fate to decide," Lucien replied, "and for destiny to reveal. Approach the moment without hesitation and accept what comes for what it is. What remains will determine your course." As he spoke he clapped a long fingered hand on his son's shoulder, gave it an affectionate squeeze, then walked away toward the small campfire and the women grouped around it.

When the night grew quiet and the others settled down to sleep, Charanditha came to Alexander and sat down beside him. "I am here for you, my love," she said quietly as she drew open her linen blouse. She closed her eyes and let her hair fall to one side, revealing her throat to him. "Take me, and let me feel the ecstacy you have given me before."

Alexander hesitated. The scent of her blood was compelling, but his guilt dampened his hunger. He groped for the proper words.

"Charanditha, have you mayhaps wondered what we are to each other?" he asked finally.

It was as if a spell had broken, and her head came down again as her dark doe eyes rested on his. "What doubt is this which troubles you so?"

"I..." and here he stopped as his tongue seemed to tangle itself into a knot. He experienced a burst of sudden fear as he said, "I want to know your heart. You and I have shared only a few moments alone together on our long journey through the desert. You have not told me your hopes and desires, your thoughts about the world. I have only taken your blood when you have offered it to me, and not shared myself with you. Do you not find it strange?"

The woman next to him looked down and shrugged thoughtfully. "I thought it prudent to watch you, and learn from your acts of bravery and kindness. You know my life from what I do. Is that not enough?"

"No," he replied. "There are other things which pass between a man and a woman which we have not done. I cannot say I love you, for I do not know you. As a person. As a kindred spirit. As all those things which are important for me to regard you as a lover."

"You... do not?" she asked, with a charming but trembling pout pursing her generous lips.

Alexander turned to her and took her hands in his, trying to soothe what looked like a growing bout of tears. "Do not misunderstand me. You are a young, beautiful woman. I am older than I appear to you, and have lived a long life already. I am trying to tell you that you should not place all your trust in me, for I am not a man like other men, and my own life is yet unknown to me."

"Ruthinda thinks I am a fool for loving you the way I do," Charanditha replied soberly. "But, can you not accept that I do, without reservation, without a claim, and take me as I am?"

As she spoke she drew the blouse off, and turned her head so that the spots of feeding were clearly visible, the strong pulse surging beneath.

Alexander's mouth grew moist at the thought of tasting her blood, and his blood pushed at him to take her again. He took her into his arms and kissed her, clamped his mouth to her throat and bit her gently, then with forceful greed as she threw her head back with a soft gasp.

In a flash of sudden desperation he followed through and made love to her the human way, then collapsed onto Charanditha's warm body and laid still, deliciously drunk on blood and passion, half blind and barely aware of the world around him. He felt much better now than he had in weeks, and he did not want to stop feeling that way.

Elsa's face disappeared from his memory as it was supplanted with Charanditha's, transformed by the will of the dragon's blood in his heart and mind.

Charanditha moaned gently and shifted, but did not try to remove him. They laid still like that for several minutes, silent but joined together in their passion; breathing hard, tingling, hot, delirious. Then a zephyr of cool desert breeze stirred him aware again. Alexander looked up and around, then eased himself out slowly, laid down next to her, and used his fingers to gently stroke her face and hair.

Charanditha opened her eyes. "Now I am complete," she said. "And you have made me so."

He replied, "you have awakened me to the passion you have felt with me. I am glad to be the agent of your happiness."

"There can be more of what we shared this night," she said. "You need never doubt that I will give you what you need, whenever you need me. You need never tell me that you love me, for our passion will tell me more than mere words can ever do."

"Charanditha, you are far kinder to me than I deserve," he said.

The sound of Ruthinda's voice calling in the night drew their attention. "I must go to her," Charanditha said, then gathered herself together and stood up. "I will come to you again when you call. Until then, I will carry the memory of this night in my heart."

Alexander took her hand and kissed it. "Sleep well."

Then she was gone again, and as he laid back on the short grass and looked up at the bright milky band of stars twinkling above, he felt all his doubts flow away into the night like a river of darkness.

127

Turkmenistan

June 1646

36

The next few days were each the same as the last as the small caravan passed through the scrub desert marking the southern quarter of what was called Turkmenistan by those they encountered on their way.

Most of the area was marked by vast herds of musk oxen, cattle, sheep and goats, driven from place to place by whole families in a land constantly on the move. Through brief and often tense conversations with the nomadic shepherds, Alexander and Lucien learned that the place was a hotbed of conflict among the Turkmen, Seljuks who occupied the mountains to the west, Persian moghuls from the south, and Uzbek kahns from the north.

Roving bands of raiders from various tribes exacted an ever escalating campaign of revenge upon one another. Fields of crops were devastated by fire. Cattle were plundered, and the small groups of resistors were put to the sword to set an example for the others.

Concern for the peasants caught in the middle was never brought into the conversation among their leaders, and the peasants in turn did not care a jot about who was in charge, remaining stoic about distant rule. But they were the first to suffer when any of the involved parties chose to single out this or that tribal chieftain for daring to act independently.

Thus they were rendered virtually homeless, unable to settle anywhere in their own land for fear that their homes and lives would be destroyed.

Their plight was further punctuated by the sight of vast plumes of black smoke rising from the distant horizon during the day, and deep suspicion accorded strangers until they were clearly identified as peaceful. Starvation was rampant, and cannibalism was practiced with little restraint among the isolated enclaves in the mountains.

The Arkanons spent their rest stops wisely, pausing only to obtain food and water for the women and then moving on, following the line of the mountains and the hard won scraps of information given them until they reached the first hillock at the edge of the desert overlooking the town of Ashghabat.

There, the group made camp outside the city gates along with a crowd of other families and refugees dotting the landscape around them, as it grew too dark to move on.

Ashghabat itself was little more than a few hundred Turkmen and displaced Uzbeks occupying a central hub around a ramshackle palace, which looked deserted most of the time. Alexander wandered the marketplace, where he found nothing but misery among the shopkeepers and travelers.

Even the most prosperous traders complained of having less to sell than ever, exascerbated by the lack of shoppers. These in turn were guarded by men with faces of hard determination and grim purpose, and whose presence only served to intimidate the shoppers and drive them away.

Alexander asked among the merchants if a caravan would be going to the sea, and found a group of travelers who were making their way toward the port of Turkmenbaşy. They spoke of taking a ferry ship toward the western edge of the sea and the port of Baku in the land of Azerbaijan, and pointed him to their leader.

Alexander talked to a short squat Uzbek named Sarkasy, who agreed to let them join the caravan if his palm was generously crossed, explaining that the risks were great and his costs onerous. Alexander offered Sarkasy a deposit of a gold coin to hold a place in the train, and promised the rest when they were ready to depart. That transaction did not please Sarkasy, as he wanted the sum up front, but Alexander said his word was a good as his bond, and emphasized that with a quiet suggestion in mindvoice.

Reluctantly, Sarkasy agreed to the terms and promised to wait for him before starting out.

Alexander returned to camp with the good news. "Most excellently bargained," Lucien said. "Once we reach the other shore, we may find shelter there for a time until the child is born."

"I would not wager a drachma for the prospect, as things stand now," Alexander replied. "I have heard that the Turks are everywhere now."

"Fear not. A full century has passed since I escaped the attention of the Turks. I am no longer a threat to the designs of the Sultan, and he and his sons are long dead. I do not think they are even looking for me."

"Even if they did, they cannot really find you, can they?"

Lucien turned to him and smiled. "Not even if I am there. You have not yet learned to use all the abilities you have at your command, have you?"

"I am keen to learn," Alexander said. "You make it appear so easy. I have not a tenth of your ability."

Lucien chuckled. "It took me years to learn, and even more to become an expert. It is a skill like any other skill. All our natural powers are realized with patience and practice. They do not suddenly appear, or manifest by magic. Think of the eagle, who must fledge by flapping his wings. He cannot take to the air until the time is right."

"But any man with a strong will can resist mindvoice, can he not? I confess it does not come as easily to me as it does to you."

His father grunted softly. "True. But one also hopes that a man with a strong will is also gifted with the strength to resist his own reckless impulses. Therefore there is no need to overcome his mind. Our powers must be used only when they are needed, or we would fall prey to the ease of their use and rely too heavily on them when other ways are better and more effective overall."

"You speak of the abuse of power," Alexander said.

Lucien nodded. "One could gain control of another man's mind, but it is not the proper way to treat him."

"Then, even if the powers are part of my nature I must never use them? Then of what use are they?"

The older man sighed patiently. "You must not let them define you, but to help you to survive."

Alexander considered for a long moment, then said, "if I can live among men without the need to use them then I am better off."

Lucien clapped his hands. "I could not have said it better. The lesson is over," he said. "Now, what else would you know?"

"Suliman spoke to me of wanting to use machines to better the lives of his people. He struck me as a man desirous of peace among all men. Indeed, I am surprised that he did not call for revenge against Aurengzeb for the hurts and insults he suffered."

"His wisdom was in his restraint," Lucien remarked. "Though he may continue to suffer for the wounds in his mind long after the wounds to his body heal."

Alexander bowed his head with sudden shame. "I meant to seek you out and bring you to a world ready to accept peace, but it appears I have failed."

"Do not blame yourself. I do see good in even the meanest of lands, and that compensates me," his father replied.

"Thank you, father. Your words restore me," Alexander replied.

Lucian smiled. "And now, I think it is time to depart, before other men find fault with our appearance or manner. I sense that the way forward will be just as difficult as the way we have come."

37

That much was true. The caravan going to Turkmenbașy was a group of men hoping to find work there as shipmen and sailors, and their families were a meager scattering of women and children; rough beggars all with few possessions among them.

They were suspicious of all things foreign for the fact that they were foreign, and far less friendly to each other than Suliman's pilgrim army. They all appeared to be running from something, judging by their circumspect behavior, but Alexander could not tell what.

After bearing a certain amount of hostile scrutiny, Alexander and Lucien were accepted among them with grudging reluctance, made less so only when Alexander bartered one of the asses for a few articles they needed to make Sarasvati more comfortable.

For most of the journey the Arkanons kept to themselves, and Lucien chose to keep their wagon rolling well to the rear, putting a short distance between it and the end of the file. At night, he and Alexander took turns keeping the watch through the night while the women slept inside fully dressed and equipped against any sudden call to action.

The next day, Charanditha went to trade with the other women and was rebuffed for her trouble. She returned to the camp in tears, saying that the other women were scornful of her because she was Hindu, while they were mostly Moslem or Christian. She said they spat on her and told her that her art was trash; that they had seen finer things in other places. Finally, they drove her away, throwing rocks and whatever else they could find until she fled with her wares as fast as her legs could carry her.

Sarasvati and Ruthinda told her that if the other women would not trade she was better off keeping her goods for more appreciative buyers, and that the value of their coin was not enough to compensate for her labors of love and her skill. Alexander and Lucien discussed what to do, but concluded that the best course was to do nothing at all.

Charanditha vowed to stay close to the campfire and concentrate on making more and better things to trade, and soon forgot about the upset of the day.

A full plodding week later, the caravan reached the shore of the Caspian Sea and Turkmenbaşy. The port city was something of a disappointment, consisting of a series of rough docks and loading platforms surrounded by warehouses and shanty houses, inns and taverns; and a crowd of half starved refugees from villages burned out by raiders.

The ships anchored in the port were leaking ramshackle wooden barges sunk up to their scuppers and overloaded with goods and travelers with better coin trying to escape the wars. Others were fishing boats; some little more than dinghies with one sail and no room for anything else but fish and nets.

Of law and order there was none. Men with tempers scraped raw by desperation and greed assaulted each other openly on the streets, while others watched or tried to avoid being drawn into the altercations. Thieves and looters went through the marketplace and stole whatever they could. If things were not tied down or watched constantly they disappeared.

The whole place was poor, so a fair amount of violent recyclng went on as the inhabitants jockeyed for living space and resources. In the light of day it was one city. At night it transformed into a different place altogether. There was little governance by the authorities, and some of the officials even participated in the looting.

The caravan came to a complete stop in the middle of the main square and its members scattered like cockroaches in the late afternoon sunshine, moving kits and sacks quickly until there was literally nothing left of it.

After collecting his toll, Sarkasy turned his horse and rode away toward the nearest tavern without saying a single word of goodbye, leaving all to their own destinies.

"There goes a disagreeable host," Alexander murmured quietly as he watched Sarkasy dismount and go inside.

Lucien glanced all around him and made an uncharacteristic noise of disgust, his nose wrinkling. "I blame him not, for this is a most uncharitable place. I shall be glad when we are well out to sea and have left it all behind."

Alexander and Lucien sequestered the wagon in a quiet cul de sac off the main road and told the women to stay inside for their protection while they went to transact for the trip to Baku. As they walked along the dock they examined the boats anchored there and discussed their weak points.

The single ferry boat which passed between the two ports was a rather large ship, with three decks open to the air and one reserved for steerage. There was already a good sized crowd gathered on the first deck. But the way it listed slightly to port was distasteful, and the unsavory expressions on the sailors' faces drew doubt into going by sea.

"Look at her," Alexander remarked. "She is unbalanced. She will sink before she reaches Baku."

"Aye, but what alternative is there?" Lucien replied. "It will take yet another month to go around by land, and we do not know what kind of trouble we may meet on the way. Come. Let us obtain our passage before she sails."

They went to the gangplank and were met by a man who stood by to collect the toll and allow passengers aboard. He looked European; tall and thin, with fair skin, long features and small narrow set blue eyes; dressed in a long capecoat with a fur cap covering a rough thatch of brown hair.

"What is the fare for five of us, a covered wagon and four horses, my friend?" Alexander asked him.

The man looked him and Lucien up and down with a cynical smile, revealing a mouthful of crooked yellow teeth, and his voice came out a deep lazy Slavic drawl as he said, "you are different from the others. I have never before seen such skin. Whence came you, tovarish?"

By now Alexander's own temper was raw with the journey, and he was not in the mood for evasion. "What has the color of our skins have to do with the price of a place on board?" he asked, frowning slightly.

"Alexander," Lucien chided him.

"Borzhe moi," the man replied, rolling his eyes. "A comedian are you. I was only curious. For you, two gold dinar, and another two dinar for wagon and horses. What other three are you? I see only you."

"My wife and her maids, good sir," Lucien said. "They wait for us close by. Come. Will you not favor us sailing with you to Baku? We cannot travel by land, as my wife is heavy with child."

"The sea is no place for woman with child, but that is for her to say. So then you are six," the Russian replied. "Unborn child is added weight. Another half dinar."

"It is more than fair, sir," Alexander said, as he drew the coins from a pouch at his belt and handed them over. "Here are seven. The difference is yours to keep."

The tall man's eyes lit up with a brief flare of delight, then tamped it quickly as he looked at the gold in his hand. As was the habit of the day he took one of the coins and bit down on it, then smiled again.

"As you say, tovarish," he said, nodding. "Your family may come aboard. We do not sail until an hour from now. But hurry, as there may not be room for you when you return."

"You have our thanks," Lucien said, then led Alexander away quickly. As they hurried to the covered wagon, he remarked, "he seemed friendly enough, but I sensed a small degree of chicanery. All is not as it seems."

"The thought had occurred to me also," Alexander replied. "A pirate, perhaps?"

"Mmmm. An opportunist. He is a shrewd man. He may not have larceny on his mind now, but the prospect of gold is attractive to him, and is difficult to resist in his present circumstance."

"He might try to rob us, then," he ventured.

Lucien's face was grim. "Aye. If he is going to try it will be when we are well out to sea and where we are most vulnerable. That concerns me greatly. But we have no other choice."

When they reached the wagon Alexander and Lucien told the women what they would face.

Sarasvati's nose crinkled with distaste as she said, "We are lost to the elements, my husband, blown about like leaves in the wind. What can we do now?"

"I gave you my promise that we shall make an end of our

134

journey," Lucien replied. "But we must face many more obstacles on our way before that day. Do you regret your choice to stay with me?"

Sarasvati closed her eyes for a moment, and when she opened them she replied, "nay. You have not deceived me, nor given me cause to regret. I am your wife and will stand by your decisions, whatever they will be."

She turned to Ruthinda and Charanditha, who sat watching her quietly. "My position brought you to this, my sisters. You too have a choice in this matter. What say you? Do we go on, or do we go back?"

Ruthinda was the first to speak. "Mistress, I know that I was foolish to dream of returning to Lahore, but I know I cannot go back. Alexander was right to remind me that the way forward is the only choice we have." She looked to Charanditha, who said, "Ruthinda is right. Let us face our destinies together and united as a family."

Sarasvati turned to Lucien and Alexander. "You have our thoughts. We will continue on our journey together."

38

An hour later, the Arkanons were safely ensconced on the second deck of the ferry, having earned a place among the more prosperous passengers with the weight of their gold. They took a spot a short distance away from the others, and ignored the curious stares cast in their direction. Alexander was so used to their eyes roving over his face and dark clothes by now that it was like breathing the air, and ignored the fear and suspicion charging the atmosphere.

Lucien stared out over the dark water ahead like a pilot, taking the measure of the horizon and a sky now covered with dark clouds. In the half light his grey eyes took the aspect of sparkling silver with a hint of red flame. But while his face was calm his spirit projected a visible discomfort with the prospect of meeting with trouble, manifest in the way his gloved fingers gripped the railing in them like a steel vise. Alexander could easily imagine what was on his mind at that moment, as his own thoughts were of a similar bent.

The Caspian Sea was really an inland lake landlocked on all sides by mountains. The far shore lay beyond the western horizon. The water was dark and choppy with froth.

As the creaking overladen boat plowed its way through the waves, the passengers clung to the railings and the sail rigging like monkeys, trying to keep their food down and their hats on their heads. Some were not successful when the gusting sea breeze plucked their hats away before they could fasten them more securely to their heads, while those with weaker stomachs bent over the railing and discharged their cargo into the water.

Ruthinda and Charanditha took to the sea like seasoned sailors. Like their male companions they avoided the crowd and kept to themselves. Though their clothes spoke of feminine charm the swords and daggers they wore warned off anyone with the mind to provoke them. They stayed close to the wagon and stood guard while Sarasvati remained inside, struggling to maintain her composure against the tossing and heaving of the deck beneath her.

When the ship was out a fair distance, the wind changed direction and started to blow strong and cold, as spray kicked up from the surface of the water. Apparently this did not happen often, and the passengers became nervous as the dark storm clouds to the north grew even darker.

Alexander squinted upward and said, "I think it will be a squall."

"Aye," Lucien replied. "There is little to do now but weather it." He pushed his broad brimmed hat lower on his head and added, "I must check on Sarasvati and make sure she is comfortable. With all this upset she must be very ill by now."

He slowly made his way toward the wagon, his dark clothes billowing about him in the wind, while Ruthinda and Charanditha drew their rough cloaks closer about their bodies and retreated inside ahead of him.

Alexander clung to the railing and looked around at the crowd huddled in the center of the deck. There were no escape boats in case the ship foundered in the growing swells. There was no choice but to swim for the nearest shore, and he did not know what kinds of sea beasts swam beneath his boots. He had seen what a shark could do to a man, and his thoughts grew ever darker as the sky lit up with the first flash of lightning.

Several of the women screamed with sudden terror. A moment later, a blast of rolling thunder shook the deck. Alexander's feet picked up speed toward the wagon as he thought to help his father, but it turned into a drunken stumble as the planking shifted and bounced beneath him. He managed to reach it and duck inside just as another bolt lit up the sky, followed more closely by another clap of thunder.

Lucien had his wife bundled in his arms while the other women clung to each other for warmth. The air was supercharged with ionized atmosphere, and Lucien's luminous skin glowed blue in the darkness of the wagon while his long white hair seemed to stand away from his neck.

"I cannot sustain this," he said to Alexander. "I must discharge the excess or I will burn."

"The excess what?" Alexander asked, puzzled.

Lucien held out his bare right hand and showed a thin film of blue flame flickering in it. "It comes from my body, but it is more than I can carry. Those of us who are of pure blood must touch something metal and ground ourselves to it, or the power will destroy us from within. I had not expected this. Come and take charge of Sarasvati. I must go outside."

Sarasvati's face reflected her concern as she gazed up at him. "You are going outside?" she asked. "But, the storm..."

Lucien's voice calmed her. "I will return to you as soon as I can. Alexander will take care of you."

He released her and stood well away while Saravati reached out to Alexander, who took her into his arms, then tried to take Ruthinda and Charanditha as well. The four of them drew tightly into a knot for mutual protection while Lucien left the wagon.

Through the gap in the open doorway, Alexander saw him go to the iron railing and grip it hard with his bare hands, then light up suddenly into a blue flash. The halo dissipated into the metal and faded away rapidly, while Lucien fell back onto the deck and closed his eyes, breathing hard as a faint wisp of of vaporous smoke drifted upward from his clothes.

For a long agonizing moment Alexander watched helplessly, torn between staying with the women and going to help.

Unfortunately, the passengers on the deck also saw it. There was a sudden outcry, and they scrambled to put as much distance between themselves and the stranger as possible. Shouts of "Strigoi! Witch! Vrykolaka!" filled the air and almost drowned out the thunder as the rain began to fall.

Then, fear of the unknown canceled out their fear of the

elements, and they armed themselves with whatever came to hand. They surged forward toward the pale man lying on the deck, while Alexander did the same, drawing his sword quickly as he leapt out of the wagon and moved to stand between them.

Some of the men fell back, shouted with rage and shook their weapons, but the sight of the blade in his hand halted them. Alexander knew he could not handle so many at once but remained resolute. He gripped his sword loosely as Musashi had taught him to, and though it was not a katana he was prepared to use it like one..

"Come no closer," he warned them, his left hand outstretched to ward them off. "I do not want to hurt you, but I will if you do. What venom is this that you attack my father in such a way?"

One of the men declared, "did you not see the unnatural flame which covered his body? You are witches. You will bring the devil's curse on us."

"We are not witches. What of us makes you think this? Do we not share the same risk?" Alexander asked. "If this ship sinks, we will drown just as you will. Of what benefit is our deaths to you?"

"We do not want your evil among us," another said. "Magicks and witching ways are the mark of the devil."

"The only evil I see here is superstition and fear," he responded. "Come, let us speak to each other like civilised men..."

"You dare insult us?!" the leader exclaimed, clearly looking for some kind of conflict. He gave the signal to attack and led the first group of men forward.

In the same moment, Ruthinda and Charanditha left the shelter of the wagon and ran to Alexander's aid, drawing their swords quickly. The leader paused and fell back with his men at the sight of three swords confronting them instead of one. "You invite death, shedevils" he snarled. "Do you know how to use those swords?"

"You are welcome to find out," Ruthinda snarled back. She moved her sword into a gull wing pose, while Charanditha swiveled hers at the wrist and brought it down with a lazy slash toward the floor. The three of them stood waiting for the attack even as the deck kept pitching in the squall, and lit up by a flash of lightning. The deck rumbled as the sound of thunder rolled through it.

The leader only frowned and gestured his men to action. "Stop their noise," he said.

The men started forward again, and in that moment Lucien

jumped to his feet at a single bound, threw out his hand and roared, "*stop!*"

The mob seemed to freeze in place like statues, moved only by their breathing, held at bay by the force of his command. "*There is no time for this,*" Lucien continued. "*Focus your aggression on this storm which bars our way. Arm yourselves with thoughts which will save your lives, not with weapons of hate, for the storm grows apace.*"

The men seemed to wilt slowly. Then one of them threw his club to the deck, then another, until they were all empty handed. They turned away with dissatisfied grumbling and rejoined their women, who stared at the strange beings standing before them with consternation and fear.

Alexander stood down and joined his father. "It was as if you built a wall to stop them. Such force I have never seen before, and from a single word of command," he said.

Lucien did not look at him. His eyes were fixed on the nervous crowd, returning their gaze boldly. "Force is all these people seem to understand. I do not know what will embolden them next."

Another flash of lightning lit up the sky, and the thunder crashed down onto the deck like a battering ram. Sheets of cold rain fell suddenly, then with increasing force, driving everyone to find shelter wherever they could.

In the ensuing scramble Lucien and Alexander returned to the wagon with the women and secured it to a stanchion before climbing inside.

Sarasvati helped her husband out of his wet cape. "I saw what happened. Lucien, why do the others fear you so?"

Lucien sat down next to her on the floor and wrang the water out of his long white hair into a wooden pail. "Men often fear what they do not understand," he said. "It is nothing. I have lived a very long time, and have fought larger armies than this. Do not concern yourself with them. You are safe as long as I can protect you."

When Alexander had doffed his own wet cloak and dripping hat he sat down and did the same. "The question arises what they will do when the storm abates," he said. "They were in a foul mood, and spoiling for trouble for the sake of it. I only hope that we reach the shore before they decide to pursue their plan further."

Sarasvati started suddenly with a sharp gasp. "Oh," she breathed.

"The child. He is most discomfited by the storm, and has been kicking."

Lucien leaned over and placed his ear to her stomach. "He is growing far faster than I expected."

"What does that mean?" Alexander asked.

"It means she will bear the child prematurely, if she is not careful, and must rest and remain idle from now on."

"Rest!?" Sarasvati gasped again. "How can one find rest in this ferment?"

"Sarasvati, please do not worry," Lucien replied as he fluffed up the pillows around her and helped her to settle. "Come. Lie back and think of nothing but calm. This storm will be over soon, and the sun will return to warm you in the morning." As he spoke he stroked at her forehead with gentle fingers until she closed her eyes and seemed to fall asleep.

Ruthinda said, "there is little to do now but wait."

As darkness fell, the rain fell back to a steady downpour, while the boatswain made his way among the passengers with a group of men to help calm them and secure whatever was loose. Alexander watched them through the small window in the wagon's closed portal while Lucien kept Sarasvati warm and comfortable, speaking softly to her out of a need to maintain calm.

Ruthinda and Charanditha turned their attention to making more room in the cabin and polishing their swords, a clear sign that they knew well what they might have to face in the night. At length, the women put out the lantern and settled down to sleep, bundled up against Sarasvati and Lucien, and covered themselves with their rough blankets. In a short time they were in dreamland.

An hour later Alexander finally gave up the watch and settled down against the portal to sleep, using the drumming sound of the rain on the wagon's wooden roof as his lullaby.

39

Yet, in another hour he was awake again, and sat straight up listening to the rain and the noises coming from outside. It was pitch dark, and the wind had ceased its howling. He heard soft footsteps on the wet planking, and a sound of scraping at the closed portal.

He reached for his dagger and held it ready in his hand, as the door opened part way and a tall shadow peered inside. When his eyes adjusted, he could see the man's face clearly in the dark.

It was the Russian, just as Lucien had predicted; no doubt come in search of more gold. But in the dark and his human blindness he had the disadvantage, and before he was halfway into the wagon with his own dagger drawn Alexander had his hand around his neck from behind and held his blade nocked against his throat. "What mischief is this?" he hissed quietly.

"I... I came to check on you, see you safe, tovarish," the robber panted, his heartbeat strong and rapid in his throat.

"You could have knocked, *tovarish*," Alexander replied. "What. Was half a dinar not enough?" As he spoke he wrenched the weapon from the Russian's hand and tossed it out of reach.

The Russian swallowed convulsively. "You have so much gold already," he protested. "Share it with me and I will be silent to the others. It will be our secret, yes?"

Alexander gave him a wolfish snarl. "Give me a good reason why I do not kill you now."

"If you do my friends will avenge my death. Come, give me but five gold coins, and I will not let anything happen to you and your family."

"*You attempt a deadly bargain*," Lucien's deep accented voice intoned in the dark.

The Russian's eyes bugged out with sudden fear as he shivered. He tried to break free, and struggled in vain against Alexander's relentless grip. "Let me go. Please."

"*Silence!*" Lucien hissed. "You have long made your way without concern for any life but your own. Tell your friends that if any of you come near us again you will feed the sea yourselves."

Alexander let go and watched the Russian bow slightly before he stumbled headlong out the door and dissapeared from sight. As he resheathed his dagger he asked, "what do you think he will do now?"

The sound of soft laughter came to him from the dark. "If he is as clever as he thinks he will do what is best for him. If not, I will find out what he tastes like."

A sudden cold chill went through Alexander. "You are not serious!?"

"I cannot feed on Sarasvati until she has birthed the child. She needs all her strength on this journey. I would perforce feed on one of the horses, but that would only enflame the other passengers."

"I am not concerned about that, I am concerned about what he might tell the others," Alexander protested. "It is bad enough that they think us demons, or worse."

"Then the night will bring an answer," Lucien said. "Let us settle down to sleep. No one else will disturb us now."

Alexander sat down again and took his position against the wood panel of the portal, tried to relax, but sleep did not come easily until the dawn.

40

A shout of "land ho!" woke Alexander suddenly, and he was halfway to his feet again before he caught himself. He looked to the women and saw that they were still asleep. He rose quietly and peered out the small window of the portal. The sky was bright blue with sunshine and sheepy clouds. He groaned inwardly at the prospect of facing yet another day of sunburn, then dismissed it as he turned to nudge his father awake.

Lucien's grey eyes snapped open at once as if he had been awake all night. "Good morrow, Alexander," he husked quietly. Sarasvati stirred and shifted in his arms but remained asleep.

"Good morrow, father," Alexander replied. "We are still alive."

"All was quiet. How did you sleep?"

"I kept one eye open, though I think I dreamt of swimming with mermaids for a short time. I seldom remember my dreams even when I have them. Do you?"

"When I am asleep I have no sense of time passing," Lucien replied. "I am asleep one moment, and awake again the next. It is like unto a blink of my eyes, though I am very well rested afterward."

"I envy you. When I was a child I had nightmares. Brief flashes of terror and darkness not my own. But I think they were from..."

Lucien closed his eyes briefly. "I am sorry, Alexander. I never meant you to suffer so."

"How is that your doing?" Alexander said, smiling.

His father's rosy lips turned faintly upward, a sign that he was not as willing to forgive himself that easily. Then he turned to his charge and nudged her gently. "Sarasvati, my love, it is time to rise and face another day."

His wife smiled gently, then opened her eyes. She listened, and then sighed. "The storm is over," she murmured. "Thank Shiva it is so. I do not think I could face another moment of tossing."

"How did you sleep, mother?" Alexander asked. "The child has not caused you pain, has he?"

She rubbed at her belly. "He is quiet now. I think it was the storm which had him in an uproar."

At the sound of her voice, Ruthinda stirred awake and rubbed at her eyes, while Charanditha grumbled and tried to turn over. Sarasvati slapped at the younger woman's hip and said, "up with you now, you lazy girl. You sleep entirely too much."

Charanditha's voice mumbled from beneath the blanket. "Give me a bit more time and I will be myself again."

Alexander wondered if feeding from her so often had drained her of strength, but reasoned that she would have said so by now. "There will be time enough for sleep after we have our feet planted on solid ground and are well away from this leaky vessel," he said.

Ruthinda said, "Alexander is right, sister. Wake now and join us, for we must ever be on guard."

Those words drove Charanditha from her woolen cocoon, and she sat up quickly, blinking. "I am ready for whatever comes," she replied as she straightened her clothes and smoothed down her touseled black hair.

After a quick conference to plan the day the small tribe emerged from their wooden lair and strolled the deck, inspecting the horizon and the ship for signs of trouble. The clouds above were sheepy clumps of pale grey, and shafts of sunlight pierced through them and sparkled on the calm water. The wind had fallen back to a slight breeze, and the square sails billowed gently against the rigging.

Ignoring the other passengers' curious stares, Sarasvati and Lucien walked to the railing together and gazed toward the far shore looming ahead. "It is all so beautiful," she said. "I must write about this moment, so that I can remember it all the days of my life."

Lucien said nothing, but put his arm around her shoulders and held her close.

Alexander watched and wondered if there would ever be another calm idyllic moment like that again. It was during times like these when Lucien seemed more human than ever, reminding him of how little distance there was between his kind and those around him.

The rest of the passengers wisely chose to keep their distance. and watched the strangers without speaking a word while the sailors worked along the deck. There was no sign of the Russian among them. Alexander wondered if he was hiding somewhere below decks. He said to Charanditha, "you heard all last night, did you not?"

"A little of it," she replied. "You did what was necessary to save our lives. I would not have spared him."

This was a side of her that Alexander had never seen before. "Killing is a necessary evil, but cleave not to hate, Charanditha. You must not let it cloud your judgment."

"I hate all men who care nothing for others," she replied. "You saw how they were ready to kill your father, and you, for the sake of hatred alone. Never mind the gold."

"Aye. I confess I did feel that way myself at first. But I have learned to have compassion for them, for they have missed their chance to make their true mark on the world. Their ignorance makes slaves of them."

She turned to him then, and he saw a tear trickle down her dark cheek. "Yesterday I was ready to die at your side. I had never felt that way before for any man."

Alexander looked into those dark doe eyes and saw the courage and love in them. It stirred his heart like nothing she had done before. Without saying a word, he took her into his arms and kissed her gently. She did not resist, and returned his embrace.

Suddenly, water cascaded down on them from above. One of the hands had seen and decided to intervene, laughing as the two of them stood driven apart, dripping and sputtering. Lucien and Sarasvati turned abruptly and stared, then broke into laughter themselves, while Ruthinda joined them. Alexander stood abashed by embarassment, while Charanditha chafed at her arms vigorously to restore warmth, her teeth chattering.

The laughter proved infectious, and before long the whole deck was roaring. Finally, Alexander joined in, then Charanditha. For a brief hilarious moment, the venomous atmosphere of distrust was banished. "Come," he said to her, chuckling. "We must dry you off before you catch something."

He escorted her toward the wagon quickly and went inside with her in search of a towel. Their levity died off quickly as they saw the condition of the interior. Someone had entered unseen and rifled through it, turning out crates and drawers and scattering their things all over the floor.

"The devil take them," he breathed. "You stay here and change into warmer clothes while I inform the others."

When Lucien heard, he said, "I am not surprised. No doubt the Russian, or one of his men, took the opportunity in hand when we were distracted by our merry making."

"What shall we do about it?" Sarasvati asked. As she spoke Charaditha approached, dressed again for battle and armed. Lucien turned to her and asked, "did you take a count of the funds in your possession?"

"I did, my lord," she said. "No more than two gold pieces are missing, which I had out for incidental expense. The rest remains hidden and untouched where no one else would think to look. I found a nook beneath the floorboards, where I cached them in a leather bag. It lies there still."

"You are a clever girl," Lucien smiled.

"You honor me, my lord," she replied, smiling back.

"Come," he said to Alexander. "We will speak to the captain or his mate and find the truth of the matter. If they are indeed pirates, we may have to fight our way out of it."

He led the way toward the captain's cabin, where they were confronted by a large bald man with a dark moustache and sporting a gold tooth. He had dark eyes, and his clothes were shabby and ill used like all the others, but he had the air of authority among them, drawing himself up straight as he met them. "What business have you here?" he asked.

"You are responsible for the passengers' welfare on this vessel, are you not?" Lucien asked. "Someone has entered our wagon and gone through our things."

The man looked him up and down with a surly expression, then spat on the deck as he said, "the storm was most violent last night. Many things were lost or destroyed. How do you know this happened?"

"It happened but a short time ago," Alexander declared, frowning. "After the storm was long over."

"What was taken?"

"Nothing of value, good sir," Lucien replied quickly. "But we are unaccustomed to having our possessions rearranged in such a way. May we speak to the captain and add our claims to your list?"

The man blinked, but his face told them he was in no mood for complaints. "You have done so," the captain replied. "I will see to this incident. Return to your wagon and be assured it will not happen again." The gold tooth flashed in the sunlight as his mouth curled into an unpleasant smile.

When Lucien and Alexander returned to the women, Lucien said, "the captain is one of them. If they have not assaulted the other passengers it is because the storm forestalled them, but they will find another opportunity before we put in to port."

41

When the sun was high in the sky a woman came onto the deck from below and called out, "has any of you seen my husband?"

One of the men asked, "what does he look like?"

The seeker described him, but no one had seen or heard of the man. The crowd on the deck then fell into a fever of dissatisfied murmuring and discussion about similar events in the past. All agreed that it happened far too often to be coincidence.

Alexander threw aside his apprehension and approached her. "When did you see him last, good woman?" he asked with a gentle tone.

She started, and her eyes went wide with fear as she looked up into his eyes. But concern for her absent husband quickly canceled it out, and she said, "since this morning, when the sun was but a handsbreadth above the sea. He said he was going to obtain our breakfast. But when I asked of the cook his whereabouts he said he had not seen him. No one has."

It seemed the best moment of any to speak of it, and he said, "I think he may have met with violence and gone over the side. There may be piracy afoot among the crew." At this, the crowd settled to quiet and listened.

"Pirates?" she murmured with a fearful expression. "Think you they murdered him?" Alexander nodded. She burst into tears and said, "oh, I am lost. Lost. I cannot live without my Vlisi. I am alone in this world without him. Whatever shall I do now?" She crossed herself, then laced her hands together and began to pray fervently, trembling as she spoke.

Alexander saw the opportunity to turn the tables on the pirates materialize before him. "There is a way to avenge him," he replied. He pitched his voice louder and said, "everyone draw near and hear me."

"We do not want any trouble," one of the men said. "But we will not allow ourselves to fall victim to this treachery as did her poor husband. What would you have us do?"

"You must tell the other passengers what I tell you, and prepare them for action All must arm themselves with any weapon they can secure discreetly and out of sight. Upon my signal, you must find every member of the crew and hold them prisoner. The pirates must not suspect what we are about, or they will gain the upper hand."

"I will inform the others on the first deck, and wait for your signal," the man said. "Are the rest of you with me?"

"Aye," the others replied quietly, nodding.

Alexander turned and watched the deck, where two of the crewmen were checking the rigging. They appeared too engrossed in their work to notice the crowd gathered together, and were too far away to hear what was said. He waited and watched as they passed on to climb up the ladder to the top deck without stopping. "Go now and prepare. Quickly now."

As the passengers scattered to their tasks, Alexander returned to the covered wagon where Lucien stood guard. "We are become pirates ourselves, it seems," he said. "There is a man missing, probably murdered, and the rest of the passengers are willing to take matters into their own hands for it. We are going to take the ship."

Lucien's pale eyebrows crept upwards. "I could not have thought of a better way to avoid drowning," he remarked. "Well played, Alexander. What would you have me do to help you achieve your success?"

"I would perforce avoid using your phenomenal skills and invite another witch hunt."

Lucien pursed his lips. "And I was so looking forward to a bit of swordplay. Ah well. I will remain here and look after the women, and leave all in your capable hands."

147

"I do not want to concern Sarasvati overmuch. She is in such a condition as to warrant its avoidance. It is no reflection on your skill as a partner in combat, but you may have a front seat before the stage."

"Thank you. I will observe and take note. Good luck."

Alexander smiled in reply. "Luck has nought to do with it."

As the day progressed, Alexander glanced out across the water and saw that the ferry was but another two leagues closer to the dock, marked by the line of the mountains rising above the horizon by degrees. If anything was going to happen, it would have to happen now. The storm had delayed the pirates' plan, but not by much.

He did not have to wait long. A group of men climbed down from the top deck and took positions close to the ladders, while the big man climbed up onto a large crate and called out, "everyone, draw near and harken to me!"

Alexander noticed that the Russian was not among them.

The passengers turned to give their attention to him and fell silent.

"You will turn over any gold and valuable trinkets in your possession to us, or you will be tossed into the sea," the captain said.

"What betrayal is this?" yelled one man, while another said, "you cannot do this. I gave you everything I had for my passage."

"That matters not," he replied. "My men will go among you and collect the bounty. Surrender all your valuables, and we will consider sparing your lives. If you do not cooperate your bodies will feed the fishes soon enough."

There was a moment of frozen silence. The crowd on the deck returned his gaze like hounds straining at the leash. Then a whistle sounded from nowhere and everywhere at once.

The passengers launched themselves forward yelling with heathenish abandon, brandishing sticks, belaying pins, and whatever else came easily to hand. Their numbers grew as the other travelers came up from the first deck and joined them.

The pirates were caught off guard at this sudden display of brazen courage, and they were outnumbered ten to one. Three of them were disarmed and went into the water at once. The rest made a fighting retreat but were cut off from the ladders and driven toward the bow sprit, where they were trapped against the spar and could go no further. There they were forced to submit to capture, sustaining hammer blows and rough handling as they were tied up and hauled away.

The captain managed to create a gap between the passengers and himself with vicious swipes of his cutlass until he found himself face to face with Alexander, who blocked his blade with his own. After a desperate round of fighting, Alexander struck the steel from the captain's hand and drove him back against the railing, pinning him there with the tip of his sword pressed against his heaving chest.

The crowd fell back and stood down until Alexander stood alone in the eye of the storm with his captive. "Your days of piracy are over," he said. "Surrender now and we will hold you for questioning by the authorities in Baku. Refuse, and the sea will have you now and forever."

"Who are you?" the captain asked.

"It matters not who I am," Alexander replied. "I speak for the passengers you sought to harm, and is all you need know. Your callous disregard for the lives of others has doomed you already. Shall I hand you and your men to these people to do with you what they will, or to the proper justice you deserve? Speak quickly, for my patience grows thin."

The captain returned his determined gaze and his eyes grew wide with uncharacteristic fear. "You are not one of us, demon," he breathed uncertainly. "I am a sinner, and I know my path to hell, but I do not want to die. Come, I would make a bargain with thee..."

Alexander frowned. "You mistake me, sir. I want nothing from you. The evil you have done is for your own profit, and your faith is too easily cast aside to suit your greed. Your hands are already covered in blood, so all your prayers will not avail you now." He stood back, sheathed his sword, and said, "take him."

Several men detached themselves from the crowd and took the captain prisoner, bound his hands behind him with rope and pushed him toward the center of the deck, where he was tied securely to the mast among his men.

One of the passengers said, "the stranger is right. We should form a court and hold justice on these men according to law."

"I say they should die the way they planned our deaths," said another. "Toss them over the side and let God sort them out."

"Nay. We should hand them over to the port authority and not soil our own hands with their punishment," said a third man. "We have the evidence of their guilt by their own admission. Let us try them, but allow justice to do its will in the proper hands. Whatever happens, this man and his crew will not return to the piracy they once waged."

"What say you, stranger?" the first man asked. "What do you think we should do with these men?"

"If a court will satisfy you, then you are most welcome to try him," Alexander replied.

The first man looked around, then said, "let us put the matter to a vote. How many want to throw them overboard?"

At this there were only a few sounds of agreement from the men, which were quickly squelched by their women, as the notion of revenge was not popular among them. Alexander found that encouraging. "How many here agree to hold court on these men?" There was a loud roar of approval from the crowd, Then he asked, "how many want to give them to the authorities?" and an even louder sound went up.

"You have an answer, sir," the man said. "And we will honor it."

Alexander said, "where is the wife of Vlisi?"

The women came forward, and said timidly, "here, my lord."

He bowed toward her and asked, "what say you, lady? Your husband was used badly by these men. Therefore it falls to you to decide their fate."

She hesitated. "You want me to... ? I have always looked to Vlisi to make our decisions."

"Come. You will have to make your own path from now on. Your word will honor your husband's guidance."

The woman took a deep breath and then replied, "I want them to be tried by the court in Baku."

The crowd applauded, but the matter was not finished. The other men came forward, and their leader said, "we must find where the pirates have secured our belongings and restore them to their owners."

Alexander replied, "look to the Russian for answers. He is the bursar, and knows where he has cached them."

The passengers went en masse to their group of captives. "We seek the Russian," the leader said. "Where is he?"

The pirate captain laughed grimly. "He is sleeping with the fishes now. I caught him pilfering my own stores, and slit his throat for it. You will not find the treasure no matter where you look."

"By that you admit that you know yourself, so tell us now, or you will suffer greatly," the man insisted.

The pirate remained tightlipped and glared back, pouring all his hatred into his gaze; foolishly defiant.

The passenger stepped back, and two of the other men came forward and hauled the big man to his feet. One tightened the knot to his bonds, and was rewarded with a grimace of pain. The other placed a small length of rope around the pirate's neck and drew the loop taut. He twisted the knot gradually until the captain's air was cut off. Alexander saw his face turn red and his breathing grow faint, until he finally stamped his foot and nodded vigorously.

The men released him and let him drop to the deck, where he wheezed and coughed for a few precious seconds. "It is in my safe, secured beneath my bunk," he rasped as he gulped for air.

Thus armed with this information, Alexander and some of the passengers went down the ladder to the lower deck, where the captain's cabin was tucked among a store of grain bins, hidden from sight. There, two men went inside and found the safe and, with the help of two other friends, brought it out onto the deck. It was heavy, and dented the deckboards as it landed. The box was a large chest with a big lock and a chain wound around it. "The key," the leader said. "He still has it, I'll wager. Go back and get it."

"I will get it," Alexander said, now suspicious of their designs. If they were capable of torture, they might be equally capable of murder, and he wanted no part of it. He made for the ladder and shimmied upward to the second deck, then went to the pirate. "The key to the strongbox, captain. Give it to me, before the others have your blood."

"Why do you want to protect me from them?" the pirate asked. "You want to kill me too, no?"

"I simply want to avoid more bloodshed. I care not what happens to you once we are in Baku. Now give it up or I will search you for it."

"You are welcome to try," the pirate replied. Ignoring him, Alexander patted him down, and felt into his pockets, his waistband, everywhere, until he had searched the man's clothing thoroughly. Forced to give up, he asked, "where is it?"

The man's gold tooth flashed in the sun as he smiled with a broad grin. And the moment he did, Alexander knew instantly where the key was. There was no reaching it now. "You swallowed it?"

"Now you will have to wait until we land at Baku to get your things back. And I will be able to escape the dungeon anyway, because my brother is the magistrate there. He will free me, and you will hang for your assault on my ship. You get me, now I get you." He dissolved into freakish laughter at the irony he projected, with the confidence of a man at peace with himself.

"Then you have sealed your fate, and nought can help you, for you have signed your own death warrant."

Alexander backed away and returned to the waiting passengers. When they learned what the pirate had done, they were sent into a frenzy of anger. Shouts about hanging and dunking filled the air along with slitting of throats and worse. Alexander had to hang back and watch, helpless to stop them, as the mob stormed toward the ladder.

He heard the pirate scream with terror among the shouting, then go silent in an instant. The pain in his mind was so strong it filled his soul with anguish. He had never felt such a horrendous bout of empathy before. He crumpled over the railing and finally let go, discharging the knot in his stomach in coughing waves.

When Alexander finally recovered, he returned to the chest and tore the lock apart with his fingers, drew the lid open, extracted the two gold coins the Russian had taken from Charanditha. Then he sealed the box closed, picked it up and went up the ladder to the second deck.

He found the passengers gathered around the body of the captain, whose body was sprawled on the deck and gutted open like a fish. The other pirates were silent as they tried to avoid antagonizing their captors. Two were sobbing with open terror, while another had fainted dead away.

A wooden missile crashed down onto the deck in front of the passengers and broke open, spilling its bounty. Everyone froze, startled, then looked up and saw Alexander standing above them on the poop deck. "You did not have to kill him to get the key," he declared. "Now, your hands are just as covered in blood as his."

He turned his back on them, walked away and joined Lucien at the door to the covered wagon, leaning heavily against it with his head bowed. "I had no power to stop them. They murdered that man. I brought death to him just as he accused me. I relied on the others' capacity for compassion, and instead I am rewarded with pain and horror."

Lucien's face was sober as he replied, "Alexander, there was nothing you could have done to prevent it. They were already out for blood, and they got what they wanted."

"Did the women see this happen?"

"No. I bade them to remain inside." Lucien placed his hand on his son's shoulder and patted it gently. "You should rest now, and try to put this day behind you."

Alexander nodded, then went inside and shut the door.

Charanditha confronted him with concern. "Alexander, what happened?" she asked.

"Justice has teeth of her own, and a hunger for blood like no other," he replied sadly as he sat down on the floor quietly, then began to tremble, and finally burst into sudden uncontrollable tears. She reached for him and took him into her arms, and Ruthinda and Sarasvati watched with quiet sympathy as he cried out the anguish in his soul.

✧

Kartli (Georgia)

42

When the ferry finally entered the port of Baku the port authority officers were patiently waiting on the dock just as they always did. While the dock men secured the lines to the ship, the passengers made ready to disembark. The officers watched each man and family haul their belongings down the gangplank toward the dock and made a careful count of them. There seemed to be more passengers leaving the ship than usual.

The officers greeted them one by one, and were promptly inundated with stories of piracy, greed and death, told in angry indignant tones. Some passengers even wagged their fingers in their faces and told them that on no terms would they be persuaded to use the ferry again.

The port officers were so distracted by the passengers and their tales that they never noticed the wagon and horses going down the cargo plank behind them. Alexander lashed the horses and drove it away toward the north at a gallop before anyone could sound an alarm or stop them. Lucien brought up the rear; and they did not slow down until the houses lining the road thinned out into farmland and they were certain there would be no pursuit.

When they were well into open country Alexander slowed the horses to a gentle walk to afford Sarasvati a respite from the violent jostling, and turned onto a broad road following the foothills. It was well used, and there were deep ruts marking where carriage wheels had made them for many years.

Several wagons and travelers on foot passed them by going toward Baku and paid the strangers no notice. This seemed to assuage Alexander's concern that they might be set upon by bandits.

The countryside here seemed peaceful enough. Fields of crops ready for the harvest gave way to vast herds of cattle and sheep. The natives barely noticed the little caravan passing them by as they bent over the vegetation and plucked up their bounty. There was a smaller population here than in Turkmenistan, and all seemed to be at relative peace.

At twilight of the second day the small wagon crossed a bridge near the walled city of T'blisi, nestled in a valley at the foot of the Caucasus Mountains. But Lucien chose a spot to make camp just within sight of it and would venture no further.

"I know this place. The last time I was here, the Turks were using it as a stronghold, and I would not invite their notice if I can help it," he said.

"Then I will scout ahead and discover the lay of the land," his son replied. "Stay here and tend to the women, and leave the danger to me."

Lucien examined his face carefully, then said, "the ferry still weighs heavily on you. You have hardly spoken since then and I sense great sadness in you. The fire of adventure does not burn in your eyes as it did before."

"You know my heart as well as I do," Alexander replied softly.

Lucien placed his hand on his shoulder and said, "I am your father. I knew you before you were born. How can I not know you now?"

Alexander sighed. "It is not an easy thing to set aside like a worno out glove or a broken vessel. The memory of that pirate's death is forever etched into my mind. Even now, I have flashes of remembrance that come unbidden at the most inopportune moments and blot out all other thoughts. I fear that it will happen when I must be ever attentive to some event critical to our lives."

His father glanced at him. "Alexander, all men feel as you do at one time or another. Even I..." he paused to close his eyes and take a deep breath. "It will take time to pass, but you must not dwell on it, or it will take you down a path you cannot return from. You must forgive yourself for that which was beyond your control."

At that, Alexander shrugged and smiled bravely. "I have come full circle, it seems, for I gave you the selfsame advice in Shangri-la. I will try."

"There is my boy," Lucien replied, smiling. "Off with you then, and return soon with good news."

Alexander spurred his horse with a spirited kick and galloped away down the road toward the city.

As he rode past fields of long grass and well tended crops he worked to convince himself that Lucien was right, and that the man's death was ultimately the result of his own profligate thieving ways. When he felt the weight of mourning start to lift from his mind, he dismissed it to the back where it belonged; and focused on the present and on finding a way through the pass.

The mountains were now covered in heavy caps of snow, a sign that winter was coming. Alexander realized that he and his father had been on the road from Tibet for almost five months. He thought back to the day he left Nihon and marveled at the great distance he had traveled already. Now it would take travel of an equal distance to achieve more civilised climes.

Alexander was halfway to T'blisi when he caught sight of a great hulking ruin tucked far back on a hillock overlooking the road. He drew his horse to a stop and studied it intently for a long while.

The place looked like a palace, a mere shell of stone blocks three stories high; surrounded by a swath of charred timbers and flagstones, possibly the remains of a village.

Curious, he turned his horse into the grass and made his way slowly toward it, alert for every movement among the brush around him. There had been a carriage drive here, but the brush had grown through the cobblestones and turned them aside. He followed that closer to the ruin.

The palace had a vaguely oriental aspect in its architecture. The friezes carved into the stone lintels were foreign to him but they looked vastly old, and dark streaks marked where rain had dripped and left a deposit of fertile soil from somewhere else. Where the fire had not ravaged them the carvings were broken or completely obliterated. Here he could see an eye, there an arm. Faces stared at him from the eves where broken gargoyles no longer channeled the rain. The flagstones in front were made of colored mosaic tiles, now broken into pieces and scattered about like a jigsaw puzzle.

Alexander had seen such vandalism before in Rome, but not with such callous disregard for the values of art as he saw here. The Ottoman Turks seemed determined to erase the history of the region and supplant it with their own, a version which allowed for no other gods or heroes to exist. He did not know what people or nation existed here before, but their culture was slowly disappearing into the earth with time and age.

He sniffed about and found the scent of charcoal on the air, suggesting that the house had burned but recently. The marks of hoofprints all around it showed that it had been besieged by a large group of men. If there had been any animals kept here, they either ran away or were consumed by the invaders. Old marks of bloodstains littered the weedy landscape, but no evidence that any bodies had lain there long. Even then there was something of an invitation to investigate the interior.

It would make an excellent home for the child to come, his blood suggested quietly.

Alexander caught his breath and frowned. Oh, there you are, he replied. Where were you when I was in dire need?

We made the choice to let you guide yourself. And we are well satisfied with the sustenance you have brought to us.

Why then do you emerge from hiding now?

You are entering dangerous territory, his blood replied. *All your resources will be needed now, if you are to survive the journey.*

You remind me of that which I know already, he replied. Save your advice for the day I am rendered witless. Begone!

The presence in his mind vanished as if it was never there. The dragon's blood could be demanding at times, but he would never submit to its rule entirely. Freed from the trance, Alexander took a deep cleansing breath, then dismounted and led his horse with him around the ruin. He tethered her to a ring post near the burned out hulk of a stable and walked the rest of the way.

His steed whickered and snorted, and he turned to see her looking askance at him. "Calm yourself, my good friend," he replied. "I will return shortly."

The creature stretched her neck out, shook her head, then leaned down to crop the grass.

Alexander went in at a side door and looked around. The roof had collapsed into the center, but the ground floor appeared intact. The sound of wings flapping above his head told him that pigeons and bats had found good nesting sites in the eaves on the second floor. There was no sign of anyone living or dead within.

The ground floor boasted a great central hall with a fireplace and grate bigger than any he had seen before. The floor was made of the same marble he had seen on the supporting pillars. Lumps of molten metal which were the remains of hanging sconces were scattered down the center of the hall. The fire had been fierce and burned every bit of wood and textile to ash. The other front rooms were in a similar condition, and the narrow windows stood open to the elements. Shattered stained glass laid on the floor beneath them, where the Turks must have destroyed whatever images they found.

Alexander probed deeper into the back and found a generously large kitchen, two crude indoor privies and other rooms for storage. They were disused, and whatever was left in them was blackened with soot or shattered beyond saving.

Here the air was distinctly pungent with human waste and mildew where standing water gave it a chance to prosper. A solid layer of cobwebs across the small windows gave testament to the spiders waiting patiently for the flies and other insects in this fulsome feeding ground. Water roaches scurried away at every step he took, and the screeching sound of rodents came from gaps in the walls.

Alexander made sure not to touch anything as he went toward the rear portal, which was blocked by tumbled burned out timbers. He kicked the charred wood aside and emerged to stand on a short terrace overlooking a large plot of ground, surrounded by a low rear wall. Beyond that the land stretched away toward the marshland marking the river's edge. At least here was a source of fresh water, and from where he stood he could hear the current rushing past at a goodly pace, leaving no place for mosquitos to breed.

Several graves had been dug and filled in, marked by staves of wood with indistinct markings scrawled upon them. They were set to the left of the yard, while the rest was devoted to rows of crops now plucked of its harvest and trampled into an indistinguishable mass of rotting vegetation.

Alexander thought that with a good cleaning the house could be rendered habitable in a short time. He made a quick assessment of all he had seen, then secured his horse, remounted her, and rode quickly back to the camp.

When he returned, Alexander slid from his horse's saddle and walked the rest of the way. "We should not make camp here," he told Lucien. "I have found shelter but a short way up the road, where we would be safe from discovery."

He described the palace in as much detail as he could, including its vantage points and benefits. "We could rebuild the roof and other parts as needed, and leave the front in its ruined state so that no one passing would know we lived there."

"Deserted, you say? What of the former owners?" Lucien asked.

"I found a graveyard in the rear acre. The Turks were in that way most gentle in their respect for the dead. It is a pity that they had no such respect while those who lived there were alive. I suspect that it has been years since anyone has lived there."

As he spoke, Lucien stroked his chin. "Aye, your suggestion has merit. Sarasvati must have a temporary home until the babe is born, and the other women are exhausted with travel. Let us move there for now, and make the house ready to live in."

By the time the stars came out from behind the clouds in their millions, the travelers had moved quietly into the palace compound and the covered wagon was stowed away in the center courtyard out of sight.

43

Over the course of the night and the next day, Lucien and Alexander kept busy clearing the burned timbers from the rooms of the lower floor, while the women worked to make the living area ready for Sarasvati and her unborn child. She remained in the wagon and slept well for the first time in weeks.

Lucien found a hand pump to a well dug beneath the floor to the kitchen, so there was no need to bring water in from the river. This pleased Ruthinda, who had taken a tour of the river bank and said that the distance was too great to haul it in. Alexander suggested that collected rain water would also do well, and spent the next hour in search of barrels able to hold water without leaking. His search turned up only two, and she set them up near the kitchen door for easy access. Lucien suggested that they dig a channel to redirect water to the field so that the winter crop would have good irrigation, and a latrine to serve as a standby until the privies were usable.

The two privies took a good deal more than water to clean, having been befouled by vandals and the outside elements. Lucien made up a bleaching cleanser from herbs and minerals he found on the grounds in order to disinfect them, saying that tiny animals he called "germs" infested the surfaces and were the cause of disease. He stressed the need for cleanliness for the sake of the child to come.

The women saw the wisdom in his words but could scarcely stand the chemical smell the cleanser exuded, and Sarasvati kept clear of it saying that it made her feel sicker than she was already.

Lucien thinned the mixture out with water and distributed it liberally, instructing them to scrub using sticks to which bundles of rags had been attached instead of going to their knees in the filth on the floor. In this way, he explained, their labor would be less tiring but more effective, saving time beside, and they would better avoid contracting disease from touching the surfaces or inhaling the foul air.

Next, they worked together to clear out the kitchen and prepared it for cooking. The kitchen had its own fireplace, and judging by the condition of a kettle left on the hook the contents had burned and turned to sludge long before the fire went out, indicating that the inhabitants had been surprised while preparing a meal. Lucien looked for another pot and other utensils among the scattered remains and built a fire; first to burn the ruined food stores he found in the pantry, then to prepare the grill for cooking, while Alexander and the women swept the stone floors clean of leaves, ash and dust.

Ruthinda and Charanditha moved their things in from the wagon and made places to sleep in the adjoining rooms, probably the servants' quarters. Charanditha found a cache of linens covered in fine embroidery, secured in a cubbard which had somehow escaped burning; and used some of them to make up her bed, handing off the rest to the others.

Lucien and Alexander then set to work clearing the vegetation from the yard and made it a garden again. Alexander hunted for deer, ducks and geese, while Lucien and the women combed the surrounding forest for wild vegetables, fruits and nuts. In this way they grew a well stocked larder to live on when the wind turned bitter cold and snow began to fall in the valley. Then they settled down for the long winter to come.

During this time no one disturbed them. Small groups of Turk soldiers passed by on the road without noticing the palace, while other travelers avoided it. None dared to come closer to it and explore or to use it as a hostelry. And, as many humans of that time were wont to do, they regarded the night as a time for the devil. No one but Alexander and Lucien traveled by night, so no one ever saw them enter or leave its dark shelter. A blanket of snow made the road impassable at times, and that only served as more camouflage.

During his forays into the city for supplies, Alexander learned that many thought the place haunted by ghosts, citing the plumes of smoke which rose from the chimneys, or the occasional light at a window as evidence. As time went on he learned that the house had long been deserted, and the former owners were rumored to be nobility taken prisoner by the Turks almost two decades before.

Beyond that, however, no one knew anything about the past or what people had inhabited the valley before the arrival of the Turks.

No one had been there long enough to cultivate an appreciation for its history, nor did they stay long enough to learn.

44

February, 1647

Sarasvati's time came while the snow still shrouded the palace in a layer of white. Ruthinda and Charanditha sequestered her in her room and tended to her, insisting that this was woman's work and that Alexander and Lucien were only in the way. Now banished to wait for news of the birth, Lucien adopted the habit of all new fathers. He paced back and forth in front of the door while sounds of fierce anguish and words like "push!" and "yes, breathe!" emerged through the wood.

Alexander had never witnessed a birth before, and was forced to sit patiently and wait for the event to conclude. The sounds were grievous and loud, and the pain in his mind intense. He hoped that Sarasvati would survive such suffering intact. He had no inkling of the mechanics involved, or the joy or sorrow afterward. Other thoughts about his own past crowded out any thought of the future until the sound of wailing cut them off and the pain lessened.

A few minutes later, Lucien stopped pacing and watched as the door opened, and Ruthinda's dark face peered out.

"Your daughter is born, my lord," she said. "Sarasvati is weak, but she suffered little."

"When may I see my child?" he asked, wide eyed with anticipation.

"In a moment," she replied, smiling, then shut the door again.

"Such mystery!" Lucien exclaimed with a patient sigh, then resumed pacing.

The next few minutes were agonizing. Alexander felt Lucien going through several different states of anxiety at once, then asked, "father, what is amiss?"

Lucien turned to him. "The last time I was present for a birth, it was I who tended to the mother, and helped her to bring the child into the world alone. What a joy it was to hold you in my arms, Alexander, no matter that your mother was beyond saving. But you were exceptional, and I worry that your sister may not be. Her mother endured much on the journey here."

The door opened again, and Charanditha said to him, "you may come in now. Mind you be quiet or you will disturb the child." Her air of authority was quite charming, and Alexander smiled. She smiled back as she stood aside and allowed them to enter.

Sarasvati was laid beneath a pile of blankets, holding a bundle of swaddling in her arms. The baby squirmed slightly and made a vague noise of protest. Sarasvati looked beautiful despite the violence she had just suffered, and her long hair had been brushed out into a black veil across her shoulders. "Lucien, my husband, come and look at her," she said. "She is so beautiful. You were right to say it would be a girl."

He went to her bed and sat down, smiling. "What have you thought to name her?" he asked. "The choice is yours alone, my sweet."

"I have thought much about the choosing of a name. I was named after the wife of Shiva. I have thought about continuing the tradition, and as Parvati was the daughter of the goddess, I will name her Parvati."

Lucien smiled, and stroked her hair. "Very well. Parvati it is." He reached out toward the baby and drew his finger gently across her forehead. "You are Parvati. May you enjoy a long life in gentleness and good fortune."

The child shifted and opened her eyes, which were a startling shade of grey. She reached out with small pudgy fingers and grabbed the digit, squeezing it, feeling for the first time. Lucien said, "ho. She is very strong, just like her mother!"

"You had a hand in that," Sarasvati replied with a smile. "She is as strong as Alexander was when he was born, isn't she?"

Just then, Lucien's smile fell for a split second. It did not escape Alexander's notice, and he puzzled about it, even as his father renewed it with a grin. It only reinforced his doubt about his own origins and the secret of his own birth, about his father. What about it was Lucien hiding, that he should respond in such a way?

He did not dare ask, thinking that the question might drive a rift between them that could not be mended with mere words. And it was already clear that Lucien's mind could not be read easily. There was a mental wall which remained erect through everything no matter what Alexander tried to do to penetrate it, so he determined to bide his time and ask when it was prudent to do so.

But even as he thought it, Alexander felt the strange sensation of change cross his mind. He wondered where his place in the family would be now that a child was brought into the mix.

Sarasvati's voice broke through his thoughts. "Come closer, Alexander, and greet your baby sister."

Alexander moved closer and looked down. He saw that the baby's tiny face was active with a myriad of expressions. Her skin was lighter than her mother's and her nose was a cute little button, while her lips were pudgy and a froth of bubbles decorated them. A small wisp of dark hair sprouted from her forehead. "She is beautiful," he remarked with a smile. "As beautiful as her mother."

"Come, Alexander," Lucien said. "Let us leave Sarasvati to rest and bond with her child."

Once they were outside and the door closed, he continued, "I sensed your uncertainty. I am not blind. What were you thinking, that such sadness should fill your heart so?"

"Am I that transparent? Faith, you hear my thoughts as if I shouted across the room. I feel... useless. There, I said it. I feel that I will have no place in the family now."

"Alexander, you speak nonsense," Lucien insisted. "I would have need of your companionship now more than ever. Your participation is of greater importance than you might think."

"How so?"

"I would ask what you have to protect, apart from yourself? You are fully grown but you are still my child, and I would miss you if you departed from my side. What is the haste in your need to be gone from me?"

"Nay, I can think of no haste which would part us so easily. But my traveling heart is chafing at the bit, and you have your family to occupy you withall," Alexander replied. "I feel quite like a fifth wheel on the wagon, which has no purpose save to replace the one already in place."

"You are my right front wheel, the one which steers all the others, if you are to use such an analogy. You should never feel so ill used, or used at all. You are as much a part of my family as you have ever been, and I would keep you at my side as my cherished son and companion. You have never needed to prove your worth to me. You have helped me to see the world anew, and for that I am ever grateful."

At that, Alexander felt that he had misjudged things, and said so. "I am sorry, father," he concluded. "It is how I feel, not as things are. I will wait on your word until Sarasvati and the child are ready to travel."

"You say what is in my mind. This ruin is not a fit place for my daughter to grow up in. Shall we wait for spring to move on?"

"Aye, father," Alexander said.

45

During a break in the weather, Alexander ventured out on horseback to scout out the valley, and found that the eastern shore of the Black Sea was only thirty miles away. It was still iced over close to the shore and there was no way to safely cross it. Further exploration revealed that there were small towns dotting the region along the shore, but they were fully ensconced in Turkish rule.

When he returned to the house, he told his father about what he had seen. "If we travel again by sea we will have to take a boat from the port of Bat'umi, but the Turks control the docks, and we would be easily recognized," he said to Lucien. "Word of what happened to the ferry has spread inland. Those who tell the story speak of demons who incited the passengers to riot, and caused them to perform unspeakable acts of torture on the crew with magic. I heard also that the Turks have taken an interest in the story, and are hunting for a wagon very much like our own, two men and three women who took part."

"Hmmmm. The passengers were quick to deflect the blame for their crime to us," Lucien replied, musing. "That means we must change our mode of transport. One of us will have to risk discovery and obtain a different wagon for the rest of the journey."

"There is no room for chance in it," Alexander replied. Then an idea came to him from somewhere within. "Oh. What if we transform it into a caravan wagon such as the gypsies use for travel? I have seen how they cover their wagons with all manner of device and decoration, making them bright and colorful to see."

The gypsies called themselves Roma, an ancient tribe driven from India by the Kushans. Alexander was familiar with their plight as outsiders, having seen a number of them persecuted by Dutch and

English settlers throughout Europe. But their status as outsiders was also excellent camouflage for alien castaways from another planet.

They were itinerant by necessity and never settled in one place for too long, earning their living with circus acts, fortune telling, dancing and song wherever they went; an ideal lifestyle for someone like Alexander, who felt more at home sleeping under the shade of a tree than in a warm comfortable bed.

They also attracted suspicion and scorn for their wild lifestyle and their belief in the power of magic; as well as their failure to convert to whatever religion was dominant. They kept to themselves, and as a result became easy scapegoats; accused of stealing, murder and other wrongs which were never really proven. Once accused, however, they moved on rather than try to prove their innocence, which in the eyes of the "gadjos" only served to reinforce their guilt; and they roamed the land one step ahead of the "witchfinders" who were the real criminals.

The witchfinders were men who traveled from village to village, taking free food, lodging and the occasional favors of the local virgin in exchange for their talents at identifying and drawing out witches. Too often, they created chaos and disharmony instead, using religion like a shield, declaring the hapless women they deflowered to be witches so that they could preserve their fame as men who got results, and also to prevent a trail of bastards from being born.

As the years went on, however, the age of reason put a stop to their predatory careers when too many of them appeared at the town council meetings with their hands out and a rather arrogant sense of entitlement.

Lucien's words brought Alexander's thoughts back to the present when he replied, "and hide out in plain sight? A clever strategy, Alexander. Then let us set to work and be ready to move on as soon as the leaves are on the trees."

46

It was not until late April when the palace was abandoned, and a small gypsy caravan drawn by two horses trundled up the road toward the shore of the Black Sea, while Lucien and Alexander followed it to act as a rear guard. Ruthinda and Charanditha sat in front, and while Ruthinda held the reins, Charanditha watched the hillsides for marauders with her sword balanced in her lap and a loaded arquebus laid within easy reach.

The Arkanons wisely avoided T'blisi altogether, and it was not until they reached the foothills of the mountain range at twilight when Alexander and Lucien dismounted and took the drivers' places. Ruthinda and Charanditha then retired inside to join Sarasvati and take their evening meal.

Sarasvati stayed inside and tended only to her baby, who had grown fast and had a mature look about her. Parvati's large grey eyes were wise beyond their years, and her small fingers kept her busy exploring the world around her with gentleness and care. She could already speak several words in Hindi, English and Romani. She kept silent unless she had something to say, and babyspeak to her only made her frown.

Sarasvati plied her with toys Charanditha had made for her of canvas stuffed with sweet maple leaves: a bear, a lamb, and a duck. Parvati never threw them, and slept with them grouped around her in the cradle Lucien had made for her.

She smiled whenever she saw Alexander, and called him "Lex", reaching for him with her tiny arms. And Alexander would return her hugs with a kiss on her button nose. Her affection for him only reinforced his need to protect her, and his sibling jealousy soon faded into dim memory because of her sweet innocence.

The Arkanons traveled for two days without meeting anyone on the road until they arrived in the port town of Sokhumi. One of the horses had thrown a shoe, so the Arkanons made camp near the guard outpost marking the entrance to the port, concealing the wagon in a grove of elm trees. They took the horse into town and had to wait for the blacksmith to replace the shoe. They were not challenged by anyone in authority so they felt it safe to be visible among the townsfolk.

While they were there they took on supplies for the next leg of the journey, attracting curious stares wherever they went. The people in Sokhumi were paler in skin color and there were more blondes among them, so Lucien was simply an oddity, and Alexander blended among them quite well. Here, either news traveled slowly or the people were determined not to let the Turks have their way.

But the sight of Hindus traveling through their town was also a source of curiosity. Charanditha quickly found herself the target of their probing questions wherever she went. They were also attracted to her wares, so she returned to the wagon much lighter and richer for it, and reported her modest success with a satisfied grin and a shake of her money pouch.

Ruthinda also returned later, but with a different story to tell. She came back with her clothes in tatters and a large bruise on her cheek where a rock had struck it. She said that while she was in the marketplace to buy food she was accosted and stoned by a mob of women who called her a witch and a nuisance. The people there were highly superstitious and prone to jump to the wrong conclusion. Once they convinced themselves of their delusion, they were not easily dissuaded from it.

"Truly, they saw me for a danger, and would not honor my coin," she said.

Alexander told her not to go into town alone again. "You should have taken me or Charanditha with you," he said to Ruthinda. "We are strangers in a strange land, and you most of all should know that the people here are not as easy to befriend as your own."

Ruthinda sniffed back tears, and held a moist piece of cloth to her cheek. "I know. I will stay close by the camp from now on."

Sarasvati remarked on her clothes and disheveled appearance. "One can only think what is ahead of us now," she said. "They are barbarians. Where are the people you describe, Alexander, that would welcome us with open arms and more friendly words of greeting?"

"They are yet another thousand leagues away," he replied softly. "But do not let these people destroy your faith in a better place to live."

Once their horse's shoe was replaced, the small tribe of six rolled away into the wilderness under the cover of night.

47

The road north narrowed somewhat and turned into a rough trail following the mountains along the shore of the Black Sea, and when rain threatened to swamp the wagon the Arkanons found a large cave set on a bluff overlooking the water.

There, Lucien and Alexander made a fire close to where they found a more ancient hearth which had burned out thousands of years before. A further exploration of the cavern revealed a small group of scattered bones and human skulls, which Lucien insisted on moving deeper into the dark so as not to frighten the women.

The firelight illumined the cave walls and revealed a painted panorama of primitive yet compelling images of men and animals frozen in action. The women looked at them with wonder and mused aloud like patrons in a museum, but neither Alexander nor Lucien knew more than they did about the prehistory of the earth.

Later, and when the rain had stopped, Alexander went to the shore to collect water. It smelled strange, like oil, so he took a taste to sample it. The water tasted bitter and vile, and he spat it out. He stood, looked out over the mass of dark water and felt the strong sensation of loss. No, not just loss. Absence of life, total and clear, like a hole sunk in the universe.

He stood puzzling until he heard Lucien's quite approach. "What kind of place is this?" he asked.

"It disturbs you," Lucien replied.

"Aye. There is no life here," he said, then looked around at the shore. "It is as if the water is poisoned. I have seen no shells on the beach. No crabs, no mussels, not a single trace of animal life. No animal has approached to drink of it."

Lucien nodded. "The lamas told me that once, long, long ago, water from the great sea overflowed the banks of the Bosporus and created this sea. That it had once been a lake of fresh water before it was overtaken, and that a great many people and animals living along its shores were drowned. When I fled Transylvania, I took a more northern route through Cimmeria, and did not pass this way. Now that I look upon it, I well understand what you feel. It is dead. Nothing we know lives in these waters."

He bent over, picked up a pebble and chucked it into the water. The splash barely made a ripple. "I think it best we not stay long and move on in the light of day. I would not even venture to bathe in it, for it may be polluted beside."

"We still are in need of fresh water," Alexander remarked.

"If I am not mistaken, I spied a spring near the road but a short way back," Lucien said. "We should gather as much of it as we can, and keep it aboard the wagon in those wineskins we found in the palace. I will caution the women to avoid the shore."

As he walked away, Alexander looked again toward the west and thought it so far away. In the darkness, he looked up at the stars marking the Milky Way and felt as if the journey was as distant as the lights in the sky.

✧

The Ukraine

May, 1647

48

After another three days of travel, the Arkanons arrived in Sebastopol, on the Crimea. This was the last port of call on the Black Sea along their route. After a brief stopover for supplies and whatever news they could learn about the way ahead, they turned inland and entered the Ukraine, a vast river valley populated by a mixture of western Slavs, Poles and Ugric Cossacks. But wherever they went they found that the Turks had already been there.

Villages stood ruined and burned out, and the people were scattered into the hills without their herds or possessions, forced to hunt for food wherever they could. The Turks had left little behind.

As the wagon passed them by, hundreds of refugees came begging down the hillsides toward it. There were so many at one point that Alexander was forced to lash the horses into a run to escape them. Their pitiful cries for succor were haunting as they pursued the wagon and were left behind. Lucien hung back to make sure that none could overtake the wagon and raid it until he was nearly set upon for his horse. Finally, he scattered them into disarray with a spoken mindvoice command and a wave of his sword, and left them all to their fates.

The sight was so pitiful that Charanditha burst into tears of sorrow and sympathy. Ruthinda put her arm around her and hugged her close as she drove, telling her that she was good for caring about strangers, but that there was nothing she could do for them. "There are too many, sister, and we have little to give them."

Another day later, the small tribe passed near a battlefield, where hordes of ravens and other hungry animals picked their way through the bodies of thousands of men and horses, accompanied by a small crowd of human scavengers in search of anything they could find to barter or sell. Upon catching sight of the wagon, the poor creatures left off from their work and nearly set upon it.

Charanditha was forced to lash the horses into a run while Ruthinda yelled and waved her sword in the air, and Alexander and Lucien created a barrier with their horses and swords to deter any pursuers.

When it was finally safe to slow down, Charanditha handed off the reins to Ruthinda and retreated into the wagon in tears, saying that she could not bear to see any more death.

The only shelter the Arkanons could find was among the darkness of the forest lining the road, where no man dared to go even during the day. Yet the two alien vampires kept watch through the night for fear of a surprise visit from any band of men who might think to brave that barrier.

The next morning, the only visitors they had was a skittish band of wolves, who were so thin that they could barely keep up with the deer they were chasing. Lucien took aim with his bow and shot the deer so that the wolves could catch up and have their hard won meal at last. "I found them pitiful to behold," he explained. "No creature living should be so deprived. It may be the only meal they find for a long time."

When the sun went down against the jagged shadow of the mountains, they finally stopped on the west bank of the Dnieper and made camp for the night. Here was open country for miles around, and the forests were darker and thicker where they grew along the river banks.

After a short tour to reconnoiter and make sure that the area was safe, Alexander and Lucien constructed a wood blind formed of small trees and branches and concealed the wagon from sight a half mile from the main road.

That night, the women dined on biscuits and honey, fried fruit and mead, rather than make a fire. Then after Sarasvati fed the baby they settled down to a quiet and uneasy sleep. There was little to fear from the Turks because they rarely moved by night, but there was still a chance they might be set upon by other travelers.

No word passed between Lucien and Alexander for an hour or more as they listened to the wolves howling among the rocks above the river, and the bats flitting about in their erratic aerial hunt for insects and mice. The flowing water passed through a narrow channel of rocks and the sound of burbling liquid was accompanied by a chorus of crickets and frogs.

"Father, do you regret your decision to come with me and see the world?" Alexander asked.

"No," Lucien replied. "You have asked me that before, and my answer is still the same. If I wanted to return to Shangri-la I would have done so already. I made my choice then, and nothing since has made me regret it."

"It seems the world has become less civilised than when I departed from England," he continued.

"It may be that only pockets of civil men have survived," Lucien replied. "The Turks and their incursions have erased any trace of what was here before, just as Genghis Khan and Attila did before. They wish to make all men like themselves, but that is impossible, for the world is far greater and more resistant to their dominance than they think."

"They are isolated by their faith," Alexander said.

Lucien nodded with a small grunt. "These men have no knowledge of the world beyond what they see in front of them. They are remarkably incurious. Therefore it does not exist for them."

"I am not like them, father. I want to know what the future will bring, what wonders lie beyond the horizon."

"Ah. You will see such things as dreams are made on," Lucien said.

"Will men ever conquer their ignorance?"

"I cannot tell from what I have seen so far. One can only hope. Your mother saw a time centuries from now, when men will try to restore what they have lost. She spoke of vast libraries, and machines which would make life easier for mankind. She spoke of prosperity and enlightenment, conditions mankind could have now if they would only stop making war on each other."

Alexander grunted. "She was wise."

"Aye. But she spoke only of things which might happen. Time will tell whether she was right."

Alexander turned to him and asked, "how did she divine these things? Did she have visions?"

"It is difficult for me to explain," Lucein said. "She may have been in touch with my thoughts of the past, and may have had a connection with my memories. Dreams were what powered her knowledge, yet it was as if she could read my mind."

"Your mind?"

"Aye. I will never know the truth of it." Lucien shifted and sighed. "I will give you by example a dream she claimed to have one night, but which seemed to pluck a memory. "

Alexander leaned toward him, "I am listening."

Lucien replied, "your mother spoke of a machine which could store information better than any scribe, employing a a small wafer of ..." here Lucien trailed off as he seemed to grope for words. "A tiny square of artificial material, etched with patterns and melded with molten pieces of metal. It is so small that it can rest on the tip of my finger, yet it can hold thousands of bits of information as can the largest library of books in the world."

Alexander's wonder grew exponentially. "Tiny? How tiny?"

Lucien brought his thumb and forefinger together and stopped just short of touching them, as Alexander laughed quietly. "Aye. Tiny, yet embued with such power that it is formidable in its use," he continued. "That power is knowledge, enough and of such form as to liberate these people from their slavery to superstition and fear, and gathered by men of science and literature. The more they learn from reading what is published, they will understand their world, and fear it no longer."

Alexander's mouth fell open. "You speak as if you have seen this also. Tell me more. What would one gain from its use?"

Lucien held his hands up a small distance apart. "Mankind will create boxes to hold many of these parts, and erect thin wafers of glass on them so that they might see what is stored on them. They will be able to change what they see, like moments of time frozen in place, or whole pieces of time preserved to look at later. They will use it to control other machines, and to make objects and goods which are identical in every way, in measures of quantity greater than an army of men could ever achieve alone. They will even communicate across vast distances as if they stand together in the same room, by voice and by appearance, without the wall of time between to delay their discourse."

"But, what agency would give one access?"

"Such devices would be powered by lightning," Lucien replied.

"Lightning?"

"Aye. Lightning, controlled and harnessed so that it does no harm to the user, and guided by means of the metal filaments attached within. It is too complex a principle for me to explain fully without teaching you the whole of science which makes it possible. It would take a year or more to give you such understanding, even if I were to start your instruction now. And, as I am not one who worked with such devices extensively, I am not sure I can explain all without error. Suffice to say that one day they may exist, and all can benefit from their use."

"It is most wondrous to hear," Alexander said. "I hope that one day I will be able to use this machine you speak of."

"I have no doubt of that," Lucien said. "And, as you have lived longer than mortal men, it is only a matter of waiting patiently for the world to catch up with you, then joining with it in the joy of such discovery."

"Were such machines used before, perhaps in antiquity?"

"I do not know," Lucien replied. "If men ever used them before there is no evidence, and no oral memory among the generations. That is for time and history to tell. Along with the usefulness of such alchemy and science, there is an equal risk that mankind will use it badly, and hasten his own downfall into another dark age such as was told to me. And we do not know how many times it has happened, or how far in the past it has been so. Man has been on this earth only recently since the earth was formed, and is only now emerging from the darkness yet again."

Alexander grunted. "I did advise Suliman that such knowledge could enable men to wage war through the use of machines. He understood my caution, though his desire was one of peaceful intent. Now you say that they are not only possible, but that man is more prone to use them to destroy what they create."

"Aye. Mankind must learn their proper place in their world, and to avoid the temptation to use their machines in such a way. But I fear that there will ever be men so tempted, and without regard for the consequences no matter that they do themselves the same harm. They will learn to harness such energies as are beyond their understanding and control, but misuse them from ignorance and greed."

Despite the sadness evident in Lucien's voice, Alexander was encouraged by his remark. "Then I will be patient, and, and in time I will be a man of the future, with a voice to change it for good." He looked up at the stars. "What a brave new world, that has such a challenge and destiny to fulfill."

Lucien turned and ruffled the top of Alexander's hair. "Good evening, Alexander. Dream well."

Before long the sounds of night lulled Alexander into a deep but satisfying sleep as all the hurts he had suffered before seemed to slip away like ghosts.

49

The next morning, clouds covered the sky and threatened rain. After breakfast, the wagon was made ready for travel again, and by the time the first drizzle began to fall the Arkanons were well on their way up the road.

When the rain stopped and they had gone a few more miles Alexander volunteered to scout ahead and see what obstacles they might have to face, partly to assuage his sense of adventure and discovery, and partly out of a need to be alone with his thoughts. During previous scouting expeditions he found the solace a good way to sort them out.

"Have a care, Alexander," Lucien said. "I have a sense of the Turk lodged close by."

"They will not even know I am there," his son assured him. Then he urged his horse into a canter and went on alone.

The valley was a vast grassland dotted with small stands of forest. The road skirted the treeline as if the darkness therein was meant to be avoided. As he walked his horse past acres of oak and ash, he sniffed and caught the scent of ancient wood and wet soil, bringing with them memories of times past. The trees were like silent giants standing next to the narrow path, neither welcoming nor inviting in their aspect as they seemed to watch him ride by like spectators.

Alexander shook himself loose of the image, thinking he would work himself into genuine fright if he kept indulging his creative spirit in such a way; but determined to write the experience down as soon as he returned to the wagon.

When he came to a crossroads, he found a stone highway marker set in the center next to a small shrine to the virgin Mary. To the left was marked a town called Chisinăo. To the right was a place called Krywy Rih. But to Alexander, who could not read Cyrillic, their place names might well have been in Chinese. He puzzled for a few moments, then thought to ride back and tell Lucien what was ahead.

But as he turned his horse around Alexander spotted a plume of smoke rising above the trees to the east, and an orange glow coloring the grey sky close to the horizon. Curiosity overtook him. He rode toward it through the high grass, slowly to allow his horse to negotiate her way.

When he rounded a group of boulders he found the entrance to a village, and grew appalled at the sight that greeted him.

Bodies of men, women and children, horses, cattle, chickens, pigs, were strewn through and around a cluster of burning hovels, speared with lance and sword, mutilated and broken. The ground was soaked with dark red pools of blood, and the strong scent of iron blended with a myriad of other odors into a horrid miasma of death.

His horse shied and neighed, reared back and tried to run away from the horror. Alexander was forced to dismount and tether her securely to a tree, then ran the rest of the way, looking for anyone who might be left alive to render them aid. He wandered through the ruins, dismayed at the waste and violence; looked about for signs of movement and could barely make out a faint heartbeat here and there, but when he went to help them he found the owners were far beyond saving, clinging to life only long enough to see a friendly face or to utter a few faint words before they succumbed.

Then when he rounded a turn in the common causeway Alexander heard a soft moaning sound among the rubble. The men lying here were soldiers of a different group; more elegantly dressed and caparisoned than the rest. Knights fallen while defending the village, or agents of its destruction, it mattered not to Alexander. Any life fighting for survival was worth saving.

He moved swiftly and found a horse lying on its side, dead from a lance driven into its side. He detected a pulse lingering underneath, took hold of the animal's carcass and pulled it off, revealing a man pinned beneath it.

The soldier was a fair young man with pale skin, almost a boy compared to the other men around him. His cheeks were stained by dried tears and muddy blood. His helmet covered a wool lined fur hat, which hung askew and threatened to fall off. His long straw blond hair tried to escape its leather tie. He wore a thick coat with wide sleeves and a cuirass concealing a heavily embroidered linen tunic. There was a deep gash in his side, staining his armor with dark red, and other lacerations bleeding through thick dark baggy woolen trousers tucked into high leather boots.

A sword lay near his right hand, broken close to the hilt. The other part of the blade rested among the other bodies nearby. He must have fought very bravely before going down at last. His life force resonated weakly within the thin chain maille surrounding his torso, threatening to go out like a candle's small flame.

Carefully, Alexander seized the man's left gauntlet, unlaced it and pulled it off, then felt tenderly for the pulse. It was weak and thready from loss of blood, hovering on the brink of silence. He dipped his finger into the pool of blood oozing from a shallower wound and brought it to his mouth to taste it. The blood was healthy, and brought understanding to his mind. The dialect was Russian mixed with Ugric, a heady mix of vowels.

Using that knowledge, he ventured to speak, his voice soft. "My friend, can you hear me?" he asked.

The young man shifted and slowly opened his eyes, which were blue grey, dark as the sea after a storm. His blond lashes fluttered as he blinked upwards, then his eyes widened with sudden terror. "Borzhe moi!" he exclaimed, and moved to escape, but Alexander held him down firmly and made the effort impossible. He winced with pain as he struggled until the stranger's warm voice said, "Please, do not fear me. Do not move, or you will die of your wounds."

The young man subsided gradually. Then another lance of pain contorted his face, and he coughed. Each spasm brought more pain until he fell back exhausted and closed his eyes again. "Are you the angel of death, come to take me to Heaven?" he breathed. "Blessed virgin, please tell me it is so."

"Nay," Alexander replied. "You are far stronger than you think you are. But your wound is grievous and you have lost a great deal of blood. I can help you, but you must trust me. Do you want to live? Will you do what you must to survive?"

Silently, the young man considered for what felt like an age, then swallowed, coughed, and nodded.

Alexander stripped off his left glove and bit deeply into his own wrist. When he was sure the blood would flow he placed it over the youth's lips and allowed it to drip into his mouth.

His patient coughed and started to turn away, clearly shocked by this. "No!" he rasped roughly.

Alexander told him, "you must drink. It will heal you and give you strength. If you want to live to fight another day, you will. Fear not. It is the only way I can help you, for your wounds are so deep that I cannot move you now. Trust me and drink."

The young man hesitated, then seized Alexander's wrist and brought it to his mouth, closing his eyes. He sucked gently, then with increasing force. Alexander permitted this for only a few moments before he said, "that is enough now. Rest, and let my blood do its work."

His patient fell back weakly and began to smear the rest of the red bounty from his lips. Alexander licked at his wrist, then waited for the wound to heal over before drawing his glove back on.

The young man's voice was soft and gentle, filled with the Slavic inflections of the Crimea. "My thanks for your aid," he said. "I am named Count Karel Nikolai Arkelin, a Zaporozhian Cossack of the Ukraina. Who are you, sir, that you have the face of an angel, but the blood of a demon? Faith, it tasted like fire and ice in my mouth, yet like sweet ambrosia also. I am restored to life, though I was surely at death's door."

At this Alexander smiled. "I am no demon, but a man with special gifts. I am Count Alexander Vincent Corvina. I am the scion of the house of Arkanon, from Transylvania."

"The country is no friend of mine," Karel replied. "But as you saved my life, I will make an allowance for your kindness. I could never repay it adequately."

"What happened here?" Alexander asked.

Karel had just enough strength to raise his head and look around. "It would appear that I am the only one left alive among my retinue."

He flopped back weakly. "We were on our way to Kyiv from Sebastopol when we did see the destruction and joined the Turks in battle. We sought to defend this village, but the day was not won.. There were too few of us, and too many of them. We could not hold the line."

"I know of the Turks from my father," Alexander replied as he carefully unlaced and pulled the armor from Karel's wounded body. "We fought them in Wallachia, and drove them back to the Black Sea." He reached for the dead horse's saddle blanket, pulled it loose from the carcass and placed it on Karel, tucking him among its rough woolen folds, then reached for a dead soldier's cape and folded it up into a makeshift pillow which he tucked under the count's head.

"Wallachia, you say," the young count replied. "Are you related to the prince Vlad Tsepesh Dracula? I have read the legend of his boundless courage. He was a terror to Mehmed, who dared to lay his eyes on the forest beyond the river. I have seen his painting."

"He was my... great grand uncle," Alexander replied as he searched among the ruins nearby for clean pieces of cloth, which he tore up into strips. When he returned he helped Karel to sit up, then began to wrap the strips around his torso to bind the wounds tightly and prevent more bleeding. The wounds oozed fresh blood, and the iron scent of it was tempting, but Alexander ignored his hunger and continued to work.

"I heard that he drank blood at the execution block," Karel said. "And that he impaled one hundred thousand people. They say he was murdered. They never found his bones, did they?"

Alexander froze. How to tell this stranger that the whole affair was more complicated than anyone could believe? "Those were only stories told to frighten children at night, my lord count. He was betrayed by his own countrymen," he replied carefully. "They were in league with the Turk, corrupt and easily swayed by gold and power. But they could never truly kill him at the end."

"He was immortal?" Arkelin ventured with an eager tone.

"He is remembered as a hero," Alexander corrected him gently. "Only his memory lives on."

He began to wind the bandages tightly around Arkelin's arms and legs. As he worked, he tried to avoid the storm blue eyes studying every inch of his face. "Yes, I see a certain resemblence," the soft voice said, "around the eyes and nose. Even to the color of your hair. Your lineage shows in every angle and every curve. He was a handsome man, too, as I remember."

Alexander was not sure how to take that and said so. "You flatter me overmuch, my lord count."

"Nay, I am not inclined to find you winsome in bed," Karel chuckled as he winced. "Give me two well endowed women with healthy bodies and I will be well satisfied." He emphasized his remark with his hands, making sinuous strokes in the air, then dissolved into another fit of coughing which he fought to suppress. He felt carefully at his chin where a bruise darkened it. "I still have my teeth, thank God. I thought the brute broke my jaw."

"Do not think of such things while you are so ill disposed. Wait while I find something for you to eat, for blood alone will not sustain you."

"I am hungry," Karel agreed. Then he fell back and went instantly to sleep.

Alexander watched him carefully for a few more moments until Karel's heartbeat calmed to a steady rhythm, then left him to search the ruin. He picked his way among the dead until he found a good sized cow, took it by one hoof and dragged it into the plaza. He piled wood near the carcass, then lifted it with an effort and placed it carefully on top. He lit the pyre with a burning log, fanning it with a large piece of leather until the fire grew large. There came the sound of snapping and sizzling as the cow's fur was burned away and the meat started to char slowly.

To anyone else it was a bounty of grilled beef, sizzling and bubbling with juice and fat, delectable and delicious. To Alexander it was a noxious odor of decay like that in a charnelhouse, and death did not feed the dragon's blood. He held his sleeve against his nose to blot out the stench.

In an hour, Alexander had a good sized portion of ribs piled onto a large serving platter and brought it to Karel, who was just rousing himself. The count sniffed and said, "mmmmm. It is a rich feast you lay before me."

"I will find you something to drink, if there is anything left," Alexander replied.

"If you can, see if there is vodka. Or better still, slivoviska," Karel said. He rose carefully to a sitting position and reached for the meat, picked up a rib and began tearing pieces away with his teeth, chewing with ravenous abandon as the juices mingled and dripped down his chin.

Alexander searched carefully around the vicinity of what looked like a tavern, found a cellar and went down into it. There he found a few ceramic bottles scattered intact among the tumbled pieces of a winerack and broken glass. The Turks avoided spirits according to Qur'anic tradition, so they were left behind untouched.

He snatched them up and took them back to his patient, who opened one of them with relish, tipped the bottle and chugged the lot. Then he stoppered the bottle and chucked it aside, wiped his mouth on his sleeve and punctuated his satisfaction with a pronounced burp. "Ah, that is better," he said.

He turned his head and noticed Alexander watching him. "You have touched nothing," he said. "Are you not hungry?"

"I have no appetite in this place of death, but I may indulge in one of those bottles myself later," Alexander replied carefully. "Eat your fill."

Karel smiled briefly and held up the rib, then resumed eating.

While the count was thus occupied, Alexander began clearing the village of the corpses, gathering them together carefully into a pile for burning. It would not do to leave them as they were, and there was the risk that disease might spread from this village into the next, borne by the scavenging animals already picking their way among the dead.

He stripped the corpses of both coin and jewelry and tucked the loot into his pockets and his pack for Charanditha to sort through.

The horses and other animals went into another pile. He set fire to the pyres and silently watched them burn, feeling a mixture of sadness for the villagers' deaths and anger at the Turks for their murderous behavior. When another hour passed he left them and returned to Karel, who had eaten his fill. The young man watched the flames and said softly, "what a tragedy."

"I fear it will be even more of a tragedy if the Turks return and find us here," Alexander replied. "How are you feeling now? Do you feel ready for travel?"

"Where are we going?" Arkelin asked.

"I have been scouting the way ahead for my family. We travel alone, and have been on the road for many leagues. Do you know the safest way to Transylvania from here?"

The count shook his head. "I would guide you there myself, but I must return to Kyiv and give an account of what befell us. I would be remiss if I did not obtain reinforcements to force the Turk back to his own ground." Then another twinge of pain assailed him, and he was forced to lie back again with another bout of coughing racking his small frame. "Though I find myself unable to do anything now."

"Then rest," Alexander told him. "That is all you need do. I will return to my father and bring all to you."

Karel did not hear him, fast asleep again. The dragon's blood had resumed its work. Alexander stepped away on silent feet and retrieved his horse, then rode away and down the road as fast as she could gallop.

50

When he returned to the camp in the forest, he told Lucien and the others what he had found. When he had finished, Lucien said, "it is fortunate you found a guide, but what did you learn about the Turks? It is possible that they may return to search for their wounded."

"I saw no Turks living," Alexander replied. "There was nothing left of that village to salvage. Count Arkelin is not strong enough to move on his own, and I would perforce not abandon him, nor to hasten his death."

Sarasvati said, "what of his character as a man? Think you he will be an agreeable companion on the journey? Or will he change his allegiance once he is on firmer soil and among his own people?"

"Mother, he is a man like any other man. I cannot vouch for his loyalty, but only for his gentle manner from what I have seen of him. I will bear the responsibility for anything he does which does not please you. The wagon must bear him for some time, as his wounds are most grievous. Can you make room for him?"

"I see that you regard him as a friend already. I will not deny you that," she said. "Very well. He may travel with us."

"It will be a tight fit," Ruthinda said. "But if he is as gentle and noble as you say, we will welcome his company."

"And we will care for him as if he were one of our own," Charanditha added. "All life is sacred."

An hour later, the young nobleman was picked up and loaded into the wagon, and placed in a comfortable space close to the front where he could sleep in safety, while the others could come and go unhindered through the back. He bore Lucien's careful handling without a sound of protest, and only answered his questions with one or two words. But all through the examination and treatment he looked tense and anxious.

Sarasvati told him, "you are safe, and among friends. No one will harm you." She shifted closer and began to stroke his hair. Something about her soft touch and her gentle smile seemed to reassure him, though he understood nothing she said, and gradually he relaxed against his pillow.

"Your wounds are deep, but none of your organs are damaged," Lucien said as he applied a poultice of herbs to the cuts and lacerations. The mixture was pungent, and stung by degrees, at times prompting a wince of pain. "I apologise," he said. "The ointment bears a modicum of astringence but will deaden the pain in a short time."

Karel found his voice, and replied, "it is far better than the pain I have endured so far. The vodka cut it down already. Is there any more?"

Lucien said, "it will do for now as an anesthetic, but I fear you may lose more blood if you drink too much. How much had you?"

"I drained a bottle soon after Alexander found me. I have drunk far more than that before," the count assured him.

"Then you are already prepared for what comes next."

Karel's face took on a distinctly puzzled look. "What comes next?"

"How do you feel now? Is there any more pain?"

He sat like a statue and closed his eyes, then opened them again. "No. This is wondrous. The pain is all gone."

"Good," Lucien said. "Now, to the stitches." He produced a long needle made of bone and already loaded with fine white thread. The sight of it caused Karel to go suddenly pale. He flinched and started to move away but fetched up against the wall with nowhere else to go. He exclaimed, "what are you going to do to me?"

"Alexander, hold him," Lucien replied calmly. His son obliged, and held down the struggling, yelling count easily while the stitches were put in place. But by the time the operation was finished, Karel had subsided again. He looked down at the crisscross pattern across his ribs and felt at it with trembling fingers. "What have you done? What magic is this?" he asked.

Lucien slapped his hand away and said, "do not touch it. Let the wound heal cleanly. You have no knowledge of the medical arts, do you? How do you treat your wounded?"

"We do not have leeches to tend us on the battlefield," Karel replied, his voice soft again. "Our wounded often die before they can be helped. I have never seen such a wonder before. Will you teach me this magic?"

"It is not magic. It is science. Rest now, and let your body heal. Do not touch the stitches, nor move about too quickly, or the thread will break, the wound will open and you will start bleeding again."

The count laid back on his pillow and replied, "then I will do as you say, and you have my gratitude." In a few moments, his eyes drifted shut and he fell asleep again.

Lucien nodded, then patted him gently and stood. "Alexander, I would have a word with you. Let us go outside, and leave our guest to his sleep."

Alexander followed his father as he walked away to a place some distance away from the camp, and was taken aback at the grim face which turned and confronted him in the dark. "What possessed you to give him the dragon's blood, Alexander?" Lucien asked.

His son stood dumbfounded. "Father, what have I done wrong?"

Lucien said, "It is not for outsiders. Our blood is given only to those worthy to receive it, not spread about freely like water or wine. The dragon's blood can be a danger as well as a boon to those who take it. Given to the wrong man or woman, it can also make them into monsters. Nosferatu. Come, I would have your reason for this recklessness."

Alexander looked down. "He was bleeding unto death. I had no time to find another way to save him, and I was not thinking about the future. It seemed the logical thing to do, and my blood did not tell me nay."

At this, Lucien stood down from his outrage. "Logical, you say. One cannot argue with logic. But you acted with emotion, not logic.

Logic dictates that you should have left him to die as he should have done, not bring him into a world he has no understanding of. How can this thing be undone? It is too late for him to make the choice of his own free will."

"I do not know," Alexander said. "But I disagree. There was no time to consider the consequences. Therefore, it fell to me to act as my conscience dictates. I would shed more of my blood to others if they have need of it, for I have seen too much suffering and death already."

"Then you had better speak to your new friend of the rest of his life, for he will turn before his time. His wounds made it easier for the dragon's blood to inhabit his body and prepare him to weather his transition. You said you would be responsible for his behavior while he is with us. You are responsible now for helping him through his transition, and preparing him for his life afterward."

"Yes, father," Alexander replied with equal force. "You need not concern yourself with his care from now on. I know he will need my guidance, and I accept the burden gladly." With that, he strode away into the darkness out of sight, leaving Lucien standing alone in it.

"Alexander," his father said to the night, his voice filled with contrition. But the darkness did not reply.

51

An hour later, Alexander returned to the camp. He said nothing, and took up his usual post to stand guard for the night. Lucien wisely stayed clear and let him have his solitude.

Charanditha joined Alexander a few minutes later and sat down next to him. "You have been so quiet, my love," she said. "I could not help but see you arguing. What trouble has driven you from your father's side?"

He started to reply, but instead looked down and sighed. "It is complicated," he said finally. "Nothing you need concern yourself with."

"I would know my lover's heart better," she insisted. "I see that these last few days of travel have affected you as deeply as it has affected me. I want to know your mind."

"You are human. You would not understand," he replied.

She reached out, turned his face to her, and said, "make me understand. I have seen your suffering, though you strive to show it not. I am a woman, and I see things in a man's heart more easily than does another man. You have not been yourself since the ferry."

"It is not for a man to show his feelings as easily as does a woman," he said. "Men live in much denial of their own hearts. And I would perforce be brave for all in my care, no matter if my heart is broken in twain."

"What did your father say that hurt you so?" she asked.

"It is not what he said, but what I did," Alexander replied. "I erred on the side of caution, but now I fear I have made things worse. I may have caused harm to my new friend in doing so, and now I cannot take it back no matter what I do."

"What did you do?"

Alexander turned to her and took her hands in his. "You know how I must feed on blood to live, and what I must do to obtain it."

"Aye," she said. "What has that to do with Karel?"

"I did give him some of mine own blood so that he may live. He was at death's door, so weak that there was no time to do anything else. My father reminded me of the fate which awaits Karel now. He will become like me in time, and no choice has he in it. He will suffer much for wanting to live for the rest of his days."

"And you punish yourself for wanting to help?" she asked. "Alexander, what you did was most kind and noble. You cannot fault yourself for wanting to save another, no matter your method. Your desire to do good cancels out all that is evil in your nature."

"Think you my nature evil?" he asked, taken aback.

"Nay. You mistake my words. True, your ways are foreign to all other men, and that they see nought but evil in them. But I have seen no evil in your heart, nor in your deeds. Evil is that band of pirates who did invite their own deaths for their murderous ways. I give my blood freely to you because it is what you must live on to survive, not for any other reason. But when you take it from me I feel loved, and give you my love in return, and that feeling is more valuable to me than anything else."

"Charanditha, you are a gift from the gods," Alexander replied, and kissed her full on her lips. He felt a stirring of his manhood, and finally acknowledged that what he felt for her was indeed love. He set aside his sword and took her into his arms, kissed her with growing hunger, then made love to her with his teeth.

The dawn brought more rain, and the wagon moved north into the veil of falling water with caution. Alexander led the way on horseback while Lucien stayed to the rear. The road was filled with mud, potholes and rocks, making the way forward more than difficult. There would be no way to escape the Turks if they set upon the wagon now.

While Karel slept in relative comfort, the women sat in front and guided the horses in silence. Even Parvati, infant that she was, seemed to know that quiet was essential and remained mute.

They met no one on the way. Here and there they could see light glowing among the trees where small villages lay hidden among the light stands of oak and ash. Twice, they passed places on the hillsides where they could see the campfires of the Turks laid out in their thousands. During the day they stayed hidden among the rocks above the road to avoid detection, and evaded one Turk raiding party successfully by rolling on through the night without stopping.

As the Arkanons followed the course of the river toward Kyiv they passed through wild untraveled country. The next day they saw more ancient ruins perched on a hillock above the road, but there was no shelter to be had there. The only portion left standing was the burned out shell of a front wall and part of a tower, long grown over by weeds.

While they traveled, Karel told his hosts tales about the history of the region. He spoke of the incursions as if it happened yesterday and he was an eyewitness to history. He spoke of empires forged of steel and blood which faltered and fell to yet greater armies, and of the resilience of his own people throughout.

The Cossacks of the Ukraina had held back the Tatars and Mongols, and the word itself meant "borderland", long the southernmost province of Cimmeria. Russia had conquered the northern portion a century before, and had her eyes on the south. Despite their relatively small number the Cossacks were skillful fighters, and their courage was legendary, all born of generations of Attila's huns and ruthless Cimmerians. Even their women, he boasted, were formidable fighters and horseback riders whether they were of royal blood or not.

He boasted of their attacks on Constantinople and the Anatolian Turks by land and by sea to throw them into confusion and to deter invasion, but as history showed, only slowed down the Ottomans' relentless desire for territory and the destruction of Christians in their path.

Then Karel explained his role as a diplomatic representative to preserve the uncertain peace between the two lands with the full understanding that he was really a hostage to placate the Tsar and forestall his ambition to be emperor of all the provinces he claimed.

"We have long been fought over by this or that warlord like a lamb thrown to the wolves," he said. "We are a nation of refugees in our own country. First Poland, then Lithuania, then Hungary. All set their eyes upon our land and called it their own. But we!" he pounded his chest proudly. "We are Cossacks, and our own lives and fortunes do we own. This is our land. We have been here since the beginning, and will be here long after the conquerors have gone from our midst. Now the Russians claim us, and the Turks, but we will outlast them until they have all fallen to dust!"

The effort of speaking suddenly proved too much for Karel. He fell back coughing against the pillows while the women rushed to his side to make him comfortable. "It seems my body is not in concert with my mind," he laughed, then fell instantly unconscious.

Alexander took note and thought that the day of his transition was near. Sooner or later he would have to tell the young count the truth.

52

When the travelers made camp for the night near the river, Karel woke. He was quiet, and made little effort to eat, in contrast with his healthy ravenous appetite the day before. "I am not hungry," he said. When Sarasvati insisted "you must eat," he dashed the dish from her grasp with a sweep of his arm and declared, "take that filth out of my sight! The smell sickens me."

She retreated quickly, scooped up Parvati into her arms and left the wagon. "He is ill," she said to Lucien, looking frightened. "He has no hunger for food. What is happening to him, my husband?"

"His mind is not his own," Lucien said. "Alexander and I will help him now. Take your sisters and go for a walk. Do not go far, but some distance as safety would warrant."

"Very well," she said, then went to the others and ushered them away. When they were gone, Alexander and Lucien climbed into the wagon and confronted their surly guest.

"You frightened the women," Alexander said. "What did my mother do that you would shout at her so?"

The young count sat on the floor looking miserable with contrition, and fidgeted nervously with his blanket. "I apologize. That was not like me. I feel ill. Different." He looked away and took a deep breath. "Faith, I feel the cold of death moving through my veins like water."

"It is time to tell you the truth," Alexander said. He looked to Lucien and said, "I would speak to him alone."

"As you wish," Lucien said, nodding, then left the wagon.

Karel was nothing if not observant, and he said, "what would you tell me which are for my ears alone?"

"My father is well acquainted with what I would say to you, my lord Count," Alexander replied softly. "You recall that I gave you some of my blood, that you might live through your injuries. It has given you enough strength to heal and restore your body to strength. But there are other things you must know to prepare you for what is to come."

Karel's eyes widened slightly, and his forehead furrowed as his shapely eyebrows rose. Clearly he had no memory of the event or shock had blanked it out altogether. "What!?" he exclaimed. "What did you do?"

"You are changing. Soon you will feel a hunger for blood yourself. I am sorry, Karel. It is my fault it is so, but I could not leave you to die."

"You... you are vrykolaka?" he asked. "Borzhe moi! What have you done, Alexander? You made of me an abomination, that none will look upon me as a man again!"

He made an effort to rise and leave the wagon, and his hand went to his side feeling at the bandages aroung his torso. A wince of pain contorted his features as he pushed at Alexander to get past.

But Alexander pushed Karel back easily and held him down, making shushing noises as he struggled to get free, until he subsided and sat trembling in profound silence.

"Nay," Alexander insisted. "It is only your body which changes, not your soul. It is nature which changes you now, not magic or necromancy. When we took you up and cared for you, you were at death's door. The dragon's blood has preserved your life."

"Am I not dead already? Vrykolaka are undead," Karel insisted, panting for breath. "The living dead who prey upon the innocent, young and old, weak and strong. They are demons from the pit of hell, made from God fearing men and women who sinned much in their lives, or killed themselves and thus separated themselves from the love of God. What had I done to deserve this punishment, that I should be doomed to walk the earth in purgatory, suspended between forgiveness and utter damnation?"

Alexander bowed his head with sudden shame. "Nothing. Nothing at all, my young friend" he said. "But, given the choice between leaving you to die in that village or helping you to live, the error is mine. I had no thought of your immortal soul at the time. I had to act quickly. You may lay all blame upon my shoulders and I would welcome it gladly. But please, listen to me, for I must explain all to you before it is too late."

Karel's blue eyes filled with tears, but he sniffed and pushed them back bravely. "What will happen to me now? What could happen that has not happened already?"

"You are not dead but changing, and it may seem most unnatural but is a natural state. Your body will be taken with a fever, which will course through you like flame. Your ears will hear all manner of sounds. Your eyeteeth will become longer and sharper, like the fangs of a wolf. Your eyes will see the life force of everything living, and your other senses will grow sharper, too. Your fighting arm will become stronger than those of other men, and your reactions more rapid, so that no man would easily defeat you in battle. You may even be able to hear a man's thoughts, and so know what he plans to do. Those are the advantages."

When he finished he sat still and watched Karel's face. The blue eyes glowed slightly in the dark, the pursed lips trembled. Karel brought shaking fingers to his long blond hair and pushed it back away from his high forehead. He looked up at the ceiling as if he could see all the way to Heaven, then closed his eyes. "And, the disadvantages?" he asked quietly.

That was an encouraging sign to Alexander, who thought he would begin screaming in terror or die from sheer fright. "You would not be able to stay in the sun for very long without your skin burning, nor eat your favorite foods again, for they would be like ash in your mouth. You must forsake your love of vodka, as spirits will affect you not. You could never again find the love of a woman without feeling the hunger and the temptation to take blood from her. And, you must feed on others for your strength at regular intervals, or you would die or go mad ere long."

"But, my soul would still be my own, would it not?" Karel ventured.

"The dragon's blood is generous, but to a point," Alexander replied. "You may find that it will speak to you as another being from within you. It will impart advice and knowledge to you that will guide you through life, ever with the intent to preserve you. It can even take control of your body and make you do what must be done. But if you stray from the path of moderation or make an unwise choice it can also punish you."

"Have you ever strayed yourself, Alexander?"

The question sounded more like an accusation. "Often enough that I know its effects. Your stomach will enjoy pain, and your blood will churn in your veins. You will feel unpleasant in so many ways that you will obey in order to escape it."

"And your father?"

"His blood is pure, so the dragon's blood rules him even more than does mine. He has been able to go longer without blood than me. But even he must feed eventually. There is no other way."

"Then there is no hope for me, is there?" Karel said. "I would still turn into this creature, and live as you do?"

Alexander nodded.

"Borzhe moi. It might as well be as if I had died. When will it happen?"

"You spake of your blood turning to ice. Soon. But I do not know how it will affect you. My father has said that each man responds according to his gifts. Your own experience may be vastly different from mine."

"What must I do now?" Karel asked.

"Lie still, and let it happen. It is all you need do. The dragon's blood will do its will in the fullness of time. Then, we will see."

"What if the dragon's blood does not accept me?"

Alexander hesitated. It was strange to hear that from a human. How much understanding was already flowing through his veins? "I have never heard of anyone feeling such rejection. I have never met any others of our kind before who were. There is nought for me to think it possible."

"Leave me, then, and let me pray for my soul," the count said.

When Alexander emerged from the wagon Lucien approached and asked, "does he understand now? You told him all?"

"Aye, father, and he appears to accept his future," his son replied. "Now, only fate and the dragon's blood will rule his destiny."

For the women's safety, Alexander and Lucien constructed a small log cabin for them to stay in set some distance from the wagon, and took turns keeping Karel under a strict watch.

A day later, the young Count complained of pain in his stomach, then fell unconscious again. He was soon consumed by the blood fever and covered in sweat from head to toe, and all they could do was to swab his body down with water from the river and wait for his transition.

Karel tossed and turned fitfully, crying out at times in an agonized, pitiful voice, reaching upward with clawed fingers toward whatever he saw in his mind. His breathing became labored and stentorous as if he was fighting for his life. At times he seemed defiant; at others penitent. Alexander's mind was bombarded with snatches of emotion: terror, anger, confusion, ravaging hunger, abject misery. Then, after an hour, nothing. Karel subsided again, and fell into a deep and paralyzing sleep.

"Is it over?" he asked Lucien.

"Not yet. He must not be disturbed by any sudden noise, or he will wake too soon," his father replied. "Come, let us leave him to rest."

Once outside, Lucien crossed his arms and looked off to some middle distance, then said, "he is taking it better than anyone I have ever seen before."

"I have the memory of my own transition to give me the example," Alexander replied. "I would not wish it on my worst enemy."

"Was it that terrible?"

"Nay. It was what happened afterward which I have no desire to repeat. There was no one there to tutor me through it, so that I did not have a clear vision to exercise restraint."

"Elsa."

"Aye. Elsa."

Lucien turned to him, and said, "I faulted you for an error which I realize I might have commited myself. Can you forgive me for being so concerned for your welfare that I did admonish you without thinking? You are fully grown, with your own mind and spirit. My own fears fueled my reserve, and tempered my judgment with caution beyond all sense."

"I forgave you the night we argued," Alexander replied. "I had to spend some time alone to debate myself. In the end, rationality and common sense won the battle, and it was Charanditha who pulled me out of my darkness."

Lucien drew his son into his arms and hugged him tight, then let him go. "Thanks be to Charanditha," he said. "You and she are well matched. Is it too forward looking for me to see a grandchild in your future?"

"For a man who has seen over six thousand years you are most impatient," Alexander replied with a rueful grin. "But surely we cannot plan for such an event until we reach more civilised ground."

"Take as much time as you need," his father replied. "I only expressed a wish which I have long had since we left Tibet."

"Father, why did you not tell me this before?"

"I felt that a more propitious time would come. I will leave it to you to decide when and where to accomplish it."

"I cannot see you as a grandfather. Faith, sir, you do not look old enough to be one," he said.

"That is your human half talking," Lucien replied patiently. "But make no mistake that I still look upon you as a mere babe in my arms, and I constantly think of the future for our family. Creating a dynasty takes a long time to do, and to do well, so that time is nought but a fleeting barrier to that end."

At that Alexander laughed again. "I will ever cherish that image in my mind. Let me broach the subject with her, and bring you an answer."

But when he talked to Charanditha, she took the question with a grave look on her face. "Alexander, I love you very much," she said, "but I know that your traveling heart would never accept such imprisonment to a family life. I think that children should wait until we have established a proper home for them."

It was ironic that Charanditha's approach to motherhood was now diametrically opposed to her stance before. When she and Alexander first talked of affection, she hinted that she wanted to start a family. Now it appeared that she had grown more mature, and was not willing to rush headlong into a permanent situation as things stood now. He now feared that she had seen enough of him and his father to reject the life of a consort.

"Charanditha, my love, you speak wisely. But my father is an old man, despite what you see of him. His heart yearns for grandchildren."

"Yes, but what do you yearn for?" she asked, with a questing expression on her face.

"I have given no thought to myself," he said. "Of late, I have thought only that the road ahead is more difficult to travel than the way before. I would not say I was tired of travel, for I am not. But if you want a family, and to give me a child to father, I would be willing to wait for you to make the decision and make a home for you wherever you want to be."

"Then let me think on this, and when I am ready to settle I will tell you," she said. Alexander seized her hand and kissed it.

Later in the day, as the sun went down behind the mountains, Charanditha announced that she would go down to the river and hunt for herbs and wild onions to make a salad for supper. With luck, she said, she would also find carrots and berries to enrich the stew and sweeten the bread.

"I will go with you," Ruthinda declared.

"Nay," she said as she reached for her sword and buckled it securely to her waist. "I will not go far. Stay here and protect Sarasvati and Parvati. I would be alone today."

Ruthinda blinked at her with sudden consternation. "Sister, what weighs so heavily on your spirit that you would leave us so?"

"Let her go," Sarasvati said. "Let her have her solitude, for you two have been inseparable since Baku. Have a care, Charanditha. Mind you do not go into the woods, for there may be wolves in there, or worse."

"Worry not about me," she replied. "I will be watchful, and call for help if I find I need it." With that, she plucked up her gathering basket and walked away through the grass toward the river's edge.

Ruthinda watched her go feeling as if that was the last she would see of her. "I should follow her and make sure of her safety. I have a bad feeling about this," she said to Sarasvati.

"Sister, you have not been yourself since the ferry either, and for the hurts you have suffered since," Sarasvati told her. "But you should not find fear in every bush and tree."

"Aye, but something tells me not to lose sight of her. There is no telling what will happen. The Turks could be out there, close by."

"Well then, as you are so determined, follow her, but do not let her see you. If you are wrong she will be cross with you."

"She will not even know I am there. I promise," Ruthinda said as she reached for her own sword and laced the scabbard on her belt. Thus armed, she ventured into the tall grass and disappeared from sight.

Ruthinda followed the trail of trampled grass down to the river's edge, where she looked about carefully for some sign of her sister working along the shore. She finally spotted Charanditha standing a few yards away, plucking about the bushes and pulling up wild onions and garlic, tucking her bounty into the basket as she hummed a small snatch of song to herself.

Then Ruthinda looked beyond into the growing darkness and spotted a campfire burning less than a mile away. And beyond that, another, and still another, stretching to the far horizon. She could see dark figures of men moving about among the peaks of canvas pavilions. Tall poles were erected above them sporting black pieces of cloth, each with a white crescent moon and a star, fluttering in the mild summer breeze. Fear froze her as she realized that her fears had

194

come true. The Turks were camped nearby, so close that they would spot her sister easily if she moved from the shelter of the thick brush.

"Shiva protect us," she murmured, then moved quickly forward to pluck Charanditha away.

But it was already too late. Voices came from nearby, then footsteps stomping past, halting her. Ruthinda ducked down as low as she could and became invisible as a small group of Turkish soldiers marched by within mere yards and then stopped.

She watched in horror as three of them ran forward and seized her sister, relieved her of the basket and threw it aside, scattering its contents on the ground. Charanditha was disarmed even as she drew her sword, and the blade was tossed into the water far out of reach. They held her, struggling, as they tore at her clothes, exposing her breasts and legs. Finally, she screamed for help as the men began to toss her about, laughing at her fight for freedom.

Ruthinda instantly drew her own sword, yelled a Hindu battle cry and waded into the Turks, slashing about like a samurai with skill and courage. She killed two instantly, but she was quickly outnumbered and surrounded by the others and was forced back by a wall of scimitar steel. She watched Charanditha go down into a pool of her own blood even as a flash of white hot pain pierced her back from behind and silent darkness closed in suddenly.

Sarasvati heard the screams and stood up to listen. Alarm surged through her. She took up Parvati in her arms and ran to the wagon as fast as she could go, then pounded on the door with desperation until Alexander opened it. "Quickly, Alexander, to the river's edge!" she exclaimed. "Charanditha and Ruthinda are caught by the Turks!"

He looked at her askance at first, then felt ice cold run through his veins as her words sank in. "My stars," he breathed. "I will go at once." He ducked back inside and closed the door. "We have all been so lax in our attention," he said to Lucien as he drew on his outer clothes and armed himself. "Now are my true fighting skills put to the test, and I may not spare those men if the women are murdered."

"I cannot leave your friend now, as this time is critical if he is to survive," Lucien replied. "Do what you must, and return safe."

Alexander's outrage froze his blood as he waded through the tall grasses rapidly until he reached the site, and found several soldiers rifling among Charanditha's riven clothes looking for anything of value they could take for their own.

She laid where they had thrown her, limbs in disarray, her body half naked and bleeding. Her throat had been sliced open from ear to ear. He could not see or feel her life force, nor Ruthinda's, who was half immersed in the water with her sightless eyes staring upward. Their life auras were dark forever, like a candle's flame snuffed out by a waterfall.

The sight filled him with blind feral rage. Alexander drew his sword and plunged forward silently like a wraith. He laid the Turks to waste before they even had time to draw their own, nor any chance to raise a cry of alarm. One tried, and was quickly rewarded with a slashed throat for his trouble. Alexander was silent and swift, deadly accurate wherever he struck them, and they were dead long before they hit the ground.

When the last man fell still, he stood among their bodies and fought to quench the fire of red rage which had seized his mind. He trembled from head to toe. His sword hung from his hand, dripping rubies, but he was numb beyond feeling. And as the rage slowly subsided, he went blind again, caused by tears of grief.

He dropped his sword, went to his knees next to Charanditha's body and gathered her gently into his arms. "Charanditha," came out a quiet reverent sob. Gone was the hope of children, or even the sight of her patient loving smile. Gone was her kind and loving spirit, sacrificed to the selfish cruelty of men. Now she was a pitiful shell of lifeless flesh and bone. "I will avenge you," he husked. "They will pay for what they have done. I will not stay my hand till the rest are dead."

"Nay," came his father's voice nearby. "Think not of revenge, for that way lies true perdition. You have already meted out your just punishment on the men who took her life."

He looked up through bleary watery eyes and beheld Lucien holding Ruthinda's drenched and lifeless body in his arms. "Father, how can you forgive this evil?" he asked.

"I forgive it not," Lucien replied calmly. "But taking on an army as you think to do is folly. Justice calls for more careful planning. Now is the time to mourn and mend your heart, and in time we will defeat the Turk on his own ground. They camp but a mile hence, and are large enough in number that you could not take them all. Now come away before the next patrol discovers us."

When Alexander and Lucien returned to the camp Sarasvati met them, and her eyes grew wide as she saw her sisters lying still and limp in their arms. She fought back tears as she asked, "what happened?"

Lucien laid Ruthinda down gently on the ground and composed her limbs, pausing to stroke her hair gently. "She fought bravely to defend her sister, but could not prevail against them," he said.

Alexander was too consumed by grief to listen, and stood silently with his lover in his arms.

Lucien approached and said, "let me take her."

His shocked son jerked back and said, "no! You cannot have her. Not yet!" Then he dissolved into tears again. "Not yet," he sobbed quietly.

"Alexander, you must let go," he replied. "Take your own advice for once and mourn her, but she is beyond saving now."

The words penetrated his outraged mind slowly, and he finally surrendered Charanditha's body. Lucien laid her next to her sister, composing her limbs into something more dignified. He covered her mutilated body with a blanket as he asked Sarasvati, "how are the dead disposed of among your people, my wife?"

Sarasvati was too mortified by sorrow to speak at first. But she finally said, "we build a pyre, and burn the body to ash, that the soul might take its place in the heavens with Vishnu."

Lucien stroked at his chin. "Hmmm. That may not be possible with the Turk encamped so close by. May I inter them in the earth as the Christians do? A fire would bring the Turks for certain."

"By all means, do what you must, my husband," she replied sadly. "I will prepare the bodies for burial, and decorate them in the manner of my people. We dress them in their finest clothes and jewels, that their souls may ascend with dignity."

"I will help dig the graves," Alexander said, as he snuffled back bitter tears.

54

In another hour the graves were dug, and the bodies laid to rest with their possessions gathered around them. Alexander was certain that the Turks were not beyond defiling the graves, having no respect for any traditions or customs but their own. Lucien suggested that when they were filled in, the earth was to be tamped down and brush gathered over the graves to render them invisible.

Once that was done, the remaining Arkanons struck camp in silence and moved on, just as a crescent moon and the planet Venus rose above the highlands to the east.

Morning came with flowers splashing bright colors across the green meadows. Poppies, lilies, crocuses, all made the countryside gay with fragrance and blooms as the travelers found shelter in a stand of oak trees, close to the road but well concealed from sight.

Here, the road was well traveled, and from his vantage point on a tree branch Alexander watched peasants going to and fro, merchants bearing their wagons loaded with grain and other foodstuffs toward the capitol city; and a small group of orthodox priests, escorted by a large regiment of mercenaries, moving south toward Sebastopol. He judged it a good sign that the Turks had not gained any territory this far north of the old camp. But once he imparted the information to Lucien and Sarasvati, he resumed his ritual habit of sitting on a rock to watch the horizon again.

He had grown morose and could not find a quantum of solace within himself. He mourned quietly like a widower, wallowing in his grief for Charanditha without any desire to work his way out out of it. The only thought which stuck in his mind was the desire to find and kill more Turks, which only made him feel even more miserable. He knew that Lucien was right about revenge. But revenge, he felt, was precisely what he needed to honor his lost love.

Even when Sarasvati came to him and asked him to join her for tea and find a little cheer, he politely but firmly refused with a small shake of his head. She then offered him a freshly plucked daisy to put in his hair. He could not look at her, and said not a word, brooding silently.

"Alexander, you must not let grief pull you down into darkness," she said. "What can I do to help?"

He hesitated before speaking, feeling as if the words would turn into maggots in his mouth. "Mother, I do not know," he replied. "I cannot shake this, nor do I want to. It is as if my heart was ripped from my body, and I deserve this, for I was not there to protect her as I swore to."

"Your father told me about your advice to him when you went to draw him out of his sorrow. Your mother's death kept him from finding joy again for a very long time. Now you must take your own advice and let go of Charanditha. She is passing through the bardo into a better world, and will be reborn anew one day."

Alexander remained mute, awash in futile sentiment.

After a few moments, she finally relented, drew his hair softly behind one slightly pointed ear and tucked the flower in it, laid her hand on his shoulder and rubbed it to give him comfort, then walked away quietly.

He finally broke his solitude when Lucien came to his side and announced that Karel was awake. "It is time to feed him," he said. "And he is asking for you. Go to him, Alexander."

Reluctantly, he unrooted himself from the rock and dogged Lucien in silence all the way back to the wagon, where he found Sarasvati sitting on the steps and cradling his infant half sister. She gathered Parvati up in her arms and walked away a short distance to sit on a boulder, where she drew her sari aside and allowed the baby to suckle.

Lucien told him, "I must stand the watch in your stead. I trust you to handle him alone."

Alexander nodded quietly, then entered the wagon. He found Karel sitting up on his makeshift bed with a calm expression on his face. The young Count's blond hair was plastered to his forehead and neck, but he looked stronger than he had before, and his teeth flashed points as he smiled gently and reached to him. "Ah, there you are," he said. Then his smile fell as he looked at Alexander's sad face. "What have I missed?"

Alexander told him what happened, and as his story concluded Karel's face became a reflection of his own.

"I am sorry," he said. "What a terrible thing. I grieve with you." Then a sound of rumbling came from his stomach and he said, "my hunger, it seems, grows apace. What happens now?"

Alexander drew off his coat and rolled his right sleeve up. He sat down next to Karel and oferred his bare arm to him. "You must continue to feed from me. I must stay your hunger until we reach Kyiv. You may not find it to your taste, but it is necessary to feed from another man's veins when there are no females available to draw from."

Karel stared at the pale arm held before him with unease, then took a deep breath, seized it gently and brought it to his mouth. His lips clamped to the cold dry skin as he bit down.

Alexander felt a sharp sting, then nothing. It felt odd, but in a few moments all the sorrow and self recrimination flowed away into the background, to be replaced with a strange exhiliaration. He closed his eyes and started to drift away, until a sudden warning twinge in his mind and throbbing pain rippling up his arm told him to stop Karel from taking it all. He opened his eyes and looked down. The Count was feeding like a lamprey.

He said, "you must stop now. You have had enough."

But Karel kept on sucking as if he would drain every drop. Alexander tried to pull away. Karel pulled back and sucked harder, until the arm was wrenched away from his grasp and he was flung back roughly against his pillows. His face filled with indignant rage, and his eyes flared red. "Why did you stop me!?" he snarled. "How dare you!?"

"*Enough, I say!*" Alexander declared, and his voice was rich and magnificent, echoing in the dark as he said it. "*When I tell you to do a thing it shall be done!*" His eyes became bright red points of merciless anger as they bored into Karel's.

The boy swallowed hard, backed up against the wall and threw his arms up to shield himself. "Please! Do not punish me. I did not mean it! I was not myself!"

Alexander's eyes damped down to small embers as the anger drained from him like a receding tide, leaving him trembling from head to toe with the shock of it. He had never felt such darkness fill his mind before. "I was not myself, either," he said. "Forgive me."

He kisslicked the wounds and rolled his sleeve back over them, quickly relacing the cuff.

The young count stared at him with wonder. "Borzhe moi. You were like the dark prince himself. It is said that he..."

"You do not know what you are talking about," Alexander said, cutting him off. "I am not Dracula, for if I was I should have thrown myself to the wolves years ago. Think you that I wished to be this way? I was born to it, and it has taken me a very long time to reconcile myself to this life."

At that moment, Lucien threw open the door to the wagon and climbed in. "I heard shouting," he said. "What happened?"

"Nothing," his son replied as he rose to his feet. "Merely a small disagreement, which has been rectified. Karel has fed. I beg leave to rejoin mother and give her my assurance that all is well."

He made to pass his father but Lucien stopped him. "I will speak to you later," he said. "We have much to discuss."

"It would seem inevitable," Alexander replied, then left the wagon.

55

That evening, Lucien ventured to light a fire to cook porridge for Sarasvati and Parvati, who had cut her first tooth. By now, the baby found everything around her fascinating, and Sarasvati was kept busy stopping her from putting things into her mouth as she crawled around the campsite. Pillbugs fascinated her, and the small balls of yarn that were part of the fringe on her mother's shawl, as well as the leaves and the colored rocks littering the forest floor. All came to her thorough probing examination, and she laughed and clapped her tiny hands with delight at each discovery.

Alexander watched her, and for a few moments forgot his sorrow as his wonder grew. He saw her look up at the stars and laugh as she pointed upward with a pudgy digit and said, "toys!"

He abandoned his post and sat down crosslegged before her. "They are pretty toys, aren't they?" he said.

Parvati looked at him and said, "Lex is pretty, too!" and reached out to him. He scooped her up into his arms and hugged her, kissing her small cheek. Parvati kissed him back, then said, "Lex be happy."

This in itself was remarkable. Recognition and response as cogent as an adult in an infant less than a year old. Her vocabulary growing fast. Dumbfounded at her perceptive remark, he said, "as you wish."

Then Parvati squirmed free, climbed off his lap and crawled back to her mother as if nothing had happened.

Later, during a quiet interlude Parvati started to squirm in her mother's arms. "Parvati," Sarasvati said, struggling to restrain her, "how big and strong you have grown. Oof!"

The effort proved worthless. Parvati began to chafe and strain, then to cry, until Sarasvati relented and let her sit on the ground again. The infant looked at the dirt around her, then started to climb to her feet. Sarasvati looked to Lucien, who was stirring the porridge slowly, and said, "Lucien! Parvati is trying to walk!"

Lucien left the spoon in the pot and came to her side to watch Parvati as she went on all fours, then climbed to her feet. She stood, tottering, then sat down again with an expression of surprise. Her grey eyes lit up and she burbled with a smile, then pushed herself up and remained standing, grasping at her mother's skirts for support with her pudgy questing fingers.

"That's it," Sarasvati said, smiling down at her. "Good girl!"

Parvati looked up at her mother and smiled again, then took a faltering step. Then another. She swayed and looked about to fall down again, but seemed to correct herself and remained on her feet as she began to toddle. She took a few more steps, then stopped and stared into the darkness of the forest as if she could see everything. She smiled and then squealed with laughter as she clapped her hands. Something about the dark made her happy, and as at home with it as she was in the light.

"Parvati," Lucien said, smiling gently.

She turned her dark head and looked up at him, then said, "da."

Lucien squatted down and opened his arms. "Come to me, sweet little one," he said. "You can do it."

The baby smiled again, then started to toddle toward him. She went a few more steps, reached out and grabbed Lucien's fingers with her own, and he closed the gap as he swept her into his arms and held her close, kissing her pudgy little cheeks with unbridled joy.

From where he sat, Alexander watched and found a certain comfort in the event, and the hope of more nights like this one. The sight gave him a renewed sense of purpose. He made a vow to protect his half sister at all costs, and began the work of purging himself of his widower's grief.

56

The next day the camp was struck and Lucien drove the wagon out of the forest and onto the road north toward Kyiv, with Alexander riding behind. They traveled without incident for another day and a half until they reached a bend in the river where it broadened into a small lake. Kyiv was closer now, just beyond the next hill, but Sarasvati was very tired from riding in the wagon and both Alexander and Lucien needed to feed. Lucien thought it prudent to make camp in a copse close to the river's edge.

It was here that Alexander helped Karel out and let him stretch his legs. After relieving himself and bathing in the river, the Count let Alexander help him to dress in some of his old clothes, then asked to be alone for a little while.

Alexander replied, "aye. I imagine you have much to think about. But do not go far, as we may have to uproot ourselves at any moment."

"I will not, I promise," Karel said. Then he walked away along the shore, keeping to the shade of the trees. Alexander watched him go feeling as if a part of himself was going with him. But that, too, was the magic of the dragon's blood at work. Now that Karel was one of his own kind, Alexander was as bound to him as he was bound to Alexander. They were now brothers, pledged to protect each other by the link of the dragon's blood.

Lucien appeared next to him and said, "we must talk about the future. I am not sure that Count Arkelin understands fully what he is. Have you told him yet?"

"Some of it," Alexander replied. "At times I can scarcely understand it myself. Sometimes it frightens me, what I can do and what I cannot. It is as much a mystery to me as it is to him." He looked down at the ground and scraped a bit of clinging mud from his boot. "And when I fed him, for a moment I thought I was someone else."

Lucien's eyes widened, and his pale face seemed to grow even paler. "What happened?"

Alexander told his father about the spell of sudden anger and impatience that frightened Karel into submission. "It was as if I was thrust aside in my own mind, and someone else had taken my place."

At this, Lucien said nothing.

"Father, what does it mean?" he asked. "What happened to me?"

"I know not," Lucien replied. "Mind that you tell me if it happens again." Then he walked away swiftly, as if he was frightened, too.

Alexander watched him go with the feeling that change had taken over all their lives. He stood expressionless, but his mind was churning with a myriad of possibilities and questions. He had never felt so strange and uncertain before. Now, only the future would tell what was going to happen next.

"Come. Not as bad as that," Karel's voice said next to him. "We make our own destinies, do we not?"

Now it was Alexander's turn to be startled. The mild soft voice sounded different, as if it was channeled through a tunnel. The young count's step was noiseless like his own, and he had to remind himself who made him that way. He turned and looked down into the dark blue-grey eyes studying him with a singular intensity. "We are at a crossroads," he said. "I was just thinking on the future."

"As was I," Karel replied, his voice calm. "While I was walking just now I had a heart to heart talk with myself. But just now your doubt was reflected in your face. I have a faculty for reading the hearts of other men by observing their faces. I find myself better able to accept my own fate than I was before."

"What did your heart tell you?"

"Alexander, you saved my life. You gave me more than any other man would have done. No matter what happens now, I will accept the life your nature has given me, and not abuse it. I owe you a duty to honor. Will you accept my friendship and protection as a token of my gratitude?"

"You owe me nothing. You were my friend the moment I laid eyes upon you," Alexander said. "But I am glad for your friendship."

The Count laid a small hand on his shoulder. "Good. Your father told me of your skill with the sword, and what you did for your women. I hold faith that what I tell you now will give you strength of spirit, for I bear knowledge which will grant your wish for revenge against the Turk without having to stain your hands with more blood yourself."

"Aye? What would that be?"

"There has been talk in the court of a rebellion growing among the nobles to throw out anyone who would usurp our birthright."

"Indeed? When do you think this might happen?"

"I confess I am uncertain," the young Count replied. "But it must happen soon, or the Turks will overrun the country and take Kyiv ere long. I shudder to think what would happen then."

"Are you a part of this movement?" Alexander asked. "Are you not also a soldier?"

The blond head shook vigorously. "I am meant for the court and politics, not war. I am nothing more than a diplomat. I fight with my mind and my skill at gentle persuasion and strategy. But if my news sways the nobles into action, my participation in the war is assured as if I lifted my own sword again. I will do all I can to make them listen to me, and I must not fail or it is disaster for us all."

"Then it is imperative that you continue there, and take your place at court," Alexander said. "Feel you well enough to travel on your own?"

Karel felt carefully at his side and uttered a sigh of frustration. "My wounds tingle and ache still. I cannot sit a horse in this condition," he said. "How long until they will heal?"

"Not long," Alexander replied. "I dare say you will be whole again by the time we reach Kyiv."

"The citadel lies but a few leagues away from here, in a glen on the eastern bank of the river. We have made good time since the marshlands, and I can guide you hence as I know these lands well. When will we move on, think you?"

"That all depends on the day and the conditions of the weather."

The count grunted, then squinted upward into the reddening sky, now dark with eastern stormclouds. "The wind bodes ill," he said. "Here, it does not rain often, but when it does the rain falls hard and the road turns into an impassable bog. I know of an inn close by where we could learn the news of the day and the safety of the road ahead. There, your lady and child can find a good meal and the warmth of their fire."

"What do your people think of Hindus in their midst?" Alexander asked. "We have passed through lands where superstition rules the people's sentiments for strangers."

"Hindus are no strangers to us. The Maharaja of Kashmir visited us at court nought but ten years ago, and the nobles greeted his visit with warmth and pomp. Why do you ask?"

"My stepmother is the daughter of the Maharaja of Kashmir. I would have her treated with respect and gentility according to her station while we are in Kyiv. Have I your word that she will come to no harm while she is your guest?"

Karel nodded. "You have my word. She will be treated as my own sister, and no one would dare impugne her under my flag. It is the least I can do for the man who saved my life."

"Those words alone redeem you, and give me hope," Alexander assured him.

When the rain started falling again, the wagon was already safely parked behind a small traveler's inn perched on a hill above the river, just beyond the far shore. The place was cozy but crowded with travelers seeking the same protection from the elements.

Lucien and Alexander accompanied Karel inside, where the innkeeper recognized him immediately, having served him and his men before, so that in short order the Arkanons were given the largest room on the top floor, which had three narrow beds and an extra large chamber pot.

Karel threw his weary body on the bed near the window and claimed it for his own, falling instantly to sleep, while Alexander opted to sleep on the floor and laid out his saddle blanket to lie on it. Lucien took the bed next to the door, and strung up a blanket across the space between his bed and Sarasvati's so that she was accorded a little privacy.

She made a bed for Parvati in the drawer of the bedstand next to her. The baby promptly curled up and went to sleep, quiet as usual, while her mother threw off her concealing robes and climbed under the thin blanket to sleep.

Alexander laid back and listened to the rain drumming on the roof over his head until he fell into a long, restful sleep; the first one he had in what seemed like an age.

206

57

Sometime later, Alexander woke suddenly and sat up straight. The dream was vivid, but already fading away into the past like a zephyr of smoke. He caught his breath and looked around.

He heard gentle breathing in the dark and knew it was Sarasvati, accompanied by a small snatch of wheezing from the chest drawer. Karel's bed was vacant. So was Lucien's. It seemed odd.

He climbed to his feet, drew on his boots and ventured out into the vacant hall, where it was dark as pitch, but he could still see easily. He followed a filament of blood scent down a creaky flight of wooden stairs and into the main lobby; then passed through that into the deserted tavern, where he found them both sitting at a table playing chess. Karel played black, while Lucien played white. They were studying the board like generals, planning out their battle strategies in silence.

"There you are," he said.

Lucien ignored him, reached over and picked up his queen, then placed the piece down in front of a black knight guarding the king. "Check," he called.

The young Count also ignored Alexander, and moved a bishop in place next to his king. "I do not think so," he said.

Alexander reached over to touch Lucien. His hand went through his father's body as if it was a ghost. Startled, he watched as Lucien picked up his queen and used it, taking the knight. "Check," he said again.

But it was clearly the wrong move to make, and Alexander wondered why his father should choose to play it.

In response, Karel picked up his bishop and captured the queen. He grinned, and said, "your move was weak, my lord. She is mine now." And as Alexander watched he placed the queen off the board on its side. But now it was not a piece of carved ivory. Sarasvati, dressed in white, laid on the table, her hands and feet bound in rope. She looked unconscious. Suddenly alarmed at this pass, he asked, "father, what is happening?"

Lucien ignored him as he rose to his feet and faced his opponent. "She is not yours, nor will she ever be," he said to Karel. And as Alexander looked at Karel, he too had changed. He was the mirror image of Lucien, with dark hair and amber golden eyes. He smiled, then laughed, his voice filled with devil's mirth. He reached over and picked up the tiny figure of Sarasvati, then popped her like a morsel of sweetmeat into his mouth.

Alexander came up suddenly with a small cry of distress, breathing hard. He found himself sitting on his saddle blanket where he had collapsed the night before. His hand still gripped the scabbard of his sword, and had his blade halfway out of it before he stopped himself. He caught his breath and looked around in the gloom.

Nothing had changed. Karel was still in his bed, as was Lucien in his. Karel's chest rose and fell gently, a sign he was still immersed in dreamland. Then he gave out a small snort, stirred and turned over, and settled again into sleep.

Quietly, Alexander breathed a soft sigh of relief as he eased the sword back into its sheath and laid it aside.

His father raised his head to look at him, and whispered, "Alexander, what is amiss? I heard you cry out."

"I had a dream, nothing more," his son replied, and brushed his hair out of his face as he glanced out the shuttered window and saw that the sun had set some time ago, a warm glow on the western line of the mountains still visible beneath the mantle of emerging stars.

Karel stirred again and turned back over, then opened his eyes. He looked around and rested his gaze on Alexander as he pushed himself up. "Have I slept all day? Faith, I am more of a morning sort myself." He scratched at his head and yawned, then placed his hand over his mouth to suppress the sound. He winced briefly at the pain in his side and swept his bedraggled hair into order as he laid back down carefully.

"You will grow more accustomed to it as time goes on," Lucien told him. "We are creatures of the night. The light of day is not our time." Then he turned back to regard Alexander with a neutral expression. "You told me that you seldom remembered your dreams," he said. "What of this one was so different that it woke you in such a fright?"

Alexander searched inside himself and found no help from his blood. "I... It was so strange that I scarcely want to tell you for fear that it would alarm mother," he said.

Sarasvati's warm female voice came from beyond the wall of blanket. "What dream is so strange that you do not want me to hear it?" she said. She emerged from behind the blanket with Parvati in her arms and set her down on the floor. "I have some understanding of dreams, as was taught to me by Dharshiva's fourth wife Indira. She could read the signs and tell the truth of them very well."

Alexander turned to look up at her, and said, "I have already said too much. I do not want to frighten you."

"I too have had many dreams," Sarasvati replied. "I do not speak of them, for what harm can come from a dream?"

"Mother, your insight is refreshing. But what I dreamed was of a future which has not yet come to pass, and I feared it would be so."

Sarasvati leaned down and placed a warm hand on his cheek. "It will only come to pass if you do such as would bring it to that end. Now, what did you dream?"

Alexander took a deep breath, then related it to all. At the end of his speech silence descended in the chamber, and Sarasvati's eyes had grown large and round with consternation.

Then Lucien spoke. "That is quite a dream," he said.

"I do not understand any of it," Karel said. "Why would I do harm to such a sweet lady?" He smiled at Sarasvati, who smiled back.

"I know not," Alexander replied. "I only tell it as I remember it, and understand it not. I am more of a habit to sleep the day through without recall."

"It may be that some kernel of your mother's talent has emerged," Lucien remarked.

"But, why should I begin dreaming so vividly now?"

"I do not know, my son," his father replied. "But I think it is a dream which is better forgotten."

Alexander blew out his breath. "Aye. Perhaps my mind has gotten the best of me. I am still in a shock from all which happened in the last few months. Forgive me," he said to Karel.

To his credit Karel took no offense. "You have done nothing to forgive, Alexander."

Lucien rose to his feet and reached for his coat. "Now, as we are warmed by the terrors of the day, I dare say we face a challenge in the night. I must go in search of blood. Will you join me, gentlemen? And afterward we will bring you a feast, my wife, so that you will not have to mingle with those rough men who frequent the tavern."

Sarasvati looked as if she was about to protest her confinement, but said nothing of it. "As you wish, my husband," she said. "I must bathe Parvati and mend some of my clothes. Do not stay out long."

"I will return to you as swiftly as I can," he said with a smile.

The three vampires descended the stairs and entered the tavern. The place was already loud with cheery conversation, laughter and feasting. Wenches and boys dressed in peasant clothes passed among the customers bearing trays of grog and platters of food; some to be grabbed at intervals by the men and used for other amusements while still others laughed and roughhoused with boisterous abandon.

The hall was not brightly lit, and the only warmth came from body heat, Cossack cheer in the face of a certain doom, and a roaring fire burning in the hearth. A few minstrels had found a cozy place in the corner near it and played a lively tune with lutes and balalaikas, plucking and laughing at the occasional note played out of tune, and were on occasion showered with both coins and vegetables depending on the mood of their audience or how well they played.

The air was redolent with food and alcohol odors, turning into an incense of gluttony that nearly drove Lucien and Alexander back in distress. But it appeared that Karel was completely inured to its effects, so that when they hung back with faces of distaste he asked, "what is amiss?"

"The smell is somewhat... overpowering," Alexander replied. "I have been in taverns before where there is some fresh air to be had. Nothing like this."

"I must admit that I never had a good sense of smell," Karel replied. "Is it that repellent to you?"

"Aye," Lucien said, as he brought a small kerchief to his nose. "Give me but a moment to accustom myself, and I will overcome it." After a few moments had passed he nodded to Alexander, who nodded back, and together they passed through the crowd, who barely took notice of them.

They found seats at a table in the shadows under the staircase into the mezzanine, there to watch the activity from the shelter of darkness. "Faith, I have never known such noise before," Karel remarked, wincing as he clapped his hands to his ears. "I am like to go deaf."

Lucien's powerful voice penetrated the din easily. "Concentrate, and your hearing will become less acute."

The young Count sat silently with his eyes closed, then relaxed and gave out a sigh of relief as he opened them. "That is better," he said. "What comes next?"

"Now, we hunt," Alexander replied. "Focus your gaze on whichever woman you desire, and she will come to you."

Karel seemed quite accomplished at this already and became the instant attraction for several of the women. He allowed their blandishments with all the gusto of a tavern snipe, winning their sympathy easily when he told them of his injuries. Then one of them sat down next to Lucien, and another next to Alexander, while Karel took a third in hand. The others saw that there was no chance with them and wandered away to accost the other men for their favors.

Lucien subtly nuzzled at his woman's neck, gave her a soft fragrant puff of his breath to seal her compliance, then bit her before she could react. She stiffened and then settled quietly into his arms.

Alexander followed suit, and Karel watched them for a few moments before he managed to enchant his woman with all the clumsiness of a novice, then finally bit her throat, his hand fondling at her breast as she fell into a languorous swoon.

The room danced and laughed and drank and ate around them as the three silently drank their fill. Then Lucien withdrew carefully and murmured a quiet command into his feeder's ear, kisslicked her throat to heal it and watched her get up and walk away as if nothing had happened. Alexander did the same.

But Karel clung to the wench in his arms as if she was the only thing he prized. It took Alexander's guiding hand on his shoulder to make him stop. Reluctantly, he pulled out gently and kisslicked her throat, then said "my thanks," and let her go.

The wench smiled gently, kissed his nose and then walked away with a drunken swagger to join the other women. The spell woven in their minds made them forget the incident in a few moments, so that in short order they were soon occupied with someone else.

Then a short but decisive tussel between two brothers over a woman drew everyone's attention, until the tavernkeeper broke up the fight when he saw knives appear, and intervened with his arquebus to threw them out, all accompanied by music and a boisterous appreciative crowd. "Take your business elsewhere!" he shouted. "Or feel the burn of iron in your backsides!"

Reluctantly, the brothers stood down and left the tavern. Several of the women detached themselves from the crowd and followed after, including Karel's wench.

Karel stared after them with a wistful glance, then sighed and leaned up against the back of his chair. "Ah, Alexander, that was wonderful," he said. "I never knew blood could be so stimulating. I felt as if I would never stop. I did not want to stop. To feel her warmth against me, her energy, her life force. To hear her breath and her heart pounding in my ears. Her blood was like vodka, intoxicating and full of fire and ice, more delicious than the finest food I have ever eaten. It was like ambrosia."

Alexander regarded him with quiet concern. He had never heard anyone describe feeding quite that way before. Finally he said, "you wax poetic over a common need, my lord count."

"Is it not that way for you?" Karel asked.

"The first time for me was very different," he said.

"Each of us experiences our needs differently," Lucien added. "Each time that I feed it brings me a brief thrill, but often it is over so quickly I scarcely notice it."

"I have heard from the traders from China that the juice of the poppy is very much like this," Karel said. "Some men smoke it in pipes, and I am told the effects are like dreaming. One could easily become ensnared in its charms. Is that what will happen to me?"

"Only if you partake too much or too frequently," Lucien replied. "We take only as much as ensures our survival, nothing more. Your blood will counsel you of this. Do not allow yourself to become too enamored by the taking of it, or your spirit will fall prey to temptation. It is especially so with a loved one. You must exercise self-restraint at all times, and you will find that only willing blood will satisfy you in the end."

The blond young man stared at him with a sober expression. "I value your counsel, Count Arkanon. You have not led me astray. But then, what shall I do when I go home?"

"If you act in such a way which keeps your nature secret, you will be able to conduct your life as you did before. For a time you may claim that your limitations are a result of your injuries. But after that you must be circumspect in your dealings with friends and family alike, or they will learn the truth and judge you according to their beliefs. They may think you mad, or a monster, if you reveal yourself too soon to them."

"I find it most difficult to lie to my father and mother," Count Arkelin said. "I have never done so before. My life is nought but an open book to them, and by my faith it is a sin to lie."

"If times were different I would applaud you for it," Alexander replied, "but now you must lie to them also. The truth would kill them as surely as if you had put them to the sword."

Karel bowed his head. "Thank you for your warning. I shall take it in the spirit of its intent."

58

After an hour or so had passed, Lucien bore a platter of chicken and potatoes, greens, and a pitcher of warmed goat's milk up to their room, while Karel and Alexander lingered behind and began to talk to some of the men about the conditions in the countryside. Some were from various parts of the province and beyond, and the subject of Turks soon occupied the whole assembly; so that the room grew sober, quieted down and turned into a town hall on the spot.

"Aye," said one of the men. "The Turks have been on the move since last month. I have seen them camped not ten leagues from here, on the marches. They took Odesa and Chisinao. They're the devil's spawn, for they spared not a single man, woman or child on their way."

Another man asked, "what is the word from the nobles in Kyiv? Are they raising an army?"

"If they are, they've not told us," said a third. "Think you the Turk will come this far north?"

"My men and I were overwhelmed by their numbers," Karel said, and he winced as another twinge of pain assaulted him. "I alone survived. I must ride on to Kyiv myself to bear the council of nobles my news, but I cannot, for I am injured. Will someone here take up the gauntlet and ride for me?"

"Aye!" A number of the men raised their hands in response. "Someone must go now, tonight, or all will be lost!" an old man replied. "Let us arm ourselves and stand ready to fight," said another.

"Thank you all for your aid," Karel replied. "Let me write for you what must be told. Parchment and ink at once, good landlord!"

When they were brought to him, the count inscribed a brief message in Cyrillic and poured tamping powder on the letters, then blew it off and folded it into a neat square, the corners of which met in the middle. He took a candle and dribbled wax onto them, sealing them closed, then stamped his ring seal into the wax. "Now, who will take it?" he asked, holding it up.

Three of the men stepped forward with their hats in their hands and bowed. "We will, my lord Count," the middle one said.

They all looked like native Cossacks for certain, and Karel had the good sense to examine them closely before he handed it over. "I have given instructions that you will be paid well for your loyalty to our motherland," he said. "My seal will be my bond. Ride like the wind, and may God and the blessed virgin go with you."

The men crossed themselves, bowed and exited the tavern swiftly, while the other men and women turned to converse further. Karel said to Alexander, "if luck is with us, my word will turn the nobles to action. If not..." He shrugged with the acceptance of fate, then glanced up at him and smiled. "The hard part is yet to come."

59

When they finally returned to their room, Sarasvati and Parvati had retired behind the blanket for the night, and Lucien sat up waiting for them, reading from his book in the dark. "How did your evening go?" he asked, as they entered the room. "What news have you?"

"I have sent word to the council to warn them of the advancing Turks," Karel said, as he slowly doffed his overcoat. He felt at his rib where the stitches held him together and said with a faint frown, "I had expected to heal from this by now."

"Each man heals differently from another," Lucien replied. "Your wound was deep, and you were close to death for it. You have survived it better than another man would."

The Count eased himself carefully down on the bed and said, "I admit that I am a smaller man than my cousins. But I hate to be delayed by an inconvenience such as this. Perhaps the blood I drank will heal me faster? I should have ridden ahead and warned the nobles myself. I feel useless."

Alexander helped him pull his boots off and laid them aside. "You did all you could do. It is no fault of yours. Rest now, and allow the blood you drank to help heal you. If you need more..."

"Nay. You have been more than generous," Karel replied with a sharp glance. "I must learn to stand on my own, or I will be less than a man to myself. I am like to be ashamed for it."

"As you wish," Alexander said.

But as Karel started to lie back on his bed another wince flashed across his face, and he fell back holding his rib. "You are right. There is much more healing for me to do."

"Then it is time for you to find more sleep," Lucien said. "Alexander, will you come with me? I must go down to check on the wagon and make sure it is secured safely for the night."

"Yes, of course, father," Alexander replied, puzzling at the strange expression on Lucien's face.

Once they were outside and some distance down the corridor, Lucien turned abruptly and grabbed Alexander by the arm. "What possessed you, that such a man could beguile you in such a way?" he asked with a menacing low tone.

Alexander's mouth fell open. "What? Why now do you protest? What do you see in Karel that I cannot?"

"Your dream furnished me with a warning, which I did see clearly but could not give voice to in his presence," Lucien replied. "You saw him as your uncle. Julianus could use another man's mind as a vessel so that he might travel unseen among his enemies. Your friend Arkelin may be such a vessel, and you did see him so in your dream, but your human half did not recognize the signs."

"Father, I cannot fathom your suspicion," Alexander protested.

Lucien's face relaxed, and his voice came out smooth velvet. "If it truly is nothing more than a dream, I shall be glad to be wrong. But if I am not, and Count Arkelin becomes the monster I see in my mind, it falls to you to rid the world of him. Do not fall too far into friendship with him or trust him. Under that frail child's exterior lurks something else, which may emerge tomorrow, or some years hence. Nosferatu. An untamed killer, with no remorse or regret, ever consumed by the lust for blood."

Alexander's dark eyebrows drew together. He replied, "I cannot believe that, now or ever. He is a good man, father. I have faith that he will never be such a creature. If I pledge to you now that I will watch over him when we are together, and guard against such an event, will you then let me keep him as a friend and blood brother?"

Lucien considered, then placed his hand on his son's shoulder. "I have no wish to stand between you and your heart's desires. Just be of care. Go back to the room and watch over him, for I would not allow him to be alone with Sarasvati for very long in his present condition."

With that, he left Alexander standing alone while he glided silently down the stairs.

When Alexander returned to the room he found Karel already sound asleep and bundled under his blanket, and there was a gentle sound of snoring coming from it. The candle next to his bed was extinguished. Alexander listened for sounds beyond the blanket wall and found the calm heartbeats of mother and child.

Breathing a quiet sigh of relief, he settled down onto his saddle blanket and sat quietly for a few minutes to absorb the shocks of the night before he removed his boots and settled down again to sleep.

60

As the sun rose above the foothills and bathed the river in gold, an outcry outside the window stirred Alexander awake. He listened to the sounds of horses and wagons rolling away, and shouts of urgency among the men and women in the courtyard below, causing Karel and Lucien to raise their heads and listen.

There came a pounding on their door. Alexander reached for his sword as he called out. "What is it?"

A man's voice penetrated the wood. "Rouse yourselves and flee, for the Turks approach from the south! It is an army too large to defend against!" Then the sound of running footsteps receded down the hall.

"God curse them," Karel declared as he swept his blanket aside and rose carefully, feeling at his side.

Lucien went behind the blanket wall and found Sarasvati feeding Parvati. He said, "hasten and make ready with all speed, my wife, for we must be gone from here."

"I have been prepared to leave since last evening," Sarasvati replied softly. "Give me but another moment, for Parvati is hungry."

Ten minutes later, Count Arkelin and the Arkanons went quickly down the back stairs and emerged from the inn to find the courtyard deserted, laced the horses to their faithful old wagon and rolled away northward, to join a small crowd of other travelers chased by the rhythmic sound of drums coming from the south.

For all its fame and notoriety as the capitol city, Kyiv was only a medium sized town with a high wall to keep out invaders, and had already been destroyed more than once in its storied past.

The wall surrounding the city had four gates oriented to the cardinal points of a compass. Each gate was a massive rampart built of thick stone and brick, well guarded by a force of soldiers posted in small tower rooms overlooking their approaches. The south gate was already opened to admit a stream of refugees fleeing the marauding Turks advancing toward the city a scant five miles behind.

At Karel's request, Lucien drew the wagon to a halt a mile from the gate bridge and behind a small hill out of sight, and held the horses while Alexander aided him onto his saddle.

"I must be seen to be in command, or at least in good health," Arkelin explained. "Leave all the negotiations to me. Most of these men know me well for all my coming and going, but some do not."

"I leave all in your capable hands," Lucien replied with a smile and a small gracious bow.

Alexander thought it odd, contradicting all the thunder Lucien dealt him the night before, but knew there was little choice but to trust that Karel knew what he was doing.

When they drew close to the gate, several of the soldiers came forward on horseback and intercepted the small caravan. One of them recognized the young nobleman readily. "We thought you were caught by the Turks, my lord Count," their lieutenant said with a salute. "God grant you good health, and I am pleased that you were not harmed."

The man was short and stocky, wearing a huge overcoat trimmed with regimental braid that draped over thick woolen trousers tucked into black riding boots. His dark hair was tied back into a braid under a thick bear fur hat that made him look a little taller. His mouth was hidden beneath a thick dark moustache and beard, and his smile revealed crooked yellowing teeth behind a vaporous fog from the morning cold.

"And you, Lieutenant Koshokov," Karel replied. "Did you admit the three men I sent to you in the night?"

"We did, my lord Count. They bore their news to the palace directly, and I sent one of my men with them."

"Good," Karel said. "These people are my personal guests and are under my protection. They are to be treated with respect and are to have freedom of access to the city."

"Their names, my lord Count, so that I may have a record of them," Koshokov replied.

"May I present to you Count Lucien Arkanon of Transylvania. His wife and child are with him also. And his son Count Alexander Corvina, who is a good friend of mine."

The man betrayed a moment of puzzlement in his eyes as he smiled at Alexander and Lucien. "All who are friends of Count Arkelin are most welcome in Kyiv," he replied with another salute. "Come in quickly, and we will bar the gate." He turned his horse and led the way in.

Lucien chucked at the horses and the wagon rolled into the courtyard of the gate, while the soldiers took up the rear. Behind them, the giant wooden gates swung closed. The portal was set with a massive iron bar which swung down into brackets on both sides, lowered into place by a hand cranked winch.

As they passed into the main road a man stood on the battlement and blew on a large ram's horn. "Ay!" he yelled. "The Turks approach! Make ready for battle!"

Another man took up the call and rang a bell set in the tower. Other bells began to ring, and those in all the churches. Townspeople began to hurry away to their homes in the early morning sunshine to secure them, arm themselves and hide out from the invasion.

Other men in the guard ran for the stairs to the battlements while Koshokov remarked, "God curse them for the heathen devils they are." Then he barked orders, and the guards took their stations at the top of the gate armed with their muskets. Two small cannons were maneuvered into place and aimed at the road, while a large contingent of armed men brought forth horses and mounted them, arranging themselves into military order. At his signal, a cutout portion of the gate opened and the cavalry rode through at a gallop, making south toward the enemy's position.

"Unless they have cannon with them, they will not get beyond the gate," Karel assured Lucien. "Follow me and I will take you to my home, where you will be most welcomed. Then I must report to the council."

He guided the horse at a fast walk into the city proper, where the sight of him entering the square attracted a great deal of attention from the people on the street. A crowd approached him and began cheering, and shouts of "welcome home," and "we thought you dead," and "god be praised," followed him as he led the wagon toward a large house surrounded by a high wall at the end of the commons, and through the gate into a small driveway where a squad of servants came running to greet him.

A pair of men ran to the gate to the compound and shut it to to keep out the wellwishers, while Alexander helped Karel from his horse, setting him gently on the ground.

A giant approached. He looked Mongolian, and he wore a large sheepskin coat which made him look even larger. His head was shaven but for a long black braided topknot. "Truly, master, we feared the worst," he said in a thick voice. "Welcome home."

"I am glad to be home," Karel replied. "I would have been dead if it were not for these good people, who rescued me. Treat them as you would your own, for they are my guests."

"We will do as you command, master," the large man said.

The sight of Lucien alighting from the wagon brought a few gasps from the servants, and they edged back nervously as he stood in the weak sunlight fighting its way through the gray clouds, a tall pale figure in black resembling the ghost of Death himself. He paid no mind to their curious attention as he calmly slapped the dust from his cape and adjusted his hat when a gust of wind threatened to remove it.

But Karel would have none of this. "Come, come. One would think you had never seen foreigners before," he said. "Back to work, all of you, and stop gawking like so many dolts."

Sarasvati emerged wearing her finest sari and a hooded cape over it, bearing Parvati bundled up in a large blanket in her arms, bringing even more gasps, this time of admiration. Lucien smiled as he offered his hand to her and helped her down the stairs.

The Mongolian took the initiative and silently climbed aboard the wagon; then drove it away toward the stable followed by the stewards with the other horses. The other servants fell to whispering to each other as they broke up into small groups and drifted away to their routine tasks.

"Unforgivable," was Karel's only comment as he led his guests into the front parlor of the house.

There, another servant was waiting for them, and he seemed very much calmer than the others. He was tall and lean, with gray hair tied back into a short queue and dressed in a long black cassock like a priest. He said, "please to give me your coats, that I may hang them in the vestry."

As Karel shed his coat he said, "thank you, Vasili. Where are my parents?"

"In the council chambers, at the palace," Vasili replied. "Your grandfather has taken a turn for the worst and is near death. His leeches are with him now."

"Oh, no," Karel replied with a touch of sadness coloring his voice. "I must go to him. Please see my guests to the apartment in the west wing, and tend to their needs. If you will excuse me, my friends?"

"It appears we came at an inopportune moment," Lucien said.

The young count looked up at him, and Alexander saw tears brimming over, held in check by the determination to look strong in front of the house man. "My grandfather has been ill for a very long time, and I fear he may have heard the wrong thing." As he spoke he started to walk, then run toward the stairs, holding his rib gingerly.

The servant Vasili led them on an exploration of the house to an alternate set of stairs, then up to the second floor. There, he opened the west wing door and led them through a short hall to a door near a tall stained glass window at its end. "I hope these accomodations are acceptable," he said. "It has been a long time since we had guests grace our house."

He produced a keyring from his belt and selected an ancient brass affair which he shoved into the lock. The door squealed open and revealed an entryway to the inner rooms. There were three: a common room and two rooms to the side, with a small privy.

"I beg pardon for their condition," he continued as he led them in. "These have not been opened for a very long time. But there are no leaks in the roof, nor gaps in the walls. I will have someone make a fire in the grate for you, and put some grease on the door hinges."

"Thank you, Vasili," Lucien said as he looked around with an appraising eye. "This is quite acceptable."

"Is there anything else you require before I go? Hot tea?"

"Some warm goat's milk?" Sarasvati asked.

"I will have a woman draw it," the servant replied. "And you, my lords?"

"Nothing, thank you," they both replied in unison.

The servant started with sudden fear, then nodded quickly and left the room.

When the doors closed, Lucien glanced around the apartment, then strolled over to the casement and looked outside. He wiped his glove along the frame and stirred a pall of dust into the air, sniffed, then turned to the others. "The Arkelins are not a prosperous as they would have us believe," he said. "Young Karel must keep up appearances for the court, but his family appears unable to sustain their fortunes."

Sarasvati took one look around and declared with uncharacteristic force, "it matters not to me. After the roughness of the road, this place is a sumptuous palace, not to be belittled because of a bit of dust. And did we not make a home of a ruin ourselves but a month ago?"

Alexander swiveled his head to look at her. She stood with both feet firmly planted, as if she was arming cannon against her husband. She was angry, and with good reason. "Mother, what is wrong?" he asked. "What has made you so discontent?"

"I am just tired," she replied. "My sisters are dead, and the world is no longer the bright and wondrous place I thought it was."

Lucien abandoned the window and went to her. "I apologize, my wife," he said. "You have endured much, and I am to blame for it. Will you forgive me?"

His words seemed to drown her ire. She sighed deeply and relaxed, her shoulders slumping. "No, my husband, I cannot blame you. It is my fault for asking for more than the world can ever give me. I was so..." Then her words caught in her throat and she began to cough, softly at first, then with increasing force. Lucien reached out to catch her as she fell back, but she pushed his hands away.

"No, give me a moment," she coughed, then turned away and sat down on a divan nearby, her small hand clutching at her heaving chest. "I cannot breathe," she wheezed. "I cannot find any air."

Lucien went and dropped to his knees before her, seized her left wrist in his long fingers, then placed his palm against her forehead. "You are burning up with a fever. How long have you been like this?"

"Since the inn," she replied. "I feel cold... Dizzy..." She coughed some more. "My very bones ache."

"You are ill," he replied, swept her up in his arms and laid her onto the thin mattress. "Alexander, will you go find me some water, and some clean towels? We must bring down her fever."

"At once," Alexander replied, then left the rooms quickly.

His thoughts were in turmoil as he wandered down the stairs and found his way into the kitchen, where he encountered a large woman bustling about preparing dinner. At his approach she looked up, and a small noise escaped her generous lips as she drew back.

"Borzhe moi," she breathed. "Who are you?"

"There is no time for introductions," he declared. "Quickly. I need water and clean towels. My mother is ill."

To her credit, she recovered her wit quickly, and said, "there is pail in back. There is pump for water next to door. I will find towels."

Alexander drew a full pail and brought it back in, then armed with the cloth he fairly sailed back up the stairs and into the apartment, where he found Lucien still seated at his wife's bedside. "How is she?" he asked.

He placed the pail on the floor and handed the towels to his father, who took one and dipped it in the water, wrung it out carefully and placed it carefully on her forehead. Sarasvati reacted as if she was burned by the cold wet, and moaned as he dabbed gently at her skin.

"She is very ill," Lucien said. "I am not certain of it but she may have the ague. She cannot be moved for several days and she must be isolated. She never told me how she was feeling. I could not sense it. Why did she try to hide it?"

"I do not know, father," Alexander replied, puzzling. It seemed so sudden and unexpected, as if a spell was put on her. But he knew the answer laid in science, not in superstition.

"I did not want you to know," Sarasvati said, her voice weak. "I wanted to be strong for you. I wanted to be like you."

Lucien's voice came close to breaking as he looked down at her and said, "tush, my darling. You are stronger than most women, and have endured much for my sake. You made me happy through our long journey together, and I have much to be grateful for. Now rest, and sleep a bit, and I will bring you some soup in a little while."

Alexander watched her settle back against the dusty pillow and close her eyes. Lucien rose carefully, scooped Parvati up into his arms and kissed her, then set her down again. The infant tried to climb into the bed with her mother and her father had to hold her hand tightly to restrain her. Parvati had the good sense not to struggle.

There was a soft knock at the door, and Vasili entered bearing a tray with a pitcher and pewter mugs. "I have brought the goat's milk," he said. Then he saw Sarasvati lying in the bed and asked, "is the lady ill?"

Alexander quickly took the lead. "We have been on the road for a very long time, and the arduous journey has proven too much for her."

"Then I will light a fire, and pray for her," the servant replied. "The Count's grandfather passed away but a few minutes ago. There is much sadness in the house today."

As he spoke he bent to the grate and shifted the logs there closer together, then took his lantern and lit a length of wick he had in his pocket. He shoved the wick under the logs and waited for the flames to catch, then crossed himself and asked, "is there anything else you require, my lords?"

"Nothing, thank you," Lucien replied. "Please leave us."

The house man bowed, then left the room quickly.

"I will go to the Count now, father," Alexander said. "He will need a friend to stand by his side in his time of grief."

Lucien nodded. "By all means. Do your own will," he said with a soft tone, then pulled up a chair and sat next to his ailing wife, picked Parvati up and placed her on his knee as the flames in the grate grew and danced.

223

For the first time in his life, Alexander felt a wall go up between himself and his father, as if it was constructed of granite. It was not anger, but something like disappointment. The memory of Charanditha bubbled up to the surface, reminding him that he was not there for her either. He wanted to stay with Lucien, but he also remembered his promise to Karel, and if he could tear himself in half to help both of them he would. Silently, he surrendered to his duty and left the room without saying another word.

61

Alexander was admitted to the bedchamber by a servant and found his young blond friend cowering by his grandfather's bedside, weeping openly. His pale hand gripped the lifeless arthritic fingers like a vice, and his face was buried in his sleeve, while a middle aged woman dressed in a dark gown knelt on the other side of the bed and was also immersed in tears as she prayed fervently over a rosary.

The doctors standing nearby conversed in latin about the fee they were to extract from the family fortune. Suddenly, their cold pedestrian attitude incensed Alexander, and he bounded forward. "Away with you, you creatures of pain!" he exclaimed. "Is gold all you care for? Leave these poor people to mourn in peace and begone!"

He emphasized his anger by drawing his sword halfway from its scabbard, and at the sight of him the men fled from the room in terror.

Karel looked up at him, startled at the sound of his voice, and so did the older woman. She stared at the tall interloper like a lioness on the prowl. She was of indeterminate age, with a lean physique and dark hair shot with grey hidden under a mantilla of lace and pearls. Her face betrayed no fear at all, as if she had awaited his entrance all her life. But as her eyes failed to make contact with his, Alexander suddenly realized that she was blind.

Her voice was deep and heavy as she asked, "Karel, who is this man?"

"Forgive me, little grandmother," he replied, snuffling. "He is my new friend and savior, Count Alexander Vincent Corvina of

Transylvania. Alex, this is my grandmother, the grand duchess Mareska Vilanova Arkelina."

Alexander affected a short bow. "My apologies, my lady," he began. "I overheard the leeches counting coin before your husband was but a few minutes cold. I..."

"I heard what they said," she replied with a stoic tone. "We have coin enough to pay for his care as well as his funeral." She dabbed at her eyes with a lace handkerchief. "They did nothing to help my husband keep his life, so what do I care for their indifference and greed? A word from me and they will not find work anywhere in Kyiv."

"I beg your forgiveness," he said, properly chastened.

The older woman drew back and dabbed at her eyes again, blinking rapidly. "You are forgiven," she said. "Now, what mischief has my grandson brought you to?"

"Grandmother, I owe the Count my life, for he rescued me from a cruel death," Karel explained. "The Turks overtook the village of P'risi. My men and I tried to drive them away but I was gravely injured, and my men were slaughtered along with the rest of the villagers. Alexander came upon me when I was at death's door, and he and his family nursed me back to health. They brought me home to you."

"Indeed? Then it is my turn to apologize," she said. "You are most welcome to our house."

"My thanks, my lady, and may I convey my family's gratitude also," Alexander replied with another bow.

"What of father and mother?" Karel asked her.

"They are at the council, trying to sway the other nobles to arm themselves and defend the wall," she replied. "They think that they can ignore the trouble brewing in our country, but they are naught but children. They know nothing about how to govern the state."

"Then they must act quickly, for the Turks are at the gate even now," Alexander said. "It is too late to debate about it."

"I sent men with a message, a dire warning from the inn down the road," Karel said. "They delivered it in the night when all would fear to travel. Surely the nobles will not ignore it if it comes from good and God fearing men."

"Then the answer will come in due course," his grandmother said. "I sometimes wish I was a man that I might join in the defense

225

of the city. But I cannot. And you cannot, my Kashka. You stay here with me, and let those boasters on the council prove their worth."

A warm kernel grew in Alexander's heart. She was brave and spunky, like Queen Elizabeth, like Elsa Blanchett, Charanditha and Ruthinda, and perhaps like his mother. "Lady, your courage gives you credit," he said.

"You honor me, sir Count. But I am naught but a sightless old woman, and I know I have no place among the men. So I will let them fight and die, mourn them, and pray for their souls when they are in their graves."

If only I could tell you how wrong you are. Alexander thought. *We need the courage of our women to give us the strength to fight.* But now was not the time to argue the point, and he vowed to tell her later about the women in his life, and how they fought and died like men, as bravely as men, with hearts full of courage and honor.

"If you will permit me," he said, "I will go and fetch such arms and armor as will fit me and my father, and we will go to the wall for you. Stay with her, Karel."

Karel started to rise, but felt a twinge at his rib and sank back. "But..."

"No. Do as your grandmother bids you and stay with her. Protect her. Do not worry about me," Alexander assured him. "I can defend myself. I have been in battle before. And my father..." he shrugged.

To Alexander's surprise, Karel almost cracked a smile. "Then go," the young count said, "and may God's love go with you."

Alexander returned to the apartment, where Lucien was busy directing a group of young women who had come with clean linens and blankets to prepare Sarasvati's bed and make her more comfortable. Parvati sat on a small cushioned chair next to the bed and watched her mother with an anxious expression on her small pudgy face.

When he stepped over the threshhold there came a sound of pounding outside, then scattered gunfire. Two of the women started at the sight of him and crossed themselves quickly, but it appeared that the rest were more frightened of the battle raging at the city wall than of him. One covered her face with her hands and began to weep.

"Sweet virgin, we are all lost," she sobbed. "If the Turks breach the wall they will not spare us."

Alexander took no notice as he declared, "father, it would appear that our skills at warfare are needed."

It was as if the wall between them was torn down by those words, and a flood of reassurance came from his father's expression of calm acceptance. Lucien turned to him and said, "aye, and I will relish the blood shed for the sake of these good people today."

62

They went down together to the stable where the wagon was parked and went inside, found their arms and then went by horse to the wall, where an army of men were already busy repelling the invaders.

Koshokov saw them and came running. "Have you come to play with us?" he asked, puffing with fatigue as they dismounted and checked their weapons. "The Turks have cannon set on the hill across the river. How are you at running an assault to extinguish those wicks?"

Lucien clapped him on the shoulder and replied, "we can handle the cannon alone. You hold your men back and protect the wall. Help us by picking off any man who tries to stop us. But, whatever you do, do not let them open this gate."

"How will you do this alone?" the lieutenant asked, appalled. "Just the two of you?"

Lucien smiled the way Karel had before. "We will find a way."

He took the lead, grabbed at a hawser attached to the gate winch and climbed it rapidly like a lizard on fire, Alexander following at his heels. They paused to reconnoiter and saw the line of cannons placed across the river, aimed directly at the gate.

One of them discharged, and a whistling red hot ball came sailing toward them. They ducked as it landed on the rampart close by and exploded, scattering men and bricks all over the soldiers working below. The blast was accompanied by cheering from the enemy across the river.

"They mean rough business this time," Lucien declared, drawing his sword. "They will break the wall down soon. There is no more time to waste."

Alexander drew his sword and said, "I am with you, father."

Together, they leapt the twenty feet to the ground, landing on six Turks trying to set fire to the gate, scattering them like bowling pins with swift slashing strokes of their swords. Then they kicked the pitch pots and the firebrands from the bridge into the water and sent up a cloud of spitting steam which provided a good smokescreen.

From there, they mowed a running path before them, slicing and hacking their way across the bridge through the line as the startled enemy soldiers tried to cut them off and defend the artillery. But the dark demonic shadows passing through their ranks were too swift to be caught, and by the time another cannon discharged its deadly cargo they had already dispatched three of the wick men and two of the ball men before more fuses were lit.

The third ball man screamed in terror and tried to flee but was cut down by his own platoon sergeant for his cowardice, who in turn was struck by an arrow from the wall. He went down screaming the glory of Allah before he went silent.

From that point on, the cannons were indefensible. The men on the ramparts saw this and started shooting, picking off the men closest to the gate and concentrating their fire on the cannon men on the rampart.

The Turks tried to surround the enemy intruders, but Lucien and Alexander seemed to vanish one instant and appeared the next somewhere else, always with deadly results, moving like ninjas among the troops. Two lieutenants and six more soldiers bearing fire pots fell to sudden slashing death. Men and horses went down dead or wounded among the others without warning.

Others fell back from their positions and fled in terror, while their commanders scattered about in disarray and confusion, shouting frantically but unable to bring them back, or shooting the deserters as they ran.

Riderless horses trampled several men as they galloped away from the battlefield into the safety of the woods, never to return.

When all the cannon men were dead, Lucien took a loader, used it to pry loose one of the cannon tubes and rolled it from its caisson. The hot weapon bounced down the hill and rolled, gathering speed as it scattered the Turks in its path, maiming the slower ones, until it reached the boulders at the riverbank and cracked open with explosive force, sending up a pall of steam.

Alexander followed suit, and found himself straining from its weight, but managed to tip the cannon off its caisson and onto the grass. He jumped clear just as the hot tube set fire to the scrubweeds next to it and also cracked open, hissing and sputtering like a snake on fire. The fire spread through the grass toward the kegs of gunpowder standing nearby, and soon there were explosions scattering cannon balls and anything else close by into the air.

Alexander walked away calmly as the flaming debris behind him began to rain down on the fleeing enemy and limne his figure in fire.

When the Turkish general saw this he gave the signal to retreat, and the soldiers broke off to run back down the road behind the remains of their cavalry. Behind them came a cheering roar of approval from the wall as the defenders saw that they were defeated. Arrows and musket balls pursued the retreating army. while Lucien and Alexander stood alone on the hill watching the rout, surrounded by bodies and wreckage.

The white haired demon held his sword at the ready, and he stood straight as a mast. But Alexander bent over and wheezed faintly, feeling an ache in his lungs. "By the stars," he panted. "I have never fought that many before!" Then he looked up at his father, and saw that the red fire in his eyes had not diminished. "What is wrong?" he asked.

"I am just hungry," Lucien replied. "The scent of fresh blood is overpowering my self-control. I must feed before we go back to the city, or I cannot answer for what happens then."

Then he clutched at his chest as if he was in pain and winced briefly as he fell to his knees, gasping for breath.

Alexander looked down and saw the dark blood oozing through his gloved fingers. "You're wounded!" he exclaimed, his concern turning to alarm. He caught his father by the arm to steady him as Lucien swayed and started to fall over.

Lucien closed his eyes and gasped, "it is nothing. It will pass. I was simply not fast enough."

Alexander helped him sit down on a cannon brace. "Come. Feed from me," he insisted. "You should not drink the blood of these men. It is dead and you will poison yourself."

"Ah. You remind me of that which I know so well. But you have already given so much to Karel. You will weaken yourself."

"That matters not to me," Alexander replied. He went to his knees before the man in black and opened his cuff, baring his arm. The signs of Karel's feeding were still fresh.

"I have strength enough to stay your hunger until you can obtain more in safe shelter," he said. You are my father. I would not be a dutiful son if I did not give you that which you need to live."

Reluctantly, Lucien lifted the wrist to his mouth. Alexander betrayed only a small wince of pain as the sharp fangs sank in and stayed, and surrendered to the euphoria once again. But the moment was short, and Lucien withdrew quickly, kisslicked the wounds closed and sat silently with his eyes closed, then opened them again.

"It is sufficient," he said. "I hold you not to your bondage as my son."

Those words gave Alexander a moment of further mystery. But as he looked into the red fire in Lucien's eyes it damped back down until it was virtually gone. Lucien was his calm, peaceful self again through the grime marring his pale cheeks. Alexander reached for his coat and drew it open, tore aside the cuirass and unlaced the bloody shirt carefully to examine the wound. "You were lucky," he said. "It is lodged in bone and missed your heart. I must take it out, or your wound may become infected."

"The dragon's blood will not allow that," Lucien reminded him. "But do what you must. I have no desire to go through life as a pincushion."

Alexander drew his poniard and probed at the pale skin with its point, prompting a wince and a brief noise of pain. "Sorry," he said. Then he carefully pried the musket ball out and threw it away. He watched as the wound healed closed on its own to a small red pock. "Thank the dragon's blood for its power to heal," he said, as he laced the blouse closed.

"Indeed, I am thankful every day of my life," Lucien replied with a small smile. "Else I would have died long ago."

"We will not tell Sarasvati of your injury. She need never know, for she has enough to burden her already."

"I agree," Lucien said. He stood with Alexander's help, and together they walked slowly back to the wall, where the soldiers were busy picking up the wounded and preparing bodies for burial.

Once they had passed through the gate into the courtyard, they were met by a happy crowd, and escorted with boisterous jubilation back to the house, where once again the Mongolian footman drove the crowd away with a snarl and a pronounced curse as he and two servants closed the gates to the compound.

Karel met them on the porch with youthful excitement. "What have I missed? How was the battle?" he asked, then saw the blood on Lucien's clothes. "You are wounded!"

Alexander drew a finger to his lips and said, "Shhhh. We must not let my stepmother know. He was struck by a musket ball but it missed his heart."

"'Tis but a mere inconvenience. I will heal soon enough," Lucien added. "But I must have your silence for I fear that in her frail health she will be hurt by this news."

"Of course, my lord Count," Karel replied softly. "I will abide by your discretion. Come inside and rest while I will send word to the council that we will meet them."

As he turned away to lead them into the house, Alexander noted that the young nobleman's shoulders were still slumped with sorrow, and said nothing when he called to his steward for pen and parchment.

When they returned to the apartment, Alexander and Lucien slipped inside silently and changed out of their clothes into fresh ones without disturbing Sarasvati, so that when she woke she would not notice anything out of the ordinary.

63

Over the course of the next day and a half, Lucien was hardly focused on matters of war as he tended to the needs of his wife. On the evening of the second day her fever broke, and she took some soup while Parvati toddled about with her bear clutched in her small arms. The maid assigned to her seemed quite happy to indulge the child's every need as if she was her own. Lucien watched over them quietly while Alexander paced back and forth, eager to hear from Karel about the state of affairs in the country.

There came a discreet knocking at the outer door. Alexander admitted the steward, who said, "you are summoned to meet with the council of nobles at the palace, my lord Count. They wish to congratulate you for..."

Alexander clamped a hand over his mouth and replied softly, "thank you, Vasili. We will prepare to go at once," with a meaningful glance toward Sarasvati, who appeared to be asleep again.

To his credit the man did not protest, and nodded silently. When Alexander removed his hand, he continued, "Count Arkelin awaits you both in the sitting room."

When they had dressed in their finest of clothes, Alexander and Lucien went down the stairs to the main hall and met their host, who was dressed elegantly and stood looking into the fire burning in the grate. At their entrance he looked up, and Alexander saw that his storm blue eyes were glowing slightly in the firelight. He looked confident, and all sadness for his grandfather's death seemed to be gone; or he was putting up a very brave front for the benefit of the household.

"Ah, there you are," he said. "The council would like to meet with the heroes who saved all of Kyiv. Perhaps they will listen to me now that I have the backing of two worthy examples of bravery and skill at my side."

"My lord Count, we did only what was necessary," Lucien protested mildly. "Why should they not listen to you?"

"I am still young, and some of them are older seasoned men and are not ready to listen to new ideas," Karel replied. "Some are Poles, and some Lithuanians, and some Russian. They are not all together in their opinions, and by their enmity and alliances with each other, not willing to hear in peace that which they have avoided in war. It will take all my skills at persuasion to change their minds. But I must, or it will be too late for all of us."

"You speak with great eloquence, my lord Count," Alexander said. "I can scarcely think why you would have such doubts."

"My mother and father are but minor players in politics. There is only one among them all who can be swayed by reason," Karel replied. "If I can reach him, I may be able to gain some measure of rationality, and by doing so, unite the council. It will be a shaky endeavor at best, but better than standing by and letting things go to ruin. He is hetman Bohdan Khmelnytsky, my second cousin on my mother's side. He has called for unity before, and will be a welcome ally in my call for action."

"Is it possible to meet with him before we meet with the council?" Lucien asked.

Karel shook his head. "Nay. He is most secretive in his affairs outside of the council. He keeps his lodgings separate, and only appears when the council meets to discuss anything. He has many enemies who desire his death for reasons which I cannot divulge. Now come. The day is growing late."

The palace was a huge square cut three story building enclosed by another high wall and a large courtyard, standing near a white and gold onion domed cathedral named for the archangel St. Michael. It abutted a large central square where bronze statues of various Cossack heroes lounged and played intruments accompanied by their horses. All had faces frozen in grim purpose, and even the minstrels looked serious about their world.

Karel, Alexander and Lucien picked their way on horseback through the milling crowd toward the front gate, which was made of wrought iron pinions and wedged in the center of a white stone portcullis emblazoned with the crest of the Zaporozhian clans.

At their approach the gates were opened by the palace guard, and the three entered the courtyard leading to an elaborately carved front entrance. They dismounted and let the stewards lead their horses away as they walked up the steps into the front of the hall.

"The entire palace was rebuilt since the war," Karel explained. "These walls are new, but our country remains as old as it has always been."

Lucien suggested, "but the people are what keeps the country whole. Not the buildings."

"One would not think so, given the way the council reacts to crisis. But that will change one day, I am certain," Karel replied. Then he paused to consider. "Odd. It is as if the world has opened up to me since I turned. All is displayed before me with a clarity I have never known before."

"And so it should be," Lucien replied. "The dragon's blood is wise as well as demanding of tribute. We owe it all for our existence."

The blond Count smiled softly and said, "how well you put it." Then he led the way through the main hall toward the chamber where the council sat. Once there, they passed through a brace of armed guards and into a large meeting hall. There Alexander saw a long table made of oak set at the center, where an assembly of men

233

were already seated; drinking, eating, laughing and arguing, punctuating their speech with sharp emphatic gestures.

A group of women were ensconced in a gallery overlooking the table and busy engaged with their mending and embroidery, pausing only to take note of the newcomers' entrance with hushed murmurs and admiring glances. Alexander observed that they were not participants in the discussions themselves.

Then one of the women started when Karel entered the room, and waved to him with a smile. She had dark blonde hair like him, and she wore a circlet and wig of small pearls over a short wimple, as was custom. She looked to be about forty years old but had fine cheekbones and skin, and almost looked a mirror image of her son.

Karel looked up at her and waved back. "That is my mother," he said. "She counsels my father in all that he does, and sometimes tells him what to say. She is his equal in mind and temper, and no better advisor than she can be had in times of importance."

"But, she does not have a vote on the council herself," Alexander ventured.

Karel shook his head. "There is no need, for they are in concert with each other in all matters of policy. I have never seen them disagree with each other before."

A grey haired Cossack detached himself from his conversation with his companions and approached. He grabbed Karel and drew him into a tight embrace. "Thank God and the Blessed Virgin that you were spared, my boy," he declared. "When I heard from the men of the inn about your courage in P'risi, I prayed for your swift return."

Karel replied, "my thanks for your prayers, father." He turned to Alexander and Lucien. "This is my father, Count Nikolai Illyanov Arkelin. Father, this is Count Alexander Corvina, and his father Count Lucien Arkanon, of Transylvania. I have taken the liberty of extending the welcome of our house to them, that they may bide in comfort while they are here in Kyiv."

The older man's expression betrayed sudden surprise as he stared up into two pairs of grey eyes. But he recovered quickly with a smile. "My thanks for your aid, that you brought my son home to me safe and sound."

Lucien replied, "it is our duty to render aid wherever we go. Our thanks for your hospitality."

Before the older man could reply, a tall older man dressed in dark but elegant clothes in the Cossack fashion approached Karel, and opened his arms to beckon him into his embrace with a hearty laugh. He had rough cut blond hair that brushed his shoulders, and a well shaped beard which did nothing to conceal a heart shaped face creased with years spent in the outdoors. His brown eyes twinkled with mirth. "Come. To my arms, sir. I was told you were dead, yet here I see you again."

Karel allowed himself to be smothered and clapped on the back as he smiled in reply. "They could not kill me," he said, with a meaningful glance to Alexander. "But let me introduce you to my companions."

The bigger man released him and studied the two pale men standing before him closely. "So. These are the men who saved us from a pounding at the wall?"

"Aye. May I present to you Count Lucien Arkanon of Transylvania, and his son Alexander Vincent Corvina. This is my cousin, Bohdan Khmelnytsky, of whom I spoke."

"You are most welcome, in that you did much to forestall the Turk wolves howling at our doors," Khmelsnytsky said. "I have a report of your courage." Then he turned to the others. "You should make room at the table for them. They are strangers but shared in our defense, and are welcome to share our words, for I will vouch for them." He gestured to the stewards standing by and said, "bring chairs for our guests so that they may sit at our table."

While the servants did as he commanded, the nobles shifted and jostled to make room. But when he took a seat among them, Alexander had the sudden impression that he and his father were less than welcome to the discussion, and his conclusion was reinforced by a soft comment from a corner of the room. "Are our discussions now privy to outsiders, Bohdan?"

All eyes turned to the dark haired man sitting near the end of the table. He appeared already bored with the proceedings though they had not started yet. He sat picking at an apple with a small poniard to remove the seeds before taking a bite. His black eyes rested on Alexander's, and his face betrayed nothing as they glanced away again. Then he bit, and for an instant Alexander thought he saw fangs pierce the apple's flesh. Juice dribbled from generous lips, and a long fingered hand brought up a linen napkin to catch the sweet ooze before it found a home on his black velveteen jacket.

Alexander knew there were vampires living among the humans in secret, but he had never met one who lived in the open as he and his father did. The man did not have the familiar blood scent of a human. It smelled almost pureblood.

His thoughts were interrupted by Khmelnytsky's gruff voice. "You find the dark side of everything, don't you Ostap? Accept these men in the spirit of this day. Now let me introduce you to them. This is Ostap Kuryan, who speaks for the Cossacks of the Bucovina. A lone wolf among the sheep, eh?"

"You have such a dark impression of me," Ostap protested lightly as he chewed. "I merely asked the question." He tossed the apple's core toward a servant, who caught it and put it in his pocket.

"I welcome them because we have all been remiss in our duty to plan well against the invaders," Bohdan replied, prompting sounds and words of protest from the others. "No, it is true. We have all been asleep at our posts, have we not? And you, Stopan Stopovich. You Poles thought yourselves grand at taking us over, but now that you have it in your grasp you do not know what to do with it."

At this the other men laughed, but the Pole frowned at that veiled insult. "And you, Khmelnytsky," Stopovich replied. "I did not see you go to the wall with these men. Where were you?"

"I was engaged with the dark devils in a different part of the city, and was not there to see what the others told me of. But what a grand play it was. The cannon are still there to examine, if you but venture across the bridge to the hill. I have seen them myself. Split open like so many chicken bones. It is a wondrous thing. And where were you? Hiding underneath your wife's skirts, no doubt."

"Please, my friends," Karel ventured. "We should not consume our time in accusations. We must decide what to do. The Turks were driven away today, but they will return, and in greater numbers. Surely you read of my own situation in my letter. My men were slaughtered before my very eyes, and I could do nothing to stop it. I was wounded myself, and would not have survived were it not for these worthy gentlemen."

Another man spoke up. "You are but an envoy of the Russian ambassador, and not empowered to speak yourself. Where is this grand Tsar Nikolai who you talk of, who cannot bring troops to our aid? When will we see him step forward?"

"You know that I hold the position with great reluctance," Karel replied. "I am a loyal Cossack. For eight generations my family has been the center of the city. I love nought else but my family and my country. Can I not hold the same opinion as all of you? I know not the reason for delay. My position is sometimes compromised in that the ambassador does not tell me everything. So I must wait on his word as do all of you."

"You are Nikolai's lapdog," one of the other Poles said, and the other nobles fell to murmuring amongst themselves. "Yes. You alone survived the battle? Perhaps you fell in with the Turk to spare yourself."

"My son is not a coward," the elder Arkelin declared with forceful resolve. "When he speaks, he speaks only the truth, compared to some." He concentrated his steady gaze on Stopovich.

"You say that because you are his father," the Pole replied with a patronizing tone and a smirk. "Why should we listen to you?"

Karel's small fist came down suddenly on the table like a sledge hammer, threatening to topple the goblets, and the sound of it caused the nobles to fall silent and stare at him with astonishment. His voice was strong and clear, ringing echoes against the stone walls as he stood up and said,"*because as long as we continue to bicker, we will lose to the Turk!*"

Alexander felt a small flush of pride at this. He had fledged a chicken hawk, small but deadly quick.

"So, the boy has acquired a backbone at last," Kuryan remarked.

"You should listen because I am right," Karel declared. "The Turks are not reasonable men. Their purpose is driven by greed and faith. They would turn all men to the grace of their Allah by force. And they do not acknowledge the alliances we have signed amongst ourselves."

"Aye," said another man. "We are God fearing Christians, and they have never forgiven us for Constantinople, have they?"

"But that was a long time ago, and yet they make war on us just the same," a third man replied with a helpless shrug.

"That matters not to them," Karel replied, taking up the reins again. "They care not for history or for peace. They will consume all of Ukraina if we do not ask for aid from the Tsar. A blind man could see that we are but few and scattered, and they are many. The assault on Kyiv but a day ago should be evidence enough of their intent. I beg you, in the name of the Blessed Virgin Mary, to come to an agreement among you, or to seek help. Else we will dissolve into the ruin I saw myself in P'risi. I... I nearly died there."

"Yet, here you are," said the Pole. "And in the pink of good health. What wounds have you?"

Karel's eyes seemed to pin him to his chair. "I recovered. What, are you suggesting that I made it all up? I lost my men, my horse, my..." Here he seemed to hesitate, and collected his wit before he said something he should not have, "yet I went through the fires of hell to warn you. The Turks were at our heels every step of the way here."

"Well said," Bohdan said. "How can we all unite and forge a union which will give us the independence we seek, when we are not in union over the slightest idea amongst ourselves?"

"May I speak?" Lucien said.

Bohdan turned to him and replied, "the word of an outsider will be honored here." To emphasize that he gazed around the room with a challenging look. Any coming word of protest was quickly squelched.

"You must make one decision or another," Lucien said. "And stick to it once you have done so. You cannot change your minds later. If you are so desperate to rid yourself of the Turks, you may have to capitulate to Russia, as Count Arkelin suggests. You will have no choice in the end."

Just then, a soldier entered the hall and handed a piece of parchment to the supervising steward, whispered something in his ear and went back out. The steward in turn brought the packet to Bohdan, who looked at him askance as he took it.

"A letter from the Sultan of Turkey," the steward said, and stood by out of the way.

Khmelnystsky opened it and peered closely at the script. "I cannot read this," he said, as he flapped it around with impatience. "I am familiar with Turk sign, but this is in Arabic."

"I can," Lucien replied quietly. The nobles stared at him, and it seemed to Alexander as if the room had just become ten degrees colder. "I can speak and write in ten languages, and Latin and Greek," he continued.

Silently, Bohdan passed the letter to him. Lucien's silver grey eyes glanced briefly over the text. Then he took a breath before he said, "it is a demand for your surrender."

"Our surrender!?" yelled one noble.

Bohdan gestured for silence and said, "go on. What does it say?"

Lucien began to read the letter verbatim. "To the nobles and administrators of Kyiv, in the land of the river Dnieper, I send greetings to you in the name of Allah, who is the lord of all things and the master of Heaven."

"Hah!" exclaimed Stopovich. "He would kiss us, would he?"

"You must give up your lives to him and submit to his rule. I am but his humble servant, who obeys him with all my love and who desires not to shed more blood in pursuit of a needless war."

"He attacks us, and yet he says this?" Karel's father replied, followed by a bout of murmuring among the councilmen.

Lucien looked up and waited patiently for silence before continuing. "If you will but accept the destiny for which you are fated, we will allow you to continue your lives without further turmoil. You must destroy the idols you worship, and the churches that defile the earth in defiance of the almighty god which is Allah. You must not be deluded by the teachings of your priests, who seek to enslave your souls and prevent your entrance to Paradise. Make your obeisance to him who is the most perfect of all beings, and accept the prophet Mohammed, blessings be upon him, as your savior."

Lucien paused to take another breath, though to Alexander it sounded more like impatience with the message. "If you do not," he continued, "we will make such war on you from which you may likely not recover. I await your reply with all love and comradeship, that you may become blessed in Heaven with me in the union of all people of the world under the love and grace of Allah. With all sincerity and friendship, Mohammed triad."

Stopovich snorted, "what sublime nonsense."

"Grrrrr. A load of road apples," another man said. "How dare he insult us like this?"

"He is trying to play for time with which to reinforce his garrison," Lucien explained patiently. "His weakness is in his words. He cannot afford to wage war with the men he has now, and would preforce delay you until he can obtain more. But he will make war upon you, you may be certain. He would make an end of your Christian faith by commiting a sin greater than all, but he would also destroy all the things which make you different as a people. Your art, your culture, your skill as horsemen and most of all, your freedom to worship or not as you will. All tokens of independance are abominations in his sight."

"It is true, my lords," Alexander said. "I have seen the ruins of many beautiful places between here and the Caspian Sea. All burned or broken. Nought remains but death and sorrow in their wake. In P'risi I saw a thousand people killed, man, woman and child, and not even the animals were spared from the lance."

"So had I, on my way there," Karel added. "P'risi is not the only village to fall. They took Odesa, Chisinao, and are even now camped to the south of Kyiv. The upset of yesterday is not likely to stop them if the Sultan decides to send them back to finish what they started."

The first man protested, "his words are an offense to us all, who have loved and prayed to the Blessed Virgin and her son all our lives. We are not base sinners who pray to the devil. What cause has he to tell us what to do?"

"He is the Sultan of Turkey," Lucien reminded him simply. Silence descended in the chamber as the words sank in and stayed.

"My lord Count, what would you do if you were I?" Bohdan asked. "We crave fresh ideas."

Lucien paused to consider before he gave his answer. "First, I would ignore this letter and continue to fortify the city against attack. Then I would summon all the chiefs of the surrounding clans to the city and make them understand the mind of the enemy. Without further debate on the matter, I would assemble every able bodied man and train him in arms, from the humblest peasant to every son and daughter of noble birth, because you will need an army greater than that which you have now to defend your land."

"But, what of aid from the Rus?" Bohdan asked.

"Only as a last resort, and when all else is lost," Lucien replied. "When every man is trained to defend his own cot and field, the land will be protected. But if they come to you and you are not ready to repel the Turks, this city will see ruin and every man, woman and child will be put to the sword. Your walls will come down and no one will escape the cruelty of these men of war."

"You speak as if you have seen it all before," Ostap said.

"I did," Lucien replied. "And I have no wish to see it again. I am a man of peace, but I fought against the Turks in Wallachia, and it was a festival of blood fit for the sight of Ares. For twenty long years, my lords, we fought them in every field, in every tree, until they could not sustain their numbers and fled."

"Then it is all true," Karel murmured softly.

"What?" Bohdan asked. "Speak up, Kashka. What mean you?"

At this Lucien's gaze seemed to pin Karel to his chair, and the fair countenance wilted quickly. "Nothing," he replied. He appeared to squirm and then fell silent, leaving the subject hanging in the air.

"Well then, we are left with a momentous decision to make, and we should retire to our chambers to consider all we have heard," Bohdan said. "But we must first fashion a response to the Sultan so that our resolve cannot be mistaken. Are we agreed on that, brothers?"

"Aye!" the other men shouted. "Bring pen and paper, that we will reply with the same politeness he gave us," said one. "Where is the scribner? Steward, summon him at once!"

"Yes, my lord," the steward replied, and left the room quickly.

"You are an intelligent man, my lord Count," Khmelnytsky said. "You speak well what is on my mind. I know that a well trained militia is necessary to accomplish our defense but we have never had the resources, and we waste time making war on each other instead of making common cause. But now, as there is a great need, the whole land will have a singular purpose for uniting under one banner." He reached for a goblet and poured a measure of slivoviska into it, took a hearty gulp of the wine, then set the goblet down and smeared at his lips and beard with his sleeve.

The steward returned with a cleric, who bore a tray with sheets of sheepskin and a hawk feather quill, a small bottle of ink, and a perfunctory attitude. "Here is little father Ambrose, who will take down your words," he said. "Mind you be gentle with him."

At this, Khmelnytsky threw his head back and laughed, and the other nobles joined in. "We will not harm a hair on his head," he said.

The man was small compared to the men surrounding him as they gathered to watch, and he looked intimidated as he sat down at the table and prepared to write. "What do you wish to say, my son?" he asked.

241

Bohdan cleared his throat roughly and said, "let me see. Uh... thou Turkish devil."

The cleric looked up at him, startled, and asked, "you want to start with that?"

"Why? What's wrong with it?" Bohdan replied.

"Uh... nothing. Nothing. Go on."

Lucien and Alexander exchanged cautious glances while the other nobles laughed. Karel started to laugh, too, then thought better of it and fell silent while Khmelnytsky continued to dictate.

"Brother and companion to the accursed Devil, and secretary to Lucifer himself, greetings!"

Ambrose appeared to hesitate, but the laughter was infectious, and he fought off the urge to join in as he hastily scribbled what was said. The other nobles became more boisterous as the hilarity of Khmelnytsky's words rang clear in his contempt to the Sultan's person rather than his station. It would certainly demonstrate the Zaporozhian Cossacks' strong defiance of his will.

"What the hell kind of noble knight art thou?" Bohdan continued, "Satan voids and thy army devours it. Never wilt thou be fit to have the sons of Christ serve under thee."

The other nobles laughed and clapped their hands with renewed glee.

"Thy army we fear not," he continued. "And by land and by sea in your chaikas, we will do battle against thee." At this Khmelnytsky paused to reflect, and gestured to himself as he groped for the next words. "Ah...thou scullion of Babylon, thou beer-brewer of Jerusalem, thou goat thief of Alexandria... thou swineherd of Egypt... both the greater and the lesser..."

At this the chamber roared with laughter. Some of the nobles began to wipe tears from their eyes. Even Lucien smiled faintly, and Alexander watched the cleric's smile broaden into a chuckle as he continued to dip and scribble. The meaning of the joke was lost on him, but he tried to find the humor in it and laughed pleasantly with the rest.

"Thou Armenian pig and Tatar goat. Thou hangman of the Kamyanets... thou evildoer of Podolia..."

At this, Stopovich shrieked with mirth, slammed his hand on the table, and held his stomach as he quaked uncontrollably, his eyes squeezed shut. Alexander was just able to see a gold tooth flash in the candlelight.

"Thou grandson of the Devil himself, thou great silly oaf of the world and of the netherworld, and, before God, a blockhead..."

At this, Karel could not help himself and joined in, while Alexander found himself chuckling at his choice of words.

"A swine's snout," Bohdan continued, "a mare's ass, and a clown of Hades. May the Devil take thee!"

There came a rousing cheer while Ambrose continued to scribble. But Khmelnytsky was not finished. "That is what the Cossacks have to say to thee, thou basest born of runts!"

Another bout of cheering rang against the stone walls.

"Unfit art thou to lord it over us true Christians!" he proclaimed. He paused while Ambrose hastened to catch up, then ended with, "the date we know not, for no calendar have we got."

"Poetry now, Bohdan?" exclaimed another noble.

The big man smiled and replied, "it does rhyme a bit, eh?" Then he tapped at his forehead and added, "the moon is in the sky, the year is in a book, and the day is the same with us here as with ye over there."

More laughter ensued, but he ended the letter with, "and thou canst kiss us thou knowest where!" and that sent the whole assembly into a paroxysm of giggles and applause.

While the nobles laughed and shared jibes, Ambrose finished up and offered it to Khmelnytsky to sign.

"Nay," he laughed, "give it to Ivan to sign, for he is the true leader of the council. Ivan Sirko, come over here and sign this letter, for I have given it a flourish of pretty words for you!"

More laughter followed the man as he got up from the table and ambled over. "I could not have said it better," he laughed, as he grabbed the feather from Ambrose, dipped the point in the well and then signed his name at the bottom, finishing with a fancy squiggle underneath.

Ambrose picked up the parchment and blew on it, then fixed the ink with powder and set it aside to dry. By now his fingers were black, and he stood up from the table. "Is there anything else you wish of me, Bohdan?" he asked.

Khmelnytsky drew a copper coin from a pouch on his belt and handed it to the cleric. "Give this to the church, little father, and light a candle for me," he replied with a grin. "Thank you for your most excellent service today."

Ambrose bowed slightly and crossed the air at him. "God grant you mercy," he said, then plucked up his instruments and fled from the room.

"My confession will entertain his brothers, of that I am certain," Khmelnytsky said, prompting another bout of laughter. "But now, let us be serious for a moment and think on what we have done today. Are we all in agreement, my brothers, that we must unite and drive the Turks from our homeland?"

"Aye!" they all declared, with thunderous applause.

64

Later, after the council meeting and a short bout of feasting and partying were over, Alexander, Lucien and the Arkelins returned to the house. It was late, and the full moon was already high in the sky, shining through a break in the clouds scudding past in a stiff cold wind. The compound was silent and dark as most of the household had already gone to bed.

As they dismounted, Karel and Nikolai dismissed the servants with cheery words and allowed them to lead the horses away.

"Thank God that is over," Karel remarked with candid relief. "Do you think they will stay united in one accord?"

"I hope it will be so," his father replied. "But the hour is late, and only the morning will bring better news."

After saying their good nights, Arkelin and his wife went up the steps together into the house. Lucien waited until they were inside before he turned to Karel and asked, "how fares your wound?"

Karel felt carefully at his rib. "The pain is gone," he said. "I feel no more discomfort, and can move with greater ease than before."

"Then it is time to remove your stitches. You do not want to go through life looking like a rag doll, do you?"

The young Count betrayed a mild wince of distaste through his rueful smile. "There is little choice to be had, is there?"

Alexander said, "come, there is no more need to fear. My father is most gently skilled, as you have seen before. And there is no more pain to feel, for you should have fully turned by now."

"Then I await your pleasure," Karel said to Lucien, "and after that, you will continue my education in this new life. I must know everything."

He took the lead as he marched up the steps into the house.

While the rest of the household slept, and after Lucien removed Karel's stitches and pronounced him healed, the three stayed together in the study and talked quietly of many things, and of tales told about demons and vampires and the plague, so that Karel obtained a better understanding of his new world in short order. Karel seemed less fearful of Lucien than he had before, even paying deference to him as a mentor instead of a constant source of intimidation. Alexander found that encouraging given what his friend had to go through to achieve his ascension.

It was not until the moon had cleared the tops of the towers in Kyiv that they broke up to go to bed.

And yet, something stirred Alexander awake again an hour later when he heard the door close gently in the front parlor. Instinct brought him to his feet, and he listened carefully as soft feminine footfalls padded away down the hall. Instinct told him it felt wrong. Puzzling, he threw on his houserobe, shod his feet in slippers, went to Lucien's room and eased the door open but a crack.

The cradle furnished for Parvati's comfort was still, and he could hear the infant's calm breathing from under the thick blanket covering her. Lucien appeared to be sound asleep, but the space where Sarasvati slept next to him was bare. Alexander reasoned for a moment that she must have gone to relieve herself, or to obtain water, and thought to return to his bed; but some nagging concern told him it was too simple an explanation for her leaving the chamber in the middle of the night. He had never known her to do so before.

He went to the front door of the apartment and opened it carefully so as not to wake Lucien, then slipped out into the hall. It was silent and dark. He could not easily find her with his heightened senses, and the concern changed to alarm as he ventured quietly toward the stairs. At the top of the landing he caught a short whiff of her blood scent at last, and he followed it down into the dark warren of the house and toward the outer door to the east wing, where Karel's family kept their rooms.

He sniffed about, thinking she might have gone toward the kitchen or the library, but the trail grew stronger as it led him straight to their door. Even in the safety and relative sophistication of Kyiv city life, people were prone to lock their doors and shutter their windows at night to keep out the vrykolakas and demons they were afraid of, as the undead were said to return to their homes and kill their relatives; and the superstition was never challenged though it was never yet proven.

That was no deterrent to Antellans because they were not undead, and they had such strength and speed that no door would be an effective barrier. Being civilized beings, however, they preferred to be welcomed in before entering. But in this moment of urgency there was no room for it.

After a moment's hesitation, he took hold of the handle and pushed gently to test the lock. The door was unlocked and opened easily, another unexpected surprise.

He poked his head in and saw that the candles in the sconces had been extinguished, but he could see the faint glow of moonlight through the crack of one door. Alarm surged through him as he presumed the worst, and closed the gap in a few seconds, pushed it open and found Karel Arkelin standing near a window, holding Sarasvati in his arms. His face was buried in her throat, and by the limp attitude of her limbs and body he could see she was caught in a sleep trance, unaware of the feeding. Her face was devoid of emotion or pain.

Alexander hissed angrily. *"Release her at once!"*

Karel raised his head, startled. His eyes were filled with red fire, and his fangs were stained with blood. A small drip of blood ran down his chin. His face was not his own. He was like the revenent described in the worst of humanity's fear.

He snarled at first. Then he smiled with demonic mirth as he rasped in a deep, husky accented voice, "it is too late, Alexander. She is mine now."

It summoned the memory of that terrible dream. It was then that Alexander realized with sudden horror that Karel's mind was not his own. He had been taken over, and was but a puppet to the unseen master pulling at his strings. *"Devil! Begone from this child and use him no more!"*

He bounded forward and wrested Sarasvati from the young Count's grasp, hugging her to him with one arm as he shoved Karel back and threw him hard against the window frame with the other.

Karel collided against the panes and went to the floor, then smiled again and began to laugh. "You cannot stop me," the young Count replied in Julian's voice. "You cannot compel me. I will have my revenge for the hurts my brother has done to me."

"Leave us alone, you murderer of women, or I will hunt you to the ends of the earth and kill you myself!"

Those words seemed to dispel the charm, and Karel snarled yet again, then wilted quickly and slumped to the floor, unconscious. His face softened and returned to its quietly angelic state, marred only by the blood smeared on his lips and chin.

Alexander turned to examine his stepmother. Sarasvati's throat was bleeding, and he kisslicked at the wounds carefully to close them. She remained asleep and unaware. He thought to waken her, but had second thoughts. How would he explain to her this assault on her person? and to his father?

Lucien's quiet voice came to him from the doorway, startling him. "Come. Let me take her, Alexander."

He turned, impressed again by Lucien's capacity to approach without warning like a ghost. "Father, I can explain all," he began, as he handed Sarasvati over. "Karel was not himself."

Lucien took her into his arms and picked her up as he replied, "she must not know this happened. If she does it will harm her mind. Remain here and tend to your young friend."

When Lucien had gone, Alexander picked Karel up in his arms and placed him on his bed, and began to draw the covers over him when Karel stirred awake. Karel looked up into his eyes and asked, "Alexander, what are you doing here?" His gaze was all innocence and honesty again, as if it was all a bad dream.

"You do not remember what happened just now, do you?" Alexander replied. He reached over to fetch a cloth from the washbasin and handed it to the count. "Here. Wipe your chin."

Karel obeyed, perplexed, then stared in shock as he saw the blood smeared on the cloth. "Borzhe moi," he whispered. "Blood? What did I do? Whose blood is this, Alexander?"

"Sarasvati's," Alexander said. "I caught you just in time. You were feeding on her. You were not yourself."

247

"Not myself?" the blond Count asked, pushing back a lock of his tousled golden hair. His fingers paused on his high forehead as he lay there thinking. "What was she doing here? I can remember nothing," he said finally.

"You remember that dream I told you of, where she was a pawn in a game of chess?"

"Of course I do. But, that was nothing more than a dream." Karel pushed himself up to a sitting position, frowning with puzzlement as he struggled to remember. "I feel so strongly as if I have been somewhere else, but I have no memory where."

"Those of us with the power to cloud men's minds can alter the memories of those we control, so that they will not remember. My uncle took over your mind long enough to reach Sarasvati. You are not at fault."

"Sweet Virgin," Karel replied, his eyes growing large and round. "I did not... hurt her, did I?"

"My friend, it is painful to hear but I must tell you. If I had not found you when I did you would have drained every drop until she would not have revived from her sleep."

Karel paused to lick his lips, and closed his eyes. "What can I do, Alexander? How can I prevent this from happening again? Will I become what I fear most, an instrument of the Devil, with neither will nor strength to make my own destiny in this world? An excommunicate from the love of God? Nosferatu?"

Alexander closed his eyes. "I do not know, my friend," he replied. "This is far beyond your control, and I blame you not."

Karel's hands bunched into fists, and he said, "if that day comes, you must kill me. I do not want to become an undead thing with no remorse or purpose for living. My soul is damned already as it is for all the sins I have commited, large and small."

"We will make sure you will not, for we are not undead, my lord count," his friend replied gently. "We are not of this world, but of another, as my father told you. Your blood has not spoken to you, has it? I do not know what is the delay, unless you were fully human, and resistant to its power somehow."

"I feel my blood go cold at times, frigid as the Dnieper in winter, and at other times hot as a raging inferno. My blood sings to me, but I have been trying to deny it," Karel replied.

"It... sings... ?" Alexander asked, wondering.

"Aye, a chorus of angelic voices in my mind, a sound as pure as the choir at high mass, the divine music of the spheres. I understand it not, but I know it is trying to speak to me. It is most wondrous to hear, and tranquil in its sound. Is this the dragon's blood, Alexander?"

"Perhaps," he ventured. "But, does it also compel you to do things against your will?"

"Nay. Or perhaps it is content to let me do things my own way. I may be lucky in that respect."

At that, Alexander finally cracked a smile. "May we all be so fortunate. But, now we must be circumspect. You must tell no one what you have told me, or we will all perish."

A rooster crowed outside, the first alarm against the growing dawn. Alexander glanced out the window and saw its gray light begin to banish the stars. "It is late," he said, "and you must get some rest." He rose while Karel laid back and settled himself to sleep.

As he went to the door, he heard Karel's voice telling him, "Alexander. Promise me."

Alexander's hand hesitated at the handle. Then he said, "I promise. Pray that the day never comes."

65

It was not until late afternoon the next day that Alexander woke. He looked up at the ceiling above him and listened to the sounds outside: of birds singing; the voices of men and women working on the grounds; of horses making sounds in the stable; of insects buzzing about on the still air. For once, no alarm was raised, and he did not feel his blood stir him to rise. He uttered a sigh of relief, then rose to his daily ritual of shaving and dressing.

When that was done, Alexander looked in on Lucien, who was already dressed and seated by the window reading from his small book. Sarasvati remained sleeping with Parvati tucked in next to her. He started to say his good evenings but Lucien laid a finger against his lips.

Alexander nodded, then took a seat next to his father. "She has not suffered harm from last night's adventure, has she?" he whispered.

"Nay. But, she has not woken since," Lucien whispered back.

"I make no defense of Karel's behavior, but his mind was not his own," he explained.

"I know. Is he aware of what happened?"

"He is now. But then, he was not in control, and unaware until I woke him. My uncle was responsible for the attack, not Karel. But I fear he may fall prey to another spell."

Lucien grunted softly. "There is always that risk. Once touched by one of us in such away, it opens the avenue to taking control again, and my brother is not beyond availing himself of the opportunity. It takes a strong will to resist his commands, and your young friend is but newly turned and not yet familiar with his own person. All we can do now is to observe him and watch for the signs." He closed the book, marking the place with its ribbon, and laid it aside. "And now, we must go in search of our host. It is time to plan for the next leg of our journey."

Quietly, they slipped out of the apartment and went down to the main hall, where they found the Arkelin family arrayed around the hearth and deeply engaged in serious discussion. Upon their entrance all looked up at them with the expression of dismay found on those notified of bad news.

"Ah, there you are," Karel said, to break the ice. "I trust you had a good day of rest?"

"We did, thank you, my lord Count," Lucien replied with a small bow, and Alexander mimicked him. There was a long moment of silence, during which an ember sparked and sailed upward into the chimney. Then he continued. "Has something happened?"

The elder Arkelin replied, "we have been summoned to attend court in Moscova. It was Karel's task alone, but the Tsar now commands that we all go, to show our good faith and to demonstrate that the Cossacks are willing to negotiate an alliance with the Rus."

Alexander recalled Karel's remark about becoming a royal hostage to save the fortunes of his country. "Ah. That is good, yes?"

"It is not good for the whole household to uproot and venture into a strange land, but it appears we have no choice," the Count's wife replied. "I have my son back again, but now we must lose our ancestral home to political convenience."

The deep warm voice of the Grand Duchess came from the other corner of the room, where she sat behind her embroidery frame clad in mourning black. The frame contained a cloth, and she applied methodical stitches in the silk using her fingers and thimbles like a sighted person. "Veska, we have discussed this before. We knew it was our fate," she said.

"Yes, mamalika," the woman replied with a chastened tone.

"Karel has told me how much you helped him," Nikolai continued. "How may we repay your generosity?"

"We interrupted our journey to bring your son safely home. Now that he is restored to you, we must continue on toward our destination," Lucien said. "We require only fresh horses and some provisions to sustain us as far as Suceava."

"All that you require, and more, will be amply furnished," Arkelin replied. "And you will need an escort to the border, no? There are some in our land who will not allow strangers to pass through without collecting a toll. Now that the council has decided on a course of action, the members must depart and carry their news to the clan chieftains. Let me send for my friend Ostap Kuryan, who knows the territory. Kuryan is a man of integrity and honor, and I am sure he would enjoy your company. His retinue is large and well armed."

"That would be quite suitable," Lucien said with a small bow.

"Then we will make the preparations, and depart together in the morning," Arkelin said.

That evening was spent with the house in a quiet state of uproar as the servants gathered together the essentials the Arkelins would need for travel. A quiet supper was shared in the dining hall with all the somberness of a funeral wake, and afterward the family members took turns giving confession and saying prayers in their small chapel under the ministration of the local bishop.

The Grand Duchess would remain behind and care for the house while they were away. And having just buried her husband, she would be the only Arkelin to remain in the Ukraine. Once she died there would be no more to carry on the family name.

Karel acquainted Alexander with the clan and its extended family, boasting that the blood of Matthias Corvinus, a past king of Hungary, ran through a cousin's veins, and that in many ways the blood royal ran through many nobles' veins, connecting them together no matter where they were by intermarriage and alliance, so that he could even claim cousinhood with the first king of France,

Charlemagne. "And the blood of Attila is strong in every one of us, just as he is strong with you," Karel insisted. "So while we are separated by great distance, we are all of one blood."

Alexander replied, "by extension then, we are brothers by more than blood, and I will defend your name to any who tries to besmirch your honor."

"And I yours," Karel replied.

They clasped arms and shook them to seal the bond between them.

Alexander and Lucien wisely left the women alone to commiserate together and spent the time preparing their wagon, inspecting the braces and the condition of the wheels, making small repairs in its fabric where necessary, then examining the horses and judging their worthiness to pull it.

"This old thing is becoming like home to me," Lucien said softly as he patted the old woooden door. "I care not for a soft bed and walls to hold me in. You are right, Alexander, to crave the open sky and the fresh mountain air. I had taken all for granted in Shangri-la. Yet, one day soon I must settle and give Sarasvati a proper home or she will lose all patience with me. The upset of the other day acquainted me with her feelings more than all the days we have spent together in travel."

"We will find it," Alexander replied. "I hope it is Transylvania, but if it is not mayhaps Hungary will do just as well."

Lucien shook his head. "I do not think so. Hunyadi did not welcome us there."

"There was talk of prison before. Is that what inhinged my uncle's mind?"

"Nay," Lucien replied with a regretful tone. "Julian was never stable, never... settled. Prone to moods and fits of unexplained anger at the slightest thing. He played cruel tricks on me when we were both young. And I, as his twin brother, forgave him one time too many. I will never live another day and understand the illness which took him but spared me. The blood he drank from the prince of Wallachia passed an unquiet spirit to him and strengthened his madness. Dracula was a man who was never granted a happy childhood, and I think some of his hurts infected Julian's mind with a need for revenge beyond whatever he suffered already."

"Granted, but I still cannot forgive him for what he did to my mother," Alexander said. "He was a monster."

"I would not expect you to. What he did to her was unforgivable. But one day I hope you will obtain peace of mind, for it is not good to dwell on the past."

"And Sarasvati? The event of last night weighs heavily on my mind. I vowed to protect her, but even then I could not."

"I know not his designs on her. Perhaps to punish me for leaving his side, for turning against him. For showing him that side of himself which he rejects as weak. I was ever his reflection in most respects, and perhaps that is why he despises mirrors. But what man can cleave to the path of hatred and distrust he paved, and not doubt it is the right way to live?" He scratched his head absently, then shook it with a small sigh. "It is all quite beyond me."

"Perhaps he despises mirrors because he despises himself even more," Alexander suggested. "He would avoid looking upon his own visage to avoid seeing the reminder of his own perfidy."

"Your insight does you credit," Lucien replied with a rueful smile.

A knocking sound on the stall door caught them both by surprise. Ostap Kuryan's tall lanky figure stood framed in it. "I was told by the steward that that I would find you here," he said. "I came to discuss your arrangements for travel. I understand that you need men to escort you through the Bucovina into Transylvania. Is this correct?"

"Aye," Alexander replied, taking the lead.

"As it happens I am going that way," Kuryan said. "I must stop at my father's house in Muramea. Do you know the town?"

"I do," Lucien said.

"We are leaving at dawn by the west gate. Can you be ready by then?"

"We will be ready," Lucien replied with a quick nod.

"Good. Then I bid you a good evening."

When the man had gone, Alexander turned to Lucien and said, "think you he heard our conversation?"

Lucien stared at the open doorway and replied, "I do not know. His mind was opaque, as if there was a shield thrown up. Or I am very much out of practice at reading human minds."

"Do you think he is one of us, then?"

"That, too, is a mystery. But we will have ample time to find out. Now let us return to the house or we will be missed."

66

June, 1647

When the first golden glow of the dawn painted the sky teal blue, a long file of horses and wagons went toward the west gate while the town was just stirring awake. Ostap Kuryan, Alexander and Count Arkelin led the way on horseback, with Lucien at the reins of the wagon behind them, and three coaches and four nestled among a phalanx of cavalry and a train of supply wagons pulled by mules.

When they arrived at the gate the guards ran to unbar it. Alexander could not see Koshokov among them, and reasoned that he must start the day watch well after sunrise.

Once they were across the bridge and past the hill overlooking the city, the train halted at the crossroads and prepared to divide. The Arkelins would proceed north and east toward Moscow, and Kuryan and his retinue would move southwest over open country toward the Bucovina. Everyone used the interlude to say their farewells.

"I will miss our company," Karel said to Alexander and Lucien. "You have taught me much about... my new life. But, when will I see you again?"

"You have all the time in the world now," Alexander replied. "Our paths will cross again one day, I am certain."

"And you, my lord Count," he said to Lucien. "I will make you proud of me. I promise."

"Make your father proud, and I will be satisfied with that," Lucien replied. "Distinguish yourself with heroic deeds, and live your life to its fullest. Make your mark on the world with truth and honor, and keep yourself free of sin."

"It is my duty and honor to fulfill, sir," Karel replied, and with that he turned his horse and galloped away to rejoin his father's side.

"There goes another good man," Alexander said.

Lucien said nothing at first, and his eyes were distant and cold as he replied, "that has yet to be seen." Then he chucked the reins and set the horses moving after the riders ahead.

For the next day and a half the long file of soldiers and wagons made its way down toward the leading edge of the Carpathians and the river plain which marked the border between Ukraina and the lands beyond the forest. As they traveled they were ever watchful for the Turkish regiments occupying the territory, but not a single soul appeared to greet or challenge them.

The sweeping ravages of the Turk invasions had forced the migration of the farmers to the shelter of the cities, and now the fields were left fallow. What few farmsteads remained were too small to adequately support a moving army, and those long abandoned were slowly returning to wilderness, overgrown by trees and scrub forest. There were patches of faint brown and black where the natives had pursued the tactic of burning everything to deprive the enemy of provisions and shelter before they fled.

Ostap Kuryan proved to be an enigma. During rare moments of conversation he was not quite evasive, but shared no useful information about himself either. He could be called taciturn, and his face was as cold and inscrutable as that of any gambler. He took to smoking a long pipe with a tiny cup from which emerged a fragrant sweet smoke, and he left a trail of it behind him wherever he went.

Alexander continued to believe that he was really a pureblood making his way in the world as a human, but so far Kuryan had done nothing to prove or disprove it. He soon found it a diverting challenge to discover the truth of the man, and kept one eye fixed on his every word and movement as they traveled slowly through the wild verdant country he called his homeland.

The retinue Kuryan led was a hodgepodge of soldiers and servants, all descended from huns or sons of huns, and all well armed to the teeth. They moved down the road with barely a word spoken between them. They made no attempt to engage Alexander or Lucien in conversation, and a few even crossed themselves at their approach. But a quick word from Kuryan made them move on.

On the evening of the first day, the group made camp on the bank of the Prut River, which marked the territorial border with Romania. There an uneasy spirit descended on the men, who behaved with all the nervous hesitation of bridegrooms.

Lucien and Alexander helped Sarasvati out of the wagon and prepared to erect their own shelter among the tents going up on the marshy ground. Upon seeing her dark skin and grey eyes the women shied back and crossed themselves, and fell to muttering imprecations to their virgin.

When Kuryan saw this he barked, "cease your prattling! Mind your own business, and save your prayers for the church." The sound of his voice raised in command caused the women to retreat inside their tents without a sound raised in protest, while their men turned away and kept their conversation quiet and furtive among themselves.

"Forgive them," he said to Sarasvati with a small bow and an unpleasant, off-kilter smile. "They are nought but superstitious fools." Then, without further ado, he made his way into his own tent and closed the flap.

"I know not what these people will do, husband," Sarasvati said quietly. "I feel most unwelcome here."

Lucien took her hand up in his and kissed it gently. "Do not concern yourself with them," he said. "It is best you stay close to me and avoid them. No one will harm you as long as I am here."

From then on, Sarasvati kept to herself in the wagon and did not venture out except to relieve herself or to take Parvati for short walks. Kuryan told one of his men to take his weapon and go with her, but Lucien interceded quickly. "I will protect her," he insisted. "Save your shot."

"As you wish," Kuryan replied with a short bow and a smile.

On the evening of the second day, the train made camp on a hilltop overlooking a shallow canyon, where a vast herd of wild horned sheep wandered aimlessly cropping the grass. After the other men settled down to sleep, Alexander and Lucien walked down into the flock and found blood among the animals, then brought the carcasses back to be butchered and stored in the larder.

Ostap seemed to accept the ration without a word of curiosity or consternation spoken in their direction. This in itself made Alexander ever more curious about him. But he knew that too much curiosity would ruin the uneasy camaraderie they shared, and it was difficult enough to watch the man without alerting him to the scrutiny. He resolved to spend less time in nosy speculation and concentrate on learning more about the land they traveled, and after a short time was able to distract himself with the beauty of the country.

But as they approached the head of the Siret River, Alexander noticed that most of the men and women were now wearing silver crosses on chains around their necks, along with garlands of garlic flowers; and votive candles were lit near where the people sat or slept. Wolfbane sprigs soon decorated the wagons and the women even tucked them in their bosoms for nosegays. When they spoke, it was of demons and vrykolakas, and their talk soon made him feel self-conscious. Through them he learned that a man had disappeared in the middle of the night on the way to Kyiv a fortnight before without making a sound of alarm.

"A deserter," an older man said, following up with a generous dollop of spit on the ground. He looked like a veteran of many battles, and had a generous scar across one cheek. He wore the attitude of practicality.

"Nay, he left everything he owned behind," said another. "Would a deserter do that?"

"Maybe a vrykolaka got him," said a third, as he shoveled a spoonful of ham porridge into his mouth.

"You and your vrykolakas. Where are they?" said the older man. "I have never met one. Have you?"

The third man frowned, then jerked his head in Alexander's direction. All heads turned with deliberate care and looked at the tall young man in dark clothes as he watched the horizon.

His face was stone, but he was listening to every word.

"Then where do you think he went?" said a fourth man.

"He went to do his business and got lost," said the first man, sniffing with disgust. "We have seen no one in the woods. No one."

"Then where is he? Did you see him come back?"

"No. No one did."

"And what about Tuporza, the week before?"

"He probably got lost, too. Kuryan did not care."

"Why should he? The man was an ass."

The conversation ended abruptly when a long mournful howl came up in the darkness among the trees, then another. The group broke up and moved nervously toward their tents. Wolves were common in the forests of Romania, but they were feared as "devil dogs" and servants of the "evil one" nonetheless. When there was little to hunt they were known to attack horses or the odd hunter caught alone after sunset.

But they seldom ventured near places where more than one human lived for fear of being skinned. Their pelts were prized for the color of the fur and their suppleness.

Alexander withdrew from his post near the wagons and drew Lucien aside, speaking to him in a quiet voice. "The men are talking of comrades vanishing, and they are buried in silver and other decorations to ward off the evil one they fear. They grow more frightened with every mile we have traveled. It is not a good sign."

Lucien blew out a short breath and looked down. "They fear what they do not see, what they do not hear. They stink of fear, Alexander, and we are the cause of it."

"Then we should not stay. We should go, now, and leave them in peace. Kuryan cannot defend us from them, and I am much reminded of that day on the ferry. I would not care to repeat it."

Lucien turned to him. "We will not get far alone in these woods. I do not fear for myself but for Sarasvati and Parvati. I will not see my family harmed for the sake of haste, or an unwise decision we may regret."

"We invite their aggression if we stay longer," he replied. "They are like dogs straining at the leash. If we cannot control them..."

"Aye," Lucien agreed with reluctance in his tone. "Let us broach the subject with Kuryan, and see what can be done."

Romania

67

That evening, when the travelers were finally bedded down, Lucien and Alexander went to see their host, who was seated on a folding chair before a small table, writing something on a piece of parchment paper by the light of a candle. On their entrance, he looked up, startled, then rose and asked, "gentlemen, good evening. Is there something you wish?"

Alexander replied, "we regret this but it is unavoidable. We have decided to part company with you on the morrow and go on toward Transylvania alone."

Kuryan's cheek twitched as he stood in the gloom, considering, then placed his hands on his wide leathern belt. "Count Arkelin acquainted me with your desire to pass through our territory with all speed and caution. Have I given you some offense that you would chance the Turks rather than remain under my protection?"

"It is most admirable your discretion and attention, my lord Kuryan," Lucien replied. "But the men and women in your retinue are not of the same opinion."

"What they think is of no importance," Ostap protested mildly. "They do as I say. Is that not enough?"

"You are but one man of reason among a horde who fear the unknown. We wish to avoid an altercation. They are but a breath away from acting recklessly. Have you not observed the precautions they have adopted since we entered the valley?"

"I have. But that is for them to do, and if they gain comfort from their religion I will not stop them."

"It is not their religion that concerns us," Alexander said. "We have done nothing to merit their avoidance yet they behave as if we are a menace. They speak of men vanishing from their company like wisps of smoke, never to return."

"Those they speak of met with nought but misadventure," Kuryan replied. "They went into the woods unarmed and without a companion to keep the watch. What happened to them is a mystery, it is true, but more a result of their stupidity or their lack of experience. The woods are dark and deep at night, and as you have heard, there are wolves and other unpleasant things we can hear but not see."

Then he smiled as he continued, "I cannot vouch for your safety if you leave us now. Remain in our company and we will see you safely to Suceava. Then, if you are still determined, go as you will, and with my prayers for your safe deliverance to your destination."

"Our thanks for your caution," Lucien replied. "We will go with you to Suceava. But assure your people of our desire to travel with them as comrades, not as enemies."

"I will speak to them," Kuryan said with a curt nod.

"Then we bid you a good evening, and a safe night's sleep."

As they walked away from Kuryan's tent Alexander asked, "I have never been to Suceava. Have you?"

"It is close to the old castle, at the entrance to the Borgo. If your uncle is there, it will take all our skills to avoid his attention. There he is in his element and where his power is greatest. If we are circumspect, we may be able to make it through the river valley to Bistritza without his knowledge, and then I will breathe easier for it."

"With every step we venture further into danger, father," he replied. "I am sorry I brought you to this."

Lucien turned and placed a long fingered hand on his shoulder, squeezing gently. "You have made me regret nothing," he said. "You are a good son, and a good man to share company with." Then he asked, "have you been keeping up with your journal?"

"I feel I have scarcely had time to keep up with life itself of late, and attending to Karel was a bit of a handful," Alexander said, then chuckled. "I should be writing of our travels together, and not looking for danger in every rock and tree."

"Aye, you should," Lucien agreed. "We are well protected in our wit, and should have nothing to fear for ourselves. So. I am off to tend to my wife and child, and you must spend your hours before bed putting pen to paper of all that your imagination conjures of the day. Worry not."

"I will, father, and thank you."

As he watched Lucien walk away toward the wagon, Alexander turned his attention to the tent city around him and spotted Kuryan handing something to one of his men, who promptly mounted a pony and galloped into the darkness of the woods.

In that moment all of Alexander's senses were put on high alert, and he moved on silent swift feet into the darkness. He followed the sound of hooves in the soft soil until they reached the river, and stopped only when he was blocked by the sound of splashing water as the horse crossed at a ford. He perched on a large rock overlooking the current flowing past and listened, stretching his hearing to the limit, but the sounds of night drowned all else. There was no telling where the horseman was going now.

When he returned to the camp, he saw that everyone had retired into their tents, including Kuryan. The fire was dying, so he placed another log on the pile to stir it up again. Then he retired to his place near the wagon and laid down on his saddle blanket to keep the watch.

Yet still his mind would not settle. He tossed and turned, tried to relax, recited poetry to himself, counted sheep, his thoughts ever returning to the messenger and Kuryan's purpose for sending him into the dark.

A few moments later, Lucien emerged from the wagon and approached. "You are still awake," he observed. "What troubles you, that you cannot find rest? You think loudly enough to wake the dead."

Alexander turned to him and replied. "I saw Kuryan dispatch a messenger into the dark. I followed the man as far as the river, but could not catch him up. What event would urge such haste? Did he not say before that the woods were dark and full of risk?"

"Perhaps something dire," his father said. "I could not think else."

"Then, Kuryan is a fullblood after all. I had that impression of him when we were at the council meeting. He has been most inscrutable, and with my poor talent most difficult of all to read."

"Nay, Alexander, you were impressed by his appearance and manner but you do not see his true nature. He is a half-turned familiar," Lucien replied with a tone of disgust. "At home in both worlds. Always hungry and easy to control. What power he has emanates from his master, and I fear he may be in league with your uncle, for I cannot read him either."

"Yet Kuryan appears to have all his faculties. Was this to be Karel's fate?"

"Karel is too young and inexperienced to resist, but now that he is going to Moscova distance alone may put him beyond my brother's control. Kuryan, however, is another matter. We must remain watchful of any sign he is taken over."

Sarasvati's soft feminine voice came to them on the cool night breeze. "My husband, are you going to stay out all the night?"

Alexander watched his father's face soften with fondness, and turned to see her small face peering out from the door of the caravan. "She is most demanding, isn't she?" he asked him with a small wink.

"She is worried, and with good reason. I must return to her side. I will see you on the morrow." He placed his long fingered hand on Alexander's shoulder and squeezed it gently before walking away.

68

The dawn saw the caravan resume its slow journey through the woods toward the head of the Borgo Pass, a shallow river canyon winding its way through a low range of ancient and eroding mountains. The Borgo went west and then south toward Bistriṭa, the largest town in the area. Beyond that lay the vast dark forest and the jagged line of the Carpathians forming the backbone of Transylvania to the north. The peasants called it "the dragon's spine", and was well named, as the mountain range traced a sinuous course westward and then south toward the source of the Danube river, dividing the country from the Hungar lands beyond.

By mid afternoon they entered Suceava, a large village and coach station, and the last chance for rest and provisions before the road entered the pass. Kuryan led the train into the central square, where everyone dismounted and stretched their limbs, then began pitching their tents to make camp.

"We will stop here for the evening," Kuryan announced to Lucien. "Then we will go on to Muramea at dawn. I have already dispatched a message to my father so that he will be ready to receive us. Then after we are well rested I will escort you to Bistritza."

So that was what the note was all about. Alexander felt all the tension in his spirit flow away like water.

"You need not extend yourself further," Lucien replied. "We have imposed on your hospitality long enough."

But Kuryan would hear none of it. "Nay, I feel I would be a most inhospitable host if I did not. It is no imposition. Your wife and child will need more protection on the road than you can provide alone, and you may yet be set upon by the Turks. I will learn the lay of the land and where they may be encamped tonight. Bide with us and I will see you safely through the pass on the morrow."

With characteristic humility, Lucien said, "Your logic is compelling. I beg your indulgence to confer with my son, who is my partner in all things, and I will give you an answer ere long."

Kuryan replied with a short bow. Then he led his horse away to tie it with the others.

Lucien told Alexander, "he is most insistent. He claims all concern for our welfare. From his speech and voice I divined that some part of him is fighting for his freedom, but such a small kernel of rebellion is hardly enough to pin all our hopes upon."

"Then, what must we do?" his son replied.

"We have no choice in the matter. We cannot deny his offer, or he would suspect we know what is amiss. We can only try to reach him and cut his tether before all is lost."

"You do know how do that, I hope? For I do not."

"It is a but a simple matter. We must draw him away from the company of his retinue long enough to bite him, and then his freedom is assured. I can only hope that my will is powerful enough to overcome my brother's. There is also the risk that he will detect our plan and act to prevent it."

"What do you need from me in order to accomplish it?"

"If you will, go to Kuryan and tell him you desire to speak with him in private. Then lead him toward a place out of sight of the others. I will meet you there, and then we will grant him his wish."

Over the course of the afternoon Alexander made every effort to do what Lucien suggested, but could never quite find the opportunity to approach Kuryan without an interruption. For his part, Kuryan seemed unaware that he was being pursued, and by a string of coincidental events managed to be surrounded with a group of people demanding his attention all the time. At length Alexander had to drop his strategy and returned to Lucien bearing a load of chagrin with him.

"No matter," Lucien replied with a small smile. "We will wait him out. The perfect moment will come later. In the night. In the dark."

That evening the moon was bright and full, and the main street was deserted. The whole village looked like a ghost town. Like all those living in the shadow of superstition and fear, the villagers stayed indoors after sunset, or hurried home after shutting their shops for the night. Sentries posted at the stations and street corners kept a weather eye open for trouble, but many soon found themselves dozing or sipping slivoviska from their flasks. Dogs barked at random, then fell silent.

Kuryan and the other travelers dined in the nearby inn, surrounded by a host of decorations designed to drive away the undead. Strings of garlic bulbs hung from the ceiling, and sprigs of mistletoe and garlands of wolfbane adorned every window, shuttered tightly closed against the terrors of the dark. While it painted a picture of pastoral warmth it was also the worst place for a vampire to be in, even one as alien as an Antellan. The redolence of the atmosphere alone would have driven them out for a taste of clear sweet mountain air.

Lucien, Sarasvati, and Alexander wisely avoided the inn and remained in or close to the wagon. From where they were camped they could see the warm lights peeking through through the shutters of the tavern, and could hear the trilling sounds of a dulcimer and violins, panpipes, and a set of tabla, setting down an allegretto rhythm and a wild melody filled with gypsy romance.

Lucien indulged Sarasvati as she tried to follow the tune with dancing movements, and when the song ended he and Alexander applauded her with soft hands while Parvati imitated them with squeals of amusement.

"Ah. I miss the days when I danced for Shiva," she said as she settled down on the floor and fluffed out her long dark hair. "Will the people in France allow me to dance the way I used to?"

"We will see," Lucien replied. "And even if they do not, you may always dance for me in the privacy of our bedchamber."

While they talked, Alexander watched for some sign of Ostap Kuryan. He had learned from Lucien that the familiars' need for fresh blood was just as compelling as their hunger for human food, requiring both to survive. Sooner or later, Kuryan would have to feed.

At a break in the revelry, he finally spotted the tall Romanian emerging from the inn with a wench, who was laughing at something he said. Kuryan appeared to be drunk, and he laughed with her as they staggered along down the road toward the darkness of an alley between buildings. The moment had finally come.

He turned to Lucien and said, "the dove is flown."

Lucien handed Parvati to Sarasvati and said, "I must go with Alexander and attend to an important matter. We will return soon."

Together, they emerged from the wagon and stalked the couple a short way into the dark until they were well off the main road. They halted as Kuryan eased his prey up against the wall of a building and began kissing her. The wench appeared to be completely overcome with drink, and responded with clumsy warmth and passion to his mouth.

They watched carefully until Kuryan tugged her head back and began nuzzling at her throat. Alexander caught a glimpse of fangs flashing white in the gloom as Kuryan prepared to bite.

In another instant Lucien bounded forward and caught Ostap by the neck, holding him still, while Alexander pulled the woman away from his embrace. "*Go home, girl*," he murmured quietly to her, but his voice penetrated her mind like a fervent shout. "*Go home to sleep away the spirits, and forget this night*."

The woman giggled, then staggered away using the wall next to her as a brace to keep her balance, while Kuryan struggled against the steel grip holding him prisoner. He snarled like a wolf, and his speech was slurred as he said, "what are you doing? How dare you rob me of my repast!"

"Both drunk and hungry? How pathetic you are. I am here to free you, Ostap," Lucien replied. "You would lead us into danger with every step into the Borgo, yet you know it not. Confess that you have not been yourself since the council meeting. Confess that you are under the sway of the dark lord who has imprisoned you."

"You think me a dog of the Devil?" Ostap spat. "I am not. Unhand me, or I'll..." Strong as he was, he could not free himself from Lucien's relentless grip on his neck and arm, as if they were encased in concrete.

"You do not know yourself, sir. You are a dog of your master, but he is not the Devil. He is the one who lurks in the darkest corner of your mind." As Lucien spoke he tore away the loose collar of Kuryan's shirt, then without hesitation pulled him close and bit him in the throat.

Kuryan stiffened, fought, pushed back with all his might. But the battle was short and futile. Soon he fell back in Lucien's arms and hung limp and unconscious. And when Lucien raised his head, his eyes were bright with red fire. He kisslicked Kuryan's throat to seal the wounds and eased him back against the wall, allowed his body to sink to the ground, and composed his limbs for sleep.

"He should recover in a short time. I took only a little of his blood, but his mind is free," Lucien said. "Anyone who comes upon him now will think him in his cups and sleeping off the effects."

"You would leave him here, like this?" Alexander asked.

"He would have done himself whether we are here or not," his father shrugged. "All must appear natural to him when he wakes. Now come. We must return to Sarasvati and resume the watch."

69

The next morning, there was knocking on the door to the wagon, and when Alexander poked his head out, Ostap Kuryan stood on the stoop looking sheepish and penitent. He said, "I wish to thank you and your father for what you did for me. It is as if a dark cloud was banished from my spirit, and a great weight was lifted from my soul."

Wonder filled Alexander. "You recall all that happened?"

"Aye," Kuryan replied. "And I hold no grudge against you for it. It was a great struggle to free myself from the devilish urges which long assailed me. Thoughts and deeds came to me which I know were not my own. I know what I am, and I am repentant, but now I feel that if I pray for deliverance God will no longer deny me."

"If you rely on faith in yourself, sir, deliverance will come from your own efforts," Alexander said. "We make our own destinies in this life. So honor your faith with a firm resolve to do good."

"You speak the truth," Ostap said. "I will guide you to Bistritza as I told your father, and I will pledge my life to stand between you and all that endangers your fortunes. We depart in an hour." As he spoke his long fingers went to rub at his temple.

"Are you well, sir?" Alexander asked.

"I fear I indulged my passion for slivoviska a bit overmuch," Kuryan replied with a short chuckle, then winced. "Ah. My head feels about to burst."

"My father has a remedy which will cure the pain quickly."

"Thank you, no. I have had such pains before, and they pass quickly. But I will ask if it becomes worse," he replied, then turned and stalked away toward the others.

An hour later, the caravan of travelers pressed on into the Borgo Pass. Once again, an odd silence held sway over the forested peaks, and a cloud of ravens flew among the trees bathed in golden light, their calls and flapping about contributing to the general sense of gloom as they followed the train in search of scraps of food. In a somewhat charitable mood, Lucien tossed the remains of the last night's supper to them, and they hopped about and squabbled as they chased after the morsels among the puddles left by a predawn rain.

When the travelers approached the first turn, Alexander could see a large castle perched atop a mountain plateau: a hulking stone monster overlooking the steep approach of the river, with peaked turrets and a high wall of battlements now fallen into ruin. One of the turrets had collapsed inward on itself and the dark windows were framed with scorch marks where fire had gutted the interior. Yet, for all its emptiness, he had the impression that the windows were like eyes, watching the road from the castle's high perch like one of the great golden eagles soaring in the sky above it, and some indefinable dread sent a subtle chill up his spine.

He fell back and waited for the others to file past him as he joined the wagon, where Lucien sat with his broad brimmed hat pushed down on his fine white hair, squinting into the bright morning light as he drove the horses. "That is the castle," he said.

Lucien barely turned his head, almost refusing to acknowledge its presence. The mountain breeze whistled faintly through the trees and the ravens called raucously again before he finally answered. "Aye. It has been a long time. I had hoped never to return here, but it appears fate had other plans for me. Perhaps to remind me of the great sin that drove me from my brother's side."

"Just now I had the sensation that there is someone there, but..."

"Do not look at it for too long," Lucien insisted. "Your thoughts will guide his attention straight to you."

His son obeyed quickly. "Do you think it is him?"

His father closed his eyes, then opened them again. "Difficult to tell. He may be shielding himself. I dare not probe further into the psionic stream or I will give our position away."

"Then do not try," Alexander said. "I would not care to meet him as things stand now. He was able to take Karel over, but I am sure he cannot take me as easily. If I could smite my hate upon the ruin, and in so doing bring the stones down around his ears, I would be well satisfied with it. He deserves a coward's death."

Lucien sighed heavily, then adjusted the reins to the horses with a small chucking motion. "I had hoped I would not have to tell you this, but now that you are older and better able to bear the burden, I must. My brother and I are joined in concert by our blood, linked together in such a way that if one of us is wounded, the other feels it also."

Alexander's jaw dropped open with astonishment. "The wound you suffered in Kyiv? Is that why he attacked Sarasvati?"

"I do not know. It is hard to tell what drives my brother at times, as I told you before," Lucien replied. "He has been sedentary of late, which is fortunate, else you would see me bleeding from wounds not my own."

"What a terrible thing," Alexander said. "I never knew you were burdened by such a curse."

Lucien sighed again. "It is not a curse. True the condition is rare, but natural for twins to share such a bond. I can no more divest myself of it than one can lose an arm or an eye. I can only weather the sensations and hope the bleeding does not affect some vital organ. But I have managed to stay alive almost six thousand years at his side, and if I die tomorrow it will be no different an experience than if I had lived but twenty."

"Immortality, then, is no boon where you are concerned."

"Aye," Lucien replied, "for while I have lived many human lifetimes, it is like living one. A year to others is like a moment for me. It is all relative. When we speak of time and of life, we can only live as if we will die tomorrow."

Alexander considered that for a long minute. "Then, though I have lived almost two centuries, I can expect no more of life than from one."

"Now think, Alexander. Is your rage less intense than it was not a few moments ago?"

Alexander thought about it, and sighed with some relief. "I do feel a little better. Thank you, father."

"It was beneficial for both of us," Lucien replied. "Our conversation served as a filter for those thoughts which might attract his attention. Now we must not speak further of him, or he will turn his lion's eyes upon us."

Silently, Alexander gave him a mild salute and made his mind go blank as he spurred his horse forward to join Kuryan, where he engaged him in light banter to clear the air.

70

The rest of the day was spent in making a record of the journey through the pass. Alexander allowed his mount to negotiate her way along the trail without guidance while he occupied himself with writing in his journal using his graphite pencil. By now he had gone through several sticks already, but still had one or two left.

He wrote expansively on the beauty of the countryside, the birds and flowers, the different sorts of trees he saw, and also his memories of the way people looked and dressed in Suceava. And as he rode past the base of the castle hill he used the distraction of a flight of cranes passing overhead to center his focus, and remained calm as he wrote about them, too. It was as if the castle never existed for him.

As the travelers passed through a stand of ash and oak, Alexander saw small puffs of blue flame emerge from the ground, and the smell of rotting egg effused the air with a sulphurous fume.

The horses balked and tried to outrun it. Rather than try to keep them in check their riders let them have their heads, and the travelers gained more ground toward their destination in short order. When the caravan had gone well beyond the edge of the canyon forest and approached the open valley, the horses were reined in again and fell back to a slow walk, snorting and worrying at their bits.

The hills here were brittle and rockslides cluttered the pass road with boulders, forcing the travelers to clear the smaller rocks and find a narrow clearance past the larger ones. But finally Kuryan was forced to call a halt when their way was blocked by a giant boulder which sat in the middle of the road. To the left flowed a narrow mountain stream strewn with the same kind of rock, where the water flowed over the edge into the steep fall of the canyon, and to the right was a forested wall of more rock leading upwards. There was nothing they could do now but move the boulder aside to make room for the wagons to pass.

Alexander dismounted and joined the tall Romanian as he stood staring at the rock. He dismissed the odd suspicion growing in his mind that it had been placed there deliberately, for that would suggest planning, but there was no real evidence of that. He studied the roadblock carefully, assessing its virtues. It was about sixteen hands high and almost as many wide, made of limestone streaked with black virgin soil. "The whole group of us could dislodge it if we work together," he suggested.

"That is not what worries me," Kuryan replied. "I am concerned that we will still be here when night falls, and all manner of dangers emerge from the darkness. My comrades are not as experienced with the night as I am, and there is a belief among the peasants that those who linger in the pass and the vicinity of the castle are in grave danger from its master. Little did I realize that I had more to fear than the others, if my own example is the proof."

Alexander turned and caught the red ball of fire hovering just above the far line of the ridge, and blinked as he turned away. "We will face the night together," he assured Kuryan, placed a long fingered hand on his shoulder and patted it. Ostap's response was a slight smile of brave hope.

When the sun had long burned down behind the hills, the travelers gathered closer to their campfires, and as the sky darkened to violet, Alexander saw a cloud of winged creatures emerge from the mountain caves and take to the air, then disperse to go about their nightly task of hunting for insects and small fauna. He knew that bats were mostly innocuous, and much maligned as agents of the devil. But if not for the flying mice the planet would be hip deep in flying and crawling things. He watched them flap and flit about in an erratic pattern which was not erratic at all. For all their swiftness, none of the animals ever collided with each other, nor with any other objects in their path.

"They are on the hunt," Lucien remarked as he appeared by his side. "Sometimes I wish I was one of them."

"You would prefer to be a bat?" Alexander asked, amused.

Lucien chuckled quietly. "The night is ever their companion, and they sleep safe and secure in the darkness of their caves during the day, snuggling together in warm familiar bliss."

"I cannot picture you as a bat," he replied. "You strike me more as... a dragon. All fire and precocious wit, but gentle and wise as well."

At that, Lucien actually laughed. "If it pleases you, I will accept that as a compliment."

They fell silent when Ostap Kuryan approached them, almost at a run. "My lords, we have a problem," he said. "One of our women is missing from the camp. I sent two of my men to look for her but they have not come back."

"How long ago?" Lucien asked.

"Not long, a little time after the sun set. I told everyone not to go into the woods alone, but it was as if she has vanished like a ghost. I do not think she would have gone far, and she is one to fear the dark more than the others."

Lucien and Alexander exchanged a quiet glance of alarm. "Stay here and gather your people together. Make sure that all are accounted for. We will look for them ourselves," Lucien said. "Wait here, Alexander. I must tell Sarasvati where I am going."

So saying, he went inside the wagon, then returned armed and ready for battle. "Let us hurry, and with luck we will find them all safe."

Kuryan started to follow them, but Lucien told him to stay behind. "Your people will need your protection, for I cannot predict what will happen. Stay and arm yourselves against any assault which comes your way. And watch for the wolves. Here in the Borgo they have no fear of men. These wolves will be different, and act as one, an army of darkness commanded by their master. You know of whom I speak."

Kuryan drew his own sword, and said, "aye. And I will be ready to receive them with teeth of mine own."

Alexander and Lucien ventured up the wooded hill in the direction Ostap indicated. They soon found themselves in pitch dark, and as a full moon came up above the ridge the sound of howling surrounded them. Lucien's sparkling grey eyes grew red in the dark, and he said softly, "they are on the prowl. Watch for them, that they do not catch you by surprise."

Alexander's eyes switched to night vision, and he could see small patches of body heat and the glowing red eyes of the wolves moving among the dark trunks of the trees some yards away. They appeared to be following him and his father but kept their distance.

"They are tracking us," he said.

"They may only be curious. Our scent is less attractive to them than a human's. But I dare not think what they will do if they find our lost sheep. This pack could take them with little difficulty, no matter how well armed they are."

Alexander looked around with deliberate care. "I do not see them," he said. Then a sudden thought came to him from within his blood. "Was Ostap lying?"

Lucien came to a complete halt, and appeared to be listening to something else. "No. I would have easily divined that from his thoughts. But I sense..." His voice trailed off, and his face seemed to grow dark with anger in the gloom.

Alexander followed his gaze and could see nothing at first but the glowing lives of insects flitting about among the trees and the wolves lurking nearby. Then he saw something darker than night standing a short distance away, holding something glowing in its arms. "There," he breathed, then bounded forward toward it without thinking, drawing his cutlass.

"No, wait, Alexander. It is too dangerous," Lucien called softly.

But Alexander was focused solely on catching the villain, committed to battle. He found a tall replica of his father drinking deeply from the woman, and he could hear her heartbeat growing weaker with every second. "*Release her at once, you vile demon!*" he exclaimed.

The demon raised his head, startled, then smiled with lips and fangs rimmed with blood. His face was pale as a sheet against the fall of his dark hair, and his eyes were red fire. "As you wish," he replied, then let the unconscious woman fall. He licked his lips clean with a long pointed tongue as he turned to face his challenger. The fire in his eyes damped into pools of amber and gold. "So, I meet the hellspawn of my brother face to face at last," he continued. "I have waited a long time for this moment."

"You have much to answer for, uncle," Alexander snarled. "I will give you the same pity you gave my mother, for you deserve none. Come. My blade is thirsty for your blood."

Julian stared at him, then threw his head back and laughed. "You think you can take me, boy? I who destroyed the sultan's army and drove them back to the sea?"

As he spoke his hand went for the grip of his sword. The weapon came out of the scabbard in a flash, and before Alexander could dodge it or strike it aside the steel point nicked his cheek. He jerked back quickly and felt at the cut. His gloved fingers came away bloody, and for a moment was stunned by the sight of it and did not see the sharp blade slashing at his throat.

Then the ringing sound of steel on steel brought him back to sudden awareness as Lucien's blade blocked it and turned it away. Julian flinched and fell back, narrowly avoiding decapitation as Lucien followed through. Lucien snarled softly, "you did not do it alone, brother. If you injure him, you will answer to me. Stay back, Alexander. He is mine."

Alexander stood away quickly, but kept himself ready. He gripped his sword loosely, watching Julian's every move like a hawk as he circled, ready to strike. The monster smiled with complete contempt and wicked defiance. "This is hardly the brotherly greeting I expected, Lucienantellus. What can you accomplish with your blade that I did not teach you?"

"Get used to disappointment," his brother responded with equal defiance. "Come. If it is a fight you want you will have it from me."

"You cannot defeat me, for we are equally matched. Every hurt you give me will turn back upon you," he said.

Lucien put the point of his sword against his own throat and replied, "let us put that to the test, shall we?"

The wicked smile fell for an instant, the eyes narrowed, and Julian backed away slowly. "Well played, my brother," he said. "But I will have justice in the end, and you will repay your debt to me in full."

"You are a strange one to speak of justice," Lucien replied. "I owe you nothing for that which you caused yourself. You are my brother no longer, and I am well rid of you for it. Be gone from my sight, or I will do what I should have done long ago!"

The mirror image frowned, then gave out a vicious snarl of demonic anger and seemed to vanish into the darkness like a zephyr of smoke. The wolves left off from patroling the perimeter and loped off into the dark without pause, leaving the night silent and still.

Alexander's battle tension receded like a cold winter's tide and left him trembling in its wake, and the pace of his heart slowed to something more normal. He released pent up breath, then said, "my thanks, father. In another second he would have had me."

"I told you he would never allow you to gain the advantage," Lucien said. "Now, things are worse. He has seen you, and would add you to his list of enemies now that you have challenged him."

"I care not what he thinks of me, so it is of no concern," Alexander replied with a firm and certain tone as he resheathed his blade, then bent to examine the woman. "She is a pretty young thing," he observed.

"Hmmph. Just the sort of prey Julian prefers," Lucien replied with marked distaste.

Alexander picked her up and healed her wounds, careful not to wake her. "She has lost a great deal of blood," he said finally. "We stopped him before he could take it all. She will have to be cared for, or she will succumb." He looked toward the two men, who were unconscious, and noted that their pistols rested untouched among the leaves littering the ground. "He subdued them even before they had a chance to defend themselves," he said.

Lucien replied, "come. Return with her to the camp and keep a careful watch over Sarasvati for me, eh? and I will bring these men back myself."

"By your command, father." With that, Alexander carried his charge carefully through the dark down toward the warm glow of the campfire just beyond the trees.

71

When he arrived, the girl's mother came forward and confronted Alexander with a look of panic on her face. "Dear God. What has happened?" she asked, crossing herself.

"She is safe now," Alexander replied. "She was wounded, and bled much. She must have rest and sleep. Have you any beef, or fruit, that she may eat of it and strengthen her blood?"

The woman nodded, then led the way to her tent, where Alexander laid the victim carefully down on a blanket and drew another over her. "Watch over her," he advised her mother, "and when she wakes, feed her as much as you can. Give her no wine but water only, which has been boiled to purify it."

"I will, my lord," the woman replied. "And I will pray for your soul. Thank you, and bless you for finding her."

"You are most welcome." He smiled gently, then turned away and joined Kuryan just as Lucien emerged from the dark bearing one of the guards slung over one shoulder.

"He will remain asleep until the dawn," Lucien said. "I will return with the other man soon." He laid the unconscious guard gently to the ground, then turned and walked swiftly up into the dark again.

"What happened?" Ostap Kuryan asked, with a puzzled expression.

"Your former master, having learned you were freed, tried to take revenge by feeding on one of your own," Alexander replied. "On the morrow we must remove the rock from the road and leave the pass or he will try again."

"We have men enough to defend ourselves, do we not?" Kuryan ventured. "Surely one man cannot take us all."

"You do not know him as well as I," Alexander said. "Make no mistake that he is more powerful alone than any army of men. Even I..." here he trailed off. "I have said too much."

"No, I would know your heart, my lord Count," Kuryan insisted. "Even when he had me in his sway, I did not know him. I would know him now, so that I may prepare for his attack."

"He is far older and more powerful than I am. My protection comes from my father, who is his equal in all things. I would gladly give my life for my father, for he is all I have in this world."

"No sisters?" Kuryan asked. "Nor brothers? Nor cousins? What about a lover?"

Alexander shook his head to each question. "All the women in my life are long dead, save for my stepmother and her infant child," he replied.

They broke off as Lucien approached with the second man, who favored his left leg. "His injury is not as bad as it looks," he remarked, as he helped the guard to sit on a log.

"My thanks for your aid," the guard said as he rubbed at his neck. "The demon was too strong for me. I fell and wrenched a muscle for my effort."

"I can give you an ointment which will warm the muscle and make it relax, so that you will experience no more than a mild discomfort," Lucien said. "Will you accept it?"

"Aye," the man said. "It is like horse linament, I'll wager."

"You are not far off the mark," Lucien replied. Then he went to the wagon and climbed inside.

"Pray, do not allow my father to know that I told you of myself," Alexander said to Ostap. "You are the first man I have confided to in a long time."

"I am honored that you shared it with me, as a friend would withal. I observe also that you have few friends to call your own."

"My travels have not allowed me the time to make them," Alexander replied. "Often I am forced to move on before such commerce is cemented in my life. I would not say that I am lonely, for I am not. But friendship becomes fleeting when coupled with distance and time."

"Aye. I know that all too well," Ostap said. :I am by necessity a solitary man myself. My life consists of soldiering for this or that warlord without allegiance to any one flag. My position on the council of nobles is merely provisional, for I have no lands or chattel of my own, no armies to command save for my personal retinue. My true kingdom is the open sky, and my bed the hard ground, and sometimes the bed of a woman," here he almost laughed, but his half smile fell quickly. "I ride from one boyar to another bearing messages, ransom demands, threats, and find value only in that I am trusted to silence, with faith only in the immunity a messenger enjoys between enemies."

"Do you regret your life as it is now?" Alexander asked.

Kuryan reflected for a moment, then laughed. "Nay. It is more life than I ever dreamed on. I now count myself blessed, for if not for the change I should have died long ago."

"You were but half-turned," he observed with a quiet nod.

"Aye, and I have not yet reconciled myself to the strange urges which course through my blood betimes. I thirst for blood without wanting it, I hunger for food without needing it. It is all a wonder to me. How do you live life this way?"

"I take each day as it comes," Alexander replied. "Though of late it has become more and more difficult to live as I am in the open. These are dangerous times."

"Then, when we are gone from here, I would know where you are going, so that I may visit one day on more civilised ground, and renew a bond I feel we share as blood brothers."

"I would be most honored, sir," Alexander replied. "But for caution's sake let us not speak of it further."

When Lucien returned with the ointment Kuryan watched with curiosity as the tall wraith went to his knees, removed the man's boot and rolled up his legging, then took a fingerful of the salve and rubbed it carefully on the twisted calf muscle, and began to massage it with earnest strokes. The man flinched and winced at first, but settled gradually and even began to relax.

When he had finished, Lucien restored the cap to the jar and clamped it closed with a device very much like a Mason jar. "I must keep the ointment hermetically sealed against contamination, or its potency would wither in the heat of the day," he explained.

"How does it feel?" Kuryan asked the injured man.

"It tingles," the man chuckled. "But the effect is pleasant. It grows warm on its own, and its scent is very like mint. Truly, a most excellent remedy. I feel as if I am on the mend already."

Kuryan's eyes lit up with epiphany, then said to Lucien, "Such a salve can have a more lucrative and beneficial value if it is dispensed in greater quantities to others. If you will allow me, I will act as your agent, and use my talent as a negotiator to obtain a modest sum from its sale to others. I can carry a small amount with me, and in my travels back and forth attempt to sell the benefit of it to the apothecaries I pass on my way, with a small sum retained for a commission. Would that be agreeable to you?"

Lucien paused and considered. "Truly, your proposal has merit. Let me think on it further, and we will discuss it after the evening meal."

After the others settled down for sleep, Kuryan and Alexander sat with Lucien and discussed their proposition. Lucien listened, and asked questions, and in the end agreed to the terms.

On two pieces of parchment, Lucien drew up the contract, and Alexander made a copy, which both men signed. Alexander then signed both copies as witness with a small flourish beneath. Lacking a notary to record the event, they rolled the parchments into small tubes and tied them closed with lengths of sinew, and then sealed the knots with candle wax.

Ostap Kuryan was now the proud owner of a small business of his own. "But, how is this wondrous ointment made?"

Lucien produced a worn scrap of vellum from his weskit pocket and said, "you must obtain these ingredients and mix them exactly as written, or they will not work together. I entrust you with the alchemy of it, and you may produce as much of the ointment as necessary to sell. But I charge you, sir, that you must not share it with anyone else, or you will find yourself in competition in short order."

"Agreed," Kuryan replied, "and I pledge to you that whatever income comes from the sale of the ointment will be invested and paid with a dividend. But, where shall I send it?"

Lucien replied, "I will send a letter to your home in Muramea explaining when and where, when we have found a place to settle."

"It is where I rest my head when I am not on the road, my lord Count." Ostap agreed. "I will await your word."

When Kuryan said his good nights and went to his tent, Lucien and Alexander faced each other in the dark. "All in all, a good end to a frightful day," Alexander said.

"And a profitable one," Lucien replied. "Now, let us stand guard and watch through the night. I would not trust that things are as they are until the dawn."

Alexander knew better than to question that, and said nothing, but took up his customary watch a short distance away and kept his mind focused on staying alert, while fighting a renewed bout of blood hunger.

72

The next morning, the travelers struck camp and prepared their wagons for the journey, then brought forth rope and shovels to dislodge the rock. All hands were critical to the effort and even the women took part, first to help dig around the rock and make a soil ramp sloping toward the edge of the road, then to place staves made from tree branches under its bulk to help lift it from its seat.

It proved more difficult than anyone expected, as the rock was unwieldy, solid and heavy, and stubbornly refused to budge.

Even when four of the mules were removed from their wagon traces, brought forward and harnessed to it with ropes, they could not dislodge it. The mules strained along with their human partners under the lash, and after a time gave up and refused to go.

The rock remained unmoved, dug in to stay seemingly out of spite. Ostap spat angrily and kicked at the rock. "This thing mocks us."

Alexander, too, was forced to admit defeat, and stood staring at it breathing heavily from his exertions as he drew the sweat from his brow. "It is an immovable object," he agreed. "It will take a force of far greater strength to remove it."

Lucien put his hands on his hips and stood staring at, then walked around the offending boulder inspecting it with care. Everyone watched him with mild apprehension. Then he said, "perhaps not. Ostap, how much musket powder did you bring with you?"

Kuryan replied, "two barrels, only enough to supply our muskets for a skirmish. Why do you ask?"

"It is possible we can blow this rock into smaller pieces, and in so doing make it easier to shift."

Kuryan's eyebrows crept upward, and he smiled. "Aye, I had not thought of that." He turned to one of his men and said, "go and fetch one."

"We dare not go on unarmed, my lord," the man replied. "We may need the powder later."

"That matters not. The risk is the same if we remain here, whether we use it or not," Kuryan replied.

The man summoned a couple of the other men to help him. When they returned with the barrel, they unsealed the lid and opened it. Lucien dipped into the black powder with his hand, brought up a small portion and watched how it sifted through his fingers. It was black and crumbly as coffee grounds. "Hmmm. Crude, but sufficient for our need. Cut me a length of wick, yea long," and he held his hands apart about a foot, "and I shall require a half yard of cloth."

While one of the men ran to get them, the others remained watching nearby, their curiosity now piqued. "A Chinese candle?" Kuryan ventured.

"Aye. A devilish invention, but eminently useful," he replied.

When the man returned with the items, everyone watched while the white haired wraith sat down and placed the cloth on the ground before him, then scooped a portion of the black powder in his hand and drew a line with it across the closest third, adding more until he was satisfied with the amount; then rolled the tube with an admixture of coarse gravel, adding the wick end as he did so. When he was done he took a length of sinew and tied the tube tightly at each end so that the powder and wick would not fall out. When he had finished he held up a good sized firecracker.

He stood up, went to the rock and inserted the tube sideways into a fissure which ran the length of the boulder, pushing hard to work it in. "This is the rock's weakest point," he said. "It will cleave most easily here, if it is brittle enough. Now. Everyone must be a safe distance away."

Kuryan yelled, "to the trees, all of you!"

There was a quick retreat to shelter, the animals with them, and when everyone was gone, Lucien drew a flint from his pocket and struck a spark to the wick. When the cotton caught and began to smolder he retreated to join Alexander and Kuryan behind the trunk of an oak tree, to watch the wick burn down to the tube.

There was a violent puff of smoke and a cracking sound as the powder ignited and exploded. The concussion shockwave pushed at the ground beneath the rock. A flock of sparrows took wing and scattered up into the trees near the top of the peak. The sound echoed and rebounded off the hillsides like thunder, and for a long moment no one moved as it faded to silence and the sulfurous smoke cleared away to the west.

Slowly, everyone emerged from hiding and ventured closer to the boulder. It was marked with more black streaks where the powder ingrained itself, and the fissure was much wider now, but the rock appeared intact.

Lucien went to it and peered at the result. Then he slammed the palm of his hand hard against it, and the rock cracked apart violently.

A cheer went up around him, and Lucien stepped back to watch while the small crowd descended on the pieces to haul them aside. The largest pieces went into the ravine, while the smaller ones were used for target practice at skipping stones by some of the younger men, going into the stream as they bounced. The road was cleared of stones and made smooth again, and after another hour's rest the group assembled, prepared the wagons and resumed their journey, leaving the pass and its ruined castle behind.

73

At sundown the caravan entered a walled compound surrounded by fields of crops. Muramea was a small settlement of about two dozen large houses and outhouses arranged around a large central courtyard, at the center of which stood a statue of a soldier on horseback overlooking a fountain. There was a small marketplace set up to one side, where the people there gathered around the travelers to greet friends and loved ones as they entered the gate.

As Alexander rode by the statue he noted the mastery of the artist at capturing his subject in bronze, saw the soldier's face and was startled at how closely it resembled his uncle's; with a long moustache and windswept hair down to his shoulder blades, falling out from under a cap with a feather sticking up from the front of its crown. The figure wore clothes and armor cut with princely elegance, and one gloved hand raised a scimitar in the air. The horse was caught in mid-gallop about to leap from its granite base.

He dismounted and stood looking up at it with wonder and admiration, while Lucien rolled the wagon into the courtyard and brought the tired horses to a halt.

Ostap joined them when they dismounted, and said, "you are most welcome to bide with us for the evening, and we will journey on together in the morning," he offered. "My father is hospitable to many travelers who pass by on their way to Bistritza, and well prepared to receive them at all times. And he is a skilled cook of pastries beside."

"By the way you spoke earlier, I had the impression you were an orphan," Alexander said.

"My father adopted me when I was a mere babe, but he has ever been like my own, with more love for me than the woman who abandoned me on his doorstep."

Kuryan perked up when the door to one of the larger houses opened, and a stout middle aged man emerged. He was heavy set, with a bald head and a white handlebar moustache, wearing a leather apron smeared with what looked like bread dough over his clothes.

He smiled with recognition and came forward with his arms held open. "Ostap, as I live and breathe, you are a blessed sight for sore eyes," he declared. "It seems an age since you left us, yet here you are again. Welcome home."

Ostap took him in his arms, hugging him tight and ignoring the stains. "Father, it is good to be home."

The older Kuryan released him and looked to Lucien and Alexander. To his credit he did not even blink at their strangeness. "And I see you have made some more friends, eh?"

"Yes, father," Kuryan replied. "May I present to you Count Lucien Arkanon, and his son Alexander Corvina, both noble men of good character. Gentlemen, this is Giorgiu Kuryan, a boyar of the Bucovina, master of Muramea and the head of our clan."

"You are most welcome to stay with us," Giorgiu told them. "I hunger for news of Kyiv and the outside world. Please, do come inside. I will bid the servants wait upon you, and you shall want for nothing." Then he turned away and went back inside the house.

Ostap turned to Alexander and Lucien. "My father knows not the truth of my condition. Will you keep my secret?"

"We are all discretion," Lucien assured him. Then he jumped from his seat on the wagon and went around to the door, opened it and beckoned to Sarasvati. "Come out now, my wife, and bring Parvati with you."

Sarasvati emerged slowly with Parvati in her arms, and looked around at the houses. Parvati squealed and yawned at the same time, then put her head on her mother's shoulder, threw an arm around her neck and closed her eyes. Alexander observed that it seemed a good sign that she should remain so calm in a strange place.

"Parvati was very good and quiet," Sarasvati said. "I do not see how she could sleep the day through with all that noise, when I could not find a wink of it." She kissed the baby's cheek. "Now she is tired, poor little thing, and after a journey of a thousand leagues I feel as if I have traveled to the Moon."

"Both of you will find ample comfort and rest this night, my lady, for this is a good household, and well guarded. Here, you have nothing to fear," Ostap said.

"I have no doubt of it," she replied with a shy smile.

Ostap led them into the house. It was large but sparsely furnished; made of whitewashed stone and brick in the Romanesque style with an Oriental twist in the porticos and windows. The living parlor was large, designed like the lobby of a good-sized hotel. The windows were open to admit the light and the warm evening air. Flourishes of painted motifs: flowers and crosses, moons and stars, adorned the wood surfaces; and were prominent in the heavy embroidery on the upholstered furniture. Yet, all had the appearance of luxury fallen on harder times.

Alexander could not help but notice the garlands of garlic bulbs and sprigs of wolfbane adorning every door and window, as if they could keep out the demons and other unsavory things inhabiting the fevered imaginations of the humans living there. But he knew that it was all for nothing in the face of reality.

"The council of boyars once met within these walls, but when the Turks took over Bistritza for a time, meetings were no longer possible," Ostap explained. "Now we keep it as the living quarters, and our old house now serves as a stable for the cattle."

"What of the statue in the courtyard?" Alexander asked.

"Ah. That is prince Vlad Tsepesh Dracula, he who was the savior of our land," Kuryan explained. "A truer and braver man was never born. It is said that he turned away Mehmed and his army singlehanded, and helped Matthias Corvinus drive them back to the sea. Yet it was all for nought. The Turk returned in time and wiped away the past."

Alexander and Lucien exchanged careful glances as sudden understanding surfaced between them. That explained Ostap's long, lean frame, his pale skin, his intense almond shaped dark eyes, the long fine brown hair. He was descended from the son of the dragon himself, a bastard with royal blood, and he did not know it. No wonder he was taken over so easily by Julianus, as mere kinship by blood was enough to link blood to blood.

Alexander kept this observation to himself thinking that the truth would never give Kuryan a measure of comfort. No. Better to keep mum and let him go on believing in the legend. The man interred in that grave was most likely a stranger, as Lucien had told him that the prince's poor bloodless body was buried with the rest of his men the day that Julianus took his life.

"My father said he was a distant cousin," Ostap continued. "When his brother Radu and his allies murdered Vlad, my grandfather took his body from Brasov in secret and brought it here. He now lies buried beneath the statue, so that no one can disturb his rest or loot his bones. My grandfather left animal bones in their place to preserve the deception."

Lucien said with a cautious tone, "then you are kindred with us, for we are descended Draculesti ourselves."

Ostap's face took on a strange, wondering expression. "You are sons of the dragon also?" he asked. "Then it was fortuitous our meeting, for you appear the very image of the statue, save for the moustache." He turned and gazed out the open door at it. "I had long admired him since I was a boy. It is said he was a cruel man but he had to be, given his circumstances. Such a dark period could not any other man endure. The loss of his father, his uncles. Betrayed by his own brother and the Turkish devils who held his leash."

Alexander looked to Lucien, who merely gave him a warning glance to stay quiet. But if Ostap noticed he gave no sign. "An orphan like me, yes?" Ostap continued. "Still, I am proud to be of his family, for my small part."

"The past is a thing of the past," Lucien said. "You have an opportunity to forge your own destiny without the aid of his name and legend. As the Turk still longs for empire, you may yet be given the chance to make of yourself a hero like him."

Ostap's adopted father returned to them rubbing his hands together. "Come. I have prepared rooms for you on the second floor, with a grand view of the valley. You will stay with us in comfort for as long as you wish. My house is yours."

Lucien gave the living room a long appraising glance. "Tell me. Have you given thought to turning this place into a true hostel for travelers?"

Giorgiu looked around at the expanse and said, "it has ever been on my mind, but the Turk lingering close by makes such decisions difficult. One day, when the air is not so befouled with their stench, I may just do that."

He led the group up the stairs to a long corridor and to an apartment with a small living parlor. The rooms, like the lobby below, were sparsely furnished. The walls appeared to be newly whitewashed, and the windows were tightly closed. Giorgiu went to one of them and threw open the shutters to banish the smell of must. "These have been closed for a long time," he said. "The wind blows from the east, so the rooms will air out soon. We will leave you now to start dinner. Come, Ostap."

He led the way out, and Ostap obediently followed him.

Lucien threw an appraising look around the room as he stripped off his gloves, then unbuttoned his overcoat and drew it off. He actually looked tired, for all his immortality, as if the last few miles had sapped him of his strength. He said, "it is a good start to the next leg of our journey, but I will not feel better until we are well away from here."

"What is our haste?" Sarasvati asked as she let Parvati sit on the couch and gave her the bear to play with. She sat down next to the toddler and stroked at her dark hair as she looked around. "Are we not safe here?"

"We are in the midst of all hospitality and comfort, but also closest to the greatest danger of all," he explained. "My brother is not above striking back for the challenge we gave him last evening."

Alexander said, "he would not dare attack us here, would he?"

"I know well the nature of my brother's obsession, and I would not understimate him. The only thing which would prevent his acting now is the blood bond we share. I dare not put Sarasvati in further peril by remaining in the shadow of the eagle's nest."

"I refuse to be the sole source of your concern," Sarasvati declared with confidence. "There is a limit to his power, is there not?"

Lucien turned to her with a gentle smile. "You speak truth, my wife. But you are in danger as long as he has his eye on hurting me."

"And what of Parvati?" she asked. "What would he do to her?"

"He cares not for her. She would only suffer more if you were harmed. No, I would not..." As he spoke, Lucien's fingers went to his forehead, and he swayed on his feet as if he would faint. Alexander rushed to his side and tried to steady him before he fell. But Lucien straightened again and pushed him away gently as he declared, "no need to be concerned. I have not fed... is all..."

She added, "he has deprived himself of nourishment to avoid taxing me. The animal blood has not been enough."

Alexander remembered that he promised not to talk about the wound Lucien received in Kyiv, so he did not mention it.

Lucien sank down on the couch next to her. "The mere presence of my brother's dark energy has drained me of my own. I must have human blood to banish this weakness, but I dare not take it from the source of my caring. She must have all her strength to withstand this arduous journey."

Sarasvati moved to put her arm around his shoulders, and kissed his cheek. "You have been the source of all my courage and strength," she said. "You must take back a little of what you have given me. Alexander, will you excuse us, that we may have a little privacy?"

"With all speed, mother," Alexander replied quickly, and went into the adjoining room, closing the door as he did so. He found himself in a small spare room dominated by a four poster bed, with curtains of dark cloth tied back with cord. It appeared very welcoming just then, and as he slipped out of his outerwear and laid down upon it, the horrors of the last week crowded in upon him and broke apart his thoughts as he fell asleep.

74

When the stars came out in their thousands, Alexander woke at the sound of knocking. He rose and went to the door, and found Lucien standing outside. "Supper is ready, if you will join us," he said.

"Thank you, I will," he replied.

The dining room was not as spacious as the front room, and was full of cozy cheer as the guests and family seated themselves. A high chair was supplied for Parvati to sit in, placed next to Sarasvati, and a small bib was tied around her neck. Alexander observed that Sarasvati's shoulders were slumped and she looked tired, while Lucien looked hale and fit again.

There were three little boys sitting among their hosts. They all had dark hair and eyes like Ostap, but bore little resemblence among them. At first he wondered if the Kuryan household were composed entirely of orphans. Then he remembered that the Turks had an annoying habit of executing the men and boys in the villages, rather than risk letting them form an army to take back the territory. These boys must have run away to escape the pogrom, and Giorgiu had taken them into his care with a charitable spirit.

The roast pig on the table looked small, and so did the chickens, which appeared smothered in red paprika, onions and tomatoes. The nauseous aroma of cooked animal wafted on the air, and in these close quarters Alexander felt a bit queasy. But he determined to keep his composure as he always did, and managed well after a few moments of concentration and a few subtle breaths.

After Giorgiu said the customary prayer of thanks and all crossed themselves, then conversation fell to silence as they ate. Alexander took a loaf of bread and cut a slice of it, then sat chewing slowly while he watched Ostap Kuryan feasting hungrily as if he had never eaten before. He envied Kuryan's appetite, and forced himself finally to cut a chicken's wing from its body to taste it.

The bird's flesh was like ash, bland and unappealing, but he caught a taste of the paprika, salt and garlic, and was satisfied with that. He finished the wing, set the bones on his plate and sat to let his stomach savor it. It rumbled a bit, but did not reject the compound.

Encouraged by this, he next sampled a small boiled onion, and managed to keep that down as well. He convinced himself that if he could eat slowly and wait between bites he could finish a full meal. But it would never fully replace the salty sweet warmth and the tingling power of the liquid protein he needed to survive.

When the meal ended, and the servants came to clear away the remains, Giorgiu produced a small pipe and filled its cup with tobacco, then lit the cup and sat puffing away for a few moments. Then he told the boys, "and now that you have eaten, it is time for bed."

"Yes, papa," the boys said in tandem, climbed down from their chairs and ran from the room. Then Giorgiu's wife, who had not said a word through supper, said, "I am tired, Gio. I think I will go to bed as well."

"By all means," he said with a smile. "I will be up soon."

She smiled at everyone, gave a short curtsy and then deserted the room as if the devil was after her.

Giorgiu's face was all serious concern when he turned to Lucien. "Now that we are alone, I would ask what you plan to do, that I may give you protection on the road. Ostap acquainted me with your meeting, and did vouch for your reputations as men of peace. Your lady as well."

"Ostap has pledged to accompany us as far as Bistritza," Lucien replied. "He has been most hospitable."

"Is this true, Ostap?" he asked.

"Aye, father," Kuryan replied. "I did offer my protection to them for saving Count Arkelin's son from death most certain. His father charged me with their care."

The older man grunted, then puffed silently before he asked, "Where do you plan to go once you reach Bistritza?"

"We are traveling to the west," Lucien replied. "We had a mind to enter France, there to settle and make new lives for ourselves."

"I have it from others that the Turks are camped some miles to the west, near Klausenburg. Once you leave Bistritza you will no longer have our protection. Who are your friends, that we may notify them you are coming?"

Lucien and Alexander exchanged careful glances. Then Lucien said, "My lord Kuryan, there is no one to meet, as it has been a long time passing that we have been there, and our family is scattered and few. We had managed to get to the Ukraina on our wits alone, and occasionally by the kindness of those we met on the road."

"Aye. By the appearance of your wagon, you disguise yourselves to be gypsies," Giorgiu replied, and did not bat an eyelash. "This is understandable. But I doubt your disguise will serve you beyond the forest. I must warn you that Transylvania has been annexed by Hungary, so the Saxons have become many more than were there before, and they are no friends of ours. Once you enter the dark wood you will be defenseless, and I have heard there are other unsavory elements which inhabit it."

He puffed a bit more, then tamped the pipe ash into his tray before continuing. "The Turks have taken much of the southern part of Wallachia and Transylvania, and parts of the Danube valley south of Buda. Between them and the Austrians, you would have no chance to reach France in safety. There would be no protection for your lady and her child, for the Turk take their captives for slaves or not at all."

"What do you suggest we do, then?" Sarasvati asked. "We cannot travel naked." Parvati squealed in agreement, displaying a single tooth amid the fangs.

At this Ostap and the boyar smiled. "Granted, that is not an option, my lady," Giorgiu replied. Then his eyes lit up as he had an idea. "You must dress as nobles, and obtain such men at arms as can be trusted," he said to Lucien. "You may yet pass through Hungary as far as Budapesth without challenge. But beyond that point you will need letters which will identify you and your family, and such bona fides as will allow you to travel without question."

"Indeed?" Lucien said. "What other barriers may we face?"

"I have it from a man of the cloth who passed through here but a month ago that the people of the Holy Roman Empire are even more suspicious than the Austrians, and that even he was regarded as suspect until he could produce his papers of passage. You must obtain these also. Speak to the burgomeister in Bistritza, and he will furnish you with them."

"Sage advice, indeed," Lucien said with a small nod of deference. "Our capacity, however, lies only with the clothes on our backs and a few others set aside for special occasions."

"Then come with me and I will show you some things you may use to disguise yourselves." He rose from his chair and waited for Sarasvati to pick Parvati up, then led them all from the room.

The group went up the stairs into a different part of the house, then up another set of stairs into an attic, where Giorgiu and Ostap brought forward a large trunk from the corner. When he threw the lid open the trunk revealed a pile of assorted clothing, all a few years out of date but looking clean and almost new as the day they were made.

Giorgiu said, "these were left behind by our last visitors some time ago, who were so frighted by the Turk regiment passing by that they departed with all haste. They never returned for them, so I presume they may have been caught or killed."

Then he went to another trunk and opened it. It was full of hats and cloaks. One hat in particular caught Alexander's notice. It was dark suede with a curled brim, set with a single pheasant feather, and the cloak lying beneath it was dark blue. "What was the name of the gentleman who wore these?" Alexander asked.

Giorgiu took a moment to think, then said, "he was English. I think his name was... what was it? Duggens. Jan Henrik Duggens."

Small world indeed. Apparently Duggens and his party never made it back to England. "I met him in Manchuria," Alexander said to Lucien. "You remember I told you of the gentleman who did kindly allow me to join his party. They were going into the west. He said he was a trading representative for his majesty King Charles."

"How long ago was this?" Giorgiu asked.

"Almost two years has it been since I left his side," Alexander replied. "And you say he was here? How long ago?"

"About a month, as the days go. But, I have heard that Charles is no longer King of England," Giorgiu said. "The monk did say to me that a man named Cromwell has disbanded the royal family and rules with a council of nobles like we do here. I think he called it 'parliament'. But your friend must have been caught by the Turks, else why leave all these fine things here?"

Alexander paused a moment to reflect with a touch of sadness, then said, "then I will honor his ghost, sir, and wear his livery as my own."

"Did the monk impart anything else?" Lucien asked.

"Nothing of any true importance," Giorgiu replied. "He was already dotty with old age as it was, and told me only what was important to him."

He went to another chest and opened it, revealing that it was filled with arms. He picked up a flintlock rifle, examined the barrel and the powder magazine. "It needs a bit of cleaning, but will fire true," he said, handing it to Alexander. "I will obtain fresh flints and powder for you, for a musket is nothing without the shot, eh?"

"We are most grateful for your kindness," Lucien said, as he removed a dark waistcoat with a wine colored trim from the trunk and examined it. "These are far more than adequate for our needs."

"Please. Take them off my hands," Giorgiu implored him. "I have no use for them, being as I am a homebody, with nowhere else to go but the village."

There was another box opened which contained a lady's garments. "They belonged to a Russian lady who traveled with Duggens," the boyar said. "You met her?"

"Nay," Alexander said. "But I did hear him speak of Russia, so it may be he met her there. Beyond that, his life was a mystery."

While Lucien and Alexander engaged themselves with gathering ensembles, Sarasvati and Parvati fell to sorting among the feminine things, and it turned into a happy time of trying things on. A bustier puzzled them, and so did the wide petticoats of the day. "I can scarcely imagine what to do with these," Sarasvati said. "What are they for?"

Lucien smiled gently at her. "We will find out together later, my sweet," he said, even as he fingered carefully at a hole he found in an embroidered silk weskit.

When the trunks were safely removed to their rooms, and Sarasvati and Parvati retired to sleep, Alexander and Lucien held a quiet war council. "We must exercise all caution of what we say in the presence of our hosts," Lucien said. "The owners of those clothes did meet with tragedy when they were here."

"What evidence have you?" Alexander asked.

"I did find a ball hole in a jerkin, made recently by the look of the powder burns. There was also a modicum of blood left in a stain and it smelled almost fresh. Mayhaps Giorgiu Kuryan is not as honest as he appears. Your friend Duggens' party was set upon here or close by. Or perhaps Kuryan gave them up to save the village."

"But, you cannot know that for certain, from a hole, from a bloodstain alone," Alexander protested. "Perhaps he did meet with a scouting party, and those are the remains of that day. And our host could have seen all and recovered what he could when they left."

"Aye. That may be so, but these are dangerous times and we cannot afford trust even among friends from this moment on. We will take Ostap with us as far as Bistritza, but after that we must go on alone. For the present, keep a weather eye open for any strangeness in the household, and your arms close about you. Complacency or innocence could be our undoing."

"Father, what about the boyar's advice, of dressing as nobility?" Alexander asked. "I saw no deceit in that. It sounded quite sensible, as we would be afforded more courtesy for the value of our coin."

"In the city, perhaps. In the countryside, perhaps not. We will do so only when we are in Ostap's company, then return to our own traveling clothes afterward. We will keep those things for later if and when we have need of them."

Alexander remembered the money in the wagon, and said, "I will inspect the wagon when all are asleep and make sure there is no disturbance therein."

"Good. Meanwhile, I will return to my room and protect our women, that they suspect no danger, and so remain safe and happy."

At that, Alexander smiled. "Parvati?"

"She is rapidly growing into a miniature version of her mother," Lucien chuckled. "I dare say she will be a heartbreaker when she enters her womanhood. She has already captured my heart."

Alexander's smile fell. "It is a pity that Charanditha did not survive, nor Ruthinda. They were treasured friends, who left us too soon."

Lucien placed his hand on his shoulder, then said, "I know that you miss Charanditha most of all, but if we honor their memory they will remain with us, and when Parvati is older I will tell her about them. Now, I must return to Sarasvati and make sure she is comfortable."

75

After Lucien left his bedchamber, Alexander laid back on the thin bedspread and looked up into the darkness of the colorful ceiling above, trying to put the events of the day behind him. Then he glanced out the window. Through the clouded glass panes he could see the lights going out all over the compound but for those placed along the high wall.

A bonfire had been built near the statue in the center of the courtyard, and the flames lit the bronze from behind, throwing the dark silhouette into sharp relief. He did not dare dwell on it too long for safety's sake, and pulled the curtain closed to shut out the sight.

When silence descended over the household, he rose and left his room, ventured quietly down the stairs and out a side door. From there he went to the stable and wagon garage, where he found the trusty old vehicle sitting among the others. He inspected the surface of the painted wood and found it growing rough with age, and realized that it had been a good and steady companion; enduring sun, wind and rain with stoic grace through almost two years of travel.

He climbed inside the small space and inspected the interior, and was satisfied that all remained intact and undisturbed. He removed the carpeting and took up the floorboard where Charanditha had hidden her funds. The bag was still there. Letting out a sigh of relief, he put everything back and exited quickly, took a careful look around to make sure no one had seen him, then returned to his room.

The next morning, the sky threatened rain as the Arkanons left the compound and began their journey toward Bistriţa. Ostap Kuryan and a small band of his men at arms led the way, accompanied by a mule-drawn wagon carrying supplies and goods for trading in the city, while Alexander drove the little wagon and Lucien brought up the rear.

The valley was mostly patches of farmland situated among other patches of forest, denuded in places by the need for wood, of which all that were left were a grove of mossy stumps surrounded by clover. Fields and villages lining the road were dark spots of ruin grown over with weeds where Dracula had pursued his campaign against the Turks with his scorched earth policy. And the open nature of the countryside afforded little concealment for marauders; so if there were any Turks here, they must have left the area some time ago. There was no sign of their camps anywhere in sight.

Gradually, Alexander dropped his guard and relaxed into listening to the gentle rhythm of his horse's hoofbeats on the muddy road, the twittering of birds in the thickets, and the tinkling sound of the traces.

By midafternoon they came to a crossroad, where a picturesque cluster of houses, church steeples and a fortified wall lay just ahead. The city gate was opened, and a prosperous marketplace could be seen bustling with activity within. In the clouded sunshine, the town looked peaceful, and the presence of children playing on the road lent credibility to the illusion of security.

"Thank God," Ostap remarked with a sigh. "Bistritza is safe. I had thought that Mohammed's forces had taken it, too. But Bistritza has little to offer. Or perhaps the Turk stays to the south, where there is more aglitter to attract his ravenous eye."

Alexander replied quietly. "I will not assume safety until I have had a chance to inspect the conditions here."

"Aye, your caution is as mine," Kuryan agreed.

The caravan passed into the city and was an instant attraction to the people seated in the shade of open air cafes, who abandoned their tea and pastries to follow the riders and wagons as far as the central plaza. There, Alexander and Ostap dismounted and waited for the others to catch up, and stood looking around at the buildings with amazement.

None of them had suffered the damage the Turks left behind in other cities. In fact, they were in almost pristine condition, freshly whitewashed and decorated with colorful motifs, and the flowers growing in pots on the wrought iron balconies looked to be thriving and in full bloom.

When the wagon arrived, Sarasvati climbed down from the driving platform with Parvati in her arms and stood looking around at the houses. "Oh, the city is quite beautiful," she said. "Look at all the flowers. Are we staying long?"

"That all depends on what father has to say," Alexander replied. "We will discuss it later. But for now we should determine the lay of the land."

Ostap started to say something, but was cut off when a male voice behind them called, "is that you, Ostap Kuryan?"

A prosperous looking short middle aged man pushed his way through the small crowd of gawkers and approached. Ostap's face seemed to light up with delight, and he opened his arms with a hearty laugh to take the older man into his arms. "Grigori Brunwald, as I live and breathe," he declared. "I thought you were dead."

The older man clapped the younger man on the back and replied, "so did I! But those Turkish devils could not get me." Then his expressive brown eyes grew wider. "But, what are you doing here? Has something happened? How fares your father?"

"My father is safe and well. I am furnishing an escort for my new friends." He turned to Alexander and said, "Count Alexander Corvina, may I present boyar Grigori Brunwald. He is burgomeister of Bristritza and a good friend."

Brunwald looked Alexander up and down, sniffed closely, then drew back with an expression of puzzlement. "Corvina. Descended from Matthias Corvinus?"

"A cousin," Alexander replied cautiously with a small bow. "I am Draculesti, for my part. We are from Transylvania."

"Ah. Your ancestor is famous among us, almost a legend. We all know the tale of his courage at helping Matthias to drive the Turk back to the sea. The Szekelers are treacherous people, easily swayed by gold, but you do not appear to be one of them."

"The Turks took Chisinao," Ostap said. "They must have taken the southern pass through Bacau."

"Aye, that they did," Brunwald replied. "But they missed us going toward Timisoara. We blacked out our lights, extinguished every candle, and stayed silent while they went by but a league south of the city. They never saw us that night, for the sky was dark with clouds and there was no moon." He concluded by chortling with glee.

Lucien approached on silent feet. "How fortunate," he said.

Upon seeing Lucien's tall gaunt figure Brunwald took a short step back, his eyes going wide again. Alexander took the lead and said, "Grigori Brunwald, may I present my father, Count Lucien Arkanon."

"Faith, is all your family this pale?" the burgomeister asked.

"It is... a family trait," Alexander explained.

Lucien added, "we are from the north. Our stronghold is in the mountains."

"Baia Mare?" Brunwald ventured.

"Aye. May I also present my wife, the Maharani Sarasvati Shankara Todar, of Kashmir."

Brunwald leaned forward with interest. "Kashmir? I have never heard of it."

"It is a land far to the southeast, beyond the Black Sea," Ostap supplied with a helpful tone. "I am told it is a part of India."

"Forgive me. I was only curious. Lady, you are most welcome among us," Brunwald said with a short bow. "We are ready to tend to your every need."

"My thanks for your welcome," she said with a gracious nod. "It is refreshing to know that our differences are celebrated here."

"We strive to honor the gospel of our Christ, that all men and women be treated with respect and honor no matter where they come from," Brunwald replied, crossing himself. Then he added with a cursory glance around him, "but let us not stand out here in the open. There is still a chance that Turk spies might be about."

Then he saw that the curious crowd had gathered around them. "Please, my friends," he said to them. "There is nothing here to concern yourselves with. Return to your own affairs and keep a careful watch, and let me tend to my guests."

The people obliged him by scattering again into clumps of curious and open speculation, while Brunwald told Ostap, "come. I will see that your animals are well situated. You and your friends may have the hospitality of my house. An inn is not a fit place to entertain noble guests, and there is a greater chance that the Turk has spies lodged therein as well. Please."

Then he made a welcoming gesture with his hands and led the way down the road, confident that they would follow.

As they walked, Alexander asked Ostap, "what was that about the Szekelers?"

"The story here is that Albert de Istenmezo, Viscount of the Szekelers, duped Matthias into turning against Dracula," Ostap replied. "Grigori is Hungarian, and his loyalty to the Corvinus family extends to his own. The Brunwalds have been here since twelve hundred threescore and five, and they pledged their fealty to Matthias when he became king."

"Ah. I see," Alexander said, and left it at that. He knew his curiosity could never be satisfied with rumor and conjecture.

"I must confess this is as new to me as to Alexander," Lucien remarked.

"It is said that the victors write the history, while the truth is often buried or left to legend," Brunwald replied. "Dracula was a cruel man, but fair. A man of justice, who was betrayed by his need to use whatever methods he could to remove the Turks from Wallachia and Transylvania. They say he was vilified by the papists and betrayed by his own brother Radu, who was in league with the Sultan. That he sought revenge for the murders of his father and uncles with singular cruelty. But, that is all in the past. Who knows what really happened two centuries ago?"

Lucien said, "I confess that I have been on the road for so long it would seem as if two centuries had passed me by." He glanced at Alexander and winked.

Recalling what the Turk soldiers had done to Charanditha and Ruthinda, Alexander said, "I know well the cruelty of the Turks, and now Mohammed would have the rest of the world, too?"

Brunwald replied, "there is some hope to be had. I heard from a group of traders from Russia that the Tsar is planning to send an army to repel the Turks before they take Kyiv. And a man from Budapesth told me that the Hapsburgs are ready to fortify the south against their army's advance into the marches. Not since Martinuzzi's victory has there been such a push to drive the invaders from our land. It gives me hope that the Turks will be defeated soon."

Sudden hope sprang into Alexander's heart. "These traders. Would one of them happen to be an Englishman?"

Brunwald frowned. "Why would an Englishman be traveling with Russians?"

"Why, indeed," Alexander replied. "He was most private in his affairs, but he must have had his reasons. When we were in Muramea the boyar Kuryan told me he had to flee, and that he was in their company with a Russian lady."

"Ah. These men were well known hereabouts, and there was no Englishman among them, or mayhaps he devised some way to travel with them incognito," Brunwald said. "Many people have left the country at one time or another and never returned. I would like to think that they found their way safely to their destination, but in these dark times there is no warranty for it. I suppose we will never know, will we?"

"I suppose not," he agreed.

"I have also heard tell of men robbed of their homes and livelihoods by the Turks, who have now taken to robbing good people of all they have to fortify a renegade army. They call themselves freedom fighters," the boyar said. "Those brigands care not for the lives or positions of others, nor share a charitable spirit between them. It is possible that your English friend may have encountered them and met with grievous calamity."

Alexander's thoughts grew dark. Lucien glanced at him and gave him a short nudge to convey his sympathy.

Brunwald stopped at the door to a large house at the end of the commons. It was not exactly palatial, but large enough to dominate most of the other houses lining the street. "Here we are," he said, and led the way in.

The interior was cozy and charming, furnished modestly with simple handcrafted wood, and the living parlor had a large fireplace which was not yet lit. "I will have the servants take your wagon around to the rear yard, and water and feed the horses." He clapped his hands and called out, "Hans, Fritz, come to me."

A pair of boys came running in from the back. They were both of Saxon stock, with light brownish blond hair and blue eyes, looking about 14 or 15 years of age. They were dressed simply, and their clothes lacked the heavy embroidery most of the people in town preferred. "You sent for us, master?" the elder boy said.

"Yes, Fritz," Brunwald said. "Go and fetch the wagon and horses outside and take it to the stable, and see that the horses are well fed and watered."

"At once, master," Fritz replied, and with a short bow to Alexander and the others, led his younger brother out the front door.

Brunwald sighed as he looked out and watched them work. "They are an unruly pair, and must be managed with an iron hand," he said. "But they are good and honest Christians, and good workers beside."

"They are Saxons," Lucien remarked. "How come they to be here, when Hungary is yet far to the west?"

"They ran away from home when the Turks overran their village," Brunwald replied, then gestured to the floor with his palm. "They were so high when I found them wandering alone on the road, and have sheltered them ever since for charity's sake. They walked many miles from where they lived, and told me that many villages had fallen. Nothing is left of them."

"A country of orphans," Kuryan remarked quietly with distaste. "Whenever will it end?"

"That, my friend, is up to God," the boyar said. "I have a feeling that he is not done with the lesson." Then he crossed himself, and led them up the stairs to the second floor.

As with all houses of that day, it was subdivided into large apartments for family and guests, while the lower floors were dedicated to receiving visitors, the servants' quarters and the kitchen. It was also common to see houses standing empty and unused for years until someone came to live in them, especially those surviving in the wake of the Turkish incursions. As Brunwald was not rich, most of the rooms would remain shut, with the doors sensibly locked tight to keep out vermin and drafts.

He led them a short way to a large door and opened it onto a spacious apartment boasting three bedrooms and a living parlor connecting them. "I hope this is acceptable," he said. "I will have the boys bring up whatever luggage you need, and afterward they will stoke up the fire in the grate."

Lucien took a cursory glance around, then replied, "It is more than adequate, my lord boyar. My compliments."

Brunwald bowed again. "I am most honored. And you, Ostap. I have a nice room across the hall. Come with me."

When the two men left, Sarasvati went into one of the bedrooms and looked at the bed, then at the tall windows letting in the afternoon sunshine. She went to one of them and looked out. "Truly, it is a magnificent view," she said. "Come and look."

Lucien and Alexander approached and looked out with her, and they had a panoramic view of the entire valley, where huge tracts of forest rose against the ridge of the Carpathians and spread out toward the horizon. There was also a charming view of the city and the road leading into the green woods and beyond.

"It is quite breathtaking," Lucien agreed. "I know the land well. There is but a march of a few days between here and Klausenburg. Then, we will enter Hungary and travel to Budapesth. It has been a long time since I was there, but it will be a different place now, transformed by time and war."

"Will we be welcome there, do you think?" she asked.

"I do not know," Lucien replied softly, musing.

"You sound as if we would not," she said.

He looked into her face as if he could see into her soul, and replied, "that is up to fate, my wife. But we will pass through each event with calm purpose just as we have always done. Yes?"

She smiled shyly. "Yes."

Behind her, Alexander fervently hoped she would be right.

"And now, I am sure you must be very tired after our long journey," Lucien said, in that melodic hypnotic voice. "You should rest. Choose our bedroom, and take Parvati there. I must speak to Alexander alone."

"As you wish, my husband," she replied, and left the room with Parvati's sleeping body in her arms.

Lucien turned and regarded Alexander's sober face before saying, "come. I know that look. You are the mirror to my thoughts."

Alexander nodded. "I have long ceased wondering at your observance of all things. Truly, my mind is transparent as glass to you. But I was not yet born when you were in Budapesth."

"It was years before then, when I and my brother often masqueraded as the same man so he could be in two places at once. He sent me to plead for men at arms and a small fund to help provision their needs, when we needed reinforcements to repel the Turk. But in a twist of cruel fate I was imprisoned by Hunyadi for the malfeasance he saw in Julianus."

His eye grew wider, as if he could see into the mists of history. "I spent several years there," he murmured, "and marked my time surrounded by iron and stone. Confined as I was, I think I went mad for lack of blood, and I spent most of my time trying to trap animals to feed myself. Some of the guards must have seen me, and it was that moment that the word 'vampire' was attached to our family name."

Alexander replied, "I often wondered. I read things, heard things. And I did not understand until I was already turned."

"Your blood held back much for your sake, Alexander," Lucien replied. "There was so much... conflict... between my obligation to family pride and honor, and my obligation to the dragon's blood. Julianus abused his rank and privileges simply because he could. It was then that I began to question my position as his mirror image, as his avatar, as his..." he paused to take a deep breath, then continued, "I was ripe for change. When your mother came into my life I was ready for it. I was born but a short time after Julianus but I had to capitulate to him as if I was born of a different mother. It was so ever since we were boys. I worshipped him, but I always lived in his shadow."

"And now?" Alexander asked.

"Now, I am different from him in so many ways I can scarcely count them. Yet, my face and body are his, and as long as he is alive it will always be so. I cannot gaze into a mirror without reminding myself of it. And I must receive the hatred of my brother because I am his brother. Freedom from his evil is but a ghost for me."

"I can never believe that," Alexander declared. "Julianus is weak. I saw how he drew back when you placed the blade against your own throat, ready to test his resolve. He ran away to save himself. Would a strong or courageous man do that?"

"A stronger man would have taken up the gauntlet and faced him in battle. One day, I will. But for now I fear for my wife and her child, and the guilt of your mother's death. Let me determine when and how, and I promise you that one day I will honor your respect for me."

At those words Alexander drew him into his arms and gave him a comforting hug. "I will not hold you to it," he said. "Now, think of your brother no more and return to Sarasvati."

76

For the next three days, the Arkanons were treated to a rare bout of peace. While Lucien spent time making arrangements for travel or sleeping the day long, Sarasvati and Parvati wandered with Alexander into the narrow streets, which were little more than cobbled pathways between the rows of houses with barely enough room for a small carriage and horse to pass through.

At one point they passed a group of nuns from the nearby convent who walked down the road to the church like a gaggle of geese, and marveled at the wide white starched headcoverings they wore. Children played a game of football at the corner square, and their boisterous voices rang like bells against the stone walls around them as they chased the bouncing thing all over the street.

The marketplace was filled with all manner of things to see and taste, and more than one band of musicians filled the air with cheery sounds, blending one with another among the voices of merchants and buyers haggling for bargains. It was a cacophany of prosperity, rare for the fact that it went on uninterrupted in the midst of war.

Wherever the strangers went, however, they were followed by curious onlookers who watched whatever they did with great interest. Eventually, Alexander had to drive the gawkers away with a few words of entreaty for privacy. They tore themselves away reluctantly like clumps of shearling wool. But soon after that the novelty of these strangers among them slowly wore off and they returned to other pursuits.

Sarasvati found a seamstress who helped her dress according to the latest fashion, and soon she was clad in a white embroidered blouse and dirndle, and a bell skirt with a heavily embroidered band stomacher. She draped a fringed shawl over her shoulders. Her feet were clad in short hose and wooden clogs which put them some distance above the mud on the street.

Then she went next door to a hairdresser, who combed out her long black hair and braided it with ribbons into a bun, which drew it back away from her heart shaped face; while Parvati watched and made noises of approval. The hairdresser did the same with the child, who smiled and burbled but sat still with perfect patience as the ribbons were applied.

When they emerged, Alexander would not have known them but for Sarasvati's dark skin and grey eyes, and the baby with grey eyes who toddled alongside. "Truly remarkable," he said. "You are happy with this transformation?"

"Aye," she laughed. "I was so tired of my old clothes. I will wear these while we are in Transylvania, as I have no desire to stand out or attach significant notice to us. You approve?"

"Indeed," he nodded with a smile. "Though I can scarcely imagine what father will think of it."

"As he knows my mind very well, he will approve, too. He has ever let me make my own way, without much reproof or admonishment. At times we have disagreed, but every time he has given in with... a little gentle persuasion." She smiled at the memory.

Just then the bell in the church tower began to ring, sounding a knell for the evening vespers. "We had better go back to the house," Alexander said. "Father will be rising soon, and we mustn't worry him with our absence."

"There is no need for concern," Sarasvati assured him. "He told me once that he can see things in his mind which others cannot. I am sure he knows where and what we are doing. And, there are times when I can almost feel his eyes are upon me."

"I had no inkling of your perception," he replied. "Have you always had this sensitivity?"

She turned to him, and her eyes twinkled with amusement. "Always," she said. "Even before I met your father. But he opened my eyes to all I had not seen of the outside world from the moment I first gazed into his, and for that I am ever grateful. Your father is a most remarkable man. Did you know that?"

"Yes, I confess that he continues to impress me with everything he does."

"Then, whatever you do, cherish him the way I do."

That evening, supper was shared among the Brunwald family, who were twelve souls in all: Grigori, his two younger sisters and their husbands, three cousins, and a gaggle of children.

Hans and Fritz were kept busy shifting platters and dishes, and occasionally caught a bite or two of food in between or furtively tucked morsels into their pockets for later, while a younger boy carried a pitcher of wine from place to place. The pitcher seemed too big for him to carry but he seemed determined to do his job nevertheless.

Sarasvati occupied herself with spoon feeding Parvati from a bowl of thick porridge with bits of broccoli and forest mushrooms, while Grigori, Ostap Kuryan, Lucien and Alexander spent most of the meal talking about the situation on the road ahead and planning a safe itinerary based on what was known from the travelers passing through town.

According to Grigori, the Turks stayed to the south, and occupied much of Croatia and Serbia, southern Hungary and parts of Wallachia. It appeared that all of Dracula's attempts to keep the invaders out had met with failure years ago, and this was the third such incursion in a decade.

"I know not the situation in Buda proper, but I think it will be safe if you keep to the north road," Grigori said. "Beyond the dark wood is the gypsy camp, and beyond that is Klausenburg. That is the extent of my knowledge, for I have not had time to explore the hinterlands beyond."

"Gypsies?" Lucien asked, his interest perking up. "By what name are they called?"

"Let me see..." he said, while scratching at his balding head. "Ah. They call themselves Cecescu. A large tribe consisting of several families, all linked together by blood. They claim to come from the north, too. They are marked by their large eyes, which come in all different colors as if someone dipped them in paint. Some are blue, and some green, and some, if you will permit me to say, are grey like yours. But none exactly the same from one to another. And one of them even has one blue eye and one brown, and another one grey and one green, as if God could not decide what color they should be and left it up to fate. They apply black to their eyelids, all around, and in that way their eyes appear bigger than any I have ever seen."

At this, Lucien raised a pale eyebrow. "Indeed? I am intrigued. Tell me more."

"They are a superstitious lot, yet they do not practice any religion that I know of. I do not think any of them have come closer than the river at the edge of the wood. They keep to themselves in their camp and have stayed in the same place for over a year, as if they were waiting for something. There is nothing remarkable about the land they occupy. There is no abundance of fish or game to feed them all. Yet they stay nevertheless, caught there like a cloud of flies in tree sap."

"I wonder what keeps them there?" Alexander said.

Brunwald replied, shrugging, "it is all a mystery to me."

"Hmmm," Lucien said, looking straight ahead as if he could see through the far wall. "Fascinating."

This prompted the boyar to ask, "what is?"

The question jogged him loose from his reverie, and he took a deep breath before answering, "oh, I was just thinking, and lost my way."

Later, as the Arkanons were preparing for bed, Alexander approached Lucien. "Father, what was that about the Cecescus? I sensed that you were keeping something back."

Lucien regarded him with a sharp look. "If I tell you, you must tell no one else. On your honor, swear you."

This mystified Alexander even more, but he said, "I swear, father."

"What I know of them is not known to these people. The Cecescus are of an ancient line of Szganis, whose name means 'raven'. We met them when we crashed to earth in the mountains. A proud people they were, and fierce warriors beside, claiming to have the blood of Attila in their veins. We bided a short time among them and learned all there was of mankind. They may have among them progeny of our kind mingled with theirs, for there was a time when we found them fair to look upon."

"Is it possible they may know us if we meet them?"

"Aye. There is also a risk that they may find us not to their liking. You must understand that I was not as you know me now, and in all ignorance I partook in their enslavement. I can only hope that their capacity for forgiveness is great. We used them most shamefully, and for that I hold all regret."

"But it has been two centuries since that time. Surely they must have forgotten by now. What will happen if we meet them?"

Lucien made a small noise and shrugged. "We will cross that bridge when we come to it," he said.

77

Almost another two days came and went while Grigori Brunwald gathered a group of men together to escort the Arkanons to Klausenburg. When they were fully provisioned, they prepared to leave Bistrița by the west gate.

Ostap Kuryan came to Lucien and reported that a pair of apothecaries were prepared to receive a small shipment of the salve Lucien had developed for sale in their shops, and gave him a small bag full of coins.

Then he reached into a different pocket in his tunic, and extracted a small sheaf of papers tied with a red ribbon. "And this is from Grigori. I acquainted him with your needs and he did create these letters of marque for you, that they will see you into Holy Roman lands with all safety."

"Thank you for your most excellent service, Ostap," Lucien said. "Say your goodbyes again for us to your father, and I hope our paths cross again. But I think it will not be for a very long time."

Ostap gave him a short bow. "I will await your letter when you arrive in Paris. Journey in safety."

Lucien gave him a smile in return. Ostap turned to Alexander and smiled, bowed to him and then turned and left them to rejoin his retinue.

"There goes a very good man," Lucien remarked. "And Brunwald also. These are men of honor."

Alexander watched the tall Romanian mount his horse and signal to his men, and soon they were on the march back toward Muramea. When he finally left off and turned his attention to mounting his own horse, he spied Grigori Brunwald approaching at a jog.

"Gentlemen, I bring you news," he said, puffing slightly. "The Turk have moved on toward Sibiu, which is far south of Klausenburg. With luck you may pass through the wood safely, and arrive without meeting trouble on your way."

"That is good news, indeed," Alexander said. "Thank you for your hospitality, and good fortune to you."

"May God protect you all, and speed you on your journey." He bowed slightly, then stood by as Alexander mounted up, and Lucien took the reins of the wagon horses. With a short signal to their hired retinue, they left Bistriţa through the western gate and followed a winding road into the unknown.

✧

Transylvania
July 1647
78

For the whole day long, the men escorted the wagons without speaking a word. The forest was vast and quiet. Patches of silence were broken briefly by another group of ravens calling raucously and unseen, and at irregular intervals the distant sound of a woodpecker's beak on wood gave out a rapid staccato tattoo for a few precious seconds before fading away.

Alexander looked for movement in the branches and saw nothing. A steady breeze ruffled the trees' leafy heads and moaned faintly through the branches like a tired ghost. The horses' hooves clopping and the tinkling of their traces; the occasional snort or belch, and the sound of the wagons' creaking wooden wheels only seemed to add to the great emptiness of the forest. If pressed to give his impression he would have called it eerie.

When they stopped to camp, a pecking order of sorts had been established among the men, and only one of them, a tall older Hungarian calling himself Bela Ragosi, relayed Lucien's orders to them. He looked solid as iron, a war veteran with dark curly hair and blue eyes, and spoke such a strange dialect of Hungarian that Lucien resorted to giving his instructions in Latin in order to be understood. Ragosi was also the only man among them who did not appear to be afraid of Lucien.

Like Ostap Kuryan he kept much of himself private, but compared to him Ostap was a chatterbox.

That night the watch was kept by a few men armed with flintlock rifles, crossbows and swords arrayed at the edge of camp, while the other men slept with their horses, fully clothed and armed against a sudden attack. They maintained their silence just as they had during the day, and Alexander felt the sensation of raw untrammeled fear wash through his mind more than once that night as he settled down to keep his customary watch.

But as he took a look around he spotted Ragosi reclining on his saddle blanket, watching him intently. His eyes seemed to glow in the dark, then flared briefly red. Then, with an odd smile on his lips, the Hungarian turned over to show his back and settled down to sleep.

Alexander fell back against his saddle with amazement as if he had been struck in the face. He caught himself staring and looked away quickly, thinking that he had been dreaming, then stole another look. But Ragosi remained prone, and the sound of snoring soon drifted to him on the cold night air. When he convinced himself it was a trick of his own fatigued spirit, he finally closed his eyes.

In the morning the chill in the air was banished by the warming sun as the travelers stirred themselves up to begin their morning libations. One of the men was a fair cook, and when the campfire was stoked he set to work cooking sausages and onions, loaves of fresh bread and sticky buns made with honey. His makeshift kitchen was briefly assaulted by a group of curious bees until he was able to drive them away with a generous application of slivoviska to the campfire.

The eruption of flames and smoke startled the other men at first, but they broke into laughter, a sign they had all seen this before. Then they set themselves to searching for the nest and found it nearby. With a little judicious poking with a long spear, they brought the hive down and began to divide up the waxy honeycomb among them in the midst of a swarm of angry insects.

When he saw the men were thus distracted, Alexander left his blanket and went to the Arkanons' faithful old wagon, knocked on the door quietly, and waited for the door to open. When it did, Sarasvati's brown face peered out at him. "Good morrow, Alexander," she said.

"Good morrow, mother. Is father awake?"

She looked within, then said, "he is asleep now. Shall I rouse him?"

He started to say what was on his mind, but hesitated. "Nay, it can wait."

Sarasvati examined his face closely, then said, "something troubles you. What is it?"

"You are most perceptive, lady, but it is of no concern," he replied. "I am seeing shadows, is all."

"What shadows? Pray, tell me all." As she spoke she came out onto the first stair and closed the wagon door quietly, then sat down and drew her shawl closely about her shoulders to banish the chill. Just then she looked tired as if she had also been awake all night.

"Mother, there is something strange about these men we hired to escort us to Klausenburg," Alexander began. "One in particular, the man called Ragosi, is more than he appears to be."

She narrowed her grey eyes, much as Lucien was wont to do. "Yes, I have seen that in him myself."

"I am not entirely sure of him. Father appears to trust him, but I do not. Be on guard with him. That is all I can say."

She reached out and stroked at his cheek. "Alexander, you have been through a great deal since we started out from Srinagar," she said. "I know we have not spoken of the past, but you must confide in me now and again, that I may know your heart. I have grown to regard you as my own son though I did not bear you myself. I am also not of your kind, so it is not easy for me to know your mind, or to feel all the things you do. But I am ready to listen whenever you need surcease from the world."

Alexander smiled gently, and replied, "I thank you for your caring heart, mother. I will come to you later and share what is on my mind."

She smiled back, then gathered herself and reentered the wagon.

Alexander returned to his blanket and placed it on his horse's back, then the short saddle, and cinched it tight. His new horse was a blue roan filly, about three years old, and she watched him work with a strange curiosity. Finally, she reached back and nipped gently at his sleeve.

He turned to her, smiled and said, "what is it, girl?"

The horse turned back and shook her head. This mystified him even more, and he went to her head, ruffled her bangs and looked into her large brown eyes. As he spoke he stroked at her velvet nose. "You are different from the others," he observed. "You have not been broken long, have you?"

She whickered softly and pushed her nose into his hand for more.

The Hungarian's deep sonorous voice came suddenly from behind him. "You have a way with horses," he said, in accented Queen's English.

Alexander turned suddenly, startled, while the filly gave out a shrill bleat and edged away but did not get beyond his grip on her bridle. He stared at Ragosi with consternation, marveling at the big man's capacity for stealth. "Who are you?" he asked.

"I would ask the same of you," the Hungarian said. "You saw me last night, though it was almost pitch black. Few other men would have seen that far in the dark."

"You know me only from my father, I presume," he replied. "We were not properly introduced. I am Count Alexander Vincent Corvina."

Ragosi affected a light but courteous bow. "Ah. A Corvinus. Also a Draculesti, if I am not mistaken, like your father. How long has it been? One, or two centuries?"

The statement rocked Alexander back on his heels, and he almost gaped. He pitched his voice lower as he replied, "you do not know what you speak of. What perfidy brought you to us, that you did not reveal yourself to my father from the first?"

"None, apart from the need for discretion. Like you, I have lost my lands and position, and desire to travel to the west. There is nothing for me in Transylvania any longer."

He reached out to touch the horse's mane, but she shied back and continued to watch him with the whites of her eyes showing. "Charming creature," he continued, "but a trifle skittish. You would be better off turning her loose now, and I will furnish you with another, more docile creature."

Something about that urbane wit put Alexander off. "She is more intelligent and perceptive than most animals, that is all," he replied, putting more emphasis into his words with his voice.

Ragosi stepped back briefly as if he was struck, then shrugged. "I meant no offense. Later, I will come to you and we will talk. I must also explain myself to your father, else he will take my head off, no?"

"That is up to him. Above all he values the truth."

"Then the truth is what he shall have," the tall Hungarian replied, then smiled, bowed and walked away to rejoin the others.

79

When the sun dipped low behind the hills, Lucien approached Alexander and spoke to him in a low quiet tone. "Sarasvati conveyed your concern to me. What of Ragosi has ruffled your feathers so?"

Alexander explained his encounter with Ragosi and finished with, "he is willing to explain himself to you, but I caution you, sir. I cannot trust him. He..." and he groped for the right word. Finally, he managed, "he frightens me."

At that Lucien looked at him askance, then dissolved into chuckles. "He frightens you? Alexander, you have the strength of ten men. You move like the wind, and no one can catch you without losing a limb or an eye. He frightens you?"

Alexander felt his cheeks flush hot with embarassment. "Father, please."

The pale alien's smile fell slowly, and he placed his long fingered hand on his shoulder. "You are right. I should not find levity in your concern. Now come with me and we will sort this business out."

Together, they walked across the compound to a group of men who were playing a game of dice. Ragosi was among them, and upon their approach rose to his feet and met them. Lucien spoke to him in his customary Latin. "Come with us. Let us walk some distance as privacy would warrant."

As they walked into the sheltering darkness he continued, "I understand that you are not at night what you are in the day. Tell me what you are in truth, that I would know you better."

Ragosi nodded, then said, "for safety's sake then, we should continue in Latin, as I do not want the other men to overhear what I would say to you."

"That is easily done."

The three penetrated the darkness of the wood and found a tall hedge of buckthorn separating them from the camp. Lucien halted and faced the tall Hungarian with a serious expression. "Now speak. What is the truth? Why do you disguise yourself in such a way?"

Ragosi looked back toward the camp and made sure that no one had followed them before speaking. "I am what you would call an immortal. There are few of us, compared to the teeming thousands whose lives are cut short too early. I have lived over a thousand years, and in that time I have seen many things. Things which would freeze your blood if I told you of them."

Lucien raised a pale eyebrow and replied, "Indeed? Then you are of a rare breed. Humans are ephemeral creatures, are they not?"

"I have lived long enough to know that they shorten their own lives through their embrace of all things sinful, and time wasted in war and the lust for power."

"Granted, sir, but that does not explain why you chose to play this role," Alexander said.

"Like you, I would journey into the west and toward calmer lands. I am not from this place. I was trapped here by the Turk and have lived here ever since, forced to serve, to hunt, to carry for whomever would have me. I wish no harm to you, sir, or your family. I seek a place of my own, where I might live out my days unmolested."

Here Lucien studied his face for what seemed like a long time to Alexander, but was really only a second or two. Then he said, "I will not ask where you come from, but I caution you, sir. I will not abide further deception. Had you been more open with me from the beginning I would have been glad to lend you my trust, but I sense you have more to hide."

Ragosi made a humble bow. "I apologize, my lord Count. I took you for an honest man myself. But I was born of this earth, whereas you were not. I know you have as much to hide as I do."

Lucien's eyes widened slightly, and that was the extent of his reaction. But his voice slipped into echoes as he said, "*you are not to speak of this matter again.*"

Ragosi blinked, and for a moment his eyes grew blank. Then he blinked again, and smiled like a possum. "As you wish." He bowed again, then turned and walked back toward the camp.

Alexander stared after his receding figure, agape with utter shock and amazement. "Father, what happened just now?"

Lucien turned and replied, "some men do not respond to mindvoice as well as others. He is but one exception. I will be glad when we part company, for his knowledge of us will be a danger as long as we remain joined together as travelers."

"It concerns me that we have relied on him for this long. Are there others like him ahead, that we must ever be on guard?"

"Such men are rare, Alexander. There are no more than a dozen like him, men and women who cannot die in a natural way. I do not know what force of nature made him so, but we must trust that he is at risk himself if he reveals us to the others. We need not fear a betrayal from him. But what drives his heart is yet to be understood. I can only read some of him. There are other parts of his mind which remain hidden from probing."

"Then, how must we treat him?" Alexander asked. "As a friend, or as an enemy?"

"I have found that sometimes they are interchangable. If you will, regard him as a friend with an alterior motive. As Sun Tzu once said, 'keep your friends close, but your enemies closer.' Watch him, Alexander, but do not forget that he is not like ordinary men."

"Aye," he replied. "I will not turn my back to him."

80

The next morning the caravan packed up and proceeded on toward the source of the river Krudd and the meadow where the gypsies were camped. Ragosi and two of the men scouted ahead and reported back in the afternoon with news that the Turks had moved on toward the south, and that the bands of freedon fighters had followed them, leaving the road clear for a time.

The caravan went on toward the meadow, and from the top of a hill Alexander spotted the painted wagons grouped close together around a common bonfire. There were eight in all, and near them there was activity among a group of women doing their laundry in the river, pounding cloth against rock and singing a plaintive melody, while several children ran and played close by.

When they spotted the approaching group of riders and wagons, the children broke off from playing and disappeared into the shelter of the camp like ghosts, while the women dropped their bundles of wash and followed closely after them. They all appeared well acquainted with danger.

When the caravan arrived at the camp, a small group of men confronted it armed with sticks and swords. But they were too few in number and the men in the caravan would have been able to overpower them easily. Ragosi commanded them to stand down and wait, dismounted some distance from the gypsies and walked the rest of the way to meet the leader.

After some words were exchanged between them, he walked back and explained to the others that the gypsies wanted no trouble, and would be willing to host them for the evening in exchange for a few coins of gold.

"They value peace above all," Ragosi remarked to Lucien. "They are also very curious about you, my lord Count. It seems you are well known to them."

Lucien narrowed his gaze as he studied the men assembled on the road for a few long moments. Then he appeared to relax a bit and declared, "their welcome is enough for me. Bid them make a space for us among them and we will accept their hospitality. Are your men amenable to this arrangement?"

Ragosi shrugged. "They will do what I say. It matters not what they think. If any raise a word of complaint I will remind them where they stand."

At that Lucien nodded, and at Ragosi's signal the file moved forward again, then off the road into the meadow and toward the group of wagons.

The leader of the gypsies was a thinner man than the rest, wiry and lean with a dark moustache and a large gold earring piercing his left ear lobe. His neck was bedecked in gold chain and charms, as people in that area were wont to carry their fortunes with them in the form of jewelry, easily bartered for the food and goods they needed to survive. He also wore a large gold ring which looked like an old Roman seal ring, no doubt passed down to him from antiquity and received from his father as a badge of office, or retrieved from the body of a less fortunate comrade. Alexander caught sight of his eyes, which were a strange shade of hazel, reminding him of a lion's eyes.

He met Alexander and Lucien with a deep bow and a bit of a flourish of his broad brimmed hat, and with a voice which boomed out of his chest, he said in broken Romanian, "welcome, my lords. We have been waiting for you for a very long time. I am Velin

Cecescu, named after my grandfather. All these Cecescus are part of his tribe. It is fortunate that you return to us now, when we have much need of your guidance and protection. Your return was foretold by our brudja, who saw your coming in the bones."

At this Ragosi threw a sharp glance of surprise at Lucien, but said nothing; while Lucien tied off the reins to the wagon horses and jumped down to face the Szgani leader.

"I am not the man I once was," Lucien replied. "I stand before you older and repentent of what passed between us before. The past must never come between us again."

The gypsy drew back at this, then smiled. "Then the tales my grandfather told me are true," he remarked. "You are the man himself. We have not forgotten, my lord, and stand ready to be your humble servants yet again."

There was a long moment of awkward silence. Alexander studied their faces and was rewarded with reconciliation of a kind. Lucien never elaborated on the time he and the remnants of the fugitive Antellans spent with the Cecesçus; it seemed too painful to discuss beyond what he had said before. But Lucien also seemed to have suffered along with them, both the blessing and the curse of being emotionally empathic and the common trait of beings alien to this primitive preindustrial world.

The gypsy moved forward and embraced Lucien like a brother. "Welcome home, master," he said. "All are ready to receive you. All we have, our lives, our fortunes, is yours."

Lucien returned his embrace for a brief instant, then stood away. "My humble thanks to you, my friend, but I do not require more than a space for our wagon, grazing for the horses, and the warmth of your fire. And perhaps, a tale or two to while away the hours. Then we must move on. You need not uproot yourselves on our account, nor sacrifice anything for our sakes."

The gypsy stared at him, his eyes betraying his puzzlement. But he nodded his acceptance. "As you wish. It shall be as you command."

"This is my son, Alexander Corvina," Lucien said. "My wife and child are with us also."

Velin's kohl lined eyes seemed to grow even bigger as he said, "they must be tired and hungry after so long a journey. Please, come and take your place at our fire, and we will bring them whatever they wish. Your manservant has told us of your journey to the west, and we will do all we can to make you comfortable."

Velin turned and began shouting orders in a strange language, almost impossible to follow for Alexander, and the entire camp began an uproar of moving things and vehicles to accommodate the crowd of men and horses.

As they watched, Lucien turned to him and said, "I must admit I did not know the elder Velin that well, but I must have left a better impression on him than I remember."

"One would almost think you were their king," Alexander replied.

"We were, for a brief time. We ruled them like kings. We were their hearts' blood, their swords, their masters. Then we abandoned them when Julianus decided to take on the mantle of princedom in Wallachia. My own life was measured in finding blood among them in his shadow. It was not an easy time for me then."

"Yet, his grandfather found you kind and fair, far kinder than your brother. That must have counted for something."

"At the time it was far from my thoughts," Lucien replied quietly.

"And love?" he asked.

Lucien shook his head. "Before your mother came into my life, love was the least of my passions, and at the time one could not tell one brother from another. As I said before, she changed me into a better man. I will never forget that." He clapped his hand on Alexander's shoulder and then walked away to help with the arrangement of the camp.

That evening, the stars were bright in the sky, and the campfires among the wagons were bigger than usual. The men and women ate and conversed and laughed, while the children sat and listened to the tales brought them by the adults. This was the only way anyone learned about the outside world apart from brief contact with the villages on the valley floor.

Then everyone grew intently silent as Bela told their parents the news of the Turk armies ravaging the rest of Europe, of the situation in Ukraine and Wallachia, and warned them that if they did not act to fortify themselves, the godless ones would come and swallow them all up like sweetmeats. The children's eyes grew bigger at that, and some actually broke into tears.

But Alexander could barely listen, as he became the instant target for a pair of young women who found him a handsome catch, and before long they began to argue over him like fishmongers. He could only understand a word or two as they plucked at him, stroked at his long dark hair, kissed his cheeks and pushed at each other, each trying to win him over. He sat quietly, grimly determined to ignore them both, and endured their tussling like a mannequin until Velin saw this, walked over to them and shouted, "cease your noise and leave him alone. Can you not see he is our guest?"

Startled, the girls left off arguing, glared up at him with sullen faces, then got up and ran away into the darkness, arguing and pushing at each other as they went.

Velin watched them go, then turned to Alexander and said, "I am sorry, my prince. Their behavior is most shameful. I should have them whipped."

"No harm done," Alexander replied. "They caught me off guard, is all. I am not used to having such attention paid me by such winsome creatures. Please, do not whip them for my sake."

"Oh, then perhaps you would find one of them to your liking? Are you not married?"

Alarm bells sounded in Alexander's mind. "In truth, sir, I had no such thought in mind," he replied carefully, sensing that the man was eager to see one or both married off and out of his hair as quickly as possible.

"No sweetheart? No romantic entanglements?"

"....no," he said, recalling with a sharp pang of regret the sweet face of Charanditha smiling beneath him that night in the desert, when they cemented their bonding. "Not for a long time. With respect, sir, I am not ready yet to accept a bride. Perhaps... in another year..."

"But, you need someone to take care of you," Velin insisted. "Someone to cook and clean for you, and bear your children."

"One day, but not now," Alexander replied firmly. "It is too soon..."

Velin's eyes and face suddenly grew calm. "Ah. She is dead. I could sense it. You have an aura of tragedy about you, as if death has visited you before. How long ago?"

Alexander looked down at the meadow beneath him and plucked a dandelion, sighed, and with his breath scattered the seedlets into the cold night air. "Almost a month has passed since I buried her. Yet it seems to me as if it was only yesterday."

The old man sat down on the grass next to him and said, "then you must cast off your sorrow and embrace another. Nothing is as precious as the love of a woman, to have children playing at your feet, to see them grow into strong sons and daughters, and to see your tribe go on. We all accept that as a part of life. Do you not?"

Alexander turned and looked into his eyes. "You are kind to say that, but you do not understand. Love with one such as myself is to court death. I am... not like other men."

Velin blinked, then placed a tentative hand on his shoulder. "Nothing is more important to a man than family," he insisted. "It is as much a part of his life as is death. Even those who fight on the battlefield understand what that means. You are different, but you are part of this world, just as we are. You are as much a part of our tribe as your father, as his ancestors, as his kind. Do not think of yourself as separate but as a part of the whole, for we are all the same under the stars."

The wisdom and kindness in his words was hard to deny, and Alexander said, "You speak kindly. I will think about it. Thank you."

"I will leave you now. Only consider what I have said," the gypsy replied, then returned to his feet, bowed and walked back toward the campfire, where he was instantly leapt upon by two of the children who wanted to play with him. He picked up and swung the youngest boy around in a circle, laughing with him as the child giggled with delight.

Alexander laid back on the grass, looked up at the bright milky band of stars above, and beheld a light which streaked across the sky, flared briefly and then went out. Even with the sounds of music and laughter in his sensitive ears he could hear and feel the cold breeze stir at his hair and clothes; and just at that moment he felt free to be himself. Then he closed his eyes, and dozed lightly until the sound of crunching grass coming closer opened them again. It reminded him of that night when Charaditha declared her love, and he sat up with her name caught between his lips.

But it was not her. Sarasvati sat down next to him, adjusting her sari carefully as she did so. Her customary gold jewelry was absent, and her expression was sober as a judge. "Here you are, Alexander," she said, as she tilted her head up to look at the stars. "It is a most pleasant and peaceful night, is it not?"

He contemplated her exotic brown features and spotted a streak of white among the black hair, now tied back into a matronly bun. She looked older, tired and worn out. It was a result of giving blood frequently, and he wondered how long it would be before she would tire of feeding his father. She seemed quite happy with the arrangement between her and Lucien, or that she had long ago accepted that she would lose her youth and beauty faster than most women. Yet now there was an expression on her face of tension and hopelessness at the same time, and a droop to her large grey eyes which spoke of despair.

"Mother, do you regret marrying my father?" he asked her.

She turned and gave him a startled look. Then it softened again. "Nay," she replied. "But sometimes I do wonder what kind of man I am married to. He is betimes like a child in need of comfort. He has fits of dreaming, and they are most unpleasant for him, enough that he will cry out and sit up wet from head to toe, trembling like a leaf. And at other times he starts and feels at his limbs, and on his skin a red mark appears here and there, that I am hard pressed to know what magic is responsible for it. He talks in his sleep also, and makes such grievous sounds as to wrench my heart with pity. He speaks of Melanthea, and of his brother, as if he lost them both in the same instant. Then he speaks of you as if he would lose you too..."

She paused and took a deep breath. "Yet he is all peace and love when he is awake, with a great strength of spirit beyond any ordinary man. How could I leave him? I love him more than life itself, and my only desire has been to make him happy. Yet I know he needs much more than I can provide."

Alexander listened and grew alarmed. This insight about Lucien betrayed a side of him he had never known before. "Mother, that you should bear such a burden alone... I had no inkling..."

"Hush. I would not have you thinking that. I accept that it is my task to give him my love and comfort as his wife and lover. I give him my blood willingly, so it is of no matter to me. Swear to me that

318

you will not tell him that I confided this to you. Swear that it will be our secret, that he would not lose an ounce of assurance from us both."

Alexander sat up and took her hands in his as he looked earnestly into her grey eyes. "I swear upon the star I saw just now, that passed so bright above me and died into the dark."

Sarasvari sighed again, and said, "and, there is one more thing, dear Alexander, that I would have you know. I have been to see one of the gypsy women, who is a midwife and apothecary. I do not know what to tell Lucien of what I have learned. Will you help me to keep my secret?"

He studied her face. It was grave with concern. "Are you with child again? Why would you keep that from him?"

"Nay," she said, and bit back sudden tears. "Alexander, I am dying."

The words took a long moment to sink in, and Alexander could not believe his ears. "What?" he asked quietly. "Dying?"

Sarasvati then bit her lip again, and nodded silently as a tear drifted down her cheek. She reached up and wiped it away with an impatience born of the need to maintain her composure, then sniffed.

"When? For how long have you been ill?" he asked.

"Since we were in Kyiv. You remember that I fell into a spell of weakness and cold, that it did give me a fever."

"Aye."

"The woman told me that it was the first sign, that I may have fallen ill at the house in the marches, and that it would grow worse with time if I did not reclaim my strength. Something in that lovely place caught me, a humor or strain of evil, I know not what. And the more blood I give your father to live, the weaker I will become, until death comes to claim me one day. And I fear now it will be sooner than I expected."

Alexander stared at her, aghast. "Why would you keep such a thing from him? We must tell him at once."

He moved to rise, but Sarasvati's grey eyes grew wider, and she looked genuinely frightened at his suggestion as she grabbed his hand and pulled him back down. "No, please. You cannot make me do such a thing. I fear it would only drive him away from me. I want him to think that everything is as it should be. I will tell him when I am ready. I do not want him to mourn for me before I am gone."

"How long will it be until the end?" he asked.

"Three, perhaps four passings of the full moon," she replied.

"No," he said. "We should not wait so long. I cannot keep this from him. We should tell him now."

Her face went hard as stone, and she declared, "you swore to me that you would not tell him. Will you violate your oath and tear your family apart? Think on it, Alexander. My death is foretold. It is in my karma. I cannot change that, and neither can Lucien. Please. Let me tell him in my own way and in my own time."

She had offered to hear him in confidence, and now he felt as if all his own concerns and sorrows were superfluous. It must have been agony for her to keep her illness from Lucien all this time, and then to confirm what she had feared all along.

"Mother, Sarasvati, you are the most patient woman in the world, and you have been a comfort to me even when I denied it," he said. "This is a grave matter that you have confided in me, and I respect your need for discretion. I will keep your secret as long as I can. But you know that Lucien will learn all from me before I say a single word. He will not be so easy to deceive."

"I know," she said. "But please try for my sake. It is all that I ask of you. I have watched you go through much sorrow in this world, yet you have a spirit which I admire. That of the adventurer, who is always looking toward the far horizon. I had that spirit once myself, but now I must think on the next bardo, which is waiting for me at the end of my days. I will be rewarded in the next life for all that I did in this one, and I am content to accept my fate. Only, do not mourn long for me, but find comfort in the love of a woman like Charanditha, that you too feel the happiness I have shared with your father for the rest of your days."

She gathered herself and rose to her feet, then swayed unsteadily as if she would faint. Alexander jumped to his and reached out to give her support, but she pushed his hand away. "I will be all right," she insisted. "I am going to the wagon and to bed. If he asks for me, say only that I am tired from the journey. Good night, Alexander."

"Good night, mother," he replied, and watched her walk slowly back toward the campfire with a heavy heart, helpless to do anything else. Just at that moment, he felt all the years of his age weigh down on him like a mountain.

81

The sun rose a fierce red ball of withering fire and pierced the clouds with arrows of light. Alexander started awake suddenly, and had the sensation of danger as he opened his eyes with deliberate slownesss, ready to catch the intruder unawares. But there was nothing but cursory movement among the men stirring themselves up, and he felt the sensation slip away, the final note in a long dream now fading so fast he could not recall what made him feel that way.

One of the men said, "it will be hot today." Alexander realized with some chagrin that it was close on to summer now, and he had lost all track of time and the passage of seasons while traveling. A hot breeze brushed through his wild dark hair and tossed it about, and he reached into his bag for a ribbon to tie it back.

Before putting on his hat he brushed off a mote of lint and examined it. The pheasant feather looked ragged and old, so he plucked it out of the band and threw it away.

Duggens would not mind this, he told himself. I will find another much grander feather to put in its place.

He paused to reflect on the odd memoriam he kept about the man, and reasoned that he had been something like a friend, even at arm's length. Then he shrugged off the sensation as he rose and began to gather his things together.

While he was thus occupied, Alexander looked across the compound to the old faithful wagon and spotted the tall figure of his father just emerging from it. Lucien threw up a hand to shade his eyes from the harsh sunlight and drew on his hat, adjusted his clothes, then approached Bela Ragosi to speak with him. As he did so, he gently drew the immortal into the shade of an oak tree. They appeared to agree on something, then Ragosi went toward Velin Cecescu's wagon and knocked on the door.

Lucien approached Alexander and said, "I have an alternate plan which will satisfy our need for safety on the way through Hungary."

"Aye?" Alexander replied.

"It came to me in a dream, but I would have thought of it anyway, methinks. If we were to disguise ourselves as mummers, or a theatrical troupe, we could escape to more friendly climes without attracting attention to our true natures."

"As mummers? Father, I am not an actor, and cannot see myself wearing greasepaint and a large nose, can you?"

"Ah, you propose an even better idea. A circus. Alexander, you have outdone yourself once again," Lucien replied with a grin. "I provide you with the seed of an idea, and you always return with a fresh green shoot."

"You flatter me, sir, but I am confused. What skills have these people in such things?" he asked.

"Velin reacquainted me with the tribe's profession before the Turks came to trap them in this place. They were all gifted with music and other performing arts, so they are natural to this alteration. We could take them with us and we would be assured of a safer sojourn for it. I would not like to have Sarasvati and Parvati traveling into a strange land without all the protection I can provide them. Our numbers alone would provide it, and Velin presented me a profound loyalty I cannot easily abandon."

Alexander considered long and hard, then said, "I could... try to find some skill in me somewhere, and I will have to think what to do. I have some knowledge of the mandolin, but I will have to practice."

Lucien clapped him on the shoulder and said, "there is my boy. Now help me hitch the horses to the wagon and prepare the others for the journey."

Through the hot afternoon the camp was a abustle with preparations, while some of the men in Ragosi's troops made it known they were going home. This was not surprising, as many had only come to provide an escort to the border with Hungary. They were deterred by the fact that they were not Saxons, and they had families waiting for them back home.

As the meadow was only about 20 kilometers from the river, the caravan reached it when the sun dipped below the peaks of the Carpathian Alps, and made camp in the shelter of a stand of oak trees.

When the fires were lit, Velin, Ragosi and Lucien took turns sorting out who could do what, what their little circus would be called, and so on.

Through it all, Alexander watched and listened and noted that Lucien had not mentioned Sarasvati once during the day, and there was a strange glint in his silver grey eyes which spoke of a deep sadness beneath his smiles. He seemed to behave as if nothing was wrong. But Alexander concluded that she must have told him the truth of her own volition. He resolved not to mention it until Lucien brought it up.

There was an audition process, where members of the tribe showed off their skills. There were several musicians, a juggler, women who sang and danced to a series of old folk tunes. Sarasvati appeared among them wearing her old veils, performing a sinuous temple dance that left her audience roaring for more. But then she stood down modestly claiming that she was tired and withdrew into the shadows to rest.

It was then that Alexander realized she could not possibly do this every day without draining whatever life energy she had left. He watched as Lucien got up and followed her quickly into the dark, the tight urgency in his pale face showing his deep concern, and resisted the urge to follow and satisfy his curiosity. He reminded himself that whatever they shared was for them alone and that he was far too curious for his own good.

He was briefly distracted by the debut of the quarreling sisters, who showed off their abilities; one as a contortionist and the other as a sword dancer. Several other men and women proclaimed their skills at fortune telling and divination, another at sleight of hand with playing cards.

Bela Ragosi then came forward and said that he was developing a magic act, but needed a volunteer to be an assistant. Apparently he was just attractive enough that the younger women jumped at the chance, and for a while there was a frantic chaotic commotion as they jostled each other to be in front and better noticed.

"Wait," Ragosi said with a coy smile, "you do not know yet what I require. This will entail some risk, and I need someone of a serious mind and discipline."

"I am serious," one insisted, and the others echoed her like magpies.

"Serious enough to do whatever I ask?" he asked.

"Oh, yes!" said another. And "me, too!!" echoed her.

"Very well. I must have a pretty young woman to enter a cabinet, and each night to disappear at a certain time, and to reappear at a certain time. Which one of you can do it the same way and in the same time at every performance?"

"Me!" "No, me!!" "Don't listen to her, choose me!"

"Wait, there is more," he said, and the sound of his voice brought them all to silence. "I must also enchant her so that she is oblivious to all sight and sound, and must do my bidding with all trust, so that the illusion is accomplished faithfully without error."

"You speak of the devil's work," said one of the men. "Witchcraft."

Ragosi looked at him over the cloud of female heads and replied, "nay, there is no evil in it. No harm is done, therefore how can it be the work of the devil? It is but an illusion only, the appearance of magic without magic, to fool the eye and amuse the audience. It requires the utmost discipline and skill to produce, therefore must the subject be acquainted with it. I will train her to act on cue and with perfect timing, like a water wheel which fails not."

"Ah. So none of it is real magic," said another.

Ragosi nodded. "For me to perform real magic is... beyond my abilities. But to project such an illusion is not easy without rigorous preparation, and some trial and error." He turned back to the women and said, "I will question each of you in turn. Come to me when I call your name."

The women broke up into clumps of animated conversation, curiosity and speculation as they wandered away. Then Ragosi turned to Alexander and said, "you have not said what you are going to do."

"That is because I have not decided yet. I have some small skill with a mandolin, and I am somewhat skilled in the art of the sword..."

At that Ragosi began to laugh. "That long thing dangling from your belt? It is too long to be of any use. Or perhaps you let it do your thinking for you." His remark sounded at once derisive and ignorant, and his smile curled into one of scorn.

Alexander frowned. "This blade is a katana. The steel was forged in the fires of Mount Koroda, in a far off land called Nihon. I learned from a master swordsman who earned his title with a life of simplicity and skill."

Bela Ragosi's eyebrows crept upwards, and his skeptical smile grew even broader. "I have been there."

"Yet you laugh like a man who respects not tradition." Alexander jumped to his feet and placed his right hand on the woven grip. "I am at your pleasure, sir, and I'll whittle you down to a more proper size for your insult."

Ragosi's eyes grew sardonic as he drew back and drew his own sword, a crooked piece of Ghurka steel etched with a cursive design, and made ready.

The crowd saw this and moved away to form a rough circle and watch. They grew so silent that the only sound heard was the fire crackling in the nearby rockpile. Then Ragosi plunged forward, aiming the point at Alexander's heart.

The katana swept out of its scabbard in a flash and blocked it, and on the return swing sliced off one of the wooden buttons holding Ragosi's coat closed.

The immortal's eyes widened with surprise, and he jumped clear before the sharp curved steel slashed through the leather and caught the skin beneath. After that he was on the defensive, deflecting blow after determined blow until he was backed up against the side of one of the wagons and vigorously fighting for survival.

"*Alexander!!*"

Lucien's alien voice cut through the rage filling Alexander's mind and stopped him. He came forward and interposed himself between the men, his silver grey eyes sparkling as he studied his son. "What has possessed you?" he asked, frowning. "What ferment bids you to draw your sword in good company?"

"He... he insulted my sword," Alexander replied hotly, never taking his eyes from the immortal's, his words emerging from his lips like daggers. "He called it a 'long thing dangling from my belt'. I wear it for Musashi's sake, and he would soil it with such words that shame me..."

"You would dishonor Musashi even more if he saw this," Lucien declared. "Come, this is beneath you, Alexander. You would let a few misplaced words damage the trust we have forged with this man?"

"But..."

"Retire, I say, and let your temper cool, before you do something you will soon regret," he insisted.

Gradually the words penetrated Alexander's rage and damped it, and as he slowly lowered the katana and returned it with reverence to its sheath, he wondered where it all came from. It felt alien, as he was not prone to sudden flashes of temper. He remembered what happened with Karel and felt as if he had been thrust aside once again. Shame and embarassment filled the darkness in his mind. He said, "I... I am not myself. I do apologize, herr Ragosi. I do not know what came over me."

Ragosi exhaled the breath he had been holding and resheathed his own. "No harm done," he replied. "I think we are all tired, and what is needed now is a good night's rest. But I capitulate to your superior skill with the sword. I have never been bested like that before. Will you teach me something of the art?"

"If I have any time," Alexander muttered, then strode away into the darkness beyond the trees.

"I have never seen him lose his composure before," Lucien said softly. "He has ever been a good son, with an even humor and a ready wit. I know not what has possessed him of late."

Ragosi observed, "perhaps you do not know him as well as you think you do. Or he shelters some concern which he will not share."

Lucien sighed. "I fear so."

82

The morning brought a calmer mood, and Alexander strolled across the common space between the wagons, watching the preparations being made.

There were fewer wagons now, the others having departed during the dawn's early light. The train was now composed mostly of the brightly painted gypsy wagons, some now covered with sheets of painted cloth proclaiming their arts; and several of the gypsies and men at arms were busy practicing various tricks and stunts under the supervision of Ragosi and Velin. The two men seemed to have reached an accord between them, and stood discussing the finer points of the program they had arranged.

Alexander joined them and said, "good morrow."

"Good morrow, my lord," they both said in tandem, each with a short bow. Both behaved as if the upset of the last evening had never occurred.

"When do you think we will be ready to depart?"

"As soon as your father gives the word," Velin Cecesçu replied. "We have not seen him since last evening."

"Then I will ask of him the delay," Alexander replied. He had not seen Lucien emerge from the wagon since he woke, and was now more curious what might have happened to Sarasvati. He returned to their faithful old wagon and rapped gently on the door. He waited, and it seemed an age before the panel swung open.

Lucien's pale face greeted him this time, wearing an expression of exquisite sorrow. "Yes, Alexander?" he asked.

He paused, speechless for a long moment, not knowing how to broach the subject. Then he said, "father, Ragosi and Velin would like to know when you would like to go? They are waiting on your word."

The pale apparition appeared to waver with distraction, then said, "tell them to gather the wagons and wait for us, and we will be there to join them directly. I must take care of something first."

"As you say, sir," Alexander declared, as brightly as he could, then turned on his heel and walked back to them, his thoughts thrown into turmoil yet again. When he reached them, he relayed Lucien's decision, then added softly, "I fear my stepmother is gravely ill, and that the travel has affected her health. May we travel slowly, so that she is accorded some comfort during the journey?"

"Aye, indeed," Velin replied. "She did declare she was tired last evening."

"It may be nothing serious," Alexander said. "She took sick in Kyiv, you see, and we were delayed almost a week for it. I would caution against straining her health further."

"We will accommodate the lady, but that may be yet left up to fate," Ragosi said. "I have it from one of the men that a band of men calling themselves 'vampire hunters' have been roaming the area near Klausenburg looking for fresh prospects."

Alexander drew back suddenly, his pale face blanching at the words. "Vampire hunters?" he asked.

"Aye," the Hungarian replied. "He spake of a rumor that a wasting disease has struck Klausenburg, and that vampires were said to be responsible. These men have already killed many good men and women whose only sin is that they died and were buried too soon."

"Too soon?" Alexander said. "What do you mean?"

Ragosi said, "it is more likely that the poor wretches fell into a sleep so deep that they were mistaken for dead, and in their helpless state were buried. Then, when they woke, they clawed their way out of their graves and were discovered wandering in a daze. Such a death I could not wish on my worst enemy, for these men would dispatch them with all haste and with little concern for their station or gender. I have heard that they even staked children to the ground, then mutilated them in such a way that their little cadavers were desecrated most shamefully. They claimed that in this way their souls would be released to ascend to heaven, and they would not return as revenants from the grave."

"And you say they search for anyone who matches their perception?"

Ragosi nodded. "Many men are too willing to believe whatever they are told, no matter how fantastic or impossible it is. When combined with religious fervor, their beguilement is complete."

Alexander could not argue with that. "Then we must proceed with all caution and watch for these hunters, that we do not lose our own to their predations."

"Think you they will attack the camp?" Velin asked.

"That, I think, is up to time and opportunity," Ragosi said.

Ragosi and Velin gave Alexander a short bow of agreement, and then turned to their task, while Alexander quickly returned to the wagon and told Lucien what they told him.

The taller man nodded soberly, and replied, "as I feared. The way forward is far more dangerous than the way we have come. We are entering another world, Alexander, and all our instincts will be needed to survive. We must avoid Klausenburg and enter Hungary by another route. We will go north and take the road to Oradea, and hope the Turk has not taken it again."

"What about mother?" Alexander asked anxiously. "I gather you have learned of her illness."

"Much as it saddens me I must weather her loss just as I have weathered all else," he said with a small shrug. "The thought of not having her by my side all the way to Paris is something I had not considered before. I had not turned her as I wished to, so now it is too late. I cannot save her from the disease which wracks her body. It has eaten too far. Her blood is thin and polluted, and I have not drunk from her since we left Bistritza."

328

"You sound as if you have known all along," Alexander replied.

He shook his head sadly. "No. Sarasvati kept her illness from me as long as she could, but I only learned it from her body when I fed the last time. Her scent had changed, so I knew before she told me anything. Even if I give her my blood now, the dragon's blood cannot change her in such a state. It preserves life, but cannot restore it entirely, nor raise the dead from the grave. If she turned now, she would remain an invalid for the rest of her days."

Then he leaned over and ruffled the hair on the top of Alexander's head. "I know that she told you what she could not tell me, and you took her confidence most admirably, but now that I know all you may be more open with your thoughts to me. Perhaps that was the source of your temper last evening? It would be natural for any man to chafe so with such a heavy burden placed upon him."

Alexander searched inside himself and realized Lucien was probably right, drew a breath, and replied, "I was not trying to deceive you, father, but she made me swear not to tell you."

"I know," Lucien replied patiently. "You are a rock, in that none can sway you from your purpose or commitment. I will always remember that, and be thankful for you as you are. You have not disappointed me, and exceeded all my expectations as a father."

"Thank you," Alexander said, feeling a flush of quiet pride. "But mother... how is she now? May I see her? And Parvati?"

"Wait for a little, as she is asleep now, and you may visit her when she wakes. Parvati, sweet little thing, refuses to leave her side even when I tell her to, so I must wait on the both of them for my direction."

Then, Lucien drew the wagon door closed and shut Alexander out, leaving him feeling rudderless as a small boat drifting toward a waterfall.

An hour later, Lucien emerged from the wagon's back door and climbed up onto the platform, took up the reins and guided the horses toward the front of the file. There he joined Ragosi, Velin and Alexander, and his face was stone cold as he said, "we are ready. Signal the others and we will go."

Velin turned in his saddle and waved his arm, and the long file started down the meadow toward the road.

329

83

By the time the sun went down three days later, the gypsy train passed through the last leg of the forest and approached the northern wall surrounding Klausenburg. The road passed by uncomfortably close to the watchtowers, and there was a tense hour when a squad of uniformed men intercepted the train at a checkpoint.

They were soldiers of the Hungarian army, and they occupied the road with their horses to form a living blockade, resplendent in Prussian blue and gold, wearing helmets resembling those of Roman centurions, but with pony tails made of horse hair at their crests.

The caravan halted about a hundred yards down the road. Lucien and Alexander peered ahead and discussed what to do next. "What do you think they will do?" Alexander asked.

"We cannot leave the road, and they have seen us already," Lucien replied. "We must rely on their generosity. What do you think of them, Ragosi?"

In answer the Hungarian stared at them for a few seconds, then spat on the ground. "We do not have enough men to give them a good fight, and there is no easy way to make our escape. We will have to talk our way out of it. They may be reasonable, but it has been many years since I was here; therefore I cannot be certain."

"We have never been this far into Hungar lands," Velin said. "Will they welcome us, or fire on us?"

Their discussion was cut off when one of the soldiers detached himself from the blockade and approached, stopping about fifty feet away. He was Saxon blond, and he sat on his horse with his sword in his gloved right hand but held the point down, a gesture of cautious peace. He shouted in German, "who are you? Fled from the Turk, are you?"

"Nay," Ragosi called back. "We are but a humble traveling circus from the Ukraina. We are traveling to Oradea."

"Oradea? Whither else would you go?"

"We would go on from there to Budapesth," he replied. "Are the Turk lodged nearby? We have no desire to meet with trouble on our way."

The soldier ventured a few feet closer, and gave the wagons careful scrutiny. "A circus," he said. "You look like vagabonds and gypsies to me. What do you do?"

"Nought but this and that," Ragosi said. "We perform with tumbling, and juggling, trapezzio, music, theater and other such entertainments."

"And magic? The Emperor Ferdinand has forbidden all acts of magic. It is witchcraft in his eyes," the soldier said.

Alexander groaned inwardly. Ragosi's neutral expression wavered. Then Lucien said, "we assure you that we have no magic, good sir. We create illusions only, which are pleasant to the eye but do not capture a man's soul." As he spoke, Lucien raised his hand to display his pale thin fingers, then produced a pair of gold coins between them from seeming nowhere.

The soldier's attention was seized instantly, and he studied the count's pale features for a long moment with wonder and amazement. Some kind of connection was established, though what it was Alexander could not fathom. Then the young captain relaxed in his saddle. "And we have no Turks here," he declared confidently. "You may pass."

He turned and signaled to the others to open their makeshift wall. Then he rode closer to the wagon and asked Lucien, "what do you know of men roaming about in search of vampires?"

"We know only as much as rumor has supplied," Lucien replied.

"Then guard yourselves, for the king has given no saction for these acts. Those men are sought for murder and desecration of the dead, and we would apprehend them all if we could."

"We will look out for them," Alexander said. "Do you know them by name?"

"Their leader is a man from Austria who calls himself van Helsing. Nicholaus van Helsing. He is tall, with light brown hair and blue eyes, as others have described him. He wears a leathern coat with a fur collar, a broad brimmed hat, and carries a large leather bag. He has been seen with other men seaching places of the dead, and even attacks people on the road if he finds fault with their manner or appearance. On your guard from here to the river, mark you."

"We will be careful and watch for these men. Thank you for your warning, captain," Lucien said.

The young soldier then saluted him quickly, turned his horse and galloped back to his squad. As soon as they passed over the hill and returned to their checkpoint, all four men breathed a sigh of relief. Ragosi remarked, "the day was easily won."

"The day is not over yet," Lucien replied, in a stoic tone laced with sadness, waited until Ragosi signaled the others, then chucked at the reins of the horses and drove on.

That evening the camp was quiet, and everyone made a show of going through their acts, blocking their routines and rehearsing, but kept their weapons on their belts or close by in case of attack.

During a short interlude, Alexander went to the Arkanons' faithful old wagon and knocked on the door yet again.

Lucien opened the door and peered out, then said, "come in Alexander, but pray, be quiet about it. She is weaker than ever now, and must have no excitement to stir her poor heart."

Alexander nodded, then climbed in carefully, and went to his knees beside Sarasvati's prone body, marking how wan and thin she looked. The disease was advancing more rapidly than anyone had expected, and she lay under the blanket with her eyes closed but she was not asleep. Her breath was so faint and light that she seemed to be dead already.

Sitting nearby, Parvati clutched her stuffed lamb in her tiny arms and watched with grey eyes sober with the adult knowledge of death.

Sarasvati stirred, and her eyes opened as she looked up at Alexander with a weak smile. "Alexander, how nice to see you again," she said, her voice barely audible.

"Mother, I am glad to see you," he replied gently. "How are you feeling?"

"It will not be long now," she said. "I am not afraid."

"Father, what can we do for her?" he asked Lucien.

"I... do not know. I have no skill to prevent this. But I will not see her die this way, on the road and in this rough place."

Sarasvati shook her head. "This is home for me," she said. "This poor old rolling wooden box has been my comfort, and the memories I cherish most are here with you, my husband. I am richer here than any palace could make me feel. Even in that lovely place on the river I did not feel at home unless you were close by. But here with you, I am happy."

"What of Parvati?" Alexander asked.

"She will have to go on without me, and I feel certain that in time she will grow into an accomplished, intelligent woman like her aunts Ruthinda and Charanditha. I look into her eyes and see a wisdom beyond her years, and for that alone I am compensated. Promise me you will protect her then as you protect her now."

"I am doubly honored, lady," he replied, feeling strangely detached, almost numb, resigned to the inevitable. He looked to Parvati and picked her up, hugged her close and kissed her cheek. But the child was too keenly aware of the solemnity of the moment and did not respond at first. Then she threw her arms around his neck and turned away, and for the first time began to cry in earnest.

Lucien turned to Alexander and said, "take her out for a walk. She has not left her mother's side once since Bistritza, and I must have a few moments alone with Sarasvati. Please."

Silently, Alexander carried the weeping toddler out of the wagon, and endured the piercing sounds of her shrieking in his ear as she cried out and reached toward the wagon, calling to her mother.

But he was not prepared for the sight confronting him as he emerged. A sea of candlelight surrounded him in the dark, and the gysies' somber faces glowed above the flames as they stood a silent vigil. He looked around in wonder and astonishment as one of the gypsy women approached him and said, "let me take her for a time, and relieve your burden. She is so like my own child, whom I lost to a palsy last year. With your permission, my lord?"

He looked down into her eyes and saw the truth in her words, and reluctantly handed his weeping half sister over. "Your name, lady, that I might know you?"

"I am called Erzebeta Cecescu. Velin is my uncle," she replied. Parvati gradually seemed to surrender, and curled her hands around her neck as the woman's warm arms sheltered her with a tender hug. "Do not cry, szusheska. I will take care of you."

"I am grateful, lady," he replied with a short smile. The woman nodded, and carried Parvati away with her, whispering soft words of endearment in her small ear to calm her down.

Then his own heart grew dark with sudden solitary grief as he joined the others to wait. And as he watched the old faithful wagon, he vowed to honor Sarasvati's memory with deeds of kindness and courage from then on.

After another three hours had passed, the humans gradually took to sitting down where they stood, and the candles had burned down almost to the bottoms of their wicks. Alexander sat silently in the midst of them, his focus centered on the door to the wagon.

Then it opened slowly, and Lucien carried his wife's limp and lifeless body out of the wagon. "It is ended," he intoned, his voice deep and sonorous as a funeral dirge. "Pray, prepare a pyre, so that she is burned in the tradition of her people."

Slowly, the gypsies rose and went to gather wood, and in a short time a stacked pile of timbers appeared in the center of the clearing. Alexander watched while Lucien laid Sarasvati's body on top of it with tender care. He composed her limbs, bent and kissed her cold forehead, brushed his long fingers along one lifeless cheek, then took the burning torch from Velin Cecesçu and thrust it into the logs.

The wet wood sputtered and almost refused to catch. Then Ragosi stepped forward, unstopped a bottle and sprinkled liquid on the pyre. "A toast of slivoviska for the lady," he explained quietly.

The fire flared upward and spread rapidly into the center as the pyre began to consume the body. At length, a woman started singing a plaintive folk tune, and gradually everyone joined in. When they finished, all grew silent again.

Alexander watched from a short distance away as Lucien stood silent, stiffly at attention like a soldier. In the warm firelight he caught sight of a tear glistening on his father's cheek and the solemn expression of a man left alone in the world. Though he wanted to take Lucien in his arms to console him, something told him that he could not possibly share in his father's grief by any measure, so he remained where he was.

As the flames rose high into the sky and finished its work, Lucien stood back farther to escape a sparking ember, then turned his back on the conflagration and walked away into the woods alone. And as the flames ascended into the dark, it seemed as if an age had come to an end.

At that, the assembly broke into murmuring, sorrowful groups and returned to their tents.

Lucien returned sometime later in the night without a word to anyone. Alexander wisely said nothing when Lucien entered the wagon and closed the door gently.

84

The morning brought a somber mood when the carnival of lost souls stirred awake, but as the sun rose all went about their tasks as if nothing had happened the day before.

Alexander joined in where he could and helped them prepare for the journey, partly to banish the sorrow threatening to drag him down, and partly out of a sense of duty to his father.

Sometime in the afternoon Lucien emerged from the wagon with Parvati in his arms. The child clung to his neck, still crying, still in need of her mother. Lucien spoke to her softly, and kissed her wet cheeks, but she was inconsolable.

Alexander left his saddle blanket and approached. "Let me take her," he insisted. "You have enough to burden yourself."

"Will you be her mother, too, Alexander?" he replied with a sad smile as he handed her over.

Parvati's intelligent response was another shock. "Momma gone!" Then she dissolved into another bout of tears. Alexander could only hold on to her and let her cry. "We cannot travel with her in this state," he declared. "She has had no time to mourn her mother's loss."

Lucien stood considering for a long time, then said, "Erzebeta. Velin's niece did express an interest in Parvati's welfare last evening, did she not? If she were to take Parvati into her care until we have established a home for her, she will be in safe hands."

So together they went to the Cecesçu's wagon, and Velin met them at the door, his face still wet with shaving lotion. When they proposed their idea to him, he barely took time to think before he turned his head and called, "Erzebeta! Will you come to the door?"

A few moments later, the woman appeared at his side. She looked as if she had been crying through the night. Timidly, she asked, "you called, uncle?"

Velin said, "the master and his son are not able to care for Parvati while we are traveling. Will you be willing to undertake her care, that she has a home and mother to raise her until they are well situated?"

The woman's eyes betrayed tears of both sadness and joy as she said, "aye, uncle. I will, and she will be most welcome!"

Reluctantly, Alexander handed Parvati over, and Erzebeta cooed softly to the toddler as she hugged her close. "You will have the love of a mother, szusheska," she soothed. "I know that I could never replace her, but I will give you all that I have to make you happy. Yes?"

Apparently they had formed a special bond during their brief time together, because Parvati snuffled and sniffed, and the tears stopped flowing. The toddler threw her arms around Erzebeta's neck and said, "yes, Beta. I wuv oo."

"I wuv oo too," she sobbed, then retreated inside with the toddler before she started crying again.

Velin looked after her and said, "I think it a good arrangement. Parvati will have my niece's love and care, and you will be free to go on to wherever you are going. Will you leave us here, or will you journey on in our company? It seems that all our fortunes are linked together."

Lucien replied, "you will always have our protection and our gratitude for your hospitality. If you cherish your freedom and wish to go elsewhere, you have only to tell us."

"You are generous as you have always been, my lord," Velin said with a short bow, then retreated inside and shut the door.

"His words strengthen me with hope," Lucien said with a sigh. Then he turned to Alexander. "It may take some time, but once we are in France it may be possible to create a good home for Parvati, where she will enjoy all that her heart desires."

Alexander looked at the wagon, studied its worn appearance, and asked, "and what about the wagon?"

Lucien turned and stared at it for a few moments before he replied, "It seems that part of my life is over, and it is now only a reminder of the love I shared with Sarasvati. It was hers, and hers alone. Now that she is gone, it must go with her. I will take my place at your side as your companion and father and sleep outdoors, for I spent far too much time away from you. Will you have me so?"

"Father, you never had to ask," Alexander replied, somewhat amazed at Lucien's humble mood.

Later, when Lucien had distributed everything Sarasvati and her sisters had owned to the women in the camp, he chose one of the horses for carrying luggage and gave the other to Velin. Then he took an axe and began to destroy the old wagon, rendering it into shivers of kindling with methodical, determined strokes. It appeared to be a cathartic experience for him.

Thunk. Thunk. Thunk.

Alexander watched as the blade penetrated the wood and sent the pieces flying. It was almost painful to see, as brief snatches of happy memory, of hot tea, Charanditha sorting through beads, and Ruthinda's loyalty and determined courage, of Sarasvati's charming smile that afternoon in Bistriţa; flashed through his mind like lightning and disappeared again. But these, too, had to be let go.

The rest of the camp watched quietly and did not offer their help knowing that this was Lucien's task to do alone. When there was nothing left, Lucien dropped the axe and stood breathing heavily as he appraised what he had done. Then he silently stood by and watched while the others began to sort through the shivers for good firewood.

85

August, 1647

Over the course of the next few days, the little circus traveled slowly through the thickest part of the forest, following a small creek which meandered toward the marshland of the river marking the border between Transylvania and Magyarland, also called Hungary.

Lucien had resumed his monkish demeanor, clad in his usual black, and read from his little book while Alexander and Bela Ragosi kept a watch on the road ahead and behind. It was here that the danger of being set upon by bandits was greatest, because the wood only thinned at the river's edge and the road. But again the forest was empty.

Alexander remembered what Lucien had said about the plague, and was reminded that there were now fewer people in the world than there had been before. The new world of the Americas that Sir Walter Raleigh had spoken of was yet to be fully explored. He wondered if the forests there were just as wild and bleak as Transylvania's.

Twice they passed through clearings where the Turkish armies had left ruins and remains of burned out villages, but judging by their overgrown condition the attacks must have taken place years before.

The Szganis stopped long enough to search for whatever could be salvaged, burned the ricks to the ground, and rounded up the wild sheep grazing among the ruins. After all, milk and meat were ever needed, and the children were already complaining of hunger.

That evening, everyone dined on roast mutton and flat bread, and drank the last of a cache of wine found in a cellar. Alexander and Lucien feasted on the blood of an old ewe gone lame, then donated her flesh to the cooking pot.

Days later, when the woods thinned out and turned into pastureland, the first signs of farming and crops gave the travelers some measure of hope. They set up their camp near the last turn in the road before the approach to Oradea, out of sight of the castle and the city ramparts. Lucien wisely advised Velin that it was best to find out what they could of the condition of the city before they entered it.

When they saw the tents go up, some of the farmers on the fields ventured closer to watch, and before long the word was spread that a circus had come to town. As more people from the surrounding area gathered together on the center lane they shared what they knew of the road ahead.

The news was grim. Oradea was still occupied by a Turk regiment, and by all accounts the Sultan Mohammed was negotiating a treaty with the voivode Stephan Bathori of Transylvania, whose intercession was the only thing preventing the Saxon lands east of the Danube from being totally overtaken.

There were bands of Hungars, Magyars, Saxons, Hessians, Austrians, and even Swedes roaming the countryside and getting into heated skirmishes with each other, the Turks, and the local population.

Anyone suspected of being foreign, Protestant and/or undead fell under close scrutiny from all quarters and were made to identify themselves. But according to the locals, Transylvania was not at the center of the conflict. Everything was said to be concentrated at

Budapesth, and there was no telling when that would change. Yet the city continued to operate as it had for centuries, Turks or not.

The whole picture resembled a jumbled hodgepodge of rumor, fact, inuendo, and just plain conjecture.

"And, you say this has been so for thirty years?" Lucien asked Ragosi. "Remarkable. One would think there were no more Turks left to fight."

The tall immortal shrugged. "They breed like rabbits. From what I have heard, there is little time for one noble to make his mark on the world before he is removed from it and replaced with another. I have heard of brother turning against brother, mother against son, child against father, and all for the sake of royal caprice. And the Turks are busy negotiating treaties which fall apart at the drop of a hat. It is sheer madness to travel openly in these conditions."

"Then let us be circumspect from now on, and question anyone who does not belong," Lucien suggested. "I should not be surprised if there are already spies of one camp or another in our midst. Pass the word, but do it quietly."

Ragosi grinned like a possum, then gave him a short bow and strolled away.

86

That evening there was a prosperous crowd in attendance, and the circus performers were in good form. The night air was warm and dry. While the tumblers and other artists kept the audience rapt with attention, a tall man wearing a broad brimmed hat and a leather coat with a fur collar walked aimlessly among the crowd looking as if he had lost something. He carried a large leather bag which looked heavy.

His companions walked nearby, dressed in similar leathers, looking battleworn and seriously grim as they filtered their way through the crowd.

One of the boys noticed them loitering too long among the living tents. He slipped away toward the main wagon, entered it and went to Lucien, who sat counting the day's receipts.

"M'lord, there are armed men on the center lane," he said. "One of them is the man you described to us, a tall stranger wearing a hat and a leather coat. He is carrying a large valise with him."

"Thank you, Aric," Lucien replied softly, "you have done well. Here is a copper for your alertness. Now go back to set the watch, and do not let anyone see you."

Clutching the coin tightly in his hand, the boy ran to obey while Lucien finished counting the stacks of coins, recording the figure on a piece of parchment. Then he put everything away in a strongbox, which he locked up and stowed away under a pile of clothing. He drew on his sword belt, found his flintlock pistol and tucked it into his belt, then drew on his overcoat. Thus armed, he emerged from the tent and walked silently toward the center stage.

Alexander met him quickly on the path, sensing something was amiss. "Father?"

"Van Helsing is here," Lucien replied softly.

Their nemesis was not that hard to spot. His hard, stern Hessian face stood out like a banner among the laughing, delighted faces of those around him. His blue eyes scanned the crowd and the rigging near the stage, not the stage itself or the performance.

"I see him now," Alexander said. "What is your plan?"

"I will go and introduce myself to him," Lucien declared.

Alex's mouth dropped open, and he said in a shocked whisper, "have you lost your senses? The moment he sees you, all is lost."

Lucien's mouth curled into a faint smile. "Calm yourself, Alexander. I know well what I must look like to others. It will be the only way to bring him and his men out into the open, and if they resist they will only reveal to the crowd the source of their trouble."

He placed his hand on his son's shoulder, patted it, then moved on toward the hunter.

Alexander swallowed his initial shock and dogged him, but not too closely; and signaled to Ragosi and Velin what was happening. The two of them then followed after Alexander, arming themselves as they went.

When they arrived, they saw Lucien come to a standstill right behind van Helsing. There was a pause of perhaps five seconds as the unaware vampire hunter continued to observe the crowd. Then Lucien said, "good evening," close to his left ear.

Van Helsing turned suddenly, startled. His eyes went wide as he looked the tall pale man up and down, and he backed up a step as if he had been burned. "Gott in Himmel!" came out of his mouth before he could stop himself. "Where...where did you come from?"

"Right behind you," Lucien replied calmly. "Come. Shall we speak privately where these good people cannot be disturbed?"

The thick lips curled into a frown. "Why should I fear you? You are but a servant of the devil, not the devil himself. Who are you?"

"I am Count Lucienantellus Corvinus Arkanon, a prince of Transylvania," Lucien said with a bow and an elegant flourish of his hand. "And you are...?"

"Baron Nicholaus van Helsing," the Hessian replied with a stiff curt nod of his head. "My mission here is one of the utmost importance. I seek out the undead, nosferatu, who plague the living in the land."

A pale eyebrow elevated skeptically. "To what purpose?"

"Why, to rid the world of them," van Helsing snorted. "Heard you not the stories of their bloodlust? How they murder their loved ones in their beds, and cause much sickness and ruin wherever they go?"

Lucien studied him with steady sparkling grey eyes, and said, "let us speak as man to man, and you will tell me what you have learned, but not here in the open. I would not have you destroy the peace. The people here have already seen so much war and strife in their oh so short lives, and they have need of the diversion. Do you agree?"

Van Helsing considered long before he finally answered, "aye. I well know the truth of that. But if you are lying to me..."

"Then come." With that, Lucien deliberately turned his back and walked toward the darkness. To Alexander's relief the hunter followed him, and he slipped through the gathered crowd trying to stay abreast.

When they saw van Helsing walking away into the shadows, his men abandoned their posts and followed after as subtly as they could, until all were entirely swallowed up by the darkness and beyond the perimeter of the camp.

There, Lucien turned suddenly, and confronted the hunter with a stern expression on his pale face. "I have heard many things about you, too, my lord Baron, and they have not been complimentary. They say you dig up the corpses of loved ones and desecrate them in a shameful way. They say you even mutilate children who were taken so tragically before their time. What mandates you to perform such horrendous deeds?"

"I was instructed to do so by an angel of the Lord, who did come to me in a dream," van Helsing replied. "The angel told me that it was the only way to restore their souls to righteousness. The families seek me out to do this, as it is their custom, and that they find all comfort in it."

"And for the gold, perhaps. Was there ever any doubt in your heart?" Lucien asked, his eyes threatening to flash red.

"Never," the hunter replied with certainty. "As for the gold... I have needs, just as any other man does."

"Granted. Yet, you believe so firmly that your cause is just."

"The angel told me that it is for the good of their souls that I do these things. The undead are servants of the devil, and the demons which inhabit their bodies must be cast out."

Lucien frowned as he replied, "there is no evil in those poor unfortunate wretches who find themselves in the midst of a sickness which renders them into a deep sleep, that they cannot be wakened easily and so are interred before their time. Thought you to inspect them for proof of life before you drove the spikes into their hearts, or did you do them in with all haste and carelessness in your holy certainty? Were you to but wait a little, you might have saved their lives as well as their souls."

"You speak blasphemy!" van Helsing exclaimed. "What I did was for the good of all. I freed their souls from bondage!"

"And now you seek out the living, to dispatch them also in such a way, do you? Have you no conscience or compassion, sir?" Lucien asked. "You will not find what you are looking for here."

Van Helsing paused as if his power of speech was cut off, then asked, "and you, Count? Are you a witch or necromancer? What gods do you pray to? Have you no love of Christ?"

"I am a man who believes in the truth, and whose god is far greater and more wondrous than yours," Lucien replied. "That god is science. My soul is free to explore wherever my heart takes me. If your prophet Jesus were to witness your deeds, he would cast you out from his heart. I pity you, Nicholaus, for your spirit is enslaved by the delusion which has possessed you. You are become the very thing you fear "

"I fear nothing!" the hunter replied, stepped back and reached for his waist, where a large flintlock rested at his belt. But before his fingers even touched the grip he found a sharp blade nocked against

342

his throat, and Alexander's low growling voice intoned in his ear from behind, "touch that and you die."

Slowly, he lowered his hand and let it go slack while Alexander relieved him of the weapon. "I may have miscalculated your determination," van Helsing continued. "But if you kill me, my men will avenge me. Each is sworn to protect me and my cause."

"Then your men will meet a similar fate," Lucien said. "Alexander is excellently skilled in the art of the sword, and if he had wanted to kill you you would be dead already. Even then, had you drawn your pistol I am more than capable of defending myself without his aid." As he spoke, he drew open his black coat and showed his weapons. "And I have other skills you would not be able to overcome. We are not innocents, Baron, nor did I trust you from the moment I learned the truth of you and your quest. Your thoughts are transparent as a pane of glass, and I saw all reflected in your eyes. By your very words you confess yourself a soldier of fortune and a murderer."

"You are a witch!" van Helsing cried out. He looked around with growing desperation and found that he was completely alone among the four men who surrounded him.

Ragosi laughed harshly as he declared, "your men are out cold. Did you think we would let them roam freely among us like wolves among the sheep?"

"Now I will tell you what you are going to do, my lord Baron," Lucien said. "You will collect your men and go back to Austria. This is Transylvania, and our ways are not your ways. The emperor does not look kindly on your desecrations and there is a price on your head, which I would be tempted to collect were I infected with your lust for gold. Think on your deeds, that they have made of you a marked man, with no place to lay your head in safety."

He jerked his head, and the blade disappeared from van Helsing's throat.

The vampire hunter stood quietly rubbing at the spot where the sharp edge had nicked it. "Yes," he said finally. "I will think on your words. Good night." Then he turned and walked away into the darkness.

Ragosi and Velin, Alexander and Lucien watched him go until he disappeared from sight. "Think you he will return?" Velin asked.

"That, only time will tell," Lucien replied.

87

The next morning, two of Ragosi's men were sent to reconnoiter the condition of the city, and brought back news that the Turks had established a garrison in Oradea, but it was relatively small and posed no significant threat to a large force of any kind.

"If we are circumspect, and confine ourselves to the marketplace, we may escape their notice as nought but minstrels and players," said the first one. "Then we may purchase our supplies and move on before they can even blink an eye," said the other.

"I wish I had your confidence," was Alexander's quiet remark. "Thank you. I will pass your news on to my father."

The two men bowed and walked away to do other chores, while he went to Lucien and relayed what he learned.

Lucien looked somber as usual, and said, "we must obtain more food for the others," he said. "There is little choice to be had in the matter. Very well, let us broach the subject with Ragosi and Velin, and if all are in accord we will move into the city."

By late afternoon the odd circus packed up, assembled into a neat line, and set off toward the main gate of the high wall.

Oradea was built around its castle, which sat atop a high promontory overlooking the small riverside village crowding its base. The road cut straight through the center of town and passed across a Roman bridge built in the 3rd century to span the Danube where it passed through the lower Carpathian ridge. Parts of the bridge had already seen damage from previous incursions by Huns, Saxons, and now the ubiquitous Turks, but it continued to serve as a passage through the invisible boundary between Hungary proper and Transylvania, and the division between two distinctly different cultures.

Once across the bridge, however, the Germanic influence of the Hungarians transformed the rough countryside into something resembling idyllic charm and pastoral grace. Aside from the frequent skirmishes between warring clans, life went on in spite of the war. Or perhaps it was simply that the peasant and merchant classes accepted that the high risk of being utterly wiped out in pitched battles was part of it. In any case, the goal of reaching France was much closer now, and Lucien was adamant about moving as fast as possible in spite of everything.

When they approached the gate, Lucien signaled the travelers to come to a halt, as several soldiers dressed in the colors of Hungary came forward on foot and blocked their way. Their leader approached almost timidly. He was unarmed, and his uniform looked as if he had slept on the ground in it. His blond cheeks sported the rough stubble of a beard, unusual for a guardsman. His hair was also rough cut, and his thick lips betrayed a slight gap between his teeth. His blue eyes looked tired, as did his entire body. He asked in German, "Gut tag, my friends. Who are you? What business have you in Oradea?"

"Gut tag, mein herr," Lucien replied, "We are but traveling performers, and desire to pass through on our way to Budapesth."

The guard studied him carefully, then the rest of the train behind him. "How do I know you speak the truth?"

"We have our families with us, and our sole task is to give all we encounter brief moments of respite from the war and entertainment to those in need of a diversion from their sorrows. Come, sergeant. Will you not give us shelter for a night? I pledge that if anyone is harmed by our presence we will move on and trouble you no more."

The sergeant glanced about and then leaned forward. His voice went low and urgent as he said, "it is difficult enough with the Turks sitting on our chests and pushing their arrogance on us. They have made slaves of us all. What can you do to help us?"

"By ourselves, or as one man, perhaps nothing," Lucien replied. "Where is your commandant, your burgomeister?"

"My commandant is dead. So is our city council."

"How many of your people share your view?"

"All of them," the sergeant said simply, shrugging.

"Then you are well fortified, and need only to organize to repel the enemy. But wait until the opportune moment, and when the Turks are off their guard, you must act as one body, and be of one mind. All the people of the town must work deeds of such complexity that the Turks will be easily divided and overwhelmed. Then is their rout certain and assured."

Something in Lucien's warm melodic voice washed away the tension and mistrust barring his way. The sergeant almost came to attention, then said, "you speak like a soldier, sir. What campaigns have you seen?"

Lucien replied, "more than I care to count or speak of. If you are keen to hear my story, I would feel more content to tell it if I am not sitting on my horse. Will you let us pass in?"

"A moment, if you will, my friend," the sergeant said, and rejoined his comrades to discuss the situation. They appeared to agree, and the sergeant returned to Lucien. "You may pass in, and I would consider it an honor if you would meet with me at the inn of The Dragon and The Phoenix, at mid evening. Many of us are hungry for news of the outside world."

Alexander almost gaped with quiet amazement. The dragon did seem to be everywhere, in every part of the world, and by an odd coincidence appeared to be central to moments in his life where he was at a crossroads, or taking another turn. Were he the superstitious sort he would have thought it predestined, but his experience told him otherwise.

Lucien nodded, and said, "I shall be there. May I bring my son, who is my companion and confidant in all things?"

"Aye. Your name, sir?"

"Lucien Arkanon, Count of Baia Mare. This is my son, Alexander Corvina. And your name is?"

"Sergeant Hamar Multenyi. Welcome to Oradea," he said, saluting, then signaled to the others, who ran to open the gate. He followed after them, shouting orders as he did so.

Alexander leaned over and asked, "father, are we now adding rebellion to our list of heroic deeds?"

"The town is already ripe for it," Lucien said. "I have no desire to stay longer here than absolutely necessary." With that he turned and signaled the caravan to start moving again.

When they passed through the gate, the road became almost instantly lined with people who came to stand and watch the file go by. Then something strange happened. A man and his wife began to clap their hands, then a few more, and still a few more, until the whole crowd was cheering and applauding their approval.

Alexander looked around him and felt both confusion and astonishment. It was if a conquering army had returned home, not a ragtag circus of performers and illusionists. He could hardly fathom the source of this welcoming noise. He asked, "father, what is happening?"

"It appears we are the first ones to penetrate the wall without being challenged since the Turks first occupied the town," Lucien replied. "Sergeant Multenyi was right in that they are starved for news, but even more for hope that their liberation is at hand. Perhaps he was in his own way demonstrating his defiance of the Turk by allowing us in. Notice that there are no soldiers to prevent our entrance. Their forces must be stretched thin indeed, that they cannot control the people or prevent their assembly for any purpose."

"The question arises whether the Turks will allow such open defiance to go unpunished."

"That, my son, shall be answered by time," Lucien said. "Worry not, and focus only on that which is necessary to protect our own."

88

The circus established a compound on the waterfront near the bridge, and soon the center lane was again packed with visitors; all clamoring for entertainment and eager to hear news of the outside world. Somehow skin color, race, or cultural distinctions disappeared as the throng moved along the course sampling the wonders the circus had to offer, and shared their gossip furtively as if they had all been imprisoned behind bars.

The Turk soldiers keeping guard could only watch, but could not prevent the crowd gathering and did not even try. For all their menace they were in fact quite impotent against the greater numbers of the people under their control.

While Ragosi and Velin kept an eye on the operation of the circus, Lucien and Alexander found their way to the inn.

The place had seen better days, but now all the windows were dark and the shutters closed; and a sign on the door proclaimed that it was closed for business. The door gaped open a crack, meaning that someone had already gone in. With their usual caution, Lucien and Alexander cased the vicinity for a short time to make sure they were not followed or observed, then slipped inside.

The inn was completely empty, and no candle or torch was lit within. They stood looking around at the shabby interior, the worn out furnishings, when an older man carrying a small candle came in from another room and greeted them. "You are the men Multenyi told me were coming?" he asked.

"Aye," Lucien replied, nodding. "Where is he?"

"Come this way," the man said, and led them through the empty foyer into the tavern area, then down the stairs into a wine cellar which had been turned into a crude meeting place with a long table and chairs, dimly lit by small lanterns. There were no bottles, and the racks were folded up or broken into piles of kindling on the floor.

A large group of men, some in Hungarian uniform and some in civilian clothes, sat or stood waiting for the meeting to begin. One of them was Multenyi, who had changed from his uniform into civilian clothes.

When he saw Lucien and Alexander come down the steps Multenyi said, "welcome. Please, sit and share a tankard with me. These are my compatriots, who are men of good birth and fortunes. Gentlemen, this is Count Lucien Arkanon, of Baia Mare, and his son Alexander. They have come from Transylvania."

"Baia Mare?" said one of the men. "I have heard of it. I heard tell of a great explosion in the mountains many years ago, which did set the forest on fire. The people were scattered and driven away by the flames, and never returned to the village. Yet you say you came from there?"

"It was rebuilt anew, and taken over during the war some time ago," Lucien explained. "There is little left of it now."

As he and Alexander sat, the innkeeper placed tankards in front of them. "It is water only, for here we are forbidden from dispensing spirits," he explained. "I must keep the inn closed unless we are meeting."

"Water is quite acceptable," Lucien said, and raised the container to his lips. Alexander smiled and mimicked his father. The water tasted barely potable, and smelled vaguely of leaves and mold. He pretended to sip and then placed the tankard on the table without drinking.

Suddenly, the whole picture became clear. Like Multenyi, the other men in his company had a lean and ill-favored look, and he sensed that they had not shared a single prosperous meal between them in weeks.

"We wish to know what the conditions are in the countryside," said Multenyi. "You spoke of organizing, and dividing the enemy so that he can be easily defeated. I have no gift for strategy, but I and my comrades are eager to learn what we can do to free ourselves."

"So you are not as interested in what I might have done before, but in what I can do to help you plan your strategy," Lucien said.

Multenyi nodded vigorously. "We need new minds, and fresh ideas. Everything we have tried has met with disaster, and we are closely watched at every moment. Even our wondrous instant of greeting on the road today is being picked apart by those Turk devils up in the castle. Every moment is fraught with risk that we may be set upon and imprisoned, or worse, executed for daring to defy them."

"By a show of hands, then, may I know how many of you have been outside the wall in the last six months?"

Multenyi raised his hand, and six others. "I have only been beyond the wall as far as the large tree you passed on the approach to the gate," he added. The rest shook their heads with glum futility.

"Then I bear you good news," Lucien said. "We have not seen Turk regiments anywhere in the last month, and the captain of the guard in Klausenburg told us they had already moved on. In Bistritza we learned that the Turk have all moved south to Sibiu and on toward Serbia. Prince Stephan has arranged a treaty to keep Transylvania from being overrun yet again. This garrison is isolated, cut off from all hope of securing reinforcements."

The men exhaled their relief. "That is good news, indeed," said another man.

"What have you tried before that has met with failure?"

Over the next hour, each man spoke of tactics which were planned well, but failed due to the timing, the place, or the opportunity vanishing amid random events. Three told their own harrowing experience of escaping capture by hiding out among the populace, who were more than happy to shelter them because they were all related by family or clan allegiances.

Another talked about his frustration at being kept under close scrutiny by units of soldiers stationed in the most advantageous spots around town, which rendered ineffective any attempt at an insurrection. All agreed that they bore a grave risk just by attending this meeting, where the Turks could easily scoop up all their rotten eggs in one basket. Each man had pledged to keep his association with the group a secret even if tortured.

When they were finished, Lucien sat considering for a long moment, then said, "each of you are working independently in a place where there is no coordination, communication, or an authority to rely on. Who among you is the leader?"

"We all agreed it would be Sergeant Multenyi," said the second man. "We pass notes to each other wherever and whenever we can. But plans are often not acted upon, or there is some ill timed delay in their execution. Three days ago, one of our group was roused up in the middle of the night and escorted to the castle by a troop of Turk soldiers. We never saw him again."

"How many are the Turk? I count but twenty of you."

"Uh... they do seem to be everywhere," Multenyi replied. "The number changes day by day, but I estimate they are but two hundred two score, or perhaps a few more."

Alexander asked, "two hundred two score, in a town of thousands? Where are the rest of your militia?"

"Most are dead or injured beyond fighting," he replied. "The others went home to their wives and children to wait. We have all been waiting for someone to come and save us."

"The Turks have all the guns, all the cannon, and all the horses," said another man. "We have nothing. Each of them is protected by his fellows, and none has ever been caught alone."

"That may still be in your favor," Lucien said.

"A man can turn anything into a weapon," Alexander added. "Even his hands. And one man can inflict great damage to his enemy using his mind alone."

Multenyi leaned forward. "How? We have tried everything we can think of. Please, my lord, I beg you. Teach us this new way of fighting, that we may become better at defeating the Turk."

"There is no time for me to teach you all," Alexander replied. "But you can use what you know already to your advantage."

"The journey of a thousand miles begins with but a single step," Lucien added. "Each of you must decide what you are going to do, and then do it. Do not wait to confer with each other, but act independently. Each of you must be prepared to face the consequences alone if you fail, and to sacrifice your life for the good of your community."

"Aye, we well know the price for failure," said one of the men, and there were noises of agreement all around him.

"Now, perhaps we may achieve success," said another.

The man assigned to keep a weather eye out for the enemy came to the trap door and called softly, "the patrol is coming."

Quickly, Lucien blew out the candle in the lantern in front of him, and the others extinguished the other lights in the room. All grew quiet and dark, and Alexander could hear the sound of marching outside. But the soldiers did not stop, nor did their steps falter on the cobblestones as they passed. They marched on down the lane and turned the corner.

Even then, no one moved to light the lanterns even as the sound of marching feet faded, and in the pitch dark Multenyi's voice said, "we must disband for the evening. Good night, gentlemen. Safe journey home."

There was the quiet shuffle of footsteps as the men went up the stairs, through a rear door and into the night, dispersing quickly until all of them were gone. "This much we have been able to manage," he added. "Can you find your way back to the circus?"

A hand landed on his shoulder, startling him, and Lucien's smooth accented voice replied, "do not worry about us, Sergeant. Come, Alexander."

"Wait," Multenyi said. "Please tell me you will stay and help us. Tell me how I can lead my people better. They are afraid, and must have something to restore their spirits. Hope is all we have left."

Alexander said, "I will stay and talk more with him. I can find my own way back. Can we stay longer until this matter is settled?"

Lucien replied, "I must confer with our people, so that all are in accord with this. We must ensure their safety, remember. I will take your vote with me to the others, so choose now."

Alexander weighed the options, and came back with, "I could not abandon these people if their need is so dire. If we must leave, I could stay longer, and then catch you up on the road."

"Then I will convey our answer to you in the light of day, Sergeant," Lucien said. "You will know it when you see it."

Then he was gone as if he was never there. Alexander could see Multenyi grope around in the dark for an anxious moment, then said, "he is gone. I am still here."

"I did not hear him leave. I could not see him. How did he do that?" Multenyi asked.

"That... is not easily learned," Alexander replied. "If you wish to know how to conquer the Turk, you must conquer your fear of them first. You must begin by going home and making an inventory of all your possessions. Divide those you value most from the rest, and discard all else."

"What will that accomplish?" Mutenyi asked, when he had recovered his wit.

"You must know what you are prepared to leave behind, and what you are not. It will unburden your heart of those things which have no meaning, and remove all distractions from your resolve."

Alexander then recited the nine principles of the way Musashi taught him to assign priorities to his life. "Above all you must accept death as a fact of life, and be prepared to face it calmly, no matter what happens."

"This is marvelous," Mustenyi gushed. "But, how may I use this knowledge against the Turk?"

"You will serve your people best by showing them how to behave in the face of death. It will strengthen them to conquer their own fear and to overthrow the enemy with each act of simple defiance. You took the first step this morning, by allowing the circus in. Never before have I seen such courage."

The young soldier considered for a moment, then said, "I agree it was a bold move. But I was desperate..."

"What you saw as desperation was an act of true daring. In that moment, you forgot your fear of being shot or imprisoned and went on instinct. The fight for survival makes us do very strange things betimes, but it is the result alone which shows a man's quality, in every aspect of his life."

Multenyi ran a hand through his bedraggled blond hair and finally said, "all our lives we are taught to fear God, to avoid sin, but to obey orders even when they do not make sense, to fight and die without questioning. But you say there is better way to live, and if we are all to survive we must learn to govern ourselves. Is that right?"

Alexander smiled. "You have always had the freedom to choose how you live your life," he said. "But when you commit to fight, or choose what else to do, you must know in your heart that it is the right thing to do, and why you are doing it. Do not allow others to choose for you. You chose to be a soldier, so fight like one."

Multenyi's hopeful smile fell. "Eh... I did not," he said. "I am but a conscript, forced into service because Emperor Ferdinand needed troops and I was of the proper age. When I was younger I wanted to be an artist. In whatever brief moments of freedom I can find I scribble, or manage a drawing or two. But of late there has been no time, and the Turk has confiscated all works of art saying that they are marks of the devil."

Alexander bowed his head. "I sympathize, for I am heart a writer, and keep a journal of my travels."

"Then you know my travail." The Sergeant drew himself up straight. "But you are right. I am a soldier, too," he said. "And because the others look up to me I have a duty to lead them. You say that a man can use anything as a weapon. How?"

"If there was any time, I could teach you how to use your bare hands," he replied. "But let us start with your mind, and that can wait until the morrow, for now it is late, and I must go."

"Yes, of course," Multenyi said. "Thank you..."

And suddenly Multenyi had the strange sensation that he was completely alone in a dark room. He looked around frantically, trying to get his bearings, but could see and hear nothing. Shivering with the chill moving up his spine, he said, "he has got to teach me how to do that!" and quickly ran up the stairs into the night.

89

When Alexander returned to the circus, he could see that it was in full swing and there was a generous crowd gathered around the main stage, where Bela Ragosi stood dressed in a rather elegant outfit and performed a wondrous magic act using one of the Szgani women as an assistant.

It involved two cabinets. He helped the woman enter one of them, closed the door, spun it around once, then opened the door. The cabinet stood empty, and the crowd murmured in hushed tones as he went to the other cabinet and opened its door. There the same woman stood, and there were gasps and applause as she stepped out.

Then she removed a handkerchief from her bosom and fluffed it about to show that it was just a square of cloth, bunched it in her hand carefully, waved her hand over it and fluffed it again. Out flew a white dove. The amazed crowd applauded again, and both Bela and his assistant took a deep bow as they were showered with coins.

Alexander had never seen the entire act from its inception and had to admit to himself that it was quite a feat, though he could hardly understand how the people could afford to be so generous in their dire straits. Or perhaps that, too, was an act of defiance toward the Turks, and normal behavior in the face of certain doom was seen as a mark of courage.

He went on to the main wagon and climbed in. There, Lucien and Velin sat together talking, while Erzebeta sat with Parvati on her lap.

At his entrance, Lucien looked up and said, "ah. Alexander, we have decided to stay until the Turks have been dealt with."

"That is good," he replied. "I gave our friend Sergeant Multenyi some advice he would find of great use for the time being, but he is distracted by the heavy burden of so much responsibility being placed on his young shoulders. He is modest and inexperienced in matters of subterfuge and war."

"Such distraction could be his undoing," his father said. "I sensed he was fearful and confused."

Alexander snorted. "More like terrified witless. He is an artist."

Lucien's eyes grew larger as his brows crept upward. "No. Truly? It would explain much."

"He spoke of having to be something he is not. He is no soldier of fortune but a conscript forced to serve his king the best way he knows how. Now he is looked to by the others for leadership. I told him how to conquer his fear, but it will take something truly magical to help him retain his courage. I can scarcely think what."

Erzebeta looked down at the grey eyed toddler sitting next to her and asked, "Parvati, what do you think we can do?"

The toddler smiled, then threw up her hands and said, "boom!"

"Boom?" Lucien said, looking puzzled. Then his expression turned quite devilish as he smiled. "Aye, boom indeed."

The next morning, the circus went about its daily routine of rehearsal and trying out new things, and everyone practiced more vigorously than ever. Twice, Turk patrols stopped to watch. One of them even divided itself and made a more thorough inspection of the camp.

Everything seemed perfectly innocent, and they were assured that everyone was present and accounted for.

Just then one of the ramparts at the outer wall exploded, sending bits of rock, flame and black smoke up into the air. The closest patrol unit ran to see who would dare set incendiaries, and when they were thus occupied another part of the wall exploded clear across town.

Sergeant Multenyi was busy trying to calm the rage of hunger in his stomach when the noise startled him. He spat out a mouthful of dry biscuit before he choked, and stood up slowly when he saw the plumes of dark smoke drifting upward into a blue sky.

He breathed with a happy smile, "dear God," abandoned his post and began running. As he passed a shopkeeper, he called out, "round up the others and start making a loud noise."

Another explosion went up in yet another part of town, and still another, until the Turks were scattered and on the run trying to identify the source and put out the fires.

As if on cue, a crowd assembled in the central square and the adjacent streets. They started dancing, shouting, and drumming on anything they could find. Their mantra was a frenzied chant, "freedom! freedom! freedom!"

The Turk soldiers tried to stop them, but each of them was outnumbered ten to one, and before they could take aim and shoot they were overwhelmed, disarmed and thrown down. Those who fought back were beaten and dragged away, tied up and thrown into a makeshift prison made of an old pig pen which had been emptied of swine long ago.

Then the angry crowd gathered together and armed themselves with pieces of wood, the Turks' swords and muskets, even crockery, and ascended the hill to the castle. There the mob was barred by a platoon at the gate. Several men went down when the guards took aim and shot them, but others relieved the guards of their weapons and turned them on the rest, putting them on the run.

The pressure of their bodies against the iron grill pushed the gate down as the villagers flooded the grounds and threw rocks at the windows, broke them, pushed down the doors and invaded the castle keep. The Turk officers in charge were shot trying to defend the breach.

When the battle was over, and every Turk was accounted for, Multenyi and his comrades declared victory, shouting to the crowd that the enemy was routed and Oradea was free. A great sound of triumph went up among the mob.

Lucien and Alexander sat across from each other, playing a game of chess. While the shouting, screaming and gunshots filled the air and echoed across the compound, Lucien calmly reached over, moved his knight in front of his queen and said, "it worked. Multenyi is a true champion of his people, and Parvati has proved the source of his success. Out of the mouths of babes, indeed."

"She is the daughter of a queen," Alexander replied, as he moved a pawn forward a square to block the knight, planning to take it en passant.

"Then, as there is no barrier to our remaining a few days longer, you may indulge yourself with training sergeant Multenyi to become a true leader of his people. Oradea must be rebuilt from the ground up, and he is the one to do it."

"I would find that an interesting diversion," Alexander replied, then frowned when the knight jumped and landed on his bishop. "Oh. I did not see that. I am out of practice. It has been a long time since I played this game."

"We all learn from our mistakes, Alexander," Lucien replied with a gente smile.

70

Later that afternoon, the young Hungarian came into the compound looking for Alexander, and found him practicing calmly on a mandolin.

"I bring you great news, my lord Count. We have taken the town and castle back from those Turkish devils," he said.

"Yes. We could hear it from here," Alexander replied. Strum.

"A stroke of genius, it was. The element of surprise was quite keen and sure, our victory glorious. The Turks were thrown into confusion so that they were easily defeated. But I must know who was responsible for those wonderful explosions. Did you set those charges at the wall?"

"No." Strum.

"Did your father?"

"No." Strum, strum. Alexander paused to tweak a string at a fret, plucking until the tone rang clear.

"Then who did? I would like to thank him."

Alexander turned to face him, and said calmly, "it should not matter who set them. The deed was done."

In his shock Multenyi's mouth fell open. Then he said, "this is another lesson, isn't it?"

Alexander smiled again and shook his head, but said nothing. Strumm, strumm, strummm, plink, plink, plink. The tune was random, aimless, yet always returned to key.

Multenyi stood thinking furiously. "No," he said, when he came to the end of his rope. "This is madness. I cannot fathom by your silence what you are trying to teach me."

"I am not 'trying' to teach you anything," Alexander replied, and continued strumming. "Take a deep breath through your nose, breathe out through your mouth, and then count to ten."

When the Hungarian did as he was told he appeared to relax, then shook his head with frustration and said, "I am on fire to understand, sir!"

"The whole is greater than the sum of its parts," Alexander said with deliberate calm.

Multenyi frowned in concentration, then ventured, "you are saying that each man is a part of the whole community, and that united, the community is greater than any army of men."

"Aye," Alexander replied. "You demonstrated that more than adequately this day."

"But, the people say I am a hero. They are thanking me for that which I did not do, and I feel strange for accepting their thanks."

"That is because a hero requires no thanks. His satisfaction comes from the result. No reward can ever replace the feeling of success for a good cause. Each man can make a difference in this world, but he must let go of the notion of thanks or rewards, for they feed the basest part of a man."

"You are saying that some men claim to be heroes, and do heroic deeds for the rewards alone. I would call them hypocrites. But then, who do I thank? I feel flushed with success, but I could not have done it without your help."

"Now you are being too humble. If you must be grateful, then thank your comrades for staying loyal to you in spite of everything.

Thank your people, who placed their faith in your leadership though you were stumbling blind in the dark. You must lead them by example and become what you were destined to be."

"What is that?" Multenyi asked, frowning with puzzlement.

"Why, Burgomeister of Oradea, of course," Alexander said. "Someone must begin the work of building the town anew. Who better than the man who opened the wall and permitted a wandering band of players to enter, and who displayed his brave defiance of the Turk oppressors with a simple act of hospitality?"

"I? But, I am no politician," Multenyi protested.

"Policy is a necessary evil. The position does carry the risk of being judged for your decisions and the burden of being responsible for the lives and fortunes of others."

"And what about the rest of it? You said you would teach me how to fight, and plan, and I want to learn how to move soundlessly as you did last eventide."

Alexander looked into his eyes and replied, "I will do as much as I can to teach you, but it is up to you to learn. Are you prepared?"

Multenyi swallowed as his gaze darted away, then nodded vigorously. "Aye, I am ready. But, how much time have you? Your father said..."

"We are staying for a few more days, if you will have us."

"You are welcome to stay as long as you like," the young sergeant gushed with enthusiasm. "When can you begin?"

"Gather what men you trust who wish to learn the art of self-defense, and I will teach you all together. You must build a worthy militia to defend the town, no?"

"Yes, of course," he said. "I will go at once and summon the others. Where shall we meet?"

Alexander glanced around at the open square and replied, "I think here would be ideal, where a man can gain some distance from another and have room to practice. We will start this afternoon, if that is agreeable."

"This afternoon," Multenyi nodded. Then the sound of growling emerged from his stomach and his hand went to his waist.

"And eat something, will you? A man cannot learn anything on an empty stomach," Alexander said, giving him a wink.

"I will do that right away," he said, then fairly ran toward the marketplace.

Alexander lowered the mandolin and sighed heavily, thinking that he was making a mistake, but could not find an excuse to change his mind. True, Hamar Multenyi was no politician, but inside that timid exterior lurked the heart of a lion, if he could only find it.

91

Two hours later, a small group of men assembled in the square, Hamar Multenyi among them. They all looked tired from the excitement of the day, but were eager to learn. The moment Alexander entered the square they all came to attention like soldiers.

He stood looking them over for a long moment before he commanded them, "come to your ease, gentlemen. There is no need. I am not a general."

They laughed in tandem as their bodies relaxed again. "We thought you were going to make us march up and down the square," Hamar added.

"I may just do that," Alexander replied, and the laughter resumed. He waited until they had all quieted down before he said, "line up together and put your arms out, like this." He stood with his arms outstretched on either side of his body. "Stand apart as far as your arms are stretched."

Puzzling, the men did as they were told. Then Alexander told them they could put their arms down. "In order to prepare you to learn the art of self defense, you must learn to tone your bodies first. Which of you has an ache or pain anywhere?"

Three of the men pointed to their backs, two to their necks, and another toward one knee. "Good," he said. "Go home, gentlemen. Have your wives rub your aches away and do all else which will banish your discomfort." At that, the other men laughed and winked at each other. "Then return on the morrow. I cannot teach you now."

The injured men nodded, then limped or ambled away as best they could. Hamar watched them go, then asked, "why?"

"When there is pain anywhere, it is likely to get worse," Alexander explained, "and I cannot teach a man who is not focused on the lesson."

"Ah," he said, nodding.

Alexander then addressed the others. "I am going to teach you all how to stretch, and to resist, and also to breathe. In this way, your bodies will unlearn all that they have learned about combat. When you know how your bodies work, you will know how to fight using nothing more than your bare hands. Then I will show you how to fight with other objects, and then with a sword. Is there any man here who does not accept this regimen? Speak now, or hold your peace."

To their credit, he was greeted with silence. One man coughed, but no word of denial was said. "Very well," he said. "Let us begin. Remove your coats and weapons and lay them on the ground. You will not need them."

Over the course of the afternoon he went through a series of moves of yoga, demonstrating as he explained the purpose for each move. The men followed him and were clumsy at first, but soon became more comfortable with the routine as they discovered they were more limber for it.

When the sun went down behind the hills and cast the square in long shadows, Alexander ended his instruction. "That is all for today. If after a time you find that your limbs ache, take a hot bath so that your joints may loosen. Come again tomorrow after midday."

As the group dispersed Multenyi approached him, and said, "that was invigorating. Where did you learn this way of stretching?"

"In Tibet," Alexander replied.

"Tibet. Is it very far away from here?"

He clapped the younger man on the shoulder and smiled. "It is on the other side of the Moon."

Taken aback at his remark, Multenyi said, "you speak strangely, m'lord. Surely it is not so far away as that."

Alexander laughed. "Nay. I say it in jest, but it is truly very, very far away. A year of travel to the east over land, at the very least."

"I should like to go there some day," his friend replied. "What else do they do there, besides practice this... yoga?"

"They live their lives just as other men do. And I will tell you more about it later. But now I must return to the circus. Good evening."

The next day, Alexander resumed the lesson, and there seemed to be more men in attendance than the day before. He accepted them all with equanimity and placed them with the rest, told them to learn what they missed from their brothers, then reviewed the lesson of the day before.

He then moved on to a more physically demanding routine and began to talk about dodging, blocking blows, and footwork.

He used Multenyi and two other men as demonstration dummies to show where the vital spots were, how to do the most damage using the blade and the palm of the hand.

At the end of that day he watched as the men practiced on each other, grappling and throwing, blocking and dodging and hitting, though not too hard. He cautioned them to avoid letting the blows rattle their composure or take them too personally, and not to think of revenge as a motive for fighting.

Then he dismissed them for the day and watched them walk away, observing that a certain comradeship had formed among the classmates.

Over the next few days, more men arrived, and those who had been injured returned. Among the newcomers were farmers, a few more sons of merchants, and even a pair of sisters orphaned by the war who worked as barmaids. The students kept coming until Alexander had a full regiment on his hands.

Before another week had passed, Alexander had the regiment moving in lockstep through a series of fighting steps using quarterstaffs, and when he returned to the circus compound at the end of every evening, he related his day to Lucien. "I find it invigorating to guide them through the difficulty of what feels quite natural for me," he remarked.

"Truly, Alexander, I think you have found your calling," Lucien said. "And when you have lost interest in their training, what will you do?"

"Father, you know that I am only doing this for the good of Hamar Multenyi and his people. I do not seek to delay us further. How fares the circus? Does it prosper?"

Lucien's smile was gentle as he replied. "It is doing very well, and a small fortune has been earned in your absence, but soon we must move on to more prosperous climes. The good people of Oradea have a limit to their resources and are showing signs of boredom with us. We must resume our journey to France before the first snow lays on the ground, or we will be trapped here through the winter."

"As you say, father," Alexander said. "I have not forgotten."

Still, Alexander had promised to show his students the art of the sword. The next day he began to demonstrate the principles of Musashi's use of the katana, and how to use their own rapiers in the same way. Through the afternoon he took the faster learners and used them to demonstrate, then guided the slower ones with individual instruction, until they could fight with the best and maintain an equal footing.

At the end of the week he told Hamar Multenyi that the circus was moving on, and that he must leave with it. Multenyi took this news with his usual angst. "But, my lord Count, we still have so much to learn from you. You cannot leave us like this!"

"You know already that which you need to survive," Alexander replied. "It is your task to use what you have learned and to continue your own education, for which you need no more than your eyes and ears and the good sense to sort good from bad. And you must practice your skill with the sword every day until it becomes an extension of your own arm, that you could even fight sightless if need be. You recall that I spake before of crossing at the ford?"

"Aye," Hamar grumbled. "I just did not think it would be so soon. You are a fair man. You did say you would would bide with us but a short time, and you have taught us well how to fight. But I have found also a good friend in you, and I will miss your company."

"And I will miss yours. One day I will return, if I can, and look in upon you and yours. Pray that fate will allow it. But if I cannot, I wish you all prosperity for the future."

"My thanks to you," Multenyi said. "I will pass on your news to the other men." He removed a small pouch from his belt and offered it to Alexander. "We have gathered a small sum to recompense you for your efforts. I hope it is enough."

Alexander accepted the pouch but did not open it. "Truly, I had not thought to ask for anything."

Multenyi said, "a teacher learns from the student."

Alexander smiled as he hefted the bag. "Well said. I shall put this to good use, then."

Muletnyi stretched his right hand out to shake. Alexander hesitated, then took it. Hamar started at his touch and said, "your skin. It is cold as death itself."

"It is my nature to have such skin," he replied. "Think nothing of it. But now I must warn you. There is a man who purports to be a vampire hunter, and who calls himself Baron Nicholaus van Helsing. He is wanted by the authorities for desecration of the dead. He claims to obey the will of God, but his deeds are an abomination and given no sanction by the church or the Emperor himself. If you see this man come among you, give him no shelter nor accept his coin, for he is but a pariah in search of gold and seeks only to disturb the graves of your people."

"I believe I have heard of him before. Indeed, then I will watch for this man," Hamar said. "There are no such things as vampires, and if he is caught disinterring the dead we will prosecute him for it."

Alexander found that encouraging. "Farewell, then, and good fortune to you and the good people of Oradea," he said.

"Farewell, and convey my goodbyes to your father. Until we meet again," Hamar replied, saluting smartly. He caught himself, smiled a sheepish grin, then turned his back and walked away toward the marketplace.

Content that Multenyi would take his advice, Alexander returned to the circus and began packing.

Hungary
September, 1647
92

The next day, the circus was already across the bridge and ten leagues down the road when they entered the marshlands, and beyond those the countryside opened up into a flat bowl of farmland, light forests, and meadows surrounded by mountains. The heat was less oppressive than expected for late summer, and gave way to colder nights than were normal.

Alexander felt more content with life than ever before, as if all the troubles of the last year were nothing more than a bad dream to be forgotten. Even then, he was assailed by flashes of memory: of the ferry, of Elsa, Ruthinda and Charanditha, of Sarasvati. He wished fervently that he could find someone to love who would live longer than the average human. But where to find her?

At length he removed his hat, swept his hair back out of his eyes, then put it back on; and with the motion banished the thought from his mind and rode on.

The fall harvest had already begun. The growing season was shorter this year. Groups of farmers were bent low over fields of cabbage, cauliflower and broccoli, busily plucking the heads before they would begin to rot. Others swung their scythes among crops of wheat and millet, hops and barley, gathering up sheaves which they tossed onto wagons pulled by oxen. Pastureland as far as the eye could see was dotted with cattle and sheep roaming free in the sunlight, driven by horsemen and dogs under a blue sky filled with white sheepy clouds.

As Alexander rode along he could smell the change of seasons brewing in the air. The scent of fall on the light breeze and the sight of leaves turning brown, orange and red stirred him to write of the maple trees seeming to catch fire without burning, and the sounds of fresh water all around him made him wax poetic again about rhythms and patterns on the river, about the stars, and finally the Moon.

He paused to look up when he heard the sounds of honking. The geese were already winging their way south, and he watched wave after wave of V formations pass by overhead. It was an ominous sign, their migrating this early in the fall. It meant that the winter would be harsher, colder and longer than ever in decades.

Next to him, Lucien spoke for the first time in the day. "We may have to stop somewhere to spend the winter before we move on to France," he remarked quietly.

Alexander grunted. "I had hoped we could make it as far as Vienna, but we do not know what other obstacles stand in our way. If we must stop, what say you if we tarry there? I was told that it is a bigger and grander town than it used to be, and that all the buildings are now like castles."

"I will leave that to the others," Lucien replied. "I would welcome a place to put my head which is not under the open sky for a change. The chill in the air bodes ill, and while you and I do not feel the cold as much as the others, they must have a safe place to stay until the spring. Erzebeta has said that Parvati cut her fifth tooth last evening. She has outgrown all her old clothes, and the woman cannot mend them from what fabrics she has. It is time to go shopping. After all, we too must follow the fashion of the day."

He glanced down at the used jerkin he wore and plucked at it with an impatient gesture, then turned to Bela Ragosi, who rode alongside in silence. "What say you, Ragosi? "

The immortal squinted toward the far horizon to the west, then tied his hat down as a stiff gust of wind threatened to blow it off. "It is up to Velin. He has already said he and his people desire to find a place to settle for a time. They are not nomads by choice, my lord count, and they are tired. He said he would be content to settle wherever you choose."

Lucien replied, "then we will find a place in Vienna and winter there. I am sure he will be pleased with that. The circus would fare far better there than in Budapesth."

One of Ragosi's men galloped toward them from the rear of the file. He brought his horse to a halt as he exclaimed, "riders, m'lord! They trail us but five leagues behind! I recognized the leader as the one you call van Helsing!"

Ragosi growled and spat on the ground. "Van Helsing? Curse him for the dog he is! I'll split his skull in twain!"

"We will wait until night falls, then deal with him in his element," Lucien said. "Let us continue on as if nothing is amiss, then when we are camped and the women secured away from harm we will confront him together once and for all. The road is no place to fight a battle we cannot win so encumbered."

He told the messenger, "take two of your brothers and fall back, then report to me if they decide to advance."

"Aye, m'lord," the man replied, then spurred his horse around and galloped back. He beckoned to two of his comrades, who followed him as he rode back down the road and took up a middle position between the circus wagons and the hunters.

"Think you he will attack us on the open road?" Ragosi asked. "He would not dare!"

"If he is clever he will wait. If not, Alexander and I can deal with him and his men alone."

"You two alone, against that army?"

"You have already seen what Alexander can do," Lucien replied. "You do not know what dangers we have shared alone before, and emerged unharmed."

"True there was that perilous moment in Oradea when I thought you would lose all composure against that brigand," Ragosi mused. "But I have never seen you lift a hand to your weapons."

Alexander insisted, "you did not see what he did to the Turk in Kyiv. My father could carve you into pieces before you could blink an eye. Yet he values peace above all. Think you he is weak for it?"

"I will not debate you, sir. You are your father's son, forsooth!"

Lucien spoke up. "Thank you, gentlemen, for your confidence in me. But let us speak of me no more and I will be grateful." He waved his hand with an expression of faint disgust, kicked his horse's ribs and rode on ahead to escape any further praise.

Ragosi watched him go and remarked, "he has not been the same since he lost his lady, has he?"

Alexander replied, "she was the center of his life. But we both lack the skill to raise a child properly. Parvati is a handful to mind on the calmest of days. She has entered the terrible twos, methinks, far too early to be natural for any child."

"Nay. Your sister merely needs the firm hand of a mother to guide her," the immortal ventured. "What about Erzebeta? The woman has cleaved to the child as if she was her own."

Alexander looked down at the ruts in the road and sighed. "They may be parted sooner than both would like. Parvati is one of us, not of the Cecescus. It cannot be helped, for when we move on we must take her with us. There may come a time when we must part company."

"What about the circus?"

"I am confident you and Velin are quite capable of handling it on your own. I have invested less time with it than my father."

Ragosi reached up to stroke at his chin, musing. "The Count has been managing our funds fairly. All have prospered, and his honest guidance will be missed. I had not planned to manage a circus myself, but I have found it diverting. I will think on it, discuss it with Velin and give you my answer in due course." He gave Alexander a quick salute and then reigned in his horse, falling back to join the Szgani leader.

93

When night fell, the circus retired some distance from the road and made camp in a copse of oak trees. While the women prepared supper and fed the children, the men assembled a war council. Van Helsing and his men had not appeared yet, but it was only a question of time.

The men spent the time polishing and sharpening their swords and axes, mending crossbows and restringing them, checking the bolts and counting the supply as well as the worthiness of their muskets and pistols. Three of the men were posted as sentries to keep the watch at the perimeter, and were told to send a message if the enemy were sighted.

Meanwhile, Lucien and Alexander sat perched in a tree overlooking van Helsing's camp, watching the hunters checking their weapons, eating and drinking with furtive haste. They did not speak or share a glance among them, but occasionally raised their heads to listen to the children of the night and to watch the darkness for signs of danger.

Nicholaus knelt some distance from the others, deeply immersed in prayer. Apparently his angel had deserted him and he looked worried. His voice was barely audible as he murmured fervent invocations to the dark.

Two of the other men watched their leader nervously. One of them made a small face, while the other frowned and shook his head.

Alexander was reminded of the story of Jesus and his apostles, on the night the prophet was betrayed by his best friend of all. But it appeared none of these men were so loyal as the twelve. He could not tell if it was because they were worried about van Helsing or because they feared him. It seemed to be a mixture of both, or that his behavior had changed since Oradea and they did not know why.

At length, one of the men got up from his seat on a log, wiped his greasy hands on his trousers, and ambled over to him. His voice carried easily on the still air as he said, "my lord Baron, what troubles you so? You have not eaten."

The vampire hunter started, and turned around quickly. Then when he saw the source of the voice he exhaled his breath and said, "it is nothing, Klaus. Rejoin the others."

"You should not be out here alone, my lord Baron," Klaus replied with a solicitous tone. "There are wolves nearby. I saw a group of them nearby, not an hour ago. They were tracking us."

"They will not bother us. They fear our muskets." He turned away and gazed into the forest. "No, something much worse than wolves awaits us this night. Those men in the circus, the Count and his son, are the very demons we seek. Now is our mettle tested, now must we be resolved to rid the earth of all their kind."

Alexander's hand tensed on the limb it rested on, his fingernails digging into the bark like iron nails, but Lucien reached over and patted it. "Do not allow his words to anger you," he whispered. "Let us send them a message to remind them where they stand."

He raised his head and uttered a long mournful howl into the night. In answer, there came a chorus of howling all around the camp. The men dropped their plates of grub and rose abruptly to their feet, arming themselves with whatever came to hand. They looked around into the dark and found themselves surrounded by still more howling.

"Dear God," said one, crossing himself.

"Steady," another one replied. "They would not dare attack us." Yet he looked around as if he doubted himself.

Nicholaus marched back to the campfire, his aide behind him. "Do not let the noise rattle you," he said. "Make ready, and fire on anything which moves."

The howling went on for ten minutes. The men stood together, tensed, ready but unsure. The howling soon fell to an eerie silence but no one moved.

Then Nicholaus relaxed his guard and returned his sword to its sheath. "You see?" he said. "The wolves were merely singing to their goddess, the Moon." He pointed to the bright orb shining overhead.

The men laughed at that.

"Wait," said the first man. "Where is Durban?"

The laughing stopped. Then another man said, "mayhaps he went to do his business."

"Did you see him go?" van Helsing asked.

The man said, "no, but..."

"Look for him. Now."

For a long while they searched the camp and the surrounding forest for their man, but could not find him. When they met in the center space they were in a more somber mood. "Nowhere! Nowhere at all! How?" the first man asked.

"It is magic," another said. "Magic like what I saw at the circus but a few nights ago. Witchcraft, more like."

Apparently it did not occur to any of them that the man may have collected his things and gone, having found ill favor with following a madman. None of them appeared connected to van Helsing by more than the promise of gold at the end of a very long rainbow.

"Now are all the devils arrayed against us," Nicholaus declared.

"Then we should attack the circus now," the first man replied. "How many more of us will disappear before we act?"

"It is night," van Helsing declared. "They are in their element in the dark. We will wait until the dawn, then take the demons in their sleep, when they are weakest."

At this, Lucien gripped Alexander's arm and whispered, "we must warn the others."

Together, he and Alexander leapt silently to the ground and ran back to their horses, then rode back to the circus as if the devil was at their heels.

94

The dawn brought gray skies. The trees dropped leaves at random, and a ground fog shrouded the trunks with a weaving white mist. It swirled around the men's legs as they walked toward the campsite arrayed under the trees. They entered the camp quietly, looking for signs of life among the tents, but no one greeted them. It was deserted, and ravens flapped about in the branches overhead, chattering and crowing in the gloom.

"There is no one here," a man said, looking around.

Another asked, "where did they all go?"

Nicholaus brought a gloved finger to his lips. "They are here," he said. "I can almost sense it."

He pointed to the main wagon, where he guessed Alexander and Lucien would be fast asleep in the imagined torpor of the undead. His men moved to surround it, and waited as he went to the door. He pulled it open, carefully, and climbed inside.

369

The wagon was completely empty. He stood looking around at the stripped walls, the bare floorboards. Not even so much as a torn curtain was left behind. The circus must have gone in the night and left these things behind to delay him finding the vampires.

Roaring with frustration, he exited the wagon. "They have deserted it," he declared. "Fan out! Search the woods!"

He froze at the sight of his men being held at bay by a crowd of armed Szganis. A calm, accented voice replied from behind him, "there is no need."

Van Helsing whirled, startled, and was confronted by Lucien Arkanon, standing not ten feet away from him, sword in hand. "You thought to ambush us in the light of day," Lucien continued. "You thought we were weak and helpless. Once again, you understimate us, Baron. I warned you what would happen to you and your men if you pursued us."

The hunter drew his sword quickly. "You must die for the good of all. You are not of this earth, you are a bloodsucking parasite, with no love of God!" He charged forward, aiming the point for Lucien's heart.

The white haired demon deflected it easily with his blade, then followed through with a slicing motion so quick that van Helsing was forced to jump back to avoid it. Then the battle was on, and raged on for several minutes.

Lucien stayed on the defensive, making van Helsing do all the work until the human was sweating heavily with his exertions. He danced and minced, teased his opponent on with quick furtive strokes of his blade, never once yielding ground. And van Helsing had no chance to draw his pistol as Lucien left him little time, dashing in and touching his blade yet again before he could reach for it.

Anger spurred the vampire hunter to try new tactics, and Lucien answered them all with small cuts on his arms, legs, torso, until his clothes were stained with fresh blood. Lucien himself remained untouched and unsullied, and his grim smile only goaded van Helsing even more.

From his vantage point on the hill with the women, Alexander watched with admiration at his father's uncommon restraint. This was different from battling the Turks that day in Kyiv. He was like

Musashi reborn, though he doubted the old swordmaster would have stayed his own hand for mercy's sake.

Lucien delivered the coup de grace by striking the sword from van Helsing's hand. The blade flipped upward high into the air and fell, burying itself point first in the moist earth.

The exhausted hunter sank slowly to his knees, breathing heavily. "Kill me then, as you will. You have bested me," he panted.

"Nay," the white haired demon replied. "I will spare you, and let you think long on your deeds, for they are many and without honor. The asizes await you wherever you go." He resheathed his weapon and stood back to give him room. "Go now, and plague us no more."

The hunter remained on his knees, staring intently at the long white fingers curled around the sword's grip, the pearlescent fingernails gleaming, the thin film of blue light surrounding them. Then without thinking he grabbed the pistol from his belt, aimed it and fired.

One of the women screamed, "look out!" but too late.

Startled, Lucien ducked back and dodged it as the ball tore through the space where his chest had been and struck one of van Helsing's own men. The man yelped, clutched at his side and fell. The others waited until Velin signaled the Szganis to lower their weapons, then ran to him to check his wound, leaving their leader to face his nemesis alone. Van Helsing frowned at their betrayal with disgust.

Lucien's smile fell to a grim tightlipped line as he reached down and picked the hunter up by the throat with one hand, lifting him high above the ground until his boots were clear. His eyes were blazing with red fire. *Give me a reason why I should not dispatch you like the dog you are!*"

"I will never stop hunting your kind," van Helsing replied. "You are the devil's undead. Kill me, then. My kin will avenge me."

"You will die a murderer's death at the execution block as you deserve, and your god will not save you. I do not have to stain my hands with your blood. You are already marked by madness." Then Lucien dropped him, stepped back and said, "take him."

The crowd surrounded the hunter and took him prisoner. At first van Helsing struggled, but thought better of it as he looked into the faces of his jailors and found no pity in their eyes. The other men

371

surrendered quickly, and all were herded into a small hut built especially to hold them and put under guard.

Lucien turned his back and marched away into the fog until he disappeared, a flare of white hot anger trailing behind. Alexander thought to follow him, but did not know what he would find. He stayed instead to help the Szganis build the circus anew.

95

When the circus was restored to some semblence of normalcy, Alexander finally went looking for his father, and found him sitting on a large stone by a burbling brook, chucking small pebbles into it. Instead of a raging demon, Lucien looked completely and utterly spent. The expression on his face told Alexander of the war going on in his breast.

Alexander approached carefully. "Here you are," he said. "I thought you were sleeping. This is a most tranquil place for meditation."

"We must go, Alexander," Lucien declared softly, without preamble. "We must go, and leave these good people in peace. I... we have already imposed on their hospitality long enough. He made me angry, enough to feel murder in my heart. I never wanted to sink to that level again. I did not want you to see that, nor the others. No. We must go, before I do something else to lose their trust."

"What about Parvati?" he asked. "You said Erzebeta could have her until we found a home for her in France."

Lucien's answer was more misery, and he chucked another stone into the cataract. "Yes, I agreed to that arrangement, and you have no inkling how it pains me to think of tearing them apart. But she is my child, Alexander, and I am responsible for bringing her into this world." Then he added, "I know you think I was foolish for fathering a child with Sarasvati, but you know she wanted children. I could not deny her greatest wish, and I promised her father it would be so."

"I remember what he said," Alexander said, nodding. "All men are faced with a decision such as that at least once in their lives. But it is a matter of good sense, surely, that we must let them go on a little longer together. The road ahead is beset with many more brigands and soldiers of fortune like that creature van Helsing. If at long last we cannot find a place, how can we make Parvati go through the same test of endurance her mother did? Have you discussed this with Erzebeta? What said she?"

"I have not," Lucien said. "I am now so uncertain how she will react that I have been avoiding it. You saw how she was in tears the day we handed Parvati over. The woman lost her child and saw redemption in the care of another. She was teetering on the brink of all despair. Now will I be the monster who robs her of her reason for living? It is farthest from my own wish."

"Let me talk to her, and guage her response for you," Alexander offered. "I am certain we can reach a compromise which will satisfy everyone."

Lucien turned to him and smiled faintly. "Alexander, you always elevate my spirit when I am in sore need of it. Again, I bow to your superior ability to wage converse with the fairer sex and gain a good result. I recall very well your convincing Ruthinda to remain with us. I could not with all my power do it alone. She was a stubborn child who needed nothing more than a word of encouragement to change her mind, and you gave it to her."

Alexander shrugged with a rueful smile in return. "I seem to have the gift of understanding women," he said. "Though I have no understanding how or why myself. Charanditha found me fair to look upon, and that was enough for me. But she was the one who told me it was so, and I never forgotten her love and generosity to me."

Lucien smiled gently. "You are blessed with humility, and that is a gift few men possess. It will serve you well in the long years to come."

"I would rather think I received it from you for being your son," Alexander insisted. "You comport yourself with honor even when your reserve is being tested beyond another man's limit. I am not certain that I would have let van Helsing live."

Again, there was that moment of hesitation, of guarded secrecy which he could never understand. "Then I am in good company," Lucien replied finally.

"Come then. Return with me to the circus, and we will sort out what needs to be done together," he insisted.

Lucien shook his head. "I must be alone for a little while longer and sort myself out first. I will not be long."

Alexander relented. "Take as long as you like." He rose and walked back to the camp.

96

That evening everyone huddled closer to the campfires than usual as a cold dry wind blew about among the trees and threw embers high into the air. Then the air became gusty in spots, and soon turned into a fierce gale which drove everyone indoors. They poured buckets of water onto the fires to prevent the embers spreading to the surrounding forest and moved the wagons and horses into the big tent, where all would be sheltered from the wind.

After making one last check on the prisoners for the night Alexander fought his way through the stiff headwind toward the main tent and went inside, securing the door flap with a ribbon of sinew to seal it.

Above him, the canvas shuddered and pitched as the wind changed direction several times. The supporting poles and rigging rocked a little, dangerously close to collapsing were it not for the ropes binding them together at the top, but the ropes held fast.

Alexander's thoughts returned to Lucien. He had not seen his father again all afternoon and into the evening, and now he was concerned. True, Lucien was 6,000 years old; certainly old enough to take care of himself. But the feeling kept nagging at Alexander that there was something wrong. He just could not divine what.

He walked across the floor to the wagon set off to the side and climbed in. There, he joined Velin and Ragosi as they played a game of cards, while Erzebeta had Parvati on her lap, combing the toddler's hair carefully as she cooed in soft tones to her. Parvati responded to her older half brother's entrance with a smile, displaying a ragged set of white teeth. Among them were a pair of small sharp canines. "Milk teeth", Erzebeta called them; remarking once how much the toddler reminded her of a cat.

Velin slapped his cards down on the small table and admitted defeat. He said, "curse it. How do you do it, Ragosi?"

The immortal chuckled and grinned like a possum as he reached across the table and gathered his winnings into a small pile. "I do not cheat, if that is what you are thinking. It is all done with numbers and luck." He took the coins and tucked them into his vest pocket. "Another hand?"

Velin grumbled, "no thank you. I cannot afford to lose so much all at once. One can milk the cow only so long until her udder runs dry."

Ragosi laughed. "Then I will grant you a reprieve until the next paypacket." He spotted Alexander watching and asked, "my lord Count, would you care to play against me for a small wager?"

Alexander said, "thank you, no. Have either of you seen my father? He has not returned."

"Nay," Ragosi replied. "No one has."

Alexander gazed toward the unseen brook. "He said he wanted to be alone for a little while, but I have never known him to stay out so long." He did not say that he had lost his blood connection with Lucien, and that in itself was concerning.

"You worry overmuch, my lord Count," Velin said. "I feel certain he is somewhere nearby, but had the good sense to shelter from the wind. And you should not be out looking for him in it, either. It is like to tear a man's skin to shreds, and to make his teeth chatter from the cold."

"I beg leave to speak to your niece of a delicate matter," Alexander continued. "Might you leave us for a little? And take Parvati with you."

"Certainly," Velin replied. He beckoned to Parvati and said, "come, little one. Lex and Erzebeta talk, yes?"

The child nodded soberly and climbed down off the woman's lap, then took Velin's hand and walked out of the wagon with him and Ragosi. When they were alone, Erzebeta asked, "what would you tell me which are for my ears alone, my lord?"

"Erzebeta, I must ask your thoughts about Parvati. My father and I are thinking of leaving the circus here, and going on to France on our own. He has expressed a reluctance to impose further on you and would take Parvati with us. What say you?"

"He is not pleased with me," Erzebeta said, snuffling. Her eyes teared up and she wiped the liquid away with impatient hands.

"Nay," Alexander replied gently. "He finds no fault with your care for Parvati. He lays all blame on himself, that we have spent far too much time with your people. That we have brought the trouble of this morning upon you all, and would avoid revisiting the moment for your sakes, or to place any further burden upon you."

"But, my lord Lucien said you would travel on without her until you have made a proper home, that she may live there happily without enduring the hardships of the road. I know she is not my child, and yet I love her just the same. You and your father cannot care for her alone. She requires a mother still. She has been no burden to me and is not one to be left in a convent or counted an orphan. Life is hard enough."

"My father is aware of that. But as he is Parvati's father, he feels all responsibility for her care rests with him."

To her credit Erzebeta did not fall into hysterics or grow angry. "I understand. Then let me ask you, please, to let the child stay with me through the winter in Vienna, and that she be allowed some measure of peace until it is time to move on."

"I will convey your thoughts to him, and you may rest assured that his decision will be in consideration of your boundless generosity and maternal spirit, with which you are blessed in abundance."

She smiled and nodded in return. Alexander said his good nights and exited the wagon thinking he had won some measure of rapprochement. Now if only the wind would pass quickly so that Lucien could return in safety. He reminded himself that he could also look for his father without moving a single inch outdoors.

Velin, with Parvati perched on his shoulders, approached him and asked, "is something wrong, my lord Count?"

Parvati sneezed, a small puff of sound, and wiped at her nose with the back of her hand.

"Nay," Alexander replied. "All is well. I will remain out here and mind the rigging, and you may return to the warmth of your wagon. We must not have my sister catching her death of the cold." He reached into his jerkin and extracted a kerchief, which he used to wipe her button nose clear of snot. "There. All better?"

Parvati simply smiled her charming snaggletoothed smile.

"Aye," Velin replied, chafing his arms. "It is colder than normal for this time of year. Good night, then. Parvati, say good night to your brother."

Parvati smiled again and said, "goonight, Lex."

Alexander could not help the smile which crossed his lips, and he reached up to stroke her hair. "Good night, little one. Sleep well."

Velin turned, walked to the wagon, lowered Parvati into his arms and went inside. Ragosi remained, and asked, "what has happened to your father? I had never seen him so angry before."

"It is not his habit to lose his temper in such a way, and he imparted it so to me this morning. He also asked for some time alone to meditate."

"Then perhaps we should oblige his humor."

"Perhaps. But it is also not his habit to stay out so long." He paused briefly, then continued, "now the hour is late, and you must have your rest also. Good night."

Ragosi hesitated, as if he had something else to say, but said "good night, m'lord," and walked away.

Alexander retired to a corner of the tent where several set pieces were assembled for easy access, went behind them and sat down in their shadow crosslegged, composed his limbs into a half lotus, took a slow deep breath and closed his eyes.

His mind entered into a light trance as he searched among the myriad sensations bombarding him for the psionic link he and Lucien shared, spotty and weak as it was.

And he found it at last, merged with the sound of water. Lucien was still there, next to the brook. Naked, exposed to the elements, using the wind as a lash to punish his body for that which he could not change. Alexander was made conscious of Lucien's agony, his sorrow, and realized with shock that his guilt was greater than anything he projected to the outside world. He visualized Lucien reaching up to the sky and howling into the wind like a wolf, then throwing himself into the storm to be lashed yet again.

He tried sending a thought through the link to Lucien. *NO! You do not deserve this. Do not do this to yourself. Fairness and justice will serve you in the end. Father, please!*

But even if Lucien could hear him there was no response. Alexander tried again, then yet again, and finally gave up as a spasm of pain passed through his pineal membrane. No, I have no power to penetrate the veil, he thought. I cannot reach him, he is too far away. Or he is blocking me yet again. Why?

In answer, a chorus of the multitude in his blood sounded in his ears. *Lucienantellus has a great burden to bear which you cannot relieve him of. Grant him his moments of human weakness, for he cannot abandon his past and his sorrow is great. He bears it for you, Alexander.*

But, I want to give him comfort, not punish him for that which he did not do. Why must he be punished, and what part had I in it?

He will be harmed all the more if you try. Let him have his privacy, halfling. It is not meet that he shows his true feelings among the others, for they have no understanding of them .Were they to know, they would not be equipped to provide him a remedy. Let it be, Alexander. Let it be.

Reluctantly, Alexander relented, took another deep breath and settled back, then opened his eyes. The outside world rushed back again, and he went to his feet listening as he heard a noise outside. Something had fallen over, or was blown away.

Another creeping sensation up his spine told him it came from the vicinity of the cabin outside.

He drew his sword and ran out into the wind, was buffeted briefly and almost pushed off his feet, then regained his balance and ran toward the cabin. There, he caught the vampire hunters en flagrante, emerging one by one through a hole in the wall made by removing a plank. He cudgeled the man standing the watch before he had a chance to raise the alarm, then stopped a third at sword point as his head and shoulders appeared.

The man raised his hands slowly, and Alexander pulled him out, gripping him tightly by the arm as a sharp blast of wind swirled around his legs and in his hair.

"Where is your master?!" he shouted, then bared his fangs in a furious snarl. "*Speak to me now, or my words are the last you will hear evermore!*"

But the man was too terrified to speak. Then he raised one hand and pointed, his eyes going wide as he stared past.

Alexander turned and looked. His mouth fell open and his hand went slack, allowing the prisoner to jerk free and escape. He stood agape with shock as he saw a dark shape standing on a hillock above the trees, holding Nichaolaus van Helsing tightly in its arms.

The dark clothes billowed like wings, the white hair danced and swirled around its head like serpents, as the long taloned fingers moved from the hunter's arms to his neck. Above them, the air glowed with superionized static, and a flash of lighting lit up the sky above both as they were immersed in a strange halo of blue light. Van Helsing's body jerked and shuddered, and the sound of his agonized screams for mercy filled Alexander with sudden pity even as Lucien clamped his lips to the man's throat.

Alexander screamed, "father!! *No!!*" but the answering thunder drowned out the sound of his voice. He moved as fast as he could through the trees toward the hill, and when he arrived he saw Lucien drop the body from the rock and back away. Lucien's eyes were bright red spots of fire as he turned to face his son. "It is too late for me," he said. "My blood calls for vengeance."

Then his eyes damped back to normal and rolled up in his head as he fell back unconscious on the rock like a rag doll.

Alexander sheathed his sword quickly and climbed up to join Lucien, fervently hoping he was not dead. He knelt and listened to his father's heart for a pulse, slapped at his cheeks gently to rouse him, but there was no response. Lucien's clothes smelled faintly of bleach, and smoked just as as they did on the ferry. He seemed as one dead.

Alexander bit back tears as he sobbed, "father, why?"

Seconds passed. Then he was rewarded with a faint drum beat, about one every two seconds, and he breathed a sigh of relief. Then he looked for van Helsing, and found a charred, smoking ruin of clothed bones lying at the base of the rock. Nicholaus van Helsing would never unearth anyone to wreak bizarre murder again.

Carefully, he picked up his father's body and carried it back to the circus, marking how light it was for such a tall and powerful being. But Lucien was dead to the world, and Alexander vowed to learn what made him so.

97

Bela Ragosi paced back and forth, chewing on his corn cob pipe, and stopped when he could find no peace with his thoughts. "No, Alexander," he said. "I do not know what has possessed your father, but I also know that he will not withstand anymore shocks like the last one. One more like that and he will go mad, mark me."

Sitting next to Lucien's unconscious body, Alexander had to agree. "You were not there," he replied. "You did not see. He frightened even me, sir, and you speak of madness?"

He bit his tongue to still the next remark, that he was so much like his uncle at that moment. "You speak of possession? He was like..." like a god? Aye, and that would certainly bring even more madmen out of the woodwork to hunt him down, he thought to himself.

"Like what?" Ragosi asked, trying to make him finish.

Velin chose to speak up to quell the anger brewing in the closed space. "Let us not speak so loudly in the presence of the Count," he remarked. "He could be listening to us even now. You know not my lord Lucien the way I do. He is not like ordinary men, he is different. My grandfather..."

"Your grandfather was a superstitious old fool," Ragosi cut him off sharply. "That was over a century ago. I was in Wallachia and this man is not the demon I heard of then. Dracula was far worse, you know this. So what if he killed van Helsing? I would have done it myself, given half a chance."

"My father is not prone to these fits of temper, of anger beyond all sense," Alexander interjected. "Of such implacable rage that it burns white hot like an iron which has been in the fire too long. Until now. He surprised me, too. But he is ill, and I would he have ample rest and time to recompose himself. So now, gentlemen, I beg to be alone with him. I will undertake his care myself, and if he does wake insane, you may lay all blame upon my head if I... fail to stop him."

"As you wish, my young friend," Ragosi replied. "Come, Velin. We must discuss this with the others. All must know what awaits us if the count awakes and is not himself, or perhaps the creature van Helsing described in his mad rambles."

"He is not undead, Ragosi," Alexander replied, his eyes hot. "He is one of your poor unfortunates who lost their hearts to the spike and the headsman's axe, a tortured soul bearing much misfortune. Think of him that way, I beg you, for he is not a monster."

"I will take that as your warranty, then" Velin said gently. "Let us be away." He and Ragosi exited the wagon, and left Alexander alone in the dark with his father.

Alexander watched Lucien's paper white face and the translucent skin looking dry and careworn, with small cuts and marks where the wind had bombarded it with grit and twigs, sand, dead leaves. The white hair seemed even whiter. The long slender fingers were still, and the fingernails had grown long, tapered to points like eagle talons. The lips blushed and smeared with the hunter's blood, barely hiding the sharp points of extended canines. He did seem not quite dead, but not quite alive either, like the vampire van Helsing spoke of.

"Father, you must fight this," he said softly. "I am here, and I will help you. You are not alone." He reached out and grasped one of Lucien's hands, gripping the fingers gently to convey his presence.

The sound of thunder rumbled through the tent outside, and the air grew fragrant with the tincture of moist soil. Rain was coming yet again. Alexander pleaded to the recumbent form. "Father, please. I am here, ever faithful, ever waiting. I promise that I will do all I can to make you happy, if you will just return to me."

Nothing. Lucien remained corpselike, unconscious of the world around him. After a few moments, Alexander fell to his knees, threw his arms across the sleeping body and wept until he fell asleep.

For the next day and a half the rain fell cold and strong, forcing everyone to remain sequestered in their tents and makeshift cabins under the big top. During this time, no one came to see the sleeping master and his son.

Alexander remained at Lucien's side, rarely straying far except to relieve himself, and did not feed on any of the animals to quell his gnawing hunger. Even his blood did not press him and remained quiet.

Then, as the evening of the second day grew dark, Alexander was awakened to the sensation of a hand resting on his head. He raised it and saw that Lucien's face had been restored to normal, and his eyes were open.

"Thank the stars," Alexander breathed. "Father, how do you fare?"

Lucien squeezed his eyes shut, then opened them again and reached up to press against his temples. "What am I doing here? How long was I gone?" he asked. "Ah. I feel an ache."

"Almost three days, by the passing of the sun," Alexander replied. "You were as one dead, and had me most severely worried. What happened?"

"That... is not easily explained," Lucien said. "That blackguard van Helsing caught me on my way back to the camp, and pursued me from the river to the perimeter. All that I can remember being consumed by a black ferment of fury, but nought else afterward. Where is he?"

Alexander hesitated, not sure how he would react. "He is dead, father. You killed him."

The pale eyebrows rose. "Dead?"

"Aye. You were like a dark avenging angel, father, at the height of his power, magnificent with anger. You and he were fighting. A blue flame did I see, which covered the both of you. Then you fell, and the villain rests at the bottom of the plateau as a pitiful pile of ash and bone."

Lucien pondered that with the sobriety of a judge. "I have no recall of the event. But I know not why. My blood is strangely silent about it."

"I think I do," Alexander replied. "The man goaded you beyond all human endurance, and you only acted as any other man would have done. But, you were Antellan at that moment, and your spirit could not abide the shocks he subjected you to."

"Who would suggest such a thing?" Lucien asked, his glance sharp with suspicion.

"Ragosi himself averred that he was sore tempted to dispatch the man himself. And Velin reminded me of his grandfather's memory..."

Lucien's face softened. "Ah. Yes, of course."

"Yet it is justice, is it not? That he should be destroyed by the very thing he feared?"

A glimmer of humor returned to Lucien's eyes. "A long way from a bat, no?"

Alexander smiled gently. "I will always cherish your description of them. But you are still a son of the dragon to me."

Lucien licked at his lips, felt at his clothes, and he trembled from head to toe as his hand went to his stomach. "I fear the villain's blood has given me an ache all over. I need to feed."

Alexander quickly unlaced a cuff and drew it aside, baring his wrist once again. "Here. Take what you need, father."

Lucien looked away with a weary sigh. "Alexander, I cannot."

"But why?"

His father said simply, "I dare not. You have given me so much already, and I must have female blood to heal from this."

"There is no one here more willing to give you that which you need," Alexander said. "I know you, and you would not hurt me or anyone if you could avoid it. Here, feed but a little, and later we will find someone to persuade. Besides, you look a terrible sight. What woman would have you with this disarray?"

He punctuated that by plucking at Lucien's bloodstained weskit. The blood had dried long ago, but the stains now marred the smooth black cloth with patches of dried brown.

Lucien looked down. "Ah. You do have a point."

Alexander stood up and then sat down next to Lucien, and allowed him to fasten his lips and teeth to the vein in his wrist. There was a moment of hesitation, then Lucien bit down. He fed for almost a minute, then pulled out and kisslicked at the wounds. "It is enough for me," he said. "Thank you."

Lucien then stood, trembling; then with more surety, shrugged out of the overcoat, the weskit, and the torn white undershirt. He stood half naked in the cold looking a little lost at first, then chafed at his arms and said, "I hope I have aught else to wear, or I shall have to wear the livery of a mummer."

Alexander smiled at that, then went toward the cases stored among the clutter and drew one out. "Here," he said. "Choose among these. I kept a small assortment against the day we should change our appearance."

Lucien spent some time sorting through the clothes, finding some of them too elegant for traveling, and settled on a dark ensemble in deep grey, with an undershirt of soft muslin. When he tried them on he found them to be a little larger than his usual size, but he seemed satisfied.

"These will do, I think," he said. "And I will wear the trousers tucked in with the fashion of the day." Then he changed the subject. "How fares the circus in my absence from this world?"

"They wait upon your word, father," Alexander replied. "Erzebeta has said that she would like to keep Parvati through the winter, so that the child will not have to brave the elements. And, judging by the storm which blew through here these past few days, they will be most unforgiving from now on. What shall I tell her?"

Lucien appeared to hesitate, then said, "one cannot counter her logic. Therefore, grant her permission to keep Parvati through the winter. As I am not yet whole, let us also remain with the circus until April, then move on toward France. Are we agreed?"

Alexander sighed with some relief. "She will be happy to hear the good news." Then as the rest of Lucien's words sank in, his smile fell. "You spoke of needing female blood. What can I do to help you?"

The white haired demon cast his eyes to the floor, then said, "I will hunt on my own. One of the Szgani women must suffice, else I will lose all control of my will. My blood will take me over if I do not feed."

"Yet?"

Lucien smiled as he looked again into Alexander's eyes. "You are far too perceptive. You know my heart, you are my conscience. You think as I do, so do not be alarmed. I will be subtle and swift, and none shall know what I do until it is too late. And with luck I will obtain what I need without causing harm to the lady."

The two vampires clasped arms. "I have no doubt," Alexander replied. Lucien nodded, then left the wagon.

✧

Austria

Vienna, April 1648

98

The winter was not quite as harsh as everyone expected, though for a time no one stirred outdoors through a particularly long blizzard which lasted for almost a week. But the Christmas celebrations outshone the weather, and the little circus enjoyed a long bout of success and relative prosperity.

The war outside the city's walls did not seem to concern the populace. Outsiders entering the gates told of grim skirmishes between Austrians and Turks, Austrians and Germans, even Austrians and Dutch. But the city remained untouched and untouchable. Beyond that, no one wanted to talk about the war for any length of time, as if ignoring it could make it not exist.

Lucien and Alexander found lodgings in an inn nearby and used their small apartment as a headquarters, while the Szganis maintained their camp in a courtyard near the city's cathedral. As usual, the "gypsies" kept to themselves but had the good sense to stage their performances on any day but a Sunday.

Bela Ragosi found himself in a good position to start a small business trading in furs, and used his spare time to hunt for wolves and other pelt fauna in the surrounding countryside.

As Parvati grew older, she grew more precocious and willful, and Erzebeta found a governess to help her manage the child. But the woman disapproved of the living arrangements and the strange way the child acted, and soon turned in her notice. Then there was another, and still another.

It was not Erzebeta who made them uncomfortable, it was the way Parvati looked at them with her probing grey eyes, the way she spoke as if she knew their language fluently, and other strange behaviors. It was the way she seemed to appear suddenly as if by magic, and threw a fright into them more than once because they never heard her coming.

Finally, the fourth governess packed her things quickly and fled, and her last word on the subject was "the child is bewitched, and possessed of the devil. I'll not stay another minute in this house!"

She did not even stay to collect her week's wages, asking Erzebeta to send it by messenger when the funds were in hand.

When he heard of the upset in the household, Alexander grew concerned. "Truly, I thought the good people of Vienna were more refined than this."

Erzebeta sighed and shook her head. "If they knew Parvati the way I do my lord, they would not be so afrighted. I know not what to do. I have had four women come and go, and all too soon to suit me. I can barely manage to keep up with her on my own."

"Let me have a word with her, then, and I shall set her straight," he replied.

Erzebeta laid a fond hand on his arm and said, "you have always had more sway with her than I."

He laughed as he patted her hand. "I? Hardly. Where is she now?"

Parvati's small voice caught him from behind. "here, Alex."

Startled, Alexander turned and beheld her standing in the doorway, holding a bunch of flowers in her small hands. It was true: she was as stealthy on her small feet as Erzebeta said she was.

"Ah, Parvati," he said. "Come. Walk with me."

She thrust the flowers toward him and said, "for you."

He took the bouquet and sniffed at the blooms. "Thank you. They are very pretty." He held out his other hand, and Parvati took it as he guided her out into a small patio at the rear of the house, where he found a seat on the ground under the shade of a linden tree. Parvati sat down next to him and promptly occupied herself with a dandelion within her reach.

At first he could not find the words, then decided on the direct approach. "I am told that you have been frightening your nannies," he said. "Why did you do that?"

Parvati frowned with a small pout. "They were mean," she said. "They did not want to play with me. I made them go away."

"Parvati, they are older and wiser than you, and they were supposed to teach you things you did not know. They were not meant to be playmates."

"But, I have no one to play with," she declared, shrugging.

Alexander realized then that she was probably very lonely. "I know. I have not had time to come and play with you. Are there any other children living nearby?"

"Aunt Beta won' let me go outside," Parvati said. "She says I must be p'tected. She says she's scared for me, like Mamma was."

Alexander thought about that. "Aunt Beta loves you," he said. "There are many scary things outside. Big things that would eat you up." He tickled her stomach until she squirmed and giggled. "But, I know you are lonely. I wish I could make a friend your age for you to play with."

"Not like Bela?"

"Yes, not like Bela. But now, you must let the new nanny teach you, or I shall be very cross with you."

"No, Lex," she replied, pouting again. "I won't do it again, I promise. Papa told me to be good to ev'body."

Alexander drew her into his arms, gave her a hug, then sat her on one of his knees. "Papa is right. It is important to be good to everyone. But, there will come a time when you must choose how

386

to be good, and there are many people who choose badly. Those are the ones you must stay away from."

"The last lady called me a witch," Parvati declared. "What is a witch?"

"Oh, that is not important," he said. "What is important is that you are not what she thinks you are."

Parvati's expression was wistful. "She was afraid of me."

"Yes, I would suppose so," Alexander replied. "She was afraid of you because she did not understand you."

"Unnerstand?"

"It means, to know something well," he explained. "Like, how you feel when Aunt Beta combs your hair, or your favorite toy, or like the stars up in the sky. You know those things even in the dark, do you not?"

"Yes!" she squealed, delighted. "I unnerstand!"

"Good," Alexander smiled. "Then when the next lady comes, you will not try to scare her, and you will be good to her. And then when you are older, we'll try to find some new friends for you to play with."

Parvati's face grew sober again. "When?"

Time was always the issue. Alexander realized that he would have to explain what he and Lucien were planning to do, so that she would not feel entirely abandoned when they left Vienna.

"Perhaps I should tell you now," he replied. Papa and I will have to leave soon. We are going to a land far away, and we may be gone for some time. We are looking for a new home, where you and I and Papa will live together, and you may have as many friends as you want."

"Going away?" she asked, and her eyes grew bigger.

"Only for a little while," Alexander insisted gently. "Then we will come back for you."

"Aunt Beta too?"

"That is up to her," he said. Clearly he was out of his element, as Parvati was not as easy to reason with as Charanditha or Ruthinda had been. He could feel the tears brewing in her eyes even before Parvati shed the first one.

"Nay, it is nought for tears," he insisted, and hugged her tight. "We will never leave you behind, dear Parvati. We just want to make sure that you have a good home, and in order to do that we must travel. Then we will come back for you. Do you understand me now?"

Parvati sniffed and snuffled, and finally pressed her small face into his neck. "Yes, brother," she said. "But I'm scared for you. I'm scared something bad will happen."

One would have to be heartless to withstand her sorrow. Alexander's heart melted like an ice cube in the sun, and he said, "nothing would please me more than to say it will not, but I do not know what the future holds. What can I say which would make you feel happy while we are gone?"

Parvati silently shook her head. Alexander could do nothing but hold her tight and reassure her with soft entreating words, until Lucien's deep accented voice broke through the bird song surrounding them. "Come. Not as bad as that."

Parvati relinquished her hold around Alexander's neck and jumped off his lap, ran to Lucien and hugged at his legs. "Papa, don't go," she sobbed. "Don' leave me."

Lucien placed a long fingered hand on her head and looked up at him with a half-shocked smile. "Alexander, what have you been telling this child?" he asked.

"Only the truth," he replied. "It seemed the logical thing to do. Parvati is dreadfully lonely, and has no one to play with. Erzebeta must have told you what happened to her governesses."

Lucien nodded, and sighed heavily. "Aye. I had no inkling of her travail until today. I have been quite remiss of the whole affair." He knelt to put himself at eye level with Parvati. "I have neglected you terribly. I should have visited more often, so that you would not feel the way you do."

"Lex said you are going away," the child replied. "For a long time!"

"Aye, but it cannot be helped," he said. "Alexander and I are going to France. We planned this since before you were born. Mamma must have told you where we were going? Why we were traveling?"

Parvati nodded soberly, and wiped at her cheek.

"You are my daughter," Lucien assured her. "I love you very much, but I must sometimes do things that may seem cruel to make you happy, just as I did with your mother. She died knowing that you would be happy in a new home. It is all I have striven to do all these many months."

"Then you will come back for me?"

He nodded, and kissed her forehead. "No more tears, little one. You have no need to fear, nor to feel sorrow. Now, go in to Aunt Beta, as she has milk and sweatbread laid out for you to eat."

"Yes, Papa," Parvati said, then promptly ran into the house.

Alexander watched her go feeling as if some of Parvati's anxiety had been dispelled along with his own.

Lucien turned to him and said, "it is always so difficult when reasoning with a child, but methinks she took the news better than I expected. Once again, she has surprised me by being more mature than other children her age. Was it not but a year ago that she started to walk?"

"I remember the day very well," Alexander said. "But I still think she is far more like you than me. Like me she is but half Antellan, but she surpasses me yet again. She will be most formidable when she is older."

"She may not need more than a firm hand, and the guidance of a wiser woman. Poor Erzebeta is yet unable to match the demands made on her. For all her boundless love for Parvati, she is uneducated beyond what those other women understand or appreciate. And from what I have heard I would not have them teach my daughter anything, for they are ignorant of that which lies beyond their imaginations and would have her believe whatever they do. Yet it must be so for now. My hope is that they do not corrupt Parvati's little mind with superstition and fear while we are away."

"The weather has not been inclement of late," Alexander suggested. "Mayhaps if we leave now, we will return sooner."

Lucien smiled, for the first time in weeks. "You make an excellent point. Then, let us make the arrangements, and depart on Monday next."

Later that day, Alexander and Lucien, Bela Ragosi and Velin Cecescu held a private council, where they discussed the disposition of the circus.

"It is not for me to say," Lucien explained, "but as we must scout the trail ahead and establish a place for our family, the welfare of the tribe is yours, as it always has been."

Velin replied, "we will tarry in Vienna as long as the people will have us. And if they do not, we will move on to the next town, or return to Transylvania. You need not fear on our account."

Bela said, "I have found it both amusing and rewarding to help Velin with managing the circus. I would be content to stay on longer, if you would have me."

"Indeed, you have been very helpful," Velin replied. "You may stay on as long as you wish."

"Then it is settled," Lucien said. "On Monday next, Alexander and I will depart, and we will send word when it is time to collect Parvati. Erzebeta knows well what we have planned."

For the rest of the week, the circus continued to perform to large crowds as usual. On Sunday, the circus remained closed as usual. During that time Lucien and Alexander packed and dispersed some of their wealth among the children, then spent the afternoon communing with Erzebeta and Parvati. Afterward, they passed the evening looking for blood among the animals, and by the time the sun colored the dawn golden, they were already riding on the road west toward Linz, towing a pack horse with them.

✧

The Holy Roman Empire (Germania)
April, 1648
99

The road was wide open as it passed through a patch of wild forest. The river Rhine rushed by just beyond the trees, running a meandering course alongside it. The sound of the ice breaking apart on its frozen surface was like gunshots in the cold still air, and twice the spooked horses shied and worried at their bits. But they calmed again at the sound of Alexander's patient and compelling voice.

Alexander Corvina was heavily dressed, as was his father, Lucien Arkanon, since the chill of the long winter had not yet gone from the spring air. Alexander felt the cold less than others, but recalled that there had been times in Vienna when he could have done with a thicker coat and boots. He could not hear the birds yet, and he saw icicles dripping among the fresh green shoots on the bare branches.

There were few travelers along the way. A hay wagon passed by going in the opposite direction, and the driver was more occupied with nursing a flask than paying attention to the road. Women walked along the weed covered shoulder of the road toting baskets, headed toward another village. As they passed the two riders, they looked up, and their startled faces reflected some nameless dread. Alexander was forced to do something to assuage them. He opted to tilt his hat toward them and smile. It seemed all he needed to make them relax their guard. After another moment, the women nodded their heads in return, then shyly giggled as they walked a little faster.

All through the morning Lucien had said nothing, and spent some of the time reading from his little book. As the sun climbed higher in the sky, he put the book away and sat sleeping in his saddle, his hat drawn down over his eyes, while his horse walked on unguided.

Lucien looked tired, something almost unheard of in the two long years they had traveled together. Alexander had never seen him do that before, and wondered if his encounter with van Helsing had taken more out of Lucien than he wanted to reveal. He also seemed somewhat morose. Alexander fervently wished it was more about leaving Parvati behind in Vienna than anything that passed between Lucien and the vampire hunter.

At one point Lucien's horse wandered off the road into the thickets and began to crop winterberries from the bushes. The pack horse followed suit. Alexander had to turn back, seize the reins and pull them back onto the road. Even as Lucien's horse offered a moment of resistance, Lucien never stirred from his repose but never threatened to fall off either, as if he was glued to his saddle.

A breeze started to tip his hat off, and Alexander was obliged to replace and tie it under the waterfall of white hair. Even that did not disturb the tranquility of that sleeping form. Alexander finally tugged at the reins and led horse and rider on behind him.

After a time, the way down the hill revealed a pleasant valley, greener than the one they had passed through before, and the air was warmer here. Alexander occupied his thoughts with observation of the forest surrounding the road.

Birds twittered and fluttered among the thickets, and the sound of water rushing among the rocks along the course of the river was scented with flowers. Spring was gentler here in the Tyrolian countryside than in the grim and silent darkness of Transylvania's wooded plain.

The urge to write it all down led him to draw some parchment from his pack and record the impressions before they evaporated like the mist rising from the ground. Yet Alexander maintained his caution and stayed on guard for any attack.

The word in Vienna was that the war between Austria and the Turks had heated somewhat in the form of a Hungarian rogue named Miklós Zrinyi, a poet and local hero, who led raids against Turkish garrisons in the firm belief that the Ottoman Empire was weakened financially and not able to enforce its reach, and who also claimed that God was on his side.

Alexander recalled that Lucien had once said, "those who claim to speak for God were not chosen by God." But the claim alone was enough to make him cringe with distaste. He had already seen enough of false prophets when he learned of the Spanish Inquisition, which he had barely escaped but a century before. But Zrinyi's only wish was to expel the Turks and restore his country to the freedom it deserved. Alexander could not fault him for that.

Zrinyi was also said to visit Vienna frequently, trying to rally the emperor Ferdinand III to action, but most of his entreaties fell on deaf ears. The country's resources were already stretched beyond their limit and the people were tired of the war, which was now thirty years long. The emperor was probably mindful of that and did not want to be drawn into funding another fruitless expedition into a prolonged and expensive conflict.

Zrinyi's followers were known to set up vigilante outposts in the territory to "protect" travelers, but with that there came the risk that highwaymen pretending to be the same vigilantes took advantage of travelers on the road and "liberated" their valuables almost with impugnity.

Alexander recalled discussions among the local merchants that "puritanism" ruled the lands to the west, and that the protestants infected everyone with their austere requirement that men should not wear lace or bright colors and other decorative restraints. Having always been frugal with his own appearance, Alexander found those rules somewhat rigorous but acceptable. But what other religious rules would they then impose? Would he have to attend church or in other ways capitulate to custom in order to keep the peace?

He suppressed a brief shudder of dread and egged his horse on with a gentle nudge in the ribs.

A short time later, Lucien finally shifted, sighed and raised his head. He glanced around and said to Alexander, "I must have dozed off. How long was I asleep?"

"Not long," Alexander replied. "It thought it prudent not to disturb you. You seemed..."

"Tired? I do not deny it," he said. "I can never forget that evening, and the blood of that half mad creature still flows through my veins. It will take time for me to rid myself completely of the sensations, of mad, vain righteousness and murderous intent also."

"You said nothing of it in Vienna," Alexander said. "Why did you not tell me? I..."

"There was nothing you could have done," Lucien declared with a faint smile across his lips. "I did not want to disrupt the peace there. It is my concern, and mine alone." Then, to end the conversation he urged his horse onward and took the lead. Alexander kept his peace and followed him.

100

At midday, the pair of travelers retired to the shade of a small copse close to a crossroad and on the bank of the river, where Lucien quickly dismounted and laid his blanket out on the grass next to the water. He laid down down on it and covered himself with his riding cape, then his head with his hat. Then, he seemed to wink out entirely.

Alexander was helpless to understand these changes in Lucien. The bouts of fatigue and alacrity were alien to Lucien's character, he of the swift, certain sword and ready wit. The word "depression" had not been invented yet, but Alexander refused to believe that Lucien was prone to melancholy. He tied the horses to the low branch of a tree as he pondered that.

After a few moments Alexander regained his composure, laid his own blanket down and after brushing out his long hair with his fingers, restored his hat and sat brooding for a long time; lulled by the gentle breeze which stirred the branches above his head.

For a short time he warred with himself whether he should write or nap, but gradually he began to doze off. He allowed his limbs to take the lead and drag him onto his back, where he finally relaxed into a deep and dreamless sleep.

For a long interval of peace, the only sounds to be heard was the tattoo of a woodpecker somewhere in the dappled shade, while shafts of golden sunlight pierced the clouds and the trees.

Alexander's darkness violently wrenched him awake as the tranquility of the afternoon was shattered by the sounds of gunshots and men shouting, collisions of wood and iron, horses neighing their distress, the noise echoing chaos among the trees.

He stood up quickly and scanned the forest for some sight of the conflict, thinking that the sounds were far too close for comfort if he could hear them at all.

He turned to Lucien, and found his father sitting up. "Did you hear that?" he asked.

"I did," Lucien replied. "We must do something to help those travelers, or they will all die." In a instant he was on his feet and leapt onto his horse's saddle with a single bound, startling the beast. He gazed expectantly down at his son and asked, "are you coming, Alexander?"

Amazed at his father's sudden flare of energy, Alexander followed suit with "I am right behind you!"

He charged his horse into the thicket after Lucien as he pursued a straight line through the trees toward the sounds of battle. By the time he caught up he and Lucien emerged from the wood onto another part of the road, which had curved around the bend like a hairpin.

A band of men had secured themselves in a thick grove of oak trees, occupied with loading their muskets and shooting at three men of means who used a nearby boulder as a shield. Their coach was pitched off the road into a narrow ditch, and there was a tumbled mess of cases and boxes scattered in the mud behind it.

Their driver was already dead, his body sprawled haphazardly in the middle of the road like a lost piece of luggage. Another two servants were wounded and trying desperately to crawl away from danger, but were pinned down by small explosions erupting in the mud around them.

The coach horses were caught in the crossfire, bucked about and strained at their yokes to free themselves. Another horse laid on her side in the mud along the road, kicking and struggling on the ground as she whickered and groaned with pain.

A man inside the coach reached out and fired a pistol at the enemy, then ducked down quickly as return fire shattered the coat of arms on the door. Alexander saw him push his way out the other side of the coach and go down out of sight behind its bulk as a volley of hot lead tore open the curtains.

Lucien took point, charged his horse forward and approached one of the assailants, struck the gun from the man's arm and in the same swing coshed him on the head with a solid fist before he could even react. The man went down in an instant. Without pause, Lucien went on toward another two and scattered them apart using his horse as a battering ram. He pulled a third from an overhead branch and flung him roughly away into the woods. Through all the action, he never gave the men a moment to recover or react, and his horse nearly stumbled twice trying to keep up with his mental commands.

Alexander followed his lead, drew his sabre and began mowing the gunmen down, aiming his blows for their hands and arms so that they could not hold their guns or shoot. That left only three in defensible positions among the branches of the trees, where they continued to fire on the coach as if their lives depended on it.

Alexander leaned over in his saddle in mid gallop, plucked a musket up from the ground and used it to shoot another sniper before he had a chance to finish reloading.

Lucien then turned and pursued the other assassins as they abandoned their posts and fled on foot into the sheltering darkness of the woods. "Hold the line, Alexander!" he called back. "Defend those men!"

Alexander quickly turned his horse around and rode into the shade behind the coach, dismounted with a bound and went to the carriage horses to cut their traces, allowing them to bolt for the trees and out of firing range. Then he ducked down with the besieged travelers behind the boulder.

Lucien returned, reached toward the last man and caught him before he could fire, rendering him unconscious with a single squeeze at the neck. Without stopping, he turned his horse and went into the wood after another fleeing bandit. Soon after that, silence reigned over the forest.

Noting that the coast was now clear, Alexander turned toward the strangers and asked in English, "are you well? Are there any injured among you?"

The man crouched next to him turned to Alexander, his eyes wide with amazement. He looked to be about thirty years of age, clad in a plain waistcoat, weskit and and a muslin shirt with lace at the collar and cuffs. His long curly hair and eyes were dark brown, and he sported a small thin moustache under a straight thin nose. He said in French, "mon Dieu! Qui c'est vous?"

Alexander's blood supplied him with language, and he replied with a small nod of his head, "je m'appelle Alexandre Vincent Corvina, Viscomte d'Arkanon, a votre service, monsieur."

The man crouched next to the questioner was dark blond, and his curly locks were ragged with sweat as he leaned over. "Mais un hero, monsieur," he said. "You and your man have saved our master from those brigands. I am sure he will reward you handsomely."

Alexander smiled modestly. "That man is my father, monsieur, but no reward is necessary."

The second man seemed to blanch. "Your father? But, he looks no older than you are."

The first man nudged him in the rib and crossed himself. "Do not question the aid God sent to us today, Armand." Then he addressed Alexander. "I am Jean-Louis Sevigny, Baron de Neuvillette, and this is my cousin Armand Richard Bourgoyne, deputy parlementaire of Beaugeraux."

"Oh, yes? and your master's name is...?"

"Eh... the Baron *is* our master," Armand replied with a sheepish expression. "The other man in the coach is our footman. He was our decoy for today."

Alexander was taken aback as he addressed the Baron. "Today? How many times has this happened? Who are you, that so many men desire your death?"

The Baron smiled. "I am appointed ambassador to Bohemia by His Majesty Louis quatorze. Rather than drag a long train of soldiers with me, I chose to travel incognito, though now I must live to regret it."

Alexander grew conscious of Lucien's presence in the shadows among the trees, but he had not come out to greet them. It was almost as if Lucien had been struck by doubt. Ignoring the prickles he felt, he stood and called across the road, "father, come join us."

What felt like a long few seconds later the tall dark figure emerged from the shadows like a ghost and walked toward them as he calmly brushed leaves and dust from his riding cape. He replied, "there was no need to shout, Alexander. I could hear you very well."

Lucien paused to wipe something dark from the corner of his mouth as he straightened his clothes, and adjusted his swordbelt as he resheathed his blade. He gave a courtly bow as he said, "good afternoon, monsieurs."

The young man from the coach emerged from a tree's shadow as he doffed his curly wig and brocaded overcoat, handed them over to the ambassador and said, "Monsieur le Baron, I will not repeat this masquerade for all the gold in Provence. Mark me. I was nearly killed myself." To punctuate his remark he plucked at the lacy cuffs to his undershirt with short impatient strokes.

He looked no older than about 14 or 15, but was already considered an adult. His dark hair and eyes made him ideal to impersonate the Baron, though his moustache was no more than a thin brushy line applied using a crayon at the last moment. Then he placed his hand on his chest and with a short bow said, "I am Gaston de Vrais, bond servant to Monsieur l'Ambassador. I am most pleased to meet you."

De Neuvillette smiled as he exchanged garments with the boy. "There will be no need after this, Gaston," he said. "Those were probably the last of them."

Then he turned to Lucien and Alexander and offered them a courteous bow. "Monsieurs, I owe you my deepest gratitude. Who are you? Whence came you?"

Alexander introduced Lucien to the men, who gave him a polite bow. He explained, "my father and I have just come out of Vienna and are bound for France ourselves. We were camped nearby when we did hear the upset."

The Baron said, "I praise God for His grace, for I am on my way home to Paris myself. You will be my traveling companions, yes? After what I have seen, I must beg your protection, for you surpass all standards of guardianship. Such speed and stealth I have never seen before. Such courage! Not since Cyrano de Bergerac have I seen such bravado or panache."

"You know Cyrano de Bergerac?" Alexander gushed, forgetting himself for the moment. "I have heard much of him."

"I have the honor to know of his exploits from my cousin, the Comte de Guiche." The Baron glanced to the wounded horse, and his expression fell. "Ah, ma Fleur."

He walked to her and went to his knees, put a gentle hand on her neck and stroked at it. Blood oozed slowly where the musketball had pierced a vein, and the mare shifted about feebly and whickered, trembling with weakness. "You were always my favorite," he said. "I will send you to God's loving arms, for I cannot heal you."

He put his hand over her eye, drew a small poniard and then plunged it into her heaving chest. She shuddered, stiffened once, then grew still and limp. He withdrew the blade slowly, wiped it clean on a cluster of bush leaves and resheathed it. When he stood there were tears in his eyes, and he crossed himself again. "God forgive me, and welcome her in heaven."

Alexander felt a pang of empathy. De Neuvillette appeared to be a compassionate man, so rare among all the souls he had met on the road. But that had yet to be proven.

Lucien chose that moment to speak. "If it will please you, my lord Baron," he said, "we will be most honored to accompany you and lend you the protection of our swords." Then he glanced over to the men lying on the road, and added, "with your permission, I will examine those men and judge their condition to travel."

The Baron wiped his cheeks with a sleeve, sighed heavily, then quickly forgot his sorrow as his eyes widened. "A medical man as well? Monsieur, you further astound me."

"I have many skills," Lucien replied with a small modest smile, then went to work while Alexander helped the ambassador and his companions retrieve their scattered luggage.

The coach driver was beyond saving, but of the two other retainers one was only grazed at the shoulder, and the other had taken a ball in the right thigh. Both injuries were not critical, but the second would require surgery and some bed rest to recover.

"I will treat and dress these men's wounds to make sure there is no danger of infection," Lucien said to the Baron.

Alexander said, "and I will stand the watch with your men. My experience of such matters is that where there are a few such brigands there are likely to be more."

"We should stay here through the evening, then travel at daybreak," Lucien added. "Is that agreeable to you?"

The Baron affected another slight bow. "I will place all my trust in your wisdom, monsieur. Oui, we have all had a long day already, and the horses must be watered and fed beside."

"We will take care of all, Monsieur le Baron," Gaston said, and pointed to his left cheek. "You should clean off that mud before it cakes."

"You are so bossy," de Neuvillette replied with a smile, as he smeared the brown patch from his skin and flicked it away.

Gaston went to the coach and leaned halfway in, rummaging around for something. When he finally emerged he bore a straw basket with him. It looked on the verge of falling apart. "Thank God, the food is not lost," he declared with triumph.

The Baron perked up a little. "Ah. What have you saved, Gaston?"

The servant opened the basket and drew out a glass bottle with a long neck. "The champagne is not harmed. Nor are the sausages, I think." He sniffed at one of them, made a face and said, "mais non. They have gone off. They are green already." He tossed the rancid things into the brush, then drew out a mangled loaf of pale bread and held it up. The dark smudge of a musketball had broken it in half. "Ay me!" he wailed with an air of disgust. "Think you it is edible?"

The Baron said, "taste it and find out. What has been damaged can be thrown aside."

Armand ventured to ask, "and what provisions have you brought with you, monsieurs?"

"We hunt for what we need," Lucien replied. "We carry nought else. From what I have seen, these woods are nearly bare of large game. But perhaps it will provide a rabbit or two."

"Ah. We did see a herd of sheep not far back. Perhaps we can buy one or two off that charming girl. And she may know of a patiserrie nearby."

Alexander bit off the remark that came unbidden into his mind. His blood was far too condescending toward humans at times. "Do you dare invite another attack, monsieur?" he asked Armand. "You were seen, and mayhaps that girl was a spy. It forbids returning to a place of risk for the sake of convenience."

Baron de Neuvillette seemed to accept that with a small grunt, and said with a shrug, "then we will go on toward France and leave our provisions to God."

While the men were occupied with gathering their things together, Alexander approached Lucien and murmured, "you fed, I presume, to restore your strength."

Lucien's glance was sharp as if the remark was impertinent. Then he said, "aye, but I was not able to learn anything from their blood. And there is something else. The blood was poisonous with a disease I cannot identify, and I spat it out. If you venture to feed, it is best you content yourself with animal blood for the present."

"Thank you for your caution, father," Alexander said. "I will keep it in mind."

"There is more to this event than meets the eye, though I cannot discern what. The man was mute in both speech and reason as though a cloud covered his thoughts. Therefore the secret of their mission is preserved against all inquiry."

"True, the Baron makes a valuable target, and he is a Catholic. Huguenots, think you?"

"Perhaps, or Lutherans or Calvinists. Yet something about the brigands tells me something else. Until we know why, we cannot know more." Lucien pursed his lips. "Pray, do not discuss this with the others. It would not do to alarm them."

Alexander assured him, "father, I am the very soul of discretion."

101

By the time the sun went down behind the looming peaks of the French Alps, a small camp was made among the trees. There, the men made their beds behind the trunks of the trees to conceal them from the road, and their fire was kept small behind a blind made of tree branches.

There was a perilous moment when the man with the musketball in his leg complained of severe pain, and had to be restrained by his comrades while Lucien used a paring knife to dig for the ball. But he subsided gradually once it was out and finally fainted dead away.

Lucien carefully rewrapped the leg in linens torn from the coach curtains. He then checked for the man's pulse and declared that he would recover once he had some sleep; and with Alexander's help deposited his unconscious body on a bed of moss placed close to the fire, covering him with a saddle blanket.

Lucien then wrapped the other man's arm with torn strips of linen after applying a fingerful of salve, fashioned a sling for him and told him not to move around too much or use the arm so that the muscle would heal, or it would get infected.

The man understood and said he would comply.

Lucien then announced, "I will hunt now. Stay here and fortify yourselves." Without hesitation he marched into the gloom and seemed to vanish before anyone could question him.

"Ah, whoosh," de Neuvillette remarked. "He is a man of mystery, non? I have never seen anyone so quietly composed."

Alexander smiled gently. "It is his way. Now, I must make sure the woods are free of further enemies, and count the dead before I bury them. With your permission, monsieurs."

"I will go with you," Gaston said, and made to rise from his seat.

"And I," Armand offered.

Alexander gestured with his hand and said, "monsieurs, you have done enough for today. There is no need."

The boy froze where he was, then shrugged and sat down again, while Armand leaned over and tossed a shiver of wood onto the fire.

The Baron said, "if you can, find out whatever you can from those men, if there are any left alive. I would know who warned them of our route. They did appear to know who we were."

Alexander said, "I will learn what I can," then turned and walked into the growing darkness.

He did not have to search for long. Most of the men lying beneath the trees had either died or were on the verge. He reflected that he did not strike them that hard, or that perhaps he had forgotten his own strength. He marked to himself that Lucien had been less kind, and that he would not waste his pity on men of violence, dealing as much in turn as he received.

Several of the men were wounded at the throat, but did not bleed out, revealing that Lucien had bitten them. He used his senses to search for signs of life and found one man, but when Alexander reached him the man suddenly convulsed and died in his arms, a small froth of white bubbles emerging from his lips.

Alexander puzzled at this. Who would go to such lengths to poison himself rather than live and give up his employer? What was the Baron's mission, that they should stage an ambush on his party to keep him from reaching France? He searched through the men's pockets but found little which would render a clue. Whoever had sent them to attack the ambassador's coach made sure that he or she would remain anonymous for now.

Each man had the rough face and hands of a commoner, and they must have been amply paid to go to their deaths. They could not have been mercenaries, as those men would have simply run away and returned to their master with a convenient story to cover their cowardice.

He turned his attention to digging the graves, and by the time the night covered the woods in complete darkness he had finished. Then he returned to the camp and reported what had happened to the Baron, who said, "it is for the best, I suppose. And you say the man said nothing?"

"Nothing, Monsieur le Baron," Alexander said. "All of those men went to their graves with their secrets."

There was a long silence as they digested this news. An ember sparked and floated upward into the night.

Then Armand spoke up. "Think you that the girl was complicit?"

The Baron replied, "I would not be surprised if it was so."

Alexander decided to change the subject and said, "but come, let us not speak of unpleasant things and get warm before the fire. You must tell me all about France. It has been... years since I was there last, and will feel as a stranger would once I am there again."

"There are times when I feel like a stranger there myself, Monsieur le Comte," the Baron replied with a trace of distaste in his voice. "Perhaps much of it will have changed for you, as it has for me."

The evening was spent in conversation about the state of affairs in France and the Baron's role as ambassador. He seemed quite willing to impart whatever he knew about court affiliations and the royal hierarchy, without revealing his own purpose and mission as ambassador for King Louis XIV.

His friendship with his retainers was clearly grown from their close reliance on each other for protection, their ancestry and familial connections, as well as their positions in the court. None of them were members of the peasant class, and the lowest of them, Gaston de Vrais, was bourgeoise and the son of a minor nobleman turned prosperous merchant.

Each man displayed a familiarity with their leader as comrades, but maintained a pointed adherence to the status quo. They could do as they pleased around him but paid close attention to his needs and obeyed his commands immediately. Each man was his servant, who in turn had his own servants, and all took pains to point out that they were loyal servants of Louis XIV, who was just a boy of ten but who commanded all of France. They spoke of his mother, who was queen but serving as regent until the boy's coronation.

De Neuvillette added, "he is a child now, but he is surrounded by men of culture and knowledge of the outside world."

Alexander noted to himself that it was all so similar to the culture he had seen in Nihon, but without the cutthroat willingness to take heads if someone of royal blood was insulted. Or perhaps he was so innocent of French culture that he had chosen to ignore it before. But times had changed since he was last in France

Alexander learned and observed as he watched them display an odd gaiety in spite of the violent events of the day, and that like the Nihonese they seemed to know that their mortality was meant to be short and full of selfless duty and alleigance to their king. They also appeared to have an innocent view of the world as if it was fashioned exclusively for them, and only people with a sense of wealth and privilege had that.

After traveling with so many worldly and roadwise people in the last two and a half years he found it almost charming, yet jarring at the same time.

The champagne was disposed of the moment it was opened, but as it was only one bottle none of the Frenchmen could claim to be drunk. Armand explained that his family raised Pinot Noir, and the Baron owned vinyards of his own, growing both Chardonet Blanche and Rousseau. He went on to add that no one in France actually drank the water of the Seine, as it was so polluted with runoff from the foundries, factories and sewers in the cities that it made people sick. He said that the discovery of a spring in Perierre was a boon to the sick and the suffering, but the water could not possibly heal all of France.

Alexander digested this news with some dismay, having expected that things would be better than when last he had been there. But in a century and a half, it seemed that the more things changed the more they stayed the same. "Can you not boil the water first?" he asked.

"Boil it?" the Baron asked, his interest piqued. "Why boil it?"

Alexander tried to explain what he had learned from Lucien, who had done the same thing for Sarasvati while she was pregnant. In simple terms, he said that tiny animals called germs infested the water and caused all sorts of maladies, and that boiling the water killed them and rendered the water pure.

"La, la," Gaston interjected, yawning with boredom. "It all sounds so complicated, if you ask me."

"No one is asking you," de Neuvillette retorted. "Think. Water is the most precious thing God gives us, yet we do many bad things with it. Monsieur le Comte has made a point. Why must we sicken and die every year when the simplest thing we could do is right in front of us?"

"As you say, Monsieur le Baron," Gaston said, cringing a little.

"You must not blame your men for their lack of understanding," Alexander said. "But it is not difficult at all, compared to what I have seen in my travels. Shall I tell you about what I have seen on the islands of Nihon and what they do with their water?"

The Baron perked up again. "Oui. Enlighten me. I have never been there myself."

Over the next hour, Alexander carefully explained what the natives did with their waterwheels and aqueducts, which ferried mountain meltwater into cisterns made for storage, and their waterfed machines which ground rice and millet.

He spoke of the toilets he saw in Kashmir; the search for fresh water among the mountain streams and the best places to drink. He spoke of what he had seen at Calais but did not mention the year. Through it all, the Baron and his servants sat listening, thoroughly enraptured.

When he had finished, de Neuvillette stroked the new stubble adorning his chin and said, "most remarkable! You say you have been to a great many places beyond the dark forests of Germania and Transylvania. Would that I could visit them myself."

Alexander smiled gently, thinking that the Baron would never survive the journey on his own. "Perhaps one day. But the Turk has made travel difficult for many."

"Ah, the ubiquitous Turk. Think you they will invade France?"

Alexander thought about it for a long, hard moment. "Not soon," he replied. "They occupy many lands, but as I have recently learned, they are spread far and wide in numbers too scattered to make a concentrated advance. So far they have only gained territory by means of treaties and warrants, which they violate easily if there is any resistance. If they cannot take Budapesth there is a chance to escape their reach. But if they do then there will be nothing to stop them. They took villages along our route from the land of the Mughals, and only by a stroke of good fortune did we evade capture. They approached Kyiv but were turned away for their trouble. We remained one step ahead of them, yet could not find a place to rest our heads for long."

Armand piped up. "The way you tell it, you sound as if they were chasing you," he said.

"So it would appear," Alexander answered with a small shrug. "But apart from a brief sad event on the road we simply did our best to remain unseen and unnoticed by them. We were like mice among the cats, no?"

"Your courage is surpassed by your wisdom, monsieur," the Baron said. "You appear to have seen and done many things, more than any man could in a lifetime of travel."

At this, Alexander's blood stirred up, and his guard returned as he realized he may have said too much. He crafted his next words carefully. "It is because I have been on the road since I was young, and learned much early. My father has impressed me with his wisdom also, for he has seen more than I. Wanderers are we by necessity, and survive by our wit, but we also value the traditions of foreign lands."

De Neuvillette smiled gently. "As do I."

102

Lucien reappeared at the edge of camp bearing a pair of rabbits, a raccoon, a stoat and a small deer, which he placed on the ground before the men and set to work skinning them with a long knife. The creatures all looked scrawny and ill fed, and their ribs showed prominently through their skins.

"I apologize for their condition," he remarked, "but these are the best these woods have to offer. It has been a harsh winter."

The Baron stared at the animals with a moment of consternation, and crossed himself yet again. "They are unclean, monsieur!" he declared.

"What would you have me do?" Lucien replied without pausing, as he gutted them expertly. "These poor creatures are all there is. Would you rather I threw them away?"

"Nay, you misunderstand me. God gave instruction to us which animals to eat, and which to not. The rabbits and deer, yes, but these others are not on the list."

Lucien stopped working and looked up at him, his silver grey eyes sparkling in the firelight. "You must survive on what your God has given you to eat, which are these. One cannot simply pick and choose, monsieur."

De Neuvillette stared into those eyes, gulped, then appeared resigned to the situation and declared, "then we will accept them in the knowledge that our God is good, and there is a lesson to be learned from this."

"Good," Lucien said. "Now I will cook them."

He rose with the carcasses in hand and set to work spearing them to place over the fire. He paused to rub salt and a mixture of herbs on the meat, then set the spears among the rocks so that they leaned out over the flames. When that was done, he joined Alexander while the Baron and his retainers engaged in a furtive argument over their current situation.

"They are out of their element," Lucien observed quietly. "It is as if they have never been in the world before. Innocent as babes in swaddling cloth are they."

Alexander replied, "they are isolated by their faith and their positions in the court. Luxury is all they have ever known. I wonder what else we will find in France, if the Baron and his servants are an example."

Lucien reached out and patted his shoulder. "You should not concern yourself overmuch. We will find a place. I expect nothing more than the kind of life I led at Shangri-la. Perhaps I will become a farmer and grow vegetables and grain, bake bread, and raise Parvati on the profit from my work. And if I am fortunate to find another woman as beauteous and intelligent as Sarasvati, I will take her and marry her in the custom of these people, and mayhaps sire a brother or sister for Parvati, that our dynasty will grow with the time and place. It will not change my spirit, nor should it yours. I am content to allow fate to guide my course."

Alexander turned to him. "You have ever been my source of courage," he said, "but there was a time back there in Hungary when I thought I lost you. I do not want to feel that way again."

Lucien sighed and shrugged. "I thought I lost myself for a time. I let van Helsing get under my skin. I was so outraged, so consumed with fury that I lost all command of myself. My blood took control against my will and I should not have allowed it."

"But?"

He smiled gently. "I cannot say it will never happen again. But I feel as if that is all behind me now, and I can only look forward to better days."

"Then you give me hope once more," Alexander said.

The Baron's voice broke through. "Monsieur, do you not eat?"

Without breaking his even tone, Lucien looked up and said, "I have already eaten, Monsieur le Baron, and do not sup. Please, do not save any for me."

He said to Alexander, "and you, my friend?"

Alexander replied, "thank you, but just now I am not hungry."

De Neuvillette hesitated as he digested that. "Ah. I must confess that my aversion toward eating this meat was colored by my faith, but you do not know what you are missing. My compliments on your culinary skills, monsieur. You must give me the recipe. Can it be applied to beef, or perhaps duck?"

"It can be applied to any meat you care to treat for cooking," Lucien replied. "Please, eat your fill."

With a grin, the Baron held up a second small rib, sat down again, and fell to tearing pieces of the seared flesh from the bone with ravenous abandon.

Alexander recalled that singular moment when Karel had held up a similar chunk of animal the same way and suppressed a small cringe of disgust. Half human as he was, he always felt different from other men, and the idea of eating cooked meat was as repugnant to him as cannibalism. He recalled trying the chicken paprikash in Muramea and being able to keep it down, but only just.

Then he felt the sudden urge to get away or he would vomit. He mastered his emotions with an effort, then said, "father, I do not know how you stand life among these others. At times I feel as would a stranger from another world."

"I alone can understand your sentiment, Alexander, for there was a time when I was that way myself. You must inure yourself to these things just as I have learned to do," Lucien said. "Now would be a good time. I recall you had been to France before, were you not?"

"Aye, but only long enough to change ships in Calais, and to set sail again without spending more than half a day's time there. The plague was said to inhabit the countryside so I sought to avoid the contagion, but I saw and felt much misery and despair from the dock. I dare not think what it is like now, but the Baron and his men appear to be unaffected by such matters."

Lucien placed a long fingered hand on his shoulder and patted it. "The day has strained your sensibilities. We will approach these things as they come, Alexander. Worry not."

Alexander gave him a sickly smile in return. "I will try."

Lucien rose and said to de Neuvillette, "Monsieur le Baron, if you will permit me, I and my son will set the watch, that you and your men may rest in all safety. I do not think the night will be disturbed, and you have a long day ahead of you on the morrow."

The Baron smiled and said, "you are most kind, monsieur. Merci."

After they finished eating, de Neuvillette and the servants gathered their things together and settled down where they were to sleep with their boots aimed toward the fire, using their saddle blankets as mattresses and their overcoats as blankets.

Lucien and Alexander armed themselves with the muskets they had found and settled down with their backs to each other so that each had a 180 degree view of the forest.

Soon, the sound of snoring joined a loud chorus of crickets and frogs beneath a rising half moon.

103

The next morning, the sun rose above a layer of grey stormclouds to the east and stirred the men up with its light. The Baron woke first, sat up slowly, yawned and stretched. The chill in the air was bearable, but he drew on his overcoat anyway.

The air held an aroma of cooking. He sniffed and turned to look around. To his surprise, he found a small buffet consisting of scrambled dove eggs and bacon made from strips of smoked stoatflesh laid out on a plank. The champagne bottle sitting next to them was full of fresh water drawn from the river.

"Praise be to God," he said, as he rose and stretched his legs. He crossed himself, reached for the crucifix hanging on a chain around his neck and kissed it, then looked around for his hosts to thank them. They were nowhere in sight.

He turned to see Armand lying nearby, just rubbing the sleep from his eyes. "Come on, up with you, you slugabed," he said. "Have you seen our angels?"

"Non," Armand grumbled. "I have been asleep." He felt gingerly at his side and added, "I feel as if I have been sleeping on a pine cone." He turned and found a piece of exposed root where his ribs had been resting. Then he turned to Gaston, who was still asleep, and shoved at him roughly. "Wake up! You shall not sleep another moment if I cannot, you lazy creature."

Gaston cracked open one eye, then the other, then tried to turn over to avoid further abuse. "Leave me alone," came out a faint mumble of disgust. "I was dreaming of Giselle, and you cut me off in mid..."

"Paahh!" Armand replied with a kick at his boot. "Stop thinking about her. Your lust is beyond insatiable." To punctuate his displeasure he slapped the boy on the shoulder.

"Ay. Monsieur, you are so cruel," Gaston declared, then rolled over again and sat up, blinking with surprise. "We are still here. I thought yesterday was but a bad dream, but it was not."

The two injured men remained where they were, completely senseless and looking peaceful in sleep. Gaston looked to the Baron, who waved off his coming remark and said, "let them sleep until it is time to go."

A bluejay pursued his mate through the branches of the trees as a small gust of spring breeze stirred their heads. The Baron looked around at the silence and the ground fog curling just beyond the brush. "Oui. Our hosts are absent as if they were never here. Where have they gone?"

As if in answer, Lucien appeared at the perimeter of the camp bearing a large box. "Good morrow, monsieurs," he said. "I have brought you more of your luggage. The rest is damaged and cannot be retrieved intact. Are there any important things I should look for?"

The Frenchmen gazed at him with silent astonishment. Then the Baron broke it. "Monsieur le Comte, you must be very strong. Two men could not lift that box the way you have."

Lucien set it gently on the ground. "Aye? It did not feel that heavy to me, or perhaps it is not as heavy as your servants have told you."

That seemed to be a logical argument, and the Baron did not pursue it further. "What of the horses?"

"Alexander is gathering them together. Two escaped injury and ran away, and the four pulling the coach did not go far. If you will forgive me, I took the liberty last evening of using the coach as a pyre for Fleur, as there was no way to repair the damage done to it. An axle was broken, and as it was made of iron..."

The Baron had grown tense upon hearing this, but then relaxed slowly as understanding sank in. "Ah. That does make things simpler."

"Monsieur le Baron, I do not understand," Armand said. "How then are we to travel? All our luggage, all our things..."

"We have no need for the coach, Armand," de Neuvillette replied. "We must sort through our things and take only what is most important with us. We will disguise ourselves as merchants or pilgrims and ride on without the rest."

Gaston asked, "you think the coach was a hazard?"

"That coat of arms alone was like a red flag," the Baron replied, rolling his eyes for effect. "I forgot that it was there. One might as well have put a sign on my back with the words 'shoot me' on it." Then he winked toward Gaston and Armand. "Just do not tell anyone. Please."

Armand and Gaston laughed. "We are all discretion, Monsieur le Baron," Armand replied.

"Well, then. We had better eat our breakfast before it turns to ice," he said.

While they ate, Alexander returned on horseback, towing the other horses with him by their reins. The horses all looked as if they had been terrified witless, and showed it in the whites of their eyes. He dismounted and worked to calm them down; reached out and stroked at their noses, their necks, while he spoke to them in soft tones.

Gradually, the horses became docile again. Alexander then looped their reigns around an overhead branch and allowed them to feast on the underbrush. He turned to the men and said, "the night was kind to them. Methinks the wolves were occupied elsewhere."

"You appear to have a way with horses, monsieur," the Baron said.

Alexander turned to him and smiled. "So I have been told before," he replied. "But my father is far more gifted with horse sense than I."

Lucien bowed to him with humility, and said, "you are far too kind, Alexander."

"But, monsieurs, you are both most excellently skilled at many things," the Baron gushed. "I am certain that His Majesty would value you for your good and honest service, for he has great need of such men of quality. If you please, let me vouch for you, and propose to him that he give you a position at court. As it happens, I understand that he is looking for a stablemaster for his horses at Rouen, as the old stablemaster has died of old age. He needs someone with a firm hand at the reins. Would either of you care to fill his shoes?"

Lucien replied, "let me discuss it with my son, and we will render to you an answer. But now, please finish your breakfast and prepare to depart, as the sun is high and it will be perilous to remain here too long. I have no doubt that the men who pursued you may have associates who may come looking for them."

After breakfast the men fell to sorting through their damaged luggage, which contained a large assortment of elegant dress, extra wigs, and also extra shoes.

None of them wanted to forego this or that favorite article of clothing, until the Baron exclaimed, "stop this! we must dress as the peasants do, or we will be set upon the moment we enter München. When we reach the embassy house we will obtain reinforcements and fresh clothes. Take only that which is most important to you. Your traveling papers, money, the clothes on your backs and one change. From now on, we will travel light."

"Oui, Monsieur le Baron," Armand replied with a short bow. Then he turned and ordered Gaston to move quickly for safety's sake.

"Find the strongbox," de Neuvillette told him, cutting him off. "I must know that my badge of office is not harmed or missing."

Armand ran to the midst of the boxes and found it, opened it, then extracted a smaller box made of iron. He brought it to the Baron, who drew a fine chain of gold from around his neck and used the key pendant to unlock the box.

Inside it were several papers wrapped up together and tied with a ribbon; and a large medallion bearing the seal of Charlemagne and the Carolingian kings. The Baron said, "I will wear this on my person from now on, and keep the papers in my pocket. Put the box back where it was and leave it."

Armand ran to obey.

Lucien approached him. "We must conceal your things in the thicket, and cover all so that no one will know you were here. I have restored the appearance of the road so that anyone likely to pursue you will think nothing occurred to change your route. To them, it will be as if you had vanished from the face of the earth."

The Baron stared it him in mild astonishment. "Monsieur, you exceed all expectation," he gushed. "You are far wiser in affairs of espionage than I."

Lucien placed his hand on his breast and gave him a short bow. "You honor me, Monsieur le Baron. To the horses, then, and let us depart with all haste."

104

The small group of men galloped along the river road without encountering a single soul until the sun went down. They stopped to make camp next to the river within sight of Linz, and the next morning ventured into the town to obtain supplies and learn the lay of the land.

The Baron sent Gaston ahead to München with word that he would need help getting across the border without interference from the Austrian and Hessian troops occupying the border lands. This would take time, he explained, so for now it was best to keep a low profile and stay ready to leave Linz at a moment's notice.

They bided their time at an inn at the edge of town until the sky grew dark with clouds. As Armand and the other men kept watch for danger, they made their way toward a large house at the end of the main square.

"It is our embassy outpost," de Neuvillette explained to Lucien and Alexander. "I will confer with the envoy and determine what can be done to avoid another embuscade."

A clap of thunder sounded in the distance, and the moist wind picked up pace as the first drops of rain began to fall. They reached the gate to the embassy wall just as the pattering turned into a sudden downpour, as if nature was determined to drown them before they reached shelter.

The guard leader spotted them coming and waited until they were within hearing distance before he marched to the gate, hefted his lantern higher and called out, "come no closer, friends. Identify yourselves."

The Baron gestured to the others to wait, then ventured closer. "Come, Lieutenant. Do you not know me? I am Jean-Luis Sevigny, Baron de Neuvillette, Ambassador to the kingdom of Bohemia."

The soldier narrowed his eyes as he looked the man up and down, and did the same with his companions. "How do I know you are telling me the truth? Where is your retinue?"

"We were set upon by highwaymen on the road from Vien, and did only escape with our lives. I bear the seal of His Majesty King Louis. Will you not open the gate and allow us to shelter?"

"Let me see it," the guard insisted.

De Neuvillette reached into his overcoat and drew out the chain bearing the seal, holding it up. The coat of arms gleamed in the lantern light like a beacon.

The sight of it drove the guard back a step, crossing himself as he drew himself to attention and saluted. "I beg your pardon, Monsieur le Baron, but I thought you a highwayman yourself by your disguise. I am Lieutenant Phillipe Fachon, squad leader of the embassy security force. Welcome to Linz, monsieurs. Wait a moment and I will admit you." He came to the gate and unlocked it, then drew it open.

The men and horses entered a small courtyard leading to the front door of a modest two story mansion set at the center of the grounds. There, they dismounted and led their horses under a long veranda toward the stable at the rear of the compound.

On their approach, three other guards posted near the open double doors were interrupted at their game of cards and nearly tipped the table over in their haste to stand to attention.

"This is the Baron de Neuvillette," the Lieutenant explained. He pointed to two of the guards and said, "post yourselves at the front gate while I see to his needs myself."

The men ran to obey while Fachon led the ambassador's group into the stable. When the horses were secure, he led them to the back entrance of the embassy house and through a long hallway toward the front.

"I do this for your safety, monsieurs, because we have had reports of spies watching the embassy," he explained. "I do not know who they are or what they plan to do. I myself have seen one of them keeping watch in the doorway of the house across the avenue. No doubt they have already seen you."

"I quite understand," the Baron replied. "Where are the rest of the staff this evening?"

"The envoy and his secretary are at evening mass, and the rest of the staff are all occupied with errands elsewhere. Let me show you to your rooms myself, as we are very few here in Linz and there has been very little to do. You are the first Frenchmen we have seen in over a fortnight."

He fell silent just as a flash of lightning brightened the night and another clap of thunder rattled every loose pane in the windows. All except Lucien and Alexander flinched, as the lieutenant blinked up at the rain battering at the windows and declared, "it will last the night, methinks. Come with me."

Fachon led them on a short tour of the house, then up the stairs to the second floor. He ushered them into a spacious apartment, where he quickly set to work drawing the thick curtains while the men removed their hats, scarves, and cloaks. He then rushed to set a light in the hearth to warm the room. When he had finished, he asked, "have you eaten, monsieurs? I will have the cook bring you something."

"Oui. Merci. I am certain we are all famished," the Baron replied.

When the Lieutenant had gone, he turned to Lucien and asked, "what do you think we should do? Stay here and wait for reinforcements, or go on to Paris as we are?"

"What does your heart tell you to do, Monsieur le Baron?" Lucien replied, as he studied the building across the way through a narrow gap in the curtains. A coach and four passed by, obscuring the view. But when it did nothing changed. Lucien drew the curtains closed and turned to the ambassador. "I am for staying through the night."

"Alas, my stomach is doing my thinking for me for the moment. Perhaps after we have fortified our bodies our minds will be free to plan." Then de Neuvillette scratched impatiently at his neck. "I will be glad to get out of these clothes. I swear to God the fleas are eating me alive!" He crossed himself again.

"Then, perhaps you should bathe and eat first. Alexander and I will do a bit of exploring and return after supper."

The Baron gushed, "monsieurs, it is raining outside. The way it is going now, I fear you will drown."

"It is no concern to us," Lucien replied calmly with a small smile. "We have weathered worse storms than this."

Armand began to laugh, but it quickly died when no one joined in. De Neuvillette then said, "as you wish, monsieur. Do as you will. Bon chance."

Alexander was quick to catch on to Lucien's suggestion, grabbed his cloak and weapons and followed him out of the apartment and down the stairs into the main foyer. "What is your plan, father?" he asked.

Lucien replied, "I think it is time to hunt for rats."

"Think you they are still there? I saw the house as we passed. It looked abandoned."

"We do not know how many of them there are in that house, but they must be removed from the scene, before they send word of the Baron's presence to his enemies. I resist killing, but will do what is necessary, no? I will take the rear, while you advance from the front so that they cannot find an avenue of escape. Agreed?"

Alexander smiled at the prospect of action. "Agreed."

After they dressed again in their outerwear Lucien led the way outside into the curtain of rain. The guards had retreated into the small rampart rooms at the gate and did not see Alexander and Lucien dash for the wall and climb it like lizards. They dropped to the ground in front and stopped to reconnoiter the street and its layout.

As was expected, no one was on the narrow cobblestone lane in the steady downpour. Alexander blinked into the veil of water and could see that there was a light set near a window. Shadows moved back and forth in the curtained windows and eclipsed it like planets. "There is someone in there after all," he said. "I cannot tell how many."

"I can sense perhaps five or six. I am out of practice. Let me go first, then follow me after a count of three."

Lucien crossed the narrow cobblestone lane as a dark blur and moved like a shadow around to the back of the building, while Alexander strolled across at a languid pace and approached the front entrance, ignoring the cold water drenching his hat and clothes. His eyes had already shifted to night vision, and he studied every inch of the door and windows. The door was not quite flush with the wall but slightly recessed, with a small portico the only shelter from the downpour.

But as he walked toward it there was subtle movement of the curtain in one of the windows to his left. He caught a glimpse of a metal tube extruding through the opened pane. The pistol discharged and a lead ball exploded toward him. Instinct shifted his senses until it came toward him in slow motion. He ducked aside quickly and let it pass, the insult of that shot charging him with sudden anger.

Drawing his sabre, Alexander slammed his way through the front door and entered a small warren of rooms linked by a single hallway. He took a path to his left and pushed down that door with a violent kick, catching three men by surprise. Two had already drawn their swords, while the third frantically worked to finish reloading his pistol. The two men said nothing, but rose and attacked him at once.

Alexander leaned into their assault and slashed at their arms, disarming them quickly, while the third man raised his pistol and fired again. The ball penetrated the wall next to Alexander's head, and he paused for a moment to see smoke curling from the wood. By the time he turned his head again the man had dropped the pistol and fled down the hall toward the rear of the house.

Alexander wasted no time and went to one of the injured men, hauled him roughly to his feet, and growled into his face. "Now, you will give me answers."

The man struggled against his stone grip, but refused to say a word. Alexander shifted to mindvoice as he said, "who are you? Who is your master? Speak!"

The man's eyes went wide with surprise and terror, and it seemed an age before he finally gestured toward his mouth, signaling that he was mute. Whoever had employed him took pains to remove his ability to reveal anything.

Alexander narrowed his eyes and said, "they took your tongue? Horrors. Find pen and paper and write it down. Now!"

The man shook his head and mimed a writing gesture. By that, Alexander guessed that he could not read or write, either; only listen and do as he was told. Defeated by this, he slowly relinquished his hold. "Stay there and do not move, or by Morga's sword I will gut you," he declared.

The man slumped back against the wall, where he rubbed furtively at his throat and gasped for breath, coughing.

Movement out of the corner of his eye alerted Alexander as the second man eased his way carefully toward the door. He pounced, grabbed the escapee by the scruff of the neck and hurled him back. "You will go nowhere. Are there any more of you in this place?"

Both men shook their heads. It felt true, but he would take no chances. "I do not trust you," Alexander said. "When your comrade is returned we will know the truth of your plan."

They both looked miserable and in pain, but he would not let pity into his heart. The blood staining their arms and the tantalizing scent of their fear kicked up his thirst, but he refused to succumb to the temptation. There was a touch of rancidness to their bloodscent, signaling that they engaged in visceral activities which left their health in doubt, like the men in the woods. Whether deliberate or not, the coincidence alone pointed to something more devious afoot.

Lucien entered the room and propelled the third man forward like a missile. The hapless spy collided with a nearby end table before he went to the floor, where he lay sprawled, heaving with exhaustion and sobbing with terror.

"This one was not able to speak," Lucien said with a trace of disgust. "Are they all mutes?"

"Aye," Alexander replied. "Nor can they read or write. Therefore, their silence is most profound."

Lucien considered. "A pity. Let us conduct them across the way to the embassy house, where their jailors will be less kind than we have been, and we will have to learn their secrets the hard way."

"The hard way?" Alexander echoed him, puzzled.

"It is... a colloquial phrase. Pay it no mind, for I am prone to speak of things in a different temper betimes."

Alexander stored the phrase in memory as another revelation of Lucien's life on the home world, which he spoke little of; and reasoned that his own blood would instruct him further as time went on.

105

Later, when the rest of the embassy had bedded down for the night, the Baron, Alexander and Lucien held a short conference over the events of the day in a small parlor off the sitting room.

After he was filled in about the house across the way, de Neuvillette said, "I have never known such things before. Men who poison themselves, and whose tongues are cut out to prevent their giving their confessions? What agency would resort to such measures?"

"As I recall, the Turks ensured their agents' silence in that manner," Lucien replied soberly, "and for me that was not so long ago. It is a new world, monsieur, and in my travels I have seen it change, yet remain the same. This is only a foretaste of things to come. Those men who assaulted you on the road are part of a conspiracy which has no name, and may endanger your life and all your good works."

"I know of spies, monsieur. What I do not understand is the sheer deviltry at work here. There is no sign which enemy has done this, and it is not for me to accuse without proof."

He shrugged with a helpless expression. Then he leaned back and sighed as he gazed blankly out the window, which was still being battered by the relentless rain. "As I have been concerned with avoiding a scandal in Bohemia, I have been utterly ignorant of such chicanery. Was this why my delegation was attacked? To whom have I given offense?"

Lucien studied him with a calm expression, then took a deep breath and said, "there is another possibility. I know of... others... who may have a vested interest in keeping the state of affairs in an uproar."

Alexander understood well what he was talking about. He had avoided thinking about Julianus to forestall revealing their location to him, but it was not beyond his uncle's ego or character to do something like this. But, how did France and the Austrian emperor figure into his plans, and what were they?

Lucien continued, cutting off his thoughts. "These are men who delight in instilling chaos for its own sake, or to gain control for their own ends," he told the Baron. "Such men will employ lackeys to achieve their goals and do all to enable them. They also use religion as a foil to beguile the faithful and to justify their deeds. And were the king not protected by his armies, his life would be ever in danger from their schemes."

The Baron's face became sober and resolute. "Novus ordo seclorum," he muttered softly. "Aye, I have heard. But, to threaten the king? They would not dare!"

"Then let me ask you this," Luicen said. "Is your Cardinal Mazarin a trustworthy servant of the king, or of his church? Which master does he serve best, God or the crown?"

The Baron looked both shocked and outraged. "You think Cardinal Mazarin is behind this?"

Lucien raised his hand. "Nay. I do not accuse. If he is rational, he would want to follow the rational course. But such decisions may be out of his hands, and your young king Louis is vulnerable. Is he not?"

The Baron swallowed. "But Monsieur le Comte, my instructions are most specific. Beyond that I am powerless."

"A diplomat must employ all his skills to serve his king well," Lucien replied. "But you are French first and the king's loyal servant second. Kings will come and go, but the country endures. All you do, you must do for France, or there will be no country to govern and no king to serve. Such a conspiracy as I have described could destroy all you have built, and it can begin with a single event."

The Baron turned to him. "You put it very well. How can I stop this conspiracy?"

Lucien considered for a moment. "That is not easily done without knowing who is behind it," he replied with a soft smile. "But you are tired. I suggest you get some rest, as it has been a long day. Allow time to sort the pieces and render to you an answer."

De Neuvillette started to yawn, then caught himself. "I confess I am tired. I will go to bed, then. Good night, monsieurs." He rose from his chair and walked out of the room, his shoulders slumped as if all the life was drained out of him.

Alexander stared after him, perplexed. Then, when the door was firmly closed, he turned to Lucien. "Why did you send him to bed early, father?"

Lucien raised his hand again. "Alexander. No command was necessary. He did look tired, so my suggestion was natural."

"Oh." Then he smiled. "I find it a challenge to keep pace with you, for you are quite unpredictable betimes."

Lucien's lips curled upwards into a small catlike smile. "I sometimes enjoy being so. And now we must also go to bed. It will not do to have us caught pacing these halls through the night. From now on, we must be ever discreet among these people."

He waved back languidly as he walked out of the room. "Good evening, Alexander."

106

Gaston returned a day later, exhausted from walking, with news that the embassy in München was destroyed by a mysterious fire in the middle of the night, and that it was a smoldering ruin by the time he had arrived. The envoy was missing, presumed dead, and the embassy staff had all fled.

He concluded his report with, "and there were many men assembled within the city walls, armed as if they were preparing for war. I lost my horse to thieves and was forced to shelter in an abandoned hut outside the city until it stopped raining. I found my way out by sneaking onto a rick pulled by a farmer. I walked all the way from his farm back to Linz. I walked all night, Monsieur le Baron. Mordieu, I was terrified that the very trees were plotting against me."

He plopped his tired body down on a seteé, and fanned himself with his hand. "Ay me. Je suis trés fatiguéd." His nose wrinkled, he sniffed, then gave out an explosive sneeze. He wiped his nose with his coat sleeve, then reached up and plucked a straw from his ragged brown hair, which had grown matted and limp.

The Baron would not be put off. "But, how did you leave the embassy, the city, without being caught by the soldiers? Was there no challenge?"

The boy looked down and plucked at his clothes, now darkened with sweat and mud. "I admit I am small but it worked to my advantage. I kept to the side streets and talked to no one. No one would notice or stop me looking like this. And see!" he gushed, dug into one of his coat pockets and held his hand out. Resting in his palm were a cluster of red beans. "Two of the soldiers stopped me at the gate and asked me where I was going," he said. "I said that I traded a cow for them, that they were magic beans, and I must return home to plant them or their magic would not work. And everyone thought me a fool! They laughed at me and let me go."

Alexander and Lucien smiled, while de Neuvillette laughed and clapped his hands "Very clever, Gaston," he said. "But now, I think you should get out of those clothes and take a hot bath, then go to bed. I need you ready to march again soon."

Gaston sniffed, then sneezed again and held his nose to stop another explosion. "I think you are right. I cannot smell anything. Lala, I must reek! My apologies, monsieurs." He rose slowly, sneezed again, then walked out of the room.

When he had gone, the Baron turned to Lucien and said, "this bodes ill. If we cannot find safe haven in München, what will we do? Our path to the border will be treacherous from now on. Must we find nothing but enemies in every bush and tree?"

Lucien replied. "We must all be as clever as Gaston. If we remain circumspect, and continue on the road in disguise as we have done, we can stay on the road and need not enter München at all. We will only stop to obtain such provisions as are vital, and camp in the wood rather than occupy any inn on our route."

De Neuvillette walked away slowly, considering. Then he nodded. "Agreed. We must pack our things and leave tonight. I will inform the others as soon as Armand returns from his errand." Then he started as if confronted by a horror as he looked out the window at the reddening sunset. "Dear God. Now I fear some calamity may have befallen him."

"When did he go?" Alexander asked.

"I learned of his absence from Lieutenant Fachon this morning. He did not say where he was going, and when I spoke to the embassy secretary he said that Armand had a personal assignation. I cannot think where he has gone to or why."

Lucien said, "let us wait a little more time for him. If he has not returned when the sun is down, Alexander and I will search for him ourselves. Lieutenant Fachon must know where the deputy might have gone. For your safety, pray remain on the embassy grounds and wait for us. Linz is not so large a town that he can have gone very far."

The sun was soon blotted out by evening clouds, and when its rosy light dimmed and the sky turned indigo, Lucien and Alexander slipped out the rear entrance to the embassy house and met Lieutenant Fachon near the back gate, which was a narrow file in the thick wall and barred by an iron grille. "There is no more time to waste," Lucien declared. "Where is he most likely to have gone?"

Fachon replied, "I do not question the comings and goings of the embassy staff, as my task is to secure the grounds and the household." Then he leaned forward and spoke softly. "However, I have seen some of them going into a brothel or two in the town. If he went anywhere, it would be to visit one of them. I have heard that the entertainment is... em... most attractive."

"Have you been there yourself?"

The Lieutenant seemed to blush and threw up his hands to ward off the suggestion. "Not I personally. I am married, you see, and I would not be unfaithful to my wife. We have... an understanding."

"Thank you," Lucien said. "Then, you need not accompany us and spare yourself a dressing down."

Fachon's eyebrows elevated. "But I must go with you, monsieur. Monsieur le Baron told me to aid you in your search. I cannot disobey a direct order."

Lucien appeared to waver, caught by a moment of indecision. Then he said, "very well. Come with us, but be prepared to fight if the moment presents itself."

Fachon drew his sabre out halfway and resheathed it in an instant. "Let me lead you to the first one, which is called 'The Dusty Rose', and hope that the deputy is there." With that, he led them out the gate into the twilight.

107

The Dusty Rose was a cabaret, as the sign proclaimed, and when the three men entered it was fully alive with partiers. The back rooms were set up to receive gentlemen of means, and the others for more common regulars. Judging by the cut of their dress, most of the customers were fairly well off. A group of musicians played the latest gigues and ballades in one corner of the front parlor, while scantily clad women laughed, drank and caroused with their guests.

As he entered the front parlor, Alexander was instantly seized with a sense of familiarity, as if he had been there before; but that was impossible. A chill ran up his spine as the sights and sounds of the house rushed at him like a sudden torrent of emotion, threatening to topple him to the ground.

Used to Lucien's constant presence in his mind as an achor, the intrusion of another caught him like a bolt of lightning. He rocked back on his heels and reached back to steady himself using the door lintel. Then the inexplicable sensation was gone again like a zephyr of smoke.

He hardly had time to analyze it when the three men were met by a young woman. She was dressed more modestly than the others, mostly in black, and her neck was encircled with a red ribbon tied in a bow. She was lovely and slim, her face was pale and smooth with a hint of pinched cheeks, rosy lips, and wide set brown eyes; framed by a cloud of loose brown curls.

But there was something about the confident way she walked that said she was in charge. Her voice was warm and sultry as she said, "welcome to The Dusty Rose. Are you looking for something special? All that your hearts desire can be found here."

"We are searching for a friend of ours," Alexander replied. "He is tall and thin, young and with golden brown hair and brown eyes."

She replied coyly, "we have many customers who resemble such a man. Can you be more exact?"

"He is called Armand."

"Ah. Now I remember." She smiled. "He is not here. He met two other men here. They went elsewhere… together."

Alexander cocked his head. "Friends? Did they say where they were going?"

"I do not make it my business to know," she purred. "If I did, I would be out of it quickly."

Lucien caught her attention with, "we are wasting time, woman. Tell us where they took him."

She glanced at him, then looked up into his eyes, and her smile fell as she backed away a step and clutched at her arms as if she was caught in a sudden chill breeze. "They did not tell me, m'lord. Your friend arrived looking for companionship, but left with those men. That is all that I know of the affair."

Lucien would not be put off. "Search your memory. Some word must have reached your ears."

She closed her eyes briefly, then opened them again. "One of them talked of 'The Boar's Head'. It is a dark place at the end of the road. It has been closed for a very long time…"

"My thanks," Lucien said, cutting her off, then turned on his heel and headed out the door. Fachon followed him, and Alexander was about to go when the woman stopped him with her hand.

"Who is he?" she asked. "He is very powerful. I have not met someone of such pure blood in many years."

Alexander caught a glimpse of red in her eyes and suddenly realized the truth. It was an amazing coincidence finding another halfling, but he had no time to dwell on it. "He is the master of us all, and not one to be trifled with," he replied. "Who are you?"

"My name is Roxánne. Roxánne de La Croix."

He tipped his hat to her briefly and said, "Alexander Corvina. And now I must go."

Somehow her hand stopped him as if his arm was encased in concrete. "Come back soon. Please." Her eyes were pleading. "I crave real and honest conversation with one of my own kind."

"I can make no promises. But it is best if you leave this place, now, and restart your life elsewhere, for there is danger here. Farewell." Then he pried her hand from his arm and fairly fled through the front door.

When he caught up with the others, they marched resolutely together down the middle of the street toward the inn at its end. The pedestrians avoided them and kept to the sides of the avenue as if they could sense the conflict to come. Some abandoned their porches and went inside, shutting their doors quickly. It was clear the place had seen trouble before.

The windows were few, dark, and boarded up, only adding to its appeal as a hideout for a gang of kidnappers. There was a small sign posted above the lintel: the image of a boar's head with red letters underneath, supporting a lantern which was not lit. The door was linked through by a large chain sporting an enormous padlock, above which was tacked a small crude sign saying that the establishment was closed for business.

Fachon lifted the chain and saw that the lock was an ancient looking piece, yet attached to one link in the chain so that it only lent the appearance of being locked. He pointed to it and shook his head, whispering, "they were not even trying. What think you?"

Lucien approached the door and leaned against the rough wood, listening carefully as the cold wind stirred his pale hair into wisps. A dog started barking in the distance, but that did not disturb his focus on the sounds inside.

Finally he straightened. "It is of no matter," he murmured. "Lieutenant, we shall require a diversion, while Alexander and I mount our assault from the rear of the house."

"Aye, monsieur, and if anyone replies I will make short work of them," Fachon replied, pulling his pistol and his sabre with both hands.

While Lucien and Alexander worked their way quickly around the building toward the back door, Lt. Fachon began shouting and waving his arms, describing a peculiar dance in the street.

Lights came on in the windows overlooking the avenue. Dogs started barking, and soon it was a cacophany of sound as the neighbors leaned out their open windows and shouted at him to be quiet; while a small crowd of men assembled at a respectful distance and began showering him with coins, vegetables, and whatever else came to hand.

Fachon ignored them as he waited for the enemy to emerge, robbing them of their entertainment.

The sound of a gunshot came from the rear of the tavern, then more shots. The front door slammed open, scattering the chain. A man came running out of the darkness to aim a pistol at Fachon.

The Lieutenant shot him before he could fire, then charged through the front door and caught the other men inside by surprise. He did not waste time reloading, cut down the first man with his sabre, then engaged the other in a short battle, struck the sword from his hand and forced him back against the wall with the point aimed squarely at his throat.

"Do not move a finger, or your life is forfeit," he said with a menacing tone.

A moment later, Lucien and Alexander came in from the hall with one of the other men in tow. "This man has had a change of heart," Alexander said. "However, he is a mute also." He gestured with his pistol to the prisoner. "You will show us where you have hidden him."

The man fidgeted nervously. Lucien's voice gave speed to his movements. The word faded into the darkness as echoes. "*Now!*"

The mute led them through the house toward a door near the kitchen. There was a moment of nervous hesitation as he fumbled for the keys at his belt with trembling fingers. When he finally found the right one, he shoved it into the lock and pushed the door open.

He twisted aside and tried to escape, but Alexander nabbed him by the collar and kept hold. "You are not going anywhere," he said.

They were led by their prisoner down the stairs into a wine cellar, and when they reached the bottom, looked around in the gloom for Armand.

Lucien spotted a second door and went to it. "He is in here," he said, then wrenched the door open, revealing a small pantry where the young deputy sat bound and gagged on a plain wooden chair, half naked and shivering from the cold.

Armand looked up, and his eyes betrayed a moment of pure relief as they welled up with tears. As Alexander removed his gag and set to work untying him, he sobbed, "merci, merci, monsieurs. I thank God you found me. I thought they were going to kill me."

Alexander admonished him with, "you had the whole embassy in an uproar. The Baron is beside himself with worry. What were you thinking?"

"Alas, I was not," he said, blubbering. "I was lonely, and wanted to spend some time in good company before we resumed our journey. But those men had other plans for me." He raised his hands and added, "I swear to you before God I will never do it again." Then he crossed himself and shivered some more, snuffling the tears to silence with an effort.

"I know not what the Baron will do about this," Fachon said. "You were lucky that they did not demand a ransom, or kill you outright. What did they want with you? Who sent them?"

"That is something we can discuss when we return to the embassy," Lucien declared. "But we must go now before others come to stir up more trouble."

Alexander removed his overcoat and wrapped Armand up in it to still his trembling and keep him warm. "Are you injured?" he asked.

Armand shivered and closed his eyes as he replied. "Non. But they asked me questions for which I had no answers. They said they would kill me if I did not tell them about the Baron's mission. But only he knows what it is, so I could not tell them."

"They asked you questions? But these men are mute," Alexander pointed out.

"There was another, an older man, who had a voice. It was he who asked the questions. He also gave them orders. If you catch him, we may soon know their purpose."

Once again they were robbed of the solution to the mystery. Lucien declared, "that one is dead. Come. Let us return to the embassy." He reached out and caught his silent captive before he ventured another step toward the door, then marched him up the stairs ahead of him as the others followed.

427

108

A few minutes later, the back gate to the embassy was opened, and Fachon led the group onto the compound. The prisoners were marched to the stockade, there to await interrogation; while Armand was confronted by a very angry Baron, who was waiting for him in the foyer.

"Armand, you had me frightened to death," he declared. "Are you mad? What possessed you to go to an assignation without an escort, without telling me where you were going?"

Armand stood still with his head bowed, shivering, then ventured, "I... I simply wanted..."

"Non! Do not say another word!" the Baron commanded him. "Look at you, you wastrel, you vagabond. These good gentlemen gave up their evening to look for you. To your room, monsieur, and I do not want to see your face until I send for you!"

Quietly, and with his head still bowed, Armand shrugged off Alexander's overcoat and handed it over without looking. "My gratitude, and my apologies for the inconvenience, monsieurs. Good night," he said, then trudged slowly to the stairs and climbed them as if his feet were shod in lead weights.

The ambassador place his hands on his hips and declared, "c'est *impossible*! Now you see what I must live with. He is my cousin, but at times I question that he is part of my family. The reckless fool! I fear he will get himself killed one day."

"If I may be so bold, Monsieur le Baron, he has learned his lesson with this incident," Lucien said. "We reached him in the very nick of time. He was being held quite against his will, and was about to be tortured to reveal that which he did not know."

The Baron regarded him with an expression of surprise and horror. "Tortured? Mon Dieu!"

"Aye," Lieutenant Fachon said. "We engaged a group of men who were rendered mute like the spies in the house across the way, and the only man who could talk escaped capture with his death. If they have no speech, and no ability to write, then there is no way to learn who is behind this badinage."

The Baron replied, "I trust you will find a way. It is imperative for me to know what or who I am up against. Monsieurs, I apologize for my cousin's behavior. And now, there is much I must do to prepare for our departure in the morning. Please pardon me."

With that, he marched into the study and closed the door.

Fachon stared at the door with mystified dismay as he asked, "what just happened?"

"I am not certain," Alexander replied.

He looked to Lucien, who stood gazing at the closed door with complete concentration. Lucien finally took a deep breath and said, "it is not our concern. Now we should also prepare to leave with the morning. You were very effective this evening, Lieutenant Fachon. You have my compliments."

"You honor me, Monsieur le Comte," Fachon said with a short salute. "I will cherish the excitement it provided me, for Linz is mostly a small village with little to offer a soldier like me." He paused, as if he wanted to say more, then appeared to think better of it. "I must return home now, or my wife will be distraught with worry. It is long past supper and she is expecting me. Good evening, monsieurs." He saluted quickly, then left the hall.

After a few moments of studious silence, Alexander drily observed, "marry, he is also a discreet one."

Lucien smiled softly. "I sense that he is wasted here. In his breast beats a heroic heart, and he longs for adventure just as you do. Yet he stays because his sense of duty is stronger than his desire, and his love for his wife keeps him here. I see a large family in his future."

"He merits a promotion, after what he did this evening." Alexander suggested.

"Nay, he wants it not. A promotion would grant him more responsibility than he can shoulder, or he would be a general by now. But that is also not our concern."

Then Alexander said, "father, that woman... at The Dusty Rose..."

Lucien nodded his head. "Aye, it was a surprise to me also."

"She is half of this world, and half of another. I have traveled half the world, and in all this time I have not met anyone like her."

"It is true that there are few of us now. Most have died or fallen to a hunter's blade. But, she is more human than Antellan. Her blood has been diluted and is too weak to protect her. The dragon's blood compels her but she knows it not."

"Sarasvati was gentle and wise," Alexander replied. "Charanditha won me with her acceptance of me as I am. But this one… she is very like me, I feel a connection has been made between us, and yet… I feel nothing for her beyond a regard for a kindred spirit."

Lucien looked at him and said, "that cannot be helped. Your blood will know the one, and when you meet her, you will be seized with a fervor of longing like no other. Love is stronger than blood, and cannot be denied. I know you are lonely, Alexander, but these things are often beyond our control, and you may have to wait a little longer."

"Then, do I dare make a friend of Roxánne?"

"It is your choice," Lucien said. "Only, take care that you do not become entangled in a liaison which may break sooner than you desire. Sleep on it, then decide what to do."

But sleep did not come easily to Alexander. He tossed and turned, tried to meditate as he had learned to do at the temple, to no avail. The face of the woman at The Dusty Rose haunted his thoughts. The connection was weak and tenuous as a tattered thread in the psionic web, lacking focus, yet it was there. The questions flooded his mind until they dragged him down into a deep and gentle darkness.

109

In the light of midmorning, the small group of travelers left the safety of the embassy compound and galloped toward the west along the river road. Here, the way was well populated with travelers moving back and forth through the Rhineland, so it was hard to be completely invisible. But as the Baron and his men wore clothes which did not distinguish them from any others, they made good time heading toward the border without challenge.

As planned, they spent a night camped off the road among the dense forest crowding the river, and the next day traveling along the river bank parallel to the road. Their haste and their route made them hard to track for any but the best huntsman.

Yet Alexander soon felt that prickly sensation at the back of his neck warning him of danger, turned and caught sight of three men on horseback trailing them almost a league behind. They appeared to be absorbed in carrying on an animated conversation, and never made an effort to catch up, yet never fell too far behind.

He turned back and focused on Lucien, whose white hair was caught by the wind, and eased his horse closer. "Father," he said, "there are men following us."

Lucien nodded and replied, "they are close, but as long as there are few of them there is little to concern the Baron. Therefore, say nothing to him but continue to maintain the watch."

"That I will do," Alexander said. "But your hair is like a white flag in the sun."

Lucien dropped his reins across the pommel of his saddle, reached up and tucked the errant tresses up under the crown of his hat. "We had better catch up," he said, gave his horse a gentle nudge in the ribs and surged forward to join the others, while Alexander followed him closely behind.

That evening, the group kept their conversation to a bare minimum and their campfire small. When the others retired to sleep, Alexander and Lucien spent the night watching the woods.

The stars and clouds passed overhead, followed by a full moon, as the wolves took up their evening song. An owl hooted in an overhead branch, while small creatures rustling among the underbrush accompanied the chorus of crickets and frogs inhabiting the river bank. All was far too peaceful. Robbed of an evening of imminent danger, Alexander soon dozed off where he sat.

A moment later he dragged himself awake again feeling as if he had dreamed again, but could not remember what. He blinked to clear his blurry vision and turned to Lucien, who remained sitting up, staring into the darkness, his gaze steady as if he could see infinity.

"Oh. I must have fallen asleep," he said.

Lucien's generous rosy lips curled into a small smile. "You were tired. If there was any danger to be shared, I would have roused you."

Alexander smiled back, and thought it a rare event after all the strife they had shared. He seized the opportunity to speak about his thoughts while they shared a moment of relative privacy.

"I shall ever be grateful for that assurance you carry with you," he said. "That moment, back there in Hungary, when you were stricken. I… for the first time in my life I felt… fear. It was never on my mind before then. It was as if a hole was opened in my heart, and I could not conceive of your absence without feeling pain. And now that we are on the open road again, I find myself feeling nought but uncertain of the future, that we may be separated, or that you or I may die and leave the other to make his way in this world alone. I have left behind or buried too many friends to lose you also."

"You have not touched your journal," Lucien observed quietly. "Have you stopped writing?"

"I have stopped only because there has been little time to think of it," Alexander said. "Why do you ask?"

"You should be writing your sentiments down for reflection later, when there is time," Lucien said. "I am grateful for the depth of your affection for me, but your mind should be clear of it for now. I have no plans to depart from your side. As your father I am bound to you by blood, just as you are bound to me."

"But..."

"Alexander, you should never feel responsible for that which you did not do," Lucien insisted. "For I do not either. I have spent some time reflecting on the past, which I never want to repeat. I cannot dwell on what has been, or what could have been, or what might have been. It is done, and like the march of time I must ever move forward. I cannot promise that what happened in Hungary shall never happen again. That is for time and fate to determine. Therefore, you must free yourself of those emotions which impede your clarity of thought."

"You are saying that one day I will leave your side," Alexander said. "Even if you need my help."

"I am saying that there may come a time when you must. I do not wish to become a burden to you," Lucien replied. "If by chance that day comes, I want you to take whatever path is necessary for your survival, even if you must leave me behind."

Alexander leaned back as if he had been struck. "Father, I cannot. Do not ask that of me."

"Nay, you will. You may not wish to, but it is inevitable. There will come a time when I can no longer remain at your side, or must die to preserve your life. And I go to such a fate willingly. It is logical. Sarasvati told me the truth of her illness, and she was right.

All things come to an end. Death is as much a part of life as life itself."

"Then, you accept that you will die?"

"Aye. I have been prepared to die for a long time, and yet I am still here. But I cannot question what fate has planned for me, nor strive to avoid it. You recall that I said before that my brother and I share a unique bond, such that whatever happens to one of us, both of us are punished?"

"Aye."

"Of late I have sensed his presence near to us. He has come out, Alexander, and I have no inkling of his plan. It is possible, however unlikely, that he will do something which may be deadly to both of us. If and when that happens, mourn me not but do all you can to escape."

"But..."

Lucien's eyes closed and he waved a weary hand. "Do this for me, I beg of you, Alexander."

Chastened by that, Alexander finally relented. "Aye, father. As you command, I will try."

"There is my boy," he said, then turned and kissed him on the top of his head. "Now, go back to sleep."

110

Two days later, the Baron's group reached Strasbourg by nightfall. They approached the embassy outpost and were met by the envoy, who said he would arrange to give them an escort to accompany them the rest of the way across the border into France.

"We heard from a courier that the house in München was destroyed," the envoy explained. "We expected it would be so, as the city has been overtaken by regiments of Hessians and Hollanders. We had word that they are preparing to march east toward Austria, but that is the final communique we received."

"Then we were fortunate that we did not meet with disaster on the way here," the Baron replied. "Now is my mission most urgent that I must reach the palace and give His Majesty my news."

The envoy bowed and smiled. "Everything will be arranged with all possible speed," he said. "There is already a contingent of mousquetaires billeted in the town, and I will send word to their commandant in the morning to arrange an escort. For now, be assured that you will be safe here within these walls. Let me find you rooms and speak with the cook about supper."

When the man had gone, the Baron removed his hat and gloves and sat heavily down in a large sofachair, letting his tired body sink into its soft cushions. "We have come a long way," he remarked, then crossed himself.

Lucien and Alexander exchanged glances with the same thought. Then Lucien ventured, "I did not think it prudent to broach the subject, monseiur, but we did observe that there were men following us. Did you not see them?"

"What, more of those mute creatures?" he said, and wrinkled his nose with distaste. "Why did you not tell me before?"

"We did not want to alarm you," Alexander said. "But they appeared only to observe, and took no action. Had they mounted an attack we would have done all possible to deter them."

De Neuvillette nodded soberly. "You have my thanks once again for your diligence. I have begun to regard you as friends, though I know nothing of your family or your allegiances."

"Then we count ourselves most fortunate," Lucien said. "Your offer of friendship strengthens my hope that we will find more of such camaraderie in France. After you have completed your mission, perhaps you will visit us when we have established a home, where you will ever be welcome."

The Baron replied, "as you wish, Monsieur le Comte. I have not forgotten my pledge to you."

There came a discreet knocking at the door, and it opened slowly. Armand appeared in the gap and asked, "Monsieur le Baron, may I have a word with you? In private?"

The Baron regarded him with a sharp glance which quickly softened. "Oui. Monsieurs, if you please?"

"Certainly," Lucien replied. "Alexander?"

Alexander headed toward the door. "Of course."

Once they passed the deputy on the way out, they stood in the hallway together silently until the door closed, then walked slowly toward the end of it and the stairs.

"Armand was very quiet all the way here," Alexander said. "I hope his spirit was not broken by his captivity in Linz."

"It was not," Lucien replied. "But he is far more focused on matters of the flesh than of the spirit. He is very young and has more to learn about life. One can only hope that the event has not changed him overmuch. I believe his cousin's anger did more to subdue him than whatever those men had planned to do." He followed that with a short chuckle of amusement.

Alexander smiled. "De Neuvillette will forgive him in time. Of that I am certain."

"As am I. Now, let us find our way out and search for something to eat, as I think we will not have an opportunity to feed before we cross into France."

Strasbourg was a slightly larger town than Linz, and well populated with inns and taverns as well as a group of brothels, all surrounding the central plaza. Here, the streets were patroled by the local militia as a matter of course, since it was on the border with France and attractive to agents of several different governments as a place to meet and carry out their espionage, discreetly or not.

Lucien and Alexander went to an inn at the end of the road near the checkpoint, and soon found themselves immersed in a large crowd of travelers of all flags. The wars did not seem to affect their ability to engage in civilized conversation with each other, though they did manage to segregate themselves into groups separated by both distance and flag.

There was an air of tension throughout as tangible and sour as the scent of wilted roses. The way each group regarded the other with glances of suspicion among the polite smiles and laughter said it would take little to ignite the conflict between them, and the open display of weapons were but jeweled accents to a delicately woven pattern of deceptive civility.

The inn stewards looked well fed and prosperous, and the smell of cooked food in the air spoke of bratwurst and cabbage, roast pig and mutton, all generously seasoned with the scent of beer, wine and ale.

Lucien and Alexander found a table close next to a window and pushed the shutters open a crack to let fresh air in, then doffed their cloaks and hats and placed them on their benches. From their vantage point they had a good view of the doors to the front and the kitchen, and observed that they attracted very little attention amidst the boisterous activity of the crowd; though if pressed, they would have to fight their way out the front or dive out the window to elude capture.

The wenches circulating among the men appeared preoccupied with either fighting off their advances or encouraging them to buy more drink.

"There is nothing here for us," Alexander remarked quietly. "All the women are taken."

Lucien's reply was squelched by the sudden appearance of a young man with a tray and a towel laid over his arm. His voice and attitude was one of timidity and fatigue as he asked, "what will you have, monsieurs?"

"Bring us wine. Red, not too young," Lucien said.

"And to eat?"

Lucien looked to Alexander, who shook his head as he placed a lace kerchief at his nose to blot out the cooking odors assaulting it. "Nought else," he continued.

When the boy had gone, Lucien reached into a deep pocket and withdrew a small jar, unstoppered it and offered it to Alexander. "Here. Place a small amount under your nose and it will subdue the odor."

Alexander did as he was told, and found the sharp scent of peppermint. "The scent is familiar," he remarked, inhaling subtly. Then his eyebrows went up as he asked, "is this is the very same ointment you shared with Ostap?"

"Aye. You recall I said it was useful for many ills." Lucien's smile turned almost sardonic. "In this way, you can disguise any odor you find repugnant."

"Better than having no sense of smell at all," Alexander replied as he applied a fingertip full of it to the skin under his nose, and soon found that it did hide the cooking smell he found so difficult to bear. He handed the jar back to Lucien and sniffed heartily, savoring the sharp heady scent. "Truly, it is a miraculous potion."

"The word has spread about its benefits, and I think it came from Ostap. The man will prosper greatly," Lucien replied.

Alexander's smile fell. "Something about P'risi did unsettle my ability to weather such things. I was not so..." and he groped for the right word.

"Sensitive?" Lucien supplied.

"Aye. Not before. Is it possible to associate a scent with an event that one cannot smell it again without being so affected?"

Lucien's lips pursed. "Such events do come, regretably so. But, do not let it concern you overmuch. You will overcome it in time."

Just then, the boy reappeared with his tray, bearing a long necked bottle and two blown glass goblets. He offered the cork to Lucien, who took it and sniffed, then nodded his approval. The boy silently placed the tray on the table and poured the wine into the glasses, then stepped back and said, "compliments of the house. Your bill has been paid by the gentleman at the bar."

Alexander started, then turned his head and looked toward the long counter across the room. There were several men perched on tall stools before it, absorbed in conversation and drink, but one sat with his back to it. He was tall with blue eyes, wore dark leathers and suede, and had a pink scar across one bearded cheek. He looked familiar, though a little older, and raised his stein to offer a small salute.

Recognition drove Alexander from his seat as he fairly sailed across the room to grab the man and hug him like a brother. "You're alive!" he exclaimed with boisterous mirth.

Sir John Henry Duggens returned the hug. "They could not kill me," he replied with a broad grin.

Alexander released him and looked him up and down. "But, how came you here? We passed through Muramea, and the boyar Kuryan told me that you had to flee the Turk. I despaired of ever seeing you again. The moment which brought you here to me is the most amazing of events. Fate has been most kind indeed."

Duggens shook his head as he chuckled. "There was no time to spare, so we took what we could and fled. We rode all the way to Budapest without stopping."

He looked past Alexander toward the table and asked, "and how fares my hat? Lost its feather, did it?"

Alexander looked down and realized that he was wearing the same blue ensemble Duggens favored. He said, "I did try to preserve it, but the feather had other plans. I did take these garments as a sort of memorial to your spirit, for I had no inkling of your fate, and as the clothes fit me I..."

"And what better way to pass them on than to a friend," Duggens interjected with a gentle smile. "Your memorial to me does you credit. But, what are you doing here?"

Alexander glanced to Lucien, who watched with a mild expression of both curiosity and dismay. He said, "come, share our wine and meet my father."

Duggen's jaw dropped with astonishment. "Your father? He looks to be more like your brother."

"All our family is blessed with great youth and longevity."

"Oh? So you said before. Then by all means, lead on."

Together they crossed the room and Alexander made the introduction. "Father, this is my friend Sir John Henry Duggens, who was the leader of the caravan out of Manchuria. Sir John, may I present to you my father, Count Lucien Arkanon."

Lucien said, "I have heard nought but praise for your intrepid journey through the wilds of the eastern plains from my son. You were most fortunate that the Turks did not seize you and your party when you passed through Transylvania."

"We managed to elude them with all stealth," Duggens replied. "It was touch and go for almost a fortnight. But once we reached Vienna we were far beyond their reach. Your son was a boon to us until he left us at the border to Tibet, and saved us more than once from capture by the Mongol bandits on the Steppe. For that I am ever grateful."

Lucien reached for the glass in front of him and offered it to Duggens. "Would you care for a glass of wine? The vintage is smooth and untainted by humors."

"Thank you, I would," he replied, then sat down on the bench, while Alexander took his seat next to Lucien, who signaled to the serving boy to bring another glass.

Duggens did not hesitate, but took a sip of the alcohol and savored it. "Not as good as Bordeaux, I suppose, but adequate," he said.

Lucien took the lead and said, "then you have been to France."

Duggens frowned slightly as he took another sip. "Several times. But, why do you ask?"

"I have never been there myself. My son assures me that it may be a good and fair country within to settle."

"Not as fair as England, sir," Duggens replied with certainty. "But then, as I was born and bred there, I suppose my viewpoint is a trifle biased. It is a pity we are at war. France has much to offer in trade."

"Then, perhaps you have learned of the condition of the road ahead, for we have not."

Duggens sat back and replied, "neither have I. But as I spied a band of musketeers camped on the road I think there is something afoot. There is a rumor going about that the French embassy at München burned to the ground, and that is the extent of my knowledge. Of course, I find it a deuced bother to have to travel across France alone and without an armed escort. There are highwaymen living along the roads and off the travelers who pass them by, and only by God or sheer good fortune have I escaped their notice."

Alexander asked, "but, what of your Russian companions? Are they not here?"

He waved off the reminder with an impatient hand. "Once we reached Budapest they picked up their skirts and fled to Moscova, and I am well rid of them. They had an ill-favored look about them, and only tolerated my presence for the value of my coin, not my companionship."

"I also heard something about a lady who was with them."

"Ah," and Duggens' expression became wistful. "She was the lone exception. A beauteous and gentle lady, who was fated to be married to a foreign gentleman whose name I do not now recall. I understand that she stayed on in Vienna, there to await her intended. Once our caravan disbanded I never saw her again."

Then Alexander observed, "but, you were injured."

At that Duggens drew back and his hand went to his cheek, where the stubble was struck aside by the scar. "Aye. Got it fighting a pair of hoodlums who set upon me for my purse. Believe you me, they look much worse now than I do." He ended with a sickly laugh which told of his distaste for the whole affair. "But I'll not woo the ladies now, shall I?"

"It is not as bad as that," Alexander declared. "You look not a day older than when I met you, and that scar would sooner make you a catch than not. I think it distinguishes you as a veteran, and what lady would not prefer a veteran to a callow, inexperienced youth?"

439

Duggens smiled again. "Your insight also does you credit. I shall take that to heart." He took another sip of the wine, finishing the glass, then said, "and now, I would ask of you a boon in return for my contribution of wine. May I know if I can join you in your travels? I require no more than a place to lay my head in safety until we reach Paris, where I shall go on alone to Calais, as I am bound for England next. What say you?"

Lucien replied, "as we are traveling under the protection of another gentleman, we must ask his kind permission. But I would welcome your company."

"And I," Alexander quickly added.

Duggens's expression brightened. "Capital! When are you going?"

"That has not been decided yet. We have only just arrived."

Duggens thought for a moment, then said, "then I will await your answer here, as I have taken a room upstairs, and I shall be ready to join you at whatever time you set. If it be no, then I will be disappointed, but will not hold it against you. I count myself fortunate that I found you here at all, as it has been a long time since I have crossed words with good gentlemen such as yourselves. Do either of you play chess?"

Alexander thought the question strange, because in all the weeks they shared in traveling, Duggens never even brought out a chessboard. He caught Duggens' eyes darting about the room as he spoke, and his mouth showed a grin even as his countenance took on the cold hard edge of suspicion. He determined to learn what had the man seeking shelter among a crowd of Frenchmen instead of riding hellbent for England. Or was he also trying to elude the agents of the mysterious cadre they had encountered in Linz?

"We both do, indeed," Alexander replied. "Though my father is better at the game than I."

"Then a worthy opponent is all I seek, for I am out of practice and would enjoy a good challenge."

Alexander glanced to Lucien before speaking. "When you were traveling, did you perchance notice anyone following you, or those in your party?"

At this Duggens's eyes grew wide as saucers as his eyebrows crept upward. "What?"

Lucien said, "come, sir. You are among friends. You can be truthful with us, and with all confidence."

The Englishman said, "I have no doubt. But I have no inkling what you are talking about."

"When we were in Linz, we did encounter a group of men, all rendered mute so that they could not reveal their purpose or mission. You did not?"

Duggens frowned with puzzlement. "No."

"Then it is for your welfare alone that we impart this to you," Lucien continued. "We are traveling with the French ambassador. As it is well known that England and France are still at war, I would ask if you are prepared to travel under his banner. We will vouch for you to the ambassador, that he may know you are a man of peace."

The Englishman leaned back again, thunderstruck. "Gentlemen, you astonish me. How did you manage such an introduction?"

"That is a long story," Alexander replied. "But I will accept your denial if you say nay, as we have pledged to lend him our protection."

"Oh, hohoho," Duggens laughed. Then his face grew sober. "I will accept it if you will vouch for me as a man of peace, for indeed I seek only to return home."

Lucien leaned forward and said, "then we are in accord. We will send word to you when we are ready to leave."

Over the next hour the conversation turned to trivial matters, but when it appeared the time was growing late, Duggens finally declared that he was tired and would go to bed. He stood and placed his new hat on his head, squared the brim and said, "good night, gentlemen. Safe journey back."

"Good night, sir," Alexander said.

When Duggens had gone up the stairs and out of sight, Lucien leaned toward Alexander and murmured, "we should take his suggestion and return to the embassy. He told me more with his body than he said with words. He is in trouble. For your sake, I hope that de Neuvillette is charitable, and will accept our voucher for the man."

Alexander replied, "I doubt that the Baron would deny this man the shelter of his flag. He has declared his desire for peace also. Insofar as he is also a diplomat, of a sort, he should be accorded deference. Do you not agree?"

Lucien gathered his hat and put it on. "As always, I admire your optimism. Let us now seek out sustenance off the beaten path, then return to the embassy house."

Together, they rose and put on their cloaks, then strolled out into the darkness, went to a less prosperous inn off the main street and found a pair of wenches who for all their seeming modesty were easy to persuade with a pair of pistoles, and who gave up some of the red bounty in their veins as if they were bred for it.

Alexander observed that it was not as rich as the blood Charanditha fed him, or maybe he had grown so fond of it that he could not easily replace it with the blood of another, especially that of a stranger. But he was tired of drinking animal blood, and afterward he did not feel as if he was fighting constantly to maintain control.

111

After feeding, Alexander and Lucien emerged from the inn and returned to the road leading to the embassy. They walked silently as they threaded their way through the small crowd of pedestrians toward the gate.

Alexander soon found his attention wandering as it centered on the lanterns lining the street, the laughter of people dining under open awnings, the music played by minstrels plying their trade in return for coins tossed into their hats. Men and women laughed and shared wine under the awnings of the resturants lining the avenue. And above the activity and music, he looked up and saw the galaxy arrayed in its infinite sparkling beauty as a bright band of light. For once the universe seemed to be at glorious peace.

But after a few minutes of such pleasant distraction he found himself hurrying to catch up with Lucien, who seemed determined to leave him behind. At first he puzzled about his father's haste.

Then another sensation caught him like a broadside: that tingling sense of danger which always saved his life. He looked around subtly, and saw a group of men following not far behind, their faces grim and determined.

He caught up with Lucien and walked in lock-step with him as he murmured, "father, we are being followed again."

Lucien barely turned his head as he replied. "I was wondering when you would notice."

"What shall we do?"

"Act as if they are not there. If we confront them now we will draw attention to ourselves. Be ready for anything."

Alexander replied, "aye, father." He eased his sabre a half inch out of its scabbard with his thumb, but kept walking at a casual if somewhat hasty pace.

He did not have to wait long. The sudden shuffle of boots on the pavement and the sound of steel rustling caused him to turn abruptly and shed his cloak in the same movement, drawing his sabre quickly as the group of men came running toward him with swords drawn.

"Halt there," he said. "Stand and declare yourselves."

The men stopped only for a moment, then surged forward bristling with grim purpose and murderous intent.

In the same moment, Lucien whirled and joined Alexander with his sword also drawn. "I do not think they are listening," he said.

Alexander had no time to answer as he blocked three swords with his blade, and the fight was on. The bystanders on the street drew together and watched, or ducked aside, as Lucien and Alexander made a fighting run toward the French embassy wall, striking men out of the melee' one by one. Yet it seemed there were always more men to replace them; emerging from the darkness to join in until they were a marathon of cloaked runners fighting their way toward the embassy gate.

They were within sight of the gate when Lucien made contact with their leader and struck the sword from his hand with one impatient stroke. He reached out with lightning fast speed and grabbed the man by the throat, shoved him roughly against a brick wall and pinned him there. He growled softly, "bid them to stop."

Alexander moved to guard him, faced the others and said, "drop your weapons. *Do it now*!"

The men hesitated. Their leader, a burly man in his late thirties, made a furtive gesture with his hand, and they finally obeyed, breathing heavily. They assembled in a half circle to watch the two men.

Lucien's fierce silver gaze caught his as he asked, "why do you attack us? What grievance have you with us?"

He replied, "I am Auric van Helsing. You murdered my cousin, Nicholaus."

"I will not deny that I met the man," Lucien declared. "But his fate was already sealed."

"You freely admit your crime?" the man asked.

"Your cousin was taken with a peculiar mental condition. He pursued us for no other reason but a madness which drove him to plan our deaths. He brought his death upon himself, for I was forced to defend myself from his cowardly attack. What man would not?"

"Why should I believe you?" the man asked roughly. "Your evil has visited us many times before. My cousin was but one of many dedicated to ridding the world of you and your kind. You are a vampire. A blood sucking leech. Lucifer's undead."

Lucien frowned, and his eyes flashed red as he said, "my kind? A demon, am I? Then are you espousing murder yourself. Go and pray to whatever diety you worship for clarity, for I have no patience with your brand of piety. Your hypocrisy sickens me. *Go now*, and take your plague rats with you."

For an instant the man's eyes glazed over, and Lucien released him. The man listed to one side like a ship about to sink, then straightened again. Something flashed in the dark. Lucien swiftly reached out, caught the hand that held the knife and pulled. Auric struggled hard, kicked, flailed, but Lucien pinned him with a knee, wrested the knife from his grip and threw it aside, then coshed him hard in the head with his fist. The man went down, completely senseless.

On seeing this, the other men thought they had the advantage of surprise and attacked once again with their bare hands. Three caught Alexander, and four caught Lucien, and for a few frantic fighting moments it would seem that the fight was in their favor.

But Alexander found new strength surging through his blood after feeding, and with a roar of fury threw them off, scattering them across the street into the gutter like bowling pins.

Lucien had two down already and the other two were pinned beneath his arms, struggling and punching to get free. Then he calmly wrenched. They went suddenly still and limp. When he let go, their bodies slipped from his arms to the road.

Amidst this flurry of action two more men came forward aiming their pistols, and for a moment Alexander thought he and Lucien were dead.

Then a dark figure appeared from seeming nowhere and interposed himself, shooting them before they could fire. He whirled to face two more as he dropped the pistols in his hands and drew his sword and poinard, ready to defend himself. It was Duggens. He paused just long enough to ask, "may I play, Alexander?"

Alexander chuckled as he said, "welcome to the party."

The three men were surrounded quickly, outnumbered three to one, but they made short work of their enemies. Duggens seemed to be in his element, fighting alongside Alexander like a seasoned soldier.

Then the sound of whistling filled the air. Duggens shouted, "the gendarmes. Run!"

Without another word, the three companions made a dodging sprint for the embassy gate and climbed it, dropping safely to the other side. There, they took cover behind the columns at the gate and watched as a squad of uniformed men rounded the corner and came to a stop at the battleground.

Van Helsing's comrades scattered like cockroaches, but there were enough gendarmes there to catch them. Those who resisted were coshed like their leader, while the others were rounded up, disarmed and made to sit on the ground.

The lawmen gathered together, then fanned out and began their work of sorting out what was what.

One of them appeared to be their supervisor, shouting orders while his men scattered to examine the fallen. He soon found Alexander's shed cloak, looked down at it with newfound curiosity, gingerly picked it up. He stretched it out carefully and examined it, then turned his head to look at the embassy gate. He stared at it for several painfully tense moments, then folded the cloth and draped it over his arm. He finally turned away to confer with his men.

"By the stars, I am surely made," Alexander remarked softly when he had found his breath again.

John Henry spoke between his labored puffs of breath. "How so? It was my cloak, was it not? Fear not, Alexander, for they know me not."

"Alexander speaks well," Lucien interjected. "I would not fault his caution. Now, you travel with danger if you attach yourself to us, but I suspect you knew that already, no?"

Duggens stared at him, agape. "T'was no intention of mine, good sir!" he declared. "It was all happenstance for my part." Then he shifted his jaunty demeanor to one of sobriety. "But, please tell me now what is in front of me. What was all that about vampires?"

Alexander's breath caught in his lungs, but he tried to make light of it. "The man was mad, like his cousin. Surely you did not believe him?"

The Englishman's expression was stone. "All I know about it was displayed before me in living color," he replied with a pedantic tone. "I saw your eyes change, I saw your teeth draw down in anger. I mean no threat to you, gentlemen, but I am all aquiver with curiosity. I have heard many tales of your kind in my travels, and know well the charges made against you. But, how came you to be so? T'is not an act of God or the Devil, is it? For I have seen no evil in your comportment. 'struth, I saw uncommon restraint whereas I would have had none. I half expected you both to rend those men limb from limb in anger."

"Ours is a journey long and written in blood," Lucien intoned with a weary wave of his hand. "But be assured also that we are men of peace. We should withdraw now to the embassy house. We will introduce you to the secretary, else you will be ejected, then to the ambassador on the morrow. I will tell you all you wish to know later."

Duggens nodded his head briefly. "I await your indulgence, sir, with all anticipation."

A group of embassy soldiers approached quickly, their muskets aimed. Their leader said, "stand and identify yourselves."

The three of them turned to face the squad. Lucien said, "there is nothing to fear. It is only I, my son, and a man in search of asylum."

The leader drew himself to attention. "Ah, yes, Monsieur le Comte. We did hear the battle. Are any of you injured?"

"Nay. But I think we will not go out again for a time," Lucien said. "Strasbourg is a more dangerous place than we were led to believe."

The sergeant replied. "I have never seen such things before, but the times are different now that we are at war. It is best that you remain inside the compound until it is time for you to leave. Who is this man?"

Alexander and Lucien introduced Duggens, said that he was not a threat to the embassy and had asked for temporary asylum, which the sergeant was willing to accept readily as long as Lucien said it was so. He then ordered his squad into a neat file and escorted them to the house.

112

The next morning, Alexander and Lucien introduced their friend to the ambassador and explained that he was instrumental in foiling a plot to murder Lucien.

However, de Neuvillette's reaction to the idea of an Englishman traveling under the French flag was one of quiet reserve and reluctance.

"Monsieurs, I am not sure this is in my mission orders," he said. "England and France, as far as I know, are still at war. I would be in very serious trouble if I were to succor an agent of the enemy."

Alexander stepped forward and said in a cautious tone, "does my voucher for this man not carry weight? He has pledged to me that he simply wants to go home, and has no other faculty to do so in safety. Therefore, he can do no harm to your mission."

The Baron looked at him, and his stern expression softened a little. "I did say that I owed you a boon for saving my life. Is this it, then? For I can do nothing more beyond what I have offered."

"Yes," Lucien replied. "We ask for nothing more. If it is a burden to your embassy we will leave your company and travel with this man on our own, to ensure that he arrives at his destination with all safety."

Alexander gave him a startled glance. Was it true that Lucien would give up an estate and a fortune to shelter Duggens under his wing? It did not seem possible.

But Lucien's words seemed to persuade the Baron. He blew out a small breath and swallowed before speaking. "No, monsieur. I made you a promise and I shall honor it. You shall have the audience. And... and I shall conduct Sir John as far as Paris, where he will have to go on alone with a small squad of men to the port at Calais. Will that give you satisfaction?"

"More than possible, Monsieur le Baron," Lucien replied with a small bow.

"Is that acceptable to you, Sir John?" the Baron asked.

Duggens almost forgot himself with surprise, and bowed hastily. "Quite, monsieur. You have my thanks."

"It is granted then, that you are free to conduct yourself on embassy grounds, but the moment you venture outside that gate you will not be under our protection," de Neuvillette declared. "Kindly remember that."

"Again, I thank you, monsieur."

"Do not thank me. Thank your friends, who in their service and friendship to me have also been most charitable." Then, as he glanced over the pile of documents scattered on his desk blotter, he said, "and now, if you will permit me, I have much correspondence to take care of before we depart."

Later that afternoon, a squadron of musketeers presented themselves at the gate to the embassy and were admitted. They were all royal mercenaries, wearing black tunics with royal blue trim and tabbards, curl brimmed hats sporting blue feathers, and wide leathern sword belts and sashes. They marched in lock-step with their flintlock muskets up to the embassy door where they halted, and waited while their leader went to the door and knocked on it.

When the door opened, he introduced himself. "I am Francois Rene' Leoncour, Baronet de la Tremaine," he said, "Captain of the fourth Brigade of Mousquetaires. I am here to provide an escort for the ambassador and his party."

The secretary glanced out to see the men assembled and nodded. "I will present you to the ambassador."

The Baronet was escorted into the study, where de Neuvillette stood looking over the map of the eastern foothills beyond the border and the only road leading through them to Paris. When he was introduced, the secretary quietly left the two men alone.

The ambassador wasted no time and said, "I will be traveling with a small party of guests. They are to be accorded every courtesy. I feel I should warn you that one of them is English."

The mercenary shrugged. "My task is to provide an armed escort and that is the extent of my responsibility."

The Baron did not smile. "I crave news of home. What have you heard?"

"I am afraid I know nothing either," de la Tremaine replied. "I have been in charge of the brigade for over two years, and in all that time I have not been home once. Letters from my family speak only of the prosperity of their crops and the welfare of the cattle, or local village gossip. Nothing of the court or of Paris."

De Neuvillette blew out a small sigh of exasperation. "What a pity. I had hoped to hear more." Then he added, "I must also warn you that we are being pursued. Men attacked my carriage when we were but a few miles from Vien, and we learned of several men watching the embassy in Linz where we took shelter. The embassy in München was burned while we were in Linz. And this evening last a mob accosted my guests, who barely escaped with their lives. I want your men to be especially vigilant and to guard against any such attacks."

"I did hear of a fight in the square from one of my men this morning, but did not connect the event with the embassy. If there are spies and assassins on the trail, I have no doubt that my men are eager for better target practice. We have been shooting at trees for months."

"My thanks," the Baron replied. "Now, make your men ready to depart at midafternoon. The secretary will give you a place to billet on the grounds until then."

"We will be ready to go as soon as you are," the squad leader said, then saluted him, turned on his heel and left the study.

From his vantage point in a second floor window, Alexander looked down on the dark parade of men marching toward their temporary bivouac and said, "it appears that we are getting another army."

Lucien joined him to look, then made a small noise. "It is better than riding on to Paris alone. Yet, I have a sense of peculiar foreboding."

"How so?"

"That I, who have a love of peace above all, should become a soldier of fortune myself. That our encounter with van Helsing

449

would return to haunt us in that way. I almost regret coming out with you from Tibet."

Alexander bowed his head, and replied, "I fear I am the cause after all. I sought you out, I begged you to come with me, without knowing that it would bring you to such unpleasantness."

Lucien placed a long fingered hand on his shoulder. "No, Alexander, blame not yourself. One cannot foretell the future. It was my choice to come with you. Now, I must allow destiny and the dragon's blood to guide my hand. This world is on the edge of a precipice, and it has the choice to move forward or to fall to ruin. No matter my own fate, I am an eyewitness to history, that it unfolds before me like a flower. Should its scent be sweet or bitter? That is up to time."

He took a deep cleansing breath and added, "now we must finish packing and rig our horses for the road ahead."

113

At about four o'clock the embassy gates opened, and a long file of musketeers on horseback rode out at a gallop, flanking two coaches and their liverymen, three servants, and a wagon loaded with supplies. Lucien, Alexander and John Henry Duggens rode among them. The gatekeepers at the checkpoint were ready, and raised the wooden bar quickly to allow the parade to pass through.

The small army rode hard and fast, headed west into the low foothills through which the main road passed. When they had passed the 15 kilometer marker, Baronet de la Tremaine signaled that everyone could slow down to a fast walk.

The woods were light and the hillsides visible, allowing for a quick reaction to attack. Alexander studied the trees carefully for signs of snipers, as did Duggens. No one spoke a word during this time. Ever cautious, Lucien moved to position his horse between the edge of the road and the ambassador's carriage, while Alexander fell back toward the rear and watched the road behind them. So far, it appeared that their surprise exodus from Strasbourg was quite effective.

The group moved quickly and covered ground in a short time, so that they were almost in sight of a small town called Metz when the sun went down below the ridgeline ahead.

They did not stop to camp, but traveled on through the night until they were within the city gates, where they came to a stop in the central square. There, they dismounted and set up a billetage at the gateway inn after establishing a guarded perimeter.

The innkeeper was so happy to see the rooms filled that he declared the wine tab free of charge. The ambassador and his retinue were accorded the best rooms on the top floor, while Alexander, Lucien and Duggens were given the floor below that.

The middle floor above the tavern itself was filled with musketeers, who promptly partook of the free wine and were soon as drunk and carefree as loons.

All appeared quite innocent, but Lucien was not willing to give up his guard. Alexander agreed with his caution, and the Englishman went along with his usual affable good humor.

They were sent a tray of wine, a roast goose with potatoes and bread to share between them. Lucien dropped his avoidance of the feast, sampled a few careful bites, then pronounced it safe to eat. Duggens sat down promptly and dug in, while Lucien and Alexander stood by and kept a silent vigil at the windows. But after an hour of this, no movement was seen on the avenue and they felt they could safely draw the curtains for the evening.

A pronounced burp issued in the room. Alexander turned to see the Englishman dabbing at his bearded chin. The goose was nearly decimated, as well as the loaf of bread; as if the man had not eaten in days.

"Ah. My apologies, gentlemen," he said when he divined their expressions. "It has been a long time since I have had such good food. We English are not the best at cooking, and we envy the French for their skills. You do not know what you are missing." He picked up his goblet of wine and took a sip, then set it down again. "Please, rescue me. I am thoroughly stuffed." He pushed the platter toward them.

Alexander smiled back as he sat down. "I fear my appetite runs to different fare."

The knight cocked his head and studied him. "I confess that am curious. You must tell me how you got this way. So let me start at the beginning. Whence came you? for you are not men of this Earth. How many of you are there, and most importantly, how long have you been traveling from place to place?"

"I find it odd that you ask these questions now, when we shared so much time together in Manchuria and the Mongol lands," Alexander said.

Duggens shrugged. "You had all opportunity to kill me before for what little I knew of you, yet you did not. I am the soul of discretion, sir, and I honored your privacy. I do not betray a confidence once shared. But through you I see the future arrayed before me and would be enlightened, that I may understand."

Lucien turned away from the window and said, "you also harbor a secret which you cannot impart. Come, shall we be honest with one another? Were you not also a spy for your king Charles?"

Duggens started briefly, then shrugged with a calm chuckle. "As his trading representative I hear many things, and on occasion I may or may not share them with my king. But he is either dead or soon will be, and my fortunes have changed. Aside from your... eh... unique talents, I should think you should be a boon to any kingdom."

"I would ask the same of you. As we both have secrets to keep, and ours are on the table, it is time for you to reveal yours."

Duggens considered, then shrugged again. "I was sent to obtain a trading agreement with the king of Manchuria before the French could seal a similar bargain, but as it has been two years since that day and I was delayed much, it hardly seems important now. Would you care to hear the details?"

Lucien said, "no. I only wanted to hear from your own lips that your purpose for traveling with us was honest."

Duggens's smile fell as he said, "now I will be returning home, a stranger to my own country. All I long for now is the sight of the white cliffs at Dover, and to return to my estate in Northumberland, if it is still there. Cromwell's Parliament made short work of the monarchy and I do not know if my family is even alive."

Then he shrugged off the sentiment and perked up a little. "But enough of me. Please tell me about yourselves. I seek only to understand what is in front of me, and I am sure you have many stories to tell."

"Perhaps later," Lucien replied. "But now *you are tired*. The hour is growing late, and we must depart with the dawn for Paris. Therefore, I strongly suggest that you get some rest."

Duggens hesitated, then relaxed again. "Perhaps you are right. Answers can come later." He yawned and stretched, then stood up.

"Good night, gentlemen. Sleep well." Another burp, and then he was out the door, headed for his bed chamber.

Alexander waited until the door was truly closed before speaking. "Father, what do you think?"

Lucien stared at the closed panel for a long moment, then replied. "I think he is lost and knows it. Like your friend Ostap Kuryan, the fortunes of war and of time make orphans of us all. He makes a brave noise but his heart is truly broken, and all he yearns for is home."

Then he took a deep breath to cleanse the sentiment from his mind and added, "but come, let us go to bed as well, as we will have another long ride ahead of us on the morrow."

A cock crowed as the dawn colored the sky and the clouds golden. As the church bells rang out for morning vespers, the travelers set out once again into open country at a more sedate pace, and Alexander found himself in awe of the seeming tranquility of the pastoral scenes laid out before him.

Despite the ravages of war and povery, the farms were aglow with life, as crops stretched on in neat rows across the acres. Children were seen playing among them while their mothers and fathers tilled and raked, plowed, and in many other ways kept busy with producing food for their families and for sale in the local markets.

Travelers in carts and on horseback plodded back and forth on the wide road dressed in colors of the rainbow, looking as if they had been painted on the canvas of the world. Alexander wished he had the talent to paint, as he was tempted to sketch what he saw rather than describe them to save time. In some ways, words were not enough.

The sky above was glorious deep blue and dotted with white billowing sheepy clouds. Alexander occupied some of his time discerning shapes among the shadows; here a swan, then a small bear, then a horse head. And in one particular thunderhead, a dragon in flight.

He wondered if his traveling companions were wont to use their imaginations as he did, but in the last century imagination seemed to be at a premium. Those who revealed their innermost selves to others had a habit of meeting with misfortune, even to being branded witches and burned for their creativity. So he took the Nihonese approach and kept his imagination to himself.

As the musketeers and carriages passed them, the travelers on the road divided themselves and stood aside. On seeing the crest of arms on the carriage doors, the men removed their hats and some even bowed where they stood. It seemed remarkable to Alexander that he was at the center of such a grand procession, and vowed to write his impressions down at the first opportunity.

Toward midday, the train passed by Rheims, set a little way off the main road. Alexander could see the towers of the cathedral just above the line of the trees, and could hear the church bells tolling on the sweet spring breeze. But he was forced to do nothing more than follow the musketeers as they were determined to keep on moving, and found no more time to think about anything else.

Then, an explosion of sound shattered the tranquility of the golden afternoon. A musketeer in front of him tumbled from his horse, and in doing so set off a chain reaction of shouting as several of the musketeers took aim toward the woods and fired, pushing their horses into forming a ring around the carriages.

The carriage drivers applied the lash and the whole parade flew forward at a more frantic pace. More shots came from seeming nowhere and began to pick off the defenders one by one, even as the musketeers reloaded quickly and shot back.

Alexander looked about into the trees and spotted a whole squad of men perched in the branches, trying to draw a clear line of sight to shoot.

He kicked his horse into a rapid gallop as he drew his sabre, angled her off the road and headed straight into the grove. He caught sight of Lucien doing the same. Somewhere behind him he heard Duggens yell, "hang on! I'm coming!"

While the musketeers were occupied with defending the coach, they were thown into disarray, shouting, trying to control their horses, losing focus, fighting to aim their muskets and shoot, looking for shelter wherever they could find it. Somehow, despite their numbers the squad was ill prepared for an ambush and had become easy pickings for the snipers.

To add insult to injury, the muskets the snipers used were of a different type, easier to load and holding at least two balls with each reload, so the musketeers were quickly outgunned. Innovation had accelerated into the future, while Alexander and Lucien had struggled to come this far from a past filled with crossbows, arquebuses, pistols and swords of all kinds.

Alexander made for the first man, lopped off the branch the man was balanced on, and was already headed for the next tree as the branch and its rotten fruit crashed to the ground. He spotted another taking aim, drew his poinard and threw it. The sniper dropped his musket and fell.

Alexander barely took note as he pushed his horse into the dense thicket ahead of him, slashing at more troops with his blade to dislodge them. The thicket struck back at his face and arms and the horse beneath him, but he ignored the blows as he grimly pressed on.

He saw Lucien's horse dancing about as the white haired demon reached up and tugged other men off the branches, pulled their muskets from their hands as they fell, and used them to shoot others.

Duggens matched Alexander's path by the hoofbeat as he drew his pistols and shot two more men, then took a loose branch, tore it off and used it like a mace to cudgel the rest from the branches.

After a few more moments Alexander simply had to hang back with growing admiration for the man's reckless courage as more men tumbled to the ground.

When it seemed that there were no more enemies to fight, Alexander, Lucien and Duggens returned to the carriages and a scene of carnage.

Bodies, blood, terrified horses gamboling about or bucking to rid themselves of their saddles; wounded men scrambling to help each other, others trying to revive dead comrades. Ten of the musketeers were dead; four were injured, but the carriages were safe.

Dismounting with a bound, Alexander went to the second carriage and looked inside. "How do you fare, Monsieur le Baron?" he asked. "Is anyone injured?"

De Neuvillette raised his head slowly from his crouched position on the floor and said, "I am unharmed, Alexandre. Merci. Armand?"

The deputy raised a trembling hand and replied, "here I am. Gaston? How are you?"

No answer. Armand reached over and nudged his small friend, but this time there was no movement, no word of protest, no sound of breath. Then the small body slumped over and collapsed to the carriage floor.

"Gaston!" came out an anguished sob. "No!" Armand's words turned to blubbering as he covered his face with his hands and began weeping openly.

Alexander reached in and felt at the retainer's pulse. His skin was pale, cold and still as his heartbeat. Then he spotted a small red mark on the back of his head, oozing blood. "It is too late," he said finally.

"He pushed me down. He got in my way," the Baron said, and he reached up with trembling fingers to wipe the tears away. "He took the shot for me, poor friend." He reached over and touched Armand's shoulder to give him comfort, but that only served to make Armand even more desolate with grief.

"Then you will be glad to know that most of the enemy are dead or injured beyond fighting," Alexander said.

"Ay me. I think I will retire and keep bees in Provence," de Neuvillette replied with a heavy sigh. "This is almost more than I can bear. But I can do nothing else until I reach Paris and discharge my duty to the king."

Alexander turned and saw Lucien and Baronet de la Tremaine discussing the situation, while Duggens stood by, panting with near exhaustion, watching as the other men tended to their wounded and dying. He drew a jacket sleeve across his damp forehead and finally reached into a pocket for his kerchief, with which he cleaned his rapier. Then he sheathed the sword and stood by with a bowed head. It was the first time Alexander had seen the man so dispirited.

Determined to cheer him up, he walked toward Duggens and said, "your actions mark you as a hero, sir."

Duggens started at the sound of his voice, then turned to look at him. "And you were a demon on horseback. I could not keep up with you. You were here, you were there, you were everywhere. Your father, too. I am simply astonished beyond words. If only I had a tenth of the powers you possess, I could make a certain difference in this world, that such events as these would not happen again."

"You can make a difference as yourself, sir, without such aid. You are courage in the face of certain doom."

"You flatter me, sir, but..." and his voice trailed off as he spotted something in the thicket off the side of the road. "Watch out!"

In the same moment Alexander turned his head to look, John Henry Duggens leapt toward him, landed in front and splayed his arms as another shot sounded. The hard merciless impact of a musket ball shoved the Englishman against him.

Alexander caught him and supported his weight easily, even as de la Tremaine took aim and shot the sniper. The man ended up dangling from the branch like wet laundry before gravity pulled him to the ground.

Carefully, Alexander lowered Duggens to the ground and tore open the bloodied shirt to reveal a hole near his heart. It had pierced the artery, and blood pumped from the wound with every heartbeat. Duggens's eyes were closed, but he moved feebly, struggling to revive.

"Move not," Alexander admonished him gently. "It is too close to your heart."

"I... know," Duggens replied, his voice almost a whisper. "I had to..." his voice trailed off. Then he rallied briefly and his eyes opened, but they focused blindly. "I can see them," he continued, smiling; then coughed up dark blood which stained his lips and ran down his chin.

"See what, John?" Alexander asked, his vision blurring with sudden tears.

"The white cliffs... of Dover..." Then the knight's eyes closed again, and his heartbeat ceased as he breathed his last.

Alexander took the dead hero in his arms and wept bitter tears, while Lucien and the others could only stand by and watch, helpless to do anything more.

114

Baronet de la Tremaine had the foresight to send a rider ahead to Paris with a message for the Minister of Foreign Affairs, explaining that the delegation would be delayed while the damage done by the snipers was repaired, the dead accounted for and buried, and the wounded cared for.

The caravan moved off the road into the very woods they were ambushed from, there to make a rough camp and triage area.

While Lucien used his medical skills to repair the wounded men, Alexander and the brigade leader saw to the counting of the dead and removed the musketeers' personal effects to transport to their families. They also counted and examined the snipers' bodies, trying to learn where they came from and why they were so determined to intercept the Baron and prevent his delegation from reaching the palace. But like the previous troop of snipers, none bore any clue to their identities or their master.

Alexander was occupied with examining one of the corpses for clues when he heard the Baronet's voice, interrupting his sad reverie on the death of his friend.

"It is curious," de la Tremaine said to him. "How all of these men carry nothing to identify them. They came here to kill the Baron and his men or to die in the attempt."

"Aye," Alexander husked quietly.

"Monsieur, I also observe that you are different. Your skin, your eyes, are like none I have ever seen before. Pale, as if you are ever at death's door. Where do you come from? Forgive me, but I am blessed with an abundance of curiosity. I mean no offense."

On considering the Baronet's diplomatic approach, Alexander chose to speak the truth. "It is my nature to appear this way. I was born in Transylvania. There is nothing remarkable about that."

"Will I have anything to report to the minister, then?"

Alexander regarded him with all the sorrow in his heart reflected on his face. "Such as?"

"I heard things in Strasbourg that did give me pause. There was an altercation in the avenue before the embassy gates, the night before we were summoned to report for duty."

Alexander shrugged off the sudden urge to react with anger. His voice turned to soft velvet. "Of what concern is that to you?"

The Baron smirked. "Again, I said I was only curious. But I am wondering now if this attack was also meant for you as a form of retaliation for the occurrence of the other night. I am curious to know how many enemies you have, that you must ever travel. I have heard of your long journey from the ambassador's servants."

"As I recall, the first man to fall was one of yours," Alexander replied with a pedantic tone, "so the risk was shared by all, was it not?"

"Granted. But you have not answered my question. Do you have any enemies that we should know about, monsieur?"

"Only those which inhabit a man's nightmares," Alexander replied carefully. "I have traveled halfway across the world, Monsieur le Baronet, and with each step I have been called to question for many things I did not do, but which accorded me nought but suspicion and hostility, and all for the sake of my appearance alone."

"And, the Englishman?"

"The Englishman, for the brief time we knew one another, trusted me more than any man I have ever known, and now he is dead. All my other friends are either dead or separated from me by a great distance. All I have of them is a precious memory, an occasional curio. As for these attacks, I have no explanation save that I and my father are frequently the target of men possessed with false notions about us which we did not engender. Thus we perforce defend ourselves from their violence as any other man would."

"How came you to travel with the ambassador?"

"My father and I stopped an attack on him in Austria. We were assured by the ambassador that we would have an audience with King Louis so that he may achieve another steward. I speak nought of myself, but of my father. Would you deny your king a man with superior skills and the comportment to do his bidding?"

"Nay, monsieur," the musketeer said. "I saw your phenomenal skills displayed in the woods, and your father's. If I had ten men like you two I would see no more need to bury my comrades. And I would do nothing to deprive His Majesty of able men to carry out his wishes." He stroked his chin for a few moments, then asked, "who taught you how to use a blade like that?"

"I trained on my own, and found other techniques in my travels. I was instructed in the Nihonese method by the master Musashi, who gave me his swords," Alexander replied. "My sword master is long dead and buried. I would have others learn the art of the sword, so that his legacy is preserved."

"Nihon? Ho, ho. I would enjoy a lesson or two. The royal swordmaster, le Perche Du Coudray, has need of new instructors for his school of fencing. When we are in Paris I will arrange an introduction. What say you?"

Alexander felt all his battle tension recede slowly. He had expected derision or scorn as Bela Ragosi had displayed before. But the more he thought about it, he realized that perhaps Ragosi had been finding an excuse to test his own skills, and the tactic had turned back on him. "As I will require some kind of profitable enterprise, I would appreciate your efforts on my behalf," he said.

"Good. And now I will brief what remains of my squadron and prepare them for the rest of our journey. I offer my deepest sympathy for the death of your friend." With that, he turned and walked away before Alexander could say another word.

Paris

115

A day later, the embassy caravan rounded a turn in the road and galloped toward a sprawling cluster of spires and buildings accompanied by the sound of bells, as the cathedral of Notre Dame and the city churches rang out the call to matins under a clouding sky. From a distance, the city of Paris was a sprawling center of teeming humanity, cottage industries and commerce, planted in the middle of a circular plain through which the river Seine flowed, and where all roads through France appeared to connect like the rays of a star.

At the city's eastern gate, the caravan was greeted by a small contingent of gendarmes, who raised the gate the moment they saw the coaches and the uniforms of the musketeers. The whole train passed through without stopping and continued down the avenue in a rush, as citizens and nobles alike fell back and narrowly avoided being trampled. Some shouted insults at the riders and coaches as they passed only to be accosted by others seeking to silence them.

Alexander drank the discontent and celebration from the air as a perfume of change and a sign of things to come.

The troop led the coaches directly toward the Louvre, where they were admitted onto the grounds with flustered haste. The musketeers then retired to barracks on the grounds of the palace, there to be reassigned and await the word to go out again; while the ambassador and his young deputy were escorted to the king's chambers immediately.

The retainers and drivers were dismissed with the admonition that they should share no detail of their journey to anyone, on pain of death.

Baronet de la Tremaine lingered long enough to introduce Lucien and Alexander to the deputy Minister of Foreign Affairs, an older retainer called Chasson de Vere, then saluted them and disappeared down the hall to rejoin his troops.

The deputy minister took the two foreigners in hand with all the effulgent cheer of a man discovering a rattlesnake in his bed. Lucien and Alexander were assigned rooms in the guest wing and were told that they should wait until summoned. That it might be a day, or a week, or even a month, before anyone would be seen by the cabinet minister and an introduction to the king arranged.

He explained that while they were waiting they would be accorded every pleasure, every need, without question. He then added that they were also free to explore the grounds as long as they did not go beyond the wall which surrounded the estate, as a caution for their own safety.

Lucien did not question this, while Alexander was consumed with curiosity as to why their freedom should be so restricted. He peered out beyond the velveteen curtains onto the emaculately tended lawn and said, "everything feels out of sorts, father. What is your impression?"

"Difficult to tell," Lucien replied, and paused as he shrugged off his cloak and tossed his old beleaguered hat onto the bed. He drew off his boots and tossed them into a corner, then sank down on the damascene coverlet and crossed his legs, fell back against a pillow covered in embroidered silk and cradled his head on his hands. "There was much discontent on the avenue suggesting a conflict brewing among the citizens, and the servants' behavior is also very guarded. Truly, we are navigating in uncharted territory."

Alexander turned and saw him looking comfortable and relaxed, and offered, "yet there you are, unaffected, untroubled. How can you be so, when I feel as if I am sitting on pins and needles?"

"I prefer to call it conservation of energy," Lucien remarked softly. "All will be revealed in time. For now, I would suggest rest to cleanse ourselves of the upsets of the last day, and later we will bathe, dress again and go hunting. We did not have a chance to feed well in Strasbourg. My blood is clamoring for satisfaction." He shifted to get more comfortable with a long sigh.

There came the sound of rapping on the door, startling both of them. Then after a space of about ten seconds, more rapping. Lucien relaxed again and said, "well, answer it."

Hesitating on the brink of doubt, Alexander went to the door and opened it.

A servant stood in the hallway, dressed in royal blue with gold trim, wearing a feziwig, white gloves and high buckled shoes. He was short but regal in bearing, and his green eyes were direct as he said, "I beg pardon for disturbing you, monsieurs, but I have come to inform you that His Majesty has ordered a reception in your honor. If you will permit me, I will bring the court tailors to take your measurements and supply you with suitable clothes, and also the wigmaker to bring you and your father all such as would please you to wear."

Alexander asked, "when is the reception to commence?"

"At eight of the clock this evening. In the meantime, I will have food and drink brought to you, for you must be hungry after your long journey."

"Indeed," Alexander nodded with a smile. "We await your pleasure."

The servant bowed expansively and replied, "d'accord. Merci." Then, placing his hands behind his back, he walked away down the corridor at a calm measured pace.

Alexander closed the door, exhaled pent up breath and turned to Lucien. "Well, that was unexpected. We are to be honored guests, and we may yet gain an audience with the king sooner than I had expected."

Lucien had not moved from the bed, closed his eyes again and said, "the day is still young, Alexander."

As was foretold, a chamber valet, a pair of tailors and a wigmaker with a gaggle of servants bearing trunks, came to the chamber two hours later and proceeded to express their shock at the condition and age of the clothes Alexander and Lucien were wearing; no matter that the fashion in Vienna was as up to date as possible.

462

Over the course of the next hour the servants managed to get both their guests out of the old clothes while measuring them for the new ones; instructing them about the latest fashions of the day without mentioning their cost.

While Alexander and Lucien bathed in hot water scented with lemons, and sponged themselves with emolients, the tailors sent their servants out of the room with the whole pile of old clothes, ordering them to burn the lot.

When Alexander and Lucien emerged from their tubs and toweled themselves off, the tailors ushered them into the parlor, where they opened their trunks to display the finest of velvets and silks, and newly embroidered Chinoise brocades trimmed in gold and silver. They examined their new models with care and argued over the best colors to match their skin tones.

Lucien simply took the whole affair in stride, allowing the clothiers to fuss and pluck and get their mercurial tempers out of their systems with little objection. But in the end, he refused all but the simplest clothes in black velveteen trimmed with black silk and a simple undershirt of pure white silk.

Alexander preferred a satin ensemble in jack blue trimmed with silver to honor his dead friend, Hanry Duggens. Yet when Alexander tried it on he felt completely awkward in it. A pang of nostalgia for the old style of clothes ran through him as he considered the exaggeration fashion had come to, and finally told himself to get used to the idea, reminding himself that change was the only constant in the universe.

One of the stewards came forward and said, "monsieurs, if you will permit me, I will apply some rouge to your cheeks, for I see that you are already wearing some on your lips."

Alexander stared at him, mystified. "What rouge, pray tell?"

The valet moved closer, but timidly, and his blue eyes bugged with surprise. "Non? What rouge, indeed, Monsieur le Comte? How is it you have such lips?"

"They are mine own, monsieur," he replied firmly. "And I require no rouge anywhere."

The valet swallowed deeply, nodded and returned the rouge box to his makeup kit. "Then it is clear my additions to your natural beauty will not be needed," he declared with a short bow, then retreated a short distance and stood looking around as if he had nowhere to go. Then he collected his box and silently fled from the room.

When it came time to try on a formal wig of long curly tresses, Alexander balked when he saw himself in the mirror and whipped it back off. "It is not me," he declared. "Is this really necessary?"

Lucien looked blandly at him and said, "Alexander, be kind."

The wigmaker, an Italian named di Grazzi, widened his round black eyes and said, "Monsieur le Comte, it is required! Would you prefer to be laughed at by the other nobles of the court?"

"If they were truly noble, they would not be laughing," Alexander insisted. "No, monsieur. I will not." He crossed his arms and stood resolute.

"Lala," one of the tailors said, rolling his eyes. "Monsieur, this will not do. We have been dressing the court of France for ten years, and when di Grazzi says these things, he is right. You should take his advice. It is that or endure the gossip, which travels with such speed that you would hear it before it is even shared."

Alexander went to his knapsack and reached into it, withdrew two of the gold coins from Charanditha's cache and handed them over. "I care not for the clucking of hens, so it is of no consequence to me. Let them talk. It is no reflection on your superb skills. Here is a sum of gold for your trouble, but I require not the wig. I will tie my hair back, or some such else, and you may vend it to another."

Lucien, who had tried one on just to see what he would look like in it, removed it just as quickly, adding, "mine also, as I am not accustomed to wearing such things for the vanity it expresses. We are men of humbler cloth, who would forebear dressing as more than we are. Such things are for men of the court, while we are mere travelers who have just arrived."

"You know, Cyrano de Bergerac told me the same thing just the other day," di Grazzi replied with a sigh. "Ah, very well, but you are making a mistake, monsieurs. Mark me."

"Cyrano de Bergerac? I have heard of him," Alexander said.

Di Grazzi said, "you would do well not to underestimate him. He is one of the finest swordsmen in France. He also eschews courtly dress, but I respect him just the same."

"As you say. Will he be at this reception?"

"I know not, for I am not on the list. But my wigs will be," di Grazzi said proudly.

One of the tailors added, "we are also not on the list, but you will be our ambassadors, the both of you. You wear those clothes grandly, and no doubt the ladies will be singing your praises." He winked and jabbed an elbow at his partner, who simpered a bit, hid his mouth with a gloved hand and giggled like a little girl.

"Thank you, gentlemen, you are most kind. I think," Alexander replied, frowning with puzzlement.

When the dressers left, Alexander combed out his long dark hair and tied it back with a bit of silk ribbon, while Lucien combed his white hair until it was smooth as silk, braided two sections in front and left the rest loose, letting it fall like a curtain down his back as he had at the temple.

Then, shod in heeled pumps, they left the chamber together, headed down the corridor and down the curved staircase toward the main hall and the future.

116

They had not gone far down the stairs when everyone who had not entered the ballroom turned, beheld them in their deliberate simplicity and gasped with amazement. The conversation quickly turned to the new guests of the ambassador, and fans fluttered rapidly as some of the women watched them walk by in silent awe.

Alexander felt his cheeks flush with self-consciousness at their flattery, but kept walking as if he had not heard a word. His heart picked up pace as stage fright caught him in its grip. Lucien appeared unaffected by the sudden notoriety, but turned and gave him a small smile of assurance.

The reception was a sumptuous affair. The music coming from the mezzanine was Lully, brilliant and majestic, filling the hall with measured rhythmic cords and the application of trumpet, cello and viola. Elegance and opulence danced hand in hand as courtiers and guests described flourishes about each other on a great floor of mosaic cut marble, under chandeliers of glittering crystal hung from a painted ceiling covered in art. Alexander was stricken with awe at the beauty and grandeur displayed before him.

Then he realized that the center of civilization was here, in the palace of the kingdom, while the common people of France never saw any of it.

They met the calling steward guarding the entrance to the hall. The man was in middle age and dressed in velvets and lace, wearing a feziwig rather than a full dress wig. He barely gave them a nod of acknowledgement before he marched into the hall, rapped his long staff on the floor and called out, "mesdames et monsieurs, le Comte Lucien d'Arkanon of Transylvania and his son, le Comte Alexandre Corvina."

All eyes turned in their direction as the conversation died, and for a moment Alexander felt like a fly trapped in amber. But then there came more gasps and fluttering of fans from the women, and a little hostility from their escorts mixed with reluctant admiration.

Apparently word of the altercation on the road and tales of their heroics had spread rapidly in the court. As if on cue, one of the men standing nearby began to clap his hands, then another; and soon the whole room rang with applause. At first Alexander could not fathom this sudden noise of welcome. But, after a journey of ten thousand miles, of rough living on the road and constantly on the move, it felt as if he had come home.

One of the ministers pushed through the admiring crowd, approached Lucien and spoke to him. "Monsieur le Comte, please allow me to introduce myself. I am Chevalier Alphonse Elric von Heimdahl. I am to be your guide for this evening."

Lucien turned and regarded him with a certain reserve. Then he replied. "You are… German?"

"Swiss," von Heimdahl said, nodding. "My family holds the Schloss Ischfalen, near Geneva."

"I was not aware we needed an escort," Lucien replied. "Is this customary?"

The chevalier closed his eyes and rocked back a little on his heels. "Quite so. As you are from a foreign land, no doubt some of our customs may be unfamiliar to you. I have been tasked with making your introductions to the court."

"Ah. Then by all means, do proceed."

Over the course of the next hour, Alexander and Lucien met many of the court officials and courtesans of the day; and were treated to a variety of emotional sensations, from trepidation to outright hostility masked by pleasant and courteous smiles and speech. Alexander could distinguish little among the two. But the hostile sentiments were not aimed at him or Lucien, but rather at each other. Alexander concluded that lies and subterfuge came readily, disguised by etiquette and the need to fit in among the cliques. He found this thoroughly uncharming but told himself to get used to it.

Then they came to a man standing alone by the punchbowl. He was not very tall, dressed in simple black like Lucien. His face was pale in the candlelight, and his eyes were large and brown, framed by a cloud of curly dark brown hair. It was not a wig. To Alexander he felt like a kindred being, though he did not smell quite that way. Another halfling, or a bastard son of Julianus? Or something else entirely?

In the excitement of the moment he could not stop to find out. Du Heimdahl interrupted his reverie with the words, "monsieurs, may I present le Comte du Saint Germain."

The shorter man offered them an expansive bow, and said, "welcome to France, monsieurs. I have heard of your adventures. May I know if you are in any way related to the Prince Vlad Dracula, whose exploits have long been the toast of Europe?"

Caught off guard, Lucien replied carefully. "We are Draculesti, monsieur. How is it that you know him?"

A dark elegant eyebrow elevated as St. Germain replied. "May I venture to say that you resemble him in many ways? I have been to the court in Budapest, and his portrait hangs in the front hall. Indeed, were it not for the color of your hair and your eyes, I would have thought you were the man himself. But he is long dead. Is he not?"

Both Alexander and Lucien were struck mute as if they had been slapped in the face. There was a long moment of tense silence not shared among those who were watching. Then Lucien said carefully, "it is so."

St. Germain appeared to be fishing for something, but what it was seemed beyond Alexander's reach. What he said next was completely unexpected. "It is said that he drank blood to maintain his strength, and that he impaled thousands to protect his lands."

Lucien's lips turned flat with tension, and his eyes were dangerously close to turning red. His voice went low and soft as he replied, "there is more to the story than you know. Many of those who were there to see the truth or falsity of such deeds are also long dead. Are they not?"

Alexander had never seen his father like this before. Alarmed by the sensations coursing like mild electricity through his being, he ventured, "what you have heard were lies woven by his enemies to besmirch his honor and insult his legacy. We will not suffer them in such polite company."

St. Germain regarded him with a bland expression. "I have no interest in trading gossip, Monsieur le Viscomte. I seek only to understand. You see, I am a scholar of alchemy and folklore. If you will oblige me for the moment, I have heard many things about vampires, creatures who inhabit the night and drink the blood of the living. Have you?"

The words were said quietly, but for some reason they were transported around the room as if he had shouted. The atmosphere of tension drew others on the floor to gather around them. It appeared that St. Germain was just influential enough to command their attention simply by being there.

At that moment von Heimdahl also tried to intervene. "Monsieurs, we must move on."

"Nay, Monsieur mon Chevalier," St. Germain said. "Let our honored guest answer the question."

Lucien folded his gloved hands before him and softly replied, "I have. But they are fairy tales, surely."

"Then you must have heard of their unique abilities. How they inhabit the dark shadows of the night and haunt our dreams. The way they look, the way they appear to some and vanish just as quickly. That they take blood from us as if we are sheep to be sacrificed to their hunger. They have the powers of the gods, monsieur, but have no power to face the light of day."

Lucien's eyes narrowed, a dangerous sign. "How should that apply to me, monsieur?" he asked.

"I merely ask because I thought that in your travels you had heard more. I am keen to learn all I can. Perhaps at a later time you would be willing to share your insights with me. It is not often that I am introduced to someone who has been where it all happened. And you, being the descendents of the greatest hero in all of Europa, are the ones I must turn to for instruction."

The tension broke like a wave on a rocky shore. Clearly, St. Germain had started strange conversations like these before, and Alexander began to wonder if he was prone to do so just to keep his audience interested and entertained. He waited for Lucien to say something to put him off.

Lucien nodded his head as he replied, "it would be my honor, monsieur. I await your pleasure."

Alexander subtly exhaled, now aware that he had been holding his breath.

"Then, if it will be convenient, you may visit me tomorrow evening and we will talk. I will send a boy with the address."

"Tomorrow evening will be most convenient," Lucien replied.

Von Heimdahl insisted, "monsieurs, we must move on," and managed to get them away from the scholarly stranger long enough to mend the damage done. As the crowd broke up and returned to their own topics, he steered them toward the next person on his list.

"You must not mind him," he offered. "Le Comte du Saint Germain is always a bit... one would call him eccentric, I suppose. Why, do you know that he claims to be immortal?"

With a subtle glance at Alexander, Lucien replied, "really. How old does he claim to be?"

The knight wavered for a moment, then said, "he says he was there when Moses parted the sea to allow the Hebrews to escape from Pharoah. Mmmm....two? No, three thousand years ago. But of course that is impossible, would you agree? I think he just says it for the thrill it gives the ladies of the court. But I don't believe a word of it. I prefer to think of him as a charlatan."

Alexander turned back to look at the young scholar and caught his large brown eyes staring back it him with the same intensity and boldness that Bela Ragosi had shown when they had first met. A chill ran up his spine. Then he admonished himself to avoid getting caught up in his own imaginings, tore his attention away and centered it on the next guest on von Heimdahl's list.

Through all of this the king himself never appeared, and it seemed that the introduction would have to wait until later. Then, when Alexander was ready to give up on waiting, the doors to the inner chambers opened, and another minister emerged with a long staff, which he rapped on the floor.

The chamber musicians paused in mid song. The whole chamber grew silent as the guests turned their attention to him. He intoned, "mesdames et monsieurs, the queen, viceroy and regent of France, Anne of Austria."

He stood aside as a group of women passed him into the chamber, among them a mature young woman dressed in a deep blue gown with lace gussets and pearls, wearing a diamond tiara over a short lace veil. She had the tired expression of a woman with the burden of caring for a whole country.

She went to the empty throne at the end of the ballroom floor and sat down in it, then announced in a warm but gentle voice, "His Grace is indisposed with a humor and has been confined to bed. Please, do carry on and enjoy your evening."

The whole room bowed and curtsied, and soon afterward the musicians resumed playing.

Alexander leaned over and said to Lucien. "Ah well, it appears we must wait longer to meet the king."

Lucien studied the queen closely, then said, "patience, Alexander. The king is a boy. They have come to a disagreement of some kind, so he has been sent to bed early. She is still his mother, and charged with the management of the crown, must also supervise this reception on his behalf. I dare say she would rather be somewhere else."

Alexander glanced around, hoping to see the ambassador among them, but could not single him out in the crowd. "Baron de Neuvillette is not here," he remarked. "I have not seen him since we arrived."

"Regretable," Lucien replied. "But, perhaps necessary."

The room grew quiet when a man clad in brilliant scarlet robes and wearing a chapel cap entered the room. The minister rapped again with his staff and announced, "mesdames et monsieurs, le Cardinal Mazarin." At his entrance, most of the courtiers bowed or courtsied briefly, then returned to their conversation, while a few reached his side and knelt to kiss his signet ring.

"So, that is Mazarin," Alexander remarked.

"He appears older than I had expected," Lucien replied.

Barely five seconds passed when the steward then announced, "mesdames et monsieurs, Philipe d'Anju, le Duc D'Orleans."

A young man about 20 years old passed into the room. He was tall and thin, and wore a full cut black and brown velvet ensemble with gold trim, a lace jabot, a shoulder sash in royal blue and an elegantly curled dark wig. His blue eyes were already bright with the effects of wine, and he coughed into a lace kerchief as he surveyed the crowd giving him deference. After a brief but somewhat disrespectful nod to the queen, he began circulating through the room like a seasoned politician.

Alexander saw the queen's small mouth turn down with instant disapproval, indicating that the duke and she shared a long standing disagreement of some kind. But then a baritone voice behind him cut into his curiosity like a scythe. "I see you have been outshone by *Monsieur*. Pay him no mind."

Alexander turned and beheld the Baronet de la Tremaine, clad in the dress uniform of the Royal Musketeers, with a tabbard of royal blue embroidered with a gold cross and accented with fleur de lis. The Baronet made a shooing motion with his hand toward von Heimdahl and said, "I will take them in hand now. Go about your business."

The chevalier sputtered, "but..."

"I said, you are dismissed." De la Tremaine took on the expression of a ship's captain as he said it, and fluttered his gloved hands toward him with another dismissing gesture.

Reluctantly, von Heimdahl bowed to Lucien and Alexander and then strode away muttering imprecations under his breath.

"Good evening," Alexander replied. "How are you here?"

"Did I not tell you that I am also the king's servant?" the Baronet replied with a wink. "I see they have left you both entirely alone in this sea of pelicans. There is nothing they appreciate more than fresh fodder for their gossip. If you will permit me, I came to rescue you."

Alexander thought his description of the court somewhat artless. "How can you see your own people that way?"

Lucien chided, "Alexander. Leave such sentiments aside."

De la Tremaine leaned in closer and said softly, "all is not as civilised as your senses have told you. I agree that it appears wonderful and grand, but I know what the truth is, and these elegant trappings conceal much danger for the king. All that glitters here is far more than gold." He turned his head briefly, then spotted something in the rear of the ballroom. He added, "come with me. There is someone here I would like you to meet."

"By all means, monsieur," Lucien agreed. "Lead on."

De la Tremaine turned and parted the crowd with a brusque, "out of the way, all of you!" as he marched toward a group of musketeers standing in a corner and talking together.

One was a little younger than the rest, while the other three were in full middle age, all clad in the royal colors with their hats in their hands. They did not wear wigs, nor did they wear lace jabots or silks. All was the same plain linen with a little edging of lace, rough wool and suede. They grew silent as the Baronet approached.

"At your ease, monsieurs," he said to them. "May I present to you le Comte Lucien Arkanon and his son Alexandre Corvina. Gentlemen, le Baron Charles de Batz-Castelmore d'Artagnan, and his friends of the Royal Mousquetaires Athos, Porthos and René d'Herblay, Comte abbe' Aramis de Vannes."

"Future abbe', if you please, monsieur," Aramis replied. "I have still not decided to take my vows yet."

"I do stand corrected, monsieur," de la Tremaine said with a smile and a bow. "Future abbe'."

D'Artagnan appeared to take charge as he said to Alexander, "I understand from de la Tremaine that you were instrumental in thwarting an attack on the ambassador to Bohemia, and that you have phenomenal skills as a swordsman."

"Monsieur le Baronet honors me with flattery," Alexander replied. "What I did was only necessary."

"Virtuous, and humble beside," Athos remarked. "I have been told that you seek a position with the master at arms le Perche de Coudray. He is looking for instructors, and Monsieur de Tréville could use men of your brand of courage to train our recruits."

Lucien said, "my son is trained in an unusual form of fencing. He studied on the island of Nihon for a time, before we came to France."

D'Artagnan's eyes widened slightly. "Nihon? Where is that?"

Porthos drew himself up proudly and said, "I have been there myself. Nihon is a group of islands on the other side of the world. The people there practice all manner of heathen rituals, but they value honor above all and would sooner lose an arm or an eye, even their very lives to defend their emperor."

Aramis leaned over and asked, "pardon. When were you there?"

Caught in his fib, Porthos threw him a pointed glance and said, "it was before I met you, monsieur!"

Aramis smiled more broadly and replied, "I thought so. Say three hail Maries before you go to bed."

Athos steered the conversation back to the subject. "I would enjoy a demonstration of your fencing skills," he said. "Would you care to meet us in the Place de Hotel Troisvilles tomorrow? de la Tremaine, can you arrange it? I will invite du Coudray, and if he is satisfied with what he sees, I will vouch for your bona fides at once. I have heard of Nihon, and have met men who have been there. The steel there is made to create the finest of blades, and before God, I have heard tales of the speed and courage of demons among the men who use them."

Alexander felt a flush of pride. "You honor me and my master, monsieur," he replied with a small bow. "My thanks."

Athos winked. "Do not thank me yet, monsieur. If you are all as you are described, I will discuss it with His Grace or his chief minister about where to put you. One cannot waste such skills."

D'Artagnan was about to add something to their conversation when the Duc D'Orleans approached with a glass of wine in his hand. His voice came out with a distinct drunken drawl. "Ah, there you are, Monsieur d'Artagnan. I would have a word with you."

D'Artagnan hesitated with a look of chagrin, then took a bow with a flourish of his hat and replied, "Monsieur le Duc, I am at your disposal."

"I would like to know when you are going to reply to my pamphlet regarding the state of the State."

"When I have time to read it, Monsieur," d'Artagnan said. "As you know, I must be on hand when the king calls for me."

"The king is in bed, sent there for getting a little ahead of himself. You therefore have time to read it now." He whipped out a folded piece of fine vellum and handed it to the musketeer. "When I am king, you will not avoid me the way you have been. Mark me."

D'Artagnan bit back a surly remark, sighed and finally said, "as you say, Monsieur le Duc, but you are not king yet."

The duke turned several different shades of red, then purple. He leaned into d'Artagnan's face and snarled, "that will change one day, monsieur. You would do well to know your place."

All the musketeers present had crowded around the duke subtly during the exchange until he was completely surrounded. Athos leaned forward and softly said to him, "as long as you remember who is king now, monsieur. Come. Must I add sedition to your list of sins?"

The duke drew back quickly with a look of astonishment. "Are you challenging me to a duel?"

"If you find it amusing," Athos replied with a pedantic tone of boredom. "At what hour should we meet?"

"You would not dare," d'Orleans said. "You know that dueling is forbidden, by the command of Cardinal Mazarin."

Alexander felt a little trapped in this round robin of bitterness, but stayed where he was. D'Artagnan threw him a look of complete helplessness and shook his head. Lucien said nothing, but if he was calm it meant that all the duke said could be canceled with a single word from the queen, or the cardinal, or even Athos himself if he chose.

Athos replied, "then perhaps you should seek succor from the cardinal, monsieur, for I serve the king. I have lost patience with your brand of rancor. God ordained that child to be king. If I were you, I would seek confession and accept that what is, is. If the king dies without issue, you may petition the court for redress of your claim. Until then, kindly remember *your* place." He turned to Alexander and Lucien and bowing slightly, added, "good evening, monsieurs." Then he marched out the rear door, restoring his hat to his head.

The duke declared, "that impertinent ass!"

Then he turned and found himself trapped in a circle of royal blue. The musketeers parted just enough to allow him egress, and without uttering a word to them, he marched away, fuming and cursing as he went. The musketeers broke up to trade jibes in soft tones about his outburst.

D'Artagnan shook his head. "Athos is right. That... boy... wants the throne, and I shudder to think what he has planned for us. I apologize for his behavior, monsieurs. You have not seen us at our best."

Aramis said, "but, in his own way he is right. He is older than Louis, and by accident of fate and papal decree he was passed over. But he will not accept it." He shrugged helplessly. "What else can we do?"

Lucien finally said, "it is not our affair, but this new understanding begs the question. In time, your king will be old enough to plot his own destiny. You must be prepared to defend him at all costs if you are men of France. Even then, will you be prepared to defend the king even if he is the duke?"

"I dare say we will have to," Porthos remarked. "And *Monsieur* will not let us forget this day. La la, we are all doomed to see it turned back on us."

"Perhaps, if I had a word with the cardinal..." Aramis suggested.

"Cardinal Mazarin is not our friend," d'Artagnan replied. "He is old and has fixed ideas about the destiny of France. I survived only because he saw fit to intercede on my behalf, and were it not for that I should have been hanged for being the blind and arrogant fool that I was."

Aramis laid a gloved hand on his shoulder. "That is all in the past, mon frère," he said. "You are older now. We all are. I could not think now of having a better friend than you."

"And I," Porthos added. "After what happened to Cyrano..."

The name brought Alexander to ask, "you knew Cyrano de Bergerac? I have heard much of his exploits. Is he dead?"

Porthos turned to him. "He is not dead, but exiled from the court for making pronouncements against the duke and his friend le Comte de Guiche. He survives now on his pension and the sale of his books and pamphlets, and I hear he has just written a book in which he traveled to the moon riding on a cannon ball, where he terrorized the maidens there just as he does here. Le nariz large, non?" He paused to tap the side of his nose with a finger. "I could never get him to explain how he returned *from* the moon. 'That,' he said, 'is a state secret'."

His face then grew more sober. "But with his banishment from the court our list of allies grows thinner by the day. Talk to Cyrano and he will tell you the truth, that all is not well in France. Even the king cannot move freely in his own court."

Alexander said, "on our way here we did see discontentment with the passage of our train. What else have you heard of the country outside these walls? What of the grievances of the people?"

"That is not a subject to be discussed *within* these walls, monsieur," d'Artagnan replied quickly, as he craned his neck to look around the room. "There are men here who do more than listen."

"I understand," he replied quietly.

The group was approached by a young page dressed in blue. "Monsieurs, a moment if you please. The queen desires to speak with these honored guests."

The musketeers all gave him a small bow of deference, and Aramis replied, "of course. They are all yours."

The steward addressed Lucien and Alexander directly, bowed briefly and indicated the throne. "Please follow me."

As Alexander turned to follow him, de la Tremaine grabbed his sleeve, leaned in close and murmured, "be careful."

The steward described a beeline through the crowded ballroom toward the throne, where he introduced Lucien and Alexander to the queen, "Anne of Austria, mother of His Grace Louis quatorze and regent to the Crown."

As was told to them, Lucien and Alexander gave her a deep bow of deference and waited for her to speak first.

Her eyes lit up with curiosity as they looked the two vampires over. "I am told that you wish an audience with the king," she said. "I have never before seen men of your appearance and bearing. Whence came you?"

"We are from Transylvania, Madame," Lucien said.

"My cousin, the emperor Ferdinand, speaks in his letters of Transylvania. You must tell me more of your country, for I long to travel, but cannot as long as the regency binds me to the court."

"It would be my honor, Madame," Lucien replied with another small bow. "Your ambassador de Neuvillette did give us a promise, to which we hold him not. We seek only to make ourselves useful to His Grace as his servants. We await your pleasure to meet with him and obtain our orders."

"If de Neuvillette promised it, you must have impressed him greatly," she replied. "I will have the cabinet minister make the arrangements. You will have your audience."

"Your Majesty is most kind," Lucien replied with another bow.

She turned to Alexander. "I am also told that you have much skill with the sword," she said. "France greatly needs such skills."

Alexander replied, "my thanks for your generosity, and that of France, Madame."

She smiled gently. "Your gratitude is more than I require, for all I do, I do for France." She extended her small right hand to them, which bore a large seal ring on her finger. Lucien and Alexander knelt and kissed the seal, then drew back and stood waiting for her first command, which was, "go now and enjoy your evening, both of you."

The rest of the event turned into a freewheeling affair. Alexander was singled out by various women, all of whom were into bedding heroes without needing to learn the truth about them first. Soon it became a game of cat and mouse as he was sought after by one or another of the winsome but vapid creatures.

Finally, he escaped by hiding behind a curtain for a bit until they gave up looking for him. Soon afterward he abandoned that idea and practiced the art of being invisible in a crowded room as Lucien had taught him to do, and made his way around unseen until he could see his father standing alone near the buffet table.

When he reached Lucien's side, he said, "it appears that I am the favored target for the evening." He flapped his hand in front of his face to fan it, then ran the other hand through his hair. "They are all the most beautiful creatures I have ever seen, but I cannot decide which one to hang on my arm. And, I risk courting a duel or two in the process." He shrugged helplessly and ended with a rueful smile. "What am I to do?"

Lucien suppressed a smile. As he scanned the ballroom, he took a careful sip of what had been identified as champagne and grimaced at it with distaste. "This is not even close to slivoviska. I do not see how they can drink it." He put the glass down on the buffet table. "The ladies have found you fair in the extreme, and if I may add, some of the men. In time you will find all of it useful."

Alexander replied, "indeed? How do you mean?"

"We cannot trust what we see in this room, Alexander. Friends and enemies are joined together in such a way that one cannot distinguish between them. The Baronet is right. Perhaps I will learn more when I speak with Saint Germain. He may be a valuable asset to our settlement in France."

"And, you are proposing that any friendship forged here will have similar value. I wish it were not so. I had hoped to find a friend like Sir John among these worthies. But I must confess that I have not yet mastered the art of subterfuge or deception. Must I begin my new life surrounded by such unpleasantness?"

Lucien turned and plucked a rose from the arrangement, sniffed it and said, "you may have to sooner than later. Guard your words carefully, that you do not attract too much attention from the wrong sort of people. I am going to find something to eat."

117

The next morning, Lucien and Alexander were roused from their beds and told to dress, and soon after that they were escorted down the corridor into the west wing and the offices of government.

The chamber secretary took them in hand and led them into a sumptuous foyer. It was a gallery of marvels. One could not be bored sitting on the gold brocade cushions of the couches, and the walls were festooned with portaits of kings and queens, ministers, popes and other digitaries, all painted in brilliant colors and framed in gilt-edged wood.

Alexander strolled up and down the hall admiring the skills of the brush and the mastery of color by each artist, while Lucien sat quietly gazing out the windows onto the manicured lawn of the estate, where the gardeners could be seen strolling about with their picks and scissors, hand trimming the foliage or raking; while a group of court ladies and gentlemen were occupied with a game of croquet nearby.

Today, rather than be surrounded by a crowd of people suing for a moment with the king, the two vampires were left entirely alone. The halls were deserted. The quiet was interrupted only by the hurried passage of a steward carrying documents to another chamber, while a pair of ministers stood in the outer hall sharing a subdued conversation between them.

The sound of a swinging pendulum came from the clock on the mantelpiece of a dark fireplace, counting out the seconds with measured strokes. Alexander had grown used to the tocking sound since their days in Vienna, where it seemed there were clocks everywhere. Europe had become imprisoned by time, while the rest of the world ran according to the seasons.

He had seen many new concepts of science emerging from under the mantel of secrecy, and with it, time was necessary to keep accurate measurements. No matter what the church did to suppress the march of science, there was no way it could hold back progress. The clocks were just a permanent reminder of that fact. And now, even the churches had clocks, shown prominently below the

478

belfries. The bells had begun to ring on time, measuring out each hour, then each half hour, while the call to prayer described little flourishes of bellringing in between.

With the tinkling of chimes, the clock on the mantelpiece nearby struck eleven, bringing Alexander back to the present moment. The chamber doors parted and swung inward. A steward strode out into the waiting room, turned to Lucien and said softly, "Monsieur le Comte, His Grace will see you now."

Lucien stood up and, taking a moment to smooth down his overcoat, glanced to Alexander and gave him a subtle nod, then followed the steward into the chamber. Alexander was left to peruse the paintings alone.

A half hour later, Lucien emerged from the chamber backwards and alone, bearing a sheaf of vellum and a somewhat puzzled expression on his face, as the doors were closed before him by the guards. He stood mute with silent astonishment as if he had been slapped in the face.

Alexander approached, breathless with curiosity, and asked, "father, what said he?"

"He was… not what I expected," Lucien replied. "The king is most uncommonly shrewd and intelligent for his young age. He granted me the estates and stables of Rouen as if he had been waiting for me all his life. He told me that it was as if destiny had brought me to him. It was all quite… remarkable." He turned to him and added, "granted, I have no doubt that the Baron had told him of our adventures and prepared him for our meeting, but the child… the king, was prepared to accept me as I am."

"Even so?" Alexander asked. "He showed no fear?"

"Aye. It is most curious. He did not explain himself to me but I divined from his behavior that his family has a memory of us from a time long past, from the first generation. Therefore, it was most natural for him to expect one of us to appear to serve them once again."

Alexander was about to ask something else when the chamber doors opened again, and another steward stood in the threshhold. "Monsieur le Comte Corvina, His Grace would like to speak with you," he said.

Lucien placed a reassuring hand on Alexander's shoulder and said, "all my hopes go with you. Bon chance."

On entering the chamber, Alexander found himself in the middle of palatial opulence. The floor was solid Italian marble, and the appointments were covered in gold, while the walls were lined with more portraits of kings and queens, their children, cardinals and other nobles, going back in time to the first king of France, Charlemagne.

A large mahogany desk sat between two large windows opened to let in the fragrance of roses, gardenias and peonies lining the balcony outside, and there was a grand view of a fountain leading to a long expanse of lawn beyond. The lawn ended at a high wall lined with a hedge of bougainvillea, whose thorns could easily deter any trespass on royal privacy.

Seated at the desk was a boy about ten years of age, with long curly dark hair down to his shoulders, and dressed in dark blue velveteen cut simply. His blouse was of linen with a modest edging of lace. He had the expression of a judge, and his whole body appeared tense as he read over a document slowly; while an older man in a dark cassock bent over him and murmured urgently into his ear.

The kinglet only paused in reading long enough to raise his small hand and say, "yes, we understand. We will think about it." Then he looked up as Alexander's escort led him forward.

"Your Grace, le Comte Alexandre Corvina," the valet said, then bowed, silently backed out and closed the doors gently.

The boy's shrewd blue eyes traveled over Alexander's figure like a scanner for a few moments, yet his face remained blank as if he had no fear whatsoever. Then he glanced up at his minister and said, "merci, Monsieur Desault. Leave us. We will sign these proclamations later."

The minister's eyebrows shot upward, and he started to speak but thought better of it. Finally he replied, "as you wish, Your Grace," went to the doors and backed out with a bow, pausing only to draw the the doors gently closed behind him.

The boy climbed down off his chair a little awkwardly, rounded the desk and strode toward Alexander, walked a slow circle around him and then paused in front, placing his hands behind his back.

"I am told that you were instrumental in saving my ambassador from an ambush on the road," he began. "That your skills with the sword were exceptional, and you were the best guardian any man could hope for."

Alexander replied carefully, "I had but a small part, Your Grace. We, my father and I, were there by chance only."

The boy's lips turned up slightly. "You are too modest," he said. "De Neuvillette wove for me a tale comparable to those of Cyrano de Bergerac. He recommended you to me, and I have need of men like you, having an honest spirit, who can help me preserve the integrity of my throne, for I am surrounded by men of false ambition who would rob me of my birthright."

Alexander suppressed his astonishment at the boy's candor. But before he could answer the king continued. "It is not easy for me to rule such a large country as France, but I shall, and claim the true power of my kingship by force if necessary. I shall not allow my father's legacy to fall to ruin."

"Your Grace, may I speak candidly?" he ventured.

The boy smiled for the first time. "Say what is on your mind."

"I do not understand," he said. "Why confide all this to me? Is there no one you can trust in your government? I am but a stranger to your court, newly minted like a coin to its workings."

"I must trust a stranger before my own. No doubt you are aware of the civil war we are entering," Louis said. "The parlement is composed of men who want to destroy everything my father built. But my mother has imparted many things to me in order to prepare me for what is to come. They all tell me I am too young to understand, but I understand far more than they will ever know!"

He drew himself straighter with a heavy sigh of impatience. "In order for me to preserve *la force just* I must have men on my side with the skill and military discipline to defend the throne, but who are also altruistic in their mien. I mean to have it so, Monsieur le Comte. Do you agree?"

Alexander saw a grown man fighting to emerge from stunted growth in those large blue eyes. He bowed with humility and replied, "Your Grace, I am your humble servant. What would you have me do?"

"It is my understanding that you have traveled much, and learned much of the world beyond France. It is my wish that you enroll in the school of fencing and teach my mousquetaires what you have learned, that they may become better, stronger, and more loyal to me than they are now. And to count me as a pupil also, that I may learn your fighting style and how to more effectively vanquish my enemies when I am older. It is not enough that I must learn letters and sums. The world is marching forward into the future. You and your father are examples of that future, and I want my country to progress in step with the world."

"Your Grace, you offer me a great boon," Alexander replied. "The Baron de Neuvillette impressed in me the need for discretion in these difficult times, and I will strive to obey your commands as best I can, with honor and alacrity."

Louis relaxed a little. "It was not the ambassador who convinced me, monsieur," he replied. "It was my captain of the guard, d'Artagnan, and his three friends in the Royal Mousquetaires. I am told that you have met him. He is my confidant in all things, as he has revealed many secrets about the court to me which my ministers will not. I regard him as a true and trusted servant in whose hands I have placed my life and my fortunes. I feel certain that you would find a friend in him also, as I understand from your father that you value the power of friendship but are without friends. I heard also from him that your friend the Englishman died in your arms."

Alexander said, "that is true, Your Grace."

"Though he was an enemy of France, I am not without compassion. What you and he shared as friends is rare indeed. As your king I have had to sacrifice all my attachments in order to rule France. Such is the true life of a king, monsieur."

Louis returned to the desk, picked up a declaration, read it over and then reached for the crow quill resting in the ink well and signed it in a slightly childish hand. He then poured red molten wax on the space next to his signature, took a seal stamp and pressed it with an effort onto the wax. When that was done, he returned to Alexander and handed it over.

"This is a commission in the Royal Guards, with a stipend and lodging credit. Take it to the Commissioner of Mousquetaires de Trèville, who will give you an introduction to the master at arms le Perche du Coudray. You will find him most accommodating."

Alexander felt extremely humbled by the young king's demeanor, and took the document feeling a bit weak at the knees. "Thank you, Your Grace. I am honored to receive this, and am ever in your debt."

The king suppressed a smile. "How was your fête last evening? Did you meet the queen, my mother?"

"I did, Your Grace."

"Good. You will also find in her an ally. I know from d'Artagnan that my uncle is planning another rebellion against me. I should have him exiled, or put under arrest, but the cardinal advises me against it. What would you do if you were I?"

Alexander thought for a moment, and said, "*Monsieur* would not hesitate to put you under arrest. But I would gather the proof of his ambitions and guard it against that day."

"Quite so. You speak wisely. So I must be patient."

Alexander described a flourish and a courtly bow as he replied "a sound decision, Your Grace."

At that the young king beckoned to him with the curl of a finger, and Alexander went to one knee to put himself close to eye level. Louis spoke quietly as if he knew his valets were listening in. "I am also told that your father lost his wife but recently. I know of a lady of the court who is the daughter of the ambassador from Holland. She has recently lost her husband. Here in France it is important to marry and pass on our family blood for the generations. Do you think your father would entertain a suit from her if it is arranged?"

Alexander drew back briefly with surprise, not sure what to think. "Your Grace, he remains in mourning, as his wife has passed on only some months ago. But I know not what he will say. Does the lady have a say in this?"

"You are concerned that she will turn him down? From what I have seen, he is most fair to look upon."

"It is not that," Alexander explained patiently. "Among my people, the lady chooses her husband of her own free will. I would not have it so that she is forced to marry my father and forge an unhappy union between them."

"I would rather she was forced to marry your father than to another man with less patience and gentility," Louis replied. "Still, I will ask of her whether she is inclined to entertain his hand, once I show her his portrait. I trust you will impress upon him the importance of preserving the status quo?"

Alexander felt the tightening in his chest go slack. "Very well. I will broach the subject with him at an opportune moment."

"Good," the boy said. "Thank you for your confidence. Though I know you not well, I sense you to be a trustworthy and honorable man. I feel certain that you will do your best for France."

"Thank you for putting your trust in me, Your Grace," Alexander replied.

The king moved closer and examined his face more closely. "If the legends are as true as they are told, I have nought but admiration for your unique talents. Use them well and you will be greatly rewarded. Go now to join your father, and wait for my chief minister of estates to escort you both to Rouen. Then, when you have had time to settle your affairs, return to the court as soon as you can and take your place at the academy of fencing."

Alexander suppressed the brief shudder traveling up his spine and replied, "by your command, Your Grace."

"Good. We will speak together again soon. Thank you for coming."

Alexander stood again and bowed, then backed out of the chamber as he was instructed to.

Once the doors were closed, Lucien approached him. "Well. What do you think of our new king?"

"By the stars, he is most remarkable. He will be a formidable ruler when he is older," Alexander replied softly. "I have never met such implacable resolve before. It is as if Alexander of Macedonia never died, or that he simply passed from one body into another over the long centuries. Well read also. And, if it were not for his position, I would find a ready friend in him."

Lucien smiled gently. "I as well. Therefore, I think our journey is at an end for a time."

As they exited the foyer and returned to their apartment, they discussed what was said between them.

Carefully, Alexander related the king's concerns about Lucien's marital bereftment. "It seems to be the price for our living here in France. I know that Sarasvati is not far from your heart, but I think it a good arrangement. He will send you her portrait, and yours to her, that you might judge for yourself her beauty and gentle nature. The king wishes to ensure your loyalty with a happy life in marriage."

Lucien plucked a bit of lint from his overcoat and said softly, "Sarasvati would have approved of my decisions whether she was here or not. I will accept the lady no matter if she is ugly, if she will but accept me as I am in turn."

118

The next morning, Alexander took a carriage out into the town and headed to the Hotel de Troisvilles, where he was to meet the Baronet de la Tremaine and arrange his introduction to the chief Commissioner of Musketeers, Henri Anatole de Trèville.

He arrived in an expansive courtyard populated by visitors, cutpursers, traders, vagabonds and a cloud of pigeons begging for scraps. Chickens ran and pecked about freely in the hedges, while a rooster perched on the courtyard wall and crowed with flapping wings.

From the courtyard, Alexander could see the twin spires of the cathedral of Notre Dame looming in the distance. They were the tallest towers in the city. No other building dared to approach their height by design, as it was deemed a sin to challenge God's power or authority, and the towers served to remind everyone who walked the streets of Paris of that.

Bearing his katana and tanto in their silk swaddling, Alexander alighted the carriage and told the driver to wait for him, as he expected to be detained only about an hour or so.

He did not have to wait long. The musketeer captain came walking toward him, accompanied by d'Artagnan and Athos, and he greeted them as they arrived. "Good morrow," he said with cheer.

"Good morrow," the others replied. De la Tremaine added, "I see you have brought your swords with you. I am looking forward to a demonstration of their use."

"I am ready to show you," Alexander replied.

The musketeers escorted Alexander into the building and led him into a small foyer, where the secretary greeted them. "Monsieur de Trèville is attending to a small matter, but when he is finished he will be ready to see you," the man said.

"Thank you," de la Tremaine replied. As the man reseated himself and began scribing something, de la Tremaine turned to Alexander and asked, "may I see it?"

Athos, who had been standing at the window, turned and joined him as Alexander unwrapped the katana and drew it from its scabbard. The flash of bright curved steel caught the two men and seemed to mesmerize them. De la Tremaine gushed, "beautiful! May I hold it?"

Alexander hesitated, thinking it might be too soon, but concluded that there was no harm it letting the man just hold it. He presented it with both hands. "Be careful," he said. "The blade is very sharp."

The Baronet took it and moved his grasp to the woven grip, placed one hand under the tip and turned the blade to the light, which caught the wavy pattern and kanja inscribed in the metal. "Most curious," he remarked softly. "It feels so light and delicate, like lace. Yet I have heard it is the strongest steel ever forged. How can it be so?"

"I am told that the alchemy of the forge is a secret the sword makers carry to their graves," Alexander replied. "I do not know exactly how they are made. But their steel is better than Toledo or Damascus steel. My master showed me how one of these could cleave a small tree in twain with a single stroke."

Then he told them the story of Musashi, who was masterless himself, and of his quest to instruct all fighters in his techniques. He was telling them about Musashi's skill with an ink brush when the man they were waiting for emerged from his office and approached them.

"Ah," Athos said, cutting him off. "Monsieur le Comte, may I present Monsieur de Trèville, Commissioner and Master at Arms of the Royal Mousquetaires. Monsieur, le Comte Alexandre Vincent Corvina of Transylvania."

De Trèville afforded him a short bow and said, "I understand that you are to be inducted into the Academie Royale of fencing as an instructor. However, I would like to see a demonstration of your skills before I do anything."

"I would be honored to provide you with such a demonstration," Alexander said. "Where would you prefer to see it?"

"Come with me," de Trèville said, and led him into an assembly room already crowded with idle musketeers awaiting their marching orders. The noise of conversation and laughter was almost deafening. At first Alexander was not sure if he was ready to show off for such a large audience, but it was too late to refuse and he was already committed.

486

De Trèville called out with a deep strong voice. "Monsieurs, please be quiet. Will you give us some room for a small demonstration?"

"What have you brought us?" someone replied. Laughter accompanied his question as the men shifted toward the seats arranged against the walls.

"I am giving this man an audition," de Trèville said. "If he is as good as I have been told, he will teach you all a new way of fighting. If not, then you will have nought more than an a morning's entertainment."

More laughter came back. De Trèville rolled his eyes and muttered, "I am burdened with fools."

Then he turned to Alexander and asked, "who do you want for your opponent? De la Tremaine, will you serve as his opponent?"

The Baronet turned to Alexander. "Will you have me so?"

Alexander replied with a small nod and a smile, "of course."

The Baronet grinned, then handed the katana back to him, removed his tabbard and adjusted his sword belt, freeing his sabre from its beltlock. He drew it, went to a neutral corner in the center of the wooden floor and began stretching and bending expansively to limber up.

"Be careful, Rene'. He looks dangerous," drifted to him from somewhere among the crowd of spectators. Laughter filled the room again.

"He *is* dangerous," de la Tremaine replied. "Would you care to trade places?"

"Non, monsieur. I would not presume to rob you of the pleasure of whittling him down to size," the heckler said, and the knot of young men erupted with more laughter.

Alexander ignored the jibe and said nothing, but removed his hat and overcoat and laid them down on a chair, then removed his belt and sash to free himself of his sabre. Armed with the katana alone, he moved to the opposite side of the room and stood holding it in one hand, his fingers curled loosely around the grip, the point aimed from his waist at the Baronet's face.

At this there were murmurs and pointed remarks from the crowd, and de la Tremaine rolled his eyes as he asked, "is that all you're going to do?"

"It is all I have to do," Alexander replied as his lips turned up into a mischievous smile. "The rest shall be up to you."

De la Tremaine saluted him with his sword. Alexander replied in kind. The Baronet then moved toward him in fencing lock-step and tried a lunge to thrust home. Alexander simply leaned into his attack and swept his blade aside with a short dash, causing him to miss. De la Tremaine stumbled forward past him and nearly fell.

The noise of the crowd turned to gasps of surprise and applause.

The Baronet caught himself and turned. "Ho ho!" he exclaimed. "I did not expect that. What else have you got?"

"This is not a game, monsieur," Alexander said. "I hesitate to cause you harm."

As he spoke, the Baronet began to describe a slow circle around Alexander. "Then I absolve you of all sins and hold you blameless, for I would know the way of the sword in the heat of combat."

For the next few minutes the sparring was light but de la Tremaine kept trying every move he knew, only to be rebuffed with a few swipes of the katana. "Come now," he said finally. "I feel like you are playing with me."

Alexander matched him at every turn. "I am playing with you. Were I to demonstrate my full skills you would be dead, and I have no wish to kill you."

"How then am I to learn how good you are?"

The mercenary feinted to the left and then attacked from the right, but Alexander anticipated his move and struck the blade aside again, reached in and grabbed his sword hand, wrested the sabre from his grip and threw it aside. Then he found contact with the Baronet's collar, pulled him forward, rolled back and threw him overhand to the floor before he could react. Alexander continued to roll to his feet, turned and waited, as de la Tremaine slammed forcefully onto his back and laid still for a breathless moment, breathing heavily.

Hoots and heckling, shouts of "unfair!" and "a cheat!" echoed in the room. Then the crowd fell silent as the Baronet climbed slowly to his feet and turned to face Alexander.

"God's teeth, you were fast," he said, laughing. He stretched out his hand. Alexander took it, and the crowd of men rose to their feet cheering with applause.

De la Tremaine turned to de Treville and asked, "well, monsieur. Does he pass your test?"

"With flying colors," de Trèville replied. "But we will have to see what du Coudray says."

"Monsieur, you have to teach me also," d'Artagnan said. "This is nothing like my father's sword technique. This is almost better."

Athos said, "but what would your father say if he heard you say that? How could you shame his memory so?"

The younger man shrugged. "My father is dead, monsieur. But I am certain he would approve. He told me to learn whatever can be learned as quickly as possible."

At that, Athos suppressed a grin. Then he turned to Alexander. "I am impressed as much with your skill at not fighting as your fighting. Will you teach us how not to fight? What do you call it?"

"My master called it 'ju-jitsu'," Alexander replied. "If I am accepted into the academy, I would consider it an honor to instruct you. All of you, if you are amenable."

"Certainly," the Baron said. "I do not think that God intended us to die needlessly. Just as the sword is a weapon, this fighting technique can also be a weapon when applied at the right moment. I look forward to learning it."

"Does monsieur approve?" Alexander asked de Trèville.

The master at arms replied, "I have no objections. But it is the master swordsman of the academy who will determine what will be taught at his school. I cannot see why he should object, as he is ever looking for ways to promote it. Any techniques which add to the curriculum should be welcomed."

Another voice came from the door. "I think I have seen enough," said a tall man, dressed in a simple ensemble of brown suede and a pair of boots reaching to his thighs.

"Ah," de Tréville said. "Monsieur le Comte, may I present the man you will be working for. Jean Baptiste le Perche du Coudray."

Du Coudray was not only tall, but lean and wiry, with a high intelligent forehead and sparkling, alert and piercing black eyes. He apeared to be about 40 years old. His greying brown hair was tied back away from his face and he sported a small thin moustache much like de Neuvillette's. He walked into the room and surveyed the mob crowding the benches. "Well, what say you all? Can you bear to be beaten by this youngster?"

"We would not presume to think otherwise, else we would be skewered like meat on a spit," said one, and the crowd broke up laughing.

Du Coudray looked Alexander over with an appraising glance, and then said, "I would be interested to know what experience you have with teaching. You appear far too young to be so experienced, if I may be so bold to observe."

Alexander related in modest terms the days when he taught the civilian army of Oradea how to fight, and when he had finished, the swordmaster nodded soberly. "Very good," he said. "Then you know that some of my students are of sturdier and far more boastful cloth. I will take your appointment for a year, and if you survive it I will be grateful, indeed."

"I am not certain what you mean, monsieur," Alexander replied.

"Unfortunately, a teacher in my academy runs the risk of being challenged to a duel more often than not, and some do not last long," du Coudray said. "Mind that you try to avoid such events while you are in my employ. If you can."

"I will endeavor to do so, monsieur," Alexander replied.

Du Coudray drew himself a little straighter. "Good," he said. "Then I will expect you in the morning."

De Trèville chose that moment to interject. "If you will be patient, I understand that Monsieur le Comte's father has been appointed stablemaster by His Majesty the king. Can you spare him for a week while his family occupies the estate?"

The swordmaster's right eyebrow rose. "There is no haste if the king commands it. Then I will expect you on Monday next. I do have a schedule to keep, and I cannot waste the time."

"Monsieur is most kind," Alexander replied, and clicked his heels together with a small bow. "I promise I will be prompt."

Du Coudray replied, "from what I have just seen, I have no doubt of it. Now I must return to the academy. Good morning, monsieurs." He turned and left the assembly room quickly.

The Baronet watched him go, then said, "that went well. Du Coudray is the very soul of discipline, and when he says 'jump' his students must ask, 'how high?' He is also proud of his own technique. He has published a book on it. It is not often that one sees him so impressed with another."

Inwardly, Alexander was not so sure. "Then methinks I must not disappoint him," he replied.

De la Tremaine smiled, and clapped him on a shoulder. "Trust me. You exceeded all his expectations. Had you not he would have said so immediately, king's appointment or not."

Alexander glanced at the friendly hand. "Then I count myself doubly blessed. My thanks for your confidence in me."

"I would like to count you as a friend," the Baronet replied. "For all your foreign manner, you appear to have a generous and charitable soul. But today I must bid farewell for some time, as I have been reassigned another squadron and must return to Strasbourg."

Alexander was not surprised. "I will look forward to a letter or two from you, then. Do not let time or distance prevent friendship from taking root between us."

"Let our handshake be a seal to that bond," de la Tremaine said, and stretched out his hand. Alexander took it. The Baronet elevated an eyebrow at the cold touch that met his skin. "It is as if you were from the ice climes of Denmark. How is this so?"

"It was cold this morning," Alexander replied, and enforced the suggestion with a commanding glance.

Monsieur de Trèville, who had been watching this exchange, chose that moment to speak. "Monsieurs, please take your budding romance outside and leave me to manage this rabble."

At that, the room erupted in laughter once more, while Athos, d'Artagnan, Alexander and de la Tremaine gathered their things and marched out onto the square together.

119

The next three days were spent arranging the caravan to Rouen, which was a river port set about 20 miles from the shore of the English Channel. The port crowded the bank of the river Seine, and was the jewel of the Seine Valley.

Established in Roman times as Ratuma, Rouen was recaptured from the English in 1449. It was also the city where Jeanne D'Arc was tried and burned as a witch, and it had hundreds of churches, abbeys and a pair of castles dotting the wide expanse of pastureland.

On learning this, Alexander groaned inwardly but said nothing, thanking the stars that he did not live during that violent time.

The times being more modern, executions for witchcraft had grown fewer as more people realized that the people killed were more valuable to society alive than dead. Thus, scientists forced to hide out from religious persecution were allowed to improve on the medicines and ointments which relieved the suffering of the poor as well as those with coin enough to afford treatment.

Even monastic sects took up the task of returning to their original vision of caring for the less fortunate, the sick and wounded, so hospices sprang up in the community alongside the spires of the churches.

A renaissance of social consciousness made it possible for anyone seeking help to rely on these hospices for sanctuary and succor, no matter their status in life.

The caravan consisted of a coach and four, with a contingent of musketeers in plain dress, three servants, and a wagon with other supplies. The ride was quite uneventful, affording Alexander a chance to catch up on writing in his journal.

His small library had grown to three journal books by now, and he had been given a bible and psalms by Aramis, who thought that his religious education had up to now been poor to nonexistent. The abbe' to-be could never imagine that Alexander's time in Tibet was enough education to earn several degrees in theology. But Aramis had never been to Tibet, and was utterly ignorant about Alexander's time at Oxford.

Alexander took his religious admonishments in the humor they were intended and kept his objections to himself. At the same time, he was given a few books on the latest developments in science and alchemy by Lucien, who said he had obtained them from the Comte du St. Germain.

For his part, Lucien looked out the coach window at the scenery passing by or napped fitfully between stretches. He had been mostly silent since visiting with St. Germain. When he had returned from the visit, his demeanor had changed somewhat; from assured confidence to subdued disquiet.

Alexander wondered what had passed between them, and Lucien did not offer anything for discussion. Alexander's curiosity nagged at him until he willed it down with an effort, telling himself that it was probably none of his business in the first place.

Later in the afternoon the little caravan turned right off the main road and took a detour along a single winding path through a grove of trees. They passed a pasture filled with sheep. Then a strip of marshland intervened, spanned by an ancient bridge made out of stone and oak. Beyond that, cattle grazed on the low hillocks, and the meadow was brightly colored by flowers.

Alexander leaned his head out the window and his nostrils were assaulted by a curious mixture of perfume, livestock dung, and mildew. Yet, these odors did not disturb his tranquility as much as had the smell of cooking.

Then he saw the estate looming at the end of the road. The wall was quatre face, with small turrets where guards were posted at all times. The gate was a high rampart with a tower room very much like the one in Kiyev. As the coach and four approached, a guard signaled those within to open the gate, which parted and yawned open driven by winch and gears.

The stable itself was a large rambling romanesque style house at the center of a wide meadow, where thousands of horses wandered freely. Men could be seen working with the animals on foot and on horseback. To Alexander's delight, dozens of foals and fillies gamboled and pranced about or fed from their mothers. There were clearly enough horses to caparison an infantry brigade, but these were bred to be racers, groomed to be faster than any in all of France. He learned from Lucien that the stables were established by Louis XIII, and the boy king continued to maintain the estate out of a duty to honor his father's legacy.

The coach passed onto a driveway leading to the main house, which was a rambling two story mansion also built romanesque style, with columns and porticos in front. The coach rumbled to a stop in front of the entranceway, where a gaggle of servants were lined up in a neat row on the steps to greet their new masters.

Through it all, Lucien did not wake from his slumber, and Alex had to lean over to touch him. "Father, we are here," he said.

The eyes fluttered open, nictating membranes swept aside, and the pupils contracted. Lucien slowly sat up, blinking as if he had been asleep for a century. "Good," he said absently, then sat up straighter and smoothed his white hair back from his face.

The footman approached and opened the door to the coach, lowered the steps and offered his gloved hand to Lucien. "Monsieur le Comte?" he said.

"My thanks," Lucien replied, but avoided the man's touch and descended the short stairs on his own.

When they had both had their feet on the wide flagstones, one of the servants approached and said, "welcome to the chateau, monsieurs. I am Flandres, your housemaster."

Flandres was big as a house, and his ruddy face was framed by a cloud of light brown hair. His nose was the prominent feature of his face, flanked by small hard blue eyes and an equally hard mouth. He wore what looked like the makings of a full ensemble in dark brown, with black hose and shoes with pewter buckles. Alexander noted that his position had probably been won by virtue of his large size, then told himself not to judge the man too quickly.

Lucien looked around at the busy yard, and said, "I see. I had the impression that we would be occupying the house by ourselves."

Flandres' hard expression relaxed into a mirthless grin. "You have not had many servants before, have you?"

"Not this many; no. As we have been on the road for some time, we had grown used to doing for ourselves. But no matter. You are here, and there is no need to change the status quo, is there?"

"Monsieur le Comte is indeed very kind," Flandres replied. "We... pardon me for saying this... we assumed that with the changing of masters would come a change of servants."

Lucien cocked his head at him. "Do you feel there should be a change of servants? Did your old master find anyone here wanting?"

Flandres rocked back a little and threw his hands up to ward off the suggestion. "Nay, Monsieur le Comte. Nor have we any desire to quit of our places in the household. With respect, the old stablemaster was a kind man, and we all grew to think of him as our father. We have all grown to regard it as home."

"Then shall I, a stranger, presume to disturb your sense of family?" Lucien asked. "There is no need to fear. I pray you, go about your duties as you have done before. I only ask of you the same attention to duty you paid your old master, and I shall be thankful. If there is any question of your place in the household, do indeed consult me or my son, that you may be assured of it."

Alexander chimed in. "I must return to Paris in a few days, but for now you may rely on me as your confidant, as my father will be consumed with his duties as stablemaster. Thus will our work be divided equitably, and with harmony for all."

Flandres' smile grew gentle at this. "My thanks, monsieur. We have already prepared your chambers, and I will bring your luggage to you as soon as you are settled."

He introduced each of the servants, who were 15 in all. There were two downstairs maids, two upstairs maids, two laundresses, three cooks, a wine warden, and several gardeners, all of whom looked grateful to be staying at the house.

Alexander guessed with some chagrin that the changing of servants occurred about as often as one changed one's undergarments, and who knew how many of the poor wretches ended up on the road with little ceremony about it? He found the prospect distasteful.

The footman said, "now that you are safely arrived, I beg leave to take the coach back to Paris."

Lucien turned to him. "By all means, do, and I thank you for your service."

The footman bowed to him, then turned and signaled the guard. He climbed back up to his seat on the rear guard of the coach, and the whole parade clattered back through the gate onto the road.

Lucien turned to Flandres. "We shall rest, and tomorrow you will conduct me to the stables, where I shall inspect the facility."

"As you wish, Monsieur le Comte," Flandres replied with another small bow.

That evening, the house was opened to the spring breeze which wafted through the valley in order to banish the scent of must and dust which had gathered in the halls. Alexander spent much of his time inspecting the layout of the house and listening to the maids, who wanted a bit more leeway with their cleaning chores.

He told them about mops, and soapy water scented with lemons, and that they would not be required to scrub the floor on their knees as they had before. They were so delighted at the prospect that they danced about with glee, clapped their hands and laughed.

Then he talked to the gardeners about the grounds, and they took him to see the fruit trees and the vegetable garden. The trees looked scrawny. One of the gardeners said that a frost had taken over in the winter and may have killed the roots.

Alexander suggested that they might obtain horse dung and mix it with fresh soil, sprinkle it liberally around their trunks and then douse it with warm water which had been boiled to purify it. If the trees did not survive, they should be cut down and new ones planted in their place.

The vegetable garden was almost worse. The cabbage leaves were limp and spotted, the cornstalks nearly yellow and split apart. He instructed them to pull it all out, every stalk and leaf, and reseed; fertilizing the soil as they would the trees. The gardeners were delighted with his advice, and agreed to do as they were told at once. "Mayhaps we will have a sooner harvest," said one.

"It is a bit like starting over," said another. "As if all which was old is new again."

"A parable akin to Lazarus," said the third. "Our resurrection is at hand." Then he crossed himself.

Alexander chose that moment to ask, "how long have things been like this?"

"Oh, monsieur. Many years," their leader said. "When the old stablemaster came to live with us, he was more occupied with the house than the rest of the estate. There were times…"

Another gardener told him, "tush, Gravet. Our new master is not interested in the old stablemaster."

"Yes, I am," Alexander said. "I wish to know how things were, and to understand your lives. I am a stranger to your lands, no? It interests me to learn, that I may relay your needs to my father."

"Aye, indeed," Gravet replied. "Then you know not the way things were here. The war took many good men from our midst. The old stablemaster lost his son at the siege of La Rochelle, when the Spaniards, God curse them, dared to take the town. When he learned the news of his son's death he became a different man. He was a marechal of the nobility until then. Afterward, he softened and became more like one of us, often joining in our labors. Yet, he neglected the stables more and more, and kept to himself in his chambers, until the angel of death came for him." He crossed himself with furtive haste.

"The loss of a loved one in war would make any man humble," Alexander said.

"Nay. He blamed the king for his son's death. But what man can refuse the king's command?"

"This king, or his father?"

"His father, Monsieur le Comte. Louis treze was a hard man, determined to rid France of all heretics."

The other gardener rolled his eyes. "The king is the king. It makes no difference to me which is which."

Alexander ventured, "but, this king is a child, and has yet to learn how to be hard to his subjects, and if we are patient with him as he is with us, he never will be."

The first gardener crossed himself, and replied, "doubtless. But he'll grow up soon enough."

"I have met the king," Alexander said. "Louis did not appear a tyrant to me. He is young, but he has a strong and just heart. Will you not grant him the chance to govern France with compassion and justice? Can you blame the boy for the sins of his father?"

"I have heard from the gardeners of the Louvre that the king is a prisoner in his own palace," said the third gardener. "And that the Duc d'Orleans wants his throne."

Alexander heard this with some surprise and his eyes lit up with admiration. "Are all gardeners similarly gifted with the power to listen?"

The first one replied with a sly smile. "We feel it is our birthright, Monsieur le Comte. Gardeners have often been the front guard in any war against our homeland."

Something about these men told him they were trustworthy, more so for the fact that they had not reacted to him with fear, nor of suspicion, nor with prejudice; but with knowledge of their place in the grand scheme of life. He felt he could rely on them to keep silent about him and his father as long as they did not know the total truth. After all, open windows afforded them the privy knowledge of the court, because who would question a man standing outside clipping the verge? He laughed quietly at the notion.

"It is funny," the other gardener said with a knowing smile. "The court ignores us because we are mere farmers and gardeners, commoner folk; but we harvest their secrets nonetheless. Yet we who are loyal would never sell them to anyone, nor reveal them to the king's enemies."

"Not even under torture," said the second.

Alexander had a sudden idea. "Then, you would not think it strange if I employ you for such a purpose?"

"What would you have us do?" Gravet asked, as the three men crowded closer around him and listened intently.

Alexander glanced around to make sure they were alone, then said, "I will give to you a message to take to the master gardener at the Louvre, and you will instruct him to pass the message to the king himself, if possible. The boy is alone, with nought but four or five grown men and his mother to trust and depend upon. He will be a better king if he knows he has more friends among his people. But I cannot tell him directly. Can you arrange it?"

The first gardener chuckled. "Is that all?"

The second gardener chided him softly. "Gravet, please."

Alexander said, "on Monday next I must return to Paris, but I must tarry here to help my father settle in. I will furnish you a horse, that you may ride there and back quickly. Say, with the morning's dawn?"

"It will be even better if you furnish me with a gold coin," Gravet said.

The second gardener said, "Gravet? Are you now infected by greed? For shame!"

Gravet shrugged. "It is not for me, it is for the master of the royal gardeners. He will need more than a word from me to approach the king's window."

"Then you shall have it," Alexander said. "And I will give you more than that as a reward for your good and honorable service."

"Monsieur le Comte, you honor us," Gravet replied with a small bow.

"Then, monsieurs... mon frères, I give you a good night. Sleep well." With that, Alexander walked away, leaving the three men to talk about their new spymaster.

120

The sun climbed above the clouds crowding the horizon and cast pearly shafts of light through them. To the west, a rainbow described an arc above the river as Lucien and Alexander were led on horseback toward the stable.

The horses on the meadow varied by coat color and breed. Most chose to crop the grass close to the stablehouse as if they found comfort in its shadow, no matter the generous amount of freedom they were granted within the paddock fence. Others went running in whole packs, led by one stallion or another, and there were men standing among them. doling hay by the forkful.

Flandres was a giant astride the mare he used, and she plodded slowly no matter how much he kicked her to go faster. Alexander felt sympathy for the poor beast but said nothing about it.

"There are thirty stewards," Flandres explained, "and twelve stallmuckers. Each has a favorite among the horses, having in their time grown with them since they were borne by their mothers. There are six leeches among them, each tasked with curing any maladies, and two are in charge of aiding the mares in their labors to foal."

"An admirable division of labor," Lucien remarked. "I will look forward to speaking with each man in turn."

When they reached the stablehouse they dismounted and entered the front hall, where they doffed their hats. Flandres said, "wait here, monsieurs, while I fetch the stewards of the day." Then he marched into the warren of rooms within.

Casting an appraising glance around the hall, Lucien remarked, "this looks to be an efficient enterprise. Perhaps all I must do is allow those already so employed to go about their tasks with little need to manage them. I think I shall enjoy this new life more than I had anticipated."

Alexander saw the contentment on his face and replied, "yet it is far more responsible a position than I had thought. I hope there will be time for you to manage Parvati's growth and maturity."

Lucien turned to him. "I will have to return to Vienna soon to fetch Parvati. And you will be in Paris. I had not expected us to be so divided from each other so soon, but there is no other way for us to remain close as a family. You will write to me, and tell me all that you see in Paris. Be my eyes and ears."

"I will be faithful in that, father," Alexander replied.

Flandres returned to the hall with several other men, all of whom lined up with their field hats in their hands and their heads bowed. "These are the stewards of the day, Monsieur le Comte. With your permission, I will introduce each of them and then return to the house."

Lucien glanced to him and said, "I would have it so."

The giant turned to the men and said, "this is your new master, le Comte Lucien Arkanon, and his son le Comte Alexandre Corvina."

The men's eyes turned up to look. Two of them blanched, one's mouth fell open, and the fourth crossed himself. Finally, the eldest of them timidly stepped forward and said, "your pardon, monsieurs. We have never seen men with such pale skins before."

"Both are fair men with kind hearts," Flandres told him. "What does the color of their skins have to do with it?"

"Nothing at all, monsieur," the older man replied. "But they are paler than ghosts."

"Have you ever seen a ghost before?" Flandres asked him pointedly.

The older man appeared to weigh that carefully before replying, "non, monsieur."

"Then discard that notion at once, monsieur. Monsieur le Comte d'Arkanon is your new master, and that is all you need to know. Obey him as you would your old master and I am certain he will reward your efforts with generosity and kindness."

The older man bowed and replied, "we will take it to heart, monsieur Flandres."

Flandres then introduced each man in turn, starting with the eldest. All four bowed to Lucien, who said, "monsieurs, I will allow that I know you not well, but I hope that you will come to see me as a fair taskmaster. I look forward to seeing you at your work, and you may be assured that I will not burden you with more work than you can do in a fair day. The horses must bear some responsibility for their own lives, no?"

At this, the men laughed softly and relaxed their postures.

"Good. I will now rely on Monsieur de Cresse' to be my guide for today," Lucien said. "Flandres, you may return to the house. My son and I will find our own way back."

Flandres gave him a polite bow. "As you say, Monsieur le Comte," he replied, then bowed to Alexander. He turned and left the hall, while Alexander and Lucien were taken on a tour of the facility.

The interior of the main stable was a vast warren of stalls, each of which contained enough room for a horse to comfortably turn around in. Each stall also contained a large trough for feed, another for water, and a thick bed of straw. The ceilings were high enough to give each horse some generous head room. Given the number of horses on the meadow, not all of them would have a stall. As each horse grew older, he or she would be put out to pasture, there to grow old in a natural state and die under the open sky.

The horses were also segregated by gender so that there would be no acrimony among them. There was a house specially built for studding, and another built for foaling.

The boys in charge of feeding the animals were kept busy passing among the stalls and filling the troughs from hand pushed carts. The stallmuckers were kept busy cleaning out the stalls and distributing fresh straw. Those with this or that favorite horse spent most of their time hanging about the stalls and talking to the creatures, something Alexander had not seen since his boyhood in England; and in between, trading gossip about their wives and sweethearts.

The place was also an echoing cacophany of horses' and men's voices mixed with the sound of stall doors opening and closing, the occasional tune whistled or sung out of tune, mixed with the cooing and wingbeats of doves fluttering about in the roof eaves. The rhythmic sound was like a giant machine, in which each part drove it with fair efficiency.

A vision of metal wheels and cogs, pieces of materials falling into place or moving others, invaded Alexander's mind, and he paused to recall what Lucien had said about the boxes which housed the world's knowledge. He asked himself if this was what the future would be like for everyone.

Then he dismissed it all and took a breath to clear his mind.

When the tour was almost over, one of the boys came to de Cresse' and said, "monsieur, we have a horse we cannot tame. He is new, and came to us only yesterday. What shall we do with him?"

"Ah," the older man said, then turned to Lucien. "If Monsieur le Comte will permit me, I will show you what we do with new additions to the stable."

"By all means," Lucien replied.

Monsieur de Cresse' led him and Alexander out to a special paddock, smaller than the others, where a group of hands were having trouble with a magnificent Arabian who was determined to resist any attempt to put a bridle on him. His coat was dark bown with a black mane and tail. He was big but had a refined nose and small hooves. His eyes showed white as he pranced and kicked among the men trying to regain control of him, made noises of terror and shifted about among the stablehands, pushed them out of the way and in other ways worked to avoid that bridle; while the hands scrambled to avoid his flying hooves and teeth.

Lucien took matters in hand and said, "bid them to leave the paddock and give the horse more room."

De Cresse' did as he was told. The men backed off and climbed over the fence quickly while the horse came to a standstill, his breath labored and his mouth lathering a bit as he looked around at them. His hooves planted. His withers grew taut as if he was about to leap into the air to jump the fence, but confusion kept him rooted in place as Lucien entered the paddock slowly and drew the gate shut. The horse faced him, ready to bolt free. His tail whipped back and forth, and his nostrils flared as he panted for breath in the cold still air.

Lucien made a noise in his throat to get the animal's attention. The horse tossed his head, backed up a step, but did not do more than that. A long moment of wordless communication passed between the two beings. Then Lucien reached out and offered his long fingered hand to the beast, beckoning gently.

The horse took a cautious step forward. At this, the hands exhaled and murmured among themselves, and were at the same time shushed by their fellows.

The horse took another step, lifting one foot slowly, then another, ready to bolt.

Next to Alexander, de Cresse' crossed himself and murmured, "it is a miracle!"

"Nay, it is merely horse sense," Alexander replied softly. "The beast was terrified of your men. One cannot expect a horse to think the same way men do."

"Oui, Monsieur le Comte. You speak wisely."

The horse took another tentative step, and another, until he was about halfway across the paddock. Lucien slowly approached him until he was ten steps away. He made another noise and seemed to produce an apple from midair, which he offered to the horse at arm's length.

At this, the men gasped and made noises of approval and applause, and were shushed once again.

502

Apparently they were used to treating horses like inferior creatures without thinking that the animals had feelings or personhoods to call their own. Alexander recalled all the other encounters he had with horses and wondered how that fact could have escaped their notice.

At last, the horse slowly closed the gap and nosed his way toward the fruit in front of him, sniffed delicately, then gently took the apple from Lucien's hand. By now, no one dared to speak or make a noise for fear of breaking the fascination of that moment.

While the horse chewed on his prize, Lucien produced the bridle and carefully, gently, slipped it over the beast's head and allowed the traces to dangle freely as he spoke to the creature in soft tones.

"Truly, your father is greatly skilled," de Cresse' murmured. "Now I see why the king chose him."

"Your king is wiser than most men," Alexander said. "For that, my father is doubly blessed."

"I think things will be better now that he is here," the steward said. "Our old master, good and kind that he was, was never so blessed with such a talent. And when he grew older, he spent less time among us and more time at the house."

"My father has no such concerns," he replied. "If he is not able to administer your work himself, he will select a good representative. Of that I am certain. Fear not."

De Cresse' turned to look at the tall man in black and the horse. "Merci, Monsieur le Comte. I will keep it in mind."

Finally, Lucien picked up the traces and drew them over the animal's head, then gave them a firm tug. The horse stiffened again but did not move away, and as Lucien moved along that dark body his hand never left that shiny brown coat. The horse permitted this without moving.

Lucien then mounted the creature and sat on his bare back. The horse shifted a little, tossed his head and worried at the bit, but quieted again.

Lucien reached over and patted his neck. Then he raised his head and addressed the hands. "There will be no more spurs and no more forced bridling," he said. "You will treat every new horse with respect. They are God's creatures also, are they not?"

"Oui, Monsieur le Comte," they all said in chorus.

"If a horse fears you, he will fear you forever," he continued. "The bond between man and horse is a contract. You are partners, not master and slave. A horse has his own mind, and if you cross him, he will toss you to the wolves."

The Frenchmen laughed at that.

"Now that I have tamed this one he is bound to me. I give him the name Oberon, that he is full of mischief but he has been taken from his mother early and needs a firm hand at the reins."

A boy said, "take care that he will not turn on you, monsieur."

Lucien looked down and considered, then replied, "I hope not," and they all laughed again. "I will give him to the king, that he may have a worthy steed to ride when he is a little older. Alexander, will you take him with you when you return to Paris?"

"Think you it is too soon?" Alexander replied. "He looks too big for such a small boy."

"That is for the king to decide, and with time they may become close friends. Oberon is far younger than the king in years."

"Ah," Alexander said. "Boyhood will be sweet for both, and as they grow together, should they be drawn into battle they may be of the same mind."

"My thoughts exactly," Lucien said. He slid off the big animal and patted his back, then beckoned to one of the stall boys, who approached slowly and carefully, and handed the reins over. "Be gentle with him. Find him a place among the yearlings."

"Oui, Monsieur le Comte," the boy said, then chucked softly at the dark four footed giant and led him out of the paddock.

121

The next day, Lucien and Alexander were treated to a demonstration of the racing course, which was a dirt track about twelve furlongs in diameter. The racing horses were on the track and guided by men on other horses, which de Cresse' explained were there to give the racers some assurance. He guided his new masters to a viewing box, where they took seats under an awning and waited to see the spectacle of horseflesh which was the source of a whole new industry.

Today, the stable would test three new horses, and the jockeys were auditioning stall boys who made a show of wearing scarves in brilliant colors. None of them would know that, centuries later, horse racing would continue in that tradition with sponsors, colorful jerseys and more stringent regulations. To them, the only tradition was to stay on the horse no matter what, even if it was the horse who won the race.

Lucien and Alexander watched as the riders guided their steeds toward a small gate at the end of the course, where they turned around and presented their horses' tails to a brightly painted wooden barrier. On a signal from the gatekeeper, the boys kicked their horses into a hard gallop and leaned into the wind.

All the horses were fast, and as they flashed by it appeared to be a close tie by a nose for two of them. Then one of the boys kicked his horse to go faster, and the other two followed suit. When they reached the end of the course they reined their horses in and dismounted.

As the handlers closed in and took the horses in hand, the gatekeeper at the other end took the winner's scarf and waved it in the breeze.

"Ah, we have a winner," Lucien remarked softly.

"Indeed," Alexander replied. "He took a fair risk. It was clever of him to urge his horse on at the last stretch."

"I will be sure to give him a small bonus." Then he said, "Alexander, what would you say if, should future events warrant, we take our earnings and invest them in a stable like this one?"

"Think you there will be trouble, father?" Alexander asked.

Lucien paused again, then said, "I am always thinking of the future. I do not wish to be dislodged from this place, but if ever there comes the time, I would like to think that I have a plan in place to recover that which gives me the greatest advantage over the unknown."

"Then, you find satisfaction in being a stablemaster," Alexander ventured.

Lucien made a small noise in his throat. "It is better than doing nothing."

"Then I do not see why we should not. But I would say that you may be thinking too far ahead. The men in your employ accept you, and the housemaster Flandres said as much of the household staff."

"They are not the source of my concern," Lucien said. "But there will be others who will not approve of our presence among them, no matter the good quality of our works."

"You are speaking of van Helsing and his men?"

Lucien's smile was grim. "I have no doubt that he is searching for us still, to deal his peculiar brand of vengeance upon us. He may have more acquaintances who are waiting on his word for action."

"Father, are you afraid of van Helsing?"

"Nay. But you heard the man. Death or damnation was all he could wish for me, and it will extend to you if you defend me."

"'struth, the Baron van Helsing is a man possessed of an idee' fixe which consumes him. But, you think he will mount an assault here? We are too far out of his reach. He was in Strasbourg, and we are in Rouen. Distance alone would make him think twice of pursuing us."

"You would do well not to underestimate the forces at work against us," Lucien replied. "It is not only men like van Helsing who oppose us. Those who excommunicated my brother are not above persecuting his descendents. Van Helsing may not have been devout enough, but he was only one of those self-appointed crusaders who would stop at nothing to cause us harm."

"And the mutes we encountered?"

"I am still considering their motivations. But I feel I must warn you. My brother has come out, and van Helsing may or may not be in his employ. Or there is some other future event which they are all planning for. You may think me possessed as well, but my blood has told me to be on my guard. Your blood has not?"

"In truth, father, I have told my blood to stay out of my business," Alexander declared. "Surely I have the right to determine my own course through life, to chart my own destiny."

"Indeed, you are more fortunate than me," Lucien said. "I am pure of blood; therefore it speaks to me whether I allow it to or not, and is capable of exercising great power I cannot easily control."

"Father, I was never aware of this. Are you then its prisoner?"

Lucien closed his eyes. "Nay. It is more like... my older brother than my master. It can also push me into compliance if my life is endangered. The dragon's blood is a force which can turn to good or evil, Alexander." He opened his eyes again. "I cannot imagine what it tells Julianus, and why he cannot break free of its designs.

Or perhaps he prefers not to. Truly, it is all such a dizzying rush of possibilities that I can barely sort it all out."

"Then shall I stay on my guard when I return to Paris. The king may be in danger from those men also. I have arranged to deliver a note warning him of the danger he may face. I dare not do more than that."

Lucien turned to him and raised a pale eyebrow. "You have learned more of the men who occupy the grounds. Are they honest?"

"I... I felt that I could trust them," Alexander replied. "They were most willing to tell me of their alliance with the gardeners of the Louvre. A brotherhood are they, having among them the keen ability to judge which information they learn is worth the sharing. Such a guild of spies could prove valuable when needed."

"Indeed? Then I will trust you to manage them on your own. The raven's wing, no? I will enjoy the prospect of learning from them what you are not able to, for you cannot be in two places at once."

"Granted," Alexander agreed. "But I am far more concerned that the king has no one to rely on apart from his ministers; who are more centered on keeping their positions at court than on the king's welfare."

"True, *Monsieur* is seeking to replace him on the throne."

"Aye. And as I am charged by the king to keep an eye on *Monsieur*, I cannot approach him directly to deliver my news, as the duke may suspect. Therefore, a network of spies will help me to serve the king better by means of notes delivered from time to time, and the household guard has so far turned a blind eye to all."

"I am intrigued," Lucien said. "Are you prepared to take on such a risk when you are instructing your musketeers in the art of the sword?"

"I can only do my best," Alexander replied with a small shrug. "I give you my promise that you will be well appraised of all that I do."

Lucien placed his hand on his shoulder and patted it. "I will be content with that."

122

Later that evening, the gardeners gathered together under the eaves of a large gazebo occupying the center of the courtyard, where Gravet handed Alexander a note in return.

"His Grace has been most concerned of your welfare," he said. "A rebellion has begun, fomented by *Monsieur* and the deputies of Les Estates General against the crown. It is le Fronde, organized to dispel the king and replace him with his uncle. They have a motto which bodes ill." He said the words spoken by the Baron de Neuvillette but weeks before: "Novus ordo seclorum."

The words struck Alexander like a hand across his cheek. "You read the note?" Alexander asked.

"Nay, I would never dare. I had it told to me by the royal master of gardeners, de Foulet," Gravet replied. "He said the king is now surrounded by ministers in league with *Monsieur*, and that it will be difficult to pass such notes from now on."

Alexander pounded his fist into his other hand. "I will go to Paris at once. His Grace needs all protection."

"What do you want us to do?" Gravet asked.

"I will employ a man in town to carry my news to my father. Can I count upon you to receive him and give him shelter when he comes? Who can you recommend?"

Gravet thought for a moment, then said, "there is a warden of debtors in Paris called Rene' Dotrice. He will provide you with a servant who will not talk."

"A mute?" Alexander asked with some distaste.

"Nay, Monsieur le Comte. A man of scruples who will not betray a confidence. Monsieur Dotrice is known to select those who are discreet and honest among the wretches coming to his door with which to serve his clientele. Certainly you can find one there."

"My thanks, monsieur Gravet. I did promise you a bonus for returning promptly." He dug into his purse and produced a pair of pistoles, which he gave to the gardener. "I think you should stay in Rouen for a time, and do not approach Paris until it is safe."

"Oui, Monsieur le Comte. Bon chance in whatever you do." Then he and the other gardeners departed into the shadows. Alexander watched them go, marveling at their stealth.

When Alexander returned to the house, he told Lucien what he had learned and ended by saying, "I must return to Paris tonight. I know not what le Fronde is, but from what my man tells me, it is grave business. You are sure you will be safe here?"

Lucien smiled. "Never fear for me, Alexander."

"I do not... but what if that creature van Helsing and his men..."

"Then I will do my utmost to defend myself. You know what I am like when I am angry. Sometimes I frighten myself."

Alexander shuddered inwardly at the memory. "In truth, sir, I will never forget that night."

Alexander waited until the rest of the household had gone to bed, then went down to the stable and selected a good horse to ride. As Paris was only about 20 miles away it would be a ride of perhaps a few hours at most.

He looked in on the big Arabian and found him asleep on his bed of straw. At first, he expected the horse to make trouble, but the stallion was oddly calm and content even when roused with a quiet word. Carefully, he slipped the bridle over the animal's head and coaxed him out, mounted his own horse and went to the gate with Oberon in tow.

The master guardsman roused himself at the noise of hoofbeats and approached Alexander. "Monsieur le Comte, you are leaving now?" he asked. "But, it is almost midnight!"

"I have an urgent mission in Paris," Alexander replied. "I would have you open the gate and told no one I have gone."

"As you say, Monsieur le Comte. When shall we expect your return?"

"I will not be returning for some time. Guard my father well."

The guard saluted him and went to the others, who were leaning against the winch and dozing. "Alons'ee. Up with you. Open the gate, and be quiet about it."

When the gate was opened, Alexander led Oberon through and galloped in moonlight down the dark road toward the main highway, where he turned left.

123

When he reached Paris, Alexander stopped at the north gate. The guard was a pair of gendarmes dressed in uniform, and they confronted him with faces of suspicion.

"Ho, there," said one. "Stand and identify yourself."

"I am Comte Alexandre Vincent Corvina, an instructor at the Academie Des Armes Royale," he replied. "I have come to take up my position there."

The other man inspected the big Arabian from a fair distance. "What is this, then?" he asked. "Are you selling him?"

"I regret that he is not for sale. He is a gift for someone else."

"Where are your identification papers?" said the other.

Alexander reached into his coat pocket and felt for the packet, and had a moment of despair as he realized it was not there. He remembered packing quickly and had forgotten it entirely in his haste to be on the road. He thought desperately, then decided to to solve matters with his voice.

"*You do not need to see my papers*," he said.

Oberon shifted nervously as the men's faces took on a blank expression, their jaws growing slack. "We do not need to see your papers," the bigger man said finally.

Alexander kept his grip on the reins and said, "o*pen the gate.*"

The men obliged him, and when he was through it he said, "*now close the gate and resume your duties. You have not seen me.*"

He did not wait to see them obey and continued on down the avenue toward the Louvre.

But he did not go more than a few blocks before he was confronted with a city at war. The streets were filled with trash, furniture, and detritus of various kinds, all piled together to form barricades. Men and women marched up and down the narrow streets bearing signs, placards, clubs, muskets and swords. There was a cacophany of shouting and chanting of slogans. Graffiti adorned the walls, scrawled in paints of various colors, and exhorting the people to throw down their oppressors; meaning the king. Here and there he could see houses on fire and crowds of men on the street working in tandem to douse the flames with buckets of water.

Alexander could scarcely fathom what had happened. He had barely been away from the city less than a week, yet Paris had transformed into a battle zone almost overnight. This must be le Fronde, he thought to himself, then moved on at a slow walk with Oberon in tow. The stallion shifted nervously and worried at his bit, but kept silent as if the shadows were a welcome shelter from the noise.

Alexander made his way carefully toward the Louvre and kept to the shadows of the spaces between buildings to avoid a challenge. He turned a corner and found himself in the middle of a narrow alley where several men had taken up positions with their swords drawn, their pointed menace directed toward a tall man and his shorter and chubbier companion, back to back with their swords also drawn. The pair looked cornered but the standoff was far from certain.

The taller man had his hat on, a white plume its only decoration, and he wore clothes of the last decade which were signs that he did not keep up with fashion, or was too poor to care. His beard only emphasized the size of his nose, which angled outward and made him a shorter and skinnier version of Flandres.

His companion was somewhat overweight from eating too many dumplings, and his cheeks looked flushed as he cowered behind his taller friend and panted with near exhaustion, blade in hand.

They were outnumbered six to one. Yet, for all their menace, the gang could not get an inch closer to their victims as the taller man was a master of his blade and turned them all back with decisive stabs and slashes; while his shorter friend barely managed to keep them at bay, lobbing the occasional stone or flower pot within reach at his attackers.

Alexander wavered for a moment, wondering if he should intervene or not. Then he tossed his reservations aside as he saw more of the enemy join their comrades and surround the pair. He moved away and tied Oberon to a lamp post, dismounted, then drew his sabre.

The yearling whickered softly.

Alexander turned to the animal and replied, "do not worry. You will be safe here."

Turning his back to Oberon, he charged and hacked his way into the fray; throwing the combatants into confusion. As the men made way or fell out he reached the beseiged men and joined them. Now it was three against the many.

It was not long before the intrusion of the tall gentleman took a toll on the men, who soon broke up into pairs and threes and retreated into the dark, while others lay where they had fallen, wounded and bleeding into the mud. Some staggered to their feet and limped away, while others were hauled away cursing their pain and anger to anyone within earshot.

When the last of them was gone, Alexander flicked the blood from his blade and resheathed it, then turned to his fellow combatants.

The taller man now breathed heavily from his exertions, and he reached up with his sword arm to brush the sweat from his brow. "I have never before seen such skill," he remarked. "It is almost superior to mine. My thanks, monsieur. I think that if not for you Rageneau and I would have been killed."

"I saw that there were far too many for you to handle alone," Alexander replied. "It was not a fair fight."

"There was a time when I could have handled that many, but no longer. I am too old for this." He took his hat from its perch on his head and gave Alexander a courteous bow as he returned his sword to its scabbard. "I am Hercules Savignan de Cyrano de Bergerac, and this is my friend Porches du Ragueneau."

Alexander stepped back, struck with amazement. "Your pardon. *You* are Cyrano de Bergerac?!"

Cyrano regarded him with bland amusement. "Come, monsieur. You speak as if I am the devil himself."

"I have heard many stories of your incomparable deeds," Alexander replied. "I have read some of your pamphlets and found them both honest and practical and, if I may say, forward thinking as well."

"Practical? I have not heard them described as 'practical' before," Cyrano said, with the elevation of one eyebrow. "Ah, well. In this day and age, I suppose I can take that as a better compliment than 'reactionary'. And you are?"

Alexander favored him with a return bow. "Alexandre Vincent Corvina, Viscomte d'Arkanon. At your service, monsieur."

"Alexandre. A good sound name for a man," Cyrano replied. "I am seeing this poet safely to his home, where his wife is no doubt wringing her hands with worry. He has written a parody of the state of affairs in Paris which has netted him no good."

Ragueneau gushed, "you told me to write whatever suited me, and so I did." He put his hands to his cheeks and shook his head with chagrin. "Truly, a man could get killed for speaking his mind."

"I dabble in writing also," Alexander said. "My father and I have just come from the east, and are making a new home in France."

"Alas, France is a grand illusion to those who do not live here," Cyrano replied with a cynical tone. Then he looked around quickly and added, "come with us and share a glass of wine, if you will, and I will tell you the truth of it. If you are so disposed."

Alexander remembered his mission, turned and saw the dark four footed shadow still tethered to the lamp post. "I cannot now, but perhaps tomorrow evening. I am bound to deliver a gift to someone, and cannot tarry as long as I wish to. Where shall we meet?"

"At Ragueneau's tavern. It is in the Rue de Saint Honore'. It is where I spend much of my time now, as my room mate is fond of bringing his lovers to our apartment and makes such a confounded racket with them that I cannot find the peace to write there."

"Ragueneau's. I will be there. And now, bon soir."

Alexander remounted his horse and, with Oberon in tow, continued on his way toward the Louvre, where he was admitted quickly by the lieutenant of the guards.

"Relay to His Grace that le Comte Corvina has returned to Paris," Alexander said. "I will be at the academy if he has need of me. I give you this horse, whose name is Oberon, and comes from his own racing stable. He is a gift to His Grace from my father. Mind you that Oberon is only half tamed and has a strong will, but we hope that His Grace may find him a worthy steed in time."

"I will pass the word, Monsieur le Comte," the guard replied, as he took the reins in hand. "Mordieu, he is a big one."

Alexander leaned closer and asked softly, "how fares His Grace?"

The guard had the good sense to keep his voice low. "He is angry that such things should come to pass, and I do not doubt that he will prevail in this. Le Fronde is an affront to his majesty and his divine right to rule France. True, he is only a boy, but he will soon grow into a man. I can scarcely think what he will do to punish the instigators of this plot. The parlement has overreached its authority."

"Then, my friend, let us hope that reason will prevail and the conflict comes swiftly to an end."

"As you say, Monsieur le Comte."

Alexander and Oberon were ushered into the stable, where he saw the stallion admitted with admiration from the stewards and given the best stall on the premises.

Once that was done, Alexander said his farewell to the stewards and continued on his way to the building where the fencing academy was housed.

124

Alexander dismounted at the front steps and led his horse around to the side entrance, where he found the door locked shut. It was just around 2 in the morning, the hour struck by the bells of Notre Dame, and the only sound able to penetrate the noises of a city in uproar. The academy, however, was dark and quiet. No one had seen to approach it so far, and Alexander reasoned that perhaps the rebels sensibly feared the place which sheltered some of the best swordsmen and musketeers in France.

He lifted the knocker and pounded it against the wood, then waited. In the interval a spring breeze rustled the trees, another house caught on fire, and a group of men down the street were busy trying to keep a barricade up against an assault by a troop of the king's soldiers.

Alexander stood waiting for almost ten minutes until the door opened no more than a foot. The youth who greeted him was dressed for bed, and his breath was foul as he yawned. "What do you want?" he asked.

Alexander said, "I am the Comte Alexandre Vincent Corvina. I was admitted to the academy by Monsieur le Perche du Coudray. I am here to take my place as an instructor."

"At such an hour?" the servant asked, his face taking on a pained look of exasperation as he scratched at his tangled locks. "It is far past midnight."

It only stirred Alexander's impatience, and he leaned down and gazed into that bored face as he said, "perhaps I should return in the morning, when your master is awake. It is not your task to decide when an employee should come."

The sudden look of consternation which greeted him was priceless. "Non, Monsieur le Comte. Pardon me. I will admit you at once."

The door was flung open wide, and Alexander stepped into a small courtyard adjoining the back entrance. The servant hoisted his lantern higher as he said, "this is where you must come in and go out. I will show you where you will live. All our instructors dwell on the grounds of the academy. Monsieur du Coudray arranged it, so that there would be no delay in travel. Classes start and end promptly, as you will learn it from him."

"I understand. It is no different than when I was at university."

"Ah, Monsieur le Comte. Just so." Then the youth looked past Alexander and around. "Have you brought any servants?"

"There are no servants," Alexander replied. "I do all for myself."

The young servant tisked and said, "this will not do. You must have someone. All the others do."

"Well, I am not all the others, am I?"

The comment prompted the servant to gape. "As you say, Monsieur le Comte. My apologies."

Alexander was led down a long hall toward a wing of rooms, where the servant opened a door to a small but comfortably furnished studio apartment.

There was only one bed and Alexander thanked the stars for that, but it was a bare mattress. Next to it was a small bedstand with a candle melted halfway down. A tall chiffarobe adorned a corner, along with a chest of drawers and a standing mirror.

An adjoining door led to a small room with a wash basin and commode. The floor was of bare wood. No decoration was hung on the walls save for a small cross made of wood, which was hung over the bedstand. A small ironwork stove stood in another corner, connected to the ceiling by a broad pipe which disappeared into it. Next to it stood an empty iron cradle made for storing wood.

"Spare, but adequate," Alexander remarked as he removed his hat and cloak and placed them with his knapsack on the bed.

"Monsieur du Coudray prefers that his instructors bring their own possessions in," the servant replied. "He stresses that the comfort of the familiar governs the ease with which one may familiarize oneself with the routine."

"Your master is wise."

"Aye, but he is also very firm about other things. For example, he does not permit us to bring in women."

Alexander asked, "no women? At all?"

"None, Monsieur le Comte. In that respect we are a priesthood, shunning all other comforts. He also does not allow distilled spirits, and he will not under any circumstances allow smoking. Pipes are absolutely forbidden."

"Ah, well. I do not drink, and I do not smoke. And as for women, I can always go to them, no?" He concluded that with a wink and a smile.

"As you say, Monsieur le Comte." The servant shivered visibly as he added, "mon Dieu, it is freezing in here." He went to the stove and opened its front door. It was empty. "No wood. If Monsieur le Comte will be patient, I will bring in some wood and light it for you."

"There is no need," Alexander said. "I will do that myself." He tossed his pack onto the bed next to his cloak and hat. "You may return to your bed. Bon soir."

The servant bowed, and said, "if you require anything, just ring that little bell." He indicated the object, attached to a handle and cord hanging near the door. "Bon soir, Monsieur le Comte."

125

The twittering of birds outside his window woke him. Alexander stirred slowly feeling as if he had been on the road for a thousand years and this sleep had been his only peaceful rest since. He stayed on the bare mattress, listening to the sounds outside.

All was silence, as if the priesthood of swords was more like a monkhood. It was the dawning of a new day, and a new life, made more remarkable by the three years spent arriving to this moment.

When he had dressed and combed out his hair, Alexander made sure to tie it back with a short length of leather so that it would not get into his face. He gathered up his katana and tanto, ventured out into the long hall and walked toward the sounds of steel clashing. He found a large assembly room with the doors drawn open and secured with two chairs. Upon entering the room, he saw a large group of men dressed in tight fitting suits arranged around a large square of matting.

Standing in the center of the square was le Perche du Coudray, who took notice and walked toward him. "Ah, you returned early," he said. "Good. Please take a seat to observe my class, and I will give you a tour of the grounds afterward."

He turned to address the others. "Monsieurs, allow me to introduce you to a new instructor, le Comte Alexandre Vincent Corvina, who comes to us from Transylvania. He will instruct you in the art of the sword as it is practiced in the far east. I guarantee that he will not be as gentle with you as I have been."

Clearly, du Coudray knew his own reputation as a difficult taskmaster and seemed to revel in it. The students laughed modestly, and gave Alexander a polite bow of welcome. Alexander returned their welcome with a bow of his own. "Monsieur du Coudray flatters me," he said. "But I promise you that I will be even harder."

That prompted more laughter. He turned to the swordmaster. "If monsieur will permit me to find a good place to sit?"

"If you please, Monsieur le Comte," du Coudray replied.

Alexander went to the pews arranged around the room and selected a good seat on the third tier. There he settled down to watch an hour of the standard form: lunge, parry, riposte and other small movements. Each man was paired off with an opponent, and here and there during the practice bouts du Coudray would interrupt with the tip of his practice sword to point out the mistakes and also the improvements to his students' work. His pupils were quick to follow his direction.

As he studied the class, Alexander recalled the day that he decided to become fluid in form and relaxed in posture. He could see now that the old form was far too rigid and formal. It had become more like ballet, which was apparently all the rage among the upper classes, and gradually less like actual combat. But he recalled that among all methods of swordplay discipline was the watchword.

When the hour was over, du Coudray then told his students, "those of you who would care to observe Monsieur le Comte's extraordinary skills may take a seat among the pews." He raised his head and said, "monsieur, please join me on the mat."

There was a cursory shuffling among the young men, all of whom stayed. When they were seated, Alexander produced the swords Musashi gave him. On seeing the curved steel and the long narrow grips, the students fell into a hushed discussion among them until du Coudray rapped smartly on the floor with his staff. "Attention. Are there any questions?"

"Non, monsieur," said one, and the rest fell silent.

"Very well. Monsieur le Comte, you may proceed."

For the next quarter of an hour, Alexander told the students the story of how he came to possess the swords, his initiation into the art and the story of his master. He concluded by declaring that he had never learned how important the skill was until he studied with Musashi, who also taught him how to appreciate nature and the value of a man's life.

"When you take a blade in your hand you hold a tool with the power of life or death, and it is your judgment alone which controls it. There is more power in sparing a man's life than in killing him. Yet you must defend yourself, and in combat there is no time for compassion or mercy. Perforce you must put aside such sentiments."

"Even if it is a sin to kill?" said one student.

"Then you must ask yourself why you are here to gain more skill at killing," Alexander replied.

Another student piped up. "We learn fencing because we honor the traditions of our fathers, who fought many battles and vanquished the enemies of France. The cardinal forbids dueling only because he wishes to save every Catholic he can."

The other students laughed.

Alexander replied, "with this technique you can also. You have to know when to draw your sword and why. Then all your victories will be just and honorous."

"But monsieur, are you not also a member of the church?"

At this, du Coudray took matters in hand and spoke up. "Monsieur le Comte's faith is not a matter for discussion," he said. "Only his skill with the sword, which I have seen with mine own eyes. There is no question that he is foreign, but he is also a citizen of France, and that is all you need to know of him."

The student who asked bowed his head and replied, "Oui, monsieur. I stand corrected. "

Alexander saw that his position relied on tact. "If you will permit me, I will demonstrate a few simple moves to begin. Then if the others are sure they want to learn my craft they may enter my class."

Du Coudray nodded, and Alexander said to the student, "monsieur, please be my opponent for this demonstration. I promise you that you will not be harmed in any way."

The student nodded, crossed himself, then moved off his pew and joined Alexander on the mat, while du Coudray repaired to a seat among his students to watch.

The student was a bit gangly and tall, with dark curly hair and brown eyes, dressed in grey. He brought his foil tucked under his arm.

Alexander came to stand about ten feet from the pupil. He said, "I will not ask your name, but how much training have you?"

"I have been with master du Coudray but six months, Monsieur le Comte," the pupil replied

"How old are you?"

"I will be seventeen in August."

"Prepare."

The student swallowed a small lump in his throat and drew his blade. He saluted Alexander in traditional fashion, then moved into his first position, with his left hand loosely balanced on his left hip.

Alexander merely stood with his katana loosely held point down, and he smiled. "No, not like that. Do not hold yourself so stiffly. Stand as you would normally. Grip your foil like a friend, not an enemy."

Puzzled, the young student shook his limbs about to limber up, then did as he was told.

"Now, attack," Alexander said, beckoning with his free hand.

The youth plunged forward in a lunge and found himself stabbing at air. Alexander's blade found his and pushed it aside at the tip even as the student stumbled past led by pure inertia. Alexander stood back and waited for the student to recover his poise.

"A hit!" du Coudray said, and the other students applauded.

The young man turned to face Alexander. "You hit the blade instead of me?"

"Would you have preferred if I struck you with this blade? It is very sharp," Alexander replied.

Du Coudray remarked, "most of my technique involves avoiding the blade altogether, or affecting a quick return. How is this different?"

"By touching the blade I demonstrated that the blade is no different from the man. If I had wanted to I could have pierced his skin or a vital organ with the same move. Everything in sword fighting is movement, and one cannot predict the way a man moves, or to where, but one must anticipate the opponent's move, no?"

"Ah," the swordmaster said softly, as if he too had learned something new. "Continue."

Alexander gestured toward the student, who returned to his position on the mat. "Now, you must unlearn all that you have learned. That sword is an extension of your arm. What you see in the corner of your eye is as important as that which is before you, or the blade. But do not look at my blade. Look into my eyes. Watch them, and you will see every move I make before I make it."

"Truly?" the student asked. "How can I do that?"

Inwardly, Alexander rolled his eyes, but his face never changed. "Anticipation is your first goal. Then your attack. If you try to think as your enemy does, you will be able to foresee what is to come. Try it."

Alexander went to his first position and waited. Catching the student's young eyes, he advanced quickly and attacked. The student moved as if on instinct and struck his blade aside quickly as if his hand had its own mind. The other students exhaled and applauded.

Then one of them said, "I can do that!" and drew his foil. He pushed his armed comrade aside and made ready, but when he saw Alexander advancing toward him with a grim look on his face he flinched and backpedaled to avoid him.

Alexander continued on with merciless intent and struck the foil from his hand, then reached out and grabbed his suit collar, pulled him roughly forward and in the same movement threw him aside. The student went to the floor and rolled before he could stop himself.

Alexander told him, "never interrupt a lesson meant for another."

The young man stayed where he was, and with all the chagrin of wounded pride, said, "my apologies, Monsieur le Comte."

Alexander decided that he would stop his demonstration here, and turned to le Perche du Coudray. "I defer to you, monsieur. Do you wish me to continue?"

Du Coudray stirred abruptly from his wondering reverie and said, "I think it a good end to the day."

He turned to his students and said, "it is your choice whether you wish to partake of this new instruction. Sign up at the front desk. The lesson is ended for now. You are dismissed."

The students then rose and bowed to him and Alexander, then passed through the pews and down the stairs to the hallway.

Du Coudray returned to Alexander's side, turned to him and said, "they are hard to manage at times, but I think most if not all will sign. Of course some will consult their priests and families first. Some others are of more modest means, so the cost will be their first consideration. As for me, I learned a great deal today without paying a sou. You have my thanks."

"You may tell your students that I am not averse to an audit or two, if that will hasten their decisions. I seek only to instruct others as my master did me. You may command whatever fee you think fair, and pass to me only that which I earn fairly."

Du Coudray smiled for the first time. "You are a strange man, Monsieur le Comte. Your humility astounds me. Most of my other instructors strut about and boast of their skills like peacocks, but you... It has been a long time since I have met someone who values knowledge for what it is instead of a bludgeon of pride with which to pound others. How old *are* you?"

The inflection in his words put Alexander on his guard at once. "Monsieur, I am only as old as you think I am," he replied. Then he cocked his head slightly and smiled. "How old do you think I am?"

That only made du Coudray smile again in response. "The king thinks you are a great deal older than you appear. But then, he is the king, and what he thinks is more important than what I think."

Alexander looked into the instructor's eyes and saw only truth. "Then you and I are blessed to be friends with the king. When I first met him, he impressed me with his intelligence and strength of spirit. Indeed, he will be the finest king in Europe when he is older."

"So you would think. But his uncle and half of Les Estates General think not."

"And the other half? Surely there are those who recognize the king's sovereignty and responsibility to France. Why are they so bent on dethroning a child who all of Europe recognizes to be king?"

Du Coudray's half smile fell into a smirk of disgust. "*Monsieur* has other, more political ideas, which have nothing whatever to do with the king's age or his notoriety. I speak of the tradition of the eldest child receiving the power he is due, and the church has contravened his ambitions for the sake of its own. As his loyal servant, I have acquainted Louis with the state of affairs in France, and for that I have lost favor in Mazarin's eyes."

Alexander jerked his head toward the far wall. "So, you are saying that *you* were a ripple in that pond?"

Du Coudray nodded. "Being as I am a lowly fencing instructor, I presumed past my station. Now, I must ever be watchful that my back is not a target for some rebel idiot's dagger."

"Do your students know this?"

"Nay. If they were to know, my family name would be dishonored and my school would become a disgrace. I would be forced to close it. Such a scandal I cannot afford. Athos and d'Artagnan understand my position."

Alexander saw a new friendship materializing before his eyes; one which would never betray his trust. "You have told me a great truth. How then can you so readily confess it to me, a stranger to your land?"

"I saw no need to distrust you, Monsieur le Comte," du Coudray replied. "You speak with honor, which is more than I can say about anyone, except possibly Cyrano de Bergerac. And I am not alone when I speak of enemies. Cyrano has attracted many, and in his time defeated most with nothing more than his words. He speaks only the truth, while others shame him with ridicule. They speak of his nose as if it is a mark of disease, when his nose is nothing more than a good French nose born of its Gaelic roots. We were all Gaels when the Romans were here, and it is nothing to be ashamed of."

"You read Julius Caesar," Alexander surmised.

"Aye. Cyrano lent it to me when he was finished with it."

"The master of servants at my father's house has such a nose. But then, his roots can be plainly seen. He is fair haired, a giant of a man like Versingetorix himself. In my travels I have met people from many lands, and have a respect for their differences as well as their similarities. We all have the same love of life, do we not?"

At that du Coudray actually laughed. "Then we are blessed to have you, Monsieur le Comte, and I welcome you most heartily to the academy. I have seen the future in your words. I am loyal to the king, but I am far more loyal to my country. There are many who see science as a solution to superstition and fear. But science provides miracles, too. Of which religion are you?"

Alexander hesitated. "With respect, monsieur, I hold no religion."

"Then you are mercifully free of dogma," du Coudray said. "Do you believe in God?"

Again, Alexander hesitated. At that, the swordmaster said, "come. You can be honest without fear of reprisal."

"I find God to be the same, no matter his name or what form he takes," Alexander replied. "There is little difference between all the forms which define him. Whether one worships him in a church, or a temple, or under the open sky, to me it is all one. Therefore, I do not cleave to ritual but strive to obey my conscience, with charity and duty to others."

It was a diplomatic answer to du Coudray's probing, and he appeared to be satisfied with it. "Then are you wisely devoid of the same beliefs which can doom a man to persecution. Never capitulate to ritual, but worship or not as you choose. Truth is stronger than any lie contrived by religion. The church is powerful, but cannot stand in the face of truth."

Alexander turned to the swordmaster and studied him. The dark eyes appeared inscrutable. "You are saying that nothing is at it appears, and that there are other men and women who do as the church instructs not because they believe, but because they wish to avoid persecution."

"Aye. It is not hypocrisy, monsieur, but survival which drives us forward. Speak against the church and you will find yourself in ruin, or turned on the rack. Say nothing, but believe what your heart tells you, and there will be no retribution. Be silent as a form of protest, if you will. Let the truth sweep the old forms aside."

Du Coudray leaned back on one elbow and gazed outward toward unknown infinity and continued. "I can see a time when religion itself will be tested. But it is not for me to do it, or for you, my young friend. Only time must do its work."

"Novus ordo seclorum," Alexander murmured, almost under his breath, and du Coudray perked up to reply. "Aye, and there are others like myself who follow that motto."

"Then, I am mistaken in presuming that the phrase means some evil," he said. "Instead, I am presented with the inevitable. Time is marching forward into the future, and we are mere passengers in its wake, forced to witness whatever comes."

Du Corday smiled. "It is what we make of our lives now that will determine our future. We have the power to change the course of history as long as we do so with honor. With such power comes great responsibility. I see in you a future filled with wonders I can scarcely imagine. Tell me. Have you heard of a man called da Vinci?"

"Leonardo da Vinci? The Italian artist? I have."

"I have heard that he had designed machines of war and of flight, machines which the Holy Church had declared to be objects heretical to church teaching. But I think that he merely pursued those designs for the gold they would have brought him, not because he wanted to make them work. He was cursed with an imagination that no one of his time was prepared to accept. He looked into the future and saw more than others could bear. Some say he was obsessed with learning more, as if demons were at his heels day and night."

Alexander looked at the swordmaster. "You are saying that he was more scientist than artist. That his work was ahead of his time."

Du Corday shrugged. "Aye. Such men are out of…how can I put this?..."

Alexander groped for the proper word, but could not. He said, "I know not. My father is more versed in such science than I am. But I do understand that things must change, and for the benefit of all."

"There are also men who follow some other belief," du Coudray replied. "There is a rumor that there is a cabal who works in the shadows of Paris. I have heard little of them, but I caution you to be on your guard. I kow not their purpose, but they are like ghosts. Certain friends of mine have been killed. Others say that the cabal are to blame for it, yet there is no proof of this. My friend Cyrano can tell you more about them."

126

When the day was over, Alexander strolled down the avenue to the Rue de St. Honore' and Ragueneau's tavern. Upon entering, he was almost knocked backward by the odor of baking bread, wine, ale, and various assorted cheeses, rolled together into a warm miasma. Alexander forced himself to brace against the old nausea and managed to keep it all down.

Ragueneau abandoned his customer and came forward to welcome him. "Ah, there you are. Welcome. We're meeting in there." He pointed toward another door to his right. "I will join you when I have done with my patron." Then he hurried back to argue over the price of a large cake covered in a layer of white icing.

Alexander wandered into the side parlor and found Cyrano de Bergerac holding court with a group of men. When Cyrano saw Alexander he broke off from saying something and called to him, "ah, there you are. Monsieurs, may I introduce to you Monsieur le Comte Alexandre Vincent Corvina, who joined me and Ragueneau in putting several of the cardinal's pigeons to flight."

The men around him laughed as Alexander doffed his new hat. "I'm afraid I did very little, as Monsieur de Bergerac will tell you. I only tipped the balance another inch."

"And how are you finding Paris, monsieur?" said one, who patted the bench next to him.

Alexander found it a welcoming gesture and sat down. "It is finer and more beautiful a city than... when I was here last," he said truthfully. "Especially at night. The lights were a recent edition, were they not?"

"Aye," said another man. "The old king Louis treze commanded that the darkness be banished forever, so the standards were erected. And now, the citizens can walk at night without tripping over themselves."

At that the other men laughed.

"But you should have seen this one," Cyrano declared. "I was busy, but he was astonishing. I could have had no better man by my side."

"Monsieur de Bergerac honors me greatly," Alexander said. "And by coincidence, I have been accepted at the Academie Des Armes Royale. I was on my way there when I found him and his friend Ragueneau so inconvenienced. But I did not know who he was until he introduced himself to me. One could have knocked me over with a feather."

Cyrano leaned over and patted him on the shoulder. "And I am glad you did. I trust you are comfortable there?"

"Oh, of course. Monsieur du Coudray saw my audition. I must say that so far, France has welcomed me and my father with open arms."

"Your father?" asked the first man.

Ever cautious, Alexander glanced up at Cyrano and caught a glint of warning in his eyes. "He has received an appointment by the king," he replied. "Why do you ask?"

"Oh, I was just curious. But Cyrano has vouched for you already, so there is no need for concern."

"We must be careful how we comport ourselves now that le Fronde has been ended," said the other man. "We are the king's loyal servants, as is Cyrano. It is no reflection on you, monsieur, but since you are a foreigner you ought to know we must treat everyone we meet with suspicion since the cardinal has issued several edicts."

Alexander's guard went up. "I was not aware of this," he said.

Cyrano replied, "I was discussing this very topic when you arrived. Now that you are here, you should know that the cardinal has ordered the city's gates sealed for now. No one may leave or come into Paris without his permission. And we do not know how long this may be so until he decides otherwise."

"I see," Alexander said. "But, does the queen not have a say about it? Has there been any word?"

"She has seen fit to agree with him. But whether by duress or with free will we know not."

"This has happened before," a third man said. "All we can do is to wait until the cardinal changes his mind, or the king himself countermands the cardinal's order."

Alexander remembered that his identity papers were still in Rouen, but reasoned that if he had no need to leave Paris to get them he should still be relatively safe. "No man here plans to violate that order, does he? I shall not."

"Nor shall we," Cyrano said. "And now, monsieurs, if you will leave us, I would like to talk to our guest alone."

526

"Of course," the men said, and gathered their things together. With goodbyes and other salutations, they deserted the shop; all but Ragueneau, who stood by to collect their dinner fares.

When they had gone, Ragueneau flipped the placard over at the door to declare the ship closed for business, blew out several candles and the small overhead lanterns in front, and then joined Cyrano and Alexander at the table, which by either coincidence or design was tucked away in a corner out of sight from the front door or the side windows.

"You see that we must be extra cautious," Cyrano said. "I boast a good deal about the enemies I am somewhat famous for attracting, but it is only to throw them off balance. My friend, we are living in interesting times."

Alexander studied the chiseled features, the dominant broad nose, the warm brown eyes. That cynical charm masked a deep disappointment with the status quo. "You are warning me of that which I have known since I crossed the border," he said quietly. "I have observed the dire circumstances among the citizens. I have also seen the deep divide between the court of France and its people. Le Fronde was but a mild upset in a long standing war which has been raging for a long time, has it not?"

"You see more clearly than I expected," Cyrano said. "That is good. It means to me more than you know."

Ragueneau spoke up. "Our words, written down and recorded for posterity, speak more truth than speech alone can ever deliver."

"We are reviled by the politicians for using our words to fight our battles instead of our swords," Cyrano said. "But we have no power to change minds unless all see the truth. God gave no sanction to the abuse of power by men who twist the truth and keep the downtrodden from realizing their true potential. France was forged in the flames of combat. I fear that it will be destroyed the same way. The rabble in the streets do not read, and if they do it is only those books allowed by the church. They only know what the church tells them is good or evil. Yet I can tell you that there is not a man alive in France who does not question the edicts of the church."

Alexandeer leaned forward with interest. "Is that why the Huguenots were driven from France?"

Ragueneau nodded. "My mother taught me that all men are free to be brothers, free to be equal, but the power of the church supercedes even the power of the king. And what has happened to God? Where is he in all this? No one knows." He crossed himself.

"Are you saying that the church is godless?" Alexander asked, half in jest.

Cyrano made a noise which sounded like a chuckle. "That would be an apt description were it not for the fact that the Pope claims to know God like a brother," he said. "Are you not also a child of the church, Monsieur le Comte?"

"In truth, I have never found a reason to cleave to one religion or another. It never concerned me before. I always assumed that God resides in everything, so the rituals of worship seem superfluous; nay, even sacreligious to me."

At that Cyrano smiled. "At last, another man with the courage to speak openly about his beliefs. It does not concern me that you do not attend mass, or in other ways deny your love of God in front of others. I wanted to see what was in your heart, and now that you have told me I understand you better. I hear also that you are a descendent of the prince Vlad Dracula, who was forced to adopt the church in order to win his troops. He did not accept that bondage easily, and was excommunicated for doing his job a little too well."

"So it has been written," Alexander replied with a calm shrug. "The truth, however, is far more complicated than that. I could not put it more simply."

Cyrano threw up his hands. "I would not presume to pry," he said. "The past is the past. But myth and legend go hand in hand with history when there are no witnesses left alive to tell the truth."

Alexander thought carefully about that. "You are saying not to believe everything I hear," he said. "There are more things in heaven and on earth than are dreamt of in your philosophy."

"Shakespeare said much between the lines," Cyrano said. "You are well read, indeed."

Alexander bit off the admission that he knew Shakespeare in person and played his understudy on occasion. "I have read many of his plays. I fancied to be a thespian before I found a new role to play. That of an explorer, who learns by doing rather than by rote; and who travels many roads, learning what lies beyond the far horizon. My skill with the sword is meant to defend others, not to attack and not to harm."

"And here I thought you nought but an adventurous fool. But you are more than that. I know not where you have been but you have a wise countenance. But for your youthful vigor, I would have thought you an old man by the way you comport yourself."

"I have seen too much already. What man can see the world as it is and not be changed by it?"

"I shall take that to heart," Cyrano said. "Only think on what I have said and I hope you will add your words to ours. I am preparing a new pamphlet on the injustice of rejecting others who are different for the fact that they are different. Such prejudice harms the very foundation of the state. Do you agree?"

"I do," Alexander replied. "But, if I collaborate with you and write what is in my heart, I could bring harm to my family. Might I adopt a pen name which renders me anonymous to readers?"

"You may call yourself whatever you wish. I look forward to reading your contributions."

Alexander took a breath, then went on. "Le Perche du Coudray has acquainted me with a … cabal … operating here in Paris. I am curious to know who they are, and what they do. You should know that my father and I have encountered men who cannot speak, but who spy and kill for an unknown master. They tried to assassinate the ambassador to Bohemia. Could they be part of this cabal?"

"Monsieur, if the cabal wanted you dead you would be dead already," Cyrano replied sotto voce. "The men you speak of are too obvious in their methods. No, these villains are from some other group. There are many such cabals in Paris, each with their own agenda and their own ambitions. The rumor is that they are a rumor, and not to be believed. Yet you can find symbols of their works everywhere in the city."

"Where?" Alexander asked.

"You will know them when you see them," Cyrano replied.

A noise outside caught their attention. Ragueneau peered around the corner of the column, then ducked back and said, "I thought for a moment that it was the cardinal's guard come to arrest us. I think for safety's sake we should retire for the evening. When shall we meet again, monsieurs?"

Cyrano thought for a moment. "If it is not an imposition on your schedule I would say Tuesday next at the earliest."

"I have no objection," Alexander said. "Tuesday it is."

Ragueneau said, "then take the back door, and I will finish closing. Bon soir, monsieurs."

Cyrano de Bergerac and Alexander gave him a goodnight, then slipped out into the back alley under a half moon and split up, going in opposite directions into the dark.

127

The cloudy day drew a stiff breeze through the city the next morning. Alexander woke early, dressed in modest clothes and went down into the warren of slums bordering the edge of the river, in search of the employment office run by Rene' Dotrice.

He found it between a tanner's house and a taxidermist, lending more irony than hope to the line of men loitering on the steps of the agency building.

He entered an office furnished with a counter, a group of boys sitting on benches and several young women in the pews dominating the center of the room. They all looked impoverished. One of the women had a little girl sitting beside her, grooming a doll which had seen better days.

Monsieur Dotrice himself was a solid middle aged man who stood behind the counter reading papers, and glanced up at Alexander with a guarded expression which quickly dissolved into surprise. "Monsieur, how may I help you?" he asked.

"I would like to employ a manservant," Alexander replied. "He must be healthy, intelligent, resourceful and most of all… discreet. I was told by Monsieur Gravet that you were the man to see."

Dotrice's eyebrows crept upward, and he placed a finger over his broad lips. "Please, do not speak that name aloud, monsieur. Come with me."

He reached over and pushed the half gate open with his hand. Puzzled, Alexander walked through it as the man led him into an inner office, where he gestured for the tall foreigner to take a seat.

Dotrice explained, "Monsieur Gravet and I have an agreement. He sends me clients, and I never talk about him. So far, he has not given me cause for grief as I have never broken my promise."

"Then I shall not lead you to do so," Alexander replied, "for my acquaintence with him must also be kept secret."

Dotrice appeared to relax, and he said with a smile, "ah. Then we are both in agreement. I employ men who know the rule of privacy and confidence must not be violated. I know a few who might match your needs. I presume that you want someone who can be trusted with your secrets, and may be called upon to defend you with wit and sword, if the need arises."

Alexander studied him carefully. His blood remained quiet for the moment, and he took that to mean that Dotrice was telling the truth. "Perhaps nothing so dire as that. I need a man to do what I cannot. He would carry messages for me to my father, as I must remain in Paris to do my work. He must, however, be able to defend himself."

"That is easily done," Dotrice assured him. "Messengers are in great demand, more than any other kind of servant. I will see what I can do, and send him to you, or you may meet him here."

Alexander considered, then said, "then I will meet him here. I will pay well. Will a sou per day be sufficient?"

Dotrice's mouth twisted into a delighted smile. "Excellent! When can you return?"

"I shall be here tomorrow afternoon, if that is agreeable. I will have a letter to deliver then."

"I only have one question, monsieur," Dotrice asked. "Why are you not using the Royal Post riders? Are they not reliable?"

"I would not have anyone know when or where my letters are going," Alexander said. "I know that the Royal Post riders may be reliable, but they are also easier targets for the highwaymen. It is important that my servant not be distinguishable from any other, and blessed with the skills of a cavalryman. He must also be able to read. I trust there are veterans of the war who would fill that role?"

"Without doubt," Dotrice said. "I know one or two. I will select the one myself to remove all doubt."

"Good." Alexander produced a small bag and tossed it to Dotrice, who caught it. The employment agent opened the bag and saw the coins in it. His eyes lit up. "Monsieur is most generous!" he gushed. "Wait but a few moments. I know just the man."

He tucked the bag into his desk drawer and went out into the small lobby. When he returned, a man followed him into the office.

The man was not tall but rangy and strong looking, resembling a pit bull more than anything else. He had a closer cut of hair than was fashionable, and pale blue eyes. He was dressed in an old soldier's coat with wilted epaulets and linens, missing a button or two. But his smile was more like a cynical smirk and he appeared to be fearless as he gazed directly into his new employer's eyes.

Dotrice was perfunctory in his introduction. "This is retired squadron commander Jean Challis Reneau," he said. "He knows how to do his duty."

"He is not a pansy," Reneau remarked. "What a pleasant surprise."

Dotrice frowned at that and said, "you will not address your new employer in that manner, Reneau."

"Forgive me," Reneau said. "I was told I would be working for a wealthy man. That could only be a pansy. But look at the sword he is carrying. I'll wager a sou he is a soldier himself."

Alexander grew to like him almost instantly. "You are almost correct. I need a man to be my agent in all things, but your duties will be light."

Dotrice said, "this is le Comte Alexandre Corvina."

"I am your servant," Reneau replied, and offered a cordial bow and flourish.

Alexander said, "I am an instructor of fencing. My schedule demands that I remain in Paris. You are to deliver my letters to my father, and do all other errands as necessary. That is the extent of your service. You must also have some skill with a sword to defend yourself withal."

Reneau threw Alexander a small wink. "I shall be swift and discreet. You may rely on me, Monsieur le Comte. Is there anything else you wish me to do?"

"No." Alexander handed him a small envelope. "You may start now if you wish."

The pit bull smiled again, glanced down at the letter, read the address and said, "I will be back in two shakes of a lamb's tail," marched out the door and disappeared.

Alexander laughed quietly. "He will find it difficult to leave Paris. The gates are closed."

Dotrice shook his head. "I know I promised a reliable messenger, but that man is the best I could find. He even owns his own horse. Do you approve, monsieur?"

"More than I expected to," Alexander replied. "He is direct and outspoken. Such a man is more reliable than most. You have done well, and I look forward to his return."

He handed Dotrice a slip of paper. "When he does, direct him to this address, where I will give him lodgings or pay him a stipend to obtain his own."

"Very good," Dotrice said with a sigh of relief. "Merci."

When he emerged from the employment office, Alexander grew conscious that he was being watched. He glanced subtly around to see who would be there and caught sight of a flash of dark coat among the crowd of pedestrians and beggars walking back and forth on the narrow lane, disappearing into the alley. There was not enough detail to be gained from that glimpse, but the sensation sent his paranoia into full red alert nevertheless.

He walked quickly as he could out of the slum and returned to his room at the academy feeling as if he had been followed. It was not until he closed the door that he could relax. He tried to analyze that feeling, then willed it down as simple panic. Alexander determined to learn how to control these sudden bouts and knew that if he did not they would be his downfall one day.

He concluded that the event in Hungary may have been the source of all his fears. Clearly, watching his father dispatch the hunter in all his alien glory still weighed on his spirit.

128

A day later, the city was freed from its temporary lockdown by royal edict countermanding the cardinal's command. Once the gates were opened, the usual stream of travelers entered to carry on their usual business. One of them was Jean Reneau, who delivered a return letter from Lucien. "Your father was most generous to me," Reneau said. "He has granted me a sum to obtain better livery."

"Tell me," Alexander said. "Have you by chance seen anyone at the stables who were strangers?"

"Strangers?" Reneau asked. "How do you mean? Your father said nothing of this. What am I to look for, should I see them?"

"These men would be armed, and lack the faculty of speech. Should you encounter one, ask of them their name, or mention the weather, or in some other manner engage them so that you may know if they are mute. These men are enemies of our family, and would harm my father if they might."

Reneau replied. "Monsieur le Comte d'Arkanon already has men around him who have pledged their lives to protect him, but there is no danger if he has more. Perhaps I may be able to do more for you than deliver letters. If there is battle to be done I am your man."

"I have no doubt. But I would have you do nothing more than be circumspect when approaching my father. He may also be aware of them, and can well protect himself. But he is one man, while they are many. We are discreet for a reason, among which is that we are foreign to your land, but are men of peace."

The pit bull shrugged. "As I am a man of war, I feel out of place if I am not fighting those who would destroy the peace. Give me the charge to defend your father while I am there, should the need arise, and I pledge you my unswerving fidelity. It is not just your generosity, but my sense of justice which demands it."

"I will keep it in mind, and you have my thanks," Alexander said. He handed the man a pistole and said, "I would have you move closer to me. Find lodgings nearby, that I may call upon you when I need you."

When Reneau had left, Alexander opened the letter.

Lucien's first sentence was, "your messenger is a man to be trusted. Allow him to be more than that. His service is what he is, and without a purpose no man can live well. I have faith that you will know what to do."

The letter continued with news that Lucien was settling in and was pleased with the arrangements for all, but no word of any incursion. Rouen was a safe haven after all.

Three days later, Alexander had a full class, consisting mostly of the young men he had already met, their cousins, a pair of twins, and two older brothers of the young Catholic. He also learned from the house boy, called Herge', that the king was said to have a new horse and was seen riding it on the grounds of the Louvre, strapped to the saddle so that he would not fall off. This sparked a kernel of appreciation in Alexander for the boy's determination to manage his own affairs and demonstrate his kingship.

The uproar in the city finally died down when several parliamentarians were force marched to the Bastille through a public gathering of royalist bourgeoises. According to the the the Daily Gazette, the city's only newspaper, the crowd threw tomatoes and other objects at the politicians to express their dissatisfaction with the whole affair. A giant cartoon of the event was displayed in ink across the front page. Le Fronde was clearly over, and though the Gazette did not say so, Alexander imagined that *Monsieur* was given a stern lecture by the cardinal admonishing him to remember his place, or suffer censure by the Holy See.

By now, several of Alexander's students were becoming comfortable with his pale complexion and sparkling grey eyes, enough that they no longer stood quite so far away when he gave them their points, nor crossed themselves quite so often. Encouraged by this, he gave them more space to maneuver, and in that way opened up a dialogue which would lead to better trust. Or so he hoped. As it was, he had to tone down the use of normal strength in his swordplay, or they would see that he was more than human; and that limitation alone gave him a useful handicap.

He was thus engaged with lecturing them on battle strategy when the whole class rose as a body and bowed. Alexander turned and saw the boy, young King Louis, standing at the threshhold of the door, flanked by several men of his personal guard. He was dressed modestly in dark blue, his long dark curls concealed beneath a broad brimmed hat sporting a blue ostrich feather. The hat's band was a circlet of gold sporting fleurs de lis.

Alexander went automatically to one knee. The boy smiled and said, "please stand and face me like a brother, monsieur. It would please me greatly. Up with you all."

The class rose and stood at loose attention, and when Alexander was on his feet he said, "Your Grace honors all of us."

"I came to thank you for Oberon," Louis said. "It is not often that I receive gifts which become treasured friends. The horse and I have come to an understanding. Mind you, at first he was a trifle skittish, but once he learned who was to ride him he gentled almost at once. When you have the opportunity, please thank your father for me."

"I will of course, Your Grace," Alexander replied with a courteous bow.

The boy looked around at the students, and said, "I see that you have a full class. My compliments. I hope that when I am older you will see fit to instruct me also, as I will have to learn to fight one day."

Alexander puzzled at that. A king would normally receive a private tutor of the sword when he came of age to learn. Despite his small size Louis was almost old enough to start practicing soon. "I would be pleased to do so," he replied.

"Then I will look forward to that day. I will send for you when I am ready. Now, I have taken enough of your time. Carry on with your lesson."

With that, the king turned and strode out the door again, and Alexander was treated to a round of applause from the students. For his part, Alexander was struck speechless with wonder and abject humility.

129

For the next six months life turned routine for Alexander, and his newfound fame as a court instructor helped him avoid some of the meaner aspects of life in Paris.

He was given better quarters on the second floor of the academy even though he said he was quite comfortable where he was; and from his windows he had an ample view of the city, where he watched the standards lit by fire every night and wrote his essays by the warm glow of a kerosene lantern instead of a candle. The charms of music drifting in on the breeze led him to pause writing more serious prose and make some attempts at composing poetry, though he was not as skilled at that.

When he was not there working, he began attending to the king's lessons once a week and taught him fencing in the formal style, mixing in a few of Musashi's special moves as he did so to give the boy an advantage in combat.

Hunting for blood among the poorer denizens required stealth and finesse, which afforded him the ability to sharpen his special skills as a hunter.

He soon discovered that there were other vampires among them who had long used Paris as a central hub for their community.

At first he had to learn to blend in, then revealed himself to them gradually. The halflings among them paid him deference by the sheer power of his blood, while the older ones thought him a novelty. After that, he never sought leadership but his name alone became a rallying point for those of his kind. He accepted this with his usual humility and vowed to honor their fellowship.

Having discovered this camaraderie on his own, he wrote to Lucien twice and mentioned that there was a community on which they could rely for shelter should the need arise.

Lucien wrote back that he was pleased with this, but mentioned little about his work at the stable; only that things were going well and he had grown a circle of friends among the senior hands.

There was no word of the lady that Louis was keen to marry off. Still, the fact that Lucien wrote back at all pleased and encouraged Alexander.

"And you are sure my father is well protected," he pressed Reneau one day.

The man shrugged calmly. "As well as any other man can be. Beyond that my knowledge does not extend, Monsieur le Comte."

"My thanks, and here is a small bonus." Alexander handed the pit bull a small pouch, which he opened.

Again, his eyes lit up as if he had found buried treasure. "Oh, Monsieur le Comte. It is far more than I deserve."

"Then, save it for some future need," Alexander replied.

The man winked, hefted the pouch, then said his good nights, strode out the door and disappeared into the night.

Alexander stood watching after him, but unlike his father had no faculty for reading minds. So he guessed that Reneau would do as he suggested. He could not think that such a man should drink it all away, and as he observed, Reneau never drank anything stronger than wine.

The days passed. On the warmer evenings Alexander strolled along the river bank and shared intellectual conversations with his new friends, learned more about the city, the people and the growing businesses thriving along the banks of the river. Paris was ripe for innovation as new inventions and ideas drew entrepreneurs from other countries to set up their factories there.

For a time, the masses found employment and bettered their own lives by setting up cottage industries. Still, it was not enough. Paris was crumbling, brick by brick, as the buildings were made mostly of materials prone to catch fire or porous enough that the spring rain etched its way to the ground through wood and iron.

The warrens of the poor continued to grow like weeds.

Alexander returned home every evening and recorded what he saw, including his observations about the problems he saw looming on the horizon, with an increasing population and the need to shelter the dispossessed, the distribution of resources, and other philosophical commentary.

Everything he wrote was published under the name "Edmond Tibetin", which seemed somewhat odd but had just enough zazz to satisfy Parisian curiosity. That appeared to please Cyrano de Bergerac, who published the pamplets forthwith with little edition or criticism.

Alexander's work also drew positive criticism from various nobs among the literati, and that also seemed to please Cyrano; for it brought his own pamphlets and brochures more fame or infamy than ever.

Alexander also spent his spare time studying the architecture of Paris, trying to divine the symbols Cyrano spoke of. Here and there, he started to see connections, from the strange triangles inscribed in the cobblestone streets, to the statuary of angels and gargoyles pointing here and there.

The roads led out from a central hub, at the center of which stood a statue of a woman dressed in a Roman gown, holding a torch high in one hand and a scale in the other. The statue stood with its back to the cathedral of Notre Dame, almost deliberately. Alexander was not sure at first what that meant, but he was determined to learn more.

But soon after that, his friend Cyrano de Bergerac started receiving death threats. One of them was delivered at Ragueneau's shop by means of a flying brick lobbed through one of the new glass windows he had just installed.

A day later, the print shop Cyrano had engaged to publish his pamphlets burned down mysteriously in the middle of the night, and with it some of the galleys he had just delivered that morning. Cyrano raged at that and then withdrew into a singular funk for a while. The Gazette made light of his situation, which made him rage even more.

This campaign of hate had gone far beyond the usual rivalry Cryano and the Comte de Guiche had shared for years; so much so that de Guiche finally came to empathize with Cyrano. He did not care to call it pity, for he admired the man's determination and resolve; but he had mellowed somewhat in his treatment of Cyrano as a lifelong enemy and rival for the affections of his widowed cousin, Roxánne de Neuvillette.

He began to defend Cyrano among his harsher critics. Cautiously, of course, as those he associated with had more radical ideas about the veteran hero, and he could not afford to enflame the controversy, or he would be drawn to defend himself.

For his part, Alexander felt it was wiser to stop writing his essays for fear that Cyrano would come to some serious harm. He felt that he had antagonized the royalists and bourgeousies with his prose on the plight of the poor. But that did not stop the flow of hatred and vandalism pouring in from every quarter. No matter what he did, Alexander's loyalty to young King Louis put him at odds with the very principles of democracy he espoused, and he soon found himself conflicted.

Two weeks later, Cyrano de Bergerac was struck in the head in an altercation with a barrel wagon and died of his injuries a few hours later. His cousin Roxánne went to Cardinal Mazarin and begged him for an intercession so that Cyrano's name and reputation would not be dragged through the mud any further. The furor of criticism and hatred was shut off by decree. Hero or not, the man was dead, and that was that.

Alexander was devastated by the news, but could not attend the funeral because his position at court denied his friendship with the man. By law, Cyrano was declared a pauper and his grave was to be an unmarked plot filled with lye, of small consolation to those whose loved ones had to share a common pit. Cyrano's closer family had all died in the last century, and there was no one to intercede on his behalf but Roxánne. And despite her pleas for mercy, the court refused to reverse their decision.

At the last minute, Alexander managed to bribe the cemetery officials and got Cyrano's body transferred to a small mausoleum. The funeral was a small, modest affair, attended by the few of

Cyrano's friends who dared to show up. Alexander visited the body that evening and left a small bouquet of white roses on the coffin's lid.

Then he went to visit Ragueneau, and found the shopkeeper busily packing to leave town. He gave Ragueneau a purse full of silver as a parting gift and said his reluctant goodbyes. For his part, Ragueneau took the pouch, but declared he felt betrayed by Alexander and wanted no more to do with him. The last word Alexander had was the sight of Ragueneau walking out of the empty shop with his portmanteau, without a goodbye.

Alexander used Jean Reneau to track down the men involved in the attack. Reneau was fast and effective, and the lackeys were arrested and tried for murder, then gave up their employer in exchange for life in prison instead of a hanging. It turned out that the anonymous enemy was a prosperous factory owner who believed in acting on his sentiments with violence. The man was rousted from his bed by the king's troops and marched to the Bastille the next evening, there to be tried for murder by proxy.

After another week of deep and reflective mourning, Alexander shoved his grief over Cyrano into the back of his mind and went back to work teaching men how to kill.

130

April, 1649

Alexander began to notice a change in the audience who attended his fencing sessions. Several well dressed women sat off to one side of the room, segregating themselves to avoid harrassment by the men. They appeared to be focused on the lessons like any other man, rather than engaging themselves with embroidery or reading. And, one of them looked familiar, like a ghost from his past.

When the day's class was ended, Alexander waited until the room had cleared, then drew du Coudray aside and asked, "who are those women, and where did they come from?"

"They are ladies from the court. They came to watch," the swordmaster said. "You have drawn their singular attention, monsieur. I envy you."

"I have done nothing to merit such attention," Alexander said. "You did rule that there should be no women in the academy."

Du Coudray drew back and replied, "I meant that no women should be brought in for carnal pleasures. And you have been dutiful in that manner. Do you find them a distraction? If so, I will send them away."

"Nay. I would not want it said that they were not welcome to observe and study," Alexander replied. Then a thought occurred. "What is your policy concerning women and swords? Would you consider an exception for them in practice?"

Du Coudray shrugged. "It is of no concern to me, Monsieur le Comte. But there are no facilities here which will accommodate them. Everything here was built for men to use, and I know of no woman who was interested in studying at the academy before. Or perhaps I was too occupied to notice. It is a new day, monsieur. That much is certain."

Alexander had not thought of that before. Then an idea came to him. "If there was such a place, would you allow women to study the way of the sword?"

Du Coudray shrugged again. "If that is their wish."

"If you permit me, I will approach them and ask their intentions. I may gain a few more students, and in that way fatten the academy's purse. If so, then I would be pleased to contribute to the building of such a place. I have a small reserve which could be used."

De Coudray smiled. "I have no objection to that. Only be cautious in your selection. I am not certain but I think I saw one of them watching you with such rapture that her attention was, shall we say, not on the lesson? I would not want to offend her male companion, or husband."

"Mmmm. I too have been too busy to notice. But I will be circumspect in my approach."

"Mind that you do not bring dishonor to the academy, and I will be content with that."

"As always, monsieur, I have that at the top of my list."

The next afternoon, Alexander dismissed his class but announced that if there were any ladies who wished to learn also, they must declare their intention. At this, three of the women stood, while the others applauded their audacity.

"Come down and introduce yourselves to the class," Alexander said with a smile and a welcoming bow.

They approached most timidly from the pews. One of them was tall, willowy and had a cloud of red hair and blue eyes, seeming almost masculine in her attitude. Another was shorter and somewhat stocky, with dark brown hair and eyes; while the third -- and here Alexander rocked back with shock and surprise as he recognized her -- was the woman he had met at The Dusty Rose in Linz.

"Come, ladies, and introduce yourselves," he said.

The first one said, "my name is Elise Raveneau. I was told that your form was excellent. Now I have seen the truth in the tale. I wish to learn more."

"Then you know the art?" Alexander asked.

"My brother taught me all he knew before he was killed in a duel last year. I wish to take his place as defender of our house. My family is small, monsieur, but I am the eldest and must continue to uphold my family's honor."

Alexander bowed. "My condolences, lady. As you already have some skill, then you will learn my techniques faster."

Alexander turned to the shorter woman. "And what about you?"

She said, "my name is Genine Almandeux. I grew up with four brothers. We were close as children and learned everything together. Then they were all killed in the war against Spain. I wish to learn better so that I can defend myself and my family. My aunt is the only one of our family left alive, and she is too old to manage our property on her own. Besides," and a mischievous quirk curled one side of her smile, "I fancied that I could be a man just like my brothers. I can ride and shoot as well as they can."

Alexander smiled back. "Excellent."

Then he turned to Roxánne de la Croix. "I never thought I would find you here."

"When you told me to leave Linz, I took your advice," she replied. "Now I see that fate has brought me here to you. Like these lovely novices I have much to learn about the art of the sword, and I wish to know more. Would you have room for me also?"

"Yes, of course," Alexander said. "My ladies, please sign at the front desk. The school is not equipped at present to accommodate your needs, but I will make arrangements. We will begin after the last class of the day on Monday next. My thanks for your interest."

Roxánne lingered as the two other women rejoined their companions and left the gym. "I know you did not have time to talk before, but is there time now?" she asked.

Alexander smiled, and replied, "shall we talk over dinner? I know a club…"

"If it will please you, I am not hungry. I would rather walk by the river," she said.

"Then wait here while I change out of these clothes and make myself more presentable."

She smiled and nodded.

It did not take long for Alexander to change, and after Roxánne signed the student roll they went down to the riverside lawns, a narrow ribbon of green garden next to the water maintained by the royal gardeners. By then it was completely dark, and the lamps along the avenues filled the city with light. Music drifted across the river from a tavern nearby as they walked together along the causeway.

Roxánne appeared to be more captivated with Alexander than the sights and sounds of the city. "You appear to have become quite well known," she began. "When I first came here I knew no one, but after I found.. the others… they told me about you. Then I heard about your position at the academy."

"I must apologize for having been rude before," Alexander replied. "As I had been traveling for so long I thought that my father and I were alone in the world. When we first met I was not prepared for such an encounter."

"Granted," she laughed. "I was not prepared either."

"Who turned you?" he asked.

"Oh, that is a long story. He was a crusading knight who was turned by an ancient, or so he told me. I was but a young girl then, and he was so fair and kind that I could not resist him. But he died a long time ago. I lived as the humans did, but hunted in secret until one day I found myself in Linz." Roxánne shrugged. "I had been considering leaving Linz long ago, but when you told me to leave, it was as if my mind was made up for me. I sold everything off and came to Paris. I was drawn to this city as if you and I were joined together by a long rope, though I do not know how or why."

As they walked she had sidled up to Alexander and wrapped one delicate arm around his. Then she asked, "and who turned you?"

"No one turned me," Alexander replied. "I turned on my own."

Roxánne paused in midstep. "You were born this way?"

"Aye. It was as much a surprise to me then as it was to you. But my father told me much of the truth later."

"A half born... of a human mother, no doubt," she guessed. "What happened to her?"

"She died almost two centuries ago," he said softly. "All I have of her is a memory of pain and sorrow, and that she was beautiful and brave. I miss her as if I spent a lifetime in her warming arms."

"I was an orphan when I met my sire," she said. "I knew nothing but starvation and sickness before that day. In a strange way he rescued me by turning me, and I will ever be grateful for his mercy. But, have you never wished to be human?"

Alexander had to think hard about that, then finally said, "no. I am who I am, and cannot be anything else. I am reminded of my nature daily, but regret nothing of it. All that I do is for the good of others, and what skills I have are used only to that end."

"What an admirable sentiment," she said. "I wish I could be that sure of anything. I have never been able to shed my human side no matter what I do."

"And what is wrong with having a human side?" he asked, betraying a gentle smile.

"I do not know. I have the doubt that the good I do will be judged a small recompense for drinking blood. But it is the only food which grants me longevity and youth. I do not understand it. It drives me to do things I would never have done in my human life. I crave the taste, the color, the thrill of the hunt. Yet there is always the thought that it is an abomination before God and I will be denied entry into Heaven."

"You were religious before you met your sire. But what made you submit to him?"

She smoothed back her dark hair as a breeze stirred it into her pale face. "I suppose I was too afraid to make a clear decision. Yes, my fear of death gave me the strength to go on living. And as I have found, impossible to resist looking forward into the future, where I expect I will be when it arrives."

There was a long silence between them as they watched a pair of black swans glide by on the water. Then Alexander said, "what a pair of monsters we are. We are alien to this world and everyone in it. But I wish for a day when we will be accepted as ourselves, and not try to hide what we are. Do you think there will ever be one?"

"One can only hope," she said, then added, "oh. I have been reading some pamphlets by Edmond Tibetin. Do you know him?"

Alexander cleared his throat with sudden embarassment, then lied, "not on a personal basis."

"I find his work to be forward thinking, if a trifle sophomoric," Roxánne said. "But he always talks of the future. He speaks of a time when all men will abandon war and live together in peace."

He stowed his wounded pride in the background and said, "it is true that he is not the most skilled at words, lady..."

"What he lacks in skill he recovers well with his visions of the future. He is a dreamer. We lack such words among the thousands of pages of drivel and nonsense published every year. Yet, something about his words rings true, as if he has been to the future himself."

That caught Alexander by surprise. "The future is ever in motion, like a torrent of water; fluid in form but irresistible, driving us forward toward the unknown," he said. "Perhaps... perhaps Tibetin has found a way to freeze that motion so that one could see a single point in time and study it."

Roxánne laughed. "You speak now as if you have written his books." Then she turned and saw his cheeks now flushed pink with despair at his discovery. "Ah, ha! So it is you! No one has ever seen him, and now I find the author himself walking beside me."

"Roxánne, please..." he stopped and turned to her. "That part of my life is over. My work brought me nought but trouble, and killed a friend as surely as if I had run him through myself."

"Oh," she said, and her expression fell. "I heard about Cyrano de Bergerac, but had no inkling of your friendship. I apologize."

He looked down at her and said, "there is no need. Perhaps I have been too preoccupied with myself of late, but I would like to count myself a friend if you have need of one."

Roxánne's face was beautiful in the lamplight, but her lips had met with a small pout as if she was disappointed. "Oh."

Alexander suddenly realized that her connection with him was more romantic in scope. Perhaps he was too dense to notice more readily, but it was the same reaction Charanditha had when she declared her love to him. Now he felt as if anything more said would merely serve to tear a rift between him and Roxánne.

"No, it is I who must apologise," he said. "I do not wish to mislead you. My life has ever been one of austerity and thrift, and my choices have had to be hard from necessity. If I knew what kind of life I could give you I would be willing to enter into a bond with you. But I do not. Can you understand?"

To her credit Roxánne did not cry, or shout, or grow angry. "I do, Alexander. Perhaps my heart has governed my life for too long, but from the moment I saw you I felt as if we were fated to be together. My blood has said nothing to me since I turned. I have been forced to make all my choices alone. I would not expect you to feel the way I do, but I find I cannot be far from your side. Therefore, I will accept your friendship alone, if that is all I can have of you."

Alexander felt relief wash through him like a wave of warm water. "I respect your understanding and candor, lady. It is not often that I can share the truth of myself with another. Perhaps in time I may come to feel for you that which you feel for me. It was so with my last love, who lost her life to the Turks. My life has been nothing but battle and the risk of discovery to my peril. Can I assure any woman that I will be there to to protect her?"

"But, once you train me in the art of the sword there will be no more need, will there?" Roxánne asked. "No, that was a rhetorical question. All that I crave is a chance to stay at your side."

"The others have their collection of syncophants and disciples," Alexander said. "But you are neither one, I can sense that. Then, I will name you a partner in my enterprise. Are we agreed?"

"Agreed," she replied, nodding. "But what about your father? He was not pleased with me that day we met."

"I am certain he will turn to my way of thinking once I explain."

"And, where is your father? Is he not in Paris?"

"The king has seen fit to bestow him with an estate in Rouen in exchange for his services as royal stablemaster."

Roxánne clapped her hands together and laughed. "What a wondrous event. How on Earth…?"

"We had the fortune to rescue one of his servants. It is how we came to be in Linz. The young man we were seeking there was a deputy of the parlement and his companion at arms."

"So fate did bring you to me after all," she said. "I will cherish the moment as I would a kiss. I look forward to learning from you that which all women should, that I may carry it with me all my days, and I will take what I learn and instruct others of my gender."

Alexander said, "you honor me, dear lady."

131

So the pair of monsters walked to the tavern where the Theatre des Vampires were headquartered. It stood out among the other shops and restaurants, a garish example of extreme décor: the exterior walls were painted black, with windows trimmed in red. The sign above the door was a flag: rouge with a black bat emblazoned on it, and the name of the establishment arranged in a semicircle underneath. The door had a cross of black wood set in its center to give the place a more melodramatic appearance.

"*This* is the Theatre des Vampires?" Roxánne said with a skeptical grin. "Can they be so bold? I would call it gauche."

Alexander grinned back. "Wait until you see the inside."

He pushed open the door and admitted her into near darkness, where only small candelabra illuminated the walls and ceiling. The tavern was bigger than the outside appearance of the place: a large room with cathedral ceiling space and a restaurant area, with the windows overlooking the alley heavily curtained in dark wine red. At one end of the room stood an actual stage with a proscenium arch.

There were few patrons at the early evening hour, seated at the small tables or at the long bar stretching along one wall. They all had the pale faces and rose lips of vampires, dressed in shades of black, red and grey. A few had turned their heads to regard the front door with mild curiosity, then turned back to their hushed conversations when they saw Alexander standing in the lintel.

The barkeep raised his hand and called, "Alexandre, it is good to see you again. What will you have?"

"I have brought a visitor," Alexander replied. "May I present Mademoiselle Roxánne de la Croix, recently of Linz. Roxánne, this is my good friend and dispenser of blood, Vincent."

The barkeep set a mug down and made a small bow and a flourish with his hands. "Welcome to the Theatre Des Vampires, mademoiselle. I have the finest selection of blood liquors in all Paris."

"Blood… liquors?" Roxánne asked, with a glance to Alexander.

"He labels them so because they come from several different donors, selected for their youth, health and willingness to spare an ounce or two in exchange for a small sum," Alexander replied. "It is all quite above board. Vincent has even obtained a license to dispense blood as he does any other libations."

Vincent chuckled. "I simply 'persuaded' the license board of my desire to dispense rare and vintage spirits, using my talent as a respectable vampire. That, and a small bribe disguised as a donation to their pension fund. Their inspector only visits here once a year, and when he does, we present him only with what he wishes to see, nothing more."

"Very clever," Roxánne said with a smile.

They approached the bar, and Vincent presented her with a small shot glass filled with the dark red fluid. "Tell me what you think," he said.

Roxánne took a careful sip and closed her eyes. When she opened them, they were glowing red fire. "Paris. A girl, about sixteen. An orphan. Pregnant as well."

Vincent clapped his hands softly. "Very good. I paid her for only a pint, so that she could employ a midwife to help her deliver her child. She said she would name him after me."

"Then I will finish it with the knowledge that our charitable works are the source of our strength." She drained the rest quickly.

"But, you will stay for the performance, won't you?" he asked. "This evening we are presenting poetry by Vincent Voiture, who has recently died, accompanied by a guitar."

Alexander's eyebrow elevated a little as he asked, "Vincent Voiture? A namesake, perhaps?"

"Mere coincidence, Monsieur le Comte!" Vincent retorted. "He was killed by a mob in May while trying to make his way from the Louvre to his mistress's lodgings, perhaps to save her from them. It was a terrible time for us. We were forced to close for a week."

Alexander turned to Roxánne. "What say you? Would you care to partake in the entertainment?"

"It would be my pleasure, Monsieur le Comte," she said.

When it came time for the performance to begin, Vincent exhorted his patrons to gather closer to the stage or they would hear nothing. When they did and were settled in their seats, a man carrying a sheaf of paper and another carrying a guitar walked onto the stage from behind the side curtain.

The guitarist took a seat on the chair set there for him. A rough tripod podium was erected for the reader, who set his sheaf on it and turned pages until he came to the first selection.

"This is for Monsieur Voiture, who has left us too soon," the man said simply, then began reciting the poem, while the guitarist plinked a small hymn by Bach. And so it went for about an hour, poems recited with all the somber tones and darkness of a funeral. At the end, the reader collected his papers while the guitarist picked up his instrument and left the stage; approached the front of the stage and said, "if you wish to leave a donation, please do so with Vincent. Thank you for your kind attention."

There was a smattering of polite applause, to which Vincent replied, "come, mesdames and monsieurs. Surely you can do better than that!" The response was more applause, but the patrons were already gathering their things and preparing to go at the same time; and the man on the stage did not stay to the halfhearted accolade.

Roxánne, who had clapped her hands with some vigor, pouted at the scattering audience. "That was not what I had expected," she said. "Surely there was better to be had of it. I loved what I heard. Yet there was no warmth in the delivery; no appreciation for the words."

Alexander looked at her. "There are good days and bad days, Roxánne, even among players. Perhaps this was a bad day for them."

"Nay! It does not have to be so," she declared with some force. "What is lacking is a proper staging of the event, and with a better audience."

Then she perked up as a thought occurred to her. "What would Vincent say if I offered my services as a hostess, to greet his patrons and to make them feel welcome? I have found no employment, and while I am staying with the Baroness de Guillard, nothing to do but play cards and crocquet all day. I am bored with the niceties of the court. It is all so… human."

Alexander looked at her as if she had grown wings. "True, Vincent does not attract a goodly large crowd often."

He looked up and signaled Vincent to come to him. When the barkeep approached with his tray, Alexander said, "what would you say to a proposition from mademoiselle about the theater?"

"Ay? A proposition?" Vincent said. "What kind?"

"I see that you have a light clientele in the evenings, monsieur," Roxánne said. "There is no one to greet visitors at the door. Would you care to have someone help you who has some skill at this? I did own an inn until just recently, and were I to fill the position, your theater would bring you more revenues, and by some word of mouth, more clients."

Vincent stood still, lost in thought, then placed his tray on the table and sat down. "Mademoiselle, you astonish me," he said. "When I established this theater I had only people like us in mind, but your proposition courts another idea. What if I were to allow you to manage the front, while I manage the procurement and dispensation of all manner of spirits, and together we open a public place which is open to all of Paris? Would you care to enter into such a partnership?"

"Indeed, it would please me greatly," she replied. "But, I do have other ideas about the establishment itself which may be of benefit to you."

Vincent rolled his eyes, then sighed heavily. "As you have seen for yourself, I am no master at decoration or design. Any additions or improvements I will leave entirely to you. Alexander, will you draft a contract between us, that we have something to show the license inspector when he visits? And, please be a witness to its notary, that it was entered into by both parties. In this way I will gain a manager with a head for detail, while she gains a position she was no doubt born to."

"Monsieur flatters me," Roxánne said, with a small nod of her head.

While Alexander was engaged with drafting the contract, he paused on occasion to watch as Roxánne and Vincent discussed the walls, the drapes, the tablecloths; even the outside. She appeared to be changing everything completely around to her taste, while Vincent seemed eager to agree to everything she suggested.

Roxánne had decided that red seemed preferable to black, where humans were concerned, and suggested red brocade for the walls, with the wine curtains just as they were but tied back with ropes of gold cloth.

The wall behind the bar was to be adorned with small paintings of French countryside instead of odalisques, for the benefit of the more puritan crowd; and the tables covered in black edged with gold instead of white. Small candles in red glass cups were to be placed on each table so that the human crowd could see each other, to cut the light down for the benefit of the stage performances.

She then suggested that Vincent should remove the cross from the front door and to repaint the outside walls blood red with black trim, with the door staying black for a dramatic effect.

Alexander listened and found himself agreeing with her choices. Roxánne did seem suited for her role as a manager. Running a brothel was no different than running a public house. The money brought in must be accounted for and all made attractive to the clientele.

When he had finished drafting the contract, Alexander called for them to come and sign both copies, which he then signed as witness.

"There is only one question from me," he said to Roxánne. "How will you manage this place and still have time for your fencing lessons?"

"I will find the time," she said softly. "I have not forgotten my pledge to you. And Vincent will need protection now more than ever, now that he has a new venture, a public house which will soon attract more humans. I have no doubt that the other restauranteurs will be jealous of us and try to act on it."

Vincent's pale face appeared to blush. He smiled and said, "Mademoiselle, I appreciate your concern beyond mere words. You will begin tomorrow?"

She smiled. "Tomorrow it will be." She glanced to the small clock set on the nearby mantelpiece and said, "and now the hour grows late, and I must be back to the house before the Baroness notices my tardiness. Alexandre, will you help me with my cloak?"

He reached for the fine wool draped over the chair where she had left it and drew it gently over her shoulders. Then the both of them said good night to Vincent and walked out into the evening fog.

Alexander escorted her all the way to the house of the de Guillards, where he said, "I will expect you on Monday for lessons. I will arrange a place where you can change and store your training clothes until the facility is built. Will that be acceptable?"

Roxánne shrugged and smiled. "I will manage…that is, all of us will manage. I am sure the other ladies are of the same mind."

He bowed to her and said, "then I bid you a good evening. Sleep well."

"Bon soir," was her cheerful reply as she slipped through the wrought iron gate and hurried down the garden walk toward the house.

132

Left standing alone in the dark, Alexander looked around carefully. At this hour the street was empty. The fog hugged the outlines of the houses, punctuated at regular intervals by bright fuzzy balls of yellow light. His eyes shifted to night vision as he shifted his cloak and resettled his hat, then started to stroll back toward the academy grounds. While he walked, he fell to ruminating over what he should do to rearrange his busy teaching schedule, until a sudden creeping sensation and the sound of metal on metal drew his attention to his left.

He had come to the intersection of an alley and the street. The alley was cloaked in darkness. His senses expanded until he could see and hear about halfway into it. There were shadows moving about, sounds, but the fog would not let him find the details. He debated about moving closer to see better, then thought better of it and turned to walk on.

Caterwauling filled the spaces between the sounds and froze Alexander where he was. A cat emerged from the darkness on the run. Alexander exhaled slowly, yet instinct told him there was something out of sorts here.

There followed a shuffling sound of running footsteps as a man staggered out of the alley and fell heavily onto the muddy cobblestones. Another man followed him, and was about to finish him off with a long knife when Alexander flashed across the lane and knocked him aside with a swift kick of his boot, landed solidly on both feet and waited with his hands bunched into fists.

The assailant was big, with a swarthy complexion and unruly reddish brown hair. His clothes were shabby and smelled of a mixture of rum and other foul odors. The man struggled back up to fight back, but Alexander chopped him down quickly with a solid blow, relieved him of the knife and tossed it far out of reach into the alley. The man crumpled to the ground holding his jaw and groveling with pain.

Alexander turned his attention to the victim, who was a smaller man dressed something like a merchant. Perhaps he had foiled a burglary. He hunched down next to the victim and examined him, noting that there was very little blood, though the scent of it was strong with bile. The wound was shallow but had struck a vital organ. He turned the man over carefully. "Are you well, monsieur?" he asked.

The smaller man moaned feebly and clutched at his side, dangerously close to falling into a faint. Alexander reached for his wrist and felt for his pulse. It was erratic, threatening to collapse entirely.

The smaller man tried to rally his strength, reached for his arm and clutched it with a grip like a steel vise, drawing him closer, and whispered, "beware, Monsieur le Comte. They are here."

Thunderstruck, Alexander asked, "what? Who is here? Who are you? How do you know me?"

The man struggled to say something else when he hesitated, choking on the words, "I came to warn you…" He coughed, then fell limply back and went still.

Alexander looked around and spotted the assailant lying where he had fallen. He went to the man and roughly shook him awake, leaned into his face and demanded, "you will tell me why you have done this. Who is this man to you?"

The burglar struggled mightily to get free, but Alexander held him down easily with an iron grip. The burglar pursed his lips stubbornly and spoke not a word, as if he was as mute as those men in Linz and Strasbourg.

Suddenly, the memory of those days came rushing back to Alexander. The dead man's few words had told him the whole story. The agents of the unknown enemy were now here in Paris, and the merchant, if that was what he truly was, had warned him of the coming storm. More questions flooded to the surface but there was no more time for speculation.

He felt, then saw a pair of gendarmes turn the corner and stroll toward him, as yet unaware of the situation. Thinking desperately, Alexander concluded that he could do nothing for now.

He stood and approached them, his hands held away from his body. "Monsieurs, if you please, a moment." he said. "A man has been killed by another. I found them both just now."

The older gendarme started and drew back. "Killed, you say? Lead us to them."

Alexander led the way to the two men, and one of the gendarmes examined the smaller man's body while the other interrogated the robber. The burly man refused to say a word, or could not, which only exascerbated his situation. Cautiously, Alexander stood by and watched as the older gendarme strongarmed the assailant to his feet and fastened his hands in a pair of irons. "We will know the truth of you soon," he said.

His companion approached and and showed him the knife and the blood on it. "The other man was stabbed in his side, and bled much. He is dead."

The older man turned to Alexander and asked, "know you either of these men?"

"Nay," he replied. "I had never seen them before. I heard a noise, and at first could see nothing in the dark. Then, a patch of cloud did pass away from the moon for a moment, and they were visible."

"A stroke of luck, then," the gendarme said. "Who are you, and where were you going?"

"I am but a concerned citizen of Paris, monsieur," Alexander said. "I was on my way home."

"Will you be willing to give a statement, that we may have some testament of what occurred for our records?"

Alexander nodded, "I would be happy to. Will tomorrow afternoon be convenient?"

"Aye," the gendarme replied. "Come to the station house in Rue Saint Just and ask for Inspector Grais. You may go now."

"Good evening, monsieurs," Alexander said as cheerfully as he could, then walked away from the scene, though not too quickly.

133

In the light of day, Alexander could find no peace with his thoughts. His instincts remained at war. The altercation of the last evening made him more cautious than ever even as he forced himself not to pack and bolt from Paris.

Finally, after an hour of such doubt, he followed his schedule as usual. But he was distracted by the sense of urgency he felt as he guided his pupils through their lessons.

Soon, he became conscious of Roxánne's eyes following him all over the room. Their brown warmth were liquid as they conveyed concern.

When the hour was over, he gave the students small practice assignments so that they might be prepared for the next lesson, and dismissed them with a quiet "and now I bid you a good evening. Safe journey home."

Roxánne lingered while Alexander put his practice foil in its case. He paused, thinking long and hard about what he should do next. When he turned around he found her standing right in front of him.

Her lips trembled as she asked, "Alexandre, what is wrong? Your mind was not on the lesson."

Determined not to panic, he smiled. "What could be wrong?" he asked lightly.

"Oh, bother! The trouble is written all over your handsome face," she said simply. "One would have to be blind not to see it."

He avoided looking into those moist brown eyes, and replied, "it is a private matter. Pay it no mind."

She stepped closer and put her hand on his arm. "I think it is more than that. Please tell me."

He considered for a long moment, then said, "I stopped a fight in an alley last evening, after you left me. Something the poor man said put me on guard. I... my father and I have an enemy, a man who will stop at nothing to destroy us. A vampire hunter."

Her eyes went wide. "A hunter? Here, in Paris?"

"Yes. His name is van Helsing, a Hessian baron of an ancient order. His cousin made his living by staking the dead in their graves, and defiling them in other ways most dreadfully. His cousin accosted me and my father in Hungary. My father killed him in self defense. But, van Helsing learned of the event and has sworn to avenge his kinsman. He and his men attacked us in Strasbourg. If the king were to learn of this, our lives, our family fortune, all would be forfeit. I know I promised to instruct you and the other ladies in the art of the sword, but... I dare not put you all in danger."

Roxanne's brown eyes widened. "I thought such deeds were forbidden by Emperor Ferdinand," she said. "Now this man would pursue you in the city?"

"Aye. But now things are worse. The man in the alley tried to tell me something else, but died before he could say it."

Roxánne studied the anguish in his pale face and reached up to touch his cheek. "Family honor is more important than anything, Alexandre. Swords and fighting can wait. You must go to your father, mustn't you?"

"What can I say to the other students, and to Monsieur du Coudray? I have committed myself to their instruction, and cannot see myself running home. It is not as simple as that. I am the court instructor to King Louis himself. Were I to leave now I would betray their trust."

"You must explain to Monsieur du Coudray that you have more important matters to attend to," she insisted softly. "Your family must come first. Surely he will understand..."

A familiar voice came from behind them. "Understand what?"

Alexander and Roxánne turned and saw le Perche du Coudray standing in the open door. He looked puzzled, and had not heard everything.

Alexander took a deep breath of resignation and replied, "Monsieur du Coudray, I fear I must leave the academy."

The master swordsman approached at a casual pace. "Oh? Why? It is but the middle of the second term."

"I have had most distressing news," he hedged. "I must go home to Rouen to attend to a personal matter. I'm afraid... I cannot explain further. It is all beyond my control."

Du Coudray's eyebrow rose. "I see. When can you return?"

"In truth, monsieur, I do not know," Alexander replied. "Events are quite fluid for the moment. I must leave as soon as possible, so it stands to reason my return is also in question."

"If you were anyone else I should be cross with you," the swordmaster said, "but you have never given me reason to before.

You may have your time off, on condition that you send me some warning if it be longer than, say, a fortnight."

"Agreed," Alexander said with a sigh of relief. "I apologize for leaving you in all haste…"

"There is no need. Shall I send word to the king of your absence? He should be notified that his lessons will be delayed for a time."

"I would be most grateful if you did," Alexander replied.

Du Coudray replied, "off you go, then, and tend to your business. I will explain your absence to the other students in the morning."

He gave a courteous bow to Roxánne, then turned and walked out of the gym.

"There," Roxánne said. "It is all arranged. Now go quickly, before it is too late. Give my greetings to your father, and tell him that I send my best wishes with you."

Overflowing with gratitude, Alexander bent down and gave her a lingering kiss on her cheek, then left her to pack.

After he did so, he visited the Gendarmerie to give his statement to the chief inspector as he promised.

The man was solicitous and eager to solve the case, and asked many questions. But he did not appear to suspect Alexander of anything; choosing to believe that he was simply in the wrong place at the right time.

Through some gentle probing, Alexander learned that the assailant was known for several previous crimes, and that he was mute because he was deaf.

On his way out of town, Alexander stopped at the lodging house where Jean Reneau lived and told him what he planned.

Reneau bolted from his chair like a man possessed and said, "then you will need me. You cannot leave Paris on your own. Let me go with you."

For once, Alexander did not protest. "Very well," he replied. "Make ready, and bring whatever weapons you have with you."

His post servant gave him a devilish grin. "I was ready to go three days ago."

He went to the chest of drawers in the corner and pulled open the drawers, withdrew a bundle of clothing, a formidable looking double loaded musket, a pouch of gunpowder and a magazine of musketballs, along with a long knife in its sheath. Pausing to snuff out the candle on the table, Reneau plunged the room into darkness as he put on his new hat, a broad brimmed affair without trim, and followed his master out onto the veranda. He said, "wait a moment while I fetch my horse, and we will be on our way."

From there, Alexander and Reneau rode toward the inn where d'Artagnan lived and explained to the musketeer captain that he would be gone for some time.

"But, Alexandre, will you need protection on the road?" d'Artagnan asked. "There are highwaymen everywhere. You should let me summon my confrères and escort you."

"I managed to make it to Paris from Rouen on my own," Alexander replied. "I will be nought but a shadow on the way back, but I must go. My man here will be adequate protection."

"Something tells me the affair is dire. Then I will be discreet and tell no one where you have gone," d'Artagnan assured him. "Safe journey back."

Alexander shook his hand, then leapt back onto his horse's back, and galloped toward the city's north gate with Reneau in tow. As he went toward it, Alexander became conscious of that sensation he had before, and looked around into the shadows for some sign of pursuit. But he saw nothing.

Reneau saw his face, and cautiously glanced behind them. "Monsieur le Comte, what do you see?"

Alexander pulled his horse to a halt and looked around again. "Perhaps... it is nothing," he replied. Even then, he was not able to shake the sensation until they passed through the north gate and was well on the road into the sheltering darkness of night.

134

Alexander and Reneau reached Rouen by midnight, and just in time for a storm to discharge its load of rain. When they came to the compound gate they were already drenched, but ignored the water as Alexander glanced up and saw the guards seated in the gate tower, huddled in their capes against the wet cold.

"Halloooo," he called. "Open the gate!"

The one closest to the window heard his voice, glanced out and rose to come out into the rain. "Hallo. Who are you?"

"Alexandre Corvina."

The man gestured to the other guard, who leaned over the gate and hollered to the men at the winch. When the gate was opened, Alexander and Reneau entered the courtyard. One of the other guards ran to them and seized the reins to their horses. He said, "we did not expect you, Monsieur le Comte. There was no word of your coming."

A flash of lightning lit up the clouds above, and the thunder was deafening. The rain began to batter them in earnest. Alexander asked, "I came as soon as I could. How fares my father?"

"As well as anyone, Monsieur le Comte," the man replied, shrugging.

"There has been no one else here today?"

The puzzled look on the guard's face spoke volumes. "Non, Monsieur le Comte."

"Merci," he replied, then rode the rest of the way toward the main house with Reneau following closely behind. When he reached it, they dismounted and led their horses under the portico.

"All seems well," Reneau called through the rain.

"Aye. But I will not rest until I see my father's face." He looked around and through the downpour, expecting something, but not sure what. He had to talk himself out of the spell of unease, sure now that it was probably nervous tension.

The two tethered their horses to the rings near the front door, where Alexander pounded on it.

It seemed like an age before it opened. Flandres stood in the doorway with a look of open mouthed astonishment, clad in his nightshirt and his lantern held high in one hand. "Monsieur le Comte?" He said. "How is it you are here, and in this terrible storm?" He stood aside quickly to let Alexander and Reneau in.

"Good evening, Flandres. Where is my father?" Alexander shed his wet cloak, hat and gloves, and handed them to the house man. Reneau did the same, and stood aside to wait for an order.

"In his library, where he spends most of his evenings." Flandres replied. "I will set these next to the fire to dry."

"Merci," Alexander replied quickly. To Reneau he added, "wait here. I will not be long. Flandres, give him some food and hot tea."

He marched down the hall and walked into a large room lined with tall shelves stocked with books. He looked around at first and could not see Lucien anywhere; nor could he feel his presence, which puzzled him.

"Hello? Father? Are you in here?" he called softly.

From above his head, a warm accented voice replied, "up here, Alexander. What are you doing here? I did not expect you."

Lucien's head appeared from behind a bookcase on a small mezzanine. Then he came out bearing a book in his hand, and walked down a spiral staircase made of ornately finished wrought iron to the ground floor.

He placed the book on the desk and approached his son, pulled him into a hug and held him close, then released him again as he remarked, "you are all wet."

Alexander pushed back a strand of wet hair. "Aye, the storm caught me just as I arrived."

Lucien offered, "I will ring for some hot tea," and reached for a bellcord on the wall. "But, I thought you were happily teaching young men the art of the sword. I hear from Gravet that you and Louis are like two peas in a pod. What has happened?"

"I am...I mean I was...but I bear grave news," Alexander replied. "I came as soon as I could. Something has changed."

He told Lucien the story of the fight the night before and concluded with, "I can scarcely think what it means. I fear now that van Helsing has tracked us into France and means to do us harm. Have you heard nothing of him?"

Lucien's face was stone. "No, nothing."

They were interrupted as Flandres entered the study and placed a tea service on the desk. "Is there anything else you wish, Monsieur le Comte?"

"No, merci," Lucien replied.

"My man Reneau requires lodging," Alexander added. "Give him a room, and do close the door after you."

The houseman bowed slightly and said, "monsieurs," then did as he was told.

When his footsteps faded away down the hall Lucien asked, "did this man say his name?" He reached for a teacup and poured a measure of the hot liquid into it, then passed it to Alexander. He did not pour for himself.

"No, he was far too injured for aid and died in my arms. But what other explanation could there be?" Alexander said. "I thought at first that the army of mutes who pursued us had found me. My position as instructor to the king might also be a hazard, since *Monsieur* is so keen to replace him on the throne. I arrived in Paris in the midst of le Fronde. It was a perilous time."

He took a sip and found the tea sweetened with honey. But he did not have an appetite for it at that moment and placed the cup back on the service.

Lucien studied Alexander for a long moment, then said, "or you may be painting shadows where they do not belong."

"Why then should a stranger tell me such a thing? No, father, it is no coincidence. He was trying to warn me of a danger which remains nameless, and was murdered so that he could not."

"And the other man?" Lucien asked.

"I was forced to explain when the gendarmes found me. I had no choice but to lie, and did not know what the man who lived could have told them. As events progressed, I learned that the killer was mute because he was deaf. I could have compelled him to tell me the truth but he would not have heard me."

"But, the whole day passed and they did not come for you," Lucien offered. "This means he told them nothing useful to them. That is good for us, but not good for the poor man who warned you. Alas, this bodes ill but I cannot leave the house now."

Alexander regarded him as if he had grown a third eye. "How can you be so calm, father?"

"I must be so, no matter what happens. I no longer have the luxury of flying off like a bird to avoid danger whenever it suits me. There has been a new addition to our family and I must become a rock for her. I must provide for her comfort."

"Parvati? She is here?" Alexander asked with a happy smile.

"Nay. I have had no chance to return to Vienna to fetch her hither. It is as if fate has conspired against me. The king has sent me a portrait of the lady, which I must perforce reply to. His agents approached me on Sunday last, and asked that I deliver it within a fortnight. They reminded me that it has been almost a year since the king commanded that I entertain her suit."

Alexander's smile fell. "Oh. The lady?" He recalled that Louis had told him about her, and by a chain of circumstance had forgotten.

Lucien nodded. "La Comtesse Ingrid van der Hummerling of Holland, who is now a widow, and also a lady in waiting to Queen Anne. She is waiting for a response from me, but I am now reluctant to give her one, because I would not inflict myself upon her." He gave Alexander a rueful smile. "I recall your panic when I sued to win Sarasvati and married her. Now she is dead, and too soon. And, your mother... I fear now that any woman who accepts me into her marriage bed will suffer a similar fate. No, I am but a shadow, who lingers too long in one place and brings death with me wherever I go."

Alexander's mouth fell open. "How can you see yourself that way? It was no fault of yours."

"How can I not? I have been thinking long upon it. I would avoid endangering another woman to feed the hunger for blood which rages within me daily. And, I would not become part of such an arrangement if the lady is unwilling to accept me as I am." He sighed heavily. "My life is no longer as simple as it once was. I must follow the protocols my blood has set for me, or all that we have built will fall to ruin. I have arranged to sit for the court artist, who is to come tomorrow."

"Then, if you are so encumbered, I should go for Parvati myself," Alexander insisted. "She must be brought home to live with us, as we promised her."

"I have not forgotten. I miss her most keenly. I have recently had a letter from Erzebeta that the child misses us, and weeps nightly that we have not returned for her. It has been over a year, has it not, since we left her in Vienna?"

"Far too long," Alexander agreed.

"Yet I cannot postpone the inevitable any longer, can I?" he muttered softly. "How long can you stay?"

"My employer has said he will give me a fortnight, then only a little time more if I say I must have it. But I cannot bide here as long as Parvati is parted from us. Pray, grant me but a few hours to rest and collect myself, then I will depart for Vienna in the morning. I will bring Parvati home to you."

Lucien reached out and patted his shoulder. "Take whatever time you need, and go with my blessing for a safe return home. In the meantime, your bedchamber is laid out the way you left it. Flandres will light your way. Sleep well."

Again that impenetrable wall, which had shut Alexander out of Lucien's world on several occasions, erected itself stone by stone between them. Alexander could hardly fathom the wave of recrimination and self-doubt which came from that fearless, heroic figure standing before him. But now he was resigned to accept it as part of Lucien's need for privacy.

"Good evening, father," he said with a short nod, then left the library in search of Flandres.

As they ascended the staircase to the second floor, Alexander asked the house man point blank, "how long has my father been like that? His letters mentioned nothing dire."

Flandres paused for a moment midstep, then replied softly, "I had pledged to him that I would tell no one, but you are his son so I will make the exception. Soon after you left for Paris, he became so consumed with his work that one day he fainted dead away. He was gone for two days, then woke on the third as if nothing had happened. The leech said it was exhaustion, but was unable to explain why. He said there was no cure to be had for him but rest in bed."

The thrill of shock which ran through him was like those nights in Hungary. "Gone? What do you mean by 'gone'?"

"Monsieur le Comte... I can explain nothing of it. I tell you, he was as one dead. There was no heartbeat, no breath."

"But, you took all care of him," Alexander surmised.

"Oui, Monsieur le Comte. We feared that he was truly dead, but then he revived suddenly as if by a miracle. He has been very quiet since then, and keeps to his library as if he is trapped there, like a fly in tree sap. He goes down to the stables less often now. I have made sure to tell the stewards to go gently with him if he does. Monsieur, I fear he is very ill but tells no one. I think that he will be so afflicted as long as he stays in this house. It is not spoken of, but some of the other servants believe that the house is haunted by the spirit of our old master, that his sorrow has lingered like a ghost and caught your father in its spell."

Alexander nodded his understanding, but said nothing. He guessed that Lucien's fullblood alien empathy had absorbed all the negative energy in the house and transformed it into a deep and abiding sorrow for his dead wives. Alexander was now determined to restore Parvati to Lucien's side so that he would not feel alone anymore. "I will have to leave again soon, but will be returning soon with my sister. Perhaps that will give him some cheer and banish his loneliness."

Flandres asked, "your sister? How old is she?"

"No more than a mere babe," Alexander replied. "You will see when you meet her. Pray, prepare for her a small room with a window that opens onto the meadow so that she can see the horses, and furnish it with all that a child would need for comfort."

"All will be as you wish, Monsieur le Comte," Flandres replied. "She will be most welcome here, as it has been a long time since we have seen children in the household."

They came to Alexander's bedroom door, and Flandres opened it to reveal the four poster bed and curtains just as he had left them. Flandres went to the small desk and picked up the candelabra, blew on it to free it of dust and removed a flint from his pocket to light the candle's wick.

"I apologize for the condition of the room, Monsier le Comte," he offered, "but we were not expecting your return."

"It is quite alright," Alexander replied, and threw his hat and pack onto the bed as he went to remove his jerkin and cravat, placing them on a nearby chair to dry. He freed his long black hair from his band and fluffed it out to allow it to dry.

Flandres then went to light the logs in the small hearth. "It is going to be a cold night, Monsieur le Comte," he said. "Is there anything you wish me to bring you? A hot rum shot, or wine? Food?"

"I ate on the way here," Alexander lied. "But now I only wish to prepare for bed, as it is late and I am fatigued."

To his credit, Flandres did not press the issue. "Then I will leave you. Bon soir. Pleasant dreams." He went to the door, passed out into the hall, and closed the door softly behind him.

Alexander went to the door and twisted the key in the lock, removed his soaked boots, then collapsed onto the dusty coverlet on the bed and stared into the flames guttering in a small draft from the chimney. But he could scarcely sort out his thoughts.

He could think of nothing but the idea that a strong fullblood like Lucien was prone to humors and fainting, and Alexander remembered what he had said about his blood bond with Julian. It was like magic, or a curse. Almost supernatural.

Then he slapped at his cheeks to get the superstitious tommyrot out of his head, rose and searched for the identity papers he had left behind in the rolltop desk resting in the corner. They were just where he had left them, in a top drawer. He took them, folded them up carefully and tucked them into one of the pockets of his saddlepack, then closed the desk.

Another flash of lightning lit up the night, and thunder rolled through, rattling every pane of glass in the windows. Alexander made sure the casement was secure before drawing the curtains. As he did so, he caught sight of a shadow standing under a tree in the courtyard. The shadow was tall, dressed in dark clothes, wearing a cape and hat which obscured his features. His face was not visible.

Alexander stared, frozen with curiosity. Who would risk the storm to be out there, at this time of night?

Another flash dazzled him for a moment. When his vision cleared he looked again but the shadow was gone. He puzzled briefly, then concluded that it was probably a figment of his overactive imagination and drew the curtains closed.

He undressed the rest of the way and threw on a nightshirt, got under the bedcovers, and brooded quietly until the darkness of sleep came to claim him once again.

135

The storm passed on in the wee hours before dawn, and Alexander woke to the sound of church bells in the distance. He listened to them until the last tone faded away, then rose and began to prepare for his journey to Vienna.

His old clothes were still damp, so he searched into his closet and found an ensemble in black and brown, with a broad brimmed hat sporting a cluster of pheasant feathers tied to a band of black leather. He found black hose and a pair of knee high boots, and a brown riding cape with black trim. Thus dressed like a modest traveler, he took his pack and slipped down the stairs to look in on Lucien.

As he passed a window onto the commons he caught sight of Lucien discussing something with a guard, and went out the front door to meet them. He arrived just in time to see the guard bow to Lucien and walk away. "Good morrow, father," he said.

Lucien turned to him and smiled. "Good morrow, Alexander. I have sent for a fresh horse for you to ride."

"Oh? Was there something wrong with Matilde?"

"No. But you must admit that a horse, like its rider, attains a certain familiarity to those who might deign to follow it."

The memory of the man he had seen in the night came flooding back with those words. "Father, I did see what I thought was a ghost last evening, but perhaps he was not there after all."

Lucien's pale eyebrow went up. "A ghost?"

"Aye. When I went to draw the curtains for the night, I did see the shadow of a man standing under yonder tree. But a flash of lightning obscured my vision, and when I was able to see again it was gone. I thought it but a momentary illusion, light and dark, but nothing more solid than that."

"This man," Lucien asked. "How did he appear to you?"

Alexander had to think. "'Twas but a momentary event, so I cannot give you more than a sketch of him. He was tall, and wore dark clothes which did conceal his person. He wore a hat which obscured his face. No detail could I see which would identify him readily to me."

"Then it was not a ghost, for the guard has just told me that he saw a man lingering about in the courtyard who did not belong," Lucien replied. "I have given orders to enforce the evening watch, so that the man might be caught if he returns."

"I should stay, then, and help with the watch."

Lucien chuckled. "You cannot divide yourself in twain, Alexander. Leave the stranger to me, and ride to fetch Parvati."

Jean Reneau emerged from the house fully dressed for riding and approached. "Master, I am ready to go."

Alexander glanced at his father, then said, "a word, if you please, master Reneau."

The veteran changed direction, his face all curiosity. "Aye?"

Alexander reached out and tagged his sleeve, then drew him away from Lucien toward the shade of a tree. "I would have you remain here, and guard my father," he said softly. "A… dream I had gives me reason to fear for his safety."

"But…"

"I know you were employed for a different purpose, but nowhere better than here are you needed. I can defend myself on my own. My

566

father is a different matter. Guard him as you would me. On your oath of fielty, swear it."

"I do, monsieur. He is as much my master as you are."

Alexander reached out and patted his shoulder. "You have not failed me. I trust you to know what to do, but I must go alone. It will take me no more than three days to return. Stay here, and be my envoy in my stead."

"As you wish. Godspeed you on your journey."

Reneau turned away and returned to Lucien, who also placed a hand on his shoulder.

Just then, a steward arrived on horseback, towing a roan mare with him. "She is sure of foot, and less fearful of the shadows than many," Lucien said. "She responds to the name 'Rose'. She will carry you all the way to Strasbourg from here. I have had news that the road is treacherous with holes and that the bridge collapsed in the storm. I have found a less traveled road which will take you north and east past it toward Rheims, where you can join the road south from there to Strasbourg."

"I will follow it, father," Alexander replied, then took Lucien and a tight embrace. "Wish me luck."

"You will succeed," Lucien said. "Of that, I am most certain. Good fortune, and may the stars light your way."

With a last look at his father, Alexander cinched his pack onto Rose's saddle and mounted her. The mare shifted uneasily at first, but a firm tug at her reins calmed her. In another moment, he had her turned and headed out the opened gate at a gallop.

The north road followed the curve of the hills toward the French Alps, and was flanked by a grove of oak and poplar trees. Here the way was paved with hard slabs of marble and rough schist, the remains of an ancient Roman road long abandoned to the wood. No one was seen coming or going along its narrow length. It was deserted as a road less traveled should be.

Here and there, Alexander could see where carriage and wagon tracks had worn long grooves into the stones, and there were only a few potholes to avoid. The world turned into a fairy tale as the ground mist turned the sunlight into golden shafts piercing the shadows of the forest; and where the sun divided that veil, turned the road into a golden river of light. As he rode on, Alexander told himself to write it all down when he reached the next town.

He made it as far as Rheims by mid afternoon, where he stopped at a roadside inn to water and feed Rose. He lingered only long enough to learn from the innkeeper about the condition of the road, scribbled a few furtive words into his journal, then was back on Rose's back and headed south toward Strasbourg.

Alexander was near Metz by the time the sun went down behind the clouds gathering in the west. Here he stopped at the outskirts of town, dismounted, and guided Rose into a small copse, where he found a grotto and a small spring feeding the stream which ran through the village.

He pulled the saddle and pack from Rose's back, sampled the water and found it sweet, then let her drink her fill of it. Carefully, he examined her hooves and her fetlocks and found her legs as solid as ever. He used his fingers to comb out small twigs and bramble caught in her mane, and spoke to her in soft tones of settling down to rest. She shrugged and snorted softly as her nose remained in the cold water.

From where he stood, he could see the twinkling lights lining the main road winding through town, where the only dominant building was a church with a steeple.

Sounds wafted to him on a warm breeze as he laid out his blanket and laid down on it, placing his weapons close at hand. He listened to the laughter, the shouting, the music, the chiming of church bells; all weaving their way like tattered wool through the steady droning chorus of crickets and frogs surrounding him.

This evening, the moon rose early, a disc of pale white among the stars, peeking through the canopy of dark leaves above his head.

For once, Alexander was free of the constant impressions of human emotion bombarding him from every quarter. There was no joy, no sorrow, no anger. Only peace.

And yet, a deep sense of loneliness filled his being as he reflected on the memories he cherished, of all the men and women who had crossed his life. Sarasvati, Charanditha, Ruthinda, Arpanandra Suresh, Suliman of Arkkady, Karel Nikolai Arkelin, Ostap Kuryan, Hamar Multenyi, John Henry Duggens, and now Cyrano de Bergerac. All these people had shaped his past.

Now, all he could think of was the prospect of finding his baby sister in Vienna, and of bringing her home to Rouen. Would Erzebeta Cecescu follow her and join the household? Was there any chance?

Even the word "home" was an unexpected event in his life. When did he begin to think of the stables that way? Was it because Lucien said it was so, or because he was tired of a wanderer's life and wanted to settle down?

He thought of Roxánne and her need to stay by his side, even though he did not know if he could love her the way she wanted him to, and had made his doubts plain to her.

What are you waiting for, Alexander? He asked himself. What bids you hesitate and not marry the woman? She is half of this world and half of another, just as you are. What is wrong with you?

He could not find an answer that could satisfy his restless soul. Shrugging off these shifting, wandering thoughts, he recentered himself in the present just as Rose stirred and skittered sideways, uttering a small whicker of protest. Instantly, he was on his feet with his sabre in his hand as he listened closely to the night.

Something was moving in the bushes near the grotto, large enough to be a bear. He could see the glowing red form crawling about among the vegetation toward him. An owl hooted in the branches above him as he gripped the blade in his hand and made ready to strike.

A large porcupine emerged from the foliage, took one look at the tall creature confronting him, squealed and turned away to run back into the underbrush. No doubt it was on its way to drink from the spring and Alexander was in its way.

Uttering a sigh of relief, Alexander resheathed his sword and sat down on the blanket again, brushed his hair back and settled down to sleep. Yet, among his wandering thoughts came a dreadful notion: that the mortal danger which had dogged him and Lucien was still out there, somewhere, waiting to catch him like a spider in her web. He quickly shed the idea with a shrug of his shoulders and meditated on other things until sleep claimed him.

136

The twittering of birds woke Alexander, and he blinked up into the leafy canopy over his head. The clouds were gathered together, dark and threatening rain. He glanced over and saw that Rose was already up and cropping the brush next to the spring.

The dream was gone again like a zephyr of smoke. He ruminated on that, thinking that it must ever be his nature to dream with little recall. He thought about the one time that his memory was terribly precise, almost prophetic; but he had not dreamed like that since then.

He rose and prepared to continue his journey, then mounted Rose and charged her down the road to the south.

Alexander reached Strasbourg by mid afternoon and entered through the checkpoint. He found that the town had changed somewhat since he and Lucien had been there last. As he rode down the main avenue, he saw that several new buildings had sprung up on the side roads. The town was spreading deeper into the wooded plain surrounding it.

Then he saw it: in the distance, at the end of the road through town leading toward Germania, a large assembly of tents and wagons gathered beside it in a circle. He nudged Rose into a canter and headed toward it.

When he arrived, Alexander looked up at the sign which had been erected above the entrance to the circle in French: *Cecesçu et Ragosi; Cirque des Estelles.*

He felt as if his heart would burst with happiness and the wonder of it, and passed under the entrance into a wide courtyard where men and women, some with familiar faces, moved back and forth or lingered among their equipment; dressed in all manner of colorful costumes and dress. They looked up with his approach and scattered from the road to give him room, then burst into applause as he passed them by.

One of the men detached himself from a small group and approached Alexander as he dismounted, with his arms opened wide. "As I live and breathe, my friend, I hoped to see you again," said Velin Cecesçu, as he took Alexander in his arms and pounded him on the back.

"And I you, old friend," Alexander replied, pounding him back.

The Romani released him and looked him up and down. "But, how come you here? It has been almost a year since you left us! The stars have guided us to you and this moment as if it were prophecy fulfilled."

Alexander said, "Father has sent me to fetch Parvati from Vienna. Have you had any word from Erzebeta?"

At that, Velin looked around with suspicion, then pitched his voice low. "There is no need to ride on to Vienna," he said. "They are here with us. When we left Vienna, Erzebeta and the child joined us and persuaded me to bring the circus here rather than go on to Prague. Something happened."

Alexander studied his face and caught the hint of sorrow and anger behind those dark grey eyes. "Where are they? When can I see Parvati?"

Velin's smile fell a little more. "I will take you to them. But mind, they have been staying apart from the others. I will let them explain to you what I cannot say without bitter words."

Alexander's joy fell suddenly into an abyss. "What happened to them? Where is Bela Ragosi?"

Velin simply said, "come."

He led Alexander to a wagon set far back from the others and entered it. Soon afterward Bela Ragosi appeared in the door with a half smile on his face. "Alexander, I am so pleased to see you again," he said.

Alexander flushed with sudden anger at Ragosi's attempt to smooth over what had turned into a very somber moment. "Where is Parvati? Where is my sister?"

Bela's friendly smile fell. "She is well cared for. Wait but a moment and I will fetch her."

He disappeared inside and then reappeared with the toddler in his arms. Alexander's mouth fell open as he saw her.

Parvati's black hair had grown loose down to her shoulders. She wore a dark grey smock instead of a baby gown, and her bare feet were muddy, no longer the well dressed doll he had left in Vienna. Worse, she looked as if she had been crying; snuffling to hold back the tears flowing down her little tan cheeks, which were flushed red. Alexander felt her soul reach out and strike him like a fist, reproaching him for leaving her behind so long ago.

Parvati turned to him. Her eyes lit up only a little with recognition as she reached out for her older brother. Alexander took her small body from Bela into his arms and hugged her desperately close. "I am here, Parvati. I have not forgotten you," he assured her. "I am sorry it took so long to come back for you. Dear sweet child, have you suffered so long? What has happened?"

The waif turned her head into his dusty shoulder and burst out with a terrible wailing sound which brought him to tears. He hugged her closer and whispered soft words into her tiny ear, as he turned accusing eyes to glare at Ragosi.

The immortal shifted uncomfortably and looked down as he said, "the neighbors, curse them, set fire to their house. They fled with only the clothes on their backs, and walked out of Vienna alone to find us. We were on the north road to Prague when they came, starving and barely able to stand."

"Why?" Alexander asked. "What harm were they to anyone?"

"Parvati's ways were foreign to them, and they said she was unclean in God's eyes. Persecuted were they for being different, coming from foreign lands. Erzebeta and Parvati were accused of witchcraft." To punctuate that, he snarled and spat on the ground.

"Unclean?!" he thundered, then paused to murmur an apology to Parvati for shouting. The toddler tightened her hold. "Where is Erzebeta?"

"She is safe with me. I have married her in the Cecescu tradition, so that she has a man to protect her. Her uncle Velin and I have cleaved to each other as friends and are equal partners in all things. I love her as any immortal can. She will want for nothing for the rest of her days, or as long as she wants me. We agreed that it would be so."

That tempered Alexander's anger somewhat. "May I have leave to speak to her?" he asked.

Bela looked inside and jerked his head. "Come, Erzebeta. Mend your tears and speak to the child's brother."

A moment later, the poor woman appeared in the doorway with her apron pressed to her nose, sniffling as she did so. In another instant, Alexander could feel her fear and apprehension waft over him like a cold winter's tide. He could hardly understand how he could have caused it.

576

"Come, lady," he said. "It is not as bad as that. I am not angry with you, nor do I resent your good stewardship of my sister. I seek only to know how you have fared. I have heard how you have suffered much already."

Erzebeta raised her eyes to look at him, and replied, "my lord, I did my best to raise Parvati as if she were my own. But now, you will take her from me, and I will never see her again."

"Nay, 'tis not so," Alexander said. "You may see her whenever you wish. But my father had impressed upon you the importance of house and home, did he not? It is my sad duty to take her from you and give her that which we had promised her. I do not do this to be cruel and unjust, but for the welfare of my sister, who is as dear to me as she is to you."

"Aye, you did say that," she replied, snuffling. "Therefore, I beg leave to say goodbye to her one last time."

Bela interjected, "he is not leaving so soon... are you?"

"I can stay but another day, but must return home with the sunrise," Alexander replied. "My duties require me to and I have delayed them much. I am grateful for all you have done for Parvati."

He ventured to speak to the toddler, who had stopped crying for the moment. "Are you better now, sweet child?"

Her voice was small and sorrowful, nothing like the clear confident voice she had that day in the garden. It almost broke his heart. "Yes, brother," she said.

"I am here to take you home. We have found safety in France. No one will be mean to you there, nor bear false witness against you. I promise you it will be so. Please believe me."

A long moment of silence bridged the gap. "Yes, brother."

"Now, I will give you back to Aunt Beta for a while, and tomorrow I will take you home. Please do not cry, little one. All will be better soon."

Silently, he relinquished his hold on her and passed her to the woman, who held Parvati close and took her away into the darkness of the wagon. Velin and Bela emerged and closed the door to give them a measure of privacy, while Alexander went over to a felled tree trunk and sat down heavily on it to think about the situation.

All was silence as they watched him until he raised his head. "I do not know how my father will take this," he said. "In all my travels, I have never known such perfidy. Had witch hunts not been outlawed?"

"Aye, they were," Bela replied. "But there are places where it is practiced still, and there are witch finders about in the country, plying their trade like that vampire hunter van Helsing. Tricksters and confidence men are they all, with nought on their minds but gold and an easy night's shagging, without guilt or remorse among the lot of them."

Velin added, "perhaps it was her dark skin which had the people in an uproar. It was the same with my people when we walked out of Indus. No one wanted us wherever we went. Of foreign birth were we, and we stayed apart to preserve the peace. Her mother was one of us, of royal birth, yet she was never given her proper crown as a true maharani."

Alexander nodded quietly. "I recall her great beauty as if she is standing before me even now. She has never been beyond my thoughts, and I recall her immense patience and kindness to me. I loved her handmaidens, who died most violently by the sword of hate. But surely, there is some civil discourse to be had between people of different birth? It has not harmed me to know them as friends."

"Nor I," Bela added. "That which these people fear most they little understand. And your father is different from everyone else. He is not of this earth but of another, forsooth!"

Alexander's sharp glance told him to keep quiet about that. "That is not for the ears of strangers," he said. "But they tried to burn my sister for a crime she has never committed. A mere child! That I cannot forgive." Then he added, "if you have it in you, give Erzebeta a child, that she can be fulfilled as a mother at last."

Bela snorted with amusement. "I have already done so, but her love for Parvati does not diminish. They have a bond which cannot easily be explained. I can only hope that when she quickens and bears her own child the bond will be severed."

"Then I pray it is so for her sake," Alexander said. "The poor woman is like unto a saint for all her care and concern."

As he spoke, he became conscious of someone else standing nearby, watching them from behind a tree. He reached out carefully and gestured subtly to Bela with two fingers toward his left.

Ragosi glanced up in that direction and spotted the man fleeing into the darkness of the woods. "Stay here," he said to Velin and Alexander, grabbed an axe resting nearby on a log, and charged into the thicket after him.

"It has been that way since Vienna," Velin remarked as he watched him go. "Men come to us seeking work, and we know not which of them are in league with the hunters. We are careful, but we cannot catch all of them."

"Then, I hope that Ragosi catches that one, that we may learn who his master is and put a stop to this," Alexander replied.

A few minutes later, the immortal returned, breathing heavily. "He was fast," he said, as he buried the axe's blade into the log. "He rode out on a horse. He is the third one in a month."

Alexander studied him as Bela drew his sleeve across his sweaty forehead. "And, there is no mark which identifies them readily."

Ragosi shook his head as he smoothed his dark brown hair away from his face. "They spin a silver web of words and are slippery as ice. But, I am certain your father would make short work of them," he said. "I recall a tale a comrade told me of an attack on the Turk. They never saw Drakul's coming. A thousand men died in the dark on a moonless night. None were spared, and they say the ground was soaked in blood. It must have been a glorious battle."

Alexander's grey eyes were sharp as he said, "you would not have wanted to be there. It is a time best forgotten."

"Mark me. Your father will take up his sword again if any hellspawn ventures to make good on his threats. I did not see what happened to van Helsing, but I can imagine it so."

Alexander glanced around carefully to be certain no one else was listening. "But now we will watch for danger from every quarter and grant our enemies no advantage. Van Helsing had a cousin, who gave us trouble here in Strasbourg, and I am certain he has men looking for us even now."

Ragosi and Velin bowed to him with their hands over their hearts, even as another man who was braiding rope nearby dropped his work and slipped away silently to find a horse. He came to a mare tethered to a line next to the others, led her away into the shade of a grove of oak trees, mounted her and rode away into the dark in the opposite direction.

137

The man in black paced back and forth as he listened to the spy's report. When he was finished, Julianus Arkanon stopped and turned, his amber hazel eyes glittering with gold specks, gazed at him and said, "excellent. You have done well."

He tossed a pouch full of coins to the man, who caught it and eagerly opened it to inspect the contents. He added, "you will return to the circus and follow the young man when he leaves with the child. Let them not stray from your sight. When they reach their goal, ride back and report to me where they have gone, and there will be more gold to fill that pouch when you return."

"Aye, my lord," the man replied. He kept his gaze carefully averted, not daring to look into those lion's eyes for fear of the odd red glow within them. "I will do as you command." He hesitated, then ventured, "m'lord, I must warn you. There was another."

The man in black asked, "what other? Another spy?"

"Aye," the man replied. "I did see a man come to the circus but two days ago, who did ask for work. He may be in league with the hunters you seek. He keeps to himself much of the time. This day, the man Ragosi did chase him away with an axe." At that he paused to chuckle at the humor of it, then caught himself when he saw the tall man's eyebrows draw down. "He may have gone to the hunters' camp, m'lord."

"Could there be more of his ilk at the circus?"

"I do not know, m'lord."

The count studied him. The man was not lying, though his fear was tantalizing; a sharp wisp of urine lingering on the cold air. Then Julianus flicked his hand with a dismissive gesture, and the man quickly remounted his horse to ride back to the circus.

The moment the man was gone, Julianus looked out over the trees around the village and centered his focus on a wisp of smoke emerging from the forest across the river. Then he flashed his way toward the horse waiting for him near the entrance to the inn, mounted it and rode out at a gallop toward the source.

The other spy rode around the bend of the river and found an encampment of about thirty men, where he dismounted and approached the leader's tent.

When he entered he found the alderman and Baron Auric van Helsing conferring with some of his men. On seeing him, van Helsing rose from his chair and asked, "well? What words have you for me? Is he there?"

The spy doffed his cap, bowed and said, "my lord Baron, it was only his son, who did come for his sister. There was much sorrow and anger among them. They plan to depart with the dawn for the place where his father lives. But they spoke of it not, so I was unable to learn the place."

The Hessian pounded his fist into the palm of his hand and declared confidently, "that matters not. We will follow them. At last we shall have them all!"

He turned to one of his men and said, "bid the men make ready. We ride at sunset."

As the cohort left the tent and started shouting orders, the vampire hunter turned again to the spy. "Were you seen?"

"Aye," the man said with bitterness in his voice. "That man Ragosi did chase me with an axe. I cannot approach the circus again, or he would have my head on a pike."

"I will send another man in your place," the Baron replied. "You will ride with the others. Rest now. Eat and drink your fill, and be ready to leave with us in an hour's time."

"Aye, my lord Baron," the spy said, bowed, then turned and exited the tent.

One of the Baron's men leaned forward and spoke softly. "My lord Baron, what are we to do until it is time to go?"

Van Helsing parked his stocky body in the wooden chair behind him, lifted his stein and replied, "pray that the angels fight for us also. We will need all our strength for the coming storm."

The men bowed to him as they left the tent. After a moment of deep contemplation, van Helsing chuckled quietly as he took a sip of the brew in the mug. Then he had the sensation that he was not alone.

A voice, smooth and heavily accented, came from behind him. "I would not be so confident, if I were you."

Startled, van Helsing nearly dropped the stein, laid it aside on the table, rose and started to draw his sword.

The tall wraith in front of him was dressed head to toe in black, his pale face almost glowing in the lamplight, his golden amber eyes blazing red. He raised a gloved hand quickly, and in the same moment his voice thundered from everywhere and nowhere at once, robbing the hunter of his power to move. "*Stop.*"

It was like swimming in concrete. The Baron used all his strength to push against the force of that word to no avail. "What do you want? Who… are… you?" he rasped, gritting his teeth; panting with the effort to break free.

The man in black replied, "I am that which you hate and fear the most. You do not know what you are doing, do you? No, do not tell me." He closed his eyes and then opened them again. "That way lies a sure death for you and all your men."

Van Helsing's face turned red with anger. "You are the Devil's undead. A vampire. A demon with the thirst for blood. And your hellspawned evil kinsman killed my cousin. I will rid the world of all your kind to avenge his spirit."

Julian's face was a mask of dour bitterness. "So you say," he said. "Know then that I hold your life in the palm of my hand, to spare or crush as I will. My brother and his family are not to be touched, for they are innocents in this war between us. Turn away from your campaign of revenge for that fate which your cousin brought to himself, or you will not leave this tent alive."

The hunter's eyes turned to the closed flap and he opened his mouth to call out for help. An instant later, he was enveloped in blue fire and his senses vanished into burning pain, as Julianus grabbed his throat with his bare hands. Then he fell into a tight smothering embrace as the demon tugged his head back and bit him hard on his throat.

Van Helsing thrashed and flailed helplessly as fierce pain radiated from the bite, and his heartbeat pounded in his ears. He had no power to stop it as his heart started to slow down, then slowly fluttered to a stop. By then his mind had deserted him.

Julianus withdrew from drinking and let the half-cooked body slip from his arms to the floor. He turned to the flask of wine resting on the table nearby, took it and sprinkled the liquid all over the body and the carpet under it. He seized the lantern on the table and tossed it carelessly down, then backed away and left the tent through the rear flap just as the shattered glass allowed the oil to catch fire, then spread to the canvas walls and the drapes. The flames grew quickly until the tent was fully engulfed.

The other men came running and were driven back by the fire. Their attention diverted to putting it out, most did not see Julianus return to his horse, mount her and walk her silently into the sheltering darkness of the woods. But he was seen before he disappeared.

138

The dawn was grey, filled with stormclouds. Alexander had risen with the cock's crowing, and was already prepared to take Parvati in hand to ride with him, when Bela Ragosi came to him while he was adjusting his saddle cinches and said, "Erzebeta and I have come to an agreement. Pray, lend an ear to it and say if you will agree also."

"Aye?" Alexander replied.

"As Erzebeta requires all comfort for the child to come, and Parvati requires the care of a governess, we agreed that she should go with you to your new home, there to stay until Parvati is old enough to make her own way. And I will travel on with the circus to Paris, where I would be able to visit at the end of the season and name my child. Velin and I have agreed it will be so. I have found a wagon and two for a small sum. They will be ready to ride with you when you say the word."

"That is a suitable arrangement," Alexander agreed with a smile. "It would ease Parvati's comfort also, for I have been pondering the prospect of her bouncing about on my pommel for so many hours of riding."

The two men clasped arms. Then Ragosi walked back toward the cache of wagons resting under the shade of the copse. A few minutes later, a tiny caleche with a roof, pulled by two horses, came forward and clattered to a stop next to Alexander. Bela and Velin got down from the driving platform and helped Erzebeta out of the caleche, then Velin reached in and removed Parvati, who was bundled up and ready to travel, and set her on the ground.

The baby appeared to be in better spirits now that she understood the situation, and she sported her little milk teeth as she smiled up at her brother. Alexander scooped her up in his arms and planted a peck on her cheek, then asked, "are you ready to go?"

Parvati squealed her assent.

Erzebeta smiled at that and added, "she has been most eager now that I am going with her." Then she turned to her husband and reached to him. "I shall miss you. Have a safe journey to Paris. Write to me when you are able."

Ragosi took her in his arms and planted a kiss on her lips. "I shall miss you also, Beta. Safe journey to your new home, and you will ever be in my thoughts."

Erzebeta took her uncle Velin in her arms and gave him a tight hug, then said, "thank you for taking care of me, uncle."

"May fortune favor you wherever you go. Be happy in your new life," he replied.

She nodded to him, then climbed back into the caleche with Parvati in her arms, while Alexander climped up to the driving platform and took the horses' reins in hand. Ragosi tied Rose's reins to the rear of the caleche. Alexander waved a farewell to Ragosi and Velin and said, "I will see you when you come to Paris."

"You will be most welcome," Velin said.

With that, Alexander turned and drove out of the circus to a chorus of applause and shouts of "good fortune go with you, young master," and "safe journey home."

Yet, even with that joyous noise of farewell, Alexander could not dismiss the odd sensation creeping across the back of his neck. He drove a few more yards north around the bend in the road when he turned and looked behind him.

There was nothing there, or so it seemed. He had half expected to see a band of armed men riding after him. His guard up again, Alexander turned back and drove on as if nothing was wrong, but kept his left hand on his sword grip the whole way to the inn at the crossroad in Metz.

It was midafternoon when they arrived in Metz, and the inn was bustling with travelers, coaches and horses, coming and going in both directions. Alexander wisely drove the little caleche into the shade of the trees behind the inn and uncinched the horses from their yokes so that they could go to the river's edge and drink their fill.

While Erzebeta fed Parvati oat porridge and talked to her in soft tones, Alexander watched the road and the hedges for movement, still certain that they had been followed. But he could not see the spy anywhere, nor could his other senses reveal anything.

After about ten minutes of this, Erzebeta calmly asked, "My lord, what is amiss?"

Alexander turned and looked at her. "'tis nothing, lady."

"You turn about as if you are chasing your own tail," she said. "Think you we were followed?"

Alexander sighed. "It may be so," he replied gently. "We are but three travelers on the road, alone and with no retinue to defend us should highwaymen wish to take us over."

"Fear not for me, Alexander," she replied. "Bela has trained me well in the art of the sword, so I am able to defend myself and Parvati. I was not as prepared in Vienna to fight as I should have been. Grant me the privilege to fight at your side, if you would have me so."

Her words knocked him back on his heels with surprise. "Lady, I had no inkling of your education since we were together last. Your husband is wise, and I would not dishonor your skill. I would welcome it as I would any other comrade in arms."

Erzebeta smiled gently. "Then I shall gird my loins. Give me but a moment, and I shall transform myself into a soldier."

She handed Parvati over to Alexander and went into the caleche.

When she emerged five minutes later, she was clad in trousers and boots, a blouse of linen embroidered in red, and an overjacket in dark blue. Over this she wore a swordbelt with a heavily studded sash which covered her right shoulder and breast. The sword was an ivory handled scimitar, probably taken from a dead Turk after battle. Her long black hair was caught up into a tight braid which dangled from the crown of her head instead of her neck. She looked every inch like a Mongol warrior.

"I took this from a story my father told me when I was little," she explained.

Alexander favored her with a bow. "It suits you well, lady. Zounds, I should run from you rather than challenge you to a duel."

At this, Parvati squealed with glee.

The sensation that he was being watched returned full force. Alexander turned his head and caught sight of a dark shadow moving among the high grasses close by. "Pray, take Parvati and secure yourselves in the wagon," he said.

Without another word, Erzebeta scooped the child up and entered the caleche, closed the door and drew the curtains quickly.

He drew his sword as he peered beyond the flowing stalks of the tall grasses along the river, but could see nothing. The shadow seemed to retreat beyond his range of vision and the sensation faded quickly, as a duck and her ducklings parted the grassy veil across the river and entered the water.

Slowly, he lowered his sabre and resheathed it, took a slow calming breath, and admonished himself for finding an attacker in every bush and tree. He called, "all is well."

Erzebeta came out of the wagon alone and joined him. "She is asleep now," she said. "Let us go now, before the sun sets. It is best that we should for her sake."

"I defer to your wisdom, lady," he replied.

When the horses were rehitched Alexander mounted Rose and led the way onto the road, Erzebeta and the caleche rattling along behind him.

They made good time, and when the stars came out in their millions, they had arrived at the halfway point on the road. There, they entered a grove of oak trees, where Erzebeta parked the caleche behind a thicket of juniper bushes. Alexander dutifully watched for danger while Erzebeta fed Parvati more oat porridge and goat's milk. But he felt more confident that the shadows would not disturb them here.

He listened while the woman murmured a soft lullaby into the toddler's ear, rocking her gently until the babe fell asleep again; then watched her carry Parvati's sleeping body back into the caleche to bed her down for the night.

When she emerged again, Erzebeta sat down next to him on the log and silently gazed up toward the stars. They barely exchanged a word between them until she decided it was too cold to stay outside. She rose silently and drew her colorful shawl more closely around her, laid a gentle hand on his shoulder, then entered the caleche and closed the door silently, leaving him alone with his tangled thoughts.

139

The birds were in full twitter and the horses milled about and gamboled on the meadow as Alexander and the caleche reached the outer gate of the estate. But this time, the guard was prepared to receive him, and shouts of "open the gate!" greeted him as he approached the giant doors. Slowly, the panels swung open and admitted him onto the courtyard, the caleche following closely behind.

He led the way to the front of the main house, where Flandres met him on the steps. "Welcome home, Monsieur le Comte," Flandres said.

Dismounting quickly, Alexander replied, "thank you. It is good to be home. How fares my father?"

"He is well. And who have you brought home with you?"

Alexander turned and helped Erzebeta down from the driving platform. "May I present the lady Erzebeta Ragosi. She is my sister's governess."

Erzebeta went into the caleche and emerged with Parvati in her arms. "She has had a long journey," she said with a short smile. Parvati appeared to have slept the whole morning through.

Flandres looked down at the small sleeping face, and he said to her with a small smile, "I have prepared a nice room for the child, and there is a room next to it which you may call your own. The master has stressed that all comfort be given you during your stay."

Alexander replied, "indeed, he is the wisest and kindest of us all."

Flandres turned to him and said, "I will send for a boy to take the horses down to the stable."

Alexander asked. "Where is my father?"

Flandres looked up as if he was trying to remember and then replied, "I have not seen him all the day, Monsieur le Comte, but he may be in the chapel."

"The chapel?"

"Yes. He has been working to restore some of the frescoes adorning the walls. They had been left in a shocking state by our old master. He thinks that some of them might be saved."

"Very well," Alexander said. "I will see him directly. Please see the lady and my sister to their rooms and tend to their needs."

"Come with me," Flandres said to Erzebeta, and led the way into the house.

Alexander stared after him. If he was not mistaken, he could sense an air of prejudice trailing after the giant like the stink from a charnel house. Then he shrugged it off and, removing his saddle pack from Rose, followed them into the house.

After doffing his traveling clothes, Alexander went up to his room and deposited his saddle pack on his bed, then returned to the ground floor. He strolled down the hall toward the rear of the house and, once he had found it, followed a trail of his father's bloodscent to a short flight of stairs leading down into darkness.

The door to the chapel stood open. It was a small room, supported by a pair of columns flanking the narrow nave, and surrounded on three sides with frescoes of medieval art. What looked like a skylight covered in stained glass provided most of the illumination, leaving the rest in shadow. Candles had been lit nearby to provide more illumination.

Alexander walked in slowly and found Lucien standing in front of one of the frescoes, paintbrush in hand, contemplating a spot he had been cleaning by the light of a small lantern resting on a scaffold. He wore his usual black but the front was covered with a white apron to catch any splatters.

On Alexander's entrance, Lucien put the brush aside on the scaffolding and approached him, pulled him into a bear hug and said, "it is so good to have you home again, Alexander."

"It is good to be home, father," Alexander replied.

Lucien released him. "I trust Parvati is safe? Nothing happened to deter you?"

"Nothing at all, father. In fact, I was able to bring Erzebeta home with us, that she may remain her governess."

Lucien's eyebrows crept upward. "Aye? How did you achieve this miraculous event? What said you to convince her?"

He shrugged modestly. "I said nothing. It was Bela who did the suggesting, and her uncle Velin went along. Parvati and the woman have cleaved together as one in ways I can scarcely explain."

Carefully, Alexander related the story of their exile from Vienna, and when he was finished, Lucien stood staring off into infinity for what seemed an age before he spoke again. "I have never before heard of such a thing. My daughter, accused of witchery?"

"Had you been there, your blood would have run cold as ice, as surely as did mine," Alexander said. "By all outward appearance and comportment she is still an innocent babe, but I now fear she is more powerful than anyone can know."

Lucien tore the apron loose from his clothes and tossed it aside as he said, "then I must go to her. Now." He led the way out the door and walked up the narrow stairs swiftly, then climbed the stairs to the upper floor by threes to the landing. Alexander followed, filled with trepidation, as they went to the door to Parvati's room.

Erzebeta was busily preparing Parvati for bed, when she looked up with suprise and saw Lucien standing in the threshhold. "My lord," she said, and stood aside, bowing her head to avoid meeting his eyes. She had changed back into a woman. Alexander could sense that she was frightened, though he was not sure why.

Lucien ignored her, went to Parvati and picked her up, hugging her close. "I am here, dearest," he said. "I never forgot you. I meant to return for you, but was delayed much. It is no matter now that you are here. You are safe. You are home. No one will hurt you or be cross with you again."

Parvati's eyes teared up again, and she hugged his neck desperately. "Papa," was the only thing she said as she dissolved into sobbing again.

Alexander watched them together and felt as if the sorrow would break his heart. Yet among the slivers of pain a glimmer of joy for her homecoming emerged to banish them.

Lucien turned to Erzebeta and said, "I am most grateful to you for taking care of my daughter. From what Alexander has told me, you suffered much for her sake. You will be welcome in our house for as long as you wish to stay."

"I only wish to make Parvati happy," Erzebeta replied. "I am also quick with child. With your kind permission, I would be honored to bear it here and raise both together, that Parvati may have a sibling withal. Parvati rescued me from despair and brought me nothing but happiness. All that I have suffered for her sake I would do again, and gladly."

"Then it is agreed, and you have a place here. Welcome to House Arkanon," he said. Then to Parvati he said, "I must go for now, but be good and mind Aunt Beta. You must be tired. It is time for a nap. But I will see you at supper. Yes?"

Parvati's tears had dried, and she raised her head to smile at him. "Yes, Papa."

"Good!" He relinquished his hold and passed her to Erzebeta, telling her, "come down and have supper when you are ready."

She nodded and took the toddler as Lucien left the room with Alexander following him closely behind.

Once the door closed, Lucien turned to Alexander and said, "You are right. Parvati will have to be watched carefully, that she does not lose herself to the despair residing within her." He paused for a moment in reflection, but his face brightened again as he said, "but you must also be tired. Rest now and refresh yourself. I must finish that little piece in the chapel, then meet with my future bride's agents, who return even now with a response to my portrait."

"May I see it?" he asked.

Lucien nodded. "Come to supper at eight and I will share with you all that has happened in your absence."

Upon returning to his own room, Alexander took his journal book from his pack, leafed through it until he found where he had entered something last, then searched in the rolltop desk for a pen and ink. After he wrote of his adventures, he found that he could not keep his eyes open, went to his bed and removed his boots; threw them in the corner to air out, and fell back on the coverlet. Before long, he fell into a deep, dark sleep.

140

It was dark when he woke, and Alexander rose up quickly with his heart pounding and a cry of terror lodged in his throat. The nightmare vanished from memory almost at once, as before. He sat for a few breathless moments to find his center again, and looked around carefully with the strange sensation that he was not alone in the room. But there was nothing there.

Combing his hair back out of his face, he rose and went to the window to look out. He could see the watchfires at the wall, and a group of guards standing on the flagstones of the courtyard conversing with each other in furtive tones. All seemed calm and tranquil on the outside. He took a few cleansing breaths and worked to calm himself down before he turned to changing his clothes and getting ready for dinner.

When he had dressed, Alexander found his way down the stairs to the dining room, where Lucien sat at the head of the table. Erzebeta and Parvati were already seated to his right, and there was an empty chair to his left. There were no servants anywhere.

Lucien looked up at his entrance and said, "ah, there you are. Come, take your place at the table."

"Was I late?" Alexander asked as he obeyed. "I fear I overslept."

"Nay," Lucien replied. "I thought it prudent not to disturb you after all that you have done."

The table was laid out with food and drink, all of it for Erzebeta's benefit. A single silver goblet was all which sat in front of Lucien. He reached for another and filled it with something red from a decanter, which he offered to Alexander. "Wine?" he asked, with a subtle glance to his right.

Taking the cue, Alexander reached for the goblet and found that the wine was actually blood. He sniffed at it and narrowed the scent to sheep from the larder, then took a sip. It was rich and fresh, and he found himself drinking more. "It is quite adequate," he remarked quietly.

"I have found our cellars to be well stocked, though I think the vintage could be improved. I will look into finding more from the surrounding vintners."

"Granted," Alexander said as he drained the rest and put the goblet aside. "But, it is enough for me. I fear my head is not yet ready for… more wine."

Lucien then turned to Erzebeta and asked, "what would please you?"

"If you please, my lord, perhaps a little meat. And a piece of that glorious bread," she replied.

"Help yourself to all," he said, and handed her the serving fork and carving knife. "We do not stand on ceremony."

Erzebeta rose and reached for the platter, placed it before her and carved off a good sized hunk of beef, passed it to her plate, then reached for the loaf, which was still warm from baking, and carved a piece of that. She added two small potatoes. Smiling awkwardly, she put the platters aside and sat down again.

"Now. Would you prefer wine or water?" Lucien asked.

"Water, if you please."

He picked up another decanter and poured from it into her goblet. Erzebeta picked it up and took a careful taste. "It is very good and sweet," she remarked. "Nothing like what we had in Strasbourg."

"I am pleased you think so," he replied. "We get it from a spring which feeds the river, and it has properties you might find to your benefit. In fact, it will aid you to sleep better through the night, and help you to carry your child to term."

"My thanks," she replied. Then she drank more, and put the goblet down to eat. She paused with a forkful of the meat in midair and said, "but, you are not eating?"

"I find I have little appetite today," Lucien replied. "But do eat your fill."

Alexander reached for the bread and tore off a hunk, then sat chewing it and chose that moment to broach the subject. "So, father. Tell me of your new bride."

"Ah," Lucien said, and turned to him. "The agents sent to me were solicitous and approached the issue of my betrothal with grace and fair diplomacy. You recall that I was resistent to such a union, as Sarasvati is hard to replace in my heart. Once I saw the lady's portrait, however, I changed my mind. She is beauteous beyond compare, and they told me that she of an unassuming and modest spirit. She has been well educated in the arts and science, letters, and some music. Eh…harpsichord, I am told, and violin."

"Her portrait. May I see it?"

"I have it here," he said, and turned to pick up a miniature, no bigger than six inches across, which he handed over.

Alexander beheld a vision in blue, with a pale face and cloud of the lightest blonde hair he had ever seen. Her eyes were frost blue, and her neck was long, surrounded by a simple string of pearls and a collar of lace. Her mouth was a pair of supple and generous lips tinged with rose. She was very young and had the expression of mild apprehension, as if she was caught by surprise.

"Beautiful," Alexander said. "Yet she appears to me a trifle shy."

"It was the same assessment I had when I first saw it," Lucien said. "But, that expression may have been for the artist. I feel certain that she will be a beautiful addition to the household."

"May I see it also?" Erzebeta said. "I would know what my new mistress will look like."

Lucien took it from Alexander and handed it over. After a long moment of contemplation, she said, "I see what you mean. I hope she will be all that you desire in a wife."

"That will take time, lady," Lucien replied, then hesitated for a long moment before adding, "it will be her choice to accept me or reject me as I am. You will find that I am different from other men in many ways when you live in this house."

"But why should she reject you?" she said. "My uncle told me of your true nature, and it is of no consequence to me. By your deeds I know you to be a worthy and gentle lord, who cannot help being what he is."

Both vampires stared at her with astonishment. It seemed miraculous to Alexander, who said, "how long have you known?"

"Since the day you brought Parvati to me to care for. Uncle Velin told me the truth of you to prepare me for the moment when I should give her up."

There was a long silence among them as her statement settled into it like a fall of leaves. Then Lucien said, "perhaps that is to the good, for you would have learned the truth in time on your own. There is no reason to be afrighted of us, and if you are, you must tell me."

Alexander chose to keep his silence and returned to the subject by asking, "and when are you expecting the lady?"

That appeared to break the apprehension. "On the morrow," Lucien replied. "I am having Flandres prepare another set of rooms for her and her maidservant, that they may rest comfortably. The agents will inform me what other things I must do to complete my obligation to the king. Oh, you will stay for the wedding ceremony?"

"Aye, father," Alexander replied. "After that I must return to Paris. The king expects me to resume his fencing lessons, and I must also return to the academy, where my other pupils are awaiting me. I should not tarry longer than another day."

"I would not presume to delay you," Lucien replied blandly. "I have also been thinking on forging a sword of my own, that one day I should take it up again. I have been so consumed with my duties at the stable that I should have more practice. You will return at the Noelle holiday and be my instructor. You are the only master of the sword I have to rely on. I have heard from Gravet that your friend Cyrano de Bergerac died most shamefully. And there are... other concerns... which give me a reminder that I must be on my mettle."

"I would be happy to," Alexander replied. "The alchemy of the sword I will leave to you."

"Quite so. It will be a challenge for me to rediscover the secrets of the ancients' forge."

"But what of those frescoes?"

Lucien stared at him. "What of them?"

"You cannot divide yourself in twain, father, as you are so fond of reminding me."

"Hmmm." Lucien shrugged as he replied, "they have been there in the chapel for centuries. They are not going to go anywhere, are they?"

Alexander smiled for Erzebeta's benefit as she watched them talking. "I suppose not, but you are a better steward of your time than I am. And the stable?"

"It is so well managed now that I feel I have no place there," he said. "I settled a brief squabble among the stewards of the evening with the stewards of the day, that they should allow their duties to overlap, so that there is no interruption of care for the horses. And, the issue of increasing their wages so that they can provide for pensions of their own. I do return at odd times to inspect, and keep that to myself, so the stewards cannot know when I will arrive."

He chuckled a bit, then reached for the decanter and poured a smidgeon of more blood into it. "They are more circumspect and efficient for it."

"Then you are not drawn to remain in the house," Alexander said. "Flandres tells me you keep to it more and more."

"That is because I keep finding ever more amazing discoveries within these walls," Lucien replied with a small gesture. "They hold more stories for me than I can scarcely imagine. I hear the servants whispering about us and say nothing, nor do I try to stop them. They are like mice skittering in the wainscotting. Their gossip is even charming at times, and I learn more about their lives than they would tell me on their own. Each of them knows his or her place in the household, and each is loyal to me, whether they know it or not."

He took another sip from the goblet, then added, "and I have new books delivered to me whenever I can obtain them. There are some that I have not yet touched, so there is ever more work to be done in the library. I could never say that I am bored with this new life."

That made Alexander feel better, and now that the house would have more people in it, he felt even better about leaving Lucien alone. "I have no doubt," he replied.

"So, you need not fear that I have gone mad."

Lucien's statement caught him by surprise, and Alexander sputtered a bit before he managed, "'twas not my fear, father. I merely expressed a concern. I am told that you were loathe to manage the stable, but from what you say my concern is unfounded."

Their attention had been drawn away from Erzebeta, who made a sound of pain. By the time they looked, she had shrunk away from Parvati, cradling her right hand with her left. Parvati sat in her high chair with a strange hungry expression on her face and a small tinge of red on her lips.

Alexander asked, "what has happened?"

"It is nothing, my lord," Erzebeta replied, her whole body trembling. "I must have done something to cause her pain, and she bit me."

"Bit you?" Lucien asked, and his pale eyebrows drew down as he leaned toward her. "Why should she bite you?"

"She had done it before, when we were in Vienna. She had taken to trapping birds, mice, other small animals to feed upon, but when I discovered this she tried to hide them from me. I told her it was not meet that she should do these things, that killing them was not right. And," and here she looked down with sudden shame, "I have been giving her some of mine own blood to stop her from..."

"Your blood!?" came out of Lucien's mouth as rolling thunder.

"Please forgive me," she exclaimed with some desperation. "Parvati requires only a little. A thimbleful, nothing more, every other day."

Lucien rose stiffly, nearly tipping his chair as he backed away. "This is terrible. It explains much of her behavior. Alexander told me what happened on the road, and you.... you did not?"

"It did not think it my place to," she said, "and dear Parvati needed it. I feared what she would do without it."

Parvati sat staring at the flames in the fireplace without saying a word, as if the conversation was not meant for her. Even the sound of Lucien's voice did not stir her to make a sound.

"How had you been feeding her?" he asked.

Erzebeta raised her right index finger. Across it was a dark red scab. "I put it in her cow's milk, when I could get it. And when we were driven out of Vienna, I fed her this way so that she would not hunt and be discovered. Please, do not be angry, my lord. I did not know what else to do." She took her napkin to cover her face as she squeezed her eyes shut.

All the battle tension receded from Lucien's body, and he took a deep breath as he said to her, "it is I who should be to blame. You have done nothing to merit this. Pray, forgive me."

He turned to Parvati and said to her, "child, you know not what you do. It is your nature. But only know that I love you. In time it may mean all or mean nothing to you, but I cannot reach you now."

Alexander stared at the toddler's passive sober face and wondered what the future would bring. Would she become nosferatu or outgrow this? Lucien had told him before that children were never to be subject to turning, nor were they to be preyed upon. But Parvati had always been different since she was born. Her senses were already heightened beyond what would be natural for an Antellan.

As if she had read his thoughts, Parvati turned her grey eyes to look at him, and a small tremor passed across her lips as if she wanted to say something, but then she turned away again and stared into the flames once more.

Alexander suppressed the shudder which passed through his frame as he looked up at his father and said, "only time and the dragon's blood will tell."

"The question is now what the servants will say or do, what the king's agents or my future wife will do, when they see her this way," Lucien said. "We will have to lock Parvati away until she is older, and then we will learn which path she has chosen."

Erzebeta spoke up. "My lord, I will stay with her and teach her to avoid the darkness within her. She is all I have."

"You will have all you require to help you," Lucien said. "But pray, finish your supper before it grows cold."

She hesitated before she lowered the napkin, blew her nose into it, then dug in to eat, as Lucien put another log on the fire, stirred the flaming wood, then returned to his seat.

Alexander mentally lashed himself for having left Parvati behind for so long, and wished he could turn back the hands of time. But now it was too late.

141

Alexander was already up and dressed when shouts of "open the gate!" drifted to him on the breeze through the open window.

He had dressed in what was considered Sunday best, having found a suitable ensemble with Flandres's help among those the old master had left behind. Still, the collar of his linen blousing was a bit tight, and he kept pulling at it to loosen the ruff. His weskit and overjacket was of pale green, over trousers of dark mustard with lace cuffs; not his favorite colors, but there was little he could do about it.

Flandres assured him that the pale green set off his grey eyes, with the added note that it was not his habit to judge a man's appearance by feminine standards of beauty. "But truly you would be more fair to look upon if I were a woman," he said. "I will have the seamstress take it in for you."

Alexander found that the woolen hose were worn at the heels and toes, no doubt because the previous owner was wont to hike about on the meadows quite often.

The entire outfit was slightly out of fashion, but men's fashions tended to remain the same for decades before a subtle change occurred: the trousers went a little tighter, the length of the overjacket went longer or shorter. Trim or no trim; ribbons and lace or plain and severe; governed by whims of convention and the materials at hand. Fabric was expensive, silks and brocades especially; and recycling of used materials went on as a matter of course.

Suits were disassembled and reassembled by the tailors. As prosperous as the aristocracy appeared to be, they were no better off than the bourgeoises; prone also to be miserly with their funds and thrifty to a fault. But fashion was fashion in France, and had to be followed with strict rigor to avoid the judgment and criticism of their peers.

Alexander had drawn his hair back and tied it with a ribbon of the same color silk as his overjacket, and admired himself briefly in the glass of a standing mirror. Thus attaining a state of reasonable presentment, he descended the stairs and arrived at the front door just in time for a carriage and four to roll up with an escort of musketeers on horseback. Lucien, Reneau and Flandres were already there, waiting for the carriage door to be opened.

Today, Lucien did not wear black, choosing instead a luscious emerald green with ivory trim. His white hair was sectioned in three parts, swept back and tied neatly with a green ribbon. He looked every inch the country gentleman.

Flandres was dressed in grey with maroon trim, and his pumps were set with silver buckles. He had managed to tie back his wild curly hair with a ribbon, but it appeared to be escaping every time he moved.

Reneau wore another ensemble in golden brown which only accentuated his eyes and sturdy girth.

Lucien turned when he saw Alexander and nodded his approval, but said nothing.

The footman descended from his post on the roof of the carriage and drew the steps down, opened the door and offered his hand.

A middle aged woman wearing a rose dust coat with a hood over her clothes took his hand and emerged. When she was on the flagstones she stood aside. A smaller gloved hand preceded the vision in the portrait as she also emerged.

Alexander's breath was taken away as he saw her life sized. She looked to be no older than about twenty, wearing a modest cloak and a high collared gown in blue; and as she removed a mantilla of lace from her face and drew it back, he could see her pale blonde locks were piled up on her head and pinned in place with small diamonds.

She kept her eyes shyly directed toward the flagstones beneath her feet as the chaplain also left the carriage and joined her.

Lucien said to the chaplain, "I am Lucien Arkanon, Comte du Rouen. Welcome to our house."

The chaplain took the lead and replied, "I am the Comte abbe' des Sonnes, and it is my pleasure to introduce to you la Comtesse

Ingrid van der Hummerling and her chaperone, Madame Lucille de Petit Tourlons."

"Your rooms have been prepared," Lucien replied. "Flandres will see to your luggage." As was custom, he did not address the young countess directly, but relied on the chaplain to relay the conversation. "Emmm...I trust the journey was not long, and free of incident?"

"We had but a minor delay at the bridge," the chaplain replied. "We were forced to go around and cross at a different ford. The agents did inform us of the state of repairs, but as all things do in the countryside, they proceed at a snail's pace."

"Ah. Quite so. I too do not know when it will be repaired. The storm was unexpected, and caused much damage to it."

The chaplain said, "it is regretable. But that matters not. We are here at last, thanks be to God." He crossed himself.

Lucien glanced at Alexander and beckoned to him. "And this is my son, the Comte Alexandre Vincent Corvina."

Alexander advanced a few steps and said, "welcome to our house. I hope you will enjoy all we have to offer."

At this, the intended bride looked up subtly, and on seeing him, stifled a blush and a sudden giggle.

Alexander glanced down at his clothes and guessed that it was his appearance which caused her reaction. Embarassed by her appraisal, he said nothing more.

Madame de Petit Tourlons rescued him with, "Madame la Comtesse, please comport yourself with some grace."

"My apologies, Lucille," she said. Then she turned to Lucien. "I meant no offense," she added. "I was merely taken by surprise. No one told me that you had a son. You do not look old enough to have fathered a grown man."

"I confess that I am older than I appear," he replied. "I trust my portrait told you something more than that."

"Non," she replied. "It only touched my heart. I am a widow, Monsieur le Comte, but my husband did not live long enough for me to fulfill my duties as a wife. Will you have me so?"

"Come inside, all of you, and we will talk," he said, and led the way into the foyer.

Alexander trailed after him and watched as the women looked around at the walls and the décor. It remained simple but stylish, and

Lucien had not done more than have the house cleaned and the furniture polished.

The chaplain gave it an appraising glance of approval as he removed his cape, and said, "what a charming place." He paused to hand the cape to Flandres, who waited for the women to doff their overgarments.

Lucien replied, "my thanks, Monsieur l'Abbe'. It was in a state of disrepair when we moved in, but I have spared no expense to have it restored. I find that I cannot live in a new house, and prefer the comfort of old things."

"Then you appreciate history," the chaplain said. "That is a rare commodity in these times."

"Yet, what better time than to be here, now, on the precipice of change. The world is a better place now than in the past."

"Indeed. It was not a century ago that we were embroiled in pestilence, war, famine… and yet we survived. France goes on, thanks be to God." He crossed himself again.

Alexander paused at the lintel and listened, then said, "father, shall I tamp the fire in the parlor?"

"Aye, if you would be so good," Lucien replied. "Monsieur, precede me, if you please."

He gestured toward the door leading into the main parlor, which was decorated with couches and sofachairs covered in sumptuous fabrics. Alexander remembered when he first saw it, and was struck dumb by the wonder of it. Everything had been cleaned and restored, and the candelabras on the fireplace mantelpiece gleamed brightly in the golden firelight.

The countess and her chaperone entered the parlor and stood admiring the decor, looking for all the world like a painting of domestic peace.

Stirring himself free of fascination, Alexander went to the fireplace and stirred at the logs with a poker, added another to them and made sure it caught fire before he laid the iron aside; then went to a sofachair nearby and seated himself.

Over the next hour and a half, the parlor was filled with inconsequential chitchat, during which Lucien and the countess learned a bit more about each other, and Alexander was eyewitness to it all.

596

After a time, he came to the conclusion that there was no way that Lucien could deny himself the company of this enchanting creature, who kept pace with his discussions with equal intelligence. She appeared to have more knowledge of science than Lucien; or perhaps Lucien was allowing her to keep the lead for appearance's sake. But the illusion could have easily been destroyed by Lucien's alien knowledge of science and technologies which would have rendered all the latest innovations as primitive as the discovery of fire.

For his part, Alexander was still learning, still studying the newest concepts in science and mathematics. It was all new and amazing to him. The countess spoke of what she had read, and mentioned books newly in print. Lucien peppered her with questions about the authors, the subjects and her level of understanding. It seemed as if they could go all night about books.

Through it all, the chaplain appeared to be growing uncomfortable with the conversation, because his religion was slowly being replaced with the realm of the five senses. Alexander himself said that there was no room for religion in the world, for faith required a belief in what was not provable.

But, rather than fall to arguing the chaplain's pointed remonstrance on faith versus science, Lucien deflected it all with a few deft words in reply, "but what makes you believe that science is not an artifact of God, or that God is not an artifact of science? If all is as you claim, Monsieur l'Abbe', and God made the universe, all things within it must be from God, including science and mathematics."

The chaplain gaped without a sound, worked his mouth as if to fashion words, but was unable to. Then he said, "I will have to think about that, and consult with my monsigneur. I have never thought of the world in such a way before."

"I would not think of leading you astray, Monsieur l'Abbe'," Lucien replied. "Other men of faith have asked questions like these for centuries. We have seen advances in the betterment of ourselves by embracing the alchemies of the old. You may ask as many questions as will grant you knowledge to your certainty. I shall not strive to sway your convictions, but you must also allow me mine."

"I would not presume to rob you of them, Monsieur le Comte," the abbe' said, as he fiddled with the rosary dangling from his neck.

Lucien chose to end the parlor talk by picking up a bell and ringing it. A few moments later, Flandres appeared at the door and asked, "you rang, master?"

"Yes, Flandres. Please inform me when supper is prepared. I will see these guests to their rooms myself."

Flandres said, "ah, yes. It is the suite on the second floor, to the east side with a view of the hills and the sunrise. I have already started fires in their rooms to warm them."

"Most excellently done," Lucien replied. "My thanks." He rose and gestured to his three guests. "If you will follow me?"

Each of them was given a room, the women in a pair next to each other with an adjoining door; while the abbe' was placed in a room two doors farther to the south. When they were placed and comfortable, Lucien and Alexander left them to unpack and return to the downstairs to consult with Flandres abour the supper fare.

Today there would be squab and roast mutton, vegetables, potatoes, and sweet bread. To his surprise, Alexander learned that Lucien had baked the bread himself.

"How do you find the time to do it all?" he asked.

"I do a little at a time," Lucien replied. "I am never idle. Between managing the house and the stable, as well as devotion to my library, I find that there is little time wasted for me, and I am always finding new things to fascinate me."

"And, when do you sleep?"

Lucien turned and regarded him with a faint smile. "I do find my rest, Alexander. Never fear." Then he sighed. "I will have to rearrange my time when the Comtesse and I are married. I must make time for her also. Tell me, what think you of her?"

"She is very young and beautiful. I hope she will make you happy, or at least content with married life."

"I only hope that she will be happy with me," he replied. "Or also content. I would not have her turn away from me in fear."

"How could she? You are so like those bats we saw in Romania, full of familiar warmth and domesticity. I have seen your gentle nature, and also your fury. She will appreciate your protection alone, and I cannot believe that she would reject you once she understands the truth of you."

"I do not know her well enough to love her yet, and that concerns me," Lucien said. "It is not the same as what Sarasvati gave me. We were besotted with love from the first moment we met, as if it was all we lived for. I was her supplicant in love, Alexander, and she was my goddess. But this frail and beautiful child must be nurtured and raised like a flower, treated like a porcelain doll, with all creature comforts at her beck and call. She would be too easily shattered if she was to learn the truth too soon."

"Can you not compel her, then?"

"Compel her?" Lucien said, taken aback with shock. "I would not stoop so low. For shame, Alexander. You cannot ask that of me."

"It was nought but a suggestion," Alexander replied, retreating from it quickly. "But, what other alternative is there?"

"I will have to think on it further. But now, let us continue to be human until I find a way to win her heart without resorting to such a distasteful and devious measure."

"Then, are you not in love with her already?"

"It is hard not to be, as you can easily see. Indeed, I should be surprised if you are not also. But it is by the king's command that I take her, whether she be frail or not. These arrangements are often lacking in love when they are entered into for the good of the state. I would not have it so for her sake."

"Then I trust you will find a way to please her," Alexander said. "I am sure it was so with my mother."

"Your mother and stepmother trusted me. It may not be so with the Comtesse. But only time will tell what happens now."

142

The next morning, the wedding ceremony was conducted in the close, tomblike chapel beneath the ground floor. It was lit by a thousand candles. With Alexander and most of the servants as witnesses, and with the chaperone Madame de Petit Turlons standing by as a maid of honor, Lucien and the young countess were joined together.

Both of them wore black in the German manner, and the abbe' wore a white cassock, with a purple vestry scarf draped over it. He recited the marriage invocations in Latin while the couple faced each other on their knees.

They exchanged rings, then the abbe' draped another scarf of red and gold over their hands and tied them together. He finished with another prayer in Latin, took a pestle moistened with holy water and sprinkled their bound handclasp with it, crossed the air between them, then said, "you are now married, joined together before God as husband and wife. May God bless and keep you, and grant you many children. Now rise, kiss each other, and consummate your troth."

Together, Lucien and Ingrid rose to their feet, leaned together and exchanged a chaste little kiss, then turned to face the small congregation. Everyone erupted into cheering and applause as the Comte and Comtesse du Rouen passed among them and exited the chapel together. Alexander followed, and the rest followed him.

As he watched them ascend the stairs to the second floor together, Alexander hoped that their union would be as happy as he could imagine as he joined in the celebrations on the ground floor.

But after an hour it was as if life had ground to a slow and gentle halt. He began to feel alien, out of place once again. Something dragged him away from the others, a vague feeling of danger, and he went out onto the veranda to find fresh air and the solace to think.

He looked out onto the meadows and watched the horses in their hundreds as he tried to sort out what was in his head.

A voice, heavily accented, told him, "come. Not as bad as that."

Alexander whirled, and found himself face to face with Julianus, clad in dark clothes with a hat over his dark hair and a purple scarf which obscured his face. But the golden amber eyes were unmistakable. Alexander fell back reaching for his sabre and found nothing, realizing to his horror that he was unarmed in peace; while the tall wraith stepped forward with a beseeching hand gloved in leather.

"I come in peace," Julianus said, as if he had read his mind.

"You are not welcome here, uncle," Alexander said.

"You are not in a position to decide that," Julianus replied with a calm smile. "I came only to see for myself the truth of what has been told to me. Lucien has already claimed another bride for himself, has he not? And as is his wont, did not invite me to his celebrations."

"You call him brother, when you have tormented him all your lives," Alexander husked. "You are nought more than those baseless cowards who raped and pillaged their way across..."

The hand that cut him off knocked him back across the veranda railing, nearly toppling him over it; and stars flashed in front of his eyes as painful throbbing caught his lips. A grip of steel caught him by the arm before he fell, and the wolf's voice snarled into his ear, "quiet, whelp. Think you I enjoyed every blood soaked moment of it? I did all to survive, and by surviving, saved your father from an early doom. You should be thanking me, not insulting me."

The words were out his mouth before he could stop them. "And what about my mother? You took her life and dignity from her without compassion, and sowed the seeds of your own humiliation with the deed. You tried to kill me in the forest, not welcome me as an uncle should. I shall never forgive the dishonor you have brought our family."

The wraith released him and pushed him away abruptly as if to reject the unclean notion. "Is that what he told you? It is nought but a tapestry of lies!"

"Then tell me truly, and I may temper my reason with it. Why then do I see in my mind and feel in my heart the cruel death of my mother by your hand? Perhaps it is what you hide in the innermost part of you, and I have borne the memory of it since. You stink of murder, Julianus. Were I not unarmed at this moment I should be justified to seek revenge. It is only for the sake of my father's life that I do not dispatch you like the dog you are."

"Then count yourself in good company, Alexander, and remember that if I die, he dies," Julianus snarled again. "I have already removed an adversary of ours from the world. That craven soldier of fortune, van Helsing, will pursue you no more. Perhaps when you have dug yourself out of your self righteousness you will remember that. But only know this. The next time we meet, I may not be quite so magnanimous and spare your life, nephew or not."

At that moment, another familiar voice pierced the veil of bitterness. "You threaten Alexander at your peril."

Alexander turned, and saw Lucien standing a few feet away, Musashi's katana in his hand. He had it raised about shoulder height with his left hand ready to support it. He had stripped down to his undershirt and weskit, and stood with his grey silver eyes blazing red over a grim, set mouth.

A scant second later, the wraith backed farther away and growled, "Lucien. We meet again, dear brother."

Lucien sniffed. "As always, the air around you reeks of death. It was not hard to guess that it was you who has been haunting the compound these many weeks. But I warned you what would happen if you visited your unpleasantness upon us again."

"And, are you ready for it? I think not," Julian growled back. "You are married again, I see. Is she ready for the truth? Does she know what you really are?"

"She shall learn it with gentle words, and not with the taking of your sort of liberties. Remember this, Julianus. If you threaten me and mine again, it is I who shall hunt you down and put an end to you. Go, before I lose my temper and do something we shall both regret."

Julianus drew himself straight, seeming to tower over his younger brother. "We shall see about that. I have always bested you. Practice well, because when we meet again I shall not stay my hand against you."

Lucien shifted his grip on the katana and said, "I shall look forward to the day, nor shall I stay mine."

The wraith quickly backed into the shadows and did not come out, vanishing with the warm afternoon breeze.

Lucien lowered the katana and went to Alexander, who stood rubbing at a spot on his jaw where Julian had punched him. "It was good fortune which brought me to you, and just in time," he said. "Had I delayed I know not what else he would have done to you."

"He caught me by surprise," Alexander replied. "The fault was mine for going without a blade as my instincts foretold me. But he brought me news which may gladden your heart, if you can stand that it came from him."

"Pray, enlighten me," Lucien said.

"He said that the Baron van Helsing is dead, and will not pursue us further. By his speech alone, I divined that he must have murdered the man himself."

Lucien nodded soberly. "That is an admirable conclusion, indeed."

"But, think you he will return? Now that he has found you, will he stay away? He comes and goes as he pleases, without concern for anyone but himself and his passions. Will you and your bride be safe here if I leave you and return to Paris?"

Lucien turned and regarded him with the face of a judge. "Is that what you have been pondering out here, instead of within?"

"Aye, father," Alexander replied. "Of a sudden, I felt that I needed… space… and air to breathe, that I could calm my restless thoughts. It was then that he caught me."

"If he had wanted to, he could have just as easily killed you. But only he knows what his plans are, and I cannot think why he spared you." He looked around to make sure they were not overheard, then added, "you had better come inside and rest now, as the others have already retired to their rooms for an afternoon nap. It is a new rule of the household, as the heat of the day is often too much for their labors. We shall talk later. I must return to the Comtesse and assure her that all is at peace."

With that, he marched into the house without looking back. Alexander straightened his clothes and smoothed back a dark lock of his hair, then followed him.

143

It was not until the sun sank below the hills that Alexander woke again. He rose and dressed in something less formal, then ventured down the stairs in search of Flandres, who was busy setting the hearthfires for evening.

The blond giant looked up at his entrance into the sitting parlor with a startled look on his face. "Monsieur le Comte, you walk silently as a ghost," he said, when he had found breath again.

Alexander stroked at his chin thoughtfully, and found no more pain there. "So I have been told before, I believe."

"Shall I get you a refreshment?"

"No." Alexander shifted impatiently on his feet, then said, "I saw the way you looked at my sister and her governess when they arrived. Is there something about them which meets with your disapproval?"

The giant's eyebrows went up, and his gullet went up and down as he swallowed. "Nay, Monsieur le Comte."

"My father and I agree on our acceptance of people of other skins and faiths as kindred spirits," Alexander said. "If you are uncomfortable with this, you should have told either one of us. We have no need for prejudice of any kind in this house. Is that clearly understood?"

"I apologize most abjectly, Monsieur le Comte," Flandres replied. "It is not my place to pass judgment on others. It is a sin before God, no? I will seek absolution at my next confession."

"Good. Kindly pass the word to the other servants that all who pass through these doors are worthy of equal respect."

Flandres bowed slightly. "I defer to your wisdom in these matters. I will try to be a better man."

"Very well. What is on the menu for supper?"

"Tonight, there will be roast mutton again, carrots from the garden and endive salad. I will make sure that there is a porridge with vegetables made for the child." Then he added, "eh... I believe I can add a soupçon of lamb's blood to the porridge, that the child will have more to nourish her..."

Alexander was not surprised by the houseman's admission. No doubt the servants were slowly learning what kind of master they served, but preferred to stay silent so far. "Nay, do not. A plain porridge will be enough."

"As you say, Monsieur le Comte," Flandres replied.

Having put the fear of God in Flandres for the moment, Alexander nodded and said, "I will visit my sister now and see that she is well settled in."

He went up to the west wing of the house where Erzebeta and Parvati were ensconced, and knocked quietly on the door to their apartment. When the door opened, Erzebeta was holding a sleeping Parvati in her arms when she faced him. "My lord," she said, and stood aside to let him in.

"How fares Parvati?" he asked as he looked down at the child's face, her button nose and dark lashes. The baby's face twitched slightly, but she did not wake.

"She sleeps all the day, as is her nature, and is awake all night. She has night terrors in her dreams. It will take time and patience to cure her of the tortures she suffered in Vienna."

"Indeed, what you both endured was abominable. But I believe that time and care will cure all."

Erzebeta's large brown eyes drooped. "Bela... my husband told me much about life from his youth and his time. He is far wiser and older than me, and I have learned much. He understands me and has borne my shame better than I can ever..."

Alexander replied, "lady, you did nothing which was shameful. How can you beat yourself when the fault was with strangers, who did not care to accept you or Parvati as yourselves? Nay, Erzebeta, do not shoulder a burden which was not yours to bear. I would sooner pluck out mine own eyes rather than see you suffer so."

"You are most kind and gentle," she said, "As is your father."

Alexander added, "Flandres will send supper up to you. I would advise that you remain here in your room with Parvati until the wedding guests depart. I must return to Paris on the morrow, so for now I must say farewell."

"Must you go so soon?" Erzebeta asked.

"I have duties and obligations to attend to in the city. Do not fear. Here, you will ever be safe." He reached out and stroked Parvati's black hair. "I know she will miss me. That cannot be helped."

"But, she is with her father," Erzebeta said. "And once I explain all to her, I am certain she will understand." Then her eyes drooped. "There is only one thing I cannot do for her, which gives me great shame."

Alexander asked, "aye? What is that?"

"My lord, I cannot read or write well. How then can I raise her properly, as a child of her station?"

It was true that as a gypsy, Erzebeta's life had been confined to the shelter of her tribe and their different approach to life. Reading books was never a necessity before, as most of them practiced an oral tradition of learning. Velin and Ragosi were responsible for the signs in the camp, while the others performed tasks which required no written words.

"Your former life allowed for nothing so important to a child's education," Alexander declared. "I can assure you that my father can teach you to read and write better, that you would have a knowledge worthy of your station in the household. It would aid you greatly in managing Parvati's as well. Would you have it so?"

"Aye, my lord," she said, as her eyes brightened with hope.

"Then I will inform my father of your desires, and he will know what to do. I must leave you now. If you should require anything in the night, or help with caring for Parvati, please come to my door," he said. "Good evening."

Alexander stood aside in the hall until she shut the door, then remained there in the half darkness, pondering his next course of action. After some time, he stirred himself free of reflection and returned to the sitting parlor, where he sat on the setee near the fireplace, which was already ablaze and giving off the aroma of incense. It reminded him of his days at the temple, but he was not at peace with himself.

On the mantelpiece stood a clock with a spinning pendulum; something new to the house which made him ponder the future once more. It was unsettling, this sensation of alienation which tugged at him so. His mind told him that it was time to move on, while his blood remained quiet and passive.

At length the sensation nagged at him like an itch he could not scratch. It was as if he had no idea what to do with himself. He had never felt this way before, and could not fathom why it was so. There was ever a purpose to fulfill before, and now that he was at peace with the world, that purpose seemed to be gone.

His reverie was disturbed by the sound of voices coming from the foyer. He stood as Lucien and his new bride came in. "Ah, Alexander," Lucien said.

Alexander stood abruptly. "Father," he said.

Lucien caught the expression on his face. "You look perturbed. Is something wrong?"

"Nay, father," Alexander replied, "I was just thinking about my return to Paris. I fear to hasten my departure, as I must resume my duties at the academy."

"The academy?" Ingrid asked. "Oh, yes, your father has told me of your position as an instructor in the art of the sword. The queen said it was so. I understand you are guiding His Grace the king also. Your day must be terribly busy." She smiled.

Alexander planted a pleasant smile on his lips to mask his feelings. "Aye, I can never claim to be bored when I am there. And I enjoy the routine."

Lucien took his new wife's hand, and said, "you have told me little of your work, but that is to be expected." He glanced to her and added, "you have not told me what you did at court."

Ingrid stifled a giggle with her small hand and replied, "as a lady in waiting to the queen, mine is... was... work of a different sort. Helping her to dress, neatening her closet, picking out the color of the day, making sure her schedule is met, and so on."

"The color of the day?" Lucien repeated her words with an expression of wonder.

"Aye. You are foreign, so you would not know. France leads the world in fashion, in style. We are proud of our ability to decide what is to be worn, and the world follows us. So I and the other ladies of the court are required to select a color of the day which is not the color of the day before. Say that blue was yesterday, and red is today, for example. Then we all wear gowns and livery of that color until the day is done. We choose a color from pieces of paper which are thrown into a bowl."

"Truly, what a dizzying tradition," Lucien replied. "And what about black? Black is my family's traditional color, and my favorite. What do you think of it?"

Ingrid's grey eyes turned to him as her mouth fell open slightly. "Black is reserved for mourning and weddings, husband. No one wears black unless it is necessary. Why would anyone want to wear black otherwise?"

Alexander said, "it would appear that we must change our habits, father. It would not do to fall out of fashion."

"You are wise to suggest it," Lucien replied, "but it will be hard for me to do so readily. May I suggest a compromise, my wife, for we are not the royal court? We cannot dress a different color every day, but we will strive to be more colorful. Would you have it so?"

The young woman considered for a moment, then replied, "I said we were required to be colorful at court. If we are of more modest means here at Rouen I will not burden the household with such matters. It would not make sense to follow the court's choices if we are less well endowed with funds. My father taught me the benefit of frugality and thrift, not to indulge in excess. And I have learned to sew and embroider, so that when the cut of a dress changes I can use what I have to make my own. We should carry on as we are, now that I am part of your family."

A kernel of admiration blossomed in Alexander's heart. The Comtesse was a rare flower who knew how to be a wife despite her youth. What he had seen the day before as frivolous giggles and bold outspoken candor became the truth of her uncertainty, because she had consented to marry a stranger and did not know him well. But she had not yet discovered the family secret, and that would take time.

At that moment Flandres appeared in the doorway and said, "supper is served."

All three rose and followed the houseman into the dining room, where the table was set for three. Another fire had been lit in the nearby fireplace. Lucien sat at the head of the table, while Ingrid sat to his right and Alexander sat to his left. The table held a platter of mutton, vegetables, bread and sweet meats, as well as decanters of liquids.

Today, Lucien avoided drinking blood, as did Alexander. Today the liquids were wine and water.

"May I serve you?" Lucien asked Ingrid.

She seemed eager to let him and said so. There was an awkward silence as he filled her plate and passed it to her, then to Alexander. Then he filled their wine glasses, and paused to raise his. "May I propose a toast?"

The other two diners raised theirs, and he said, "here is to our family Arkanon, that we are finally in a new home." He took a sip and set the glass down, while the others followed suit. Then they all sat down and began to eat.

Alexander managed to avoid eating the meat and concentrated on the vegetables and bread, while Ingrid ate delicately, and not as much as one would expect.

Their conversation was intermittent but inconsequential as Lucien explained his duties as stablemaster. Ingrid listened and smiled, and asked the usual questions.

When dinner was over and as Flandres and the other servants started to clear the table, Lucien and Ingrid said their goodnights to Alexander and left him to go upstairs.

Alexander followed them only as far as his own room, where he dressed for bed and crawled under the covers in the light coming from the fireplace. As he did so, he thought he heard a scream coming from somewhere in the direction of Lucien's bedroom. The sound gave him pause: had Lucien finally revealed himself to his new wife?

Alexander listened intently for other sounds, but there was silence. The household did not stir at the sound. He laid in the darkness alone, then heard the hiss of a log splitting apart. He looked and saw the red glow of its smoldering heart. He debated with himself whether to venture out and investigate, but lost to doubt that Lucien would want to be disturbed, and finally that he must have imagined it.

It was not until the moon pierced the veil of his window that he finally fell into his usual dreamless sleep.

144

In the grey light of a cloudy day, Alexander rose and dressed, packed his valise and emerged from his room. The hall was dark; the lamps lining the walls were unlit. There was an odd chill in the air as he descended the stairs into the parlor, where he found Flandres busy setting light to a fire in the small grate.

The man looked up at Alexander's approach and said, "ah, Monsieur le Comte. You are the first one to rise since evening last. Shall I bring you a tray, that you may have breakfast?"

"No, I find myself without an appetite," Alexander replied, as he placed the valise on the marble floor. "I must prepare to return to Paris. Have you seen my manservant, Monsieur Reneau?"

"No," Flandres said. "He was given a room in the servant quarter, and I have not seen him since last evening, either. Shall I go fetch him hither?"

"Please."

Flandres finished stoking the logs in the grate as they caught fire, then walked away down the hall toward the rear stairway.

Alexander stood before the fire in the hearth and gazed into the growing flames, while the little clock on the mantelpiece chimed seven. His thoughts were tangled and unfocused, and he still wondered at the scream he heard in the night.

Reneau was dressed in his usual drab colors, and hauled his saddle pack with him as he came down the hall with Flandres. When he reached Alexander he said quietly, "I am ready to go, Monsieur le Comte. The sky threatens rain again, I fear."

Alexander said, "I can wait if you wish to partake of breakfast." He did not ask if Reneau had heard the scream. As it was, Reneau did not appear to be disturbed, as if the moment never happened.

"Nay," Reneau replied. "I am used to going without eating in the morning. It is not well to eat before going into battle. And after enjoying those wonderful pastries last night at supper, I feel that it would be bad form to eat anything now."

Alexander addressed Flandres. "Have you seen my father this morning?"

The blond giant's eyebrows went up. "Nay, Monsieur le Comte. He is wont to sleep well into the day, and rises in midafternoon."

"In that case, you may inform him of my departure. I must return to Paris, and can delay no further."

"I will fetch the steward and obtain horses for you," Flandres said, then bowed left the parlor.

Reneau scratched at his scalp and stretched himself out, then stifled a yawn. "May I know the reason for your haste to be gone so soon?" he asked.

"No reason other than that I have spent too much time here, and I did promise my employer that I would return soon to my work," Alexander replied.

"Ah. Quite so," Reneau said. Then after a moment's hesitation, he said, "I feel it necessary to inform you… Monsieur le Comte, your father did offer me a position here at the house as a retainer and guard. He impressed in me a need for someone of discipline who could keep a weather eye upon things beyond the vigilence of the guards, who must watch the gate and the wall. And since I have learned from the guards of strangers entering the compound unbidden and at all hours of the night, they could do well with another set of eyes."

At this, Alexander was taken aback. He stood silently, digesting this news for a few moments, then asked, "and who will deliver my letters? Have you tired of going back and forth? Do I not pay you well enough?"

Reneau shifted on his feet as he ruminated on the question. "Nay, it is not that, it is that Comte Arkanon, with his new wife to keep him occupied withal, asked me to do this for him. Monsieur, it would be a great honor to grant him his wish, and I have seen that you are able to protect yourself better than anyone. As for the letters… I think that the Royal Post will carry your letters here in safety now that they have armed guards to escort them through the countryside. I have seen the coaches myself, surrounded by men of conscience who are loyal to the king."

"Your argument is sound," Alexander said, then relented, diverted from his original shock. "What shall you do with your apartment?"

Reneau shrugged. "As I kept very little there, it is of no consequence to me. I will return with you to Paris and inform my landlord that I will not return."

He looked up and around at the furnishings in the room. "I… it is very strange. I feel as if I belong here, that I have a purpose here. I do not know when I began to feel this way." Then his face registered puzzlement.

Alexander divined that Lucien must have planted the suggestion in Reneau's mind, and when such things happened it was because Lucien had something in mind for Reneau. Special vigilence was necessary, and Reneau's military skills were without question. Perhaps, having seen this, Lucien must have decided that the man was wasted as a mere courier.

Alexander placed a hand on Reneau's shoulder and said, "then I accept your resignation. We will return to Paris as equals. Would you have it so?"

Reneau bowed to him. "Monsieur honors me."

Just then, Lucien came from seeming nowhere, and entered the parlor dressed in a black quilted dressing gown trimmed in red and slippers. "There you are," he said. "I see that you are ready to go, Alexander. May I detain you a bit longer, that I may have a private word with you?"

"I wait upon it, father," Alexander replied.

Reneau, seeing that privacy was in order, said, "I will wait in the foyer." And with a bow to each of his masters, left the room.

When he was gone, Lucien led Alexander to the couch in front of the fireplace and sat down. Alexander joined him. Thus settled, Lucien leaned toward him and said, "Monsieur Reneau has informed you of his decision to stay with us here in Rouen. But I sense that you had something else to ask of me. What is it?"

At this, Alexander was once again taken aback. There seemed to be no end of surprises this day. "Father," he said. "When I retired for the evening… I thought I heard a scream. But… mayhaps I imagined it."

Lucien looked away to the flames in the grate, then turned back and said, "your senses warn you well. I heard it, too. But far more closely than I would wish."

Alexander stared in shock. "What happened?"

"My new bride, upon learning of my true nature, did scream with horror at the discovery. It took me several minutes to calm her, to assure her that I meant her no harm. When I was able to convince her that she was safe with me, she calmed at last." He appeared to cringe at the thought. "Such a sound I would not want to hear again for the rest of my life. I was unable to compel her because I did not want to compel her. Such a thing would be a violation of her personhood, and I would not want to force myself upon her."

Alexander thought that a noble sentiment. "You are far too civil to others, and for that you are punished."

Lucien smiled softly. "Nay, I have no reason to think so. I was taken off guard, but I felt that it was necessary to tell her the truth, to show her the truth. I feel now that she understands enough to accept me as I am. That alone compensates me." He tugged a bit at his housegown and sighed. "And now, you will be gone from my side again."

"I pledge to you that I will come and visit when I have a few days free," Alexander replied. "And Reneau informs me that the Royal Post will be more reliable than it has been. My letters will reach you in my absence. Please try to send me more of your own, if you are not otherwise occupied. I know that you will be kept busy with Parvati, your new wife, and the stables."

"Aye, I can never claim to be bored with this life." He rose, and Alexander copied him. Lucien reached out and gave his son a hug. "Be well, and may the stars and the dragon's blood guide you."

Alexander returned the hug thinking that it was the first time in a year that Lucien had shown any affection. "Thank you for your faith in me. I will strive to honor it."

Lucien released him. "I have no doubt of it. Come. I will see you and Reneau off."

145

When they arrived in Paris, Alexander and Jean Reneau parted ways, and Alexander returned to du Coudray's fencing academy.

Du Coudray noted his arrival with some surprise. "That was quickly done," the fencing master said, when he saw Alexander walk into the gymnasium. "You have exceeded my expectations. I thought you would linger for the fortnight I allowed for."

"The ceremony was hastily arranged and rather short," Alexander replied as he saw the pupils arranged in a rough semi-circle in the room. "I thought it prudent to return as soon as possible."

"Very good. These are new trainees. I am supervising their instruction because another of my teachers has been injured in a duel. Much has been missed while you were gone." He raised a gloved hand at Alexander's coming remark. "Yes, dueling has been declared illegal, yet some do not obey the edict. The cardinal is most displeased."

"I would imagine so," Alexander said with a smile. "May I ask… what has been done about the women's accommodations for training?"

"Come and see," du Coudray replied, and led Alexander to a window looking onto the small garden outside.

Alexander saw what looked like a small pavilion erected next to the gymnasium, made of stiff canvas and leaning against the outside wall. "Truly, it looks adequate for our needs," he said. "It will serve until a more permanent structure can be built."

"Now that you mention it, I accept that it will be so, as the women you signed have been eager to begin their instruction. When can you resume your duties?"

"As soon as you say," Alexander replied.

"Then I say you can begin again on the morrow, after you have rested."

Alexander bowed. "Monsieur is most kind."

Thus left to himself, he went back to his room on the second floor and devoted his afternoon to sweeping, tidying up, and going through the mail which had accumulated in his absence. Among these was an envelope addressed to him which bore the seal of the

Count du St. Germain. He puzzled at this, and scarcely knew why the Count should want to correspond.

Curious, he broke the seal and opened the envelope, which contained a thin sheet of vellum:

Monsieur Comte Corvina,

I am anxious to speak with you. I have information which may prove valuable to you and your father. If you would be so kind as to visit me tomorrow evening, please send a note of acquiescence as soon as possible. I await your response.

St. Germain

Alexander stared at the letter and wondered how long ago it had been sent. It was as if St. Germain knew when to send it, as if predicting the future was commonplace. Then he reasoned that the mysterious Count must have been informed of his return to Paris. That alone was cause to think that St. Germain was interested in his welfare, though why was open to speculation. The envelope was inscribed with a return address which was close to the Louvre, on the Rue des Roseilles.

Alexander determined to follow through and composed a short note in return, then went out to find the housemaster and have it sent by messenger:

Monsieur Comte du St. Germain,

I am at your disposal. I will visit you tomorrow as you request. Shall we say, 8 of the clock in the evening? I will be free then.

Corvina

146

The next day, Alexander took up his classes with vigor, and saw that he had more pupils than before. There were now thirty enrolled in the class, and he was told that there were another five who wished to sign up. Having had experience with instructing a few at a time, he recalled the days in Oradea when he handled two squads of pupils, but was concerned that handling so many would be an impediment to their learning.

He took the matter up with du Coudray, who suggested that Alexander take up two classes, each with fifteen or so, so that the pupils would have his full attention.

"That will mean I will have three classes this semester, and I must attend to His Grace also," Alexander said.

"If you feel that is too much, we may have to start turning them away," du Coudray replied. "It is your choice, monsieur. I do not wish to overburden you."

"Can we then enlist the aid of one or two of my older pupils?" Alexander asked. "I do not want to turn anyone away."

At that the swordmaster laughed. "As you wish. It will fatten the academy's purse and leave you free to govern your schedule. I do not know how you manage it as it is."

"I do not know, either," Alexander quipped. "You have been most accommodating." He did not mention that he did not want to tax du Coudray's patience, having imposed on it a great deal in his own estimation so far.

Du Coudray clapped him on a shoulder. "I will let you know when you have exceeded your boundaries," he said. Then he walked away to talk to some of the students in his class.

Alexander took that as a sign that he was needed, and began his day as usual. He worked out a schedule which staggered the classes over three days, which meant he would be teaching the art of the sword more than ever. He found himself relishing the idea, and soon it became a routine he did not want to break.

The women were also pleased, and though they were segregated from the other pupils by gender and time, took their lesson of the day with proberty and discipline.

When the long day was over, Alexander put up his foil, changed into street dress and left the academy to keep his appointment with the odd Count. He walked several blocks toward a villa at the end of the Rue des Roseilles, away from the river. The evening was a bit brisk, but he barely felt it. The cool breeze invigorated him even more, as he strolled among the citizens already occupying the avenues for the evening; poor and burgeouise alike in their dozens.

When he arrived at the villa, that sensation of being watched resurfaced. Here the narrow cobblestoned street was not crowded. Most people had gone indoors to take supper, and he could hear music and laughter through some of the open windows among the buildings, where musicians were practicing on their instruments or entertaining guests.

The villa stood flush with the street, comprised of plaster and brick with narrow arrow gaps paned in glass. The short portico was at the top of a few steps, and the door knocker was a brass lion's head with a ring in its mouth. The outer walls were streaked with black mud where the rain had deposited it. In fact it looked as if the villa had seen better days. But all the buildings on the avenue looked like that. Alexander took note of this, thinking that the Count was either strained with the need to have the exterior cleaned or was hiding from unseen enemies.

Alexander drew his cloak closer around him, checked around him for signs of danger or the odd stranger loitering nearby, then went up the steps and knocked on the door.

A moment later, the door was flung open, and a wizened old man peered out at Alexander as if he had been awakened. His face was lit by a candle. "Who are you?" he asked. "What do you want?"

"I am Alexander Vincent Corvina," Alexander replied. "I have come at the invitation of your master, the Comte du Saint Germain."

The old man hesitated, and was suddenly shoved aside by the Count himself, who had come to the door closely behind him. "To your room and your prayers," he said. "I will not be needing you for the night."

Grumbling, the old man retreated into the half light of the house and disappeared down a narrow hallway.

St. Germain, clad in a black cassock like the one he wore to the gala, looked past Alexander toward the street, then beckoned him in. "Come inside, and quickly."

Alexander glanced around again before obeying St. Germain. When he was inside and standing in the foyer, he asked, "was there a risk?"

St. Germain closed the outer door and secured it as he replied, "there is always a risk. There are spies everywhere, these days. It is not wise to be complacent or lax in our attention. The cardinal has spies, the Spanish have spies, the English have spies. One cannot turn around and not encounter a spy." Then he caught himself and said, "but do not be concerned. Now that you are here you are safe within these walls."

"It is true that I felt as if I was being watched, though by whom and for what reason I cannot imagine," Alexander replied. "I have not been in the city for several days, as I attended my father's wedding this Tuesday last."

St. Germain straightened a little as he lit another candle for more light. "Ah. That explains why I did not receive a reply that day when I sent you my letter. I must have just missed you. Please, come with me into the parlor, where we can talk with a bit more privacy."

He led Alexander through the hall into a room off to the left of the front door. There it was simply but comfortably furnished, and the fireplace was crackling with burning wood. "Please, sit and be comfortable," He said, as he closed the door to the hall quietly.

Alexander shed his cape and hat and set them aside on a credenza, adjusted his sword belt and sank into the brocaded cushions of a setée, while St. Germain stoked the fire in the grate to build it up higher. When he replaced the iron he asked, "may I offer you something to drink?" He indicated the sideboard, where several decanters filled with licquors stood gleaming in the firelight.

Alexander shook his head. "I do not imbibe spirits," he replied.

"Good!" St. Germain declared. "I keep those to entertain other guests. But you are not here to drink. What I have to tell you is far more important than superficial courtesies."

He came to the setée and sat down as well, leaving a space between him and Alexander. "My manservant has the good sense to go to his room when I have dismissed him, and there are no other servants to hear what must be shared in secret. We are quite alone."

"Your letter read as urgent," Alexander said.

St. Germain shrugged. "If you wish. I felt that it was important to inform you of the true dangers Paris presents. It is a city of secrets, of lies, and of mortal danger to any who take its relative safety for granted."

"When my father visited you... when he returned to our rooms his mood was... subdued, as if he had been struck by an omen of calamity. He did not mention what you talked about. Is your news so dire?"

"No. It is the same news I gave to him, but I felt it was only fair that I impart it to you as well. You must know of strangers, men who were rendered mute to prevent their revealing their mission, their goals."

Struck by surprise, Alexander nearly bolted from his seat, but St. Germain raised a hand to calm him. "Nay, my friend. Your father told me about them, and the mystery they have caused you both. I learned of the attack on the ambassador and his party from another, and your bravery in thwarting their attackers. The truth will be sifted out in time."

At this, Alexander relaxed his posture somewhat, and relaxed against the cushions.

St. Germain continued. "And now I must tell you what I have learned while you were away. There are other men who have entered the city, and are now searching among the people for you and your father. They claim to be hunting for vampires, Monsieur le Comte."

The word crinkled Alexander's nose. "Vampires?" He recalled that night that he had walked Roxánne home, and the altercation in the alley. Were these the men the poor wretch who died in his arms spoke of?

But St. Germain was not finished. "Your father did not reveal himself to others with all caution, but he did so with me. He confessed it to me readily, as if he wished to unshoulder the burden in his heart. You are beings from another world, who came to Terra and were marooned beyond all hope of returning."

Alexander's eyebrows went up. "He... confessed?"

The Count nodded. "A most wondrous revelation. With his words he opened the universe to me. It was as if he truly wished to reveal his innermost self to someone, but feared the persecution of the unjust. I was able to assure him that he could do so in all safety. I know of the vampire community, beings like yourself who take refuge in Paris, their habits, their movements. They are at present the focus of my study."

Alexander replied. "When you asked about vampires at the gala, I took you to be a fool. What was your motive for asking then?"

"Search yourself for the answer," St. Germain said. "I am a scholar and a scientist. I would not lead you astray. I only wished to know that which I suspected the moment I saw you. It was not difficult to see the difference between you and the other guests. Your skins are paler than any I have ever seen, and your eyes regard the world with an intensity few men can ever do. How can anyone see that and not realize that you are more different than anyone encountered before?"

Alexander considered that for a long moment. "Then, you are not a fool after all. But why display yourself with such pretense? You are said to be immortal, and that you work in ways most mysterious to others. Is this to throw them off balance?"

"I do it to conceal myself. As I said, I am a scientist. The church considers science to be an abomination and heresy. As a scientist I must drown myself in religion to avoid being persecuted, for now more than ever, science is emerging from the darkness and the church wants to banish it. As long as I wear the garb of a charlatan I can work without the hinderance of the church in my affairs. Would you not?"

Alexander considered that also, then ventured, "it was only in the last century that we were burning witches. Are you saying that... witches were also scientists?"

St. Germain nodded. "The church speaks of intolerance for those who are different, who practice their religions differently. I speak of those who create potions and medicaments to heal others, who stay apart and see the stars as worlds, with beings like us living on them, and who accept the truth as evidence of a universe as rich and diverse as any before conceived. Freedom of thought, inquiry and expression are anathema to the church, because such notions grant us the power to see the truth."

Alexander nodded, "I begin to see now."

St. Germain continued. "As a scientist I wish to learn all that is learnable, and to do that I must remain apart. I allow the image of a vampire, a charlatan, a fraud, to protect me. But, be assured that your secrets are safe with me. I know what you are, and your father, but I will never give up that knowledge to anyone. Not even on pain of death. You two are unique, and presage the revelation that humanity is not alone in the universe. The church cannot deny the truth for much longer. It will come whether they do or not."

Alexander sat silently, thunderstruck.

St. Germain leaned closer and said softly, "in many ways Cyrano was right. There are many lives to be led among the stars, and now I have seen the truth. But I have even more to tell you. I and others are working to liberate the truth. Have you heard the phrase 'novus ordo seclorum'?"

"I may have heard of it on several occasions, but only in passing," Alexander replied. "I have had Latin in my education."

"It is more important than the words themselves. It stands for a new world order, in which men and women may share the world as equals, where science will banish religion and open men's eyes to the truth," the scholar said. "I speak of a world where kings and emperors must not exist, or must capitulate to the will of the people in order to rule. It is a future I know will come to fruition one day."

"Is that what you are striving for?"

"No, not I. I know it to be fact, but it is slow in coming out in the open," St. Germain replied. "I have been reading certain pamphlets that have come to me through a friend. They speak of such themes of democracy and freedom that are wondrous to read. Have you read them? The author is Edmond Tibetin."

Once again, Alexander was struck mute as if he had been slapped in the face by his own past. Then he slowly ventured, "I have, but I think he is most courageous if he has not been imprisoned already for sedition."

The scholar went on. "No one knows what he looks like. No one. Do you? If Cyrano did, he took the secret with him to his grave. Some of us think that it is a nom de plume, taken by one of Cyrano's friends. The man has managed to stay invisible against all inquiry. I want to shake his hand for his audacity, but I cannot."

Alexander tried to deflect the Count's argument. "How do you know that it was a man who wrote them? Why not a woman?"

St. Germain paused to reflect. "It is possible," he allowed, "but it does not explain the bold passion in the prose. Women are such gentle creatures that they write what is in their hearts, not what must be said. But, now that you have suggested this, I will reread them to see if there is any clue which would reveal her to me."

Then he added, "as I said before, these vampire hunters are a danger to those of your kind. There is one among them, or their leader, who calls himself Baron Stephan van Helsing. I heard that one of his cousins led a similar group of men, and was killed for it."

The name was also a surprise. "I have never heard of him before," Alexander replied. "How have you learned all of this?"

"I know of others like me, who keep abreast of the city's affairs," St. Germain said. "They observe and report among themselves, and the information comes to me when it is opportune."

"Spies?"

St. Germain started at the word, then chuckled. "Quite so. But you must be circumspect, and on guard against any attack. I am told that you are quite proficient with a sword. It is good, for the blade may be the only thing that stands between you and certain doom."

Alexander said, "in our travels my father and I had encountered such men. Each had their own reason to hunt. Mercenaries and scoundrels are they all, with much evil in their hearts. They hunt for the gold their clients pay them to desecrate the graves of the dead, to make sure that the dead stay dead according to a superstitious tradition. It was most monstrous to me, and to my father, that even children were treated with such dishonor. And now we are hunted yet again, and for murderous deeds which we did not do."

"Your father acquainted me with your quest for a peaceful land to dwell within," St. Germain said. "I understand your caution. I can only stand and maintain the watch, and when I have gathered enough information, I will tell the gendarmerie what I learn of these men. I am certain that they are capable of harming others in their hunt for revenge. I dare say that the living are in as much peril as are the dead."

Just then the little clock on the mantelpiece struck nine by the tinkling of little bells and fell silent. St. Germain took it as some sort of cue, and rose from the setee. "I think the hour grows late, and I will detain you no longer. I will send you another letter if I learn more. But for now, good evening, and safe journey home."

147

Once Alexander was on the avenue and walking away from the villa into the shadows, the feeling that he was being watched resurfaced. He eased his sabre out of its scabbard about an inch and kept the grip in his hand as he walked as casually as he could toward the academy. He expanded his senses until he could see clearly into the dark, and could hear everything. It was a long time since he had used his talents but he was determined not to be caught unprepared.

Yet the boulevard seemed to be deserted. By now, most of the population had or should have retired for bed, to sleep a few furtive hours before rising again to go to work. A dog barked a few blocks away. He shrugged off the sensations bombarding him and walked on.

He went down another small street and strolled toward the boarding house where d'Artagnan lived. When he arrived, he glanced up at the second story window and spotted a light glowing within, which meant that the musketeer was awake. After taking another close look around, he entered a small courtyard through a wrought iron door and went toward the front door. There he knocked on it.

After a minute or so, the door was wrenched open, and another dour face confronted him. Recognition lit up the face, and the landlord said, "Monsieur le Comte, the hour is late."

"I am here to see Monsieur d'Artagnan," Alexander replied. "It is a matter most urgent which brings me. May I enter?"

With some reluctance, the landlord drew the door open wider. "It is not my affair, but mind you be quiet for the benefit of my other tenants."

Alexander smiled and offered a small bow. "I will be most discreet, monsieur. You may rely on my word."

Then he passed the old man and went directly up the stairs to the second floor, where d'Artagnan kept his chambers. There he knocked gently on the door.

A moment later, it opened, and the captain of musketeers stood in it holding a candle and dressed in a housegown. "Alexander," he said. "Has something happened? What brings you here at this hour?"

Alexander replied, "I have learned something which I must share with you. I know that the hour is late, but I must give you this news now rather than wait until morning."

Without hesitation, d'Artagnan admitted him to the studio apartment he kept. Here there was no servant or companion to keep him company. Alexander noted that he kept to the solitude of a widower. He had learned from Porthos that d'Artagnan's lover, Constance Bonacieux, was murdered during an altercation ten years before, and that Charles never stopped loving her. From then on, he kept a widower's sorrow.

"Please, be welcomed," d'Artagnan replied. "I hope that I can be helpful." He gestured toward the couch in the little parlor. "May I offer you a refreshment?"

"Perhaps not," Alexander replied. "I do not imbibe spirits."

"Ah," the musketeer said. "So you said before, I believe. Well, then. What is it you wish to tell me?"

As Alexander settled onto the thin cushions, he said, "I have just learned of a group of men who have entered the city, who desire to hunt for… vampires."

At this d'Artagnan's eyebrows went up, and he rocked back on his heels as if he had been struck in the face. "Vampires? Monsieur, I am not acquainted with them. Why should anyone want to? They are mostly harmless, and remain discreetly invisible within the city walls. I know of none who have harmed anyone, unless I am severely mistaken."

"I am well aware," Alexander said. "Nevertheless, these men I speak of wish to stir up the populace and gain satisfaction by the chaos it would cause. There is one among them who is their leader, Baron Stephan van Helsing. He is on a quest to avenge his cousin, and may not be able to distinguish readily among the living or the dead. His cousin Nicholaus was known to defile the graves of the dead in exchange for gold. The Emperor Ferdinand gave no saction to this, and outlawed them in Austria and Hungary. Now they are here in Paris. I only wanted to warn you that these men are a danger to the community and may stir up trouble."

"Paris is a danger to anyone who seeks to disturb the peace," d'Artagnan replied. "And His Grace, the king. Is he also in peril from these men?"

"I know not. He is surely protected by his guards and ministers," Alexander replied. "Is he not?"

"That may not be so certain," the musketeer said. "As long as *Monsieur* continues to claim his position is just, Louis is surrounded by spies and mountebanks. Cardinal Mazarin is also a rival for the throne." He drew a short impatient breath, then continued. "We must all guard the truth against those who would plot against the king."

Alexander saw the expression coloring d'Artagnan's face. "You guard many more secrets than anyone I know. You know the king's mind. It is a heavy burden you carry."

The captain of the king's guard nodded. "And yet I cannot even confide these secrets to a priest. My friend, it is a new world we are entering into."

"Novus ordo seclorum," Alexander said softly.

The musketeer's face went pale, as if he had seen a ghost, but he pitched his voice lower also. "Those treasonous words should never be uttered in the company of the king! They are an affront to him and his divine right to rule France. They mean death to our whole way of life. What would replace it?"

"Democracy," Alexander said simply. "I speak of a world of the future, where all men and all women are equal, and there would be no more need for kings."

"Without a government? Without the protection of a king?"

"Nay, have no fear," Alexander replied. "The government would be composed of men and women of good conscience, who would render decisions of benefit to all. A government of the people, by the people, and for the people. Just think of it, my friend. Louis could grow into manhood no longer burdened with his kingship. He could be anything he wants to be, unshackled by the chains of royalty, truly free like all of us."

"You truly believe this," d'Artagnan said. "That it will be so, in the very near future."

Alexander nodded.

The captain drew another breath and sat brooding as he gazed away into the fire in the grate. "And these men you spake of stand in the way of that future."

"They are inconsequential, my friend. The future will come and they will not be able to stand in its way. They are no more but remnants of the past, where many things and events once obscured the truth. But they are dangerous to the present. We must ever be on our guard. Is there anyone you can trust in the palace?"

"A few. So very few. My friends Athos, Porthos, and Aramis, perhaps the royal guard, the royal gardener... The queen, though she is allowed to know little about it, and has been placed under a close watch by the cardinal. The rest are either in concert together or with the cardinal and the duke."

"I have confidence in your ability to wage a silent war against the king's enemies," Alexander replied. "I would be proud to play a part in it. Do you trust me to help you?"

The blond musketeer drew himself straighter and swallowed the lump that had formed in his throat. "Of course," he said.

Alexander rose and readjusted his cape, then settled his hat on his head. "Then I give you a good evening, and I hope to receive a letter from you telling me when and where to meet again. I do not think that your boarding house is safe for planning."

"As you say," d'Artagnan replied as he rose also and guided Alexander to the door. "I will think on all you have said. Good evening, Monsieur le Comte."

"Please. Call me Alexandre. All my friends do."

When d'Artagnan's door was shut behind him, Alexander tiptoed down the stairs and was out the front door before the landlord could even hear him pass his door.

148

Yet a few minutes later, Alexander was halfway to the academy when he regained that sensation of pursuit. He paused only to look behind him, and turned back to continue on, when a group of men emerged from the dark and blocked his way. They were all beggarly in appearance, and their faces were stern and menacing. Their eyes spoke of enmity and suspicion. Their swords were drawn.

He drew his sabre and made ready for battle. "I know not who you are, but you'll not stand in my way," he said.

Again, they were all silent, like the mutes he had encountered before. But they did not move toward him or away. Then a whistle sounded in the dark, and they attacked.

Alexander found himself on the defensive, and as each was struck away, another came to take his place. Thus outnumbered,

Alexander was forced to retreat until he was pinned against a wall to a garden, where he had some protection by the stucco at his rear guard.

Then another group of men clad in the red tabbards of the Cardinal's Guard intervened and began to turn the attackers away. Amid the clashing of blades another whistle sounded in the dark, and the miscreants turned and fled into the dark until there were no more.

While the guardsmen attended to the wounded in their midst, their commander came to Alexander and said, "Monsieur le Comte, are you injured?"

Breathing a sigh of relief, Alexander resheathed his blade and replied, "I am quite well, thank you."

The guardsman gave him a look over, and blanched when he saw those silver eyes gowing in the dark. Swallowing, he smiled as he said, "good! The Cardinal will want to see you right away. So you will come with us at once, monsieur."

Alexander was caught off guard. "Aye? At such an hour?"

"It is not my place to say, monsieur," the commander said. "I only obey what orders are given me to carry out."

Wavering with doubt, Alexander shrugged and said, "then by all means, lead the way."

Flanked by the remaining guardsmen, he was marched into the compound which flanked the towers of Notre Dame, where he was admitted by the castellan of the vestry.

The guard commander said, "here is your guest, Monsieur le Comte Corvina. He is to be taken to the Cardinal at once."

The castellan was a small man, who had the same reaction to Alexander that many did in Paris. "As you say, monsieur. Thank you."

The guardsman gave him a quick salute and marched away into the dark. The castellan opened the door wide and beckoned to Alexander, who did as he was told.

"You must be very important ideed, to be summoned by His Eminence to his presence this evening," the castellan said.

"I know nothing of the affair," Alexander replied. "I know not why he summoned me."

"Neither do I, monsieur," the castellan said. "Come with me." Hoisting his lantern higher, he led the way down a spacious hallway toward a decorous column in the wall, where he pressed against a cherub's tummy in the carved relief.

The cherub recessed inward and locked into place. Then the whole column recessed inward and passed aside, revealing a doorway. The panel opened inward, and the castellan led Alexander into a large room which was ornately furnished with rich and sumptuous fabrics, paintings, and a ceiling mural depicting various saints and angels. There were no windows, perhaps for the protection of the man who dwelled within.

Close to one wall sat an ornately carved mahogany desk, where Cardinal Mazarin sat studiously looking over several documents resting on it. He looked up when Alexander and the castellan entered.

The castellan bowed to him and said, "Your Eminence, the Comte Corvina."

"Ah, yes," Mazarin replied. "Pray enter, Monsier le Comte, and be welcomed."

While Alexander approached the desk, the castellan left through the secret door and vanished.

The Cardinal of France stood and extended a hand of friendship, which Alexander took reluctantly. "I have heard much of you," Mazarin said. "I do not wish to alarm you. I merely want to verify what I have heard. I understand that you have made a friend of Louis. That is good."

"I am merely his fencing instructor," Alexander replied.

The Cardinal tisked and said, "come. I have heard a great deal more than that. Your father gifted him with a horse from his own stables, and you have proved your worth as a man with scruples, who would not betray his friends. And that you have counted yourself as his friend. Your other friends being select from his own mousquetaires. Athos, Porthos, Aramis, and... d'Artagnan?"

No doubt the cardinal's spies had informed him of everything Alexander did, and he did not like the idea of being spied upon. Alexander's blood stilled his coming remark. He tempered it with, "as a man, am I not allowed to choose who my friends are?"

Mazarin raised a hand of mild restraint. "Nay, I do not wish to dictate your actions as a man. I am merely trying to ascertain whether you are a threat to the king's ambitions. He is a headstrong and willful child who wishes to attain his kingship as soon as possible. I would have men about him who would protect his interests. I understand that you and Cyrano de Bergerac were friends also, and from his cousin that you arranged his funeral with discretion and honor."

"Cyrano was also a friend to the king," Alexander replied. "But others did not think so. He spoke against tyranny, not the king. He warned that tyranny could replace the kingship of Louis, even replace Louis. None of us would want that."

Mazarin sighed. "Then, perhaps I misunderstood Cyrano's pamphlets. He spoke of the advent of a democracy, where the people ruled the affairs of man. I thought he meant to overthrow the monarchy of France, and allow anarchy to rule."

Alexander shook his head. "I knew him well, Your Eminence. He was a logician and pragmatist. He would never think of anarchy as a means to an end."

The Cardinal bowed his head in contemplation for a long moment. When he raised it, he faced Alexander and asked, "and his associate... eh... Edmond Tibetin. Do you know him?"

That name again. Alexander found himself confronted by a fact he wished to escape. After some hesitation, he replied, "I did. But he is gone from France."

"You do not know where he went?"

"No, Your Eminence."

"A pity. I wanted to thank him for opening my eyes. He is a great philosopher. His words were instructive in the extreme. I may have disagreed with him, but he did present me with something to think about. It is not often that I can find such words so stirring. They almost reaffirmed my faith in God."

Inwardly flattered, Alexander could feel his cheeks go hot. "I did read his works, Your Eminence, and found them most illustrative."

"Then I must content myself with his works alone. Think you he will ever return to France?"

"I do not know, Your Eminence."

Mazarin smoothed down his red gown briefly and crossed himself. Then he said, "I turn now to another topic of which I cam not satisfied. I understand from... others... that there are men in the city who wish to cause chaos and mayhem. My own captain of the guard tells me they attacked you this evening. Who are they?"

Carefully, and without revealing much detail, Alexander told him about Nicholaus van Helsing and his men, and about his encounter with Nicholaus's cousin, Auric, in Strasbourg; ending with the news of Stephan's arrival to Paris to avenge his cousins.

He concluded with "these are men of anarchy, Your Eminence. They would commit murder to achieve their goal, and are not concerned with collateral damage. I fear that they would harm the king if they could, if their goal is to overthrow the crown."

Mazarin said, "then I must warn Queen Anne. I will set a guardwatch over the streets near the Louvre to forestall van Helsing. The king must have all protection. And you, Monsieur le Comte, must inform me if you know more of these men."

To this Alexander said nothing, while Mazarin went over to a bellcord set near his desk and tugged on it. "I will release you now to return to your classes," Mazarin said. "Mind you be careful going home."

The Cardinal led Alexander to another panel in the wall and said, "Through here is a passage leading to the street. Good evening, Monsieur le Comte. I would like to count you as my friend. May God guide you and protect you." He pressed a button set in the wall, and the wall opened into darkness.

Alexander hesitated before replying, "and you, my lord Cardinal. Good night."

Once he was in the passage, the door closed and plunged him into Stygian blackness. Alexander used all his senses to follow it down a short flight of stairs, where the opening led into a garden next to the vestry. From there it would be a short walk through the plaza in front of the cathedral to the academy. Steeling his nerve, he managed to make it home without further incident.

149

May, 1650

It was evening when the manor house near the royal stables became alive with music and celebration. It was to celebrate Ingrid's birthday, and she was 24 today. She watched a mass of men and women who were elegantly dressed and dancing a gigue, accompanied by a small squad of lively musicians. Laughter and the tinkling of glass goblets added a chaotic rhythm to the sound of music. They had come from all over the valley, and appeared to be enjoying themselves.

Lucien, clad in his usual black, stood next to her with his arm around her shoulders. Ingrid was dressed in a gown of exquisite cobalt blue silk, and her face was radiant with the cheer of celebration.

"Are you happy, my sweet?" Lucien asked.

"Oh, yes," she replied. "I never dreamed it would be so." She turned to him and said, "I must apologize for my..."

He tugged her closer and held her tight. "Please, do not apologize. Only... forgive me for not having told you the truth at once. Will you?"

"Yes, yes, yes," she said, and turned to hug him. "You have never given me reason to fear you. You are like unto a saint for all your concern. Let me reward you."

Lucien returned the hug and kissed the top of her jeweled hair. "When all have gone home, come with me to bed and we will celebrate more privately."

"I can hardly wait," she replied, then turned up her face to kiss his lips.

Lucien accepted it with gratitude, and the assurance that their bliss was assured at last. "Then, let me..."

The words were barely out of his mouth when Jean Reneau burst through the front door. He was exhausted, and nursing a wound in his side when he stumbled and nearly fell among the dancers. The music and celebration stopped as if a cannon had gone off in their midst.

His voice was hoarse as he said, "Monsieur le Comte, the stable is on fire!" Then he collapsed to the carpet, while the guests retreated with some alarm.

Lucien abandoned Ingrid and went to tend to Reneau while Flandres joined him. Reneau was disoriented but appeared determined to stay conscious, even as blood flowed from his ribs down his torn weskit. Lucien held him up gently and asked, "who did this? Do you know?"

Reneau tried to rally his strength as he shook his head and said, "I do not know, Monsieur le Comte. There were strangers..." He fell limp as his mind left him.

Lucien rose to his feet and told Flandres, "fetch the doctor hither, and tend to our guests, while I see to this incident myself. Protect your mistress."

Flandres blanched. "Alone? Monsieur le Comte, did he not say..."

"Do as I say," Lucien commanded him, then turned to go out the front door to the villa.

Flandres bowed quickly and turned to calm the the other guests, while Ingrid approached him and said, "Lucien, you cannot do this alone. The man said there were strangers. Are these not the men you told me of those many nights ago?"

Lucien turned and grabbed her hand. "Perhaps they are, perhaps not. But now this event threatens you, and our family. And I am sure the king will not forgive me for having failed to protect his property."

"Then, take Flandres with you for protection, and I will tend to Reneau and our guests," she insisted.

In answer, Lucien seized her and planted an urgent kiss on her lips. "Courage," he said, then left her to go outside.

Ingrid turned to the guests crowding the parlor and called for Flandres, who was not hard to spot amidst the people talking among themselves. "Flandres, I would have you accompany the master to the stable," she said. "I will tend to them myself. Go, and with all speed."

"Yes, my lady," Flandres said, then stalked his way through the milling throng to the front door.

Taking a deep, calming breath, Ingrid turned to the people and called for quiet. "Your attention, please. Is there a doctor among you?"

A middle aged man came forward and bowed to her. "Here, Madame."

"You will help Monsieur Reneau. I have no medical skills," she said.

He went to his knees beside the pitbull and examined his wound. "Thank God, it is not deep," he said. "I will poultice it and bind it here, then the servants and I will take him to his bed."

"My thanks, monsieur," she replied. "I must attend to another matter, but will return with your fee."

"What can we do?" one man asked, followed by a chorus of concern.

"Can we help?" said another, younger man.

Ingrid thought carefully, then replied, "as many of you want to, you are welcome. But the rest of you should go home now."

Several young men cast off their formal coats and left through the door together. As the crowd dissipated, Ingrid followed the last stragglers through the front door and stood on the marble porch.

Down the stable road, she could see the bright flames consuming the large barns, while the horses fled en masse onto the pasture. She could see the dark silhouettes of men fighting the blaze with shovels and buckets of water drawn from the well. One of them was surely Lucien.

Forced to remain a spectator to the event, Ingrid went back into the house and told the servants to clear the parlor and gird themselves to battle. Then, she went upstairs to the apartment where her stepdaughter and her governess were housed. There, she knocked at their door.

Erzebeta opened it, and her face was a mask of concern. "My lady, what has happened? I did see the fire from my window."

Ingrid was at a loss for words at first, but finally said, "it appears that we were attacked. Pray, pack for travel, and Parvati also, for we may have to abandon the house and go to Paris."

Erzebeta's eyes crinkled with worry as she said, "will the fire come to the house?"

"I do not think so," Ingrid replied. "Still, we must prepare to leave in case it does."

632

Lucien, Flandres, and the other guests who had joined them were kept busy filling buckets from the nearby well and tossing water onto the flames, while the stable hands tried to keep control of the horses on the meadow. The flames were high and very hot, fueled by the wood and hay in the barns. Barrels of kerosene for the lanterns were in danger of igniting, and the men were driven back from them despite their efforts.

The conflagration was deliberately set, a fact made more obvious by the graffiti in red paint adorning the stucco walls of the compound: "GO HOME VAMPIRE!" and "WITCHES LIVE HERE!" and "GO HOME WITCHES!"; finally, "BURN IN HELL VAMPIRES!".

Lucien was barely aware of this. He was focused on getting the fire out and saving the horses from it. But Flandres paused to brush the sweat from his brow, and looked around to see whatever anyone else was doing. When he saw the words, he went to his master to report it. "Monsieur le Comte, the enemy has declared itself."

Lucien put his bucket down and turned to look where Flandres was pointing. After a moment of consternation, he replied, "there is little we can do about it now. Bring me the warden of the guard. I would have words with him."

He retreated from the heat of the flames and stood by until Flandres reported back with the captain of the guard, whose face was smudged by soot and grime. The man was exhausted from fighting, and he panted as he saluted the stablemaster.

"Tell me. How many men were there who did set fire to the stable?" Lucien asked.

"Monsieur le Comte, I tell you we were overpowered. There were many such men, too many to count, and they killed several of the stewards also. They attacked us in our beds, Monsieur le Comte! We had no chance to prepare, no sign they were coming."

"And, where are they now?"

The captain looked around him and shrugged his shoulders. "I do not know. They seemed to have disappeared. It is a most curious thing, Monsieur le Comte!"

Luciens shrewd eyes appraised the man and looked for complicity, but found none. Perhaps that man was telling the truth. "Very well. You may go."

When the man had gone, Lucien stood ruminating until Flandres jogged him loose. "Monsieur le Comte, you mean the fire was not an accident? It was set? Who would do such a thing?"

"Flandres, I have enemies who would see me dead. What man does not? Perhaps they saw this time as encouragement to attack me in the midst of our celebrations. But surely they would attack me directly, instead of attacking the king's horses. No, this speaks of an even bigger conspiracy, perhaps one against the king himself."

"The king? Monsieur, no one would dare harm the king!"

Lucien turned to him. "Granted. Nevertheless, it appears that I am not the target for this conspiracy. I will return to Paris and report to Queen Anne, who is his regent. I trust her to know what to do."

150

When the fire was finally out it was morning. All that was left of the stable was a pile of smoking blackened timbers, scorched stucco, and roofing tiles. The men assembled to share anecdotes on the open patio in front of them. The sun was blotted out by a storm looming on the horizon. Rain would come, but too late.

Lucien and Flandres gathered the stewards of the day and the stewards of the night to learn what had happened. Monsieur de Cresse' was exhausted but eager to explore the disaster with his master to his satisfaction.

"Monsieur le Comte, I tell you that it was as if a swarm of bees attacked us. There were men who insinuated themselves amidst us, who did keep us from doing our duties, and I hear from the others that one of these men did toss a lit kerosene lamp into the hay near the front door so that the horses could not get out."

"I presume that you had other ways to allow the horses to escape," Lucien replied. "All have survived?"

"Aye. There are three other passages within with which to guide the horses to safety, and against just this kind of accident."

"Were any stall boys or jockeys harmed? Are they safe?"

"Yes, Monsieur le Comte. They all got away, and did help the horses to escape. They are among them now."

Lucien stood thinking for a long moment as he watched the animals and humans milling about on the meadow, then asked, "did any of these invaders speak to anyone?"

De Cresse' replied, "they said nothing, as if the plan was well coordinated among them, and they tried to trap us in our quarters rather than allow us to rescue the horses. But we were able to thwart their plan. Monsieur Reneau drove back a fair number of them with his sword." He looked around for a moment and added, "now, all of them are gone."

"That is fortunate. Then, Monsieur de Cresse', I will reward you handsomely for your proberty. Go now and rest."

The man bowed and smiled. "Of course, Monsieur le Comte. Thank you for your trust in me." He bowed, then loped away slowly, as if his tired limbs threatened to drag him down.

Lucien turned to Flandres and said, "and so our small time of peace must come to an end."

Flandres' face was pale as he asked, "Monsieur le Comte, what will you do? You are not leaving!?"

"I must, or these kind people will fall under the same threat as did visit us this evening last. I trust you to take care of the house and see to the stable's management, just as you did when your old master died. When Reneau is healed, you and he must work together to protect the stable, no matter its condition."

"But..."

Lucien shrugged. "I cannot perform miracles, monsieur Flandres. I must go forward, as must we all. My family is in danger, as am I." He paused to think carefully. "I should take my family with me. I cannot leave them here undefended. Do you agree?"

Flandres placed his right hand on his heart and gave Lucien a bow of respect. "Monsieur le Comte, you honor me with this stewardship."

Alexander had just finished his last class for the day when a youth came into the gym and handed him a sealed envelope with the seal of House Arkanon on it. He balanced his foil under his arm and said to the boy, "merci," then handed him a pistole for his effort. The boy bowed to him quickly, then went out again.

Alexander tore through the seal with a sharp fingernail and opened the letter. He read:

21 May 1650
Alexander –

This letter is to inform you that we are coming to Paris. The men who cannot speak have invaded the compound and caused a fire which burned down the stable. For now it appears we are all in danger. I must ask Queen Anne for her forgiveness and mercy, and find funds to repair the stable. We will take lodgings in town near you. Do not reply, but do expect us in the next few days.

Lucien.

A fire!? What murderous intent bids these men to harass my father so? Alexander asked himself. So many more questions invaded his thoughts that he could scarcely sort through them all. He took a deep cleansing breath and closed his eyes to calm the storm, then opened them again. His focus was soon drawn to his four female students, who had gathered around him and waited for him to speak.

He had encouraged them to use their imaginations as much as possible to consider the world around them. Most innate among them was their curiosity.

When he saw their questing faces he said, "it is simply a note from my father saying that he is coming to Paris."

The four of them exhaled and clapped their hands. Then Roxánne said, "that is a happy event indeed!"

Elise Ravenneau asked, "will he also be teaching here?"

"Nay, that is for Monsieur du Coudray to decide," Alexander said. "And, he is burdened with a wife and child, so that may be impossible."

Roxánne asked, "when is he coming?"

Alexander studied the note and replied, "he says in the next few days. But since Rouen is not that far away I think it will be in a day or two."

"Good," she replied. "Ladies, let us away and leave our instructor to his thoughts."

The women said their goodbyes and left the gym, just as the master of the academy entered it. They exchanged friendly greetings. Then, du Coudray approached Alexander and, seeing the letter in Alexander's hand, raised a cautious eyebrow. "You are not leaving us again, Monsieur le Comte?" he asked.

Alexander said, "nay. My father and his family are coming to Paris."

The fencing master said, "that is good news, then."

"It... merely simplifies the matter," Alexander replied. Without divulging its contents, he slipped the letter into the pocket of his practice suit.

"Ah, yes. You informed me of his position as master of the royal stables. Has something happened?"

Reluctantly, Alexander confided the news that the stables had burned down, and that his father must beg for an intercession from the queen.

"Indeed, your father was visited with grave misfortune," du Coudray remarked. "The stables have never been threatened before, not since they were built. Now this will raise the ire of the crown. The queen will know what to do."

"These are different times," Alexander said. "Nothing is as it was before. But I fear the fire was caused by the conspirators I told you of. They must wish to drive my father from the country, or worse, kill him. They have tried before."

"Such dangers visit all of us at one time or another," de Coudray said. "But as long as he is under the protection of the crown he can enjoy some liberty to act as he must." Then the fencing master straightened himself and added, "and you, my friend, should be circumspect. They may target you next. Be on your guard."

As du Coudray left the gym, Alexander watched him go feeling that the master knew far more than he was saying.

151

A small group of courtiers and ladies in waiting were assembled and seated in the throne room, where Louis, now 11 years old, sat in the golden chair on the dais watching Lucien explain his plight to Queen Anne, who sat to his right.

Seated among them were Athos, Porthos, and d'Artagnan, whose faces were solemn as they listened to Lucien. Aramis was notably absent, but the other three were mum about it.

The story of the fire was disturbing to most of those present, while *Monsieur* simply picked at an apple with a small poinard to remove the seeds and seemed to play no part, looking almost bored with everything.

Cardinal Mazarin sat near the throne and was divided between Lucien's story and watching the duke like a hawk.

Alexander stood his near his father and watched him speak, hoping that his presence would lend more support to his plea.

Lucien concluded his story with, "I am certain that the stable can be rebuilt, and as the horses were not harmed they can be lodged under the open sky through the summer. I pledge to you that I will work to restore it using my own hands, if that will restore your trust in me."

Queen Anne's voice was gentle and warm as she said, "what you tell us is beyond any man's ability to govern all by himself. I blame you not for the incident. But these men you speak of. Do they present any danger to His Grace?"

"I know not, Majesty," Lucien replied. They may be like the men who accosted the Baron de Neuvillette. But none were captured in this event, and they vanished into the wilderness without making any sound which would reveal them. Therefore their identities are a profound mystery."

Louis piped up. "Mother, we must send the guard out to find these men. They are an affront to the crown, and I would not have them running about loose in the country. They may sow discord among the people. I dare say we have already had enough of that."

His mother turned to Louis and said, "it is true that they present a new and ready danger to France. Therefore, I will grant a small boon to anyone who can help us capture them and learn their plans. Is it agreed, then, that we shall give over funds to rebuild the stables?"

The king mulled over that for a long moment, then said, "yes, mother. But where shall we house his family until he can start again?"

"I am certain that we will find them a place on the grounds, so that they can rest easy for a time. Leave that to me."

The boy smiled. "Very well, mother. Thank you."

Queen Anne stood and addressed the room. "The conference is concluded. I will give such orders as we discussed."

As the courtiers started to leave, the Duc d'Orleans approached and said to her, "I would have had the Comte in irons and in prison for his carelessness. Instead, you give him carte blanche to do as he pleases."

At this, the four musketeers paused in the door and turned to listen. The duke was far too close to the throne than gave them comfort. Lucien and Alexander paused also, and watched the young man go closer to the queen. Louis stayed where he was and was a witness to the constant danger he was in.

Anne's blue eyes were sharp as she regarded the duke. "Then it is good that I am not you," she said. "One cannot blame someone for something which was taken out of his hands. And, you are not in a position to dictate to me what to do. If I were you, I would confine myself to my apartment and pray for the clarity you lack. Or better still, confess to the chaplain your sin of pride."

"One day I will make you eat your words," he replied.

She leaned into his face and said, "I think not. One day Louis will be a man, and when he is crowned he will be king. Do not even think you can dethrone him. He is more of a man now than you will ever be."

Her determined expression caused him to step back quickly as if he had been struck in the face. He straightened his embroidered lapels, then snarled as he tossed the half eaten apple to a servant and left the room through the side door. With a bow to the queen, Cardinal Mazarin followed him.

The musketeers relaxed their tension and resheated their swords. Athos said to Alexander, "that was close. I've never seen *Monsieur* like this before."

"He is losing patience," Alexander replied. "Cardinal Mazarin has informed me that he is having *Monsieur* watched."

"Have a care, then, that you do not become trapped in his web," Athos said. "Good evening, monsieur." He followed his friends out the door and passed down the hall with them.

Through all of this, Lucien had not moved an inch. He stood where he was and silently watched the boy king leave the room in his mother's company.

When the room was empty, Alexander approached him and asked, "father, what is it?"

"I fear the discord Louis spoke of has already occurred," Lucien said. "It has come in the form of that manchild, who has much to learn about statecraft. I recall you told me about le Fronde. Such foolishness is no way to run a country. *Monsieur* is mistaken about his place in the universe. His behavior demonstrates a distinct lack of discipline. It will go badly for him. I almost feel sorry..."

"For him? Father, he has threatened the crown before, as you recall. Only some of the parlement agreed with him, and went to the Bastille for it. If he cannot sway the others, he will fail. And the church will not intercede on his behalf. Cardinal Mazarin has told me so. Therefore, rest your thoughts that he will never be king."

Lucien gave him a patient smile. "Your optimism is so infectious. I will return to the lodging house and pass it on to the rest of us. We will await word from the queen where we are to go. I trust you will come to dinner soon?"

Alexander replied, "I will expect a letter from you telling me when and where. I have much to tell you about Paris."

152

For the next few days, Alexander was kept busy conducting his classes, and could only exchange short letters with Lucien, who apprised him of his progress.

In June, Lucien sent him a note saying that the queen had given him and Ingrid lodgings in a hunting chalet on the grounds of the Louvre. It was small but cheery, and surrounded by a rose garden. He said that Parvati was happy to explore the garden, and that Erzebeta was progressing as a new student under his tutelage. He was also having some of his books sent to him so that he could stock the small library in the chalet. So far, everything appeared quite normal and safe. They were now officially moved in.

During the summer hiatus at the academy, Alexander visited Lucien an the family often. Parvati appeared to have recovered sufficiently from her ordeal in Vienna to play outside in the warm evenings. Alexander made sure to play with her so that she was never alone, while Erzebeta studied and read books Lucien recommended to assure she retained what she learned.

At supper, Ingrid entertained by telling stories of the court and the latest fashions. The queen had accepted her back into her service as a lady in waiting, which earned her a generous stipend.

Lucien said that he and the boy king were getting along quite well. Lucien was now helping him learn his sums and other small pieces of statecraft, philosophy and science, as an erstwhile tutor.

Queen Anne was pleased with this development because she was so anxious that her son was not safe. It freed her to tend to the rest of France. So as a reward for his service, awarded him a stipend also.

Lucien said he would put it away to pay for Parvati's higher education. In the meantime he would continue to tutor her himself.

Lucien reported that *Monsieur* and Cardinal Mazarin had a talk, and that Mazarin threatened to excommunicate him if he did not cease his constant war with the crown. That *Monsieur* had reluctantly backed down to save his mortal soul and left Paris to go elsewhere, presumably his country house in Nancy. He would not be returning for some time.

Then, Lucien said that the funds for rebuilding the stables were sent to Flandres, who replied in a letter that the foundation was being laid and some of the walls shored up with wood until the stucco would set. The walls were whitewashed to erase the graffiti.

The horses were doing well despite their lack of shelter, and that the hands were all happy to sleep under tents near them. So far, the mysterious army had not invaded again.

Alexander concluded that the invaders must have learned of Lucien's relocation to Paris and had followed him, biding their time until their leader's signal to attack Lucien. Wisely, Lucien kept to the grounds of the estate without venturing into town. Surely they would not dare invade the Louvre!

As for Stephan van Helsing, he had not shown his face yet before the court of Louis XIV.

The sparring was regulation in form, as Alexander stood by to watch the boy king and his opponent, a young viscount named Bertrand de Montpassant, crossing blades on the carpet of the small gymnasium.

Alexander had chosen to match Louis with another after spending over a year tutoring him in the art of the sword. He felt it was time to break up the routine, and he feared now that Louis knew his moves better than himself. The variety would challenge Louis to use his skills rather than use the practice alone.

Their foils were buttoned, as was required during practice, and Louis appeared to be winning the bout. For his part, Bertrand seemed reluctant to show his true skills before Louis, and Alexander had not trained him, but could see that he had more practice than Louis.

After a few quick parries and ripostes, Louis clipped Bertrand's foil from his grip. The blade spun through the air and landed on the floor at the feet of a minister who had come to watch. Louis barely took note, but lunged forward and touched Bertrand with the tip of his foil at his chest.

"Touche'," Alexander said. "Your Grace, you are showing excellent form. But, you need not use such force to disarm your opponent. You could put someone's eye out. Also, remember that Bertrand is unarmed, and you should extend to him the charity of mercy."

The minister brought the lost foil forward and handed it to Bertrand. "And you should retain control of your foil, or you would lose it easily in combat," he said.

Bertrand accepted the foil and replied, "'twas not my intention, Monsieur du Fournay."

The fencers saluted each other. Louis asked, "shall we try again?"

"If you wish, Your Grace," Bertrand said.

Alexander asked, "are you tired, Monsieur de Montpassant?"

"Allow me but a moment to collect myself," he said. "And I must have a drink of water. I am parched."

A servant brought him a goblet of the liquid, which Bertrand downed with a couple of small gulps. He handed the goblet back and made ready in the first position. "I am ready now, Your Majesty."

"Do you wish water also, Your Grace?" Alexander asked.

Louis took a moment to consider. "I am not thirsty," he said, "but I may need it after."

Alexander said, "very well. Begin."

The two fencers took first position and started with the standard parry. Their blades struck and whirled rapidly, when Louis suddenly lost control of his balance and stumbled back onto his rump. The foil fell out of his hand and bounced to the carpet with him.

No one dared to laugh, as the boy king sat stunned for a moment. Bertrand lowered his foil and waited. Alexander raised his hand and said, "the match is not decided."

He went to Louis and offered his hand. "It is no reflection on your skill," Alexander said. "When I was much younger and in training, I fell down all the time."

Louis took his hand and Alexander pulled him to his feet. "But I am the king," he said. "I cannot afford to fall down." He glanced to Bertrand, and added, "I know he is better than I am. He refuses to challenge me properly. Please inform him that he must not hold back where I am concerned."

At this, the attendants gasped and shared whispers until Alexander called for calm. "Please, ladies and gentlemen. Your king has spoken."

To Louis he replied softly, "you may tell him yourself. It is time that you were more forward with your commands, as you were once with me. You are king. It is time that you showed your resolve. It is your right. Let nothing deter you."

Louis went to Bertrand and said, "Monsieur le Viscomte, I challenge you to treat me as you would an enemy. Please do not be gentle with me."

Bertrand hesitated, then bowed to his king. "As you wish, Your Grace. I will strive to do as you command."

The fencers saluted each other again, and began with the standard form. Then, Bertrand was furious with the foil, and managed to drive Louis back until he was among the small audience, who parted to give him room, Louis switched to some of the Japanese maneuvers and managed to drive Bertrand back toward the mat. After a swift and furious battle, Louis lunged and touched Bertrand on his chest again.

"Touche'" Alexander said. "His Grace wins yet again."

The audience burst into applause, while Louis grabbed Bertrand's hand and shook it. "Fear not, monsieur" he said. "For this, you will always be my friend. Thank you, for this day you have shown me that I still have much more to learn."

"Of course, Your Grace," Bertrand replied with a small bow. "I am happy to be your practice man."

Louis then turned to Alexander and asked for his purse, and took from it a gold sovereign, which he offered to Bertrand. "This is a small recompense for your skills. One day, I shall be as greatly skilled as you are," he said.

Bertrand was bewildered somewhat as he accepted the coin. "But, Your Grace, you won."

Alexander chose that moment to clap his hands twice and said, "ladies and gentlemen, the practice is concluded."

As the audience and Bertrand left the gymnasium, Louis went to the sideboard and, placing his foil against the wall next to it, poured himself a glass of water, then gulped it down. This was not normal, as a king was expected to be served hand and foot. Alexander had told Louis that he must learn to do for himself, because one day it may be necessary.

When he put the goblet down, he asked Alexander, "what did you think of my form?"

"It was much better than I expected," Alexander replied.

"I wish to be better than I am," Louis said. "That is what is important. As your king, I must be better than any man. Do you agree?"

Alexander considered that, then said, "I do, Your Grace. But, you are already better than any man. Who would challenge your right to be king?"

"My uncle, the cardinal. Who else? My mother informs me there is yet another, whose name is unknown. My father was a formidable king, who fought many battles, and yet I have not." He took a short impatient breath and added, "I am not yet formally crowned. I know not the delay for my coronation. What bids the delay?"

Alexander replied. "You are wise enough and mature enough to be crowned. All that stands in your way, I believe, is your age. The rules are archaic where you are concerned."

Louis considered for a moment, then declared, "when I am finally and legally king, I shall do away with it."

"With respect, Your Grace, you cannot. The rule was ordained by the church. In ancient times, the age at which one can be crowned king was set by older men."

"Older men. Must I grow old before I am king?"

"Nay," Alexander said, suppressing a chuckle. "All must indeed try your patience, Your Grace, but it will not be that long before you are crowned. Hasten not to be crowned so soon. Your mother has done well in executing your commands. Has she not?"

After a few more moments of contemplation, Louis replied. "Thank you for your counsel, monsieur. Though it rankles me, I shall think on what you have said."

Then the boy king collected his foil and left the room, leaving Alexander to ponder his words alone.

153

September 5, 1650

The leaves fell a shower of gold, red and brown onto the lawns of the Louvre. The palace was festooned with colored lanterns, and the color of the day was royal blue. The ballroom was filled with courtiers, ministers, and other ladies and gentlemen, who had come from the surrounding countryside to attend the young king's birthday fête. He was turning 12 today, and everyone had come to celebrate.

The music was Bach, Vivaldi, and Pachelbel, with a smattering of Lully here and there. The servants were kept busy circulating among the guests, laden with trays of hors d'eouvres, glasses of various wines, and also petit fois for those who had already dined and wanted something to chew on.

The conversation drifted from subject to subject; from the latest inventions to what was the coming thing, fashion, horse racing, and also the latest scandal, along with the attendant gossip. The roar of the crowd almost blotted out the music, but the musicians were determined to be heard and played their instruments as loudly as they could.

King Louis XIV sat on the throne and watched it all with the air of contentment. Queen Anne sat next to him and carried on a subtle conversation with him, identifying this or that newcomer to the court, while each was brought before them and formally introduced. Louis accepted them all with patience and calm, and asked the occasional question. When he was satisfied with their answers, he sent them on their way.

Nearby, three of the Royal musketeers stood around the buffet and discussed the politics of the season while seizing various sweatmeats and cheese and dipping them in sauce, chewing furtively between sentences.

Aramis was missing today. Athos explained to the others that he had contracted a cold and was told to stay home; else he would infect everyone else.

Lucien and Alexander had arrived alone, since Ingrid was tending to the queen and already seated near the queen's chair. The calling steward came forward and announced them to the crown, as was the form. When they entered the ballroom, all eyes turned to them. Amid a smattering of small applause, the two vampires approached the throne and bowed deeply to the boy king and his mother.

Anne looked them over and said, "monsieurs, you look quite handsome. The blue sets off your eyes."

Lucien took the lead and said, "we would be remiss if we did not match the color of the day, Your Majesty. My wife has taught us that it is necessary to follow tradition."

She smiled and replied, "you have taken to the customs of the court quite well. But it was not necessary."

"Madame, you honor us greatly," Lucien said. "I am told that the celebrations are already filled with cheer."

He turned to Louis and said, "and you look more and more like your father. How much older you have grown. A very happy birthday, Your Grace."

"Thank you, Monsieur le Comte," Louis replied, and gestured toward the other guests. "Please, be welcomed among us."

Queen Anne leaned forward and added, "later, there will be a cake and fireworks, and a concert under the stars. You will stay, won't you?"

"We would be pleased to stay as long as you wish, Your Majesty," said Lucien. With another bow, Alexander and Lucien turned to approach the carpet, where many of the guests were mingled.

D'Artagnan left his companions, came forward and greeted them wearing a solemn expression, while the other musketeers remained where they were.

"I am glad you are here. I have grave news," he said without preamble. "Van Helsing is here in Paris."

Alexander froze as if he was encased in ice. "Here?"

"I am told that he came with a band of men, and that he is incensed with revenge. Apparently, his second cousin Auric was killed in a fire, caused by a man who did resemble your father." He turned to Lucien and added, "I think he has mistaken you for someone else, Monsieur le Comte."

"Doubtless, captain, for I have never met the man," Lucien replied. "But, how is it that you know..."

D'Artagnan interrupted him with, "I had the good fortune to meet with the Comte du Saint Germain, who did confide in me some details of your journeys. I became curious after Alexander visited me on his way home." He paused to crane his neck and look over the guests crowding the ballroom. "I do not see him here," he said. "However, he told me that he learned of the man's arrival and warned me of his intent. You are safe here on the grounds of the Louvre, but I fear he will try something."

"Then it is good that you remain discreet," Lucien said. "You have told no one else?"

D'Artagnan's eyebrows went up. "Not even my friends, Monsieur le Comte. They know nothing of it. I would not betray a confidence once it is shared, but I felt I had to tell you that you were in danger."

"Thank you, monsieur. Think you he will come here?"

"I do not know. But he would not dare! I and my friends will protect you, and the king's guard. No army can come through the door to this palace without great difficulty. That much is certain."

Lucien regarded him with some equanimity. "Thank you for the warning, captain. I will take it to heart."

"I must return to my friends now," d'Artagnan said. "Bon chance." With that, he marched away and resumed chatting with his friends. Athos and Porthos glanced in Alexander and Lucien's direction, but were diverted by another courtier who wanted to sample something they were standing in front of. They parted and went their separate ways, but moved closer to the throne dais as they did so.

Alexander watched them while paying close attention to his father. He concluded that d'Artagnan must have told them that Queen Anne and Louis were undefended, and called for reinforcement.

"What do you think we should do?" Lucien asked. "The queen has asked us to stay. If van Helsing disrupts the party we must avoid conflict for her sake, and that of Louis. I have no desire to become the center of chaos, on this of all days."

"I would face van Helsing alone, if need be," Alexander replied. "You are innocent. He has no case against you, and has no evidence which would convict you."

The words were barely out of Alexander' mouth when the calling steward came foward and rapped his staff on the marble floor. "Mesdames et monsieurs, Baron Stephan van Helsing of Austria."

The room turned to see a tall, dark haired man in the dress uniform of the Austrian guard, standing alone at the entrance to the ballroom. He stood at attention, and his face was stone with not a hint of joy. He looked around at the guests filling the hall and his lips turned up into a cynical smirk. His empty scabbard told Alexander that his arms had been stripped from him, even as he suppressed a brief shudder at the sight.

The queen's footman approached and shared a few words with the baron, then escorted him directly to the royal dais. At this, the room hushed to quiet, and the guests gathered together to watch this stranger invade their peace.

"For what reason do you come here uninvited?" Anne asked.

"I seek justice, Your Majesty," he replied, affecting a click of his heels and a small bow. "There is one among you who has committed murder, and he is here now."

The entire court was perturbed. They murmured imprecations and shocked whispers alike, until the queen's hand raised to silence them.

"Who do you accuse?" she asked. "What are the particulars?"

Licking his lips to moisten them, van Helsing told a story of his cousin Auric's death, and was sure that the same man who had killed his second cousin Nicholaus had killed him.

"He was seen riding away from the fire. The fire consumed the tent in which my cousin slept."

Anne considered his story, then said, "you say his murderer is here. Who is he?"

The baron looked around and then pointed to Lucien. "Him!"

The guests parted to allow space between them and the two vampires until Alexander and Lucien stood alone.

Louis started to get up from his chair, then thought better of it and sat down again. "You are mistaken, Monsieur le Baron," he said. "This man is innocent. He and his son are my tutors. They have never given me reason to fear for my safety."

"Nevertheless, Your Grace, they are guilty of far more than murder. They are vampires."

The room erupted with shock and consternation, and the space grew wider still. Lucien stood where he was without moving a muscle, while Alexander gritted his teeth with fury. "You lie!" he declared.

Lucien said softly, "Alexander. Have a care, will you?"

Stephan van Helsing drew himself straighter and said, "I demand justice. I challenge one or both to a duel. I am not satisfied to see them hang for their crimes."

Cardinal Mazarin came forward and declared, "dueling is forbidden by law, Monsieur le Baron. I forbid it. You are in France now, not Austria. Have a care yourself, or you will find yourself excommunicated for your brazen behavior. What proof have you of his deed?"

"I care not for your law," van Helsing spat. "I want to avenge my cousins and rid the world of these demons. It is my right! If you do not allow me to deal with the matter in my own way, I will bring a petition to the Emperor Ferdinand and ask for war."

Queen Anne said, "You would not dare. These men are under my protection. I am France, Monsieur le Baron. Would you make war on France for a petty dispute?"

Lucien stepped forward and said, "Your Majesty, I am innocent of these events. I know nothing of his claim. For what reason does he accuse me so? I would never stoop so low as to murder anyone."

Alexander thought furiously. It was true that Lucien was different from any man he knew, and it would be ridiculous to accuse him. Then another thought occurred. But, if Lucien had a twin... Suddenly, it all made sense.

He joined his father and said, "it is possible that another may have had a motive for killing his cousins. The Baron van Helsing is from a clan of vampire hunters."

The shocked audience started to talk again, but shushed each other to silence. Alexander plunged on. "Perhaps... perhaps someone else was responsible, and he mistook my father for the one. I can vouch for my father. Where were you?"

Lucien turned to him with the wide eyes of surprise, but said nothing.

"Someone else? Pray, what are you talking about?" Anne asked.

"The Baron van Helsing and his cousins engage in the staking of dead people in their coffins, according to pagan custom. In our travels, we learned that they were paid gold to disinter corpses and defile them most cruelly. Perhaps a relative who found a loved one in this shocking condition objected to the practice, and vowed revenge. It is outrageous for him to accuse my father, who could not have been there."

The baron stood speechless. His eyebrows drew down and he bunched his fists, but did not argue the point.

"What say you, Monsieur le Baron?" Queen Anne asked. "Is what he said true? Do you engage in this... this questionable activity to earn your way through life?"

The baron worked his mouth several times, then replied, "not I, personally, Your Majesty. But I assert his guilt nevertheless."

"Then I dare say that the assizes are the proper setting for this trial, not my son's birthday party. My cousin Ferdinand has outlawed such a form of hunting, and your cousins have reaped their reward for their deeds. You will remove yourself from the Louvre, Monsieur le Baron. At once. You are to return to Austria without delay, and never darken our doorstep again."

The Baron hesitated, and began to speak again, but the musketeers stepped forward and blocked his way. Thus deterred from suing his case further, he turned and marched out of the throne room.

D'Artagnan turned to the queen and said, "with your permission, Your Majesty, I will make sure that he does as you command."

"By all means, do," she replied. Then she stood and said, "all of you, please do not let that man disturb our celebrations."

With a meaningful glance toward Alexander, d'Artagnan followed the baron out into the foyer. The rest of the court relaxed their guard and returned to their conversations and music as if nothing had happened.

Queen Anne beckoned to Lucien and Alexander, who obliged her by approaching the dais. There she spoke to them in soft tones so as not to be overheard. "Is what the baron said true? That you are... vampires?"

Lucien bowed his head, then addressed her. "It is what we are called, Madame... it is not what we are."

"Tell me the truth," she insisted. "I would understand you better if you did. I promise no harm will come to you."

Apparently she was not apprised of the situation under her own roof. Louis rose from his chair and stood by her, and listened while Lucien explained the truth.

When he was finished, Anne's eyes were wide with shock. "I had no inkling. You are alien to this world? From another planet among the stars?"

"Aye, Madame," Lucien said. "We have traveled far in order to find a peaceful place to dwell. My companions are few and scattered, and only wish to survive. We must guard our secrets to do so, and men like van Helsing little understand what we are. We drink blood, it is true, but only a little at a time, and we do not murder to obtain that which we need."

"So, what d'Artagnan has said is the truth," Louis said. "He told me of a small group of vampires living in Paris, who keep to themselves."

Alexander looked up at him. "Aye, Your Grace. Many of them are my friends. They mean no harm to anyone. But they have become targets for van Helsing's men. I fear that these vampire hunters will stay in Paris and try to kill them, or worse, try to kill us."

He told the story of how Lucien and he had rescued the Baron de Neuvillette from highwaymen who did not speak, and that these men worked for someone who was never identified. "It speaks to a conspiracy which threatens France, Your Grace," Alexander said. "I have tried to learn who is responsible but he is invisible as a ghost."

"And, you have protected me as well as you are able to," Louis said. "What will you do now?"

"We will do what we have always done, if you will accept us as we are," Lucien said. "Ask my wife of my comportment with her, and that of Alexander. We strive to be useful, and are loyal as your servants. Do not cast us out because we are different. We are as human as you are."

"And yet you are not," Louis said. "You both possess powers I can scarcely fathom. I have seen you when you have not seen me. I marvel at the things you can do. You are a superior man, and I wish to be like you. You are my role model, Alexander."

"I hope that does not change things between us," Alexander replied.

"I think not," Louis replied. "Only remind me, when I lose my way, what a better man I can be."

"Of course, Your Grace."

So the cake was produced, and a slice was given to Louis. Slices were carved for the other guests, including Lucien and Alexander. There was enough cake left to climb into, and the icing dripped from the sides.

As was tradition, Louis was obliged to silently make a wish, then blow out the candles. The court applauded his resolve, then dug in for more.

After the cake was consumed down to the platter, the court moved outside to the lawn, where chairs had been set up. There, they were treated to music from the orchestra, who played Handel while the fireworks were lit.

Blooms of fire and color filled the starry sky, and while Lucien and Alexander joined Ingrid and Parvati to watch the display, they turned to each other and smiled, content and at peace at last. ✦

Printed in the USA
CPSIA information can be obtained
at www.ICGtesting.com
LVHW041337191023
761544LV00004B/294

9 781735 238920